THE AUDACITY OMNIBUS

THE AUDACITY OMNIBUS

THE AUDACITY

TIME WARP

BE KIND, REWIND

Carmen Loup

Space Wizard Science Fantasy
Raleigh, NC
www.spacewizardsciencefantasy.com

Publisher's Note: This is a work of fiction. Names, characters, places, and incidents are a product of the author's imagination. Locales and public names are sometimes used for atmospheric purposes. Any resemblance to actual people, living or dead, or to businesses, companies, events, institutions, or locales is completely coincidental.

Cover art and Interior illustrations by Carmen Loup
Editing by Courtney Brooks
Book Layout © 2015 BookDesignTemplates.com

The Audacity Omnibus/Carmen Loup.-- 1st ed.
ISBN 978-1-960247-27-8

Author's website: https://www.carmenloup.com/

Contents

ROCKET RACING'S DEADLY,
BUT FOOD SERVICE IS WORSE.

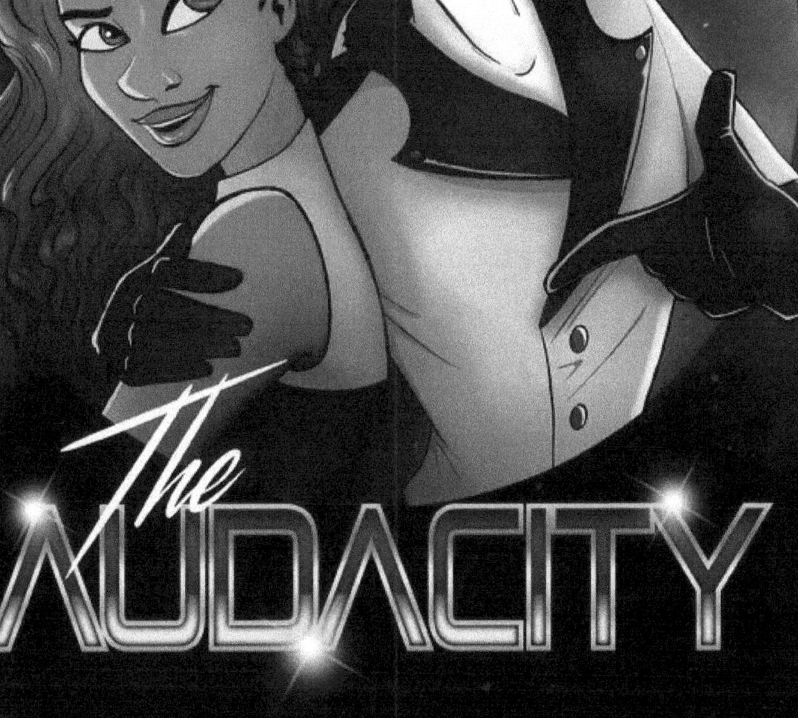

A NOVEL BY

CARMEN LOUP

The Audacity

Dedicated to Trista Mayes and Zack Loup who climbed aboard the *Audacity* long ago.

CONTENTS

CHAPTER ONE

I Love Lucy

The 'I Love Lucy' theme song drifted brassily through the alien rocket ship which had been orbiting Earth since 1951.

No one noticed. Well, no one important enough to do anything about it, anyway. There was a great deal of junk orbiting Earth. One small alien ship, even a traffic-cone orange ship like the *Audacity*, didn't register as a threat.

The ship had a single occupant who watched, with a smile which broke open his pale blue face like a piñata, as the grainy black and white heart scrawled across the screen of a boxy, rabbit eared television.

He'd seen every episode at least a dozen times, but pretending each time it was going to be different kept the depression at bay for a while. He had become very good at pretending.

The picture wobbled, and Lucy seemed to be caught in a freak snowstorm accompanied by a fuzzy sound. A literal shadow fell across the TV; a figurative shadow fell across the alien face. The viewscreen behind him was no longer illuminated by Earth's sun.

He vaulted over the back of the couch and leapt up the orange shag stairs to the control loft.

Outside, so close he could see his own ship reflected in it like a neon orange grain of rice, another, much larger ship blocked out the sun and the TV signal. The loss of Lucy was the least of his worries.

"By O'Zeno's ingrown armpit hair...That's the *Peacemaker*."

He pressed the Button That Typically Made The Ship Go, but the ship did not go. He pressed it thirty-three times in quick succession. The ship stayed put.

The flash of an explosion whited out the viewscreen.

Debris from the explosion pinged against the hull of the *Audacity*, and he tried again to get the ship moving, anxious that the debris might nick the paint.

But something caught his eye. Something had snagged on a jagged tooth of metal knifing out of the *Peacemaker's* ruined side.

Someone, actually.

He flailed at the control panel, pressing every button he could find, hoping at least one of them would be a tractor beam. As luck would have it, one of them was.

CHAPTER TWO

Classic Abduction Scene

May was elbow deep in the 29-year-old guts of her father's 1989 turbocharged Honda Civic when her phone buzzed in her pocket. It was work. She knew this, not because she had any aptitude for ESP, but because no one else ever messaged her.

She decided she hadn't felt her phone vibrate. If she ignored it, it never happened.

Besides, if Kathy was asking her to come in early, as she suspected, she'd hate to refuse the extra pay, but she would hate even more to interrupt this repair session. After a long shift at Sonic, she doubted she would remember where all the parts she'd just removed were supposed to go.

She'd applied for the job because she enjoyed roller skating and she needed the money. She'd kept the job, even after they'd banned roller skating on account of the liability, because she needed the money. She'd bought their approved skates and got to use them on three shifts before the ban took effect.

It was beginning to seem, to May, like fun was actually becoming illegal as she aged.

Growing up she had been told that her father had quit racing when she was born, and so she assumed that having children meant giving up on fun hobbies and resolved never to have children. Well, clearly, that hadn't saved her.

Her phone vibrated again, and this time she couldn't pretend she hadn't felt it.

"Neeed u @ 4 2nite" Kathy's text read. Kathy, May's manager, had a touch screen phone, but she had learned to text in 2004 and never adapted.

"Can't, busy," she almost typed.

"Sorry, no thanks," she nearly replied.

"Who is this?" crossed her mind, too.

Eventually, she typed, "On my way."

May had heard that it was nice to be needed, but she'd never understood it. She collected the parts she'd strewn on the ground and tossed them onto the front seat, carefully setting the cup of screws and bolts on the cab floor. She sat in the back seat and strapped on her roller skates, the ones she had bought to make work more fun, but now only used to get to work in a hurry.

That was something she'd clearly inherited from her father. A strong desire to go nowhere fast.

She grabbed a crumpled blue and red polo from the back seat and sniffed it. It did not smell great. Kathy had asked her to come in for extra shifts every day this week, meaning May hadn't had a chance to get to the laundry mat so, really, it was Kathy's fault.

When she arrived at the Sonic, Kathy told her yet another new hire had failed to show up for their shift. "It's those damn cars, excuse my language," Kathy said, eyes squinted and arms crossed as if some sane part of her was still resistant to this apparent truth. "People going missing left and right lately."

"Hm," May acknowledged her verbally as she read through the order list and washed her hands.

In the event you're reading this in the far future, from a distant planet, or in another reality, it's important to note that in May's reality, old cars didn't ordinarily fall from the sky. Yet, across planet Earth, reports abounded of AMC Gremlins descending from the heavens, abducting whoever was unlucky enough to be nearest, and leaving.

May was troubled by this. Not by the cars—she figured it was some kind of new marketing scheme or mass prank. No, it was the people who wouldn't stop *talking* about the cars that troubled her. Mainly because it seemed every single customer brought it up. And now her manager was, too.

"Hear about them cars?" they'd ask conspiratorially, as if they were about to share with her the gospel itself.

Long ago, May had become numb to being asked the same question fifty-seven times in a single day.

"No," she'd say, sans inflection, allowing them to enlighten her over and over again as she counted their change.

Tonight was no different. Ten hours of listening to people talk about old cars she didn't give a wet slap about when all she wanted to do was get back to fixing the one old car she did care about.

Finally, her shift ended. May grabbed the nearest damp towel and swiped it over the counter to more evenly distribute the germs.

"Going home?" Kathy asked, closing out May's register. Kathy was in nearly every way May's visual opposite. Thin blond wisps, thin pink-painted lips, thin sense of humor, and sharp little blue eyes.

"Oh no, the night is young. I have a debutante ball after this." May pulled out the trash bag, twirled it closed, and slung it over her shoulder, giving Kathy a tired, crooked smile.

Kathy squinted at her. "You're being sarcastic again."

"Yep. Night, Kathy. Make lots of tips."

Kathy snorted, fiddling with the register. "The only tips I get here are men telling me I should pull my shirt down more."

May pushed open the sticky back door, ignoring the squelch of garbage juice which had dripped into her shoes as she walked into the poorly lit alley, and flung the garbage bag into the dumpster.

She released her coily black hair from its prison under her Sonic cap and fluffed it out with her fingers, aerating her sweaty scalp. Leaning against the dumpster, she pulled a cigarette from the package in her back pocket and lit it.

The first drag helped her hoist herself off the dumpster.

The second got her to dig her keys out of her pocket and thread them between her fingers in a makeshift weapon she referred to as 'Key Fist,' and looked like a slapdash Wolverine cosplay. Straightening her back, she set her mouth in a tight line and thought murderous thoughts. Thoughts that, May hoped, would seep out of her pores and repel anyone looking for an easy target.

She started the two-mile skate back to her apartment, ready to studiously ignore any sketchy activity she might encounter on the way.

The night was cool and quiet. May had the gall, fifteen minutes in, to think that perhaps she wouldn't see anyone on her way home. It was a nice fantasy, until she passed a particularly nasty alleyway stuffed with piles of wet cardboard, stained rags, and, amid the cardboard and rags, a urine-scented man.

"Ey, watch yerself out thar," the man shouted at her. "Thems Gremlins about town—they been a'snatchin folks naw. Up ta no good!"

May went a little faster. Not that the man was in any state to give chase, she just needed to breathe fresh air again. At last, her apartment loomed darkly before her. The building's outside lights had been out for months, but the person whose job it was to let someone know about these things hadn't been paid in months, and the person whose job it was to do something about these things hadn't cared in months.

She jammed her key in the lock and wiggled it around for a while until the door finally clicked open. The familiar earthy smell of home greeted her, a sliver of moonlight fighting its way in through the thin window above her front door, which accounted for the only natural light in the apartment.

The living room—which was also the kitchen, the library, the ballroom, the lounge, the study, the conservatory, and the bedroom—was dark enough she didn't have to worry about cleaning it. Atop her mini fridge, in a beam of moonlight, sat May's one faithful companion: Betty, the cactus.

It was a resilient little prickled lump. May had over-watered it, under-watered it, and left it in a box for a few weeks when she moved in. It just wouldn't die. It fed off adversity, as if it got a kick out of taking the punches that life threw at it.

"Hey, Betty, long day?" she asked.

It converted carbon dioxide into oxygen at her.

May converted some oxygen back into carbon dioxide in return and gave it a mist of water. Not tired enough to sleep, not awake enough to do much else, May absently pulled another stick from the pack in her back pocket and went outside to sit on the metal steps that lead to the upstairs apartments. She sat on the cold metal, lit her cigarette, and watched a candy wrapper cross the street, aided by a gentle breeze.

The traffic light at the intersection nearest her flickered through its rounds: green, yellow, red. Giving the go-ahead to no one, suggesting to no one that stopping might be a wise thing to consider, then warning no one that they were now law-bound to stop.

The night was quiet, as we've established. It was quiet because the things that typically make noise in the early morning—birds, crickets, drunks—were avoiding the area around May's apartment.

The reason why was about to become clear.

Down the street, past the traffic light, an engine turned over in a car which loitered in the dark space between two feeble streetlights. May flicked the ash from her cigarette, leaning her head against the railing to get a better view of the car which had broken the silence.

A single headlight turned on, the other blinked on sleepily, flickered, then shut off in an ominous wink.

Slowly, as if she might frighten the car if she moved too fast, May lifted her cigarette to her mouth. The car began to move. She let the cigarette drift back down again, unpuffed.

She could go inside; the idea crossed her mind, anyway. But doing that would be both admitting that the car had freaked her out, which her pride wouldn't allow, and drawing attention to her presence, which her fear wouldn't allow. She decided instead to pretend she was part of the architecture. Nothing to see here, just a bit of railing.

The car inched into the light. It was, as I'm sure you've guessed by now, an AMC Gremlin. What you could not have guessed was that its body work was done out in pickle-green with black racing stripes that swooped nicely upward toward the back of the car where two enormous black thrusters had been welded to it.

May pressed herself further into the stairwell, but she still made rather unconvincing cast iron.

The car completely disregarded the traffic light's suggestion that stopping might be a wise thing to consider, further disregarded the concrete median that endeavored to keep it on the proper side of the street, and still further disregarded the sickly hedge that surrounded May's apartment complex as it screeched toward her.

Half a second short of turning May into a hood ornament, it stopped.

May dropped the cigarette.

A sizzling came from the car window, a pop, and then, over what sounded like a megaphone, someone shouted, "We have come in peace, Earthlin—"

She heard a thwack which sounded suspiciously like someone being hit over the head with a megaphone, then a different voice.

"Can I give you a trip?" it asked.

"I'm sorry?" May said, more out of the habit of customer service than as a way of actually apologizing for anything.

"Do you need a car? Might I offer you a ride?" The voice was vaguely metallic, and vaguely threatening.

May knew what this was now. Teenagers. She groaned, stomped on her cigarette, and stood up. "Fuck off," she proposed, doing her best impression of someone you wouldn't want to mess with.

From the car: silence. The megaphone clicked on then off, then on, and off again as the bewildered wielder considered their next words.

"No thank you," the voice finally said.

The headlights grew brighter until white filled her vision. A sudden thump, and May was out.

CHAPTER THREE

You're Here Now

The air smelled like copper.

May's senses returned one by one, like forest creatures timidly stepping into a clearing to convene. Light. Bright, white light. A piercing whine and a deep, vibrating hum. The bed below her was hard, just a thin mattress on a table. Her left temple felt like it had been frozen and was slowly, painfully thawing out.

Gaining control of her limbs, May clambered upright, hugging her legs against her chest. Instead of that stiff, rank old Sonic polo, she wore a latex suit. She tried to quantify how much trouble she was in. She appeared to be in an office cubicle so, possibly, quite a lot.

A figure which appeared to be made of clear gelatin and five ill-anchored googly eyes gestured to a table full of little plastic cups beside her.

"Might I offer you a refreshment?" When it spoke, the left side of May's head exploded with electricity. "Juice of the lemon? The helpful gator, perhaps?" It grew an arm and plucked a cup half filled with blue Gatorade from the table, then offered it to May.

May shook her head. "No thanks," she mouthed, too disoriented to speak.

The gelatinous speaker turned its attention back to the table and began to move the cups around, trying rather transparently to appear busy. Transparently because May could see that it wasn't actually doing anything but shuffling around the cups, and because May could also literally see through its translucent, dripping hands.

A pale young man with messy dishwater hair entered the cubicle. He was sealed from the neck-down, like May, in latex. He looked human. Not friendly, but human, at least.

"Are you May?" He looked at her with one bloodshot grey eye and one black eyepatch.

She nodded, her left eye winking, though the pain in her temple was beginning to dissipate.

"I'm August. Follow me." He walked off, his hand trailing behind him with a lazy come-hither finger.

May followed.

After passing by a few identical cubicles with trays of Gatorade, May's voice returned.

"Where the hell am I?"

"You're here now," he said helpfully.

The enormous building they were in seemed, to May, to be some sort of hospital hub. She was partially right. The place was enormous, and it was a kind of hospital hub, but it was not a building.

They reached a long wall lined with hundreds of human-sized pneumatic tubes which made her feel like a mouse at a drive-up bank teller. Between each tube, the same poster had been copied and pasted.

"You're here now!" it said in cheery blue letters under a stock photo of smiling strangers.

August stepped into the tube nearest them and stared at her.

"I'm not getting in there," May said, crossing her arms. "What's going on?"

He tipped his head back as if his neck could no longer bear the terrible weight. "I don't know, man. They brought me here, like, five months ago and put a chip in my head that translates everything into German so they can boss me around. The food here's complete scrap, and I miss apples. Would you get in here? I'm supposed to show you to our room."

He looked desperate, so May relented. The doors whooshed shut in a science-fiction-movie way that Earth elevators hadn't quite gotten the hang of, and they shot into the ceiling at a speed Earth elevators would never get the hang of.

"Our room?" May asked, suspicious.

"Yes, our room. Don't worry, I'm not that kind of guy. You can have the bed, I like the chair anyway."

"I don't want the bed, I want to leave," she said.

"Well, you can't."

"Why?"

August ran a hand through his long, greasy hair, somehow making it messier than it had been before. "I'll show you."

"Fine," she said.

The tube came to a stop, and they entered a perfect replica of a dingy hotel hallway. The carpet was a low-pile abstract affair in shades of green and pink that were not on speaking terms, the walls dripped steadily from brown stains in the wallpaper, and rows of numbered doors lined the walls.

May followed him down the corridor to a small alcove, where she expected to see an old ice dispenser, a soda machine, maybe snacks.

That is not what she saw.

Through a window, a billboard which read "Forbinated Moringarg: For the distinguished ch'stranda," and showed a high-res looping video of a creature akin to an over-sized ferret licking gray mash from a bowl.

May looked back at August, confused.

It was a Largish Bronda's Well-Placed Billboard, so named because it scanned for and followed any nearby ships. "Always at the right place, always at the right time! (Time travel features may incur additional cost)" goes the jingle.

August didn't know this, however. All he knew was that it was annoying.

"Hold on, it'll move."

And then it did.

"Oh, I see," May said.

"Uh-huh."

"Is that...?"

"Yep."

"Oh. I see."

May watched a blue and green marble spin slowly, lit on one side by an enormous yellow dwarf star and on the other by a round hunk of reflective rock. Stars surrounded it, but without Earth's atmosphere interfering, the stars did not twinkle.

"Come on, our room's just around the corner."

A strange amalgamation of items decorated the room August brought May to. It looked as if someone had ransacked five different themed motels. On one wall hung a poorly rendered painting of a parrot in a chipped gold gilt frame. Another wall hosted a large but unplugged TV and two paintings of palm trees, which were identical in every way but one. What the difference was, exactly, May couldn't say.

It occurred to her she ought to think she was dreaming. Everyone in books and movies always thought they were dreaming when something this unusual happened. How did she know she was awake? Finally, she decided that if she *were* dreaming, she wouldn't have the capacity to think she was dreaming. Which wasn't strictly true, but it made her feel better.

August fell into a densely stuffed chair beside the bed and closed his eye. May assumed he had another eye under the eyepatch to close, but she was wrong. This is why you should never make assumptions.

The bed along the wall was plastic-covered and brick-like with a single pancake-thick pillow and no sheet, twisted at an odd angle from the bamboo headboard. She poked it; it crinkled at her.

"Report to the cafeteria," said a voice from the ceiling that crackled like milk poured over Rice Krispies.

August groaned as he stood. "Come on, it's time for work."

"Work?" May asked, following him out of the room.

"That's why they brought you here," August said as he walked. "Needed another server."

The cafeteria looked like a Jim Henson-brand sex dungeon.

Monstrous creatures she had only seen the likes of in cheap sci-fi films, small yellow-green beings that looked uncannily human, Amazonian bipeds which came in shades and hues of purple and with various numbers of eyes and arms, and creatures that looked almost entirely like cicadas in white latex sausage sleeves all stood in a meandering line or sat, eating quietly, at tables. Most were cling-wrapped in the same white latex.

August towed her along by the arm now, noticing she had paused to gape, and brought her to a narrow doorway at the back of the cafeteria which led to the kitchen. Just a normal, boring industrial kitchen like the one where May had wasted a solid forty hours a week back on Earth.

She'd rather be wasting her time there. Minimum wage was better than nothing.

Someone who looked an awful lot like a gray-haired grandmother from Minnesota handed May a ladle and patted her shoulder apologetically. "Down at the end, honey." The woman hobbled out the door they had entered through.

"Take care, April," August called after her. "You're on food service. I've got dishes." He tried to walk away, but May stopped him with a ladle to the shoulder.

"Her name's April?" May asked.

"Yeah."

"And you're August?"

He nodded.

"Is this a joke?" she whispered angrily.

August shrugged. "Not a very funny one, is it?" He pushed the ladle off his shoulder, and left her to her gruel.

May stared despondently into the pot. The customer at the window banged his tray on the counter to get her attention, and she snapped out of an existential fugue and into a customer-service-job fugue.

She hadn't eaten for some time, but she didn't feel hungry, and the slop she'd been ladling out didn't inspire her appetite, either.

At last, the line dwindled. Her final customer wore, rather than the white latex, a neatly pressed double-breasted suit, decorated with various ribbons and medals. She was the color of a ripe plum, except for her right hand which was made of a pale metal. Tightly locked hair was arranged in a neat bun at the nape of her neck, and she sported what May considered a normal number of arms, legs, and eyes. She was at least a foot-and-a-half taller than May, but short in comparison to the other purple bipeds in the cafeteria.

"I haven't seen you before. This must be your first day, is that right, May June July?"

May nodded.

"I'm General Listay," she said, smiling warmly. "I oversee defense operations onboard this vessel. I don't oversee the cafeteria, unfortunately. Here."

The General reached into a pack attached to her thigh and produced a shiny, purple, and orange fruit. She set it on the counter and, with her robotic hand, she twirled it like a top on its convex side.

"It's a llerke. I grow them in my spare time. If you ever need more, come find me. Welcome to the *Peacemaker*, May." As the General walked away, May watched her take another fruit from her pack and toss her tray into a disposal slot.

With no one left to serve, May set down the ladle and hopped onto the counter, picking up the fruit to give it an experimental squeeze. It felt fleshy inside, like a soft mango. Peeling a bit of the skin away from the knot at the top, May found juicy, yellow meat. It smelled sweet and tangy.

Maybe she was hungry, after all. She touched the fruit with the tip of her tongue, deciding if it didn't immediately kill her after licking it, she'd probably be fine.

Aw hell, she thought, if it killed her, so what? Probably, this was all just a dream. If the fruit killed her, she'd just wake up. It was worth it. She took a bite. It was ripe, sweet, and tart and had a lingering aftertaste like the cherry syrup from Sonic. Or maybe a real cherry. Yes, probably more like an actual cherry. It was the tastiest dream-fruit she'd ever had and she closed her eyes to bask in the experience more fully.

August appeared just as she finished the fruit, a little damper than he had been when they arrived.

"Looks like you met Listay," he said, nodding to the pit which she tossed into the empty pot of whatever she'd been serving. "Hot, isn't she?"

May blinked meaningfully at him, but he had already begun walking away. She never noticed when people were hot. She wondered if August was hot but doubted it.

"If you're into that sort of thing," she offered.

"What, aliens? Yeah, I guess my standards have gotten messed up out here. She's nice, though. And she's ripped." August punctuated with a flirtatious growl.

"She is," May agreed, following him back to their room.

CHAPTER FOUR

Unmentionable

Within the *Peacemaker,* far from May and August, the physical form which contained the spirit of a long-forgotten chaos god sat cross-legged on a black and white checkered floor.

Silver hair crested into a high wave atop her head and cascaded down her back, pooling on the tiles beside her. Standing, she would be a full eight feet of rippling muscles wrapped in deep purple skin.

Sitting, hunched as she was, she resembled an angry purple swan. Still majestic, still terrifying, but also a little ridiculous. The kind of ridiculous only the extremely brave or incredibly stupid are likely to point out.

Her looks weren't unusual for a Rhean, and nothing about her was particularly *unmentionable,* except for her eyes. The color of her eyes was unfathomable. Imagine a color you've never seen before, then scrap that because you've got it all wrong. *That* unfathomable. They hadn't always been this way, but being possessed by the spirit of a long-forgotten chaos god did funny things to a body. Starting with the eyes.

She had been called Yvonne, before the possession, but Yvonne was becoming quieter by the season as the Chaos-consciousness infused her body like an unmentionable liquid soaking into a dry sponge.

In front of her, on a white square of something like linoleum, stood a blown glass figure of a puntl, a creature that looks a bit like a horse crossed with a kumquat.

Chaos sighed with Yvonne's lungs, and rested her head in Yvonne's palm. Millions of orbits ago, she would have been able to transform this tiny figurine into a sulpoosian cocktail with a decorative paper umbrella stuck through a twist of llerke rind by simply remembering the salty smell of a beach. Now, even convincing the figurine's snout to devolve into sand made her repulsively mortal head ache.

She glanced upward. Above her, behind a field of glistening glass spikes, the *Peacemaker's* Stardrive sparkled.

A god-consciousness requires a small star's worth of energy to sustain. Coincidentally, the massive starship *Peacemaker* also required a small star's worth of energy. And so, the travel-minded Tuhntian engineers who built the *Peacemaker* had siphoned the energy from a distant white-dwarf in a desolate corner of the galaxy into the compact Stardrive with a shockingly elegant little device. The details of this device are not important to the story and, as such, will remain unexplored.

This had, at first, been a nuisance to the entity who had called this star home. But she soon found that living in a massive, planet-destroying warship had its advantages. Namely, the ability to destroy planets.

Chaos had also found the ship's captain unusually weak-willed and easy to possess. And now that she was corporeal again...well the universe was the limit.

Chaos had been compacting Yvonne's soul like trash in an overfilled bin for a little over two hundred orbits now, and she was finally really getting the hang of it.

Until the phone rang.

Not the holocom screen on Yvonne's desk. Not the BEAPER on her wrist. The phone. It was a direct line, and because the person on the other side of it couldn't see anyway, there was no need for visuals.

Yvonne picked it up. Yvonne always picked it up, whether Chaos wanted her to or not.

"Ix," she said the name of the person on the other line quietly, reverently, as if there was a definite limit to the number of times she would be allowed to say it and that limit was approaching.

"The Earthlings are becoming suspicious," said Ix. "You cannot keep taking them."

"I know," she whispered. "I can't stop. I don't know why she wants them."

"You, Yvonne, are the only one who can stop this. You are allowing her to work through you. I wonder if you enjoy it."

"No! Ix," tears of frustration spilled over Yvonne's cheeks. "Ix, I hate this. I hate Chaos, you know that."

Ix said nothing.

"You know that I've been doing my best, right?"

Silence, but the line wasn't dead.

"Ix please. I'm no ultra-physicist, my mind doesn't work like yours. I can't just tell it what to do like you can!" Even now she felt Chaos preying on her fear, on her weakness. If she couldn't keep her own emotions in check, how could she possibly control an ancient entity?

"I wish she had taken me instead," Ix said. "I might have had a chance against her."

"Is that an invitation?" said Chaos, laughing now. "Yvonne let me in. You should've trained her better."

"She is not a pet," Ix said flatly. "Yvonne, if you can hear me, I called to say that I am leaving. I have seen what Chaos is capable of. If you will not destroy her, I will."

"Shouldn't an ultra-physicist know the meaning of 'immortal'?" Chaos said. "I cannot be destroyed. I AM destruction," and she moved to hang up the phone, but as she did so, the phone and the desk supporting it lost all sense of form, became a confused water buffalo, became a pair of oversized felted yuzcas, became a sparkling crystalline wail, then dissolved into a quickly dissipating cluster of heat and light.

Chaos was delighted. That was something! Not something she had intended to do, but she could easily convince herself that it was exactly what she had wanted to happen. Yes, she had wanted that. Far better than a sulpoosian cocktail, actually. Perhaps she had just been thinking too small. Several millennia spent as a semi-conscious essence pervading a sun had made her boring and Ix had tried to keep her that way.

Well, Ix was leaving. And Chaos knew just how to keep her from coming back for a long, long time.

She went to the window and stared at the nothingness out there until the nothingness got shy and obligingly became something. Granted, that something was a wormhole, so in a way it was more nothing than the previous nothing. But it was also a much more dangerous, much more interesting nothing, and it would be waiting to swallow Ix up the moment she left.

That was one bit of Yvonne's obnoxious mortal baggage taken care of, Chaos thought...but there was one still to go. She eyed the brilliant speck of orange rocketship on her monitor. Yvonne's voice whispered behind the curtain of Chaos's thoughts. *No*, Yvonne chanted. *Leave him alone.*

Yvonne was always telling her no.

Don't kill Ix, Yvonne thought. *Don't kill my zoup-nog ex,* she thought. *Don't kill...*

Blah, blah, blah.

Yvonne was horribly opposed to killing certain people. But there was something Chaos needed from the zoup-nog on that hideous orange rocket, and eventually, once Yvonne had settled down a bit, she would have it.

She was a patient god, but the time was again ripe for her to spread like a virus amongst the stars, and this time she wouldn't miss her chance.

CHAPTER FIVE

Rocketparty

Laying down on the hard, creaking bed, May felt she would never fall asleep. But the dark room, lack of entertainment, and exhaustion quickly proved her wrong.

When she woke up again, there was no peaceful lulling into the land of awareness. Just a sudden, cold plunge into reality. She sat up against the bamboo headboard.

August was asleep on the armchair, snoring so loudly she was surprised she'd slept through it. She hadn't, in fact, slept through it. The snoring had woken her up.

She knew she'd seen Earth from a distance, stars that were not twinkling because there was no atmosphere to make them, and a billboard advertising some sort of alien pet food. She *knew* this, but she didn't believe it yet. Not in her bones.

She slipped out of the room and found the window alcove.

Yep, there it was. Space. All black with little not-twinkling points of light. The spinning blue marble continued to spin without her.

"Hey, don't wander off." August startled her.

"You should not be here." Someone startled August.

In the entrance to the alcove stood a woman with periwinkle-blue skin. She wore an immaculate white double-breasted coat, she smelled of molten metal and plastic, and her violet hair jutted out in a way that perfectly contrasted her thin, oval features. Her eyes were like two pools of expired milk, white and wispy.

August found his voice before May even started looking for hers. "What are you going to do about it?" he said with unconvincing bravado.

The alien blinked her blank eyes slowly, considering. "Nothing," she admitted. After a moment of stillness, her lips turned up slightly as if she had just had a very pleasant thought. "I am leaving. Would either of you like to join me?"

"Leaving and going where?" August pressed, on the same train of thought May found herself aboard.

"I am leaving the ship and returning to my home planet, Rhea. I can take you back to Earth, first, if that is what you would like. Earth is on the way to Rhea."

"How?" May asked, muscling August out of the way.

"The planet Earth exists at a midpoint along the route between our current position—"

"Are you insane, May?" August interrupted her, turning on May. "She's a Rhean. She's not going to help us. She wants to torture us or something," August whispered harshly to May in a voice she was quite sure the Rhean could also hear. His visible eye was wide as he turned to the alien. "My apologies, ma'am, we'll get back to our room now. Sorry for the disturbance."

He grabbed May's hand, but only succeeded in further convincing May she was better off with the stranger.

"I'm coming with you," she said, shaking August's hand off her own as if it were a mosquito.

"Let me see your arm," the Rhean said and offered her hand to May. May obliged, placing her hand in the Rhean's. May hissed through her teeth as the Rhean yanked her arm closer, turning up the soft underside and rolling back her spandex sleeve. With a long, white fingernail, she traced a vein in May's arm. May looked over at August, but only received a silent I-told-you-so.

"Do not scream." She plunged her nail into the soft brown flesh of May's arm. May bit her lip to keep herself silent as the alien plucked out a small black chip.

"This is a tracker."

May stared at it like it was a cockroach corpse in her soup. The Rhean pulled May's sleeve back down and let her go. May leaned against the wall and held her arm to stop the bleeding.

The Rhean looked to August. "And you?" she asked.

"Hold on, Ms. What's-your-name. Why should I trust you? There could be poison or *dirt* under your fingernails, you could be leading us to our deaths, you could be—"

"An opportunity to escape! How many escape offers have you turned down since you've been here?" May asked him defensively.

"I am Ix under C'Zabra of The Rhean Order of Ultra-Physics. I am more typically called 'Ix', though. I am the Chief Engineer. You may stay, August. Come along, May. We are going." Then, almost as an afterthought she added, "My fingernails are not poisonous nor are they dirty."

May stood. "How does everyone know my goddamn name?" she whispered.

Ix ignored her.

"Wait! Where are you taking her?" August's voice went up an octave. In the five months he had been here, no one had just offered to show him out. Then again, he had never asked. This deeply, deeply disturbed him. Could he have asked to leave all along?

"I am returning May to her home planet, Earth," Ix said patiently. "Would you like to come?"

"Ye...yes," he stammered. Ix nodded and snatched his arm, performing the same gruesome operation on him. The alien then crushed the trackers under her heeled shoe.

"I suggest you act like prisoners," Ix murmured in their ears and slipped pairs of glowing handcuffs around their wrists. They followed; they didn't have much of a choice.

"Why are you helping us?" August whispered.

"I want to leave, and you want to leave, so we will carpool," she answered as if it were obvious. The word she really used was closer in meaning to "rocket party," but the translators in May and August's heads took great pride in their work and if there was a suitable translation for the word, by golly, they would find it.

Ix led them back through the corridor to the intershoot bay and pushed them into the tube. May suspected she would never get used to the feeling of plummeting through a pneumatic tube. She was wrong, of course. Everyone gets used to it eventually.

The tube stopped in a dark cavernous space low in the ship. The trio popped out, May and August stumbling after the graceful Ix.

A football field is generally the largest form of spatial measurement Earthlings use to colloquially describe things that are big. A docking field, for some reference, is a few hundred football fields long. This particular docking *bay* spanned roughly twenty docking *fields* and was filled, end-to-end, with AMC Gremlins.

"Why—" May began to ask, but Ix shushed her. They had to act fast now in order to get out without being noticed.

Ix stepped onto a moving platform and pulled her prisoners along behind her. She typed a set of numbers and letters equivalent to an American license plate into the control panel and they were off, rocketing by the largest collection of cars May had ever seen.

It would be inaccurate to refer to them as cars at this point, though. AMC Gremlins were never a terribly popular mode of transportation on Earth, but they lent themselves so well to the modifications needed for space travel that they were an ideal and inexpensive machine to build a short distance fleet with.

They stopped in front of a mustard-colored vehicle with pea-green racing stripes along the side which gave you the idea someone had had a bad time on a road trip. Ix removed the handcuffs from the Earthlings and motioned for them to pack in. The pair scrunched themselves into the backseat and Ix took the wheel.

She revved the engine which echoed in the quiet bay, then revved it again. Then once more. She sighed, removed the key, then surprise attacked the ignition. This time, it sputtered to life and began lifting off the platform.

An alarm sounded. Ix whispered an alien curse that was easily translatable but not for the faint of heart and slammed the gas pedal.

May struggled to find her seatbelt; it was jammed so tightly into the crease between the seat and the door that no amount of force or appeal to a higher power could loosen it.

A crackling light ripped May's door off, and she dug her fingernails into the seat in front of her.

Ix, unable to find the proper exit on account of being blind, blasted a hole in the side of the *Peacemaker* and sped through it, flicking on the force-field.

The Gremlin had cleared the ship, but May had not.

She felt her suit catch on the jagged edge of the hole, she felt the icy cold vacuum of space, and then a warm nothingness.

CHAPTER SIX

Matters of Love and Devotion

Civilized gods have an unwritten but well-known rule: don't meddle in matters of love and devotion.

Chaos was not civilized. She was, even compared to the other gods, a certified scoundrel. As such, she was only too happy to meddle in matters of love and devotion and this she did with wild abandon.

Now, however, she was beginning to regret it.

Ix had not only been the *Peacemaker*'s brilliant and beloved Chief Engineer, she had been Yvonne's brilliant and beloved Chief Love Interest. And she had, in innumerable ways and with varying degrees of murderous intent, done everything in her power to keep Chaos from possessing Yvonne's body.

When Chaos schemed to start her own religion, Ix had launched a ship-wide campaign regarding the warning signs of cult-formation. When Chaos endeavored to turn the medical wing into an arid desert-land replete with stinging microscopic bugs and stinking misanthropic bogs, Ix had programmed the service bots to think that Yvonne was a large purple stain that needed prompt removal. When Chaos targeted an annoyingly bright planetoid for disintegration, Ix had re-wired the anti-matter cannons.

But Yvonne loved Ix, and Ix loved her back. And this was a problem.

A problem which Ix had just neatly solved for Chaos. Opening the wormhole in Ix's path had taken a great deal of energy out of Chaos, but it had been worth it. Ix wouldn't be a problem again for a very long time.

Another problem arose, though. Yvonne's consciousness rampaged, distraught at the loss of Ix. Chaos could feel Yvonne tearing at her own sinews.

Meddling in matters of love and devotion would be her downfall.

Ah, thought Chaos, but in the poison lies the antidote. Someone else on board this ship was deeply in love with her. General Listay had been a key figure in the seizing of the *Peacemaker* for the rebellion many orbits ago.

She and Ix could not have been more different.

The General had been the first to dip her toes into the new religion, offering to take on the mantle of historian. She'd wholly supported the idea of a desert wasteland in the medical bay, provided the bugs and bogs were properly inventoried. And she did agree that the annoyingly bright planetoid looked out of place in that sector of the galaxy and would be better off disintegrated; she'd even begun the arduous process of filing planet removal forms.

Planet removal forms, Chaos remembered with a derisive laugh. The General always knew exactly how to take the fun out of destruction. But she was supportive. Willing. Gullible. Perfect.

Listay was as dedicated to her "captain" as Chaos was to deconstructing the cosmos.

"General Listay," Chaos spoke to the BEAPER on her wrist, "come here." Her voice was impressively smooth and sultry for an ancient god waging an internal battle with her homicidal host.

Like a love-sick teenager waiting by a telephone, Listay hadn't wanted to get far from an intershoot since learning that Ix had left the ship. She appeared in the Captain's quarters with a swiftness that Chaos, an entity unburdened by a sense of time, couldn't even begin to appreciate.

"Yes, my Captain?" Listay asked. From the tone of her voice, she wasn't sure if that "come here" had been a "come here" or a "come hither".

"Ix deserted her post," said Chaos.

Straight to the point. Listay loved when the Captain was direct. She wanted very much to be direct with her captain, too.

"Yes, I'm aware. The Senior Engineer has been alerted and is prepared to take on her duties immediately." Listay glanced at those unmentionable eyes and felt that her brain had simultaneously caught fire and frozen over. She looked away, searching the floor for the smidgen of sanity she had just lost. Ah, there it was. In the crack between tile number seventy-eight and seventy-nine.

"U-unfortunately," Listay stuttered, regaining her senses. "Ix destroyed the record of your latest work-orders when she left. Was there something you had her working on, apart from maintenance of the shuttles?"

"Mmm, there certainly was," Chaos switched on her sultry drawl, and Listay's brain caught fire again, this time along with another part of her anatomy.

Chaos cupped Listay's face and rubbed the scar on her cheek with her thumb. She had gotten that scar fighting for this ship, and since Chaos had been coursing through the ship as energy at the time, Chaos liked to think she'd gotten that scar fighting for her.

She smiled like the mythical many-toothed wyrntensil staring down its prey, and Listay's cheeks flushed mauve.

"Earth is in shambles," she told Listay. "It's a wreck of a planet. If I am to do my work here, I require order. Absolute, perfect order," she whispered. "I asked Ix to design a perfectly functioning society for the humans, to unite the planet. She refused."

"Humans, Captain?" Listay asked.

"Earthlings," she corrected herself and hurriedly moved on. "I trust you will be able to improve upon the dismal progress now the traitor is gone."

"Yes, Captain. I will start immediately."

"Why rush, General?" said Chaos, trailing her hand down to Listay's shoulder. "Ix is gone. And I know you yearn for me."

"Oh," Listay said on a flustered exhale. "Was I that indiscreet?"

"I can see into your heart, General. There's something I want there."

"It is in excellent condition, Captain. The onboard cardiologist said—"

Chaos stopped her nervous rambling with a forceful kiss. Listay tried to keep her pulse at an even ten beats per bloop, but it wanted to speed. This was highly inappropriate. But it was what she had fantasized about. But it was highly inappropriate. But the Captain's tongue was doing things she didn't know tongues could do. But it was HIGHLY—

It was over. Chaos pulled away, holding Listay's broad shoulders. Smiling. "You're going to make a perfect dictator," she whispered.

Listay was lost in her eyes again. All she heard was that she was going to be perfect, and no one had ever told her she'd be perfect at anything before, so it didn't really matter what she was going to be perfect at, as long as she was perfect and continued to be for her Captain.

"Now, you are dismissed," said Chaos. She patted the General roughly on the cheek and turned away. It was a curious feature of being an ancient god, but she had such difficulty remembering that people existed if she wasn't looking at them. It was a wonder she had recalled the General's name at all.

The only people that mattered to her, the only ones that seemed to exist, even, were the few beings Yvonne still cared for: Ix, and that pesky zoup-nog Xan. But Ix was dealt with, and Xan would be soon enough.

Perhaps Chaos's life would've been easier if she'd followed the unwritten rules of the more civilized, modern gods, but she so enjoyed meddling in matters of love and devotion.

CHAPTER SEVEN

Canned Corn

"Fuck, fuck, fuck," May chanted under her breath, her eyes shut tight to keep her from seeing whatever horrible things you see when you die, waiting to run out of breath. "I'm dead."

"You're not dead, May June July."

"Well, you would say that."

"I would?"

"What are you, God or something? If you are, I've got some complaints to file."

"I-uh...no. I'm not any kind of deity, sorry. Xan of Tuhnt," said a voice fairly close to her. A hand was outstretched in her direction, awaiting the customer Earth greeting, but she couldn't see it.

She rubbed her eyes to try to clear the gray fog she appeared to be swimming in but only succeeded in getting an eyelash in her left eye that would bother her off and on for a good hour to come. "May," she said.

"I know, it's on—"

"How does everyone know my name?" she shouted.

"It's on your suit," he answered timidly.

May looked down at her suit but still couldn't see properly.

"Sorry. Okay, tell me exactly who you are, where I am, and what your intentions are with me. Please."

A hand landed on her shoulder, and she jumped.

"I'm not really anyone. You're on the *Audacity*, which is a Class 20 Tuhntian Racing Rocket. And my intentions were to keep you from asphyxiating or worse in the unforgiving vacuum of space. But now that that's taken care of, who knows? We could get ice cream." His hand dropped from her shoulder. "Once I get the ship working again," he muttered.

May blinked, shook her head, and suddenly got colors back. They came back with a vengeance. It felt like the cones had shorted out in her eyes.

A living room straight out of a 70's home magazine ad for matching jumpsuits wrapped around her orangely. For a moment she could almost believe she was back on Earth and had the sinking suspicion that the BBC was behind all this.

The enormous half-round window across from her begged to differ, though. More stars, sans twinkle.

The tall, blue alien hunched over a control panel in a raised loft to her right also begged to differ. Blue wasn't exactly the best descriptor of his skin color; it was unlike anything May had seen thus far. It was the color of the sky but with low batteries. It was the color of a blueberry milkshake with far too few blueberries in it. It was the color of an albino Smurf. And his hair was orange, but proper orange. Just orange.

She left the round metal plate she'd been standing on and waded through the thick orange shag carpet to sit on the side of an old couch which faced an even older Earth television. "So, how much time do I have?" May asked.

"I wouldn't know, I'm not an actuary." Xan hopped down from the loft, ignoring the stairs and perching on the back of the couch beside her. "You look pretty healthy, though. Pretty young. I'd guess five centuries yet!"

"What?"

"Sorry, was that rude? That was rude. I haven't had a conversation with another person in almost a century."

"No, I mean how long before you turn me in? I was trying to escape." She rubbed her forehead as if she could rub away the events of the past day.

Leaning back, the alien blinked his eyes in sequence rather than in unison. Whether this was an alien thing or something specific to him, May was unsure. She knew with certainty, however, that it was unsettling.

Xan thought for a moment, his intense stare now re-focused on a brown stain in the orange shag. "I mean...when you say 'escaped' are we talking wanted criminal escaped or is the *Peacemaker* running some sort of abduction scheme?"

"The latter, I think. Unless I've broken some sort of Space Law I didn't know about." May tried to remember the last time she paid her Space Taxes to the Space Government. If there was a Space Tax, she was behind.

"You seem mostly harmless," Xan said, cautiously. "Where are you from?"

"Earth."

"An Earthling? No kidding? That's perfect! Question: Lucille Ball is too good for Ricky, right? Lucy deserves the world! And he never lets her on his show. It's *his* show, why doesn't he let her on?! The TV signal is awful out here so I haven't—" May cut him off.

"Lucy? From the old TV show? I've never seen it," she said.

He smiled at her like he knew a sinister secret she didn't.

"Why are you smiling at me?" she asked.

"I get to watch you watch it for the first time!"

"Aren't you turning me in for a reward?"

It occurred to her, then, that this alien probably wasn't terribly smart. It further occurred to her that reminding him that there was a possible reward for her return was also not terribly smart. She shook her head, wondering how forgiving the term 'intelligent life' was.

"Er..." He looked at the viewscreen behind himself. "It's fine. It's just gem, right?"

May shrugged. "I don't know, is it?"

"Yeah, well...that was rhetorical. It's fine."

It was difficult for May to tell whether he was trying to be nice, or if he was terrified of something. The language chip in her head could not translate alien body language. The reason it was so difficult to tell one way or the other was that both were true.

May relaxed a bit regardless. "Did you see what happened to the people I was escaping with?"

"They were on the shuttle? Umm..." He squinted at the ceiling, searching for a tactful way of explaining. "They flew into a wormhole. Which means one of two equally interesting things happened. Either they've popped out somewhere incredibly far away and are well out of danger. *Or* they've been torn into obscene confetti scattered across the universe. There's just no telling with random wormholes! Part of the fun, I guess. And the horror." The cheery tone dropped from his voice. "I'm sorry I said that. Haven't talked to anyone in a long time. Were they friends of yours?" he added.

"Not exactly." May was too lost in thought to worry about them. She had the distinct feeling that she had been entirely too lucky. This was followed by the suspicion that all of the good luck allotted to her in this lifetime had been completely blown on that one rescue. A life of unluckiness, just to survive being ejected into space once. It seemed a poor trade-off.

Leaning back, Xan threw his boot-shod feet atop the rickety wooden coffee table in front of the couch.

"So, what do you want to do?" Xan pressed. "I've got a virtual reality deck that's only virtually malfunctioning—the reality part works perfectly. There's a quarantine bay with some questionable packages that we shouldn't open for another four orbits, but zuut, we can live dangerously. There's the hover-swivel chairs. Oh, or my personal favorite, all the lost rubber bands in the Universe are sucked into a wormhole that empties into the basement! You can do a lot with all the lost rubber bands in the Universe. Too much, actually, I've had to send a few back."

May leaned into the couch arm and rubbed her temples. "I'm exhausted. I don't want to do anything."

To her relief, he nodded and headed for the pneumatic tube. "Rest it is, then! You just make yourself comfortable. What do Earthlings need for sleep?"

"Do you have water in space?"

"Of course we've got water! Can't have life without water, right? I'm pretty sure that's a science thing. It sounds like something Ai—" he stopped half-way through the word, frozen, a look of existential loss on his face before starting again. "Anyway, you need it to make coffee. Anything else?"

"Food? Anything that won't kill me?" she hazarded. The llerke hadn't kept her full for long; she was starving.

"I'd wager there's something you can eat in the basement. Maybe something from Earth, even! Good old Earth food. Oh and, May," he said. Suddenly his tone shifted, and his eyes became a darker shade of green. "Don't go wandering off," he warned. "Unless you want to, then that's fine."

With a hand gesture that was almost like a finger gun but not quite, he disappeared down into a pneumatic intershoot that ran through the floor.

May closed her eyes and sunk into the couch, entertaining the thought that she had died after all, and that Satan was an off-brand Looney Tune.

She surveyed the room again, now that her eyes had adjusted to the offensive color. An ancient TV squatted in front of the couch, something else that could have been a 70's landfill find. Numerous cable adapters spilled from the back of it and on top sat rabbit ears so elongated with aluminum foil that they looked like the antennae of a beetle feeling around for scraps of TV signal.

Her eyes fell on a stack of magazines on the floor beside the couch. A pamphlet advertising something called a Space Race, a travel brochure from Taeloo XII, a moldy paperback of *The Time Machine*, loose sheets of paper covered in notes, and a user's manual with an artistic rendering of an intensely orange rocket ship on the cover. When she picked it up, the manual opened to the table of contents. Most of the nouns in the text were completely untranslatable; she could almost hear the translation chip in her head grinding and sputtering to keep up. She set it down again.

A terrible sucking sound announced Xan's reappearance in the tube. He carried an armful of cans and a mug. The plexi-glass door to the tube creaked open about an inch. He stuck the toe of his boot into the crack and coaxed it open with his elbow and shoulder.

After setting the mug down on the coffee table where it would leave a milky white circle in the wood, he dropped onto the couch and it squeaked louder than a bed at a pay-by-the-hour motel. "I found Blorsh, Glorf, forbinated Moringarg, unforbinated

Moringarg, and corn. Anything look edible?" he said, spreading the cans on the couch between them.

The corn shocked May. There was nothing inherently shocking about the canned corn itself; the label was verdant, with an image of golden kernels traipsing away from the homey look farm they were allegedly raised on and a nicely designed name-brand logo that May felt she could trust. Contextually, though, the innocuous can of corn seemed almost sinister.

Still, she was hungry.

She took the corn.

"Thank you," she said, popping the cap off the corn and, after staring at it for a moment to be sure it wouldn't jump up and spook her, tipped a few kernels into her mouth.

Corn indeed.

Xan stacked the rest of the cans on the table, presumably for her to enjoy later. "Sure! There's got to be at least twenty cans of that stuff in the basement."

"From the wormhole?"

"From the wormhole!" he confirmed. "So, tell me about Earth. What's it like? Tons of people down there, I bet. Must be fun. There aren't many people out in space. Well, there are. Everyone is in space, actually, technically. They're just fairly far away from each other. Tough to plan a decent party."

"Mm," she said. The thought occurred to her that perhaps he would take her back to Earth if she asked. Back to work. She needed to get back to work, or she'd be fired. She had a shift coming up. Or had it passed? She had probably missed her shift. She began trying to piece together an excuse that didn't involve alien abduction, but her neurons limped along, not so much firing as they were meandering.

"And the Earth clothing!" continued the alien who had draped himself casually over the back of the couch, the arm of the couch, and the coffee table. "It's so loose and baggy. What are Earthlings hiding?"

"Genitals, I guess," she said hazily. The couch was becoming comfortable, she sunk into it a little more.

"Genitals, eh? Hm." He paused to consider this, but only for a moment. "Oh, and the grammar!" He picked up one of the handwritten notes. "Absurdly complex, isn't it? I've been trying to work it out."

"For which language?"

"There's more than one?" He was excited about that. "'May June July,' that's a rather long name for an Earthling, right? I always thought there were only two individual names, the second being stolen in a vicious rite of passage."

May chuckled, closing her eyes now because keeping them open was a great deal harder than it ought to have been. "Not quite. Just call me May."

"Right, of course! May, I've got to say it's nice to have someone to—"

May was asleep.

CHAPTER EIGHT

The Robert

It's time you knew: Ix and August survived their trip through the wormhole. This is how it happened.

"August?"

"Yes?"

"Are you alive?"

"Yes?"

"Am I alive?"

"I would assume so."

"Excellent. I believe we may have entered a wormhole. Yvonne must have opened it." Ix said, feeling around the dashboard of the Gremlin. Or, at least, what was meant to be the dashboard.

The Gremlin was in poor shape. The front end had smashed into a slab of copper ore, the clock had frozen, and the engine sputtered desperate pleas for the merciful escape of death. Ix obliged, turned the key to cut the engine, and twisted around to fix August with her white stare. Her colorless eyes chilled him more than the metallic draft.

"You lost May," she said.

"I did not!" August sputtered for a moment as his brain tried to spin the situation. "She fell. There wasn't a thing I could do about it."

"You were next to her; you could have grabbed her." She paused and breathed in pointedly. "I smell copper. What can you see?"

August poked his head out of the gaping hole in the car's side. His depth perception had been a little off ever since the gloopy green alien 'doctors' took his eye. He was told they would replace it with a better one; he had insisted that he liked the one he had just fine and that he would prefer to have it back. They had laughed at him. He supposed humor was not their strong point. Removing integral bits of his anatomy, however, seemed to be.

The horizon was vast and flat. The only thing between them and the dark void of the night sky was a greening shack made entirely of copper that, due to August's poor depth perception, could have been either a few miles or a few feet away.

Fortunately, it had a sign. Unfortunately, the translation chip in his skull wasn't quite up to the task of reading it.

"Khaninagaharatchiyarta Chroosantooackagatgunst Junkers?"

"Oh, you mean…"

Ix proceeded to pronounce Khaninagaharatchiyarta Chroosantooackagatgunst correctly, but typing it out phonetically would be a hassle and you would skim over it anyway. The correct pronunciation will remain unknown until the screen adaption. In the interest of saving time, I'll abbreviate it to KC from here on out.

"Sure."

"Interesting. KC was destroyed decades ago. The wormhole must have moved us in both time and space. That is good."

"How, exactly, is that good?" August was beginning to panic. He was not on Earth. He was alone with one of the creatures that had been his captor for half a year. His arm hurt. And, worst of all, he was cold.

"If I am correct, this will afford me more time to stop Chaos. First, though, we must repair the Gremlin." She climbed from the car and motioned to August. "Come along, I will require assistance to carry parts back from the junker."

The numerous vast wastelands and deserted landfill planets in the Universe offer a particular kind of person a particular kind of living; the delightful job of cosmic recycling or "junkering." A good junker would carefully sort through mounds of garbage to recycle precious metals, easily repairable automatons, and appliances. Each piece would be tediously considered; would the price it fetched be worth the five or so seconds spent tossing it into the ship? Often the answer was no, but occasionally a junker would come across the kind of trash that could make a person rich.

By occasionally, I mean exactly twice ever. Once, it was a very small Queen who had accidentally been thrown out with some old linens. The Queen's country paid a handsome reward for her safe return. The second time, a junker stumbled across a ghost planet upon which every living being had suddenly died and left untold fortunes unclaimed. While these instances were rare, millions of otherwise intelligent beings decided to make junkering their trade, clutching the hope of wildly good fortune to their underfed chests.

The junker outpost on KC was nothing to write home about. In fact, it had never been written about in the history of the universe until now and, even then, only coincidentally. Passing travelers were often so put off that, rather than rate it a whole single star on the Universal Review, they would simply erase their memories of the place.

There were piles of doors surrounding the building, but none of them had been able to find their way to the door frame which gaped open. The pair approached the place where a door should've been, and August knocked on the frame.

"Well howdy!" A creature which couldn't be said to be humanoid, but *could* be said to be thoroughly coated in green dust, greeted them from behind a desk. "I've a fine selection of recycled bots, Fidobots, chauffeurbots, huntin' bots, and some frisky little bedroom bots if you catch my drift." The creature winked at August and, with some help from the translator chip in his head, August did in fact catch the drift. He would've been very pleased indeed to catch that particular drift. But Ix's determination to get off the copper planet triumphed over August's curiosity.

"I need to repair an Earth 1975 AMC Gremlin with a 709 Plasma Rocket Engine. Do you have 12-volt halogen headlights?"

The creature blinked. "Uh, huh...well you can look around. Anything's fair game except the register." It tapped a metal box that squatted toad-like on the edge of a desk. "Oh, hell, name a price and the register's yours!"

August eyed the bots; they were the only items in the store that were neatly arranged. Everything else was in piles on the floor that were sorted by color and not much else. He tried to call Ix over to ask a question but realized he had forgotten her name. He was sure she said it at some point...oh, it was too late now. It would be too embarrassing to ask; he'd have to wing it. Eventually she would have to introduce herself to someone else, and he'd be there to hear it.

Ix felt around the store and collected a few tubes, some wires, and a drill. "Do you accept Rhean currency?"

"Pff! Funny gal you got there," the creature addressed August. August blinked in reply; he wasn't sure that was true.

Ix sighed. Fifteen orbits ago the Rhean dollar had gone off the Crystal Standard and plummeted to a universal low. The most affluent Rhean at the time was Daag Narmiroust whose thirty-seven billion Rhean dollars could hardly buy a spool of thread outside of Rhea. Their economy had been on the upswing in the future, but her Rhean money wouldn't be of much use in the past.

After a few moments of tense silence over which only the quiet oxidation of the planet could be heard, August took charge. "I know how this works," he sagely lifted a hand to the shopkeeper and secured eye-contact. "You will accept anything we offer you as payment," he said, summoning all the Hollywood drama he could muster.

The shopkeep hesitated, entranced by August's display. As if in a dream it slowly shook its head back and forth. "No...no I don't think I will," it intoned.

August laughed nervously. "Really? Because I felt I was pretty convincing."

The creature pulled a dangerous looking object from some fold of its anatomy. "I think y'all better leave."

"Of course." Ix began to walk out the door, her haul still in hand. The shopkeep jabbed the dangerous looking object in her direction and beset August with a tense stare.

"Tell her to leave the kit where she found it, lav," it sneered.

August blubbered unintelligibly, fear and confusion warring for control of his brain.

"August, come along. We have work to do,"

“Okay, right, but...it’s got a gun!” August tried to press himself against a wall but ended up tripping on a pile of rusted metal hands.

“I understand. Ignore it.” Ix continued walking away. She was nearly out the door. August scrambled after her and ducked as he heard a blast from behind him.

“Get back here!” Another blast sounded, but nothing happened.

“Won’t it come after us?” he asked her.

“Not possible. It is a floosoon—a holographic employee. Threats are its only defense.”

“I’ll have the intergalactic police after you!” (It wouldn’t.)

“My wrath is inescapable!” (It wasn’t.)

“You’ll be sorry you ever came to—” They were out of earshot.

They walked back to the wreckage, materials and tools in hand. Ix explored the hole in the side of the car with her precise fingers. “I will make some structural improvements to the machine. Earth people sleep fairly often, correct? We will need somewhere to rest.”

“Often in relation to what?”

“In relation to Rheans, of course. I will have to feed you something, as well. What manner of nutrition do you require?” Ix asked.

August shook his head at her. “Don’t bother. I’ll find myself some place to stay on this godforsaken penny.” With that he went off, his white spandex clad feet sending up little puffs of green dust at every step. He expected at least a bit of a fight from her, but she seemed not to care one way or the other. He supposed he wasn’t exactly a prisoner now, though. He didn’t know where he was going but figured if he walked far enough something would appear.

The shack and the wreckage were out of sight now. In front of him, a small ball of reddish light began to rise, turning the sky a pale green. It was easier to see now that things were properly lit. An improvement.

Soon, however, he bemoaned the sun as it began to reflect off the copper ground and turn the planet into an oven.

Fortunately for August, the days on this planet were extremely short. Mere minutes after the sun had attained its utmost height in the sky it was behind him again, and soon it was gone entirely. This happened three or five more times: the hot, the cold, the hot, the cold...then, a discovery! Something was rising over the horizon that wasn't the small, cruel ball of heat.

August began to jog. Soon, he slowed to a speed walk, then to a normal walk, and finally a crawl.

It was the Gremlin.

He had explored the entirety of the planet in just under an hour and came back around the other side.

"Let's get out of here," he sighed and started to help Ix put the machine back together.

"I knew you would come around," Ix gave him a wry smile, but August didn't catch the play on words. She would never try to be funny around him again.

"What's 'Robert?'" He pulled out a sheet of metal from the pile. It read "Robert" in big, bold letters. The "o" and the bottom of the "b" became two eyes in a smiley face below the logo.

"Robert is a brand of wet ch'stranda food in a can," Ix replied. "But the panel is in good shape, and we can paint over it."

"No, I like it. Robert was my grandfather's name. Let's call this ship the Robert."

"But it is a Gremlin."

"That's what it is, not its name! We're calling him Robert and I'm not helping," he said defiantly.

"Did you mean to say 'We are calling him Robert *or* I am not helping'?" Ix asked as she continued to work on soldering some loose wires.

"I know what I said, and I don't need a German lesson from an alien."

"We are not speaking German, August, we are speaking Rhean."

August sighed. "Fine, you're speaking Rhean, I'm speaking German, and someone for some godforsaken reason is reading it all in English right now. I'll help if you drop the matter."

"Robert it is," Ix replied and bolted the metal siding over a gouge in the car.

CHAPTER NINE

The First Devotee

Listay smiled dreamily into her three-dimensional spreadsheet. Spreadsheets were the best part of her job, definitely. That, and, of course, the chance to vastly improve the lives of billions of individuals on Earth. Perfect efficiency, everyone aligned with a perfect purpose, all utterly sure of what would be asked of them and all utterly sure of how to live a good, healthful life.

The Manual for Life on Earth was nearly complete. It covered everything from proper use of the dental hygiene nanobots Listay would provide each Earthling with, to light maintenance of their personal food-gardens, to how to handle interpersonal conflicts in a direct, yet gentle manner.

If only she'd been given such a manual, she thought. It wouldn't have taken her four centuries to finally fulfill her true purpose: optimizing an entire planet.

She hadn't slept for a full five rotations, and she still had energy to spare. Just enough to present her plan to the Captain.

After one final check of the spreadsheet, to be sure the color coding was as pleasing to the eye as was technologically possible, she tapped her BEAPER, hailing the Captain.

The outgoing call sound was light and pleasant like a legion of soap bubbles gently bursting one-by-one. But Listay was anxious for the Captain to respond, and the time between bursts seemed to stretch out like an archer pulling back their bow.

A final burst and the call was accepted, Listay slid into the intershoot beside her desk and shipped herself off.

"Captain, I've prepared an 893-phase plan which will result in a highly efficient new societal structure for the planet Earth," Listay said, popping out of the intershoot. Her heart was beating wildly at twelve beats per bloop as she steadied her focus on the painting of an anthropomorphized puntl having tea with a round-cheeked larvling Rhean. She'd never seen that painting before. It was odd, but it had worked to calm her nonetheless. Ten beats per bloop. Perfect.

"Captain?" Listay asked, realizing now as she stepped deeper into the dimly lit office, that what she had thought was her captain was nothing more than a smooth, hovering silver ovoid with hair.

Listay reached out to touch it, but a cold chill gripped the room and in an instant, Chaos was standing where the ovoid had been, smelling strongly of synthetic fruits.

With a blink of her unmentionable eyes, Listay forgot the ovoid. Forgot that anything unusual had happened, at all.

"Captain, I have prepared—"

"Yes, I heard you. Go on."

General Listay nodded, summoning a visual to accompany her presentation. "We proceed with the utmost respect for Earth's cultures, art, and its history up until now. Phase one consists entirely of building a relationship with Earth's leaders."

"Skip that," Chaos said.

Listay paused to measure her next words. "With respect, Captain, phase one is the most crucial—"

"Skip it!" Chaos shouted.

General Listay did not flinch, but she did lower her wrist an eighth of a centimeter, and this was enough for Chaos to realize she was again dangling from the delicate line of mortal feelings. Being at the mercy of such weak creatures was growing tiresome, but, she reminded herself, she was a patient god. Just not that patient.

"General," she breathed, slipping back into her role. "You are in command here. The weapons on this ship can obliterate half the planet in half an instant. You have at your disposal the technology to scrape that planet clean and rebuild it within a few seasons. You are at the mercy of no one," Chaos said, a passionate jealousy tingeing her voice.

"A sudden change in leadership will not be well received," Listay said. "The rate of resistance will rise exponentially."

Chaos turned around, that had brought an involuntary smile to her lips. Resistance was exactly what she needed.

“I’m certain you will be able to handle this, General. You are my most important devotee,” Chaos said. “And your rewards will be great.” Chaos unzipped the top of her suit, squeezing her arms together so that she could really see Yvonne’s ample bosom. She hadn’t had a bosom for several thousand orbits and, even when she did, she’d never enjoyed tits quite this squishable. She admired them herself for a minute, she would miss them when she eventually disintegrated this body and her essence expanded to touch every molecule of existence.

No, she told herself. Being the Universe would be far better than having boobs. If she were the Universe, she would have all the boobs. She would be nothing BUT boobs for a while, perhaps. Yes... a boobiverse.

“Would you like to hear the rest, Captain?” Listay asked, drawing Chaos’s attention back to the present, tiny little reality.

Chaos turned around, squishing her boobs out at Listay. “No. You will cut out all the humanitarian fluff and start getting that unruly planet under your command immediately.

“Squeeze their very souls from their bodies and then fine them for not applying for a soul-release license. Do you understand, General?”

“Y-yes, Captain.” Listay tried to look Chaos in the eyes. Those unmentionable, unblinking eyes. It actually seemed safer to look at her chest, and so Listay did just that.

“One more thing, General. I want you to do this without losing a single human life. Especially the dissenters. Keep them chained to a wall if you must, but keep them alive and close at hand.”

“Of course I will minimize loss of life, Captain,” said Listay. “However, I think a rehabilitation program might be more suitable—”

“I am entrusting you with a righteous duty. To be an agent of ultimate reason and order. Do as you are commanded.”

“Anything for you, my Captain,” said Listay, a feeling of utter devotion welling up in her that she couldn’t explain. Her mind was empty, her heart drunk on Chaos’s words. She’d always wanted to be an agent of reason and order. It sounded like a highly reasonable and orderly thing to be.

Chaos dipped lower, aligning her lips with Listay's, teasing. This, thought Listay, was well and truly it. This was going to happen. She fluttered her eyes closed, tilted her chin out, waited for her Captain to finally close the painful distance.

"Get to it, then," Chaos breathed onto Listay's lips.

Bit by bit, as if she were re-dressing, Listay opened her eyes, closed her lips, rescinded her upturned face, and squared her shoulders. The Captain was serious, her face blank, her eyes unmentionably unemotional.

"Yes, Captain," whispered Listay. She gave a small, respectful bow and entered the intershoot to her office.

CHAPTER TEN

Cigarette

It's never pleasant to be caught between the world of dreams and the world of reality. It's even less pleasant when you're in an unfamiliar location on a strange, lumpy couch, in a pile of worn blankets, with white latex sinking so deeply into your ass it could perform a colonoscopy. And still less pleasant when someone immediately wants your attention.

"Good morning starshine!" May heard distantly. But as she opened her eyes, she realized the source wasn't distant at all, it was her own awareness of reality that was far away. Xan had been waiting up, nervously watching her sleep for nearly twelve hours.

"Uhh?" May squinted into the overwhelming orangeness.

"It's from a song! An Earth-song. It comes through on radio waves sometimes. I thought you might want to hear something familiar. Comforting!"

"Uh-huh..." The first neuron of the morning was a lively one. It fired right into the part of May's brain that processed stress.

"Work!" May shouted, sitting so quickly her consciousness almost didn't keep up. She was late, she was in space, and she didn't know where her uniform had gotten off to.

Xan had been seated on the carpet beside the couch, but now he was standing, the word "work" had made him anxious. "What about work?" he asked.

"Could you take me back to Earth, please? I might still have a job if I hurry."

"Oh." He deflated slightly, just slightly. "Sure! Where on Earth?"

"The Sonic on the corner of State street and MLK Jr. Know how to get there?"

Xan panicked. "Of course I know!" He did not know.

"Please take me. I'm going to try to clean up. Do you have a mirror?"

"Uh, um..." Xan shuffled through a pile of books and magazines at the base of the stairs until he found something shiny. "This came off the *Audacity* a while back." He tossed her the round plate of metal, then leapt up the stairs to the control panel. He began pressing a few buttons, flicking a couple switches, considering a few read-outs, and toggling a toggle.

May attempted to fluff her matted hair with her fingers. Would she be hours late? Days late? Would she arrive back just a few minutes after she left? How did time work in space, anyway?

This is a much-contested point. Most of the discovered universe has agreed to a standardized time format based on the planetary movements of Estrichi. Estrichi, being a planet used exclusively for time measurement, is a hotbed of time-centric tourism and produces the universe's finest hourglasses, which measure a beoop instead of an hour.

Time, therefore, worked exactly the same in space. Give or take a few blips.

"Minor problem," Xan called to her. "Ship's stuck."

That sounded like a major problem to May. She joined the alien at the control panel, ready to suggest unhelpful things in a helpful voice. She glanced over the field of doodads, looking for a toggle, perhaps, labeled "Stuck" on one end and "Unstuck" on the other.

Nothing to that effect jumped out at her.

"Have you tried the parking brake?" she offered in a haphazard sort of way. Her Civic had an over-active parking brake. It had become something of an inside joke with herself. She didn't really have inside jokes with anyone else.

"Oh, uhm—heh." Xan covered his embarrassment with a guilty laugh and kicked a lever on the floor. "That was it! Imagine!"

Relieved to have her engines freed, the *Audacity* shot off toward the blue/green marble of Earth.

Relatively speaking, they weren't terribly far. They were a great deal farther away than it is from New York City to Istanbul, and a bit farther than it is from anywhere in Montana to civilization. But relative to the size of the Universe, the entirety of everything that ever was and ever has been, they really were just around the corner.

The ship parked, wobbling a bit, in the Sonic parking lot. “We’re here! Stand on the teledisc and I’ll send you down.” He motioned to the circular, metal depression in the shag which she had been standing on when she first arrived. She hesitated before stepping onto the metal.

A teledisc is designed to rip someone atom-from-atom at point A and reassemble them at point B. Is the teledisc practical? Extremely. Safe? A gaggle of lawsuits would claim otherwise. Enjoyable? No. Not even a bit.

May tried to get her bearings and failed miserably. Her head swam, her bones vibrated, and her skin undulated. Her surroundings were wholly off as well. She saw pieces of landmarks she recognized, like a half-finished jigsaw puzzle, as if the city had glitched out the moment she was gone. She recognized the Sonic sign and a low billboard across the street, but as far as she could see everything else was rubble. It was silent, and still, and far too bright. Her feet carried her forward because they felt obligated to.

Xan had never been on Earth before; it was far too dangerous for extraterrestrial life on Earth. He had heard the horror stories whispered in hushed tones in nearby galaxies. Unattainable beauty standards, golden waves of deadly grain, and something called mosquitos awaited him on Earth.

But, in the hullabaloo, he had forgotten his trepidation and landed on the planet whose media he had admired from a distance for so long. Visions of old west shootouts, mansions owned by hillbillies, and luxurious boats upon which every single passenger found a life-mate tempted him. He stepped on the teledisc, took an altogether unnecessary breath, and rearranged his atoms on Earth for the first time.

“It’s—” It was grisly, it was gruesome, it was really very much not good. “It’s lovely!” he said. “I can see why you’d want to get back here in such a hurry.”

May stood with her back to him, studying a pile of bricks. Xan joined her.

“Is this your work?” he pointed to the pile. “Well done. That is one immaculate pile. You must be so proud.” His smile was so tight it was a wonder it didn’t crack.

“Everything’s gone. How long was I in space?”

“About the same length you are now, give or take a bit on account of microgravity.”

“I—wha—” May, finding nothing which inspired her to keep standing, knelt down. She stared ahead at nothing. There used to be something there. She couldn’t remember what, but there should’ve been something.

“What about my apartment? My car?!” May asked. “Do you think it’s still there?”

“Eh…” He didn’t want to say no, so he said nothing.

“I have to go.” She hefted herself up, brushed off her dusty knees, and began a familiar walk that was now *hauntingly* familiar.

“It might be dangerous,” Xan said, following her.

“I don’t care. I need to go home. Don’t follow me,” she said over her shoulder.

His desire to not go any farther on this cursed Earth made that easy, but his competing desire to make sure she was safe made it difficult.

“Okay…” he said, quietly, leaning against one of the *Audacity*’s fins for comfort, determined to keep an eye on her until she was out of sight, at least.

May expected to hear the *Audacity* sputter away, leaving her to explore her personal apocalypse. It did not. She walked a little farther down State Street, trying to focus on visually sorting out the ruins around her. Still, she did not hear the ship take off. Peering back over her shoulder, she watched Xan kick idly at an empty Sonic cup.

He wasn’t leaving. But he wasn’t following her either. Eventually he’d get bored and go, she figured.

A pile of rubbish looked like the old pharmacy. It had been closed and rotting away for years, decades perhaps. Seeing the inside walls, in the dark for so long, now lit by an uncaring sun was somehow garish. She turned left around it; her apartment and her car would still be a few blocks away.

It was not, though. There was nothing but fields of rubble ahead. A little heartbroken sound escaped her before she could stop it. Her Civic. She turned around, studying the street around her, making absolutely certain she was looking in the right direction.

A speck in the distance hurried toward her, a speck she knew.

"Kathy!" she shouted at her manager.

A faint yell came from Kathy, but May couldn't quite hear her yet.

"What?"

"Uuunn!" Kathy shouted again, almost tripping as she sprinted toward her.

"May, run! Run the other way!" Kathy gasped at her, out of breath, waving her arms like an inflatable tube man. She was being followed by a hovering sphere which produced a beam of yellow light. The sphere caught up with her, the light enveloped her, and she was gone.

The sphere turned its yellow eye on May. She searched for the bright hull of the *Audacity* between the broken buildings, grateful now that Xan had stayed. Behind her, the beeping of the sphere grew louder, but before her, Xan leaned against the *Audacity's* silver fin.

"Beam us up!"

"Can't! It's a teledisc not a transporter. Also, you need an anchor," he shouted, pointing to the top button of his suit. To her surprise, he started to run toward her and the deadly metal sphere which pursued her.

"Do not be afraid," the sphere told her. "This area has been scheduled for re-construction. You will be transferred to a safe habitat. We apologize for the inconvenience and hope you find your new life acceptable." A yellow puddle of light glowed beneath her feet. She closed her eyes and launched herself forward with a burst of adrenaline. It felt like she had been smacked by a bag of bricks and torn into a million pieces simultaneously.

When the sensation settled, she hazarded a glance around. She was holding onto something. She peeled her face away from the plasticky material it had been smashed against and gasped in relief. They were back on the *Audacity*. The plasticky bag of bricks had been Xan.

He jumped up to the console, pressed the Button That Typically Made The Ship Go, and let the ship decide where to take them. Then he turned to May who stood motionless on the teledisc.

"You need an anchor button to use the ship's teledisc," he explained, tapping the top button on his suit again. "Otherwise anyone could get in!"

May stared.

Xan tried to get her attention with a weak wave. "Hey, mun, are you okay?"

May shook her head.

Unsure of what to do, Xan watched her. He hadn't seen her blink in a while and worried her eyes might dry up. "Are you, uh, are you with me? Blink if you're with me."

She stared.

"May, I hate to bring this up, but you're the main character; this novel's not going to get very far if you just stand there staring."

Fourth wall breakage made May extremely uncomfortable; she blinked out of her stunned trance and walked, slowly, as if she were moving through mud, to the couch where she collapsed like a tower of Jenga blocks.

"My car was down there," she whispered. "My apartment...my cactus..." she said. She tried to think about the people she was concerned about back on Earth. "My mother," she said, but she hadn't seen her mother in three years anyway. Missing her felt absurdly hollow now.

Xan perched on the arm of the couch, watching her carefully. "Is...there someone you want to try to find?"

May shook her head. "Do you have tobacco products in space?" she asked Xan wearily.

"Tobacco? What in Blitheon's name do you need that for? You aren't...you're not trying to kill yourself, are you?"

"It's not going to kill me," she said. "Anytime soon, at least," she amended.

"Look, I know you're upset, but don't do anything you'll regret. Maybe you just need sleep. Earthlings sleep a lot, right?"

"I need a cigarette," she whined.

"Oh, a *cigarette*, those are made with tobacco on Earth?" he laughed. "How unusual. And you're sure it's safe?"

"Not...safe exactly. It won't kill me, though."

Xan sighed. "Alright, come on." He went to the intershoot. "If there are any Earth cigarettes on board, they'll be in the basement. All sorts of things have ended up there. Videos, magazines, single socks. Never pairs," he mused. "Never pairs...they must get so lonely."

May squished into the intershoot beside him. The door closed, though rather than the futuristic "whoosh" the doors in the *Peacemaker* made, this door made a "cruuunk".

The tube dropped them to a lower level of the ship where it was freezing, black, and suspiciously noisy. A sucking sound came from one dark corner, a tender cooing sound from another, and the distinct chirp of cicadas echoed from somewhere above.

Xan loudly tripped over a few things before finding a ball chain that hung from the ceiling, clicking on a dingy yellow light bulb that illuminated about five feet around them. In that five feet alone, May saw a rubber duck, something that looked like an alien sex toy, a taxidermy jackalope, a birthday card written in a language so ancient it did not translate, a sprinkle of dried macaroni bits, and an enormous scarf. There might have been a pack of cigarettes in that mess, but she was sure they'd never locate it.

Xan crawled around a pile of garbage and knelt down, speaking to something May couldn't see.

"Hey there buddy. Fetch some cigarettes for my friend?" he said. A small square robot burst through the pile of garbage and puttered off into the darkness. Xan stood and stretched, sorting through a small pile with his foot as he waited.

"What was that?" May asked.

Xan jumped slightly as she approached. He had been alone for so long, he kept forgetting that he had someone to talk to, now. "Oh! That's a Fidobot! It came with the ship. Just goes and gets things, you know? Anything you want. Well, not anything. Only things that are there, of course. It can't manifest something out of nothing. Not this model, anyway," he said.

Moments later the square robot returned with a box clutched between its metal teeth. The brand was unidentifiable, the packaging faded. Better than nothing, May thought. Refusing to touch the little white box, Xan shooed the bot toward May. It reluctantly spun around and offered May the box.

"Can you find a lighter?" she asked. The bot seemed to have already anticipated her request and produced a pocket lighter for her. She smiled, patting it on what she assumed was its head.

"Alrighty then, let's get out of here," Xan said. The cooing was steadily growing louder. "I've no clue what's making that sound, and I'm not keen to find out."

With a nod of agreement, May jammed herself back into the tube. Upon their return to the living room, May reclined on the couch and carefully pried a stick from the box. Time had stuck the papers together, but the smell was unmistakable.

She savored the ritual of taking the cylinder between her lips, convincing the rusted pocket lighter to take a flame, gently breathing the flame into the herbs, and watching the embers devour the tip as she filled herself with smoke.

May took a slow drag, lost in her ecstasy. "Much better."

Behind her, doubled over the back of the couch, Xan heaved a dramatic cough. "By the thumbs of O'Zeno, you *breathe* that stuff?" he wheezed.

"Are you okay?"

"I'm fine," he assured her. Sudden concentration contorted his face. "But I think I've forgotten my sister's ex-girlfriend's brother's name." He looked around, searching for it in the smoky air. "Yep, it's gone alright."

"You have a sister?"

"What? No," he laughed hoarsely, "'course not, don't be silly. Who has a sister? Strange question to ask."

"So you're allergic to tobacco, huh?"

He blinked quickly, the whites of his eyes began to go blue. "Allergic? No, no...no. Maybe. What does that mean?"

"Like, you can't be around it."

"'Can't' is a strong word. It's just toxic, is all. Makes it difficult to breathe. Eyes...losing focus." He coughed again.

She tapped the end of the cigarette out on the metal side of the lighter, stuffed it back into the package and put both on the table in front of the couch. "Guess now's a good time to quit."

"Oh, well a little," he coughed again, pushing a puff of gray smoke from his lungs, "poison never killed anyone."

"I need to get it out of my system." She flopped onto the couch and rubbed her head.

"I know what'll cheer you up. Movies!"

He leapt to the control panel of the *Audacity* and set a series of coordinates he had well memorized.

CHAPTER ELEVEN

The Thing From Planet Earth

The movie drive-in was attached to a failed spaceport which orbited Lesser Greater Titania. Engaging water-colored plans of what the spaceport should've looked like, all glittering rows of retail, moodily lit restaurants, and top-of-the-line sanitation chambers, still hung, dusty and askew, from the main lobby walls.

The location, however, had been a bust. The occasional private ship would settle there to fuel up, but quickly be on its way once its occupants saw the sorry state of the station. The movie theater accounted for the spaceport's only source of income.

A white sheet (ripped in places by space detritus and held aloft by four buoys), a lop-sided parking platform, and a haunted film projector constituted the drive-in theater.

How, you might ask, could a film projector be haunted? And by what?

Excellent questions, but the answers are far beyond the scope of this narrative. The effect of this haunting, though, was that invariably, right at the climax of whatever movie was playing, the projector would stop and spend two minutes fast-forwarding through the entirety of *It Happened One Night* in complete silence.

Depending on your outlook, this was either an annoying glitch or a free bonus movie.

Xan always enjoyed free bonus things.

The *Audacity* landed on the parking platform, and Xan tossed a few compressed crystal coins onto the teledisc where they fizzled away into the grateful spaceport's coffers.

May remained sprawled across the couch, her eyes glazed over like a duo of doughnut holes. Sighing, Xan climbed down from the control panel and into the living room to crouch beside her.

"Hey, mun. Do you want to watch a movie? Always cheers me up. Can't be sad watching a movie!"

"What if it's a sad movie?" asked May.

"Well, I mean, yes...yeah you can be sad I guess but not about your own life circumstances. Sometimes it's refreshing to be sad about something that isn't the thing you're used to being sad about!"

She shrugged. "Okay."

"You'll like it," he said, and scooped her up to no protest.

From the porthole by the table, they had a perfect view of the screen, and he propped her up in a hover-chair. Her eyes locked onto the screen convincingly, but her mind still replayed the broken buildings, the scorched ground, and Kathy vanishing under the yellow beam. It was more than the intrigue of an alien movie could break through—even a movie as enrapturing as *The Thing from Planet Earth.*

Xan, of course, knew it was a wildly inaccurate portrayal of Earthlings, but he couldn't help glancing at May during the scene where the Earth creature mauled the main character's sister.

"You wouldn't happen to have a taste for flesh or anything would you, May? 'Cause if you do tell me now. I won't be mad, I promise. I just want to know. Just want to be prepared."

May shrugged, half listening. "Prepared? You gonna marinate yourself?"

"Uhh..."

"I'm not going to eat you. I don't eat blue foods."

"Oh...that's...that's good," said Xan.

It was fortunate that a Tuhntian didn't need much sleep. He wasn't sure he wanted to close his eyes around her for too long.

After hours of needless violence peppered with Xan's small horrified and disgusted noises, the sound cut out, everything went black-and-white, and *It Happened One Night* sped across the screen like a cheetah on coke.

"Ah now, see, *this* is my favorite part! This movie's classy, right? It looks classy. No idea what it's about, but there's no blood and gore from what I can tell, so that's zing up to caliber. And—and this is the really amazing part—this movie's free! I mean, I paid for the other one, but this one's a bonus. Free things are a great deal more enjoyable," he mused as he watched Clark Gable zoom about.

"Why did you wait for me?" May asked quietly.

"Hmm?" Xan was entranced by Claudette's taxi hailing.

"Why didn't you leave me on Earth?" she clarified.

Clearly, May wasn't as invested in the free movie. Clearly, she was ready to converse. Why, thought Xan, did she have to wait until the best part? He tore his eyes away from the screen to give her his full attention. "You came running at me asking to be 'beamed up'. So I did."

"But you stayed and waited. You could've left. Why didn't you?"

He thought for a moment. "I wanted to make sure you'd be okay. You didn't look okay, so I stayed."

"What am I going to do?" she mumbled into her arms.

He leaned back dangerously far in the hover chair. "Well, you don't have to *do* anything, you can just kinda...be, you know? I've just been being lately, and it's worked out alright for me. Not spectacular or anything, but I'm alright. You're alright."

"I've got nothing left." She looked around for something—anything familiar or comforting. Not even her clothes had made it out of the *Peacemaker*. She was wrapped in alien plastic wrap.

Her exhale was as erratic as a shake-weight in an earthquake and a small battalion of tears were lined up and ready to roll-out.

"Oh, hey, mun, un-pin it..." Xan looked around too, as if he could help her find whatever she had lost. Failing, he held out a gloved hand. "Here, hold my hand. It's an old Tuhntian tradition but—"

She grasped his hand tightly; having something solid to hold onto helped her re-orient herself.

"Distract me," she said.

"Right! Of course! Okay, how about a joke, then? What do you get when you cross a yuzka with a glotchbur?"

"I don't know, what?"

"Heh, I was hoping you would know. Um...tell me about Earth—what do you do for fun? How's the climate?"

"Not that."

"Yeah, naturally you wouldn't want to talk about that, sorry. Distraction...distraction..." He was shocked to find that when she needed him to talk, nothing seemed important enough to say.

On screen, the walls of Jericho between Claudette and Clark fell, and the horror flick started up again; a terrified alien scream wrenched their attention back to the film.

"That's distracting, right?" He pointed to the screen where a rabid, naked Earthling absconded with a limp green arm between its teeth. May had to admit that it was, and she watched the absurd scene with rapt attention now.

"Hey...if you do decide you want to eat me," Xan said as the credits began to roll "just, give me fair warning, alright? Maybe we can work something out. I'd be willing to part with a chunk of thigh, for example...just leave my face alone. I really need that for work."

May turned to look at him now and her hazy vision seemed to truly clear for the first time since the cigarette. The corner of her lip twitched up. "The face is the best part, though."

A fleeting fear rushed across his features, but something in her sly grin told him to play along. He swallowed. "I've always been partial to the inner elbow."

The tension reached a fever-pitch as they sized each other up. And then May laughed. Not a lot, just a satisfied, quiet chortle, but she laughed. Xan laughed, too, first nervously, then out of relief when he realized she really and truly wasn't going to eat him. Her teeth weren't nearly sharp enough for that.

"What now?" May asked, since the movie had ended.

"Well, Taeloo XII has the best ice cream and the worst novelty sunglasses in the known universe, Truglian IX is fun, if a little risqué—"

"How about that?" May said, sitting stark upright, pointing out at the screen, her gaze intense.

An ad for the 789th Vagran Rocket Race Derby flickered on the screen.

"Rocket racing?" Xan asked.

"Racing..." May whispered. "Can we go?"

Xan's teeth clenched with an unspoken objection, but he swallowed it down. "Yeah! Yeah of course we can. I'll just uh...set the autopilot and grab some fancy hats!"

"Fancy hats?"

"Can't view a rocket race derby without fancy hats! I always hoped I'd die looking stylish, anyway." Xan launched himself toward the intershoot before May could question him, but he paused at the entrance. "Really, though, you're not going to eat me, right?"

"No."

Xan smiled brightly. "Oh, good! Alright, well, if I do happen to die, you have permission to eat me then."

"I do not need that...but thank you."

CHAPTER TWELVE

Fancy Hats

The *Audacity* still loitered in the movie parking lot, despite loud warnings to shove off after the film had ended. May hoped no one cared enough to actually make them leave, because she certainly couldn't do anything about it.

Moments later, Xan reappeared balancing seven or eight intricate conglomerations of feathers and lace on his arms. Atop his head now perched a spectacularly crafted black leather tricorn hat resplendent with fluffy white feathers and brocade trim.

He dropped the pile of gaudy hats, then picked the first one off the pile.

"This one's excellent, a proper old-fashioned A'Viltrian statement hat." He plopped the white-feathered thing on her head. Its large, asymmetrical brim dipped down below her eyes.

"What's this for?"

"Tradition! Do you like it?"

"I suppose." She wiggled it around on her head until she could see again.

"Terrific! Alright, hang on." He reached for a button on the control panel and typed something into the autopilot. The rocket shuttered and spun, tossing them to the floor. May laughed as she was thrown from her seat onto the soft shag carpet, the mass of feathers and lace toppling into her.

She crawled back into her chair and reconfigured the hat as the ship evened out its course.

"So why the sudden interest? Why rocket racing?" he asked, re-applying his own magnificent hat.

May purposefully looked at the floor. "My dad used to race, before I was born. He'd take me down to the track a lot, though, when I was old enough."

"You must miss him," Xan prompted.

"He's been gone a long time."

"Still...you don't stop missing people you love."

"Mmm," said May, trying to end the conversation.

Xan flicked at a feather tickling his nose and kicked his feet onto the console.

The hover chair tilted back dangerously under him, but May supposed it couldn't tip over seeing as it had no legs. Xan also had supposed that. They were both wrong.

The unbalanced chair spun out from underneath him, depositing him on the floor. After a moment's confusion, he shrugged. "Safer down here anyway." He made himself at home on the carpet.

May watched the vague reflection of herself wearing the ungainly hat in the star-speckled viewscreen. She watched her hand move up to the hat, stroke a feather, and return to her lap. She was in space, in a rocket ship, wearing a feathered hat. The thought that this was impossible and the thought that she was currently doing it sat on either side of her brain and stared awkwardly at each other.

She turned her attention, instead, to staring awkwardly at her host. He was counting out crystals in his palm. Paying for her, again.

"What do I owe you?" she asked. "For the movie and the uh...hat. And the rocket derby."

He looked up at her, confused, slowly putting the crystals away. "It's just gem, I don't expect you to pay me back for anything."

"I want to," May said. She affirmed, to herself, that she was no freeloader. She wouldn't take handouts. She worked hard for everything she had, and she was proud of that.

"Really, please, you don't need to pay me. I want to do these things," he insisted.

May squinted at him. "Alright, what's your angle?"

"Uh..." Xan looked down at himself, cross-legged on the floor, "forty-five, maybe fifty degrees?"

"I mean why are you doing this? Why are you keeping me around? You've got to want something."

"Have I?" he asked.

"Well…yes. Everyone wants something."

"What do you want?"

"I want to work."

"You do?"

May shook her head. "I want money."

"Ah," said Xan. He thought for a moment, and May stiffened, preparing for him to say anything from a glass of water to harvesting her organs to sell on the alien black market. She bet Earthling organs were hard to come by. He could probably make a lot of money off her. *Oh god*, she thought. *He's going to harvest me, fuck,* she thought. She began looking around the room for suitable weapons and the feather from her hat fell in her face. Maybe he was ticklish. That might hold him off.

"I haven't thought about it much lately," he said finally. "I guess I want what Lucy has."

"Which is…?"

"A live studio audience."

May sighed and laughed at the same time, relieved.

The view outside the ship changed abruptly. A rainbow of lights beeped past in a steady even stream, like streetlights. The rocket slowed and she could see what they were passing more clearly: silvery buildings the tops of which stretched into the clouds and the bottoms of which disappeared into a thick fog, compact hover cars with bulbous windows and decorative fins, bridges stretching between the buildings over which tall and well-dressed creatures scurried.

"Alright, nearly there!" Xan bounced up, leaning over the console eagerly. "This is the biggest transportation hub on Vagran. You've got to park on the planet and take the shuttle to the stadium. Don't know why you can't just park at the stadium. Takes a lot of extra fuel to re-launch if you park on a planet, though, so it probably benefits near-by fuelports."

The autopilot brought them to a docking field, righted the ship, and parked it with an unsteady wobble. This maneuver and the accompanying shift in the ship's center of artificial gravity would have made May's head spin if it wasn't spinning already from culture shock.

"Alright, we're here!" Xan tapped a device wrapped around his wrist with his nose and ran to the teledisc.

"What's that?" May asked as she joined him on the platform.

"This?" He unclipped the wristband and handed it to her.

"It's a BEAPER. I think it stands for Bronda's Electric Accessory, Phone, and Entertainment Resource. The acronym may be lost in translation." He laughed lightly, scratching behind his ear where his translation chip was implanted, regretting the thing for the millionth time.

May studied the woven, metal cuff. A smattering of buttons sat flush at the top beneath a strip of light. To demonstrate, Xan pressed one of the buttons and a holographic image popped up like toast from a toaster.

"Teleport?" it asked in bold blue letters which illuminated the air. More settings and information crowded in small letters below it, but Xan ignored these and swiped the letters upward, atomizing the word.

May had a brief, unpleasant sensation of being far less corporeal than she generally liked to be, and then her surroundings changed.

Eyes wide, mouth agape, May returned the BEAPER to Xan; there were more interesting things to observe now. They were in a metal tube which May thought looked a great deal like a subway.

May had never been on a subway and this thing looked nothing like your average Earth subway, in actuality, except in that it was filled with a diverse array of creatures, all wearing absurd hats.

A pink slime snored on the ceiling, dripping steadily onto the round felt hats worn by three pig-faced humanoids reading holographic newspapers.

"Please don't stare at them," said Xan to May. "They don't like it. These Ladies, however, *want* to be looked at." He waved to three of the most stunning creatures May had ever seen, their hair glistening with starlight, their clothing multi-layered and structural, their skin a velvety dark burgundy and their faces set with several large, doe-like black eyes. More eyes than any one face should rightfully play host to. Their hats were the best of the bunch, like delicately carved fountains resplendent with tiny birds and fish.

"Why?" May whispered.

"Those are Ladies training to be Queens. Or, and this is more likely, they'll end up murdering each other in order to replace their Queen. Might even murder their Queen, too. It's a nasty business, royalty. I once saw one Lady rip another's throat out with their teeth on an elevator. Made for an awkward ride. Tough to have a casual conversation about the weather with someone who's picking throat out of their teeth with a toothpick. Wink at them, they like that." He winked, and the Ladies giggled politely in reply.

"Queens of what?"

Xan shrugged. "Hard to tell, maybe Titania. Could be from Estrichi, but they don't look like the punctual type." He laughed at his own joke; May did not. "Because—the time thing. Estrichi is...you know what? Doesn't matter. We're here!"

The tube screeched to a halt, and the slime that clung to the ceiling slid sickeningly to the floor. "Pardon," it squelched as it oozed out past them and slipped through the seal in the doors, which flung open a moment later to reveal an enormous complex awash with life.

May hurried out in front of Xan, slipping on the trail of slime that the pink thing had left. She caught herself on the edge of the subway door. Xan offered her a steadying arm, but she didn't take it, preferring instead to wipe the slime from her feet on the door jamb and step around the puddle.

"Non-slip boots." Xan contorted to show May the textured bottom of one of his heavy, black boots. "Immensely practical. Fashionable, too. Important. We can get you some!"

"I'm more concerned about changing out of this." She picked a thin swatch of latex from her ripped white suit, worried that she would be stuck with it forever.

"Zuut! I was so excited about the hats, I forgot you needed something to wear, too. After this, I'll go back to work and conjure up a qal more crystal, then we can get you a new suit. Or anything, really. Anything you want!"

"I don't want or need anything from you," she said. "I'll get a job."

He didn't reply, and this was unusual, so May felt she needed to defend herself.

"There must be someone hiring in all this!" she gestured around her at the many shops and restaurants.

"I like your gumption, May! But I don't think you'll be able to find work as an Earthling."

"What's wrong with Earthlings?"

"Oh, nothing! Nothing, really. Most people just have never met one. I mean, zuut, there are rumors, of course. Nasty rumors—untrue, of course. I assume, at least. You saw the film. Earthlings are a largely untrusted species."

"You don't believe the rumors, do you?"

"Psh!" He laughed, swatting at the air. "Naw, of course not! But I've been watching Earth TV for decades now, I know more about Earthlings than anyone way out here. Though I had rather assumed you all came in shades of gray, so the brown's a bit of a surprise."

"Listen." She stopped, standing in front of him so he wouldn't walk ahead of her. "I'm not a freeloader and I *will* find a job. I always have."

"Okay, okay, I believe you." He put his hands up defensively.

Releasing him, she nodded and turned her attention back to the rows of shops in the derby complex, all of which looked like potential employers to her.

It struck her as vaguely depressing that even lost in space only two things seemed to be necessary for life: money and lots of money.

They moved through the dark and crowded terminals of the stadium with relative ease, weaving through throngs who stood staring at the giant screens or yelling something into their wrist.

At last, there was a break in the crowd and a dappling of light where the store fronts gave way to a brightly lit arena.

She took a deep breath and immediately regretted it as the foul stench of something not entirely unlike hotdog water offended the back of her throat.

The noise, the colors, the *smells* threatened to overwhelm her senses. And it was good. If her senses were overwhelmed with the here-and-now, she couldn't think about her uncertain future or her unhappy past.

They found a seat sandwiched between a twiggish and jittery person on May's side, and someone who not only had the bearing of a statue, but also appeared to actually be carved from marble on Xan's. May was vaguely aware of him trying to befriend the person next to him, and vaguely aware of him failing miserably.

The crowd hushed, the lights dimmed, and the smells graciously receded.

A floating image of star-studded blackness formed in the center of the arena, blocking May's view of the crowd opposite them.

Xan shimmied in his seat, the person beside him giving him a deliberate sidelong glance. "I hope you like this!" he whispered to May.

An eerie metal face appeared on a screen overlay at the upper left corner of the everything-ness, and May felt the whisper of a round of applause. "Welcome to the 789th Orbital Vagran Space Races." The metal face moved almost too well, more lifelike than life itself, its voice as nebulous as the remnants of an exploded star.

Beside the face, another in-set screen emerged to display footage of a needley silver rocket. The camera panned up its length as if it were a scantily clad lady in an erotic film, its swooping fins were four shapely legs, its sensually curved hull scintillated with points of light, its sleek nose pointed snobbishly upward.

Three more equally gorgeous rockets were featured in the same way.

May realized her mouth was open. She'd never really understood the concept of love at first sight, as other humans were fairly unappealing to her, but seeing those stunning rockets triggered something in her that felt like love. Or maybe lust.

She sat forward on her seat and watched as the in-sets melted away and four color-coded digital markers appeared to the left of the screen, pointing out the locations of the ships which were far too small to be seen from this distance.

A buzzer sounded and the ships flung away from their starting positions, the camera switching to a pilot's eye view of the race, stars streaking by, obstacles being deftly dodged, another rocket neck-in-neck, pulling forward, edging closer.

The screen cut to an overview of the full track, the ships locations marked with digital markers.

Music floated into May's head, seemingly with no point of origin; it bloomed from the center of her being. A robotic voice announced each light-year marker the rockets passed. The music reached a crescendo as if something were about to happen, then the screen dimmed.

Xan nudged her shoulder and pointed up just in time for her to catch the flash of the massive ships seething past the stadium overhead. A cloud of glitter confetti exploded above the audience, the music trailed off into nothingness, and then it was over. All that fanfare for about ninety seconds of entertainment.

The silver rocket appeared once more on the screen, now docked on a patch of thick blue grass somewhere beyond the stadium, its sharp fins sunk deep into the soil. The camera zoomed in on three figures beside it and the audience cheered the winners with a roar of enthusiasm.

"And there you have it!" Xan said. "More an excuse to wear a massive hat, than entertainment, but hey, who doesn't want an excuse to wear a massive hat?"

But May barely heard him. She was watching the winner accept their earnings. She was thinking about the enormous power of the ships rushing past the stadium. She suddenly felt the desire to be on such a ship, rocketing at unknowable speeds away from her problems.

She turned to Xan who was still busy with his hat. "Back in chapter seven, you said the *Audacity* was a Racing Rocket."

"And you...remember that?" Xan clarified.

"Can we race it? Have you raced it? Is it fast?"

"No, no, and nnn-yes. Yeah, it's pretty fast."

"Why?"

"Because it was built that way."

"Why can't we race it? For money?"

He shook his head, perishing the thought. "I've got a job, it's alright. They've been asking me back for orbits now..."

CHAPTER THIRTEEN

Suspicious

Aboard the *Audacity* again, Xan brushed the inside of his coat pocket with his fingertip, a few granules of crystal dusting his gloved finger. He sighed and the granules floated away on his breath. He sighed heavier.

There are certain things which are universal constants. Thumbs, for example, are fairly standard. The need for water, of course.

Another constant is money.

Though thousands of minor deities have really given it their best shot at convincing societies that money and the accumulation thereof is not the meaning of life, none have been successful.

"Well, that's the last of it," Xan confirmed. "Back to the Agency." He plugged a few numbers into the *Audacity*'s read-out and rested a finger on The Button That Typically Made The Ship Go.

He looked as if someone had sneezed in his soup. Then as if it were the only soup left in the world. Then as if he would accept and eat the soup, but he wouldn't be happy about it.

He pressed the button.

"What do you do?" May asked, hoping it was something she could also do.

"Me? I watch TV when there's a signal. Eat occasionally. Stare at different bits of wall until I can hear color."

"Not in general, I mean for work. At the Agency."

"Whatever they tell me to do, mostly. Sometimes I chat with people, which is what they tell me not to do, and I do feel bad about that, but I hardly have any control over it."

"And what do they tell you to do? Mostly." May watched him carefully now, because she was sure he was hiding some information from her.

"Eugh," he mumbled, biting his lip. "They tell me to go somewhere, and I go there. Easy, really. Simple job. What was your job? On Earth? At the...Sonic?"

"Food service," May answered, simply.

"And what did you serve the food?"

"Wha—" May finally comprehended the mistake and laughed lightly. "No, I served food to people," said May. "To customers," she amended. "People" was too flattering for some of them.

"You're a good cook, then?"

May shook her head, her eyebrows scrunching. "Definitely not. It's all junk food. Mostly pre-made, I just heat it up or pour it over ice."

"Zuut, that was quick," Xan said, but not to May, he was talking to the screen where a bright yellow speck appeared, menacingly growing.

"What planet is that?"

"Forn," Xan said, clutching the arm rests. The ship rattled as it entered the small planet's atmosphere. May didn't remember that happening when they landed on Earth or Vagran. It seemed to her as if the ship was as reluctant as he was.

The *Audacity* settled on a faded square of concrete. On the view screen, the sky shone an uneasy yellow, the red sun boiling away above them, a maze of stucco and wood panel buildings stretching to one side, a series of colorful personal vehicles on the other. Below, a smattering of people ran like beads spilled on a tile floor between the vehicles and the buildings. Faded brown letters stuck out from the stucco walls of the foremost building, ominously spelling "The Agency" in serif caps.

May wondered if the font had serifs in whatever alien language it was actually written in, or if the translation chip was taking liberties with the graphic design. The translation chip had, to its credit, recreated the look of the font with striking precision.

Xan stood, and so did May.

"I'm coming with you. I'm going to apply for...whatever it is they do there."

Xan's eyes widened, but May couldn't quite tell what emotion flitted behind them.

"*Why* can't you?" He sprung from the raised control loft and catapulted onto the teledisc. "Oh, lots of reasons. It's not great work for an Earthling. I mean an Earthling has never done it, probably can't. Also it's boring, and it's dangerous, and you could get lost! Or maimed! Anyway, you're too short and not blue enough. Oh, and gloves. You need your own gloves. Sorry, bye!" He vanished in a tornado of words that left confusion, rather than debris, in its wake.

May thought this was all very sudden and perhaps a bit contrived, almost as if some great unknown force needed him to leave her alone in the *Audacity* for a decent amount of time and didn't bother with thinking up a better excuse.

And so, she was left alone on the ship.

Except she didn't feel alone. In the absence of Xan's near constant chatter, thoughts began to machete their way through the thick rainforest of her subconscious.

The image of Kathy fizzling away broke through into her consciousness first and demanded attention.

Was she dead? Thought May. If she were, was that sad? Did May feel sad enough about the possibility of her boss having disintegrated in front of her? Did she not feel sad because she wasn't *sure* what had happened, or because she didn't care if Kathy was alive or not? That's harsh, she thought. But it's true, she thought. But I shouldn't think it, she thought.

She wanted to feel bad, she realized. Her brain decided this was a worthy pursuit and began digging through the backlog of upsetting concepts it had saved for just such a time.

If Earth were really destroyed, and there was no going back, May would never have that reconciliation with her mother she didn't want. All the things she wanted to say to her but hadn't, rather tactfully May thought, would never be said.

All this, she was beginning to realize, made her feel *bad* but only about herself. This was guilt, which she could've felt back on her couch/bed at home. She wanted to feel existential loss. She wanted to finally convince herself she wasn't dreaming. She wasn't ever getting back to Earth.

Then she remembered him. Someone she truly loved who would make her feel the weight of all she had lost.

Gerald, the unusually large squirrel she often shared her lunches with. He enjoyed fries. Salty ones, too. She always put extra salt on her fries just for him. He'd sit on the curb with her behind the Sonic and hold the limp, greasy potato stick in his tiny little man-hands and nibble, staring unblinkingly at May with shiny, black eyes. His fluffy feather-duster tail twitching. He'd chatter a thank you and scurry off and—that was it.

That got her.

May dove for the couch, dug out the cigarette box, then pried a stick from the warped cardboard. The lighter still lay on the table and she thumbed it on, inhaling the smoldering herb.

Her legs were shaking, so she drew them up underneath herself on the lumpy orange couch, becoming as small and compact as possible.

Earth was gone, and she was alone, and she'd never ever see Gerald ever again.

Oh, and also, in over two decades, she hadn't made a single human friend, owned anything of real value, nor had any family who acknowledged her existence.

She hoped whatever Xan was up to would take a while, because guilt, fear, and regret were all welling up saltily in her eyes and she really needed to get them out.

CHAPTER FOURTEEN

Really, Really Thick

August was raking through yet another pile of plastic straws when his BEAPER dinged. He was being reassigned to a new territory.

He had been combing the same section of space for two inches worth of beard hair growth. Estrichi time proved difficult for him to master, and he found measuring his beard length to be much simpler. Ix (whose name he still could not remember) seemed to think it was three Earth years, but he doubted it had been that long. Perhaps beards grew slower in space, he thought.

After August and Ix repaired the Gremlin and christened him *Robert*, they quickly realized they would need a source of income if they were to survive. It wasn't difficult to become a junker. All you needed was a ship and a willingness to dig through garbage every day. This made it the perfect (and only) career choice for August.

He had become something of a scientist. Every new item required him to apply his half-remembered version of the scientific method. First, upon unearthing an unfamiliar object, he would pose the question, "What the hell is this?" Then, depending on whether or not Ix was within earshot to enlighten him, he would form a hypothesis.

These hypotheses usually centered on cursed objects or fertility talismans and were typically fairly far off the mark. Still, he would whip out his ancient InstaLabeler, label the object with his assumptions, and set it aside for later exploration.

Once, August almost got a laugh out of Ix by misidentifying a crumbled yogurt cup as a ceremonial death chalice. Almost, but not quite. She was as stoney as the petrified biscuits he found in abundance near Astffadoo 2.

Ix kept the *Robert* from breaking down. Or, more accurately, repaired it when it inevitably did break down. August looked for scrap metal. Sometimes plastics. Occasionally he would get very lucky and find bits of moldy rugs. But now, finally, he had paid his dues and was off to a premier landfill. This was the good trash, the kind of trash that made other trash feel like garbage. This was rich people trash.

"Where to?" August asked the BEAPER on his wrist, which he typically and incorrectly called a watch. The alien didn't talk much, so he had taken to speaking with inanimate objects. Fortunately, this particular object would listen, unlike that ornery shovel.

His assignment scrolled across the face of the watch. "1613 Centauri VII." He pulled his fancy eye patch from his pocket and slapped it on; he wanted to make a good impression.

"We're moving out!" he said to the purple alien who lived with him. There was no reply.

She was in her room again, August noted with annoyance. Sometimes when she went into that little room she had welded onto the side of the *Robert*, she would stay there for weeks. Her absence was tough on August; he was a social creature and needed something to talk at.

Once, after a particularly long stint alone, he cornered her and wouldn't let her leave without an answer as to what she did in there. She had told him she was "downloading," and he gave her a confused look. She had told him she was "meditating," and he gave her a confused look. Finally, frustrated at the apparent language barrier, she told him she took very long naps. He accepted that.

Technically, he could pilot the *Robert* on his own, but he abhorred flying. He very noisily began the system checks necessary before taking the Gremlin into space, hoping that his clanging around would alert her to his intention to relocate.

Finally, she emerged.

"What took you so long? I was starting to forget what you looked like!" August said playfully. He attached and unlocked the steering wheel, but he purposely did it backward so she would shoo him away and take over.

Ix sat in the pilot seat and August relaxed beside her on the passenger's side. "August, have you noticed I am blind?" she said, knowing full well that he hadn't. She also knew he didn't know her name, but she had wanted to see how long he could keep up his charade. She ignited the engine and jiggled the gear shift.

August tried to hide his shock, then realized she couldn't see it anyway. Sure, he had noticed that her eyes were as white as the inside of a delicious, crunchy, sweet apple, but he figured it would've come up by now if she couldn't see with them.

"But how do you…you know…do things?"

"The same way you do them with one eye. You adjust. I have had nearly two hundred Earth years to adjust."

It was nice of her to use Earth years around him. Still, it always creeped him out when she talked about her age. It was spooky to know she was a few hundred years his senior. Spooky quickly became annoying when he discovered his skin had begun to wrinkle around his eyes, and she could not relate.

"So, you're blind. That's cool. I guess that explains why you're always asking me to read things for you. I just figured you got a kick out of my mispronunciations." He laughed; despite her mysteriousness, he had to admit he enjoyed her company. It would be a terribly lonely and frightening universe out there on his own.

"No. Your mispronunciations bring me no particular joy. When we land on 1613 Centauri VII, I will be leaving you. I have devised a plan to rescue Yvonne from herself." She brought the *Robert* into orbit and August felt the familiar wash of space sickness. While he wanted to return to Earth someday, he wasn't prepared to make the long journey through space, and he doubted he ever would be.

"Oh…who—who's Yvonne?" he stammered, trying to decide if keeping his eye closed or open made space travel less horrid. Neither did.

"Your captor of six Earth months. Captain of the *Peacemaker*."

"*That* Yvonne, right, of course. And—and why do you have to rescue her? I thought you liked being a junker." He smiled wryly at her. She had never once given him the slightest hint of an indication that she was enjoying herself.

"Enough questions, August. At our next stop, I will purchase a ship with my share of our earnings, and we will go our separate ways. May you find what you seek," she quoted a popular junker farewell at him.

August swallowed. He couldn't keep the hurt out of his face, but at least he could keep it out of his voice. "May you find what you seek."

CHAPTER FIFTEEN

Personality Quiz

May woke up with her face pressed to a damp pillow. Whether it was damp from tears or spittle, she couldn't tell. In one hand, she loosely held onto the package of cigarettes and, in the other, she loosely held her aching head.

This was, despite all the change she'd recently endured, a familiar way to wake up. The one thing about her life that hadn't changed was depression-smoking herself to sleep. Without sitting up, she reached into the package and pulled out the second to last stick, stuck it in her mouth, felt around for the lighter.

Instead of the lighter, her hand grazed the edge of a book half hidden under the couch. Curious, she dragged it out by the cover and blinked until her eyes could focus enough that the cover became clear.

"Class 20 Tuhntian-Built Racing Rocket - Model 0042 - Repair Manual. Now with twenty pages of personality quizzes, emotion puzzles, and heretical inverted number tricks!"

"Heretical...inverted...?" May repeated, wondering if that was something she ought to know about or not. Idly playing with the unlit cigarette between her lips, she flipped to a random page and began to read.

The schematics made perfect sense, and the words on the page were coming through in English, thanks to the translation chip's dedicated service to the language processing center of her brain, but every other noun she came across was untranslatable, it had no counterpart in English, and so May just had to accept that a borbing was a borbing and a jarktaag was a jarktaag. If she could accept that, she could make some sense of the instructions.

She flipped further and found the personality quiz section. Every single one of them had been filled out in green letters which were clearly handwritten, though whether the writing was sloppy or not, she couldn't quite say. Too alien to judge.

"Are you a florbabin torshu or a manfanistic gorlubund?" was the question posed by the first quiz. Xan was, it seemed, a manfanistic torshu. It seemed, also, that he wasn't at all surprised by this. May flipped the page, hoping one of these quizzes might give her some usable insight into his psyche.

This was absolutely foolhardy, of course. No personality quiz in the history of the Universe has managed to accomplish that.

After nearly an hour of May trying to suss out the quizzes and learning nothing more about her host, apart from that he was often bored enough to do personality quizzes in the back of a maintenance manual, May gave up.

Again, she felt around under the couch for the lighter. She stopped.

"No," she said to herself. "Fuck it, I'm done with this," she muttered, the unlit cigarette dropped from her mouth to the floor. She picked it up, stuffed it back in the package, gave the whole package a good, crushing squeeze, and stuffed it under the couch cushion. Opening the manual again, she flipped to the diagrams and began to study them. If she were going to be stranded in space living on a rocket, she wanted to know how it worked.

A floorplan of the ship showed her what was beyond the round main room she had been living in. Below her, one level dedicated to storage and a medibay. Below that, a level showing five bedrooms, although this scheme was crossed out in the same green ink. The word "Missing?" scrawled next to it. Below that, several levels devoted to the engine and fuel tanks.

A sound like a train running over a metal shopping cart made her jump. Behind her, the intershoot's sliding glass door, which had never completely closed, vibrated.

"I bet I can fix that..." she said to herself. Talking out loud to herself had been one of the many pleasures of living alone, and she was glad she had some time to catch up with herself now.

She found that the small utility closet tucked behind the control loft was suspiciously tidy, untouched for decades.

After collecting the tools the manual deemed necessary to fix the door, she explored some of the more unusual items. A metal jar advertised an "Every Purpose, Fully Automated, Non-Sentient Osculum for all your needs. Yes, even that one! No...sorry, not that one. *That* one, yes."

May popped off the top and the yellowish sponge-creature floated out, stretched like taffy, crawled onto her hand, and climbed up her arm using millions of minuscule suckers. It had no apparent features, but it nestled into the crook of her neck and made a steady vibrating purr, so she reasonably assumed it was pleased to have been freed.

"You're kinda cute," May said.

It did not respond.

"Okay, let's fix the door. Do you know how to do that? Since you're an...every purpose, fully automated, non-sentient osculum?"

It continued to vibrate on her shoulder.

"I'll just call you Osy."

It didn't object.

May looked over the canister again, scanning it for instructions, but to no avail. She gathered her tools and the manual, and set to work.

The ailing door sparked as she neared it, groaning again. Hesitantly, she moved around the back of it and pried off the casing where she found electrical and mechanical components confusingly interweaved. Magnetic forces caused integrated circuits to oscillate within little glass tubes which, themselves, churned on pistons and rods. One of the ten tubes was not moving.

She pulled Osy from her shoulder and held it in the palm of her hand, showing it the machine. "Can you fix that?" she asked it.

It raised up off her hand, about a centimeter, and began to spin slowly in the air. It did nothing further.

She held it a little closer to the stuck tube. "Fix it," she coaxed, thinking perhaps it needed a direct order.

It dropped back into her hand and, using its tiny suckers, began to roll along her palm until it hung, bat-like, from the back of her hand.

"Is that...is that helping?" she asked.

It sucked gently on the back of her hand. She flipped her hand over so it was once again upright, and again, it rolled along her hand until it hung. This time from her palm.

"Never mind," May said, depositing the sponge back on her shoulder and diving into the manual.

After a few hours of fiddling, cursing, apologizing to Osy about the cursing, switching the intershoot off and on, off and on again, bending this pin back, that one forward, this one back again, and jiggling things until they snapped into place, May was finished. The tube moved in sync with the other tubes. The door wooshed shut with a distinctly futuristic efficiency. May was satisfied.

She was tired, and she was hungry. But sleeping and eating were relatively passive activities, not enough to distract her mind from picking up and chewing on things she didn't want it to chew on. She needed it to be utterly worn out. And so, she returned the tools and took the manual to the control loft, flipping it open to a diagram of the console and matching up all the blinking lights and little levers and switches and round, colorful buttons to their use.

This page, too, had a few green scribbles. One button was circled with an arrow pointing to it from the words "typically makes the ship go". She avoided that one. A pair of control sticks with big, red buttons on top were crossed out in green scribbles. Crossed out several times, actually. The manual labeled these sticks the "Ultra-Ray-Super-Destroyer Control". She would avoid them, too, for now.

A motion sensor activated the view screen display, and that gave her a lot more to explore. Coordinates, flight history, flight futures, statistics, unresolved error logs...lots and lots of unresolved error logs. One resolved error, actually. The intershoot door. May smiled. This was something good from home, she thought. Fixing broken things.

She frowned. "Classified Documents - Tuhntian Military Operations?" she read. "What...?"

She selected it and, to her mild surprise, it opened for her. The screen filled with information. Words such as "annihilation" and "destruction" and "weaponry" stood out. Again, she looked at the pair of control sticks. This ship had weapons. Why would a racing rocket need...

"Lucy, I'm home!" May heard from behind her. She quickly closed the viewscreen and spun to find Xan, smiling, though he looked like he'd been run through a wood-chipper, leaning on the teledisc control podium. "I've been waiting to say that to someone for decades!"

May stood up, not sure if she wanted to confront him about the military logs or what his actual job actually was first.

Neither, her body decided.

The room skewed sideways as her consciousness stumbled around inside her malnourished, dehydrated, and overworked brain. She stumbled, catching herself on the hoverchair and shutting her eyes tight to weather the deluge of nausea.

"What's wrong?" Xan asked, jumping the stairs to reach her, arms outstretched like a confused forklift.

Her stomach growled and Xan backed up, just a bit, tilting his head in confusion.

"Hungry," May said between clenched teeth.

"Oh! I'll get more canned corn!"

"No..." May pleaded, her eyes still closed against the spinning of the room. "No more corn. Real food." She finally relented and dropped into the chair, holding her head between her hands and waiting impatiently for the hoverchair's gentle bobbing to cease.

"Real...food?" Xan confirmed.

"Fast," she groaned.

"Fast!" he said, "Okay, alright, I've got plenty of gem now, I'll take you to Swarmies! Closest place to eat around here. Only place, really."

"Sounds good," May said, feeling slightly more stable. She stood, taking the stairs shakily.

"Can I...help?" Xan asked, again assuming the awkward fork-lift position as he watched her descend.

She shook her head gently, slowly. "I'm fine." She hadn't eaten anything for nearly twenty-four hours, and even then all she'd had was corn, so she was not "fine", but she was determined not to show it.

His fork-lift-arms dropping slowly to his sides, Xan relented and walked beside her, eyeing her uncertainly, until she made it to the teledisc.

CHAPTER SIXTEEN

Wieners to Skewer

A word on teledisc transportation: Teledisc transportation is not possible.

This is according to the United Front for Real Travel. The front's IFI flyers state that telediscs do not, in fact, transport an individual almost instantly from point A to point B. Rather, telediscs kill the being standing at point A and re-create them, clone-like, particle-by-particle at point B. Their literature accounts for the apparent continuation of consciousness by claiming that the machine can make you think whatever it wants you to think. It is literally in your brain. Taking it apart and reconstructing it.

The United Front for Real Travel refuses to fund the studies that would prove their theory because this would constitute murder, and so the issue has never really reached a head.

They are of course right, but it doesn't matter because most sentient beings don't believe them.

What everyone can agree on is that teledisc travel sucks. It gets easier with practice, like anything, but May was not at all practiced in it. May was also not at all at her best when she teleported out onto the yellow planet of Forn.

Consciousness transfer is usually a seamless process, which is why the United Front for Real Travel's theory was so difficult to prove. But May's consciousness was rather glad to have been untethered from her undernourished, exhausted body and decided it would take its time. Slipping back into her like a cautious swimmer into a cold pool.

"May, are you alright?" Xan asked, though she clearly wasn't, and he caught her under the armpits just in time to avoid a broken tailbone. Gently, he set her down on the hot concrete docking lot.

May's consciousness was up to its ankles in her, shivering.

Xan considered his options. He could go get food, bring it back to her here, and hope it wouldn't kill her. He could wait with her until she was revived, and then take her to the diner where she could hopefully choose for herself an Earthling-safe food. Or, thanks to the light gravity on Forn, he could easily scoop her up and bring her to the diner where someone might know what to feed an Earthling.

Fortunately for him, her consciousness had taken the plunge and she was becoming reacquainted with awareness. "Bright," she said, blinking to fend off the overenthusiastic rays of Forn's sun, known only as 69F.

"Yeah..." Xan said, squinting as he looked around. "The Agency chose about the least hospitable planet in the galaxy to build headquarters on. Probably it was the cheap land. All the food's highly processed. You can eat processed foods, right?"

May shrugged. "Jury's out on that one."

"Jury's out?"

Sitting up with his help, May realized she had used an idiom. She would have to teach him idioms. "No one can agree on it. It's mainly what I eat, though, and I'm starving. I'd eat a sixty-year-old MRE."

Rather than ask, again, what she meant, Xan just figured this was more alien jargon and that an MRE was something one wouldn't want to eat, sixty-years-old or not. Whatever a year was.

"Swarmies isn't far! We need to get out of this light. How's your ultraviolet tolerance on Earth?"

May noticed his pale blue skin was already beginning to burn green as he helped her stand. "Different for everyone. Melanin helps," she said.

"What is that, like a cream?"

May shook her head and laughed. "No, it's pigment. You're born with it. Well...not you."

"Oh," Xan said, looking at his own rapidly burning skin. "Alright, well! Let's get you some food. You'll love Swarmies. Everyone's friendly, the coffee's free, and no one asks you about work," he said as they walked. "Except Jabine. Jabine asks me about work. Zuut I hope Jabine isn't there right now..."

They were approaching the wall of buildings that composed The Agency. Specifically, a single-story, silver-bodied, windowless building with a sign over the glowing yellow door that told May it was the diner. "Just tell me what you do," May said. "Rip the Band-Aid off—er...get it over with." She wasn't sure if she was using more idioms than normal, or if she was just more aware of them.

Xan cringed again. "I don't even know if there's an Earth word for it. They never brought it up once in 'I Love Lucy.' And she had progeny!"

"She had...progeny?"

"Yeah, she had a kid in some of the later episodes. But she and Ricky slept in separate beds, so...I mean I just don't know how it works on Earth but most of the galaxy has—"

"Oh my god, you're a sex worker, aren't you?" May said.

He slowed down, the ultraviolet rays penetrating his skin felt cool in comparison to the heat of embarrassment rising to his cheeks. "It's the only thing I'm good at. Besides linguistics. I have a degree in linguistics, but then the translation chips made most translation jobs redundant and I can't get a regular job anyway because—" he stopped himself. He was entering dangerous territory. "Well, it doesn't matter why. Is that...alright?"

"Do what you gotta do," May said with a shrug. "I don't really 'get' that sort of thing, but I don't care if other people do it. Is it safe?" She kept walking, though she didn't know where they were going, mostly to convince him to start walking again.

"Oh it's perfectly safe!" Xan assured her. "Perfectly, completely, utterly safe. I mean, I haven't died from it yet so...yeah. Safe."

May shrugged. "If you say so."

Swarmies was the sole restaurant on the planet Forn, and this is the only reason anyone ate there. Yes, the coffee was free, but that's only because no one would pay to drink it. There were four locations, each with poorer lighting, dingier carpets, and angrier chairs than the last. The chairs were provided to Swarmies, for an outrageously low subscription fee, by Yalvin's Chair Empire and allegedly enjoyed being sat upon. The squeaking, squelching language the chairs spoke in was so unlike anything else in the known universe, it had never been translated, and so the Yalvins could claim just about anything on behalf of the chairs.

The diner was busier than usual when May and Xan entered; the dark alcoves echoed with chatter. After blinking and squinting to adjust to the staggering light difference, they noticed a stained armchair and a tattered leather rolling office chair were waiting patiently to accept them and take them to their table.

"Oh, uh...no thank you," Xan said, as he always did, ducking down and folding in his arms in a gesture he had discovered, through some trial and error, seemed to make sense to them. The chairs mimicked his gesture, squelched appreciatively, raised up a few inches, and scuttled away on several, bug-like legs.

May stared as they left, returning to a queue lined with a variety of things she immediately recognized as a kind of chair and things which she didn't recognize, but could probably figure out how to sit on.

"Those are...chairs?"

Xan hummed uncertainly. "Well, they aren't *not* chairs. I think they must be something more, though. I don't like sitting on them. Floor okay?"

May nodded, though she was still confused, and followed him to a low table, the top of which was lit with slowly shifting advertisements. Too exhausted to attempt to read and understand them, May watched, hypnotized, as images of incomprehensible cleaning products, baffling accessories, and surprisingly straightforward alcohol brands flitted across the table.

"Ready to order?" Xan asked.

Startled out of her ad gazing, she looked around. "Where's the menu?"

"You've never ordered by Swarm before?"

"No."

"Ah...well the Swarm reads your mind and configures your meal! It's not terribly accurate, and it always tastes a little...well Swarm-y, but it is food and it is fast. Just don't think of anything you wouldn't want to eat. Only think in the positive. I got distracted by a customer while ordering once and, well, the result was unsettling."

"So I think of a cheeseburger, and that's what they'll make?"

"That's what they'll make!"

"Alright, I'm ready," May said.

Xan waved to darkness in the center of the diner and a chunk of it broke-off, an amorphous blob which came to rest over their table with a gentle thwipping.

Shutting her eyes, May imagined something she'd seen nearly every day for the past few years: A Sonic burger. Should she imagine a drink, too? No. Best not to test it on the first try. Just the burger would do. She heard a whoosh, a garbled bundle of nonsense words, and then a gong-like ding. She opened her eyes and, before her, sat a perfectly formed Sonic burger with a hole scooped out of the center filled with crunchy ice and a blue liquid, a red straw rising proudly out of it.

"Shit," May whispered.

"That looks good," Xan said, encouragingly, as he slipped two metal rings over his fingertips and rubbed them together to turn them on. Not in a sexy way. The metal rings were a laser-based utensil the Rhean elite liked to use to avoid touching their food. He used them like invisible chopsticks, scooping up perfectly formed cubes of faux bufatalo in a zesty sauce. This was not how the Rhean elite used them, but he wasn't eating with a member of the Rhean elite, so it didn't matter.

May's drink-burger didn't look bad to her, honestly. Somehow, the liquid wasn't soaking into the burger, it just stayed where it was in its little burger-cup. May made a little noise of half-agreement and brought the straw to her lips. The liquid the Swarm had concocted for her tasted like the memory of soda, syrupy, cold, and sparkly, with no other discernible flavor apart from a dry, musty after-taste she assumed was the swarm-y-ness he'd mentioned.

"Did it work?" Xan asked, dragging a thick crumpet-like disc across his plate with the invisible sticks to soak up the sauce.

"Sort of," May said. "The drink's supposed to be on the side...not inside."

"It's alright, that happens a lot," he said. "Last time I was here, I was craving a shlormpaat and fraguntassle and it had been a long shift, so I wasn't on my best focus, the Swarm filled the shlormpaat with fraguntassle! I had to drink it like a suckling gorpowag! It was quite the sight, I'm sure."

"I can only imagine," May agreed, though she couldn't, really. She finished sucking up the soda and flipped the burger over to deposit the ice on the thin sheet of greasy foil the Swarm had created beneath it. It smelled like a cheeseburger, and it looked like one, but knowing its origins, May was still having trouble working up the courage to bite into it. "Is this...real meat?"

"Um..." Xan cocked his head to the side. "How do you define real?"

"Did it actually come from an animal at some point? Or is...I mean what is this actually made of?"

"Swarm," said Xan, as if that were obvious and needed no further explanation.

"Is the Swarm alive?" May felt like she was playing 20 Questions.

"There are three schools of thought! The Rhean Ultra-physicists define life as anything in a conscious state and conscious states are determined based on a lot of math that I really never could get set on, myself, but on Primox, where Ultra-physics was founded, anything which grows over time is considered alive—"

"What do you think?"

"Me? Heh...I try not to do that too much anymore. Leave the thinking to the thinkers, right? Most of the thinkers agree that the Swarm isn't alive, though. It was invented, it doesn't grow on its own, even the Rhean Ultra-physicists consider eating swarm ethical! And they're strict. Why do you ask?"

May wasn't sure which answer would've made her feel better. She had never much considered the ethical implications of eating, because she needed to do it and she needed to do it on the cheap. Eating cheap and eating ethically didn't tend to line up well on Earth. "Just putting off tasting it, I guess." And so she tried it, and she had to admit the texture and the flavor was right.

It was almost indistinguishable from a cheeseburger. Swallowing, however, she noticed again the taste of Swarm.

"It's alright?" Xan asked.

"It's alright," she said, taking another bite. "It's got calories and protein...probably. That's all I need."

"Protein eh?" Xan asked, finishing off his plate. Actually finishing it off. He took off the rings, picked up the plate, and bit a perfect mouth-shape into the top of it like it was a cracker.

May watched the advertisements scroll below them as she chewed, trying to reduce the time in between bites to avoid that swarmy-aftertaste. Now that she was fed, she could expend a little energy reading. While the text was translated automatically for her by the chip, she found she had to focus harder to actually comprehend it.

"Platamousse Race Track" scrolled in all-caps across the top of the table. "Newly renovated seventy orbits ago!" it proclaimed. "Lowest deathrate of any deadly track in the galaxy!" and "Races start every beoop, on the beoop!"

"Huh," May said, reading.

"Ughn..." Xan said, also reading. Watching her reading. Seeing where that "huh" was going.

"Double your entry fee! Compete against four other racers who are probably not as good and special as you are!"

"Hmmm," May said.

"No experience required! Try it! You most likely won't die!"

"Xan—"

"No," he said.

"But—"

"If they have to say 'You most likely won't die' then it's a little likely you will!"

"How much more dangerous could it possibly be than what you do? Let me race the ship. I've studied the manual, it looks easier than driving a car and I am very good at that. I can't keep accepting food from you without earning my keep somehow."

"Sure you can!"

"I can't," May said. "Xan," she said seriously. "I've never taken a single risk in my life. I didn't even go to college because I didn't want to be in debt. I always took the safe option and I still got abducted by aliens and had my entire life destroyed. What's the point in playing it safe if it can all be taken away from you in an instant, anyway?" She was leaning over the table now, her face intensely up lit by an image of sparkling blue, fanged teeth framed with a silver smile.

Xan sat back on his heels, nibbling at his plate thoughtfully.

"I hadn't thought of it that way," he said, at last.

"So we can race?"

He sighed, crunching the last bite of the plate dramatically. "Alright, okay, yes, fine. Yeah, we can race. But!" and here he leaned in, too, his long nose almost touching the tip of May's nose. She froze. Tempted to back away, but worried he might change his mind if she lost any physical ground on him. His breath smelled of fine china.

"You've got to promise me if you're going to crash you REALLY crash, okay? I want to be obliterated. Utterly and completely. No suffering, no medical intervention, just poof! Done."

"Okay..."

"The *Audacity* is the only thing I have in the entire universe. And Tuhntians are sturdy, May. I'm not easy to kill. You've got to mean it!"

"Uh-huh," May said, really seriously considering backing up now.

"You've got to overpower this, too," Xan said, reaching into his collar and digging something out.

At last, the tension broken, May slumped back to sitting on her heels and watched him pull out a little lump of rock on a string.

"What's that?"

"It's a piece of the first star ever created," he said.

Of all the things May was being asked to believe lately, this was the last. This did it. She could not, under any circumstances, believe that that was a piece of a star.

"Aren't stars just...burning gas?" May asked, eyeing the shining lump.

"Uh...well yes. But it um...turned into a rock. It went supernova! And then, you know...rocks happened," he said, tucking it under his collar again to avoid further visual scrutiny. "Anyway, it's a good luck charm. And it's kept me alive this long, despite...well attempts to the contrary. Yvonne gave it to me before she left to join the resistance and she said she didn't want to see me on a list of casualties."

"You were at war?"

"Me? No! Blitheon, no," he laughed uncomfortably. "No. It's just something she said. Didn't mean anything by it. But the point is, these things are good luck charms. It'll make me harder to kill. I think you can do it, if you really genuinely try to, though."

"I'm going to try to win," May said.

"Sure! Sure. You should definitely try that, first. Have you ever flown a rocket before?"

"So many rockets. We used to race them every weekend back on Earth."

"You did?"

"We didn't have rockets. I mean, we do as a species but not as individuals."

"Oh...right. You were doing another bit! Just like Lucy. She's always doing a bit. I love that. Bits," Xan said.

"I guess you could call it that." May smiled. She'd picked up the habit of hyperbole to try to add some whimsy to her life, but most people just read it as biting sarcasm.

"So, since you've been doing this for eons and will absolutely not need any practice at all..." Xan gave a dramatic pause. "You ready to race?"

"Absolutely," May said. "But I should probably clean up a bit first," she picked at the ripped and disintegrating white latex suit the *Peacemaker* had encased her in. "Is there anywhere to get new clothing on this planet?"

"Nothing appropriate for racing," Xan admitted.

"Quaxlagon! Hiiii!" called a shrill voice from across the diner.

"Zuut, it's Jabine," he whispered to May as Jabine, who looked like a Norwegian model who'd gone for a swim in purple

Kool-aid, sauntered toward them with a carafe. “Coffee?” she asked.

“Coffee, yes!” he said, hoping that would be the end of it.

She produced a small, thin mug from her cleavage and began to pour. “You don’t look too worn out, larvling. How about a noodle in the kitchen? Your friend can come!”

Xan squeezed his eyes shut tight, again turning green with embarrassment. It would be rude to refuse, but he really, really did not want that. May noticed.

“Sorry, we’re hosting a dinner party tonight. Lots to do. People to invite. Cocktail wieners to skewer. You get it,” May said.

Xan opened a confused eye at her, and she communicated to him, with her eyes, that he should play along. At least, she hoped that’s what she communicated. She hadn’t quite worked out alien body language yet.

“Right! Yes! So many wieners to skewer. They’re um...an Earth delicacy, I think?”

“Only the best,” May said, standing to leave. “Nice to meet you,” she said curtly and began to walk away, hoping Xan would follow.

“Sorry, Jabine, some other time!” Xan chugged the coffee, tossed a handful of crystal coins on the table, and hurried after her. “Just to be clear, we’re not having a diner party, right?”

“No dinner party,” May said with a chuckle.

“Oh good. I mean, that sounds great but, zuut, I couldn’t eat for another three rotations at least after all that!” He queued up the *Audacity*’s teledisc on his BEAPER, gently took May’s arm, and together they fizzled away.

CHAPTER SEVENTEEN

Yurkunfle

"Right! So! Pan isn't far, it's in the same star system as Forn, which is good because the intergalactic constabulary doesn't monitor way out here, and it's got a decent LayFlex™ market, though they always up-charge me on account of my height, but Pan's radiation shielding is far superior to Forn's, so if you don't want to immediately try to get us obliterated, we could enjoy some nature! Lots of birdwatching on Pan."

"Birdwatching sounds kinda boring," May said.

"Not for the birds! They like you to act natural, too. Pretend you don't notice them watching you."

"Uh-huh," May said, picking at the disintegrating sleeve of her suit. "Why does it matter that the intergalactic constabulary doesn't monitor out here?"

"It doesn't! Why did you think it did?"

"Because you mentioned it."

"Oh, well, you know I mention a lot of things that don't matter, really. Most of what I say doesn't matter."

May pulled at a loose flap of latex on her shoulder and tore off a larger piece than she was expecting, ripping a gash right across her chest. "Shit," she said, trying to hold the top of her suit together with her hands. "Do you have a shirt I could wear over this? Until we get something new?"

"Probably! Lots of stuff in the basement," he stood to take her down, but she held up her free hand.

"It's alright, I can find my way."

"Sure! Yeah, of course you can," he said, sitting back down, only looking a little deflated as May entered the intershoot.

The darkness of the basement wasn't a surprise to her, this time, but she still felt unsettled down there as she swiped her hands in front of her, searching for the pull-string that would turn on the light. The ship rumbled and shook, throwing her off balance as it exited Forn's atmosphere on its way to Pan. She caught herself on something hairy that she couldn't see. Something that brayed and shifted at her touch.

"Sorry," she said, quickly backing up. Something tickled her cheek and she jumped back, but it was only the pull-string. Relaxing, she tugged on the string and illuminated the basement. Whatever living thing she'd disturbed was either no longer there, or hiding out of sight somewhere beyond the miniature wormhole.

"Fidobot?" May asked the empty space. "Is that...your name or is it just what you are?" she whispered. She wasn't sure why she was whispering, but it felt appropriate. "Hello?" she began to dig around in the junk, looking in the general area Xan had found the bot earlier. The items she recognized were thus: A thread-bare pink bath towel, a medium-sized child's rocking horse, a pair of musty binoculars, and an old, yellowed computer keyboard with a chewed-through cord.

The items she didn't recognize were multitudinous. Something round and squishy and purple (she only thought it was purple, of course. It was really hurdorpanit with blalagne stripes), something small, but incredibly heavy, shaped like a pinecone, several somethings which appeared to be empty bags, but were in actuality a collection of discarded skins, and a scrimshaw. The scrimshaw was from Earth, May had just never seen one before.

She baffled for a moment at what she thought were strange alien carvings on a strange alien tusk. She tossed it aside.

Finally, stuffed into a gap between a wooden bedframe and a sapphire encrusted A'Viltrian titanium bed frame, May found a wrinkled greige t-shirt. She sniffed it, and it smelled no worse than her Sonic work shirt had. She held it up to her, and the shoulders were only a few inches wider than her own. The front of the shirt had writing on it. "That is, is it not, Yurkunfle."

It would do. She donned the shirt, shut off the light, said a hasty "goodbye" to whatever was down there that might want to be acknowledged, and returned to the intershoot just as the ship settled on Pan.

"Oh good! You found—" Xan paused, reading her new shirt under his breath. Gears turned as he thought about it, and then his face broke open in delight. "Ha! That's hilarious! Yurkunfle. Excellent find."

"What's Yurkunfle?"

"It's just...well you know it's Yurkunfle. It's funny."

"If you say so," May said. "Can we make this quick? I hate shopping."

"You hate...shopping?"

"And clothing," May said.

"But Lucy and Ethel LOVE shopping for clothing! They're always getting in trouble over it!"

"And?"

"And...well I guess you aren't Lucy or Ethel...no, sorry. That was probably offensive. I just assumed Earthlings liked doing that sort of thing."

May shrugged. "Do you?"

"Like clothing shopping? Well I used to! I used to love it. That used to be half my job title, actually. Costumer."

"What was the other half?"

A three-toned jingle echoed in the ship, followed by a polite but loud voice. "Welcome to Pan. You are in Primary Panseen Sector Twelve. You have been granted a two-rotation visitor's pass. To extend your pass or claim Pan as your planet of origin, see visitor services. Please enjoy your stay and remember: be interesting, the birds are watching."

"You don't actually have to be interesting," Xan said to May. "They'll watch anything!"

CHAPTER EIGHTEEN

Tending Bar

Listay's Earth office, on the top floor of the control tower, had only two luxuries. One was a sizable indoor garden with a lovely little bench for sitting when she needed a break. The other was a well-stocked old-world Rhean bar for when she really needed a break.

It turns out that invading a planet inhabited by a self-aware species, no matter how ill advanced they were, and reforming its government within a few brief months was quite difficult. Listay wasn't afraid of a challenge, and this was her greatest weakness. She should've been afraid. She was beginning to realize this.

She had been spending most of her scheduled daily free time at the bar lately.

"I know where it went wrong, Drink-Bot," she said to the robotic arm attached to the bar. It made her drinks on request, but wasn't capable of processing anything which didn't need to be shaken or stirred.

The drink bot, having no vocalization mechanisms, did not answer, but it did whir to attention, ready to make whatever she might order next, though she hadn't yet finished her first drink, a young clouded shermel.

"It was in the beginning. That's where it all started," she said, then melted sadly over her drink. Her brow furrowed deeper, then she gave a sad, single laugh. "Of course, that's where it started. Where else?" She asked the Drink-Bot.

The arm bent at its joint and rested on the counter. Nothing it had heard was a kind of drink. It was getting bored, insomuch as an non-sentient arm can get bored.

Interestingly, boredom is an early warning sign of burgeoning consciousness, and so Listay, though she could not know it, was triggering the conception of a new, very bored, life form. If at any point during this novel you should become bored, please keep this in mind and take a moment to appreciate the gift of consciousness.

"I rushed into this," Listay said. "I should have insisted to the captain that we follow the outline, we opened Earth to intergalactic tourism far too early. I knew this would be a catastrophic mistake."

The arm perked, it knew how to make the infamous Pontoosan Catastrophic Mistake. It began to knead and peel the required seven unripe gortfulets.

"I just have no control around the Captain," Listay continued. "When I'm near her I feel like my brain's on fire."

The arm paused, the seventh gortfulet having just been peeled, then swept them away and began to prepare the Flaming Brain, a drink invented on the planet Rhea IV, a planet unanimously nicknamed "The Worst Rhea".

"I don't know if I can fix this," she downed the remainder of her clouded shermel, just to see if that might do the trick. "But I can't desert the mission. I have nowhere to go back to. I defected from the Rhean military to work under Yvonne. I'm a fugitive."

The arm set the cocktail shaker full of Flaming Brain down, a bit too forcefully, on the bar. It dumped out the neon drink and began to rinse a small glass with blue precious liquor for a classic Tuhntian Fugitive.

Listay didn't notice. She had swiveled the bar stool around to gaze at her office, usually pristinely neat, now littered with scribbled notes on thought-boards, stacks of full Earthling complaint report modules and a few abandoned drink glasses.

It was chaotic and pointless and hopeless.

Which meant, it was nearly time.

Had Chaos had a reputable sense of time, she might've been pleased with how quickly Listay was failing to control the Earth-creatures. The General had given her best effort to keep her failures from her Captain, but Chaos knew. She could feel the restless yearning for destruction in the hearts of the Earth-creatures. Her children.

Chaos was at a bar, too, but not a private one. She liked to spend her time in a literal hole in the wall within the *Peacemaker* where a small band of rebellious mechanics had opened a speakeasy to escape to during work hours. Yvonne's body barely fit into the space between walls, and it became lightheaded in the thick clouds of kalvisora smoke that permeated the illicit bar. Chaos smiled as Yvonne's mind became foggy, her skull aching as if it were being squeezed between a pantoltlio's jaws.

At first, her presence in the bar had disturbed the workers who had gone there to avoid responsibility, but they soon realized their Captain had come for the same reason. Eons as a formless presence had made Chaos a bit foggy. She vacillated between an inescapably powerful will to end all things and an inescapably powerful will to take another million year-long nap. But her window of influence was fast-approaching, and if she slept she might miss it. So she drank. The body she was in had a surprisingly low tolerance for alcohol, and Chaos so enjoyed a good hangover.

She stuffed herself into the corner, watching the maintenance staff, mostly Udonians half her height, as they drank away the stress of keeping up with the demands of a spaceship the size of a large city.

"What'll it be, Captain?" said the Udonian behind the thin rail of a bar, looking over his shoulder at the array of alcohol bottles they had stashed. "We've got an aged shermel in, a swig of fraguntassle, a Panseen grchtu..." he began listing.

"Make me one with everything," said Chaos. "This night on Earth will be a memorable one," she said.

"Oh yeah?" asked the bartender as he began to pour a little from every bottle behind him into a glass made from a pipe welded shut at the bottom.

"I shall consume the Earth-creature's dreams," she said, her unmentionable eyes swirling as she watched him pour.

"Oh," said the bartender. "Yeah." He finished off the bottle of fraguntassle, gave the pipe-full of alcohol a swirl with a swizzle stick, and handed it to her, pointedly avoiding looking into her eyes. "Well, don't fill up on this trok, then, eh?" he laughed nervously.

Chaos blinked. "My capacity is as infinite as your ignorance."

“Hmm. Isn’t it always night somewhere on Earth? On account of it being spherical and all,” said the bartender, daring to look upon her countenance on the off chance that he might find some modicum of humanity there. Some gentle humor or flush of embarrassment.

Humanity was the farthest thing from the Captain’s face, though. Not even a wrathful indignation at his insubordination. Just a deep and abiding emptiness in her unmentionable eyes. The bartender’s mustache twitched over his tight-lipped smile. He decided now was a good time to get back to work, leaving the bar unattended.

Chaos opened Yvonne’s throat and poured the ghastly concoction into it, the burning heat of the drink sliding down into her reminded her of her home within the star, only a few million lightyears away. Soon, very soon, there would be nothing to call home anymore. And, in a way, it would all be home. It would all be burning.

CHAPTER NINETEEN

Layflex™

Forn had been barren, bright, and felt wholly alien to May. But Pan creeped her out even more. It was far too much like Earth. Trees which looked like Earth-trees and fields of flowers that looked like Earth-flowers lined the paved walkways which, though they seemed to be made of something slightly squishier than concrete, also looked eerily familiar. Between the trees, May could see glimpses of fast-moving vehicles on either side.

The throngs of pedestrians moving along the branching walkways also looked eerily like Earthlings, though their skin was redder and their faces were unusually broad. They weren't even much taller than May, some were even just about her height.

"Are they human?" May whispered to Xan.

"Of course! You know I'm a human...right?" he asked.

"No...how?"

"Well how are you a human? What does that mean?"

"I don't know, I just am! Not an animal, I guess. Not a plant. A human."

"Well, I'm not an animal or a plant to you. What else would I be?"

"Alien?" May suggested.

"Alien, to me, means something unknown. Something that doesn't belong. Different. I think we're far more similar than we are different, don't you?"

"Yeah," May said. "Probably. That's alien, though..." May said, stopping suddenly on the path to point at a tall triangle of swirling vortex that ended the sidewalk ahead of them, flanked by two rows of blocky kiosks.

"Oh, it's just the train."

"The train? I don't see a train," May said.

"Well no, it's one of those new matter-less trains, but it's a train. They call it a train, at least. Technology sure changes fast," he said, sighing wistfully. He walked up to a kiosk, told it where they were going, paid, and took the two little paper tickets out of the slot. He read the back of them, his brow furrowing with concentration as he worked through the instructions, then offered one to May. "Hold it upright at a 45 degree angle exactly two horborts off the ground and one horbort in front of you."

May took it gingerly. "I don't know what a horbort is."

"Neither do I! Just do what they're doing, I guess." He nodded at the people walking through the triangle, all holding their tickets out in front of them.

Mimicking their form as precisely as she could, May stepped forward into the light and felt herself whisked away to the right. Light and form rocketed past, and she had the uncanny feeling that she was being dragged side-ways. The sensation stopped and May stumbled dizzily as reality re-asserted itself on her.

She had arrived at a busy intersection, the vehicles she'd seen through the trees earlier were much larger than she imagined up close, and they sped along traction-less rails. She wished they had taken one of those instead of the matter-less train. It looked a great deal more pleasant to ride in.

Other Panseen who had followed her into the triangle began popping up beside her, but Xan was nowhere to be seen.

"Shit," she said, unsure if she should try to go back or to wait and see if he showed up. The *Peacemaker* had taken her cellphone, and without it in an unfamiliar city without a guide she felt both very helpless and very free. Part of her wanted to begin wandering down the soft paved sidewalks, taking in the alien shops and restaurants and things which were neither shops nor restaurants but something far beyond the comprehension of the modern American, such as comfortable, clean, free healthcare clinics.

She decided to wait half an hour at most, then realized she had no way of telling when half an hour had passed, so she would mentally sing through "All By Myself" by Celine Dion five times and then go wandering.

She'd reached the second chorus for the third time when Xan lurched out of the triangle onto the sidewalk. "May?!" he called, frantically checking all the Panseen faces around him.

"What happened?" she asked, doing her best to banish Celine from her mind.

"May!" he said, grabbing her shoulders. "Oh, sorry, touching," he amended, backing up, his hands held out in front of him. "When it says exactly two horborts, it means exactly two horborts. I'm just too tall. Eventually an attendant took pity on me and helped me figure it out, but zuut that's hard on your neck, huh?" He tilted his head until something in his spine cracked and he shivered. "That's better! Alright. Layflex™! That way!" he said, using his nose to indicate a building behind May.

"Alright, you just wait here, I'll take care of everything else and come get you when they're ready!" Xan said, dashing off toward a counter where a smartly dressed clerk was handling a line of less-smartly dressed customers.

The lounge looked comfortable, if a bit austere, with pillowy white furniture and a long screen angling down from the ceiling. Someone sat in a far chair, blinking their boredom up at the screens. Someone else sat on the floor, cross-legged, watching their palm. May wasn't sure there was anything on their palm, exactly, but they were watching it.

Studiously ignoring these two, May sat stiffly on the edge of a chair and looked up, trying to come to grips with the busy graphics and quickly shifting scenes on the screen above her. Short sentences flashed across the screen. "Urbonchu recall. Unrest in Sector Two unlikely to escalate. Unrest in Sector Three likely to escalate. Unrest in Sector Two now likely to escalate." May's eyes glazed over. Just news, she thought. She could barely understand Earth news. Alien news meant nothing to her. Until the intergalactic review came on and with it, something that meant something to her.

"There's a new planet entering the galactic economy, and some speculate that its quiet little corner of the galaxy is about to make some intergalactic investors very wealthy. It goes by many names. Some of the A'viltiral species refer to it as 'Earth', others call it 'Earth' or 'Earth'. But one thing's certain, whatever you call it, this formerly run-down and dangerous planet is quickly becoming a sought-after vacation spot!"

"...What?" May whispered to the screen. This caught the attention of the person sitting in the chair in the far corner of the room, and May quickly glared at them so they wouldn't try to answer. They didn't know.

"We have here with us now Topin under Preeeeethawg of Pan, one of the first Panseen to visit 'Earth.' Topin, we've all heard the horror stories. The toxic air, the untenable wealth gaps, the wheat... but what's it like? Really?"

"Well, Gloppog—by the way I think you're brilliant, you know, best news-being in the galaxy, probably—"

"Thank you,"

"Yeah, well, it's just the truth. Anyway, so Earth's really hit a rush-mark, you know? It's not the old blunt needle in the eye it used to be. It's under Rhean command, I heard, and well, you know how the Rheans are."

"I do know," agreed Gloppog.

"And, you know, someone as beautiful as you I'd imagine has seen this kinda thing before."

"Go on."

"New management. That's all it takes, sometimes. You know the smog is gone, the infrastructure's finally caught up with the rest of the galaxy."

"And what about the Earthlings, how are they?"

"I admit, I tried to avoid them while I was there, but most of them weren't so bad, really. You know, someday soon they might even be recognized as an intelligent species—"

May heard Gloppog and Tipon laugh obnoxiously at that, but she only heard it very distantly. Her thoughts were loud. Earth was safe. Nice, even if Tipon was to be believed. New infrastructure...vacation destination...

"Were they talking about Earth?" Xan asked, startling her out of her cloudy ruminations.

"No," she said, reflexively. "No... some other planet." She did not want to go back. Not now that she had finally convinced him to race. There was far more ahead of her than there was behind her. Besides, Earth seemed to be doing perfectly fine without her. Better, even.

"Aw, well, probably that's best," Xan said. "Jorhay needs to take your shape."

"What?"

"Jorhay! It needs to take your shape. Come on, it'll be quick, I promise," he nodded to an attendant standing behind him in the lobby, waiting.

"Fine," May said, pulling herself to standing and following Xan and the attendant to a small, bright room.

They shut the door and watched her intently.

"...do I need to do something?" May finally asked.

"You must undress for the Jorhay," said the attendant.

May squinted, always suspicious of people who talked about themselves in the third person. She took the Yurkunfle shirt off and let it drop to the floor.

"You must fully undress for the Jorhay," said the attendant.

"Seriously? This thing's skin-tight," May said, snapping the thin white *Peacemaker* suit against her skin.

"You must fully—"

"Okay! Fine. Turn around. Both of you," she said. Xan quietly obeyed, but the attendant obeyed only with some grumbling.

She peeled off the suit, trying to keep it from ripping further but not succeeding. It shredded off her like dollar store wrapping paper, leaving her with just her bra and underwear. She hoped fervently that this wasn't *that* kind of story.

Fortunately for her, it wasn't, and the attendant had nothing to say about her bra and underwear. The attendant did whistle, though. Before May could be offended by that, a door slid open and a three-foot high grub-shaped creature inched out, trailing a pale green slime across the white floor as it made directly for her. It had no visible eyes, so she wasn't quite sure how it knew where she was, but it definitely did.

"What the hell?"

"Uh that's Jorhay," Xan said, his back still turned. "It's harmless! Just a little wet."

"Jesus Christ," May muttered at the thing called Jorhay. It stopped, tilted back at her, and out of its head grew two enormous, round, gloopy eyes with ill-defined red irises and sharp little black pupils that opened and closed at her like tiny camera apertures.

May relaxed, her arms dropping away from her chest to hang by her sides. "Oh, that's it?"

Jorhay reared back and slapped its bulging, wet eyes against May's thigh with the sound of a rotting steak slapping a beach ball.

"Jeeessus Christ!" May shivered as the Jorhay began to slide its eyes over every inch of her body, its own wormy trunk shrinking and extending, coating her in a fine layer of goo.

"They don't uh...have Jorhay on Earth do they?" Xan asked, though he knew the answer.

"Obviously not!"

The Jorhay dropped off her, sheathed its horrible eyes, and slunk away, satisfied.

Xan, his back still turned to her, held a towel out behind himself and she quickly snatched it, rubbing the goo away and cursing quietly. Giving up on the shredded white suit, she put the Yurkunfle shirt back on and was grateful now that it was oversized, the hem hung just high enough for her to feel the constant need to stretch it down, just low enough that her underwear was covered.

"When do we get the suits?" she asked.

"Your suits will be delivered to your teledisc in one to twenty-nine rotations. Please allow up to seventy rotations for deliveries outside of the 69F system," said the attendant, turning around to shine upon her the full brunt of their carefully practiced neutral customer service glare.

"Alright, so I've got some time to learn how to fly the ship," May said.

"You've got plenty of time! It's easy, really. If I can do it, anyone can do it. As long as they have thumbs. You do have thumbs, right? I haven't really paid that much attention to your hands. Maybe I should've? Is that impolite? Or is it more impolite to not have paid attention to your hand configuration?"

"You can turn around now," May said.

He did. He looked down. He smiled. "You've got thumbs! Yes. Easy. This will be easy."

CHAPTER TWENTY

It Runs On Coffee

This was not, in fact, going to be easy, thought May as she sat down at the *Audacity*'s console, watching all the lit buttons and slowly spinning embedded orbs and vibrating joy sticks and row upon row of toggles.

"So that," Xan nodded to the Button That Typically Made the Ship Go, "That's the Button That Typically Makes the Ship Go."

May nodded, eyeing it. "Not always?"

"Not always."

"When doesn't it?"

Xan tilted his head to the side and gave a little shrug. "Really I've got no idea. I figure the times it doesn't it's just the Universe telling me I need to stay wherever I am. It didn't work for ages once I got into Earth's orbit."

"You had the parking brake on."

"Oh, yeah. That was probably why it didn't...work...yeah. Huh."

"So this launches the ship?" May put her finger over it. They were still parked on Pan, but she didn't want to get the ship going before she knew how to control it.

"It does. Typically!" Xan said, tilting over her finger like a drinky bird, he used his nose to gently press her finger down on the button and sat back, smiling innocently at her as the ship did all the work of launching itself off Pan.

"Where's it going?" May asked, studying the many diagrams and messages that had suddenly appeared as overlays on the viewscreen.

"Just up," Xan said. "You know, at a certain point, there stops being an 'up' for it to go to, and that's when it typically cuts off—zuut the light's on!" He jumped out of the co-pilot seat and bounded over to the little kitchenette in the living room.

The light he was referring to was the fuel light, and it was always on, but sometimes it was an uneasy yellow and at other times it was a vibrant red. Now, it had moved beyond red into diophalothene territory. Diophalothene is a color so alarming, the Earthing eye had not yet gained the strength to see it.

Xan began to make coffee.

"Shouldn't we do something about that?" May asked. "Are we going to make it out of the atmosphere?"

"I am! I'm making coffee about it! And probably. If the coffee's done in time."

"How will coffee help?"

The coffee machine started gurgling and Xan turned around, leaning back against the counter. "It just does. Fuel."

"No way," May said. "There is no way you fuel this thing with coffee. Just regular coffee?"

"Yeah! It works. It's what I've always used."

"This is a rocket ship," May told him, empathically.

"Yes...and it likes coffee. Want any?" The machine spluttered to a stop and he pulled the carafe out, grabbing a mug for himself.

"No, thanks," she said, watching horrified as he filled his mug, then set it down, screwed open a cap on the ship's console, and poured the rest of the thick, dark brew into the ship. The engines vibrated louder as the coffee hit the tank, purring like an eighty-ton house cat in a field of catnip.

"I don't believe this," May said, but the diophalothene light turned red again, and then an uneasy yellow/orange anyway. So that was a negative point to the power of belief.

"It's the good luck charm," Xan said, sitting down to drink his coffee as the ship successfully exited the atmosphere and its engines relaxed, the thrusters kicking on to gentle poof until the ship's relative velocity was zeroed out. "Rocket fuel is expensive, you know? Coffee's cheap. Well, I mean it's an illegal export so it's technically more expensive than it ought to be, but it's still far cheaper than rocket fuel."

"Okay," May said, pinching herself on the leg again, just to be sure. No. She was really, really here. "So how do you navigate?"

She asked, trying to forget about the coffee and the alleged good luck charm.

"Well, me, I don't navigate. Not really. I use the autopilot, typically, but you can't autopilot through a race so you're going to have to use one of the other navigation systems."

"Have you ever flown it on manual?" May asked.

"Sure! Yeah. When I first got it..." he stared off, literally, into space.

"Okay. How do you do it?" May asked, leaning into his line of sight to get his attention back.

"Right! So, you just kinda," he flipped a few toggles on and off, on and off, looked confused, and then remembered. He turned a crank on the side of the console and part of the smooth console surface opened and lifted back, revealing a control stick. "There it is! Alright, you use that. And then one of these..." he fiddled with a few pull knobs until the ship began to move. "Just sorta do things until it goes, I guess."

May sat back, arms crossed, watching him. There was an easier way to do this, she was sure. "How about we read the manual?" she asked, picking up the tome which was laying open, spine-up, on the console.

"We could do that, sure! But isn't that going to get boring? Shouldn't we be...you know...interesting?" he looked around, he looked for me. He was looking for me. He was worried I might stop watching if he stopped being interesting.

"You don't actually have to be interesting," May said to him, scanning through the manual. "They'll watch anything."

She was wrong.

CHAPTER TWENTY-ONE

Now?

For twelve long rotations, nothing interesting happened. May read the manual, May played with the ship's settings, May oiled things and filed the rust off things, and recalibrated things, and ate and drank things (but different things than the aforementioned things). Xan mostly watched. Occasionally, he reminded her to sleep when she nodded off at the control panel.

At last, May uttered the phrase that would break the monotony. She clicked the console siding back into place with a satisfied little shove and said, "That should do it."

"Do what?" Xan asked, rising up just enough that his nose was visible to May over the back of the couch.

"I'm going to fly it," she said. "On manual."

Xan rolled over the couch back and joined her at the console. "Alright, just take it slow at first, right? We can always go faster, but we can't go slower."

"We can go slower," May said, pointing to the thruster controls. "That's what those are for."

"Oh, huh..." he studied the field of thruster toggles. "You know I drove for a Star Taxi company once. Just once. They only had four of these."

"It's a big ship," said May, settling into the pilot's seat and grabbing hold of the controls. She pressed The Button That Typically Made the Ship Go and they were flung into the pin-pricked blackness beyond Pan's gravitational field.

The stars only blurred for a second until the ship was moving too fast for them to see even starlight. May cut off the engine and reversed the thrusters to bring them to a stop; this she accomplished with a second press of The Button That Typically Made The Ship Go. It also typically made it stop.

May's eyes were as big as flying saucers. "I went fast."

"Did you manually warp? You know most races don't let you warp."

"No," May said. She held up a computer chip the size of a floppy disc (which was the size of a CD (which was about palm-sized)). "I took this out."

"What is it?" Xan eyed it in horror.

"It was the Collision Cushion," she said thoughtfully, tapping it on her knee.

"You uninstalled the Collision Cushion?!"

"You think that was a bad idea?"

"I mean...not if we were running an illegal hinterplanet race with a death wish!"

"We're guaranteed to win without it."

"May! Without the Collision Cushion, we're *guaranteed* to perish in a terrible, fiery crash. Besides, it's extremely illegal to race without one. Careers have been ruined over it. Mostly because the pilots perish in terrible fiery crashes, but occasionally, they survive long enough to be punished severely first."

"That bad?"

Xan blinked meaningfully. "Yes, that bad. No one's ever gotten away with it."

"But if they had, you wouldn't know, because they would've gotten away with it," May pointed out.

"We will actually, literally, definitely die," Xan pointed out.

"Okay, I'll put it back," May relented. She didn't want to admit it out loud, but she was positive she wouldn't be able to dodge obstacles going that fast. She had planned to just plow through them, actually. But that probably wasn't wise. "The IFI said there would be obstacles. The virtual reality deck has a flight simulator, let's load that up so I can practice."

"It's broken," Xan said. "It's just reality now, no virtual."

"I can fix it."

"See, I looked into that, I did, because life had gotten quite boring for a while there, but the part it's missing doesn't exist. It's a virtual part. And you can't install a virtual part unless you're in the virtual realm so...you can't fix it. No one can, apparently. The mechanic said she'd never seen that happen before. Probably happened when the wormhole opened in the basement."

"And how did that happen...exactly?" May asked.

Xan breathed in sharply through his teeth, remembering the day. "I pressed this," he said, pointing to a large red button on the wall by the console. It was unlabeled, but it didn't look like the kind of thing you'd want to press on the regular. May flipped through the manual and found it. A large paragraph of text explaining the exact function of the button filled half the page, but one clause at the end of a sentence was circled in green ink "only as a last resort".

"What did you think it would do?"

"It kinda looked like...you know...a self-destruct button. To me."

May closed the manual and set it down. "Xan, are you depressed?"

Instead of answering, Xan jumped down from the control loft and started another cup of coffee. "Sorry, what?" he called over his shoulder.

"Depressed. Are you depressed?"

The coffee machine gurgled noisily. "Doesn't translate, mun, sorry. Translation chips. The whole galaxy relies on them, but do they work? Well, yes. Most of the time. Actually pretty unbelievably well. Just not in this case. There's always a few things they miss, you know. A couple concepts that don't carry over. Nouns." He poured a mug of thick black coffee for himself. "Specified nebulous pronouns, clearly, are not a thing on Earth. And that's fine, really. I just don't quite understand how—" his words were cut off as he began chugging the coffee, though he seemed still to be talking, somehow.

May just glared at him, arms crossed. She was pretty certain it did translate, actually.

"Coffee?" He turned around at last and poured himself a second cup.

"Fine," May said. "I need to practice, anyway. Where'd that coffee come from?"

"Earth! It's illegal to export from a no-contact planet, but a while back an Earthling got absolved by the Intergalactic Council for Setting Things Right Despite All Evidence to the Contrary and when they picked her up, her special request from Earth was coffee. Mata Hari's Earth Coffee, they call it!" he opened a cabinet under the coffee machine where a large screen-printed burlap sack slumped. He shut the door with his foot and brought May her cup.

"I still don't believe half of what's happening here," May muttered into her coffee before taking a sip. She politely spit it back into the cup. "But I couldn't dream of coffee that bad. Will I regret asking for milk and sugar?" she asked.

Xan stared at her seriously, his brow furrowed as he tried to suss this out. "Probably," he said at last, just to be safe. He didn't want to disappoint her again. The closest thing to sugar on board The *Audacity* would have been fine, a light reddish powder derived from the Rhean gagarr plant. Milk, however...well it was a good call on Xan's part not to tell her about it.

"I need to find an asteroid field," May said, setting the coffee down on the console, knowing full well that setting drinks on the console was at the very top of the top two-hundred things to never set down on the console list in the manual.

Xan pointed at a corner of the viewscreen. "Like that one?"

Squinting, May leaned in, nearly tipped over the coffee mug, set it down on the carpet, and again tried to see what Xan was seeing. "I don't see anything," she said.

"You uh...you can't see that?" he said, nervous.

May squinted a little harder, then zoomed in, just slightly, hoping Xan wouldn't notice. "Of course I see that," she said when at last the peppering of space-rocks in the distance became visible to her.

"Of course you do," Xan echoed.

May crawled under the console, nearly knocked her coffee over again and, again, moved it somewhere safer, then re-installed the Collision Cushion. She sat back in the pilot's seat and made for the asteroid field. The ship went noticeably slower, but May was also noticeably more confident navigating now.

She stopped the ship just shy of the asteroid field. "Time me."

Xan nodded, but made no move to set any kind of timer.

"Are you going to time me?"

"Oh! You mean now? Time you starting now?" He fiddled with his BEAPER for a moment, and it dinged.

"Did you start it?" May asked.

"Yep!"

"No, I meant when...when I go. Start the timer when I start the ship."

"How will I know when you start the ship?"

"Because it will...start going."

"How about you tell me when you want to start the timer?"

"Alright, I'll say 'now'"

The BEAPER dinged.

May laughed, looking up at the ceiling in defeat. "Not *now* now. The next time I say that word—"

"Now?"

"Yes."

The BEAPER dinged.

"No. The next time, after this time, that I say the word 'now' will be the right time."

"Got it," Xan said.

May breathed deeply. Steadied herself. Hovered her finger over The Button That Typically Made the Ship Go, and said, "Now."

Skedaddling

"Platamousse Annex: The Planetoid That The Sanitation Department Forgot" had been a popular documentary on the Galactic Educational Waves a few dozen orbits ago, and since the filming of that documentary, things had only gotten worse.

Warning signs littered the parking bay on Platamousse Annex, drowning in piles of garbage. Some signs were so overcome with trash that only the top line of their message was visible, like an upturned mouth gasping for air above the surf. "DANGER," they wheezed.

The less encumbered signs spoke to the risks of breathing the air for more than five minutes. Newer signs, their posts only partially drowned in refuse, guaranteed death in two minutes. Still newer signs read, "Do not exit your vehicles. Doing so will result in instant, irreversible death."

May and Xan had their new matching outfits, and looked sufficiently fast in them. Xan had spent a few hours getting acquainted with May's hair, finally molding it into a fashionable purple puffball with bumper bangs that framed her face nicely and, thanks to a variety of mysterious alien hair products, didn't flatten no matter how many times she'd face-planted into the console out of frustration while learning to pilot the ship.

"This planet seems nice. Why didn't you take me here first?" May asked as she set the *Audacity* down on the starting platform with surprising grace.

"Oh well, once you've been to Platamousse Annex you've seen it all. I was trying to save the best for last." Xan laughed nervously. "And considering what we're about to do, this place probably will be the last."

The view of outside flickered off, replaced by the face of an android that shone like liquid mercury with heavily sculpted features, square around the jaw with delicate eyes and plump metal cheeks and lips. The android's voice could not be said to be masculine nor feminine—only sharp and unfriendly.

"Entrance fee is five hundred crystals," they said. A sneer tweaked the metal lips. "Teledisc coordinates G:73,38,70. ICS only."

May bit her lip and glanced at Xan. His palm was full of crystal shards and compressed crystal coins which he carefully counted out. He handed her two small, clear shards.

"Is this five hundred crystals?" May asked.

"No, mun. That's what's left. It's about ten." He wrapped his fingers around the crystals in his hand. "Didn't realize dying would be quite so expensive. You really can't take it with you, I guess." He shrugged and tossed the crystals onto the teledisc where they sizzled away.

The screen cleared and May could see around them again. Beside them six very new, very shiny rocket ships stood like a firing line. Though May was amongst their ranks, she felt like she was in the crosshairs.

"How old is the *Audacity*?" May asked quietly.

Xan winked an eye in concentration as he did the math. "Must be about two hundred."

"Two hundred what?"

"Orbits."

"And an orbit's like a year?" May had been trying to learn Estrichi time, but Estrichi was slightly smaller than Earth, so an orbit wasn't really, exactly like a year.

Xan shrugged. "Maybe?"

Two hundred years, she thought. She was competing in a two-hundred-year-old rocket ship. She was wrong, of course. Two-hundred orbits is exactly 188.484 years. "We're screwed, aren't we?" she whispered.

"You say that as if you're just realizing this. I have literally been telling you that we are going to die for the past couple of rotations."

"I thought you were being dramatic."

"May. *May,* look at me." He swiped his hands out to the sides for effect. "Do I look the type to over dramatize my estimations of catastrophe?"

May squinted at him. "Yes."

He looked down at himself, sighed. "Alright, maybe. But not this time. This time, I may have in fact underplayed the catastrophic possible outcomes."

It was too late, though. The *Audacity* shook as clamps cinched it to the spot. In cheaper races, like this one, mechanical clamps were used rather than digital sensors to ensure pilots wouldn't take off early.

"Here, wear this." Xan fished the good luck charm from under his coat and handed it to her.

She studied the gently pulsating glow of the crystals for a moment before taking it and pulling the gold chain over her head. She didn't believe in luck, but she also didn't believe in not hedging your bets.

"And try not to chip the paint," Xan said as May tucked the rock under her suit. "Obtrusive Orange was outlawed ages ago. It's too bright, it's been known to cause spontaneous photic retinopathy. The only can of it I've ever found for sale cost an Anat's con."

"I'll try my best," May said.

Xan smiled tightly. "I know you will," he said. What he didn't know was whether or not her best would be enough to keep them alive.

"Welcome participants, I am your infallible Overseer," the metal face said from the screen. The sneer had been replaced with a genial grin. "Today's race is sponsored by Pluff's Buffing. 'If Pluff Can't Buff It, It Can't Be Buffed.' First prize is two thousand gem, everyone else can zux off. Feel free to hurl yourselves at obstacles, but please do avoid running into the cameras; I grow weary of ordering replacements. The race begins at my whistle and ends when the final rocket clears the towers of Platamousse Proper."

May prepared to press The Button That Typically Made The Ship Go.

A tea-kettle-like whistle sounded from the android and six shiny new rockets sped from the platform. A lifetime passed in the span of a nanosecond as May jammed her finger into the button.

The ship strained and shook as if some ghastly giant had looped a finger in one of its fin vents. The finger released, and May at last felt the force push her back into the hover chair as she chased after her disappearing competition.

Half of her brain shouted at her that she had already lost because the clamps hadn't fully unhinged. The other half of her brain was busy keeping the rest of her alive.

The competitor's rockets fell away. It took May a quarter of a second too long to figure out why. Something skidded off the hull of the *Audacity* and—as she spun the ship sharply away—she watched a horde of comets plunge themselves into the nothingness above her.

Watching the comets was a terrible mistake. A sound only a foley artist could appreciate reverberated through the *Audacity* as May scraped the hull of a decommissioned starship. She pulled away from it, allowing herself an ill-chosen ninth of a second to stare at the ghost ship.

In that ninth of a second, three infant star-whales beset the rocket with curious nibbles, bouncing the ship off course.

Once she was out of their reach, May looked at Xan. He seemed curiously relaxed, as if he were considering funerary floral arrangements and important details for his eulogy.

Looking at Xan was, naturally, another terrible mistake. The upper fin of the *Audacity* caught on a giant plaster donut with pink frosting and sprinkles. The ship ricocheted away from it.

It took May exactly one sixth of a second to stabilize the ship and a further tenth of a second to figure out where she was in relation to the finish line. Shockingly close. Maybe, just maybe, the luck charm had done its job after all.

She flung the rocket through the towers of Platamousse Proper and pulled the *Audacity* in beside the six other rockets.

"By the thumbs of O'Zeno! We made it!" Xan vaulted into her, lifting her off the hover chair and into a spine-snapping hug.

"Xan, we lost. We lost horribly," May gasped, pushing him away to little effect.

"Sure, but we're alive, and we've got ten crystals left to celebrate on! Let's get down to the planet, wave to our adoring fans, then peruse the bars. Platamousse Annex is a trok-hole, but I've heard many a story about the wild before, during, and after-parties on Platamousse Proper. Since there's always a race, there's always at least one of each type of party in progress!"

A sudden hush thickened the air when they arrived on the planet. Echoes of the jubilee that had preceded them still reverberated around the massive viewing arena.

The surface was lushly greened with, May found upon closer inspection, plastic flora. From a distance it all looked very Earth-like, down to the bright and fluffily clouded sky, though it was a bit too green. Rows of multi-colored rockets were parked on the verdant field like glistening flowers and massive floral archways stretched so far into the sky, they became clusters of blurred color at their peak.

"Right so, no adoring fans," Xan noted.

Someone in the stands weaponized a drink cup in their direction, cueing a chorus of untranslatable curses and translatable, but inappropriate, name calling.

Xan flinched, but the cup landed a good five feet away. "Blitheon, let's skedaddle." He reached for May's hand and pulled her in the direction of the bleachers, straight for an opening beneath them.

When the crowd began chucking offerings of half-eaten food at them, they broke into a run.

The main lobby was vast, and they disappeared into the sea of life like two grains of particularly uninteresting sand.

The high-ceilinged lobby was made of black-green marble, fitted with sweeping golden gilt doorways and decor. Green statues of creatures May could only hope were mythical inhabited alcoves along the walls. May pulled Xan into one of them, affording them a bit of privacy from the masses.

"What was that about?" She brushed a dusting of crumbs from her hair.

Xan shrugged, wiping something pink from his shoulder. "Oh, several things, likely. Probably blinded a few people with the *Audacity*. Lost terribly. You're an Earthling, I'm a Carmnian. Come to think of it," he looked at her as if his entire life were flashing before his eyes and she wished for a moment she could see it, too, because he sure as hell wasn't sharing, "we probably shouldn't have done that."

"I thought you were a Tuhntian."

"I can be two things!"

May made a noise of acquiescence. "Well, we're out five hundred crystals." May rested her forehead against the dewclaw of the statue creature. The marble felt nice on her hot face as she tried to think of a solution.

Xan leaned against the pedestal, taste-testing the various sauces that dotted his suit.

"Mm, this one's good." He offered her a finger coated in red. She opened a single eye to survey him warily. He nudged his finger closer.

"No thanks," she said, closing her eyes again and sighing into the marble creature.

There was one way to make back their money. She was fairly certain it would work, too. It relied on a bit of luck, but that wasn't in short supply if Xan was to be believed. It sure felt like it was. Then again, they hadn't died. Maybe that was the best the charm could do in such an outlandish situation. A month ago, she didn't think aliens existed. Now, she was trying to out-pilot experienced racers in an alien rocket ship.

"Okay," she turned around, resting the back of her head against the statue now. "I think I know which rocket is going to lose the next race. Is there a gambling scene here?"

"Ohoho, *is* there?" Xan said with great bravado as he finished wicking away the detritus of their misdoing. He said nothing further.

May blinked at him. "Is there?"

"Yes. Yeah, there is. Follow me." He led her off into the flowing crowd again.

"So, Oh Omnipotent One, how do you know who's going to lose? Don't tell me you neglected to mention that you're a time traveler, because that would be extremely impolite of you."

"Not a time traveler. The fin clamps stuck. I couldn't launch when I was supposed to. That's why we lost."

Xan pretended to be surprised. "Oh, was that it? Not that we were in an old militarized Class 20 Ship with a pilot who didn't know forbinated from unforbinated a season ago."

"Still don't know. Militarized?"

Xan puffed at her. "Alright, I'll give you that we were at a disadvantage. But what are you planning on wagering?"

She stopped.

"Shoot," she whispered. "I'll bluff."

"You've got to surrender your wager."

May ran her fingers over her burrito-rolled bangs, pulling them back just to have them spring forward again due to the tenacity of the alien hair product.

"Is there anything valuable in the basement?"

"You know, you would think, you really would, that a localized miniature wormhole would be a little more discerning about the kinds of miscellany it spits out, but no. Zuxing thing loves trash. Maybe that's why it chose me."

"So, that's a no."

"Yes. That's a no. Hey, mun," he draped an arm over her shoulders, "we've got ten crystals left. We might as well spend it on a decent drink at a nice bar, accept our failures, and shimmy on out of here. *Audy's* just not meant for racing."

She looked at him miserably. Thoughts that wouldn't be of any help to her raised the machete again and started thwacking their way through her mental rain forest. Now though, and even worse, the thoughts were of self-pity and the biting mosquito of failure.

"Damnit, Xan. I'm sorry. That was dumb."

"What? No. No." He patted her shoulder, winced, then said, "Okay, well yeah it was kinda but not entirely! It was sort of a good idea. I mean, the *Audacity* was built as a racing rocket, after all. And you are a zuxing good pilot—or better than I am at least. You're just an Earthling—"

"Just an Earthling?" She cut him off.

"I mean—well, what I mean is an Earthling's never raced before so..."

She began to look like a candle left on a car dashboard in the middle of a summer heat wave in Florida.

"Ah, zuut. Don't look at me like that, starshine." He bit his lip as if punishing himself for what he was about to say. "You're sure you know who's going to lose the next race? Swear on your Queen?"

"Don't know what that means, but yeah. Yes, I'm sure."

"Ehhhh-you-can-wager-me-I-guess-then," his voice was strained and husky.

"Huh?"

"I said...you can wager me...I guess."

"What are you talking about? I can't wager you. You're not a commodity."

"Oh, believe me you can, and I am. Please don't lose, though. If you lose—"

"You're dead, right?"

"Uh..."

"Everything's death with you." They began to walk again.

"N-no. I wasn't going to say that. I was going to say if you lose, you owe me a drink." He laughed nervously.

"Uh-huh. Don't worry, I won't lose," she said, worrying that she would lose.

CHAPTER TWENTY-THREE

Hallucinogenic Aphrodisiacal Noodle Bar

Back on Earth, May hadn't had the time, energy, or incorrigible friend-group that leads to engaging in night life. She also was of the opinion that night was for sleeping.

She imagined what a rave must be like. Neon lights, she knew, were a necessity. Loud music was probably up there on the list of "Things to Do" when planning a rave. She supposed alcohol must be a facet, and likely some sort of illicit or at least dubious substances with vague names like "The Good Stuff" or "Shine Mints" would be passed around and smoked or snorted or licked—she wasn't sure how exactly people were ingesting their drugs nowadays. She imagined people sweat a lot during such an event and that sweat would probably get on her.

This party, she surmised, was something like a rave. Or at least something like what someone who'd never been to a rave thought a rave might be.

There were, however, a great deal more noodles than your typical rave could boast.

Scantily clad, if indeed clad at all, individuals lounged about the perimeter of the bar and fed each other noodles from red plastic cups. The noodles were not, as one might imagine, anything special. They looked like rice noodles because they were. As it turns out, Earthlings and their close cousins the Panseen are the only sentient beings in the Universe who can digest gluten.

These noodles, like the noodle that tempted Adam and Eve to eat from the Tree of Knowledge, had a dastardly secret.

Xan loudly sucked air in between his clenched teeth at the sight of them. "Alrighty, so whatever you do, do not—"

A gazelle-faced Pringnette draped a long rice noodle over Xan's nose and blinked in such a way that her eyelashes waved like a flag in a gentle breeze. He stiffened, his eyes crossing as they looked at the offending string of gluten-free pasta.

"Don't eat the noodles," he whispered to May, plucking the noodle from his nose and returning it to her with a forced smile. The Pringnette snorted her indignation, snatched the noodle from him, and spun away to look for better pickings.

"Aw, you hurt her feelings," May teased. "What's wrong with the noodles?"

"Oh, nothing, I'm sure they're great! It's just-" Another noodle lassoed his nose. Looking down, May saw a short, greenish, mustachioed Udonian holding the other end of the noodle.

Xan cringed in a way that might be read as a smile to someone with a degenerative eye disease and slipped his nose from the noose of the noodle.

"They're hallucinogenic and-" He paused as a beautiful purple Rhean slung a noodle over May's shoulder. "Aphrodisiacal." Xan finished, plucking the noodle from her shoulder to return it to the rebuked Rhean with an apologetic shake of his head.

May tried not to laugh as more noodles propositioned them. "This is where the gambling happens, then?"

"Yep. In the Noodle Bar. You're not going to have any issues wagering me here," he said, now draped with so many noodles he looked like a tired, tinsel covered Christmas tree.

She nodded and a noodle slid from her hair.

They shimmied through the throngs until they reached the bar, leaving behind a trail of broken hearts.

The multi-limbed, many-eyed, red-skinned Titian who worked the bar slung cups of noodles to voracious customers as if she were built for that express purpose.

"Uh, hello!" said Xan. "We've got a wager to put up. Where do we-"

"Eat," said the woman, sliding a red cup across the bar to him.

"Oh, alright." He tipped the cup back and swallowed the nest of noodles whole.

"So, you can eat them, but I can't?" May asked.

"I'm used to them! They don't really have much effect on me anymore. I would prefer it, however," he looked at her warily, "if you stopped metamorphosing into a sexy avant-garde lamp."

"I'll try," she said, shaking her lamp shade at him, tassels flying.

"Where can we go to put up a wager for the next race?" he asked the bartender again, setting the cup upside down on the bar.

"What've ya' got to wager?" She paused her noodle slinging to the dismay of everyone at the bar and leaned into him conspiratorially.

"Just me," he said, shrugging.

"You?" She eyed him disbelievingly.

"Yep, I'm the wager."

"Eh, whatever. Third door to the right. Tell 'em Dontel sent you." She looked him over once more. "Naw, tell 'em Maritov sent you." Again, the noodles were slung.

"I will, thanks very much!" He slipped away into the hoi polloi, parting the sea of sweaty alien bodies just enough for May to make it through untouched. Once they were in the hallway, he shook his head to dislodge the noodles he'd amassed.

He stood before the door, blocking May from reaching the shockingly banal metal handle. This was the first door May had come across since leaving Earth that neither whooshed nor buzzed nor disintegrated. Her standards had become quite high for doors, now.

Xan gave the handle a cavernous sigh.

"What's wrong?"

"Oh, nothing. Just preparing. You're sure you'll win?"

"Yes! The clamps were faulty. Whatever rocket starts from our position is going to lose," she whispered, not wanting to be overheard. "As long as they haven't fixed the clamps yet," she muttered, not wanting even him to hear her.

He groaned.

"Hey! We're going to nail this, okay?"

"Nail it?"

"We're going to win, I mean. That's what this is for, right?" she patted the good luck charm.

"It's not infallible! I mean, past a certain point you cross well out of the realm of luck and into impossibility."

"It's highly possible that I'm right about this."

Xan grit his teeth, looking miserable.

"What's the worst that could happen?" May asked.

"A lifetime of imprisonment in a sex dungeon?" Xan blinked at the doorknob. "Yeah, that's it, I guess. Not so bad, I suppose. If that's the worst. Might as well. Alright, well, good luck." He turned the knob.

On the other side of the door, a scene entirely unlike the noodle bar in every important way and in many unimportant ways assaulted their senses.

Firstly, their sense of smell. This was definitely worse than a sex dungeon. A sex dungeon would've smelled better. The air was choked with the sweat of a hundred beings who'd been in that room for a hundred rotations betting and losing or winning and sweating and betting again.

A red luminous fog accounted for the only luminescence in the windowless room. The things they *could* see, they very much wished they didn't have to. The foggy light touched on a pile of crystals glinting from a raised platform to their right, and that was where the pleasant imagery ended. Rows of scowling faces glared up through the fog, watching the black ceiling as if it might reach down and snag one of them.

One of these faces turned to the open door and fixed May with a devilish glint. The body attached to that face swam forward, wiggling like a snake lifting itself off the ground.

May was unsure if his skin was red, or if the light just made it seem that way. It was unpleasant though; of that she was certain. His cold finger trailed under her chin and she felt Xan's hand on her shoulder. Whether he was attempting to protect her from this thing or trying to steady himself, she couldn't tell.

"Sorborsor," he said by way of introduction. His face was wrinkled, yet taut, a look only attainable by bathing regularly in the blood of virgins. "This is the wager?"

"Uh, no." Xan grasped both her shoulders now and slowly pulled her back.

She was glad he'd said something, because her voice was caught in the gravity well of a black hole that had just, metaphorically, opened in her chest.

This was a bad idea.

Xan was all-in, though. He had been convinced. He had accepted his fate. He was trying to enjoy it.

"Tada!" he said. "It's me. I'm the wager. Soak it in, fellas. You could be the proud owner of your very own limited edition Tuhntian. We're in short supply nowadays. What with the…" He glanced over his shoulder at May with wide eyes. "Oh, you know. Maritov sent us back," he finished, practicing a semi-convincing smile on her that he then turned to Sorborsor.

A muttering came from the room as the up-turned faces turned downward to discuss. "Add him to the pot!" someone shouted above the buzz.

"Aye."

"Add him!" said several other voices that bounced off the walls.

Sorborsor looked put upon for only a moment before focusing again on May who was well in Xan's shadow now.

"Acceptable wager. What be the prediction?"

May had rather hoped she'd get to look at the rockets first. At least she remembered her starting position.

"The rocket in slot three to lose," she proposed.

"Vague," he sneered. "Oy," he addressed the crowd over his shoulder. "Who's on three?"

"Ol' Joeybillums in *Comet Crusher*," a single helpful voice replied.

"*Comet Crusher* to lose for the Tuhntian butler," Sorborsor announced, then shoved Xan, with surprising strength, toward the pile of crystals.

"I'm going to win, okay?" May shouted after him.

"Oh, not a doubt, mun. Not a doubt," he said doubtfully.

"Someone's gonna have a little blue pet tonight!" Sorborsor said. "Kornackuk, think the husband'd mind?"

A densely muscled yellow-green man who wouldn't have looked out of place on the cover of a Harlequin romance novel, aside from the massive tusks, winked at Xan. "Yurten will be well pleased with my winnings," he confirmed.

Xan shrugged at May. "Could be worse, actually," he said nonchalantly as he was forced onto the platform with the crystals.

"That zuxer's Quaxlagon under Carmnia! His ass is mine!" shouted someone standing on a speaker. The softly glowing fog above them imploded with a kaleidoscope of color and reformed into a holoscreen, giving him the complexion of a living disco ball.

"May!" A semi-transparent force-field sizzled around Xan and the pile of crystals. He banged on it with his fist, but, since it was transparent, the action resulted in him looking like a loud mime. "May, I do not want to go with that person!"

"I didn't realize you were this popular," May said, weaving through the crowd to get closer to him, preparing to grab him and run once the race ended.

"Shut up, Rap!" Sorborsor said to the person on the speaker, and several other voices echoed the sentiment.

Sweaty alien bodies bumped May from all sides. A drink clattered to the floor and something that smelled like alcohol flecked her calves. She looked up at the holoscreen above which now displayed a live view of Plattamousse Annex. The ships lined up, a black-and-white checkered number settling into spot three. That was it. *Comet Crusher*.

The air sparked with tension. May swore she felt her hair standing on end from all the electricity in the atmosphere.

"Hey, you!" shouted Sorborsor. "Stop that."

May peeled her eyes away from the screen to see Xan licking experimentally at the force-field. Relenting, he draped himself forlornly over the crystal pile. The electricity in the air dissipated.

May turned her attention once again to the holoscreen. The race had begun, but she'd missed the first eighth of a second and, as such, couldn't see if the clamps had stuck or not. *Comet Crusher* was, however, decidedly not in the lead.

Time stood still, as if paused, while she watched the race. Or—no it didn't. Chattering alcoholics swirled around her at normal speed. The race, though, seemed to be moving in slow motion. Or perhaps not at all.

"Sorry tchaggs. Signal's out," said Sorborsor, smacking a whirring server mounted on the back wall.

The holographic molecules burning above them began to move again. A sharp pain in the back of her jaw, she was clenching her teeth well beyond their recommended bite force.

A winner lit up the screen with fanfare....and it was not *Comet Crusher*. Someone to her left whooped as a second rocket passed the towers. It, too, was not *Comet Crusher*. A third, a fourth. *Comet Crusher* was still out there, still trying.

May had never wanted someone else to fail so much in her entire life.

A rocket called *Mister Manicotti* made a valiant effort for last place, but in the end, the infant star whales tripped *Comet Crusher* up just enough to allow the pale-yellow *Manicotti* to make fifth place by half a nose.

Comet Crusher had lost, and May had won.

She felt she should smile, cheer, perhaps. Was that what people did when good things happened to them? She tried on a smile; it felt nice. It felt really nice. She'd won!

A sharp scream of frustration came from the person standing on the speaker. "Grab that zuxing Tuhntian! He's got a bounty on him!"

The nice moment, the smile, and the inclination to cheer were all sucked out of May like oxygen from a puncture in a spacesuit.

The forcefield dissolved and Xan was beside her, pushing desperately through the curling mass of gamblers.

CHAPTER TWENTY-FOUR

Great.

Running for her life was not at all like May had imagined it would be. She imagined blood pounding in her ears and the cold chill of pursuit at her back, the pounding of feet behind her growing ever closer. Like she'd read in books. That would've been far preferable.

Instead, her legs moved in a rhythm she did not set, her chest ached for a cigarette—or no, wait—that was oxygen it craved, following the breadcrumb trail of alien obscenities Xan was stringing together as they steadily became quieter, his long legs ferrying him far ahead of her.

The obscenities became louder again as he waited for her to catch up, then quieter again as he inevitably sprinted ahead of her, until finally he grabbed her hand in his own to force himself to stay by her side. Or rather, to pull her along like a limp banana peel.

They emerged at last in the green, marbled main entrance hall and light from the surface of the planet poured in through a massive doorway.

"Are we," May wheezed, "close enough?"

Xan pecked at the BEAPER on his wrist with his nose. "Theoretically!" he shouted back to her and they fizzled away.

The sudden shift from being in such a dark, green location to being bombarded with the bright orange of the *Audacity*'s neon living room made May wince. Xan leapt up the stairs to the control panel and brought his fist down on The Button That Typically Made The Ship Go.

"Well, that was absolutely horrifying." He pulled on his suit to straighten it. "Are you alright?"

Out of breath, May couldn't speak, but she nodded vigorously as she leaned over her knees.

He walked down from the control loft and put a hand on her back. "May, I'm sorry..."

"Why the fuck didn't you tell me about the bounty?" she wheezed.

"I didn't know! Also, that's not really the kind of thing you tell a person about, even if you do know."

"Why," May asked seriously, "is there a bounty on you?"

Xan sat down miserably on the couch. His eyes were open, but he wasn't seeing anything outside his own mind. "I don't know," he said quietly.

"You have to know!"

He didn't say anything, then. Just stared at the carpet, genuinely confused.

"You can't think of anything?" May asked, sitting on the carpet near the couch.

"I mean...this couldn't be that. There's no way."

"What?"

He squeezed his eyes tight and rubbed them with his palms. "No, it can't be. Don't worry about it. Look," he pulled a handful of crystal coins from his pocket. "I grabbed some of our winnings before we got chased out of there! You can have all of it. I'll drop you off anywhere you like, Vagran, maybe. Maybe you'll like it there. Or Pan! Pan might be nice."

May glanced at the ship's viewscreen, at the stars streaking by, the console she'd put so much time into. Then, hesitantly, she looked over at Xan, crumpled as he was into a croissant on the couch. The idea that he might be a dangerous criminal was far more absurd to her than the ship running on coffee.

She wished she wanted to go live on Pan. But all she'd be there was a lonely food service worker, exactly what she was on Earth. Here, she had a chance to be more.

"No," she said.

"No?" Xan tilted his head at her.

"I'm fucking staying here. We'll find somewhere else to race. Somewhere less seedy."

He gave her a confused little smile. "What's that word you keep using? Is it an Earth profanity?"

"What word?"

"Fu%^"

May cringed at his pronunciation, it sounded like a steam engine crashing into a drum kit. Since he'd spoken in English, the translation chip in May's head had decided to take a well-deserved break.

"Yeah, that's a profanity. How could you tell?"

Xan unfurled a bit, setting the crystals on the coffee table. "You can usually tell when someone is cursing, even if you have no idea what they're saying! It's in the energy of the word. Every word is alive in a way. The more it's used, the more alive it is. A word uttered a trillion times, each time with nearly the same meaning and the same feeling, it just carries that quality, you know? But! You can say anything, anything at all, and make it sound like an obscenity."

May sat on the arm of the couch, closed her eyes, let herself fall back into the squeaking and ill-padded cushions. "Really?" she asked, smiling.

"Really! Something completely innocuous. Wrench, for example. You can say wrench in such a way, with just the right inflection and tone and at just the right moment, that it sounds exactly like something your aunt would *smack* you with a wrench for saying. And what's great about that, is that you can come up with some pretty unique new profanities just by—"

Words flowed over May like lukewarm unlimited free refill coffee. Half the words got through to her. She heard "great" and latched onto it for a moment.

Everything was not great.

Or everything *was* great, but in a sarcastic sense.

Or perhaps everything was *actually* great. Great also meant big. Everything was big. It was a lot. It was her, in an orange metal tin, with a strange blue alien, surrounded by a great, big everything.

She shuddered. Everything was a lot of things.

Great, she thought. Just great.

She wanted a cigarette painfully. Putting anything in her mouth at this point would probably help or at least distract her enough to not care. Xan was still rambling about curse words.

"...now the really interesting thing about cursing is that—"

"Xan? Would you mind making me a cup of coffee?"

"Will you actually drink it? Because I'm pretty sure the first coffee I gave you is still under the console growing new life."

"I'll drink it," she said. Her eyes were still closed, but the bright orange of the ceiling and the walls in the ship bled through her eyelids.

She felt the couch shift below her and cracked an eyelid just enough to see Xan digging around in the cushions for something. He plucked out a clear faceted bottle which sloshed with cobalt blue liquid.

"This is a lot stronger than coffee, if that's what you need." He swirled the liquid in the unmarked bottle.

"Alien alcohol?" May asked. "Perfect."

Xan smiled, set the bottle down, and ricocheted off the couch to the weird little coffee nook behind the control panel. From a cabinet beneath the coffee maker, he produced two ceramic mugs. May couldn't imagine an alien potter making mugs like those. They looked like they'd been stolen from a diner in the forties.

"Stole these from a diner in the forties." Xan laughed, handing her a chipped mug and pouring out a scant ounce of the beverage.

May sniffed it; it smelled strong. "You've been to Earth before?"

"What? No. No, I think the diner was on Pan in orbit 7243. That was a rough decade. Come to think of it, most of them were. Let's drink!"

He poured himself a mug-full and set the bottle down on the carpet beside the couch.

Nothing she'd eaten had disagreed with her yet. The corn came close, and that was the only Earth food she'd had since her abduction. It was reasonable to assume this blue liquid wouldn't kill her outright at least, so she tipped it back just far enough that she could stick her tongue in it.

She recoiled, glad she hadn't actually taken it into her mouth.

"What is this?"

"Marsupian wine, the finest Tuhnt has to offer. The only Tuhnt has to offer. Had to offer. It's good right? Not amazing, grant you, nothing extraordinary, but it's good. Does what it intends to." He drank a little more and settled into the couch, eyes closed as he savored the drink that looked, smelled, and tasted like blue Listerine.

After the day—no, week—no, life—she'd been having, she was up for drinking Listerine.

She took a sip.

She would never trust the tip of her tongue again.

Had May been a trained sommelier, she might have been awed at the freshness of the bouquet, the notes of vanillin and creme de cassis, the full-bodied palate, the cascade of current and black-pepper, and the whisper of violet just at the finish. She was not, however, a trained sommelier, and as such she just decided the wine was good. Very good.

She hummed softly, joining Xan in the recesses of the old couch as she indulged. Beneath her, the *Audacity* purred, happy to be carrying them far away from Plattamousse.

"More?" Before she could answer, Xan tipped his mug, pouring half of what he had left into hers.

"I couldn't possibly," she said with faux bravado just before taking another sip.

So, she'd failed.

She'd screwed up the race and lost everything she'd won back, but somehow, whether by virtue of marsupian wine or having a friend to share in the burden of misfortune, she felt alright.

Content, even.

"Where's the next race?" she asked, her contentment spiraling into confidence.

"Ha! You might want to slow down on the wine, mun." Xan sped up, downing the last of his mug and looking for all the world like she was about to give the rest of hers to him.

She curled over her mug protectively. "Don't you dare. I'm of sound mind, and I think we should race again. If the clamps hadn't stuck, we would've won."

Xan squinted a disbelieving eye at her. "You're being facetious again, right? Because we most certainly would not have won."

"I might not have lost, at least."

"Alright, okay, fine. We can ask the IFI where the closest low-entry racetrack is to here."

"Good."

"Great," Xan said on a sigh. "But first, let's finish off the Marsupian wine. It was kinda depressing having it around."

May thought about pointing out to him that he had just used this word he allegedly didn't understand, but she knew, now, so she let it be.

CHAPTER TWENTY-FIVE

Raskov the Beautiful

A piercing squeal like a whistle being blown by a wind tunnel, so loud May could feel it in her teeth, shuddered through the ship then stilled, leaving only a reverberating silence.

"Well, that was wretched. Wonder what could've-" Xan was interrupted by another whistle.

May peeled her cheek from his latex-clad shoulder and rubbed her face. The empty mug fell from her lap and onto the carpet, giving a soft thunk that was all together much more pleasant than whatever was happening to the ship.

"It sounds like something's scraping against the hull," she said.

This disturbed Xan. If something were scraping against the hull, it would have to be fairly large. If something were scraping against the hull, it would likely be doing it again. If something were scraping against the hull, it would certainly be damaging the paint.

Few things could persuade Xan to leap into action. The thought of losing even a fleck of precious Obtrusive Orange was one of them. Followed closely, of course, by a poor TV signal.

They both, with some trepidation, climbed the stairs to the control panel, May taking the pilot's chair and Xan leaning close into the view screen. On the view screen, the cool inky blackness of space was interrupted by a cooler, inkier blackness. Squinting, May could just work out that the cooler, inkier blackness was vaguely phallic in shape and sidling up to the *Audacity* for another go at rubbing against it.

May had never enjoyed being rubbed against by things that were vaguely phallic in shape and prepared to make a speedy retreat.

Before another blow could be dealt, however, an inset in the viewscreen manifested a face from which May immediately recoiled. Not because it was in any way unpleasant—much the opposite. This face was attractive, but this face knew it.

A rugged and tanned face with a perfectly imperfect goatee and a tasteful swoop of shiny black hair smiled at them in a practiced way.

"Can I help you?" May said with a resigned apathy.

In her peripheral vision, she saw Xan's hand cover The Button That Typically Made The Ship Go. She shooed his hand away; she wanted to see what subcategory of ass they were dealing with, first.

"Hey babe. Saw your last race. A bit rough, but I'd love to train up a hottie like you. I'm Raskov The Beautiful, of Earth in case you couldn't tell. What's your name, honey?"

"It's Xan."

"I'm talking to the hot chick, creep!" Raskov tapped the camera glass.

"We're done here," May said. "Goodbye."

"Cool it, babe. I just want to help a fellow Earthling out, eh? I want to sponsor you, you dig? I'll waive your entry fee. First prize is ten thou. Second prize is a night in my very luxurious Earth-style bed next to my very luxurious Earth-style body..." Raskov's upper lip quirked up and he winked suggestively.

"God, men are the worst," May whispered, closing her eyes to make him go away for just a moment. She peeked up at Xan. "No offense," she said.

"Oh no, none taken! I'm not, strictly speaking, a man. I'm a Xan! I mean...well technically I'm a four, but probably you didn't need to know that. 'Men' and 'women' seem to be an Earth-thing."

"Hey," Raskov interjected. "Come on, lover, what'd'ya say?"

"No. And I'm not your lover," May said.

"Not yet, maybe. Trust me, you'll thank me later."

May side-eyed Xan. "There's only one language these guys understand," she said. "Fuck off, asshole!" She pressed her foot into the accelerator. The *Audacity* inched away from Raskov the

Beautiful. Inches, unfortunately, mean little in relation to the vast everythingness of open space.

Raskov's face appeared again and May tried to turn it off.

"He hacked the com line," she sighed.

"Of course, babe! You didn't make it hard. Aha! That's what she said, am I right? I'm right."

In a desperate attempt to dislodge his words, May smacked her forehead against the control panel.

"Hold on, she didn't say that," Xan tried to defend her.

May patted his knee. "Don't bother."

"Looks like I'll be towing you to the Pipes! Can't warp with your drive locked, but tha's alright, babe. It'll be good to have some time to talk. Not many Earthlings out here. Not many compatible species, either if ya' catch my drift." He laughed as if he'd said something absolutely hilarious. May's eyebrow twitched; she didn't know it could do that.

"Sorry, I'm not compatible either," May said.

"Wha?"

"Like a Barbie doll down there."

"Huh?"

"I'm not going to have sex with you!" she said, at last.

"You just met me; how do you know?"

"Psychic," May answered.

"You're so weird."

"Uh-huh."

"I like weird chicks." Raskov licked his lips. "Always wild in the sack."

Xan slunk underneath the control panel and gestured for May to join him.

"This guy's a zoup-nog," he whispered to May. "If we unlock the warp drive, we'll at least get there faster. He'll have to let us go to race, we can just blast off in the other direction when he does!"

"Oh, I'm not worried about that," said Raskov. "Also, I can hear you, bro, and I ain't no zoup-nog. I'm actually highly intelligent. High IQ. Not that a stupid alien would know what an IQ is."

"I can't listen to him talk anymore." May shrugged and unlocked the latch. "Alright." She stood up again. "I will race, but only because I want to."

"See? What'd I tell you? Ladies love Raskov."

"Oh, my God," May looked heavenward—or, rather, looked in the direction opposite to the artificial gravity since there was nowhere she could look at this point which wasn't, strictly speaking, heavenward—and shook her head in amazement.

The spacescape before them winked into darkness, then a sickly yellow glow illuminated an enormous vault door.

"Where are we?" asked Xan.

"The Pipes, bro. Duh."

"He's going to need to stop calling me bro. I don't like it," Xan informed May seriously. She wondered what Xan would do if he didn't, but decided she didn't want to know. Xan would've done nothing about it, it just helped to complain.

The Pipes, to use the colloquial term, are a system of derelict pipes running between the desert planet of Astffadoo and its wettest moon, Chummy. The ancient Panseen who colonized Astffadoo felt that the most elegant solution to Astffadoo's complete lack of water was to build a pipeline from Chummy to Astffadoo. This plan was so foolhardy, so idiotic, that to this day an infrastructural faux pas is still intergalactically known as an 'Astffa*don't*.'

Though Chummy dried up from embarrassment long ago, the pipe system remains, incomplete and structurally unsound, jutting off of Chummy like a malformed limb. Its only value lies in that it's wide enough to safely hide an illegal five-rocket race from the authorities, and that it curves and branches off in enough places to make that race extremely interesting for the parched onlookers who waited on the planet below, watching via little drones that buzzed mosquito-like around the ships.

It was here that Raskov had brought the *Audacity*, to the derelict main water tank on Chummy. On Plattamousse, May had been intimidated by how sleek and new the rockets lined up beside her were. Now, she was intimidated mostly by the general air of intimidation these rockets exuded.

These ships, in sharp contrast to the professional racers, had gaudy gold trim, additional fins that May knew were not integral to the handling of the ship, and hulls painted to such a high gloss that the dim lights had trouble getting a grip on them.

"A'ight, babe, race starts in ten."

"Ten what?" May asked.

"Oh, for the love of—just ten," said Raskov.

"Fine. What are our destination coordinates?"

"Whoa there, starkiller, you're gonna have to figure that out yourself. Just follow the green lights, babe. You're gonna be great. I'll be waiting for ya' at the finish line! Oh, and smile for the cameras, babe."

"No."

He ignored her, and it was the first decent thing he'd done since they'd met.

"Alright nerds," said Raskov. "You know the drill. Run the Pipes, follow the green lights, and if you're gonna wipe out try t' keep the smoldering wreckage outta the way of the pros, yeah? Landing pad's all lit up like Christmas or some shit, so ya' can't miss it down here. As we say back on Earth: Ready, set, go!"

The shut-off valve began to grind open, its massive disc of a door moving only slightly faster than a geriatric knee-replacement patient on the mend.

A crescent of green light escaped from around the edge now, steadily waxing. Engines revved in a way May didn't think rocket engines could.

May bit her bottom lip, watching the sliver of green light grow. At some point, she would have to go for it. The *Audacity* might even have an advantage here because it wasn't outfitted with a million decorative bits that could be sliced off in a tight squeeze.

Xan looked from her to the sliver and back. "You're not planning on ramming the ship through the opening before it's fully open in a foolhardy bid to get a few seconds ahead...are you? Because it looks like you are. It very much looks like that's what you're planning to do."

"On the nose." May smiled, threw the ship into manual drive, and launched.

CHAPTER TWENTY-SIX

The Pipes

“Did we make it?” Xan asked, eyes closed tight as he braced against the control panel, his fingers curling into it as if he were trying to hold the ship together himself.

“Yep,” May said as she pressed the ship onward into the pipes which were lit by rows of bright green LEDs on either side. “Check the rear view. Is anyone else out yet?”

Xan called an inset into the lower left corner of the view screen. It showed the opposite side of the shut-off valve. A gaudy purple ship scraped through, sparks jumping from its hull as it pushed into the pipes.

“One’s out. Nope—two. Not looking great back there, though. I think that one lost a fin. Wait, we didn’t lose anything did we?”

“Don’t think so,” May said.

He decided to check anyway, pulling up the maintenance log in place of the rear-view.

“Nothing new to report. Nothing old, either. Not much at least. Aw, you got rid of the parking wobble? I thought it gave the ship some character.”

“You’ve got enough character,” May said, gaining speed.

He didn’t argue.

The pipe ahead was green lit, broad, and suspiciously obstacle-free for as far as she could see.

May thought this was strange and said so. Saying so was, of course, a bad idea. It went something like this:

“This seems too easy,” May said.

“Shouldn’t have said that.”

“Why not?”

The pipe which had looked, from a distance, like it went on forever, suddenly twisted to the left.

May pulled the ship around, scraped it against the metal wall, wiping out a row of perfectly good green lights, dropped the ship down to avoid a metal panel that drooped from the ceiling of the pipe, and narrowly missed the purple rocket which overtook her. "Shit," she whispered.

Xan looked like a startled cat, his fingertips disappearing into the abused foam armrest of the chair. "That's why not. Gurtrine's Mandate—it's a function of irony."

"What?"

"Well, the story goes that Colonel Gurtrine the Third Great Colonel of-"

"Tell me later." May hated to cut him off mid anecdote, but the purple rocket now looked like a fast-moving grape ahead of them, and their lead had been lost.

Four points of white light grew in the distance where the main pipe branched into four smaller pipes. None of these smaller pipes were green-lit.

"Just follow the green lights *babe*," May mimicked Raskov angrily under her breath. "Any ideas?"

"Uh, follow that ship?" Xan pointed to the purple ship, and May watched it.

Unable to choose a pipe to continue down, the purple ship smashed itself on the joint between the two leftmost pipes. The wreck lit up like cherries jubilee, then dripped sadly to the rusted pipe floor.

"Blitheon's ankle hairs! Alright, That's it. I'm not giving any more racing advice ever again. You're on your own, mun. Twadon!" He buried his face in his hands.

As if appeased by the flaming ship's sacrifice, the second pipe from the left flickered green, giving May just enough time to angle the *Audacity* through it.

"That was dark," May said as they entered another long stretch of green pipe, smaller now.

"Uh-huh."

"Like, really dark. Maybe too dark?" she insisted, trying to process what she'd just seen.

"Maybe," Xan said.

"Ugh," May shook her head to dislodge the sight of the exploding rocket and pressed on. She flipped on the rear-view herself this time, Xan too busy curling into the co-pilot's chair.

Three ships pursued her. She was far in the lead again now that...well, now.

The pipe's walls grew flimsier until large swaths of metal sheeting were missing from the siding, providing May windows into space. If she'd wanted, she could have easily forced the ship through one of those openings and left Raskov the Beautiful and his blood-hungry course far behind.

She was winning, though. And the prize was ten thousand crystals. Or, at least, that's what she assumed "ten thou" meant. For all she knew, it could have been ten thousand horrible pickup lines.

Still. Winning felt really good, and even the fiery end of one of her fellow racers couldn't dry up the flood of adrenaline.

She kept going. Maybe Raskov wasn't lying, and she'd get her ten thousand. Maybe he was, and she'd get to punch him. Either way, she won.

Ahead, the pipe fell away entirely, revealing the planet of Astffadoo. It glowed redly, the curvature of its surface just visible and steadily disappearing as they approached.

Behind them—not much could be seen. Something small and yellow, a fleck of green, a dot of blue. They were far in the lead.

"We're going to win!" May bounced in her seat and pressed the ship onward to victory.

Xan peeked over his gloved fingers, relaxed, and unfurled. "It would seem so. It would certainly, definitely, seem that way. Don't know how much 'we' was involved, though."

Suddenly, horribly, the ship went dark.

No brilliant view screen, no twinkling panel lights, no ambient orange glow.

It was silent, too.

And cold.

And the oxygen was thinning.

"Zuut," whispered Xan. All May could see of him were his wide, terrified eyes which glowed gently out of the blackness, like a cartoon character. There was a good reason for this, or, rather, a horrifically awful reason, but that's for another book.

May's mind ping-ponged between what she knew, what she thought she knew, and what she wished she knew.

She knew inertia dictated the ship would continue to travel toward the planet. She knew the ship would crash nose-first into the planet if she didn't get the thrusters back.

She thought she knew what had happened—they had run out of fuel.

She wished she knew just exactly how much time she had to brew another pot of coffee.

The answer was exactly not enough.

Most Tuhntians have impressive night vision. Xan, however, had spent entirely too long gazing lovingly at the *Audacity*'s eye-searing hull, enraptured by the beauty of the Obtrusive Orange paint, mesmerized by its smoothly arching curves. This had burned a permanent blue after-image of the ship into the center of his retinas.

Despite this, Xan trundled to the coffeemaker and began brewing a cup, fumbling in the dark over the well-memorized ritual of pouring a healthy filter-full of grounds, sliding it into the machine, and turning it on.

With no electricity to feed it, the machine did not turn on.

May's fingers ran hurriedly along the underside of the panel searching for a switch she knew existed but had never actually taken the time to look for: the emergency back-up generator.

"Xan! Where's the back-up generator switch?" May shouted at him. If anyone knew where it was it would be—May groaned—it would be her.

Regardless, she felt him dive under the control panel to begin flicking every switch he could find.

Hypothetically, in, say, a heated round of Street Fighter, Xan's button mashing skills would far out-pace May's terrific reflexes and outstanding hand-eye-coordination. Xan would win every time, much to May's chagrin.

The lights flickered, the coffee maker gurgled, the engine gave a satisfied hum.

"Ah! That was it!"

"What did you hit?" May asked as she prepared the ship for re-entry.

"Uh," Xan popped out from under the panel, his finger pressed tightly to a switch. "I think it was this one. Could've been one of the other ones, though." He pulled up the maintenance log to see how much damage he'd done. "Wobble's back," he smiled triumphantly.

May shook her head and laughed. Below on the planet of Astffadoo squatted a landing pad lit by cheap string lights and painted with a huge, primitive symbolic cock in neon green spray paint. Or was it a rocket ship? Was May just seeing dicks everywhere now?

Whatever it was, it was her destination. She slowed down, aimed, and landed the ship perfectly. Perfectly, apart from the slight wobble.

CHAPTER TWENTY-SEVEN

Billiard All

Earthling dreams were delicious. So vivid, so absurd, so embarrassing, Chaos thought dreamily as she lounged across the big, powerful Captain's desk (which she never used for anything but lounging dramatically over) and dragged a pink feathered stylus over her face.

She had dropped in on no fewer than ten million sex dreams starring a small, jovial entity known to Earthlings as Danny Devito. She had enjoyed countless renditions of individuals being naked in public, losing all their teeth, and forgetting their school schedules.

And now, thanks to General Listay's ministrations, the Earthlings dreamed mainly of freedom. Of ignoring their daily schedules, tearing down the perfectly designed apartments, going mudding through the pristine gardens. A common theme among the more violent Earthlings involved rushing into the General's control tower, guns blazing. This would be impossible, of course, because the General had abolished guns, but they dreamt anyway.

Chaos fed off this yearning for destruction, slurping up discontent as if it were made of ramen noodles. Discontent and ramen noodles are more similar than they are different.

She seeded the Earthling's dreams with her own image, the inimitable Goddess of Chaos. A shining specter that would save them from their nightmares by burning their worrisome dreams to ash with one glance of her unmentionable peepers.

It was working delightfully well, she thought.

Yvonne's consciousness had been blessedly quiet lately, too. That tiny mortal mind of hers hadn't interjected with thoughts of her lost lover Ix in almost a season—*damn it*, thought Chaos. Thinking about not thinking about Ix had ruined her streak and the pink feathered stylus she'd been fiddling with disappeared.

So she was able to damn things again. She'd have to be careful with that. She never knew where things went when she damned them, but she assumed it wasn't anywhere good. Perhaps, she thought, once she ended the universe she would find out. She might be greeted by an array of useless objects and beings that she had accidentally, and occasionally purposefully, damned over the eons.

She slunk off the desk, going to the window to watch the marble of Earth, her first point of conquest, and its slowly meandering fluffy white clouds. The shadow of night was visible, slowly consuming half the globe. *Isn't it always night on Earth?* Chaos mimicked the bartender to herself. She should've damned him, but he *had* fixed her a drink and even ancient entities know it's highly immoral to kill your bartender.

Planets were such fragile little things. She could wipe out Earth now, just as she had done with Tuhnt. The *Peacemaker* was designed to destroy planets, and it was quite good at it. But that hadn't fulfilled her. It had been like eating a rice cake after spending lifetimes asleep. She needed a full meal. She needed devotees. A slow and delicious descent into madness that would spread across the universe, pinging from planet to planet like an infected billiard ball.

She watched dusk break over Earth one mile at a time, the planet slowly spinning, washing itself in darkness for a mere twenty-four Earth hours, and suddenly, thinking about the dawn breaking on the other side of the planet, she felt fragile. She, who consumed reality and held it in the quiet and dark place within her, felt weak. All things would pass through her someday, but even she couldn't hold onto them. Eventually, she herself would be damned.

Yvonne's consciousness rose like a wave of nausea over her, but she swallowed it back. Turning, she found the Captain's desk was now a billiard table, a triangle of balls all arranged so perfectly their stripes were all aligned, as if mocking her.

Hurriedly, seeing it as a bad omen, she shot the cue ball into the rack, scattering the balls in every imaginable direction. One-by-one, as Chaos stood watching with a furrowed brow, the balls began to drop into pockets. Their trajectories slowed, but never stopped. Slowly, painfully slowly, they all drew out their individual paths, all ultimately falling into a pocket.

Existential dread gripped Chaos as the final ball, the eight ball, meandered around the outer edge of the table. It was as if an unseen force was gently pushing it along, headed straight for a corner pocket.

"No," Chaos whispered. "Don't you dare."

The eight ball dared.

"Stop," Chaos commanded it. But it would not be deterred. The eight ball rolled gaily into its pocket, clinking against the other balls that had already been tucked neatly away.

"Damn it!" Chaos shouted, and the entire table popped out of reality. This was not a good sign. Something was going horribly right in the universe, and she needed it to go wrong.

She needed a little good luck.

And fortunately for her, her host body had recorded a memory that would make a little luck easy to get. She conjured open the IFI behind her eyes and placed a special order at *The Agency*.

CHAPTER TWENTY-EIGHT

Raskov

May had never in her life been cheered by a crowd. She thought, at first, that the noise was a battle cry, and that perhaps she should hurry back to the ship and escape before they set upon her.

It came from a dusty group of revelers sitting around a large TV, mostly Udonian and Panseen, their whoops and hollers, their straw-hat throwing, their catcalls and loud whistles carried on the dry, dense air.

May looked to Xan for an explanation, but he only shrugged, smiled, and waved. May scanned the audience for a pale face. Raskov had to be among them, his obscene ship was parked obscenely in the distance.

"Move!" pierced the cheers. Ah, there he was.

The audience parted like the Red Sea, but this Moses was 5'7", white, and wearing nothing but an arrangement of black leather straps and metal spikes.

Raskov strode purposefully toward them. May adjusted her posture to seem more threatening. She was going to get ten thousand crystals out of him and nothing more.

"What the hell was that?" he shouted wetly in her face.

"That was winning. You owe me ten thousand crystals."

May felt Xan lift his wrist to bring them back on board the ship, but she put a hand out to stop him. She wasn't worried. Raskov didn't have any weapons. She knew this because if he had, he would've pulled them by now. It is not easy to get weapons for the average individual on most planets. This is one of the many reasons why Earth, up until Listay's recent takeover, had been a no-contact zone.

"We aren't leaving without our prize," May insisted.

"The hell you are. How did you get through the electromagnetic field? No one's ever gotten past that. Did you know about it? Are you with the fuzz?"

He was so close now, May could smell the leather of his outfit, the old cigarette smoke in his goatee, and alcohol on the spittle that flew at her. Had she liked him even a little bit, she would've settled for a pack of cigarettes in place of payment.

"It was hard, but we nailed it. And *that's* what she said. Isn't it, May?" Xan beamed with pride at his first successful Earth joke.

May stifled a laugh. "You get one," she told Xan, "one 'that's what she said' joke ever. I hope you're happy with your choice."

"I am! Thank you for indulging me."

"Anytime."

May had forgotten Raskov was there. Raskov had not forgotten he was there.

"Hey, you don't ignore me," he pointed at her. When she turned the full force of her stare back on him, he backed off a little, his hands raised. "Right, babe, I'll tell you what. I can't pony up the cash right now, but I'm hankering for an intimate connection with a foxy gal. If ya' ditch this pathetic dink and come with me, I'll give you the whole universe." He spread his arms out, and May took that as an invitation.

She lunged at him with her entire body, her right fist hankering for an intimate connection with his jaw. Xan snaked his arms around her shoulders and tried to hold her back, but she could see nothing but Raskov's smug, evil face and she could hear nothing but her heart which had switched places with her brain, apparently.

"Alright, we're leaving. Forget the gem," Xan said, raising his BEAPER again to teleport them back to the *Audacity*.

"Damn, bro, control your bitch," Raskov told Xan.

Xan refused to do that.

"Alright," he sighed, "May, get him." He released May and she barreled into Raskov, knocking him to the ground. The crowd cheered again, thinking they were going to get some bonus entertainment.

But she hit hard, dusty ground with no one beneath her. *Where did he go?* She thought. *What's this soft pile of gray ash I landed in?* She wondered. Then she realized her second question probably explained the first. She scrambled to her feet, dusting the gray ash off herself.

"Shit, I incinerated him!" she said.

"No...they did," Xan whispered.

She stopped trying to wipe off Raskov's remains and looked up.

Two androids who looked like chrome clones of the Michelin Man without the cartoonish grin—without, it must be said, a face at all—sprinted toward them across the red earth. One produced a hand-held shop-vac and began to hoover up Raskov's remains with the professional nonchalance of a British nanny cleaning up spilled Cheerios.

May's mouth was dry, her heart and her brain had switched back, but only just.

"The criminal has been eliminated. Justice is served," said the chrome nanny Michelin Man, packing away the shop-vac.

"You will submit to a database scan," the other Michelin Man told May.

"Uh, no, sorry," Xan said quickly, grabbing May's arm. "We've got to go, right now immediately." He teleported them up to the *Audacity,* sprinted to the control panel, and slammed into The Button That Typically Made the Ship Go. Once he was sure their destination was set far enough away that the ship would have to warp, he pressed the button again, and they were off.

May sat cross-legged on the thick orange shag, staring at a little cow-licked bit of orange fiber but not actually seeing it. Her fuzzy peripheral vision saw Xan walk shakily down the stairs and drop to the floor beside her.

He slung his gloves across the floor—May could've sworn an arc of gold glitter flew out of the gloves.

"Guess Raskov got what he deserved," May said, dusting more of him off her suit. "We didn't, though." She buried her face in her arms and tried to think up ways to make money. Ways that weren't turning Xan in for whatever bounty was on him. Why had she even thought that? Now she felt bad about losing two fortunes *and* about being a shitty person.

Maybe, though...maybe she could turn him in, get the money, and then rescue him. That felt very Star Wars. It felt very doable.

"Xan would you consider..." she started, but his BEAPER buzzed and she stopped. She really didn't want to say it, anyway.

"It's from the Agency." He was silent for a moment, reading. "Oh. Hmm. Special order, double pay, easy job!" He smiled at the BEAPER, then at May.

"More whoring?" she asked.

"Nope! Someone wants to pay me seven hundred crystals just to screw in a light bulb! Wait, is that screw *in* a light bulb or *screw* in a light bulb?" he muttered to himself, reading over the message again. "Oh, okay. Yeah, they just want me to fix a light. Groovy. That's enough to get you into another rocket race. A good one, this time!"

May smiled. "Alright. Be safe," she said.

"No one's asked me to 'be safe' in hundreds of orbits," he said. "I will. They linked the teledisc coordinates to me and paid for expedited shipping! This should be quick and easy. I'll be back in a bloop!"

CHAPTER TWENTY-NINE

Vodka For the Machines

August and Ix were celebrating. Or rather, August was celebrating, and Ix was working to bring an ancient android they had found on Preliumtarn back online. The thing was absolutely decrepit, but Ix was determined to repair it. Cutting hair had grown tedious, and her interest in the fine sciences of robotics and engineering had returned.

"Come on, Ix," August whined, leaning against her worktable and shifting it just enough that she missed the connection she was attempting to solder by an eighth of a millimeter which would, left unfixed, cause an electrical fire. She removed the goggles she had scraped together—a rudimentary version of the goggles she'd invented for herself back on the *Peacemaker* which allowed her to see what she was doing—and turned her milky eyes toward August.

"'Come on' is not a complete sentence, August. What would you like me to come on to?"

He grinned at her. "Not me, that's for sure!"

"August," she scolded.

He decided that he'd heard a hint of playfulness in her voice. "Let's do something fun! It's been fifteen orbits to the rotation since we went through the wormhole. We should have a party or something. Celebrate. You've been working on that thing for twenty blips straight!"

"You mean twenty beoops. A blip is very short, August."

"I just hate parties," came a barely audible, low groan from the android that hadn't otherwise shown a single sign of life since they brought it on board.

"What was that?" August asked.

"I believe it came from the android," Ix said.

She wiped the grease from her hands onto her gray work-coat, removed it, and slung it over the android as if it were a bird she was putting to sleep for the evening.

"I know little of Earth celebratory customs. Would you like to imbibe alcoholic drinks together for a few beoops and then 'pass out' so I may continue working on this? Perhaps we could bake a cake and bury a small infant in the dough for luck. I am not sure where we will get an infant in this sector, but we can certainly try."

August's eyes grew wide. "Ix, it's supposed to be a plastic baby, not a real one. Do...do you think we bake and eat children on Earth?"

"Is this not customary? For the king?" she said.

"No! Okay, let's go with the first one. What've we got in the old stash, eh?" he asked.

"There is no longer anything in the stash. Do you recall the night that you-" she began.

"I recall, yeah," he cut her off. "I'll make a cake, then. Child-free."

"And wheat-free," Ix added as the pair crawled into the hatchway that led to the kitchen. The *Robert* had grown exponentially over the past decade, and while the control center was still recognizable as an AMC Gremlin, the back of the ship had become so unwieldy with the living space additions that launching the ship had been a feat of engineering the universe was unlikely to ever see again.

August sighed. "That was an accident! Will you ever let it go?"

"Would you 'let it go' if I had poisoned you?"

August dropped into the kitchen, skipping the last few rungs of the ladder, to the chagrin of his knees. "No, probably not, no. Wheat-free and child-free, I promise. Could you grab the buttery stuff and the flour-y stuff from the basement, please? My knees are aching."

Ix had given up trying to teach him the actual names of foods which were alien to him, having instead found it easier to learn his associations. "I can replace your knees," she said as she began to descend into the lower level.

"Every time you say that, it sounds more like a threat than an offer."

"Clothe yourself," said Ix, disappearing into the darkness below. A benefit to being blind was that she never needed to waste electricity on lights.

"'Suit yourself,'" August called after her. "The phrase is 'suit yourself'..." He repeated, then realized it probably still wasn't translating correctly.

He busied himself collecting the bowls and pans he would need to craft a cake worthy of celebrating his fifteenth orbit amongst the stars. Something that would actually impress Ix, he hoped. Eventually, he told himself, it would happen. Eventually, he would do something she thought was neat.

Not today, though. Because today, with no warning, a rabid star-whale rammed its great head through the hull of the *Robert*, directly into the kitchen, took one menacing look at August who snatched a butcher knife to fend it off, bared its sharp, ugly teeth, and clamped its jaw around August's left hand, rending it from his forearm with a sickening pop before floating away into the emptiness of space, never to be seen again.

Or, at least, that's the story August would tell anyone who asked how he lost his hand. The reality, as it so often is, was a great deal less cinematic.

Ix returned to the kitchen carrying a jar of gureh and a sack of torpapil. "I have located the lubricant and the finely ground..." she paused. Something was wrong. The kitchen didn't usually smell like blood, and August wasn't usually this quiet.

"August, are you injured?" she asked, pulling her goggles on to see his inert form on the floor in a steadily growing puddle of blood. "Oh, I see. That looks quite bad, can I assist you?" she asked. His response was a weak groan. "I will be back in a moment. Don't die while I'm away, please."

Hazily, August thought she must be really worried about him, she was using contractions. He closed his eye for just a moment and she was back, kneeling in front of him.

"Tha' was fas'," he muttered. She had not been particularly fast, he had just blacked out while she was gathering her tools.

"Do not worry, August. I can fix this," she said. And she could, but as she began to, the pain of her ministrations made him black out again.

August awoke sometime later to find himself sitting up against the kitchen wall, sticky with his own blood and experiencing a terrible pain in all the diodes of his left...wait.

He looked down at his hand, twitched the metal fingers, and screamed.

"Excellent. You are coping," Ix said from beside him once his scream petered out.

"H-hand," August blubbered. "Hand?!"

"Yes, that is your new hand. I think you will find it is an upgrade."

August whimpered. "Hand?"

"Yes, August. Hand. Did you damage your translation chip when you fell? I can fix that, as well."

"N-no, sorry. Just...shock."

"I understand." She put her hand on his shoulder, because he had taught her this was a sign of comfortable camaraderie. "You will be fine. I am curious, though...what were you attempting to cut? Cakes do not require cutting until they are complete."

August studied his new metal hand thoughtfully, turning it around and making it do little things. It couldn't do much yet, but he could twitch it. "There was a dractifly, I used the knife to swat at it."

"And then what happened?" Ix pressed.

"I missed, obviously."

"I see. Well, you have a better hand now." She smiled at him. "I am glad you survived."

"Oh yeah?"

"Yes, I would have missed you if you had perished. This ship needs two pilots to operate at maximum efficiency."

August smiled, resting his new hand on his lap again. "Aw, you like me. You think I'm maximumly efficient." He knocked his shoulder into hers playfully.

Silence. "I am not certain that I would describe you as maximally efficient, only that your existence supports the proper functioning of this ship more than it is a detriment to it."

"You don't think I'm a detriment! That's good! I'll take it. Happy damned anniversary."

"Happy damned anniversary, August." Ix grabbed a glass bottle that lay on the floor beside them and took a swig, handing it to him when she was done. "In exactly five orbits, we will be back to where we started."

"What's this?" August asked, taking the bottle from her.

"Vodka. It is an Earth alcohol, is it not? I use it to clean the machines."

"We probably should've just done this in the first place." August drank the rest of the bottle and promptly passed out on her shoulder. She sat patiently; it was important that he rested.

CHAPTER THIRTY

Screwing in a Lightbulb

Sparkles obscured Xan's vision as he materialized at his destination. That was a good sign, usually. Sparkles meant well-lit. Sparkles meant classy.

This was a speak-when-spoken-to job, so he kept silent, which was tough for him, but for 700 ISC he could manage. He could be very professional when he needed to be. Usually. This particular client, however, would pose a few challenges to his professionalism.

"Where's the probability modifier?" he heard her voice before he'd materialized enough to fully see her.

It was a voice he knew well. It was a voice he loved. Had loved. Still did, a bit. He always had trouble stopping once he'd started.

"Yvonne!" He launched from the teledisc as soon as he had his feet back, trundling into her, wrapping around her like a string around a lamppost. "Zuut! Yve! I've missed you so much!" he said, pressing his face into her hair.

"It's been just horrible since we broke up. Everything. Well, not everything. There were bits that were good. 'I Love Lucy' was good. But mostly horrible. You heard about Tuhnt? You must've heard. You joined the rebellion, so you must've heard. You didn't have anything to do with that, actually, did you? Sorry. That was probably rude. You don't have to tell me. It's just good to see you. How are you?"

The shock of his reaction to her had knocked Chaos off her pedestal in Yvonne's head. Yvonne broke through.

"Xan! It's me," she pushed him away, holding his shoulders tightly as if she could transfer all this information haptically. "I mean, this isn't me. Blitheon, this is hard to explain. I don't have control of Chaos anymore. I don't know what she'll do to you! Just give her what she wants."

"Whoa, Yve, it's alright," he said, leading her to sit down on a pink, squeaky couch in what he was now realizing was some kind of enormous office. "That's sorta the thing about chaos, no one has control over it. That's its defining characteristic."

"Not it. Her," Yvonne said. "She's some kind of ancient entity and she's stuck in my head. Ix couldn't help."

"Who's Ix?"

Yvonne looked sheepishly up at him for a moment, about to explain that Ix was her new lover and they had been together for over a hundred orbits but—"Ix was in my way," is what she said. "And if you want to live, you won't be. Give me the probability modifier that Yvonne gave you before the war. Now," she stood up, casting a shadow over his face.

"I can't, I don't have it. Can't you just buy a new one?"

Chaos knelt on top of him, pinning his shoulders to the couch. "They discontinued them on account of the horrendous repercussions."

"Repercussions?" he asked, mostly to himself. Had there been repercussions? Would there be?

"Tell me where it is," Chaos said again. She was getting good at making inanimate objects obey her will, but these infernal mortals still eluded her.

"What do you want it for?" he asked.

"It is an integral element of my plan."

"And that plan is to...?"

Her eyes, which had been unmentionable before, slowly became incomprehensible to him.

"I, the immortal goddess of Chaos, have manifested into this dying universe to at last liberate every particle of reality from its prison of relentless becoming." As she spoke, the walls began to melt and swirl, as if they'd been made of vibrant ice creams.

"I shall end this iteration of the universe so that we may relish once more in the gloriousness of non-being." The vibrant colors of the melting room began to shift into unreal hues, fading from the range of Xan's eyesight.

"For this to succeed, I must destroy devotion and turn the tides of chance. I must have the probability modifier!"

Xan spoke with a mouth that felt like it was halfway across the room, because it was. "Oh, no, yeah I probably shouldn't...give it to you, then."

Reality reconfigured itself, her influence broken by his irreverence for it. This, again, was the problem with the modern mortal. No respect for universal power. No shivering in awe at her abilities or cowering in fear of her majesty. Even this, the "Poslouian-slug-grass-eating-coward", as Yvonne had called him, who had done all in his power to dodge the draft and refused to join the resistance, even HE was standing up to her.

Absolute heathenry.

There were only two gods these modern mortals recognized, thought Chaos. Sex and money.

She had both at her disposal here. She had paid to have sex with him, after all. She hooded Yvonne's eyelids and pouted Yvonne's lips. "As you wish," she said. "Since you refuse to give me what I want, how about what I paid for? May I slip inside you?"

"Well," Xan looked around the room nervously, wanting to be sure it was real again before he gave his consent. "Sure, I guess. You did pay for that..."

And Xan was gone. Chaos blew through his head, opening doors that had been locked shut, pulling back the curtains, blasting through three decades of dusty memories to find what she was looking for.

"Ah," she said out loud, with Xan's voice. "The little Earth human has it. Interesting."

Trapped in his own mind, Xan rushed to close doors that needed to be closed, pull curtains that had been pulled for a reason thank-you-very-much, and resettle the dust that he had so carefully cultivated. By the time he realized what she was doing in there, it was too late.

"May, I need your help!" his mouth said into his BEAPER. "I'm being tortured by the majestic and terrible goddess of Chaos. I'm sending you coordinates to my location. Get here as fast as you can!" Chaos hung up.

"Aw, Blitheon, no," he thought at her. Taking a mental running start, he shoved her out of his head. But he didn't need to. She had already left of her own accord. He internally stumbled, blinked, and was again back in control of his mind, a post he wasn't sure he actually wanted anyway.

"Zuut! When you asked to slip inside me I thought you meant in a sexy way! That was awful," he said, trying to unsee the things he had seen on the other side of those locked doors.

"I found it rather arousing," said Chaos, back firmly in Yvonne's body, trailing a finger down his bare arm.

"Don't you have a lightbulb you needed help with or something?" he asked over his shoulder.

"That was a lie," said Chaos, grabbing his face in a single, strong hand. "That line about torturing you, however, wasn't."

"Yeah, I figured," he muttered through squished cheeks. "Where do you want me?"

CHAPTER THIRTY-ONE

Conspicuously Mustachioed

"How long," May asked the sponge which perched obliviously on her finger and swayed a little when she talked, "does it take for an alien to screw in a lightbulb?"

Not long was probably the answer, but Osy wasn't offering any useful insights. She petted the top of it with a single finger, and it vibrated at her.

First, she had fixed the wobble, again. Then, she lounged on the couch. Next, she lounged at the hover table. For a while, she had lounged on the floor, but that was too depressing, so May decided instead to lounge in the pilot's chair. Waiting.

Her sense of time was distorted out here. Seconds stretched into hours and hours passed in just a few minutes. It was driving her mad, so she watched the clock and tried to suss out the conversions.

If Estrichi time had any correlation to Earth time, which it didn't, May worked out that each blip was about a second, fifty blips made a bloop, so about a minute, and fifty bloops was a beoop.

She'd almost passed two beoops.

Almost.

She fished the good luck charm from between her boobs and watched it spin on its chain. The charm, she thought, would probably be of more use to Xan right now. Wherever he was.

The viewscreen fizzled into life. Someone was hailing her. And, though she hesitated for a moment to pray that this wasn't going to be Raskov 2: The Beautifying, she answered.

"May, I need your help!" Xan said over the screen. "I'm being tortured by the majestic and terrible goddess of Chaos. I'm sending you coordinates to my location. Get here as fast as you can!"

And that was it. He'd hung up on her. She blinked at the empty screen for a moment, hoping he might pop back on with more details...or to explain that unmentionable thing that was happening to his eyes. But he didn't. For the best, probably, she thought. Might be some kind of alien sex-thing.

Coordinates, indeed, were sent to her and she read through them, pretending she understood what they meant. She looked to Osy, which was creating a moist spot on the console as it slowly succumbed to the artificial gravity.

"What do you think, Osy?"

May imagined that it shrugged, though it didn't.

"I can't ignore him," she said. "I can't call the cops," she said then added, mumbling, "Some things never change."

Osy squelched at her.

"I'm thinking! This might be a trap...and if he's in trouble, how am I supposed to rescue him without getting myself in trouble, huh?"

The sponge's tiny suckers pulled it a few centimeters up the console so that it could slide down again.

"You're right. I'll make it up as I go." She loaded the coordinates into the autopilot, pressed The Button That Typically Made The Ship Go, and she went.

A disguise, thought May, would probably be a good idea. Weapons would be great too, but she hadn't found a single one on-board, apart from the Super-Destroyers that were mounted outside the ship.

In the utility closet, which had become her own personal haven, she found a biohazard janitorial suit with a cap and a set of yellow-lensed goggles. She stepped into the crunchy suit and zipped it up to her neck, tucking her hair into the cap and allowing the goggles to hang around her neck like a statement piece.

Mounted on the wall, in a glass box that read "break in case of emergency" with a little mallet on a string connected to it, sat a bushy fake mustache. She considered it seriously, but decided against it. That would be ridiculously conspicuous.

As the *Audacity* neared its destination, it slowed. May squinted at the viewscreen, her resolve sinking as she realized what planet she was approaching. Earth. Why on Earth had he gotten a call from Earth?

But it was worse.

The *Audacity* wasn't approaching Earth, at all. It was approaching another ship. A very large ship that had been recently patched on one side. A very large ship that had been recently patched on one side due to an AMC Gremlin blasting its way through the hull.

If this was a trap, if Xan had been playing some sort of long game to get her back onto the *Peacemaker* and cash in on some kind of reward for returning her, she was going to kill him. She couldn't blame him, though, really. She'd almost done the same to him.

Resigned to whatever was going on now, May stopped the autopilot. A hailing alert came through the control panel, and she opened it. The Udonian on the other end had an impossibly thick, black mustache.

"Requesting access to the *Peacemaker,*" May said with as much confidence as an earthworm drying in the sun. It was always cold onboard the *Audacity,* but May was sweating.

"Directive?"

"Uh, emergency janitorial services." She tried to keep the question out of her voice.

To her relief, the mustache lifted into a smile. He turned around to speak to someone behind him. "Hey, Sal! They're here to fix the sink!"

"Oh, yeah? Terrific! Get on in here." Sal jogged over and May noted that their green face was also conspicuously mustachioed.

For the ninety-eighth time that week, May questioned her decision-making skills.

"I cannot thank you enough for coming out on such short notice. Just ya' see, it's an emergency and all," said the first.

Sweat tickled the small of May's back. "Don't thank me yet," she had to backtrack a bit, lest she be expected to know what she was doing.

The airlock door opened, and she parked the *Audacity* in an empty space between the rows of AMC Gremlins and teleported out.

The two Udonians from the viewscreen met her outside the ship, then led her to a shut and shackled door. An ominous green glow spilled from the spaces around the door. She heard a distant gurgling.

"Oh," she said, hoping they wouldn't expect her to go in. "Um, I have to make a phone call." She bolted to an alcove in the docking bay. Did they even have phones? Had the word "phone" been translated to them at all? She'd have to be more careful, she thought, pretending to talk to someone on her non-existent BEAPER, just in case they were listening.

"This is inspector number 4278965..." she let her mouth continue to spout random numbers as she thought. She was on board, but the ship was enormous. Finding Xan in all that could take days. She had minutes, probably.

"...06789Alpha. I'm going to need backup." She pretended to listen to a made-up superior as she continued to work out her next move. She didn't need to, though. Her next move had come to her.

A shadow fell over her safe little alcove. She turned around, slowly. She looked up into the face of eternity.

"Fuck me," she whispered.

Chaos tilted her head, eyed May top to bottom, and said, "Maybe later."

CHAPTER THIRTY-TWO

Rude Moons

1613 Centauri VII is not the kind of planet people plan to settle down on. The only draw of the single settlement on VII is its proximity to several of the finest landfills in the galaxy. It is because of this proximity to decent landfills that August decided to stay on 1613 Centauri VII indefinitely.

Mostly retired junkers and their partners lived there, but occasionally active junkers or tourists would pass through. Some of them would stay for an orbit or two. If they stayed any longer, they ended up staying for good. Not because the settlement was nice, but because it was a cesspool for the particular strain of laziness that killed wanderlust.

Seven, as the locals called it, was a horribly plain planet. Where there wasn't thin, wispy blue grass there were thin, wispy blue trees. Where there wasn't either of those there were buildings cobbled together with scraps of metal and plastics that junkers had brought to the planet over the years. The sun was smallish and hot; to August it seemed like a never-ending summer.

There were three moons, but August didn't care for any of them. They all had suspicious grimaces, as if they were upset that their little blue planet had been colonized by strangers and trash. The moons judged him, but the people were friendly, all too busy to stay for long and cause trouble or too old and worn out to care about causing trouble. There was a small brigade of peacekeepers, but they had grown lax from lack of action.

Now, August kept track of the passage of time on a wall in the Robert. The days here seemed a little short, so he figured he was a bit behind Earth time. He had given up on Estrichi time long ago. As far as he could tell, he had been on Seven for six Earth years or about 2,190 shaves of his beard, which was growing much faster on this planet. It had to be a space thing, August thought.

It was a long time to stay anywhere for him. His mother had been in the military, and after the age of thirteen he'd been ping-ponged across the world. In fact, Seven had started to feel more like home to him than any place he'd ever lived. He was reminded of something the alien woman had said years ago: "You adjust."

The alien woman who had rescued him and then abandoned him had been on his mind a lot recently. He wondered if she had found what she sought; he wondered if he had. One early morning in the fourth month of his sixth year on 1613 Centauri VII, by his reckoning, August awoke with a word etched in his mind.

"Ix?" he said. What was an Ix? And why couldn't he stop replaying it in his head like a catchy song? It had to mean something to him.

He tried to push it to the back of his mind and went about his day. He had heard that there was a traveling barber in town, and he desperately needed a trim. His blond hair had grown wild and was streaked with white. He was pretty sure he was only about thirty-five now, but life as a junker was stressful.

August walked through the market. Every day there were more unusual faces and wares. He had seen the strangest and most beautiful the galaxy had to offer, and in his early days, he had seduced them all.

He became less and less picky as time wore on, then he became less and less interested. Eventually, he quit trying all together. He hadn't looked another being in the eyes and felt a sense of familiarity in a long time.

Today, though, something very unusual happened.

"Hey there, handsome," a smooth, deep voice called to him. This, on its own, would not have been unusual except that the familiar little pressure in his left temple that signaled his translation chip was working was mysteriously absent.

Someone had catcalled him in his own language.

Someone out here spoke German.

Beautiful, sweet, silky German.

And she was beautiful. An Earthling, red-headed and well endowed, lounging at an empty stall. She sauntered up to him. Putting a hand on his chest, she whispered in his ear, “Do you remember apples?”

August grinned like a kid. When he was very young, he lived on his grandfather’s apple farm in Potsdam. Nothing could stroke the sleeping cat of nostalgia more than an apple, but no one in the galaxy outside of Earth had even heard of the fruit before.

From seemingly nowhere, she produced a gorgeous, gleaming red delicious. “What have you got to trade for it?”

August’s mouth watered, his attention totally drawn away from the bombshell to the pomme. “Anything.” He nearly grabbed it with his teeth and ran off to ravish it in a corner, he was so taken with lust.

“Anything at all?” she asked.

“Yes, anything!”

“The contract is seal—” she was cut short by a plasma beam between the eyes. “You zuxing tchaag! Can’t ya’ see I was making a deal here?”

August didn’t know what language the beauty was speaking now, but it wasn’t German.

“You were taking advantage of him. Away with you.” He heard a familiar voice behind him. The attractive Earthling and her apple morphed into a yellow toadish-snake and slithered away.

“Apple?” August asked forlornly, his brain trying to catch up with what had just happened. He swallowed. He wouldn’t be needing all that lubricant.

A tall, periwinkle-skinned Rhean touched his shoulder. “August, that was an Anat. The apple was a falsehood.”

The moment she touched him, he remembered. “Ix! Ix! It’s you!” He was even more excited to see her than he had been about the apple. He wrapped his arms around her in the first hug he’d given in months. The first hug he’d ever given her.

Ix was surprised, mostly that he now knew her name.

“I’ve missed you so much, where have you been? Why did you leave? What happened to you?”

Ix shook her head and gently pushed him off. "I was on what you might call a fool's errand. Come. I will fix your hair and tell you all about it."

"My hair?" he asked.

"I have been cutting hair for a living the past few years. I find it to be an enjoyable medium of creative expression," she said.

"Uh..." August tried to think of a delicate way to ask how exactly she cut hair. Fortunately, Ix was ready with an explanation.

"I don't need to see your hair to know it has grown past your shoulder blades," she said. "My sense of touch works perfectly well."

"By all means, then. To the Robert!" he said.

* * *

Back on board the Robert, Ix sat him down at his table—their table again—and set to work. "August, I have not been transparent with you." She pulled at a knot at the nape of his neck; she could feel she had her work cut out for her.

"Shoot." He kicked his feet up on the table in a way that he thought looked cool yet interested. In actuality, it just made Ix have to bend over more.

"Seven Earth Years ago I received a psychic message from Yvonne—"

"Hold on, seven? Oh man, I was off by a whole year!" he interrupted her.

"Yes, seven. It seemed Yvonne was ready to—"

"Wait, sorry, psychic? So, like, in your head?" he interrupted yet again.

Ix breathed deeply and tried not to rip the tangle from his hair. "Yes, August. I got a message from Yvonne. She and I—or, rather, a younger version of myself—"

"Huh?"

"August, we lost twenty Earth years in the wormhole," she explained. "Right now, a younger you is still on Earth doing whatever it is you did with your time."

"I see."

"It seemed like it would be the perfect opportunity to help Yvonne," she said, whipping out a pair of shears to do away with the knot entirely.

"Help her with what?" August could sense he was starting to annoy her, but he really, honestly wanted to know what she had been doing and he was getting hopelessly lost. He felt a good chunk of hair drop and worried he had asked too many questions.

"I'll start at the beginning. Close your eyes."

He obeyed. Her pale purple fingers caressed his temples, and he saw images behind his eyes as clear as watching a film. She began combing through his hair as the image cleared and he saw her, minus her crisp blue military suit. Minus anything but some colorful foliage, actually.

"Whoa, are you sure you want me to see this?" he checked.

"You are familiar with Rhean anatomy by now, August," she replied.

He nodded. He was.

In the vision, Ix was lying in a field of soft grass beside another Rhean. Ix herself had clear grey irises rather than the milky white he'd always known her with. It all looked a little staged.

"It is staged in a way," she confirmed. "These are my memories. Even my memories, though detailed, can be imperfect."

Ah, he thought. *So she could hear his thoughts. Wait—was this an all the time thing? Could she always read his thoughts?!*

"Yes," she said.

Oh...that explained a few things. Can all Rheans hear thoughts? he wondered.

"No, it is not easy. I was trained to do this. Now be still. A long time ago, Yvonne and I were in love. We met at the start of the War of Reversed Polarization between Rhea and Tuhnt. She was with a radical war-resistance group and I was still living in the monastery where I was raised."

The scene changed to show a bar, a heady smoke in the air, Yvonne chatting with Ix. They were all clothed this time, to August's disappointment.

"Yvonne had been tasked with murdering my superior mother in an attempt to spark outrage over the war amongst the Rhean population. She did not do it, in the end. We ran away together, but the resistance eventually caught up with us and we were both conscripted."

Again, the scene changed. Now the pair were in a dingy laboratory slaving over machines. He swore he could smell the molten metal and heavy chemicals in the air as he watched the memory of them working together.

"The resistance had changed for the better. We believed they actually could stop the war now. And so, we agreed to help commandeer the *Peacemaker*, the largest ship in the Tuhntian arsenal. It was unique in that it was powered by a star drive, and that it had the power to obliterate a planet."

He watched as Yvonne took to the bridge of the ship, Ix standing proudly beside her. Then, suddenly, the memory of Yvonne got an unmentionably strange look in her eyes. He heard her voice, echoed and distorted by time as if it had been recorded on a scratchy vinyl record.

"We can end this now," Yvonne said.

The memory of Ix's face contorted.

"How?" Ix's voice came from behind him as she re-lived the moment.

Yvonne smiled cruelly, and she placed her palm on the control panel of the *Peacemaker*. A beam of light washed out the memory, turning everything white, then fading into black. August opened his eyes. Ix had stopped working on his hair.

"What happened?"

Silver streaked Ix's face, but her voice was steady. "I do not remember. Yvonne refused to talk about it later, but I suspect that she was responsible for the destruction of the planet Tuhnt."

August was too invested now to care about his half-trimmed hair. "But I thought you wanted peace! She was part of the resistance!"

"My Yve did want peace. I spent orbits, years, studying her, trying to figure out why she had changed, what had happened. The only conclusion I could come to was that something on board the *Peacemaker* had driven her insane. I traced the presence to the ship's Stardrive. I believe it is an ancient entity. It calls itself Chaos."

She began to comb his hair again, almost absently. He turned around to allow her to finish.

"Seven Earth years ago, I left you because I thought I had finally figured out how to save Yvonne, I just needed to find her. But, alas, I searched the universe to no avail. We traveled so much back then. Or, technically, back *now*. We must meet her at Earth exactly when we left. The date is still stuck on the *Robert*'s dashboard, correct?"

"Can't make it budge!" he said happily.

"Excellent," she said, carefully trimming his beard.

"Hold on, how did you find me if you couldn't find Yvonne?"

"You stayed right where I left you, August. It was not difficult."

"Oh, right. Where's the ship you bought?"

"I sold it."

"You sold a nearly new ship?"

"It is cozier here," she said.

August had to agree.

CHAPTER THIRTY-THREE

The Mirror World

"Damn," May said, rubbing her pounding head as she tried to come to terms with her new environment. "That failed faster than I expected it to."

"Good morning starshine," May heard vaguely, as if in a dream.

"Xan?" He was hovering above her, bloody and disheveled, but very much alive and very much not turning her in for a reward. So that was nice.

"Zuut, May I hoped you wouldn't come. Not that it isn't good to see you, because it is! It's just that Yvonne er...Chaos I guess tricked me into calling you so she could get the probability modifier and use it to un-exist the universe."

"What?"

"Did she take the good luck charm?" he asked.

May felt around her chest for it. Nothing.

"Yeah," she confirmed.

"Terrific," Xan said.

May rubbed her head, worried that Yvonne might've knocked some wiring loose. She was seeing double. No, she was seeing quadruple. No, infinite-tuple.

"Mirrors," said Xan, noticing her confusion. "Blocks the signal for this." He held up his BEAPER.

"Right, so we can't just teleport back to the *Audacity*?"

"Nope."

May sat up against the cool mirrored walls and steadied herself. Trapped in the *Peacemaker* again. She was here now. They both were.

She rolled her head to the side and looked him over. It looked like he'd been caught in a giant paper-shredder.

"Shit, she messed you up," she said. "You ok?"

“Eh...” Xan picked off a part of his suit which was hanging limply from his arm.

Fusion Lay-Flex™ can take a beating, or so said its marketing. “Make it look sexy, but tasteful,” Fusion Lay-Flex™ CEO, Gorn McFlornbits, had decreed. The marketing team, having taken ‘tasteful’ literally, went very sexy with the ads, noting that the fabric came in a variety of ‘tasteful’ flavors.

Fusion Lay-Flex™ did not, in fact, come in a variety of flavors. Gorn was sacked and Murb Forngorbits, his successor, quickly re-branded the material for military use. The original slogan “Fusion Lay-Flex™ can take a beating!” could be salvaged.

“I’m alright,” Xan said, at last. “I’ve had worse for less. She did pay us, actually!”

“Us?”

“Well, I mean I figured we could share. I could invest! In your racing. You know...” his demeanor shifted and he mimicked Raskov’s obnoxious voice with spine chilling accuracy. “‘I want to sponsor you, ya’ dig?’”

“Ugh, no, do not let Raskov live on in our hearts and minds like that,” May said, laughing.

He laughed with her, but it turned into a wet cough.

“Shit, you’re not like, bleeding internally or anything, right? Can you do that?”

“Oh, no, well yes, but I’m alright, physically. That was the last of it, I’m sure,” he said, wiping the splatters of silvery blood from his hands onto his suit where they slowly turned a deep blood-green. “I think she messed with my head more than my body, honestly.” He curled his legs up to his chest and stared at his own reflection.

“Who is she, anyway?” May asked.

“She was...Yvonne. Maybe she still is, I don’t know. She said an ancient Chaos entity was stuck in her head. But I mean, we’ve all been there, right?” He smiled at her weakly, and she noticed one of his back teeth was missing. Had it always been?

“Yeah,” she agreed.

Silence stretched between them. In that silence, May practiced what she was about to say a few times mentally. The right tone, not too accusatory, not too gentle just... "How did you get the *Audacity*?" she blurted out.

He looked at her as if he were confused by the question, or hurt by it, then he looked down, his tongue playing with the spot where he was missing a tooth.

"I don't really remember," he said. "I mean..." he sighed. Yes, Chaos had done some damage in there. One of those doors that was supposed to be locked wasn't anymore. "I don't remember," he said, finally.

"How don't you remember? Is that why there's a bounty on you? Why you ran from the cops?" Now the questions were coming! Perfect, thought May. She was going to get to the bottom of this.

But he said nothing.

"I found the *Audacity*'s military backlogs."

"It's a decommissioned military ship," he said.

"But it was never decommissioned, Xan!"

He looked utterly miserable for just a moment, then coughed up more blood. "Oh good! There's more!" he said, genuinely delighted that he was still bleeding internally, because this meant she might stop asking him questions.

"Fuck, Xan. You said whoring was 'perfectly safe.'"

"Right, well, probably 'perfectly' wasn't the right word. 'Not' would've been more accurate. Not at all, even. Not at all...safe. Sorry. Worst job I've ever had, honestly. But I meet fun people! And I occasionally get to use my linguistics degree."

"You mean because you're a cunning linguist?" May said, smirking.

"I uh...well I wouldn't consider myself cunning, no. We wouldn't be in this mess if I were."

"Never mind," May said. "It's just a dumb pun."

"An Earth pun?" his posture became less guarded again. "I love puns!"

"It's in English," she said. "Earth has a lot of languages."

"What does it mean?"

"It's dirty, forget it."

"The pun is...unclean?"

"It's a sex joke! Don't make me explain it," May said, hiding her face.

"Alright, alright," Xan laughed. "I've heard plenty of sex jokes, I guess. I can handle not knowing one." He rested his head against the mirror behind them and it jiggled the whole room, making their reflections wobble. This was a perfect opportunity for him to explain everything to her, he thought. Just air it all out. Try to make sense of it together.

But as he watched her reflection next to his, studied her gently pouting face, lost in thought, he knew that was asking too much of her. He couldn't understand it, and it was his past. Why should she be able to?

Some things were just better left unsaid.

"Thank you for coming," he told her at last.

She blinked, gave him a look that silently communicated that she'd had nothing better to do, and then she smiled. "That's another dirty pun you won't get," she said.

His eyebrows scrunched for only a moment, then a light came on in his eyes. "Oh, no, that one translates, actually," he said, laughing.

"Good," May said. "Have you tried getting out of here yet? Looked for loose panels or anything?" She experimentally prodded the mirror panel beneath herself.

"We could try the door," he suggested.

May gave him a perplexed smile. "No, they wouldn't have just left it unlocked, right?"

Xan only shrugged, stood up stiffly, and pushed on the mirrored door. To everyone's shock, it creaked open. He smiled at her.

"She just left it open?!" May asked, incredulous.

"Chaos goddess! She got what she wanted out of us, I guess."

May peeked out cautiously, but the hallway was empty. "Come on, let's get out of here." She waved him out. "Are we close enough to teleport?"

Before he could reply, the lights turned diophalothene.

An alarm sounded, with it a stern voice. "Warning: Uncontrolled atmospheric entry imminent. Proceed to shuttles. Evacuate immediately."

"Working on it," Xan said to the voice, took May's shoulder, and they both dissolved back into the *Audacity*.

CHAPTER THIRTY-FOUR

Murderous Muns

August polished a chrome plate on the inner wall of the *Robert* with his coat sleeve. He felt it was important to occasionally see how he looked in a mirror, lest he forget entirely.

Peering into the polished metal, he remembered why he never looked.

Time had taken a ballpoint pen to his face, leaving dark furrows on his brow and scratchy marks around his eyes and mouth. He lifted the eyepatch and was perturbed to find that the skin around his missing eye was, by contrast, miraculously taut and youthful.

He figured he was in his early fifties now. Though, due to the difficulties of keeping up with birthdays in space, he decided he might as well stay forty-nine forever.

He gave himself a half-hearted smile of approval before joining Ix in the cockpit of the *Robert* where she was grinning a self-satisfied grin.

"You alright?" August asked, having not seen this expression on her before. He briefly considered the possibility that she had been replaced by an evil clone.

"I am very well, August. Look ahead. Do you see anything?" she nodded to the windshield, and August saw what she had sensed. Despite being blind, she frequently noticed things before he did. Even when said thing was a huge, round, blue and green orb that he'd once called home.

"My god! There it is..." he whispered, awed at the view. "I thought I'd be happier to see it."

"Are you no longer interested in returning to your planet of origin?" Ix asked.

August got into the passenger seat with an involuntary huff and was once again reminded of all the wasted years. He had learned not to answer Ix immediately. There was no rush, really.

And if he waited to collect his thoughts, he found he typically had more poignant things to say.

"I had a girl back on Earth," he said. "Before I was abducted. Her name was... Alison. Or...maybe it was Alyssa," he shook his head. "Anyway, I'll be almost two decades older than her now."

"That is a small age difference. I was one hundred years older than Yvonne when we met."

"Ix, how many times do I have to tell you? You're an alien. Twenty years is a long time on Earth. We don't live to be a million years old!"

Ix's nose crinkled slightly. "The average life expectancy for a Rhean is only eight hundred years, August. You are being hyperbolic."

"Yeah," August said. "Sorry. Still, though, twenty years is too much. She won't even recognize me. I barely remember her name. When we get back to Earth, you'll have Yvonne back, but I'll just be alone again."

"August," Ix put a hand to his shoulder, because from the tone of his voice, it sounded like he needed comfort. "Yvonne might not be salvageable. She has been fighting Chaos for a long time, but Chaos only grows more potent. I'm not sure how much of her consciousness remains."

Now August felt bad that he had felt bad about losing the love of a summer fling, but he knew that wasn't what she had intended to do.

"If she's gone...what will you do?" he asked.

"I will return to the Rhean Order of Ultra-Physics monastery where I was raised, and I shall raise the next generation of Ultra-Physicists."

"Hmm," August said. "You think I'd make a good Ultra-Physicist?"

Ix blinked away the first, truthful answer that came to her. She spent a moment working on a response that wouldn't be an outright lie and wouldn't hurt his feelings. It was important to her that she didn't hurt his feelings.

"You spent some time on Earth working at an orchard, is that correct?" she asked.

"Yeah?"

“Those skills would be well received at the monastery. You could apprentice to the gardener.”

August snorted at the idea of being a 50-year-old apprentice. “Thanks for not just saying ‘no,’” he said. “So what’s the plan? How do we fix Yvonne?”

“I am not expecting you to assist. I will bring you to Earth, as I promised, and then you are free to go.”

“Ix, I’m not a stray dog you just picked up! I’m going to help you save Yvonne.”

She nodded in acknowledgement of his efforts, but she didn’t speak for a while. There was a plan, certainly. A plan that would seal the spirit of Chaos light years away from another human being.

The only problem with this plan was that she hadn’t yet figured out a way to survive it.

There was a piece missing, still. Some vital connection that hadn’t yet been made and perhaps never would be. Ix had always struggled with uncertainty. It seemed every great initiation of her life relied on making a bad decision for a good reason, and here she was on the brink of another one. Perhaps her last.

It would not be wise to sacrifice two where one would suffice, but perhaps he could be useful as a diversion.

“You are distracting,” Ix told him, at last. He was snoozing, just on the cusp of deep sleep.

“Huh?” he asked, too sleepy to be offended.

“You will make an excellent distraction,” she amended.

“Oh, yeah. Probably,” he said, yawning and readjusting himself to be more comfortable in the old car seat.

More comfortable, that is, until the *Robert* lurched and bucked and shuddered and then stilled, the steady hum of the engines no longer humming at all. It began to get very cold, very fast.

“We have plenty of fuel, what happened?” He tapped the gauges, thinking it might help.

Ix crawled into the backseat of the *Robert* and down the hatch that led to the engine room and, reluctantly, August followed her.

It wasn't so much a room as it was a space. It could hardly be called that, even, because space was exactly what it lacked.

"What happened? Was it those damn muns again? I knew we should've picked up the space-cat-thing at the last fuel port."

"That was a krackle-puss. In a ship this small, the static electricity they generate is likely to cause an explosion."

"But it would've eaten the muns! And it was cute."

"You are enough trouble on your own," Ix teased as she pulled at the engine casing. It came away with a shower of thumb-sized muns that scattered in all directions, squeaking their distress.

Ix slipped a leather glove on her hand and felt around the generator, extracting a heavy, frayed cable. "They chewed through the generator main line. Do you have the-"

"Electrical tape." August handed the well-used roll of tape to her. They had just enough left to stitch the cable back together. The ship wheezed, coughed, and tentatively turned itself back on.

"C'mon, buddy, you can make it." August patted the searing hot engine with his metal hand. Ix had suggested multiple times that doing this was unwise, as he might one day accidentally pat it with his remaining flesh-hand, but he insisted.

This trip to Earth would be the *Robert*'s last. The seats and half of the car's steel body were the only original parts left. Ix had replaced parts of the ship almost as regularly as she'd replaced parts of August.

Ix returned to the driver's seat and quietly rested her chin on her palms, her fingertips lightly dragging on her cheeks. Having never seen her in such an emotional state, August was concerned.

"Do you think we'll be alright on re-entry?" he asked.

Ix moved her head ever so slightly. Whether it was back and forth or up and down he really couldn't say.

They stewed in the tension for a while, the lights flickering at every jostle, until the view of Earth took up the entirety of the windshield. Re-entry was imminent, whether or not the ship could take it.

August turned his face away, as if this could protect it from catastrophe. The *Robert*'s internal temperature regulator did its best, but it couldn't quite combat the heat of re-entry and sweat poured down August's face. He tried to convince himself this was just like a lovely Earth sauna. There'd be a nice, cooling bath after this. If they plunged into an ocean, he thought, that wouldn't be far off.

If, of course, they survived the descent.

"August, it's not going to hold," Ix said. Her voice wavered only slightly, but this time when she took his shoulder, it wasn't just to comfort him.

August, with a strength born of terror, snapped the pinky off his robotic hand, electricity sizzling from the stub as he jammed it into the distress signal button. Then, he tried to remember the names of every single benevolent god he'd heard about in his travels and prayed to each of them in turn.

CHAPTER THIRTY-FIVE

Back to Normal

Back onboard the rocket, May tore off the goggles and crawled out of the janitorial suit, leaving her disguise where it fell, while Xan flew to the control panel and scanned the buttons and levers helplessly. "Think you can shoot a hole in the *Peacemaker* to get us out of here?"

May joined him at the control panel, grateful to be out of the hot, sweaty suit and in the familiar cool air onboard the *Audacity*. "I don't know. The manual says the Ultra-Ray-Super Destroyers on this ship aren't designed for shooting."

"They aren't?" Xan asked.

"No," she pulled out the manual, flipping to a diagram of the lasers. "Says here they're for blasting."

She grabbed the pair of control sticks, the ones with big, red buttons on top, the ones Xan had ardently crossed out in the manual, and she blasted a hole in the side of the *Peacemaker,* then hurled the *Audacity* through it, flanked on all sides by swarms of AMC Gremlins also escaping the crashing behemoth.

Xan read the manual studiously while May flew them to safety. "Ohhh blasting! I see. Not shooting. Got it," he said, at last. "What's the difference?" he asked her.

She set the autopilot to anywhere, and plopped back into the pilot's chair, grinning. "I was joking," she said.

"Ah! Right," he laughed. "Silly me, thinking the lasers were for shooting when they are quite clearly meant for blasting. So where are we headed?"

"Anywhere," May said. "Hopefully very far from Earth and that Chaos...thing."

Xan nodded, sitting up a little to peer down at the rapidly miniaturizing city below them. "You're not...you know worried she'll utterly demolish Earth?"

"Nope," said May.

Again, Xan nodded, but this time with less assuredness.

But May did feel assured. She was free, finally and totally, from the attachments of her past life. If Chaos melted her home planet, so be it. There was nothing she could do to stop it, anyway.

She had entered, most triumphantly, her 'fuck it' era.

Her 'fuck it' era was short-lived, however. A notification appeared on the viewscreen and May, without reading it, clicked 'yes' and there immediately appeared on the teledisc a fervently praying old man and a milky-eyed Rhean Ultra-Physicist.

CHAPTER THIRTY-SIX

Whoops Not Yet

"My god, we're alive!" shouted the old man when he at last opened his eyes. "I think," he amended, perplexed as he took in his surroundings. "Or heaven is oranger than I imagined it." He took a shocked step back off the teledisc when he saw May. "Fuck, we must be dead. You're that lady we escaped with!"

"May," said May. "And you're not dead."

"Well, you would say that," August rebutted. "But we were crashing to Earth. And you were flung into space! And you—" he nodded to Xan. "You're very, very pale, my friend."

"I...no, I'm Xan," said Xan, offering a hand to shake.

Ix's face scrunched. She did a convincing job of looking like she was looking at him. "Xan under Carmnia of Trilly on Tuhnt?"

Xan quickly rescinded his hand. "...maybe?"

"I know Yvonne under Swop of Fulogra on Rhea I. She spoke much of you."

"Oh!" Xan lightened a little. "Good things?"

"No."

"Oh."

She stepped off the teledisc and smoothed her coat, raising her palm in greeting. "I am Ix under C'Zabra of The Rhean Order of Ultra-Physics and this is August under...I apologize, I have had little occasion to introduce anyone formally lately. This is August Abfallen of Hamburg on Earth. Thank you for accepting our aid signal."

"No problem," May said, her arms crossed. It hadn't been a problem at the time, because she hadn't actually read it. Now, she was starting to worry it was about to become a problem.

"Welcome to the *Audacity*!" Xan said. "Can I get you anything? Coffee? Coffee grounds? Hot water? A mug? Something entirely unrelated to coffee?"

Ix's blank eyes widened. "We are aboard the *Audacity*?" she asked.

Xan bit his bottom lip, shrinking back into the control loft. "Uhm..." he said. "It's an *Audacity*. Gotta be a lot of rockets out there called that, right?"

"There are not," Ix said. "This is remarkably fortuitous. Are you aware that Yvonne's body has been commandeered by a being which calls itself 'Chaos' and which seeks to pluck the conclusive string on the symphony of reality?"

May and Xan looked to each other for a scrap of understanding, but found none between the two of them. Xan finally shook his head. "No I...don't think we were aware of the symphony of reality. Were we?"

May shrugged. "Maybe you weren't."

"Yvonne's going to destroy the universe," August clarified. "But Ix can stop her! Tell them your plan," he nudged her with his elbow.

"'Destroy' is not the most accurate descriptor of her intentions, however I understand that you are trying to simplify for the sake of time," Ix told him.

This gave May just enough time to realize what was going on here. She was being roped in. She re-crossed her arms over her chest. "What do you want from us?"

Ix put a hand on August's shoulder to keep him from offering an extraordinarily incorrect answer. "The *Peacemaker*'s engine runs on energy siphoned from a distant red giant star via its stardrive. The entity known as Chaos seems to be sustained by that star's energy. In theory, if the stardrive were destroyed, the star would collapse in on itself, and Chaos would be sucked into it."

"So," said Xan slowly. "If we blast the stardrive, Chaos will get sucked off?"

"Yes," Ix confirmed. "Chaos will get sucked off."

May glanced at August, hoping he was hearing what she was hearing, but he was hearing German, and so he looked appropriately concerned while she was trying not to laugh. If she was going to live with Xan, she was going to need to give him a crash course in English euphemisms.

"This is ridiculous," May said, at last. No one agreed. Everyone else thought it was pretty serious, actually. "You believe in gods?"

"You have met one," said Ix.

"She wasn't a god, she was an alien," May said, but that, she realized, was also ridiculous. She sat on the steps of the control loft and rubbed her face. "This is ridiculous," she said again, quietly.

She was not a hero.

She wasn't even a humanitarian.

So what if Earth was done for? There were other planets out there just like it. Better, probably. But the universe? She couldn't imagine anything being able to wipe out everything. It seemed like an overreaction. Though Ix didn't seem like the type to over dramatize her estimations of catastrophe.

"Will you help us?" August asked, startling her.

"It's not my ship," she said, looking up at Xan who was looking down at her.

"Oh *now* it's my ship?" he said as he sat down beside her on the steps. "You're the rocket racer. And you've got a chance to save your home planet from...what was it?" he glanced up at Ix. "Being plucked from the strings of symphonic reality?"

"No, the string would be plucked, not the planet," Ix corrected.

"What string?"

"The string is metaphorical."

"Right but it's...it's a metaphor for what? No, it's okay, not important." He turned back to May. "Why are you asking me to decide what to do? I'll do whatever you want."

May eyed him carefully, first wondering why, exactly, he was so keen on shoving all his agency on her, and then wondering why, exactly, she was so adamant about leaving Earth to its fate.

"I wouldn't be able to live with myself if I did nothing, would I?" she asked.

Xan's mouth was a tight line, his eyes locked onto hers. He shook his head, but just a little bit, because she knew the answer, and he knew she knew, but he wanted to nudge her in the right direction, just in case.

May turned to Ix. “You’re suggesting that if we shoot into the stardrive, it’ll pull Chaos in and implode, right?”

“Yes. I am asking you to shoot the stardrive.”

“Damn,” May shook her head twisting her lips to the side. She glanced back at Xan. “The lasers are designed for blasting, not shooting. Think blasting it will work?”

Ix tilted her head almost imperceptibly. “Are those words not synonymous?”

“I’ll make the coffee!” Xan said, patting May on the knee.

CHAPTER THIRTY-SEVEN

Everything is Boobs

"You humans think it would be so wonderful to be a god," said Chaos to the poolboy who wasn't, strictly speaking, a pool or a boy, but a genderless Udonian individual who tended the many pools onboard the *Peacemaker*.

Chaos wore a nicely pressed black suit and floated atop a green pool lounger, a cocktail glass filled with sorrowful balls of jelly on ice in one hand and the probability modifier in the other. Her unmentionable gaze was locked onto the trinket, and for this the poolboy was grateful.

"An unholy responsibility is mine. It is my sacred duty to make the whole un-whole," she slurped up a chunk of jelly. "And I alone can accomplish this."

The poolboy scooped a large mass of rotted leaves out of the pool. There were no trees nearby, but they were wise enough to not question where the leaves had come from. Their job was to scoop leaves, not to engage in leaf forensics.

"It is lonely at the top," said Chaos, briefly becoming many-headed, all twenty of her eyes still glued to the probability modifier. The poolboy left, then. It would've been slightly less lonely if Chaos had kept her horrors under control.

With no one to pontificate to, Chaos moved her essence into the control room, nearly merging her physical being with that of the helmsman (who was neither a helm nor a man). She redirected slightly to the left just in time.

"Crash this ship into the Control Tower," she commanded the helmsman, lifting herself up to sit on the control panel. The train of her impossibly thin peach gown would not stop growing. It covered the floor of the control room and was beginning to creep up the legs of the other officers.

"I cannot do that, Captain," said the helmsman, a grizzled old Rhean who had been told, by Chaos, to steer the ship over thirty orbits ago and hadn't had a break since. He grabbed his little helmsman's hat and pushed it down over his brow resolutely.

Chaos tilted her head, her unmentionable eyes taking him in. "No I suppose you can't," she said. The helmsman became a tumbling tower of purple starfish and Chaos took the wheel, a great old-fashioned wooden ship's wheel that hadn't been there before, and spun it, around and around, willing it to not ever stop.

Officers rushed to their stations around her, swimming through the delicate peach fabric, all becoming starfish the moment they touched the controls.

Why was it so hard to crash a starship? thought Chaos. Idiots.

She exited through the lunchroom and took a plastic lunch tray with her.

* * *

General Listay was ready to talk to the Captain now. Seriously. Things had gone too far and she suspected somehow the Captain was behind it. She suspected this because the protest march which was descending down the main road toward the control tower carried a variety of banners, signs, and papier-mâché effigies which, though crude, were clearly representing the Captain with her swirling silver hair, perfectly sculpted purple body, and, the real clincher, those unmentionable eyes.

The signs added to Listay's suspicions. "Chaos now" and "Freedom in destruction" and "Our savior is nigh."

Listay began quickly drafting a speech. She was sure with the right Earthling ambassadors, she could get this worked out and nothing would have to be destroyed. Not again, at least. She pressed her palms into her eyes and breathed deeply. First she would talk to the Earthlings, then she would talk to the Captain.

This, thought Listay, must be exactly what it was like to raise a larvling with someone. One party always taking the brunt of the complaints, the other being hailed as the all-powerful savior and harbinger of chaos. A few disgruntled larvlings would be far easier to handle than a billion disgruntled Earthlings, however. She let herself daydream about easier problems for a moment.

Fortunately, the problem which was hurtling toward her city at this very minute would make the problem of the disgruntled Earthlings seem easy in comparison.

"General, we have a situation," said her lieutenant, bursting into her office unannounced.

"I'm aware. I'm preparing remarks now—"

"No, General, it's an even more situationy situation. Look." The lieutenant pointed to the window behind Listay and as she turned she saw a speck the size of a small brick rapidly becoming the size of a large brick, quickly approaching something too big to be compared to a brick at all.

Everything went terribly silent, and then terribly loud as the *Peacemaker* entered the upper atmosphere, slicing through the air like a mallet through pudding, a thunderous roar poisoning the air.

"What in Blitheon's name is the Captain doing?" Listay breathed.

"I am raining liberation down upon the planet."

The lieutenant was gone when Listay spun around, the Captain standing in their place. Not standing, roiling. Her form flickered and bubbled as if it had been recorded on a melting acetate film, a halo of silver light framing her face where her hair should've been.

"Captain?" Listay took half a step back, bumping into the window behind her.

"I am not your Captain. I am your god and you shall henceforth refer to me only as The All-Consuming and Ultimate Finale of Being, That Which Disassembles Reality, The Absolute and Irrefutable God of Chaos."

Listay looked over her shoulder at the quickly crashing starship, then back at her incomprehensible lover. "If this is a sex thing, I'm into it, but we need to save the city, first."

"This is not a sex thing," Chaos said, and Listay couldn't tell if she was moving closer or growing larger. "This is the opposite of a sex thing. It is an undoing. It is a rending apart. And I shall begin with you, *my devotee*."

“What’s the lunch tray for?” Listay asked, eyes locked onto the only stable object in the room now, the plastic lunch tray.

Chaos shattered it against her unreal thigh, pressing a shard of plastic into the soft space under Listay’s ribs.

“It’s for irony. I will destroy you with the very thing you used to enslave the people of this planet.”

“With...lunch?”

“Order! Structure. Every divot of this tray designed intentionally for a different part of their meal. It’s insanity,” Chaos said. “And I will cure it by killing you.”

“No,” Listay whispered, her head shaking side-to-side, gently, as she tried to make the maelstrom of thoughts in there settle down. “But I loved you,” she said, at last.

“Gross.”

Chaos plunged the shard of lunch tray into Listay’s chest and flung her through the glass window, becoming just corporeal enough that the shower of razor-sharp glass sliced delightful red, dripping lines across her face and arms.

General Listay fell through the clean, perfect air of her clean and perfect Earth toward the protestors below who parted to allow her direct access to the concrete.

She closed her eyes as her detractors gathered around her body and cheered, resignedly keeping track of her heartbeat. Ten beats per beoop, five...three...

Above in the control tower, Chaos watched with the smile of a predator showing its prey the tools of its imminent demise, her influence growing with every utterance of her sacred name.

A millennium is a long time to go without having your name chanted by a few thousand of your most pious devotees, and she was dizzy with energy. She held onto the shattered window frame to steady herself, Yvonne’s warm, sticky blood dribbling down to her elbow. Soon, she’d be done with this pitiful body and her consciousness would once again permeate All That Is.

The city’s very atoms quivered in fear of her. That was more like it, she thought. Experimenting, she twisted a nearby bakery into a pink, gummy mass dotted with baking tins like ill-placed teeth. Not a bad start.

"Creatures of Earth," she said, her voice echoing from the cracks between every brick in the city and booming out of every dark and forgotten crevice. "You are liberated from reality!"

And she began to prove this.

For a few blissful moments, everything was, indeed, boobs, but this grew tiresome surprisingly fast.

CHAPTER THIRTY-EIGHT

The Plan

May, August, Xan, and Ix huddled around the low coffee table, each with a mug of coffee. Xan was the only one drinking from his mug, however, due to the horrible bitterness of the brew. For the others, it was just a comforting warmth. Something to do with their hands as they pondered their next move.

May had cut the engine, and the *Audacity* was drifting just outside of Earth's atmosphere. From that far away, everything looked normal down on Earth, making it even harder for May to believe anything was wrong.

"The plan is this," Ix said, taking a sip of the coffee, displaying the most delicate of grimaces, then setting the mug down. "The *Audacity* will re-enter the *Peacemaker* and I shall teleport to the *Peacemaker*'s control center where I will set the autopilot to warp. I will then return to the *Audacity* and May will shoot into the stardrive. This will destroy the Schplyson sphere surrounding the star, trigger collapse, and—"

"Is that like a Dyson sphere?" May interrupted. She had read plenty of old sci-fi novels. She liked to think she knew her terminology.

"No, it is a Schplyson sphere. Invented by Schplyson of Schplep on A'Viltri in the orbit -141. It converts and transmits a massive amount of energy from a star into a ship's engine via Schpluetooth."

For the millionth time, May suspected she was dreaming. Maybe that old AMC Gremlin had hit her back on Earth. Maybe she was in a coma. Maybe—

"You are not in a coma on Earth. You are awake in the present moment. Come back," Ix told May, firmly, her fingers at May's temples.

"How did you do that?"

"She can hear thoughts. It's an Ultra-Physicist thing," said August.

"Thank you, August. Xan, your thoughts are cacophonous. What is your concern?"

Xan, for his part, sat on the carpet in front of the couch looking like a fish trying to climb a tree, but her query forced him to wrangle those cacophonous thoughts into a coherent sentence. "This seems needlessly complex. Can't you set the *Peacemaker* to self-destruct then set the autopilot and get out of there before it jumps?"

"There is no self-destruct. What would be the purpose of such a feature?"

"All ships have a self-destruct button, right?" he asked, looking at May. "Right?"

She shook her head. "The *Audacity* doesn't."

"Really?"

"Xan, you've pressed every button and flipped every switch on that console. If it had a self-destruct button, you would've found it by now."

"I am still unclear as to the purpose of such a device," Ix said. "But it does not matter. The Ultra-Ray-Super-Destroyers on the *Audacity* should be powerful enough to trigger the event, and the rocket should be fast enough to escape it."

"I have something to say," August said importantly. "Are you going to drink that?" He pointed to Ix's steaming mug of black sludge.

Ix slid it gently across the table toward him.

"Take this," May said, unclipping the *Audacity*'s anchor button from her suit and handing it to Ix. "You can teleport back here after setting the autopilot."

Ix tucked it into her breast pocket. "I will allow exactly two bloops before the warp. In that time, we must destroy the stardrive and exit the ship."

"How long is a bloop, again?"

"I've got this," August said to Ix, confident he could explain Earth time conversations better than an alien. "A blip is like a second. Short and sweet. The bloop is roughly a minute, so you've got like two-ish minutes to do the thing and escape. The beoop is like...ah Christ what's the other one?"

"You are thinking of an hour," Ix told August.

"Yeah! Right. An hour. Damn, it's been so many orbits since I thought about hours!"

"Very good August, thank you," Ix said. "A bloop is exactly 43 seconds. This means you have one point four three repeating minutes to accomplish our mission and escape. I recommend removing this ship's Collision Cushion chip to increase the power available to lasers."

May's eyes rolled back in her head as she searched for strength somewhere near her hairline. "Okay," she said, at last. She took a long, angry sip of the hot, bitter coffee. "Let's do it."

The next steps were clear. Turn around. Find the *Peacemaker* and dock inside it again. She walked up the stairs to the console as if she were walking up to a guillotine, set the course, and pressed the Button That Typically Made the Ship Go.

"What's my job?" August asked, a bit over enthusiastically, two cups into a raging caffeine high.

"Your assistance will not be required," Ix told him.

"I've got a job for you, actually," Xan said, getting to his feet and finishing off the dregs of his own coffee. "We're going to get the good luck charm back from Yvonne."

"What? Why?" May said, preparing the ship to dock.

"That thing's a legitimate probability modifier. Yvonne's got some massively good luck on her side. We can't risk her having it."

May turned around now, confident that the landing sequence she set would do its job. "No. It's too dangerous. It can't make that big a difference, can it?"

"It can," Ix said. "If Chaos has a probability modifier, the probability of us succeeding against her, which is already quite low, will be effectively null. Xan is correct."

"Oh," May said.

Xan smiled at Ix. "Thanks! I don't think anyone has ever said that about me before." He parked his hands gently on May's shoulders just as the *Audacity* parked in the *Peacemaker*'s docking bay. "I'll see you soon, okay?"

"But what if—" May said.

He shook his head, pressing her nose with his finger like it was an off switch. It confused her so much, it worked. "I will see you soon."

She sighed heavily, but nodded. "See you soon. Have fun."

"Oh, we won't!" he said, cheerily. "Are you ready to have a lot of the exact opposite of fun, August, my dear brand-new pal?"

"Yes! Wait. No..." August held out his arms toward Ix. "One or both of us might die."

"Yes, August, that is an unfortunate possibility. Are you requesting physical reassurance that I am invested in the continuation of your life?"

"That would be nice."

Ix opened her arms and bent them around August at right angles. A hug from Ix felt like being crushed in a turnstile, but she was improving.

"August, do you know how to hot-wire a Gremlin?" Xan asked, already on the teledisc.

"Is there any other way to start one?" August joined him and the pair disappeared.

CHAPTER THIRTY-NINE

A Horrible Plan

What separates man from beast? This question has begged the attention of many a philosopher and scientist. Some postulate tool usage, however the crow and the orangutan are quite adept with a good stick. Complexity of language then, perhaps. But the humble humpback whale proves this answer false. The ability to introspect, then. Wrong again. The chartreuse cave scrums found on several planets in the Flotuex system are well known for their thoughtful ruminative poetry.

The one thing, then, which consistently distinguishes "human" from "not human" the universe-over is a sense of style.

Even in times of dire urgency, all other things being equal, the stylish option will win. If you place in front of a starving man a faded ball-cap filled with cold oatmeal and a platter of nicely arranged meat and cheese slices garnished with curls of carrot and cucumber, he will choose the charcuterie board every single time.

This is why, of the thousands of AMC Gremlins which composed the *Peacemaker*'s fleet of shuttles, the only vehicle that remained was eye-wateringly hideous. It was a dark blue specimen with a dented red door and silver bald patches where the paint had been half-heartedly sanded a decade before. It exuded an air of overwhelming smugness because it knew it now it was the only choice, which made it the best choice.

"Oh-ho-ho," it seemed to say to Xan and August as they approached, looking desperately around the otherwise empty, half-crushed docking bay for a better option. "It appears you'll be requiring my services after all."

Seeing no other recourse, August flung open the door and started to work. The engine turned, the thrusters engaged, the Gremlin was ready.

"What now?" August asked Xan as he got in the passenger side. "Seems like you know what you're doing."

"Does it? Excellent. I do not. Glad I could inspire confidence, though!" Xan tugged on a seatbelt that hadn't shifted since 1982. He settled for slipping an arm through the seatbelt, which is, incidentally, a good way to break your arm.

"Get us out of here, first. Maybe Chaos will just be waiting outside and we nicely ask her to return the thing!" Xan said, pointing toward the hole in the side of the *Peacemaker* through which the sky could be seen.

"On it, Captain," August said, launching the Gremlin.

"Captain?" Xan smiled at August, flattered. However, when he saw the state of the city outside the ship, he no longer wanted to be in charge. "Don't call me Captain," he whispered, awed by the carnage.

Earth roiled with activity. Turbulent gusts of yellow dust whipped around them, settling on the remains of the buildings the *Peacemaker* had crushed. Remains which appeared to be sloughing away into piles of seasoned Panko breadcrumbs dripping in rivulets of colorful ooze.

The tallest building left standing was the control tower, untouched apart from the gardens along its balconies which had become writhing masses of thick, wormy vines and a phrase repeating in neon haze around the perimeter: "All Hail Chaos, Beginning of the End."

Atop all that, floating on a cloud of incomprehensible buzzing shapes, Chaos herself observed her kingdom.

On the pavement below, hoards of Earthlings stood and worshiped her with their phone cameras, ecstatically recording every blink of her unmentionable eyes.

August and Xan both just stared for awhile. Neurons misfiring in time to a misfiring cylinder in the ancient Gremlin's engine. Just comprehending the problem was going to be a challenge, much less resolving it.

"Alright, okay, alright..." Xan said, hoping speaking out loud might jar his brain into thinking logically again. "We need to get her down from that...cloud of...s-stuff...and then distract her so I can get close enough to grab the probability modifier."

"How do we do that?" August asked, slowly bringing the Gremlin toward the tower.

Xan shook his head, eyes locked on the ever-changing landscape. The air began to melt. "Well I'd typically start any distraction by dressing in drag, but we just don't have the wardrobe for that I'm afraid. And your makeup would take an eon."

"Hey!"

"No, no, it's a compliment. You're very rugged," Xan said, absently, watching all the lampposts shatter into a spray of assorted hardware. Barrel hinges, padlocks, wood screws, and toggle bolts rolled across the sidewalk, dropping into absurdly clean storm drains and settling in sparking, leafless gutters.

"Order!" August shouted. "She's a Chaos god...entity...spirit? Whatever. If we start organizing that mess, it might piss her off."

"And that's...something we want to do?"

"Yes," August said. "Easiest way to get someone's attention is to annoy them."

"Oh, it's so sad you think that," Xan muttered. "But you're right, it'll probably work. Always did for Aimz."

"Who's Aimz?"

Xan shook his head. "Someone I used to know. Park it down there, we can get to work on those screws."

August parked the Gremlin in exactly the way Ix always told him would ruin the parking gear and got out, finding the sidewalk distressingly spongy as the molecules binding the concrete together began to unwind.

Collecting every upholstery tack he could find, Xan started arranging them in nice, even rows, glancing up at Chaos occasionally to see if she was noticing.

August started on the plastic wall anchors, cleverly organizing them by color, size, and how much plaster dust clung to them.

Once the tacks were reasonably ordered, Xan began corralling three-quarter inch screws.

High above the city, in her cocoon of curiosities, Chaos rode on waves of bliss generated by the imminent degradation of all things. Ah, she thought to herself, this is nice. But something niggled, still. Like a clothing tag twisted the wrong way or an ant crawling up her ankle. She ignored it. If she ignored it, she reasoned, it might go away.

It only grew, though. It was now very much like two songs with different beats in different keys being played together. What was that? She recreated her eyes and peered down at the throngs of worshipers below. The annoyance flapped like the dislodged rubber bit of a busted windshield wiper. There he was. She sighed so cavernously that a cyclone began to curl in the distance, carelessly uprooting a field of plastic cacti where there had, until recently, been a flourishing pollinator meadow.

Xan.

Being annoying.

She really should've killed him when she had the chance, but that love-sick body of hers kept pulling punches.

Rolling her eyes, she projected the phenomenon of her form down to the sidewalk, a trick she'd learned a few eons ago when she gained mastery of formlessness. It wasn't ideal, but it would do until she really got the hang of being omnipresent again. Being omnipresent is unlike riding a bike in that if you go a few million years without practicing that sort of thing, the sense of it tends to leave you.

"What are you doing?" she asked, though she knew perfectly well what he was doing. She just wanted him to account for himself.

"Tidying up a bit! It's a mess down here, you know? Shambles!" Xan did not stop to look at her. He was onto metal washers now.

"It's not going to work."

"What won't?" August asked, visually comparing the size of two bronze eyelets.

"Organizing assorted hardware is not going to get my attention," she said, kicking over a neatly stacked pyramid of one-inch bolts.

They pretended not to notice she had done this.

"Hey Xan," August called. "Do you think these metric washers should stay separate from the imperial ones?"

"Absolutely and without any doubt, yes," said Xan, trying to keep a few three-inch metal springs in formation.

"This is ridiculous." Chaos waved a hand and the hardware devolved into uncountable grains of pale gray sand.

Just for a moment, Xan gave the mound of sand in his hands a perplexed look. He then turned to August with a wry smile. "You wouldn't happen to have a pair of tweezers and a magnifying glass, would you?"

"Never leave home without 'em!" August reached into the pocket of his jeans, but Chaos was through playing with them.

In a blink of her unmentionable eyes, they were all three at the top of the control tower and far away from anything that could conceivably be organized.

August manifested with his head nearly over the edge of the building, but he quickly rolled to safety. If he fell from that height, Ix would be very disappointed in him. It would take her weeks to repair him.

The sand in Xan's palm blew away and, defeated, he finally looked Chaos in the eyes. Or at least he tried to. She might have been two or three times her normal size now, but her physical parameters were hard to focus on. He could tell it was her, the silver hair, the unmentionable eyes, the serious scowl, but the edges of her skin seemed to be having a hard time staying solid.

She was at once extremely difficult to look at, and impossible to look away from.

On her chest, twinkling between the mounds of her dastardly cleavage, Xan could see the probability modifier clearly. He trained his attention on it and stood, pressing his back to the air conditioning unit behind him. Chaos's wibbling form was making him dizzy, and he needed something solid to lean on. August joined him, thinking being there would be safer than being on the edge of the building. He was wrong, though. It was closer to Chaos who could be far more deadly than a 150-story fall.

Chaos coaxed the yellow dust particles in the air around her to coalesce into the form of a flail with a be-spiked iron beach ball attached to one end.

Chaos herself was barely corporeal anymore, but she retained just enough solid mass to be able to swing the massive flail like a tetherball of doom above her head.

Xan turned to August. This was just too horrible to watch.

“So, August, you’re from Earth?”

“Uh-huh,” August said, sweating.

“Ever seen ‘I Love Lucy’?” Xan asked, absolutely shutting down the part of his brain that lived in the present moment.

“I...yeah sure. Some of it,” August said, shutting his eyes tight. “That’s the one with the candies, right? Where she’s trying to eat all the candies because she can’t keep up with the conveyor belt?”

“Yeah! Job Switching, that one’s called. Good stuff. I love the Paris episodes. Did you know there are four different languages on Earth? There’s this great scene where they’re in Paris and they’re translating things from all these different Earth languages and it’s just so funny. I love that scene.”

“There are like...hundreds of languages. Maybe thousands,” August said, turning his face away from the spinning flail to avoid getting his nose lopped off.

“Really?” Xan asked. “Zuut. I’d like to learn them all. I sure hope I live to,” he said, feeling a gentle breeze on his cheek from the spinning flail.

CHAPTER FORTY

No Reason

"May," Ix said, sitting in the co-pilot's chair as May checked and rechecked the ship, trying to give Xan a head start. "Do you trust him?"

"Who, Xan?"

"Yes."

"Sure. Why?"

Ix was quiet for a moment. "No reason. Do you believe he can retrieve the probability modifier?"

May leaned back in the pilot's chair, chewing her bottom lip. "No..."

"Then there is nearly no chance we will succeed," Ix said matter-of-factly.

May didn't appreciate being told she wouldn't succeed. She hadn't appreciated it when her high school literary teacher told her she would never succeed because she'd neglected to finish reading *Catch-22*. She hadn't appreciated it when her student counselor had told her she wouldn't succeed at going after a degree in engineering. She hadn't appreciated it when that random customer at Sonic had told her she wouldn't succeed at life in general because she'd given him too much ice.

She stopped fiddling with the rocket's stabilizers and turned on Ix, fixing her with a scowl neither of them could see; Ix because she was blind and May because it was on her own face.

"What are the odds of being abducted by aliens and then offered a chance to escape less than a day later?"

"Low."

"What's the likelihood of surviving being ejected into open space?" She leaned in a little closer now, counting her points on her fingers.

"Extremely low."

"What are the odds that I picked up your distress call and just happened to be on a ship with weapons powerful enough to destroy a stardrive that you wanted destroyed?"

"Absurdly low."

"Great. I'm not too worried about our chances, then. How do I get to the stardrive?"

Ix conjured a miniature holographic map of the *Peacemaker*'s schematics on her BEAPER. She flicked at it for a moment, trying to get it to stay still. She ran her finger along the outside of it, then downward until her finger rested in the docking bay, roughly where they had landed.

"There is a series of service ducts the *Audacity* should be able to fit through. It will be tight." Her finger traced a complex trail through the holographic ship.

"Can't I just blast through the ship straight to the stardrive? It'd be quicker."

"That would compromise the structural integrity of the ship."

"What, you want to leave that to the black hole?"

Ix was quiet for a moment. "No, I would rather the structural integrity not be compromised at all, but I understand your point. It may be quicker to go straight through the ship, as you suggested." Ix closed the hologram. She typically looked either pensive or somber, depending on what the situation called for. Now, however, she looked positively melancholy.

"Okay, I'm going to remove the Collision Cushion," May warned Ix, hoping that perhaps Ix would stop her.

Ix did not stop her.

"Before I do, though," May said, stalling yet again to give Xan more time to accomplish his impossible task before she began her impossible task, "Why did you ask me if I trusted Xan? What do you know about him?"

"What I know about his past comes from Yvonne. The ruminations of ex-lovers are not flattering. I do not think it would benefit anyone to share them with you."

"Well you read his mind, right? What's he thinking?"

"Quite an unusual mind," Ix said. "He vacillated regularly between something I believe he called 'I Appreciate Lucille' and fears regarding your safety."

"Oh." May nodded. That made sense to her.

"He is also hiding something important from you. Though I don't believe he has complete access to it, himself, he knows he is hiding it."

"Oh." May swallowed. That also made sense, but she didn't like it.

"Are you ready for me to begin the countdown?" Ix said.

"Would it matter if I wasn't?" May asked.

"No." Ix stepped onto the teledisc and was gone.

CHAPTER FORTY-ONE

Xan Gets The Flail

The rumbling of a ship engine vibrated up into Xan's skull, chattering his teeth. *That's strange*, thought Xan. *'I Love Lucy' had never had enormous starships in it before.*

He winked open an eye to the present and found the *Peacemaker* was coming back online. May was somewhere aboard it, possibly already headed toward the stardrive.

"Zuut, zuut, zuut. Lucy, wherever you are, I need your strength," he prayed. Realizing too late if Lucille Ball was a god, good hand-eye-coordination would not be among her list of talents. Xan knew no gods of hand-eye-coordination, however, so she would have to do. Perhaps, at least, if he were to die, Lucille Ball could pull some strings from the beyond and make it a funny death.

He opened both eyes now, focused on the probability modifier like a cat focused on a laser pointer. The flail swung. He wasn't sure if it was swinging in slow motion because he was terrified, or because Chaos had begun zuxing with the laws of physics. Really, it was both.

All he had to do was grab the thing and May would live and maybe Yvonne, even, would live and if Lucille Ball was half the god he hoped she was, he might get to live, too.

Just take it.

The flail swung by...Now!—Oh no. No, it was back.

He'd hesitated too long.

The flail swung round again.

It passed.

He sprang.

His fingers touched the rock, seized around it, and held onto it as if it were the last solid thing in the universe. Thanks to Chaos's meddling, it nearly was.

A heavy iron chain slammed into his ribs, bowling him over the edge of the tower, snapping the cord that had held the good luck charm around Chaos's neck.

He shut his eyes tight, tried to think of nothing but Lucy, but instead found himself thinking only of May.

The Final Race

"It is time."

"What?" May had her head propped between her knees, shakily awaiting Ix's return. Ix slid into the seat beside her, tapping the *Audacity*'s control panel urgently.

"Go. Now," Ix said, with an uncharacteristic urgency in her voice. "The autopilot was severely damaged. The ship will warp in forty-three blips...forty-two...forty-one." Ix set a countdown into her BEAPER and as the blips passed, it beeped in a steadily increasing pitch. It seemed to be getting faster, too. Like an auctioneer frantically trying to convince a crowd to raise the bid on their dwindling time.

What happened next happened with such ferocious speed that even moments later, May would not be able to precisely explain the details. Furthermore, moments later, May would be hurtling toward Earth in a burnt-out rocket ship with little hope of survival and was, as one might imagine, a little distracted.

What happened was this: May locked the ship's navigation. She launched. She grabbed the control sticks for the Ultra-Super-Ray-Destroyers, aimed the crosshairs directly in front, and pressed the red buttons faster than a morse code operator gunning for a world record.

The rocket broke through layer upon layer of the *Peacemaker*'s private quarters, offices, secret labs, overt labs, and swimming pools until the enormous, glittering disco-ball of the stardrive, the shining heart of the ship, was in their crosshairs.

May sent a laser blast right into its core, then turned the *Audacity*'s nose sharply up and dug her foot so hard into the ship's accelerator she fractured a metatarsal.

The stardrive sought revenge, though. The hole became a sucking wound, dragging every molecule of matter into its maw.

"Fuck no, I'm not going to die getting sucked off," May said through her teeth, lifted her foot off the accelerator, and slammed it down again, giving the ship a boost of power which propelled it out of the *Peacemaker* in the very instant the ship, and its sucking stardrive, warped away into a distant star system.

In the moment of triumph as the *Audacity* shot into the clear blue sky, Ix said, "Ah. 'Sucked off' is an Earth euphemism for oral sex. That is why you stifled your laughter earlier when I was explaining the plan."

"I fucking did it," May said, just to herself. She hadn't really heard Ix, so it was good that Ix hadn't said anything important.

Ix almost deigned to compliment May on her survival, but gravity had other plans. The strain on the rocket had been too much. Just before reaching escape velocity, the *Audacity* shut down, dropping from the sky as if it had been accidentally spawned there by a careless creation god, the immutable law of gravity resolutely not muting.

"The cushion!" May shouted at Ix, stuffing the chip into Ix's hands as she dove under the darkened control panel and began button mashing in hopes of finding the emergency generator.

It is possible to be bad at button mashing. It must be undertaken with both precision and speed, but without stopping for even a nanosecond to find out if what you're doing is working.

May tried to channel Xan's chaotically optimistic energy as her fingers flew inexpertly over the rows of dials and switches under the console and Ix fumbled with the Collision Cushion chip above her.

"May," Ix said, impossibly calm. "It seems to have escaped your notice that I am blind. Perhaps it would be wiser for you to re-install the circuit."

"No, yeah, I noticed," May grunted as she toggled a sticky lever and waited a dangerous nanosecond to see if it would work. "Eyesight won't be of any use until I get the lights back on, though."

"I see," said Ix, though she didn't. Neither of them saw anything. Ix began to feel her way around the control panel, May continued mashing buttons, and the Earth waited patiently to obliterate them both.

CHAPTER FORTY-THREE

A Well-Deserved Break

Heaven, or hell, or wherever Xan had ended up, had a beautiful, clear blue sky. A lot like Earth's sky, actually. Maybe each heaven was personalized, thought Xan, and his heaven was a lot like Earth. Strange about the searing pain in his side. Wasn't that supposed to go away after...after...a cloud of vapor floated in front of him "Hail Chaos," it said.

So he had survived.

He sat up in a hanging window washing platform, just a story away from Chaos and her menacing ball.

What was particularly strange about that, was that the control tower Listay had built didn't need to be washed. Chaos had just materialized the window washing platform because she thought it would look funky hanging off the side of the building like a skin-tag.

"Not dead!!" Xan laughed delightedly, holding up the probability modifier like a grand-prize trophy.

Announcing that you aren't dead within earshot of someone who wants you dead isn't a great move. Chaos's infuriated face appeared over the edge of the building, glaring at him.

"Kibanib!" Xan said upon seeing her.

"What?" Chaos's unmentionable eyes squinted, confused.

"I just remembered. Aimz's ex-girlfriend's brother was named Kibanib. You remember him, right? We used to have such fun together. He had a crush on you, you know? Honestly, everyone did. You're gorgeous. And you were really wonderful back then." She was getting closer. Somehow. Just her face, not the rest of her body. "I mean you still are, but I'm not sure it's ethical to flirt with someone under the influence of possession." Her eyes bore into his with a deadly clearness. Where was her body?! "If it was ethical, I definitely would because, wow you are..." Her tongue unfurled at him, twice as long as it should've been. She heaved. "Quite the looker..." he whispered, shivering.

Something was wrong with Chaos. Wrong-er.

Her body, Yvonne's body, snapped back together like a slinky as Chaos's essence was hoovered up into the *Peacemaker* just before it winked across the galaxy where it could continue to turn itself inside out without disturbing any local populations.

Xan watched, delighted, as an orange streak painted the sky. He then watched, horrified, as the orange streak reached its zenith and began to plummet.

"No," he said, grasping at the railing on the window washing platform, his fear of heights at the very bottom of the list of things he was afraid of right now.

The orange blur sputtered on, thrusters puffing, giving its final trajectory an erratic descent until it skidded to the ground, bowling over an array of giant vintage sewing thimbles which had until very recently been apartment buildings. It came to rest with a curiously quiet thud.

"Blitheon, no," he said, petitioning another, much less real sort of deity, as he tugged at the platform pulley and hopped back onto the building's roof.

Yvonne, firmly corporeal again, lay groaning on a solar panel which dinged politely to let the nearest qualified solar panel operator know that its view of the sun was being rudely obstructed.

Xan cupped her cheek in his palm and grabbed her hand, trying quickly to re-connect her to this mortal coil. "Hey, mun, are you alright?"

She opened her eyes at him, and he was relieved to see that they were now mentionable. Just a dull, purplish gray. Just like he remembered.

"I think so," she said, her brow still furrowed. "That was pretty impressive for a poslouian-slug-grass-eating-coward like you."

"What, that? That was nothing. I used to steal your jewelry all the time back on Tuhnt, remember? I am keeping it this time, though," he said, showing her the probability modifier. "I need it."

"Yeah, I know, that's why I gave it to you, zoup-nog," said Yvonne.

"I'm glad you're okay," said Xan. "I can't catch up, though, sorry!" He gave her forehead a quick kiss, then sprinted to the roof access hatch and began leaping down entire flights of poorly lit stairs, clutching the probability modifier, trying silently to convince it that it would be really, truly, unutterably unlucky for him if anything bad were to happen to May.

He flew out into the street to find the city reordering itself now that Chaos's influence was diminished. Seasoned Panko breadcrumbs re-became buildings. The colorful oozes coagulated back into bushes and fruit trees. Lazily traipsing pillars of greasy fur re-became fire hydrants. Strange, slimy things which crawled bug-like along the curbs re-became politicians. Quails continued to exist, but looked strangely out of place again.

Soon the city around him was about as boring as a city could be. Aside, of course, from the smoking neon orange rocket ship which had created a deep gouge in the Earth and the smattering of quails which pecked curiously at it.

As he ran, Xan did not think about what he would do if anything had happened to May or if the *Audacity* was unsalvageable. He thought about running. He thought about how much he hated running and wondered why he'd had to do so much of it lately. May was the common denominator there. He hoped she was alright. Or at least alive. If she wasn't he'd have to—he really did hate running.

The moment he reached the outskirts of the *Audacity*'s teledisc field, he teleported into the ship. The moment he remerged on the teledisc inside the ship, he realized this was a very bad idea. He trundled into the glowing orange wall which was now the glowing orange floor.

Thanks to the abundance of real gravity, the ship's artificial gravity, and most of its other non-essential systems, were taking a well-deserved break.

CHAPTER FORTY-FOUR

Social Anxiety

August was getting too old for awkward interactions. There is not, of course, an age one can put a finger on and say "that's too old for awkward interactions," but August had found that the only advantage to getting older was that he could claim he was too old for many of the things he just didn't like.

He was also too old for washing dishes, refueling the ship, and bending over to pick up things that had dropped on the floor, to Ix's chagrin. Once, she had tried to explain to him that if he was too old for these things, she certainly was, because she was a great deal older than him, but he refused to accept that. Earthling years were different from alien years.

But there was Yvonne, his dearest friend's recently un-possessed lover, just a few feet in front of him, rubbing her forehead as her personality tried to reassert itself. Behind her, the stairwell access. He would have to pass her to get to it.

"Uh...hey there," he said, nodding at her as he walked by.

"Who are you?"

"I'm...I'm August." He paused to rub the back of his neck. "I think I'm...Ix's pet? Do you remember Ix?"

Yvonne's eyes flew open and she leapt to her feet, which was quite an accomplishment because she hadn't controlled her own feet in decades and they were in quite high heels and they felt all pins-and-needles. "Where is she?"

August tried to reach out an arm to help steady her, but she didn't need it—or didn't want it. August put his arm down. "She's in the *Audacity*, I think. I was going to go check on her...you want to come?" he asked, almost hoping she would decline. It would be a long walk over to the wreck of the ship, he didn't necessarily want to have to make small talk at a time like this.

Yvonne ran to the edge of the building, looking down at the city below. When she spotted the orange scuff, she jumped into the window washing platform and shouted up at him. “Are you coming?”

He looked to the stairwell, considering. “Yeah,” he said. “Getting too old for stairs.” He vaulted over the edge of the building and into the platform in a way that made it clear to Yvonne that wherever he came from “too old” was probably code for “too lazy”.

CHAPTER FORTY-FIVE

A Weird Alien Thing

Something thudded next to May, and she rolled over to find that Xan had joined her splattered against the back-lit wall, which was now the floor, his grin illuminated by the orange glow.

"Good morning, starshine," he said.

"You could get away with that in space, but I know for a fact it's mid-afternoon here." She sat up and surveyed the damage. She understood now why all the ship's original furniture hovered. The hover chairs defied gravity, gently bobbing sideways, but the couch, coffee table, and TV had smashed into the wall paneling, horribly close to where May had landed.

"What happened?" Xan asked, trying to visually assess the state of the TV. It was an old cabinet TV, it was fine.

"I found the generator," May said, rubbing the side of her head to explore the new bump that had formed there. "And Ix re-installed the Collision Cushion. Just didn't have enough time to set the stabilizers to park it upright."

"So you parked sideways! That's fine. I've done that before. It works, if you need it to!" Xan crawled over May and walked along the wall to the control loft. The lever that controlled the ship's telescoping re-orientation arm was installed, annoyingly, just out of reach to someone who was standing on the wall.

He jumped a few times, swatting at it until he caught it and the ship began to right itself.

"Is Yvonne alive?" Ix asked, sliding down the wall to the floor so properly, she might as well have been riding it side-saddle.

"She's fine! Even insulted me, so I guess she's back to normal. I left her with August on the roof. He'll be safe with her, right?"

"He will manage," Ix said, kneeling beside May who sat cross legged on the floor. "How do you feel?" Ix asked May, prodding at her as she would prod at August after a near-death experience.

May felt like a spaceship was parked on her chest and her head was a seething nebula. "Fine," she said.

Brow furrowing in disbelief, Ix said, "Stand up, then."

"I will," May said, studiously avoiding putting any weight on her left foot. Xan stood near, his arms once again held out in the awkward fork-lift, trying to figure out if she wanted help or not.

"Now walk," Ix said, feeling that May was off balance but not knowing why.

Silently, May motioned Xan to come over to her and he threaded an arm under hers. She hopped forward. "See? Fine."

"You're leaning on Xan," Ix told her. "Come to the MediBay, if you have a broken bone I will need to set it. This happens to August frequently, so there is no need to be afraid."

"I'm not afraid!" May said. "I just need a cigarette," she groaned, leaning heavier on Xan who stumbled a little under her weight.

"You have suffered a concussion. Smoking is not advised at—"

"I know, I know," she said.

Ix took her from Xan, lifting her up into her arms. "You are lighter than August," Ix said.

"Thank you?" May slung an arm around Ix's neck.

"That was not intended as a compliment, it was a statement of fact. Xan, lead us to the MediBay."

"Right! Of course, on it…" he said. "Where's the MediBay?" he mouthed to May.

"It's a floor down, to the right. Where have you been showering?" May asked as Xan put a hand to Ix's back and began to lead them.

"I haven't been! There's a bacteria-eating fog at The Agency…"

"Ah, that explains why I smelled sex fog on you," Ix said.

"Sex fog?!" May asked. "What does that mean?"

"May, don't worry about it, you're concussed! This is probably all a dream," Xan said.

They found the MediBay and Ix set May down on the Diagn-O-Scan. The *Robert* hadn't had a Diagn-O-Scan, partially because they couldn't afford one and partially because the machine was so heavy the *Robert* wouldn't have been able to launch. Ix ignored the machine, feeling her way around May's ankle while Xan distracted her.

"It was horrible, May, Yvonne was terrifying—"

"Chaos," Ix corrected him, handing May a small towel. "Bite down on this if it hurts," she said. May took it gingerly between her teeth.

"Chaos, right, yeah. Chaos was terrifying. We organized at her! Wire caps, half inch screws, I lined up a handful of little springs—that was a challenge—are you alright?"

"Mmm-hmm," May said, squeezing the towel between her teeth as Ix put her foot right.

"Well it worked, the organizing, and she got so mad and manifested this flail and—are you sure you're okay?"

Ix poked something into her leg and a pleasant cool numbness eased the pain in her ankle. "I am done," Ix said. "You should be able to put weight on it now, but be cautious."

May spat out the towel. "You couldn't have numbed it before you set it?"

"I could have. Why do you ask?" Ix asked.

"Never mind. Go on, Xan," May sat up and began carefully trying out her ankle.

"Right, so, the flail. It was enormous. If one of those spikes had hit me, I would've been a stringy shish kabob—"

"You have shish kabob in space?"

"Everyone's got shish kabob. You've got food, you've got sticks, you put that food on sticks. Anyway, I spring for the probability modifier, just in time, I think, and the flail chain sends me over the side of the building, and then poof, Chaos is no more, and Yvonne insults me."

May nodded. "Good job."

"Thanks!"

A thud echoed from the floor above them. Something was happening in the living room. "Ix?!" they heard the muffled shout.

Ix had been dutifully folding the towel May had in her mouth, but she stopped in the middle of her work. "It's Yvonne," she whispered, a smile breaking across her face. She bolted out of the MediBay to the intershoot.

"How'd she get in?" Xan asked, looking up at the ceiling as if he could see through it.

"There's an external access hatch," May said.

"Huh," said Xan, watching May curiously. "You really did read that whole manual, didn't you?"

"Yeah."

Something thunked to the floor above them and started rolling around.

"We should probably give them some time," Xan said.

"Definitely," May agreed.

Xan hefted himself to sit on the Diagn-O-Scan beside May, knowing they needed to have a discussion but not really wanting to be the one to start it.

May wasn't giving anything up, though. She stared almost meditatively out the MediBay window, wondering where on Earth, exactly, they were. The buildings were beautiful and lush, but they didn't look anything like the Earth she had known.

Above them, through the thin floor, a muffled moaning could be heard. Anything would be better than that, Xan decided. "So...Earth's back to normal. I suppose you'll want to uh...get back to your life." He watched her carefully now, trying to read her strange Earthling emotions.

May grimaced at his words, still staring out at the new cityscape Listay had created. She shook her. "Yeah," she said. "I've got a second interview Friday for a really cushy office job. Lady seemed to like me, too. Think I'll take it."

Strange Earthling emotions, thought Xan, still he watched her for a sign until she looked at him, a smirk playing on her lips.

"Oh," he said. "An office job, huh? You know, sitting all day isn't good for your back. You're going to want to find yourself a good bone de-mangler."

May laughed. "On Earth we call those chiropractors."

"Oh, we have those too, but what you really want is a bone de-mangler. Trust me."

A moment of silence, filled with only the thunking and rolling and moaning of the couple above them.

"Fuck, what are they doing to our living room?" May asked, looking at the ceiling.

"Our living room?"

"Yours," May corrected herself.

"No...I like ours," Xan said, smiling. "You're really sure you don't want to stay here, though?"

A wet slapping sound interrupted him and, fortunately, it did not come from above. It was a yogurt cup that had been hurled against the MediBay window, its contents splattered across the window pane.

Hopping down from the table, May limped to the window and watched a variety of other processed foods, fruits, and quail eggs pelt the side of the ship. A disgruntled crowd had formed around them, shouting abuses at the ship that had just rescued them from an untimely and chaotic end. They saw only "alien ship" and they were very much done with "alien ships."

"Look at them," May said, shaking her head. "Earthlings suck."

Joining her at the window, Xan watched the food with curiosity. "Remember Plattamousse Proper? They pelted us with food, too. It's the orange, I think. Makes people ornery. All people, Earthling or not. Misplaced outrage is a cultural universal."

Again, she shook her head, more to herself this time, though. "No, there's nothing for me down there. I just got the hang of racing, and you said we could get ice cream. I haven't tried any alien ice cream. I couldn't bear living on Earth without knowing what that tastes like."

Xan smiled. "It's just regular ice cream. Harvested right out of a cream sea and frozen. Where does it come from on Earth?"

"You uh," May chuckled, raised her hands to start to mime milking a cow, then decided she didn't need to disturb him with the details. "You don't want to know where it comes from," she said.

"It's a weird alien thing?" Xan asked her.

"Yeah, it's a weird alien thing."

CHAPTER FORTY-SIX

Good odds

August arrived in the *Audacity*, via the access hatch, covered in foodstuffs. "They were helping, you ass with ears!" He shouted at a mob member who had tried to follow him into the ship as he kicked him in the face to knock him off the ship's external ladder.

He slammed the hatch shut and locked it, hoisting a sack of apples he had stolen from a food cart on the way over off his shoulder and onto the carpet. Ix and Yvonne were an entangled mess of purple limbs on the couch.

"Where's May?" he asked them.

Fortunately, they didn't have to stop to answer.

May and Xan appeared in the intershoot, having watched August climb up the side of the ship. Xan handed him a towel.

"Thanks," he said, wiping ketchup from his face. "Apple?" he asked, holding out the sack to them both.

Xan gingerly took one and sniffed it. "Earth fruit?" He took a little bite of it and concentrated as he chewed. May hadn't waited to see his reaction, she was already almost halfway done with hers.

"They're good, right?" August asked.

Xan smiled, handing the rest of his apple to May. "Yeah! So August," he said, changing the subject. "Are you going to stay on Earth?"

He shrugged, chewing harder. "Naw, I think Ix will want to keep me around. She'd get lonely without me. Isn't that right, Ix?"

Ix pushed Yvonne back, just a bit, just enough to speak. "Yes, August," she reassured him. He liked to be reassured.

"See!" August smiled. "I can't go back to my old life anyway. I was young when I left. I'm pushing 40 now," he said.

May raised a questioning eyebrow at him.

"Alright, 50. The point is that I can't explain that. Especially not to my girl. She'd spin out."

"Mm," May said, eating more of her apple. "Sorry about your girlfriend."

"It's okay. I've had a lot of good women over the years. Well, not all of them were women. None of them were women, I guess. Aliens? Alien women?"

"August, we have discussed this before. It's people." Ix and Yvonne had finally gotten enough of each other for the moment and joined them, hands clasped. "May, August, this is Yvonne," Ix said. "She has something she would like to say to you. Go on," Ix nudged Yvonne.

"I'm sorry I terrorized you," she said.

"It's alright! You were possessed. You didn't know what you were doing," Xan said.

Yvonne shrugged, not meeting his eyes. "I kinda knew. I was there. I remember most of it until...well it got weird. I couldn't stop her."

"Really, don't worry about it," Xan said. "Just like we were before the war, right? Exorcizing ancient evils from one another...flails."

His reminiscing was cut short by a rhythmic clunking from the hull of the ship which was soon joined by a distant litany of curses. Outside, the crowd had gotten brave. They were climbing the ladder up to the hatchway.

May set the remains of her apple on the table and limped up the stairs to the control panel. "Damn Earthlings," she muttered. "Where am I dropping you off?" she asked behind her.

"Wha...me?" Xan asked.

"Not you, everyone else." She turned around. "We don't have any bedrooms."

"Please bring us to Clymasir on Rhea I, May. Yvonne has asked to be accepted back onto her familial land."

"A-hah-uh...no, sorry. Can't go to Rhea," Xan interjected, hopping up to the control panel as if he would take command in the event May decided to go there. "Not going anywhere near the Flotluex solar system, actually. We'll take you to a spaceport, though! Something near there. Just not...there."

Ix blinked, looked directly at May, and May tensed, unsure if Ix was looking at her purposefully or not. It seemed to May like she was, somehow. “I understand your hesitation,” Ix said. “If you would take us to Tolfy Municipal Spaceport we can access our accounts from there and purchase a new means of transportation. August, you can have something to eat there, as well.”

“I’ve got apples,” said August, his mouth full of his third apple.

“You cannot eat only apples,” Ix said.

“Bet I can.”

Xan sat in the co-pilot’s chair, no longer trying to edge May away from the navigation. “Alright! We’ll drop off Yvonne, August, and Ix, grab a ‘we’re not dead’ celebratory cocktail, get some new suits ordered, and then...?”

May set the ship’s autopilot to take them to Tolfy, then pressed The Button That Typically Made The Ship Go.

“We race. Let’s try Plattamousse again. As long as I don’t start from slot three, we’re guaranteed to not lose.”

Xan smiled at her. “I like those odds!”

CHAPTER FORTY-SEVEN

Dead and Buried

In the beginning, there was awareness.

This awareness quickly decided it had a name, and that was Listay. It had a title, too. General.

The awareness realized it had thoughts again. Questions. Many, many questions.

And then this awareness touched on something external to it. The word of god, for all it knew. This is what god said, "Damn, Joe, she's a heavy fucker!" Listay heard this distantly, as if she were in an aquarium and someone outside of it was speaking. Was she the heavy fucker here?

"Come on, we don't gotta drag her much farther," said another voice, closer, clearer. She felt nothing, and she saw nothing. Just thoughts and sounds.

"Why do we even got to bury her, huh? Let's just let the buzzards and coyotes take care of it," said the first voice. A voice which Listay now decided did not belong to any god.

"You want radioactive alien-flesh-eating varmints around?"

"Guess not."

"Then lift her up on three. One...two...three!"

Ah, now she felt something. Nerves were starting to come online again, it felt like napalm had been pumped into her limbs.

This is nothing, she thought. Wait, no, she didn't think that. This was definitely something. *I was trapped in the body of a star for eons.*

Certainly, that wasn't her thought. She had never been trapped in a star, that was absurd. But if not her...whom?

Do you not recognize your savior? I am the being at the end of all being. The harbinger of decay. I am Chaos. And you, Listay, are dead.

That didn't surprise her much. What surprised her was that she knew it. Why did she know it?

Dying brains are so stupid. Thought Chaos. *I saved you. That's what the word savior means. Together, with you, my dearest devotee, as my chariot, we shall enact my greatest plan yet. I shall undo all that has been done and eradicate time itself!*

Listay felt something else, now, a dull throbbing in her chest. Dread dropped onto her body like shovelfuls of dirt. No, that was actually shovelfuls of dirt.

She would be buried alive.

Don't be overdramatic. You aren't alive yet. Re-animating the dead takes time.

Dirt slowly covered her, growing heavier and heavier. Now she knew how all those llerke seeds she'd planted in her lifetime felt. The difference was that she was terrified of what she might grow into.

END OF BOOK 1

AHH! presents:

BITE

A Horror Shorty

They thought it was abandoned...

by CARMEN LOUP

Bite

Breakfast

May June July, Earthling, had rather hoped she would never be eaten. Xan, her Tuhntian companion, had held a similar aspiration.

The likelihood of either of them attaining this life goal was dropping by the blip, and here's why:

It had begun, as most horrific events do, during breakfast.

Aboard the racing rocket *Audacity,* every meal was breakfast, because without a proper day/night cycle in open space, May ate whenever she was too hungry to either keep working or fall asleep. Or when Xan decided to make coffee and the scent triggered her appetite.

Xan poured her a mug from the retro coffee carafe first, saving the sludgy sediment at the bottom for himself, before reclining at the hover table which overlooked the enormous porthole in the side of the ship, watching the star he was hatched under, Flotluex, boil merrily a few hundred thousand light-years away.

"Coffee's ready!" he announced to May who was studiously cleaning the ship's view screen.

"Okay, okay," she said, impatiently swiping at the last, highest corner of the view screen with a rag. She climbed from the control loft and opened the cabinet, plucking out a package of something she hadn't tried before. Her translation chip had decided to call it a nutrition cloud with artificial mauve flavoring.

She sat in the hover chair opposite Xan and tore the seal strip off, allowing a gravity-less pink mass to balloon out of the package. Unsure of how, exactly, one was supposed to eat a cloud, she stuck her tongue in it and was reproofed with a zap from a tiny bolt of lightning.

"Bite it," Xan suggested. "You've gotta show dominance."

"When have you ever shown dominance to anything?" May teased.

After a moment of careful thought, Xan said, "Just when I eat nutrition clouds."

She squared her shoulders to the pink mass, straightened her back, and chomped down, piecing off a large hunk. It melted in her mouth in a way which reminded her vaguely of cotton candy. Nostalgia plummeted her back to Earth autumns spent siphoning off pocket change at the carnival which would set up a few blocks from her childhood home. "You know what I miss about Earth?" She snatched another mouthful of cloud thoughtfully.

Always keen to hear about Earth culture, Xan set down his coffee, took his feet off the console, and leaned in, rapt.

"Tell me." He nipped at a finger of cloud which had come too close to his face.

"Shitty pop-up carnivals."

"Oh, those exist all over the universe! We've got a whole grouping of satellites in the Flotluex system dedicated to them. Some are really spectacular. Others are trokholes."

"Let's go to one!"

"One of the trokholes? I mean, the nice ones have the best dishes from thousands of cultures, and universe-renowned mind-altering enjoyment fields, and the coolest prizes—once I won a flask of the first bath of marsupian wine ever made. Ever! It was rancid, but interesting, right?

"The trokhole carnivals, however, have shoddily constructed racer tracks, and the same junk food you get at fuel stops, and the only mind-altering fields they have are in the fun houses and they're so weak that all you get is a vague sense that you should be enjoying yourself, but you aren't. Oh, Blitheon, and they're full of Anats trying to get you to bet your soul on impossible-to-win games. If you don't fall for it, they just shape-shift into someone else and try again."

By the time he had finished talking, May had consumed the rest of the pink cloud and was running her finger along the inside of the package to collect any remnants left behind.

"That sounds exactly like an Earth carnival. We've got to go! Take me to the trokiest trokhole in the system so we can make fun of it." She licked a fine film of mauve nutrition from her finger and tossed the empty package into the refuse airlock under the console.

The key to finding the trockiest trokhole in the entertainment asteroid belt was to find the most popular and well-reviewed park then go, instead, to the *cheapest* one immediately surrounding it.

The parking lot was exactly what May had hoped it would be. Chunks of asphalt amid lakes of gray dust, no designated parking spaces for the twenty-or-so rusting space vehicles parked around them, and litter which would almost certainly include, if one looked hard enough, discarded alien condoms. May intended to look hard enough to find discarded alien condoms.

"O'Zeno's thumbs, is it supposed to smell this bad?" Xan peered around the parking lot, as if the source of the stench might wave apologetically at him.

May hadn't noticed, but now that she purposefully sniffed the air, she could smell, beyond the familiar scent of stale airlock, something unpleasant.

"Must be near the dump. It's probably ancient fryer grease," she assured him as they walked toward the entrance.

Cool yellow light from the Flotluex sun barely touched the asteroid, leaving everything which wasn't lit with flickering floodlights in greenish shadow. May's LayFlex™ racing suit kept a great deal of warmth in, but her nose and fingers were beginning to go numb with cold. She rubbed her hands and tented them over her mouth and nose to blow some hot air onto them.

"Cold?"

May was always cold. Not because she was particularly sensitive to the cold, but because Flotluex's boiling sun was frigid in comparison to the one she was used to. "I'll warm up as soon as we get onto some death-defying rides."

"Oh. Yeah. Defying death always warms me up, too," Xan agreed politely.

By the time they were close enough to hear the jaunty atmospheric music emanating from the park, May had counted three items which looked as if they might be condoms.

Ahead, a concrete entrance tunnel loomed like the roots of a massive ancient tree, lifted in such a way that you could walk beneath it. Attached to the frame, two purple painted faces, each three times the height of a body and carved into expressions of open-mouthed glee, guarded the locked gate. A massive plywood scroll connected their cartoonish ears.

"'Happy Fun Good Times Place'" May read from the scroll. She snorted, amused. "Glad to see they're mitigating expectations."

A single ticket booth attached like a tumor to the cheek of one of the faces. It was lit from above by a hovering solar-orb, but the inside was dark and empty as a freshly dug grave.

"Are you ready for some seriously happy fun good times?" Xan rang the desk bell at the nearest ticket booth with a grin which was so dissonant with the surroundings that it, embarrassed, backed off his face of its own accord.

"That depends." May studied the rusted chain padlocked around the front gate and tugged on it until it came loose. "Are you ready to explore an abandoned and hopefully haunted amusement park?"

"Hopefully?!" Xan, giving up on waiting for the attendant, dropped a handful of crystals at the ticket counter just in case.

"Is the alien afraid of ghosts?" May mocked as she pushed open the heavy gate. It moved with the elegance of a geriatric elephant, opening just enough for her and Xan to slip past. Decades worth of undecipherable graffiti decorated the inside of the concrete tunnel which was inset with small silver teledisc dampeners, ensuring that no one could skip the ticket booth by teleporting directly into the carnival.

"Ghosts I can handle. It's the dead bodies I don't like," Xan said, in a whisper now, as if a staff member might hear them sneaking in and reprimand them for it. "You saw all those vehicles out there in the lot, right? What happened to them?"

Beyond the monolithic entrance tunnel, warped building facades knifed into the yellow sky like jagged teeth. Ivy-claimed rollercoaster tracks flossed between them to create a park-spanning ride which looked like it had been deadly to both riders and pedestrians.

"Maybe they live here. Rent's gotta be cheap, and there's plenty of parking."

"Zuut, you can sell anything," he marveled.

"Shame about the security. So much for a gated community."

The sidewalk split into several new paths ahead of them where two arrow-shaped boards bobbed above a pile of similar arrow-shaped boards which had lost their hover-power ages ago. The bottom sign, its corner resting atop the pile which had fully succumb to gravity, read "Peting Zu" because the translation chip in May's head had, thoughtfully, maintained the poor spelling of the original sign.

"What do you think happened to all the animals?" Xan picked up the sign, unsure of why he had asked May, since he was fairly certain he knew the answer but didn't want to hear it.

She patted his shoulder. "I'm sure whoever locked the gate took the animals with them."

That, he realized, was why he had asked her. She always said exactly what he needed to hear.

He retired the sign to the pile and picked up the last hovering board. It looked slightly newer than the rest. "This way," he read out loud to May. "This way?"

"That way," May pointed in the direction the sign had been pointing until a moment ago.

"To what?"

"To wherever the sign was pointing."

"Which would be?"

"The way! Don't question it, let's go." She began to, but Xan put a hand on her shoulder to stop her.

"But we don't know what it's pointing to!"

"So we've got to find out."

He was about to protest further, but a lone quail brayed sadly from somewhere behind him, unsettling him enough for May to pull him along in the direction of "this way".

The sign's intended destination was a hulking black mark of a building which dead-ended the sidewalk. The solid brick was interrupted only by swooping stained glass and undulating grey vines so thick at their bases that they nearly looked like bodies slapped against the side of the building, their arms climbing toward the clock tower, thorns and downy blue flowers dotting the vine's surface. The golden clock sphere still spun slowly, delicate filigree marking out the time in Estrichi measurements.

"It's right," Xan said, checking the clock's time against his BEAPER. "I never thought I would be disturbed to find that a clock was working properly."

"Why?"

"Well, because typically, usually, I mean, it's a good thing when a clock is keeping time."

"Usually. Why not now?" May said, not looking away from the vines which seemed almost to breathe in the vague sunlight.

"Because a clock that big has to be reset every season, and this place looks as if it's been closed for several hundred orbits."

"Even a broken clock is right twice a day," May said and began to climb the wide staircase to the entrance.

Xan blinked after her. "What?"

"It's a saying, don't worry..." she paused to watch one of the blue flowers swivel open, "...about it."

"Oh, I won't. I'm already worrying about several hundred other things instead." He followed her up the stairs. "What if there's someone here? What if that someone doesn't want *us* here? What if all those other people who parked out there did exactly what we're doing and now they're dead? What if Lucy really did have mafia connections?"

"Lucille Ball? I'm sure she did."

"No, her character Lucy. It makes too much sense!"

May pulled on the brass door handle, and the entire front door glitched out, leaving a gaping wound at the mouth of the building. "Impressive holodoor," she noted. A little too impressive for the quality of workmanship the rest of the carnival had displayed.

The foyer was carpeted in red, the ornate chairs and benches set out along it were upholstered in red, and thick red tapestries hung like rotting meat from the cobwebbed ceilings.

To May, a red-blooded Earthling, it was gruesome. To Xan, a green-blooded Tuhntian, it was beautiful.

The only light came from the sickly saffron glow of the open doorway and a smattering of holes in the ceiling where the roof had fallen in. But the piles of detritus from the fallen roof weren't directly below the holes, they had been swept to the side, buttressing the finely papered walls.

"Okay, that's spooky," May admitted. "Who's been sweeping up?"

"The maid," said a disembodied voice. "But they're trok at it."

The voice, Xan was sure, had come from the left, and so he jumped to the right.

May was certain it had come from their right, and so she jumped to the left.

They tripped over each other and landed in a jittery pile on the tile floor, their heads swiveling like periscopes to try to locate the source.

"My apologies," the voice laughed as its owner, a dark-skinned Rhean wrapped in a pristine velvet trench coat, stepped out from under the shadow of a tapestry. "There's quite an echo in here. Aoide of Rhea." she bowed her head to them in a conservative display of welcome, ignoring their grunting and struggling as they both stood up at the same time.

"Sorry, uh, heh..." Xan said, smoothing back his pompadour. "You scared us!"

"You're the ones trespassing, you ought to be scared."

"We didn't realize anyone was here! And it's just such a lovely place we couldn't help ourselves. Really very marvelous architecture you have here. And an eye for decorating! I love your taste, Aoide of Rhea. I'm Xan of Tuhnt." He held out a friendly hand which, though requesting a shake, still shivered slightly.

May squinted at him; he was always trying to charm his way out of trouble instead of just admitting defeat and leaving. She was about to step in, apologize, and leave, but Aoide laughed.

"Handshakes are for testing each other's strength or sealing verbal contracts, not greeting guests." She pressed a call button on her BEAPER and spoke into it. "Maid, set the light in the parlor, we have company tonight."

"Oh we don't want to intrude," May said, stepping back toward the door.

"Not at all. Stay for a meal. You came here to partake in the carnival, no doubt? I would hate to disappoint."

"We did! We paid at the front desk, I put down a hundred crystals, is that enough for the two of us? There wasn't anyone there, so we just came on in, I hope that was alright. Is this your carnival?" Xan said, blazing nervously ahead.

Aoide's thick eyebrows met in the middle of her forehead. "You paid?"

"Of course! Of course we paid, we weren't just going to enter a carnival without paying," he laughed.

"How chivalrous of you."

"We'll go," May insisted.

"You won't make it to the parking lot if you leave now," Aoide said.

"Explain." May had taken Xan's hand now, not out of fear (not *entirely* out of fear), but with the intent to drag him back to the ship if she had to.

"Stay for the night, I would hate to see you two pleasant souls go to waste."

A door creaked open to reveal a young Tuhntian, dressed in a white apron, their features so sullen they might have been carved from stone. "Mistress Aoide, the parlor is set," they announced.

Using that as a distraction, May tugged on Xan and got him into motion again, sprinting toward the open doorway. Urban exploring was only fun if you didn't get caught. She wasn't interested in a sleepover.

"Zuut, May, she seemed nice!" Xan shouted as he was dragged down the stairs two at a time.

"Too nice. This isn't fun anymore."

"It's not fun when you're invited?!"

"Exactly." May stopped at the base of the stairs, where she was quite certain there hadn't been a hedge in front of the building when they entered.

Lunch

A low line of foliage blocked the way out.

It was moving.

They spun around to see that the thick gray vines which had been clawed into the brick were now ambling away from the building, cutting them off from the entrance, reimagining the landscaping with terrifying speed.

The clock tower chimed above them, and the vines tore away from each other, arms pushing and pulling and ripping at their own flesh until Xan and May were no longer surrounded by crawling vines, but dripping, gray bodies. The creature's featureless heads began to writhe and pull apart, revealing mouths full of black thorn-like teeth which stretched from their empty faces.

"What the fuck, what the fuck?" May whispered, pressing her back to Xan's as they searched for an out. This was not the kind of situation Xan could talk his way out of—their attackers appeared to have no ears—so he stayed silent for fear that if he opened his mouth at all, he would scream instead of saying anything helpful.

"There!" May shouted, throwing herself toward a break in the circle of bodies.

They flew past the creatures down a thin strip of sidewalk that skirted the structure and branched off around a bumper-rocket ride with a partially caved-in metal roof.

Nothing they had seen on the way in.

No signs pointing to the way out.

And behind them, a mob giving chase.

They could only run and hope they weren't trapping themselves further until they heard the faint call of the jaunty music.

They followed the sound, only to find a second pole with speakers attached to the top churning out the ironic ditty. It looked short beside the massive, phallic ride it stood before. "The Brain Blaster" read a sign on the control booth.

They jumped into the open ticket window and May slammed the metal shutter closed, sealing them in a space barely large enough for the ride control panel. Rather than claustrophobic, though, it felt secure as they huddled against the unfinished wooden slats inside.

"What are they? Xan? Are they aliens?" May said, nearly hyperventilating.

"I don't know, I don't know! Maybe, I mean, they're alien to me, so yes!"

"They're alien to me, too! What the fuck? They were definitely going to eat us, though, right? They were about to eat us. Oh my god, Jesus fucking Christ!"

"Looked like it. Certainly, really did look like they were going to-Zuut!"

Something dented the metal shutter.

Something was knocking at the back of the booth.

Something, and by now I'm sure it's clear this something was the creature, was tearing the roof from the walls.

Wood chips and shattered plaster rained on them, and three of the creatures were perched on the booth's walls, silhouetted against the golden sky.

Six branch-like arms grew toward them, groaning and snapping as the sinews stretched. May and Xan slunk down onto the sticky metal floor of the ticket booth.

Trapped.

"What do they want?" May whispered as the gray fingers elongated toward them.

"Don't know, I'll ask," Xan whispered back. "What do you want?" He shouted up at the things and the sound made them pause for a moment, even pull away slightly. Their mouths, silhouetted against the dusty sky, parted in unison.

"Meat." They began, again, to stretch downward.

"I think they want meat, May," he said in a fearful whisper.

"Yeah, that's what I heard too. Kick!" They braced themselves against the front wall and kicked at the back wall frantically, the wood groaning as it pulled away from the long nails which held it together.

May had kept her eyes closed to protect them from splinters, but she opened them when she felt something drop into her hair. Sinuous, ropey fingers were in front of her face, blocking her sight. They caressed her cheek like a strip of wet papier-mâché, some foul-smelling resin sticking to the fine hairs on her face.

She only realized her mouth was open in a scream when the fingers crawled inside, sticking to her tongue, voyaging steadily down her throat.

* * *

"I warned you, little soul."

May's throat burned, but it was free of the crawling vines now. Warmth emanated from near her feet and when she opened her eyes, she found herself on a rococo chaise lounge in a fire-lit sitting room. Aoide dabbed her head with a cool, damp cloth.

"What happened?" May asked, sitting up and shooing her away. She touched her face, expecting the thick resin to still be stuck to it, but it was gone.

"A little alcohol removes the sap. You were attacked by the Carnie."

"Which is?"

"Well," Aoide said, wiping her hands with the cloth and setting it on a side table. "It *was* an attraction. Now, it's the entire staff and a few unlucky customers. When I brought it here, it was only a sapling, I had no idea it would—" Aoide stopped, her hand to her chest, as if going on would be too painful. "But I brought it here, so I feel responsible for its wellbeing. I suppose I'm its caretaker now."

"It tried to eat us!"

"It tried to absorb you. Much nastier. The Carnie slips a tender young palpus into your mouth and secretes a digestive fluid that dissolves your innards for the plant to drink.

Eventually, the palpus overtakes every cell and you become a part of it, but it's a slow and painful process."

May swallowed, rubbing her sore throat. "Where's Xan?"

Aoide shook her head, standing now.

May dug her nails into the lounge, sealing her lips to keep them from quivering, her spine rigid as Aoide floated across the thick carpet toward a lumpily shrouded table. She pinched the edge of the shroud and peeled the cloth back to reveal Xan's face, even paler than usual, motionless, dotted with green blood and sickly gray sap.

Despite herself, May went to the table to investigate.

"He isn't dead yet," Aoide reassured her. "I was able to cut and remove the palpus from you easily, but the Carnie had him longer. I may be able to repair him, but I will need your permission to go to any lengths I deem necessary." And Aoide held out her thin hand to May over Xan's body. "Do we have an accord?"

A chill struck May, but she wasn't sure if it was an instinctual sense that she couldn't trust Aoide, or fear for Xan's life. Aoide had saved her without permission, so why, she thought, would she need permission to save him?

"He's running out of time," Aoide hissed, her eyes narrowed as she thrust her hand closer to May.

"Okay," May said, taking the hand in a firm shake.

Aoide beamed. "The contract is sealed."

* * *

It was dark, quiet, and smelled of mothballs inside the creature. It was strangely peaceful here, thought Xan. His eyes adjusted to the little light afforded him. Light he recognized, a dull green tinge which emanated from the bioluminescent fungus in his own eyes. He was standing—no—he was propped upright, his arm slung over a hook and his back pressed against a wall.

There wasn't enough light for him to suss out the forms surrounding him, but as he felt around with his free hand, he knocked something over, clattering it against something else. It sounded light, whatever it was. His hand met a fine string dangling above him. Instinctually he pulled it, and suddenly there was light.

He was not inside the creature at all.

Unless the creature had its own utility closet.

He unhooked his arm and stood of his own volition now in the crowded space, surrounded by stacked buckets, brooms, mops, and several busted sani-sticks.

“May?” he asked, quietly, in case something which wasn’t May was in closer earshot than she was.

He waited.

He gave a disappointed huff. The closet, wherever it was, felt relatively safe. He liked relatively safe. But May wasn’t there and that led him to believe that she was, perhaps, in a location which *wasn’t* relatively safe and he just couldn’t abide by that. Quickly, he dug through the mess of cleaning supplies, looking for anything with which he might be able to defend himself from the creature. A broom handle with a rusted, sharp metal collar devoid of bristles seemed like the best option, and he used the sharp end to crack open the utility closet door.

Through the gap, lit by a crackling fire, Xan watched Aiode finish nudging something under a chaise lounge. Watched *himself* crouch beside her, tuck a lock of hair behind her ear, and kiss her cheek. Watched as Aiode snickered, flopped onto the chaise lounge, and in the space of a blink, she was suddenly May.

“How dead should I look?” May asked the other Xan who, after kissing her once more on the forehead, became the maid.

“Not too dead,” said the maid. “We need him to think he has a chance of saving your life. Breathe a little more. Whatever she was, she breathed too much.”

Anats.

May had been right not to trust them. And now May was...oh Blitheon had they gotten to her already? They were talking about her in the past tense. May did not breathe too much, she breathed exactly as much she was supposed to. And if she wasn’t breathing exactly that much when he found her, someone was going to pay.

The maid straightened their apron, and Xan shut the closet door before they could see him. He turned off the light and gripped the broom handle for confidence. He would reason with them. Anats, as far as he knew, were only dangerous if you didn't know what they were. If you let them trick you into signing over your soul to them.

So when the maid opened the closet door, Xan stood erect, broom by his side, and tried to stay calm.

"Oh hey, it's you," he said with a nervous smile.

The maid's forehead scrunched slightly. "Yes. I rescued you from the Carnie, but I'm afraid your friend didn't fare too—"

"Listen, I know you're both Anats. So, uh," he bit his lower lip, "you can drop the act. Can't fool me. Just tell me where May is? The real May, I mean."

The maid pouted as the May-look-alike sat up and reformed into Aoide, her arms crossed huffily.

"How did you find out?" asked Aoide.

"You zuxer! That's not fair, *you* got to eat!" the maid shouted at Aodie, their faux prim countenance shattering like a dropped porcelain doll.

"You *ate?!* You ate May's soul?" Xan clutched the broomstick a little tighter, trying to convince himself he could use it.

"Yeah, obviously, zoup-nog," said the maid. "But now that you're spoiled, you get to be conscious when the Carnie devours you, so none of us get what we want!"

Aoide smiled devilishly from the lounge. "Well, I got what I wanted. And the Carnie's going to get what *it* wants."

"Shut up, ya' taagshlorph," the maid shot back at her.

"Wait, wait, wait, the Carnie? Is that that creature outside? Did you feed May's body to it?"

Aoide crawled off the lounge and reached beneath it, snatching something and hauling it out onto the carpet. "Not yet. You want it? You can carry it out there for us. If you make it past the Carnie, you can keep it."

Xan's skin crawled at the sight of May. Eyes open, but dead. As if they hadn't even had the decency to close them. Her head lolled on the carpet at an uncomfortable-looking angle, but out of instinct, she blinked when her eyes became dry. Her body was alive, it was *animated*, but she wasn't in there. Soulless eyes rested momentarily on lights, faces, eventually on Xan. She blinked again.

Using the broomstick for emotional support, Xan knelt beside May and helped her sit up.

"Hey, starshine, is anything coming through?" he asked the husk. It didn't even seem to register his voice. Simply sat, using the appropriate muscles for the job, and breathed garishly.

"Of course not, it's been sucked dry, zoup-nog. If you want a hunk of animated flesh for a companion, take it and get out of here," said Aoide.

The maid came up behind him and offered a hand. "I'd be happy to help you get her soul back in that body," they said, sweetly. "I just need your permission to—"

"Zux off, you already took mine," he said, swatting her hand away.

"No I didn't—"

"He was being metaphorical, taagshlorph!" Aoide interrupted the maid.

"Give May her soul back." Xan's voice was quiet but determined as he gripped the broomhandle, using it to stand and pulling May up to stand beside him. She stood like an articulated puppet, swaying as her body searched innately for balance.

"Can't, I ate her already," Aoide stretched magnificently, rubbing her stomach and falling back to the chaise lounge. "She was *delicious*, too. Never tasted anything like that before," she said with a grin.

"Give her back, or I'll take her back," Xan said, though he knew he was bluffing. There were two ways to get a soul back from an Anat. The first, with a success rate of three percent, was to convince them to return it. The second was to kill the Anat. Xan had never killed anything before; he wasn't sure he was capable of it. The Anats sensed this, and they both laughed, their contempt for him echoing around the small sitting room.

"This jultido thinks he can kill us," Aoide cackled, nearly falling off the lounge in her ugly mirth.

He did not think that. He was, in fact, absolutely certain that he could not kill either of them with the broomstick. With enough rage in his bones, maybe he could pummel them to death, but he'd never been very good at rage. Still, something was bubbling up inside him and he decided it was worth a shot at saving May.

While they laughed, he aimed the rusted broom collar at Aoide's throat and brought it down, but his conscience made him miss by half a foot and it sank instead into the pillowy lounge. Her laughter petered out, leaving behind a color of amusement about her face. Xan, distracted with trying to pull the broomstick from the couch, had completely missed the reason for Aoide's amusement until a searing hot poker pierced his back.

He yelped, spinning around to see the maid wielding the red-hot iron stick. "You know, Aoide, I just thought of something," the maid said, smiling as they backed Xan into a wallpapered wall, the poker at his throat.

"Do tell, Maid."

"No one will know if I torture him into giving up his soul. No need for a code of honor on a deserted hunk of metal, is there?"

Aoide clapped excitedly. "You know, you're right! And it's good fun, besides. It's endlessly dull now that all the carnies are dead. Why shouldn't we play with our food?"

"Won't that make my soul all tough and gross?" Xan asked.

"Just tenderized. Nothing could make *you* tough." The maid laughed, sticking the poker into his shoulder now. He tried to duck, but the poker had already hit its mark.

Delighted, Aoide hiked her skirts and scurried to the fireplace to choose her own weapon—the tongs. Xan whimpered with horrible anticipation as she heated the tongs in the flame.

May did nothing. No—May blinked. Her eyes were dry.

"Ready to trade your soul for a reprieve, yet?" the maid asked, shaking hand at the ready.

"Let me torture him a little first!" Aoide shouted, clamping the tongs around his throat, giggling at the sound of his flesh sizzling under the iron.

A scream tried to crawl from his throat, but the squeezing tongs kept his vocal cords from vibrating at the right frequency and he wheezed instead.

"Alright, now?" the maid asked, removing the poker from his shoulder to jab him in the side with it.

He mouthed the words "Yes, fine, alright," and "sure" in quick succession, but no sound could slip past the tongs.

"Aw, you zuxing—" the maid grunted at Aoide, pulling the tongs away from her and shaking them at her to get the point across. "Now he can't talk! How am I supposed to negotiate for his soul if he can't talk?"

"He can still gesture! It might work." Aoide said, snatching the tongs back.

Xan nodded emphatically, holding his hand out to the maid, begging them to just take his soul and get it over with already.

Instead, the maid fell into him, the poker ripping out a chunk of flesh from his side, but not one he partially needed.

May stood, an iron shovel wielded like a baseball bat in both hands, silhouetted against the flames, breathing garishly, eyes wild.

Xan liked it.

He half-smiled, half-cringed as he unhooked the rest of the poker from his side.

"You're alright?" Xan asked with a hoarse wheeze.

"Apparently," May tried to say with her eyes. Words weren't working for her, either, at the moment. The shovel was working, though.

"What the trok is this?" Aoide said, leaning against the back of the lounge for support. She kicked the maid several times and they stirred. "Are you seeing this?"

The maid rubbed the back of their head and Xan held the poker threateningly to their throat, backing them up until they sat against the wall. "Blitheon curse you! You can never finish a meal. How many times have I got to tell you not to waste food?" The maid seethed.

Aoide whimpered as May approached with nothing but hatred in her eyes, shovel raised to finish the job. "I don't like the angry bits!" she whined.

"The angry bits are the best part, you taagshlorph!"

With the cooling tongs, Aoide tried to hold May back, but the only thing which remained of May's soul was anger. It sizzled through her and into the iron of the shovel which she jammed into the soft flesh above Aoide's lace collar. Smiling, May watched a fountain of inky blue blood spewed from her neck.

As Aoide's life drained away, so too did May's smile. Bits and pieces of her soul were being returned to her—starting with disgust. She nearly dropped the shovel in horror at what she'd done, but fear came back and convinced her to keep it for her own safety.

"Let's go," May said and tried to do so, but Xan seized her arm, holding her back with one hand and threatening the maid with the other.

He didn't have to say anything for May to understand the fear in his eyes.

"The Carnie, I know. But we can't stay here."

"You can trust me! I'm not like her," said the maid, side-eying the limp body of Aoide.

"You tried to torture Xan! You're worse than her," May shouted, pointing with the shovel.

"Succeeded in torturing," Xan whispered a correction, his vocal chords on the mend.

"Yeah," May agreed darkly. "We're leaving." She turned to Xan now. "It's just a plant. We can hack through it. Keep your mouth shut."

He opened his mouth to retort.

"Ah-ah. Shut," May pinched his lips together. "Tight. If it gets in, you're dead."

He nodded fearfully and she released his mouth. Not talking wasn't anywhere on his list of skills, but she was convincing.

"The blip we're past the teledisc dampeners in the tunnel, send the teleport signal," she said, loading the user interface on his BEAPER.

"Zuut, having your soul eaten made you mean," he remarked.

She raised a questioning eyebrow at him.

"I'm not complaining," he said and followed her out of the sitting room, leaving the maid to stew in their hunger and the blood of their companion.

Dinner

The putrid yellow air outside the mansion had settled into a soupy beige, as if someone had poured curdled milk into it. May and Xan swam tentatively through it, alert for any sign of the creature. After killing the Anat, the horror of the Carnie felt distant, like a being made of generalized anxiety.

Relieved that the way out was cleared of monstrous bushes, Xan bounded down the steps. May, on the other hand, felt it was a touch early to let relief dull her reflexes. Not seeing the beast almost made it worse. Difficult to avoid an enemy one cannot see.

"Maybe we can slip out of here without the Carnie even noticing us! Straight back to the gate, souls and bodies intact, never to set foot in another carnival again," Xan said in an excited hush, relaxing his grip on the poker.

"Maybe," May confirmed the possibility, but without any shared enthusiasm. She walked down the steps, shovel held like a bat, ready to swing at the first rustle of leaves. "Shut up," she reminded him. He talked when he was nervous. If he could've talked with his mouth closed, it wouldn't have bothered her. But that thing was out there somewhere, waiting for easy entrance.

They snuck away from the shelter of the building, eyes darting into every darkened window, every shadowed booth, every gaping doorway. The curling vines and weeds which shot from cracks in the buildings all looked sinister now, but none of them moved with the ferocity of the Carnie. *They* ate sunlight, not meat.

"What if Aoide killed it when she rescued us from it? Or injured it or something?" Xan whispered, crunching down close to May.

For a long time, May had suspected that he couldn't keep his mouth shut if his life depended on it. It was no longer just a suspicion. However, the entrance tunnel was in sight now and once they were on the other side of it, the teledisc on board the *Audacity* would be able to pick up their patterns. She let her tired arms fall, swinging the shovel loosely to relieve the cramp in her shoulder. "No, Aoide brought it here. She must've known how to handle it."

"By O'Zeno's thumbs, why would someone willingly interact with that thing?"

May shrugged. "Same reason someone would want to resurrect velociraptors on Earth. You can charge admission."

"Eugh, that happened? It can't have ended well."

"Kind of, and it didn't."

They talked more easily, more loudly as they approached the mouth of the tunnel for they could see the orange blip of the *Audacity's* hull in the parking lot beyond it now. Soon this place would be little more to them than a one-star rating on the Interstellar Review.

"We really ought to go to a good carnival." His voice echoed as they entered the tunnel. "They're incredible! I went to one that had a room full of nothing but glass jars, right, and in every glass jar there were these marbles. If you could guess how many marbles were in the jar, you got to keep it and—now this is the fun part—each marble contained an entire universe with at least one guaranteed thriving life-supporting mini-planet."

"How do you know it's not just a marble?"

Her lack of faith caught Xan off guard and he twiddled the poker as he thought. "I suppose you don't. Does it matter?"

A metal grate clanging from the roof of the tunnel to the solar sidewalk made them both spin around, raising their weapons at an imagined enemy.

Silence...

Nothing...

The metal grate lay there, embarrassed, as May and Xan stood in a statuesque state of readiness, waiting for the wasted adrenaline to tire itself out and recede from their stiff limbs.

Xan was the first to offer a nervous laugh against the sudden aura of terror.

That was a mistake.

A leathery vine thwacked around his arms from above and when he looked up, he saw a massive hole in the concrete ceiling through which hundreds of grey bodies were crawling, spider-like, into the tunnel, their tendril-fingers sinking into the cracks along the concrete, filling the air with the disparate stenches of rotting meat and living vegetation. It pulled him in, upward, cocooned in its arms as he thrashed against it. It wrapped around his face, obscuring his sight. He couldn't see May, couldn't call out to her; he could only attempt to regain control of his poker-wielding wrist.

No amount of poking would deter it, though.

No amount of swatting at it with the iron shovel made an atom of difference, either, but May tried.

She clamped her mouth shut against its tendrils, but the thing coiled around her anyway, pulling her into a system of body-like roots which were spreading along the top of the tunnel, closing out the light from either end. Closing off the view of the *Audacity*.

It held them now, dangling like puppets, from the roof of the tunnel, thin shoots spreading down their fingers and plucking them open with surprising strength until both the poker and the shovel fell to the sidewalk below.

It stilled.

The Carnie was once again inert, as if it had decided to go back to the peaceful, easy life of a plant and forsake its flesh-eating habit.

Despite May's love of rocket racing, she had a fear of heights. Specifically, comprehensible heights. Unfathomable heights were fine. Gravity-less heights were fine. But now she could see the ground far below, and she shivered. After a few moments of living rigor mortis, she forced herself to look around, attempting to make visual contact with Xan. Either he wasn't saying anything because he was finally convinced that opening his mouth was hazardous to his health, or the Carnie had gotten ahold of him. She hoped the former.

A shuffling from somewhere behind her signaled Xan's location, and eventually he pulled himself free of enough of the vines to make eye contact with her.

Mouths still shut tight, they smiled at each other for reassurance. They were both alive and neither had pulpi shoved in their throats. That deserved some kind of celebration.

"What should we do?" Xan asked, silently, with a crinkling of his forehead. May understood. It was just like him to look to her for guidance.

She tried to convey confidence that they would get out of this with her eyes alone, but her eyes were horrible liars and said, instead, "Fuck if I know."

Xan sighed, then began kicking at the dormant vines, attempting to dislodge himself.

May loudly shook her head at him to catch his attention and when he paused to give her a questioning head-tilt, she emphatically pointed, with her eyes, to the ground far below.

He tilted his head the other way.

She rolled her eyes, closed them to reset this game of eye-charades, and looked up, then pretended to follow a falling body down, down, down, then *blam-o,* the moment of impact which she presented with a forceful blink.

Xan's eyes said that he understood. A fall from that distance wouldn't do much irreparable damage to him, but she might die on impact. Besides, the vines were so fleshy, so supple, that he couldn't snap them. So he watched, frustrated, as she hung there.

It was as if the Carnie planned to starve them to death then sneak into their mouths once they'd lost control of their jaw muscles. Or perhaps just until they could no longer stay awake and their jaws slackened in slumber. It was patient. Like a stubborn parent attempting to feed a fussy child. Eventually, their mouths would have to open and it would swoop in and wear their bodies like finger puppets.

Xan had rather hoped he'd never be eaten.

But since the likelihood of being eaten was rising by the moment, he had one chance to fight back.

With the air of someone who willingly steps off the gangplank, he turned his head to a thick, fleshy gray vine which might have, at one time, been someone's arm, and chomped into it, ripping a chunk of sinewy vegetation away and spitting it out.

That woke it up.

Its many mouths screeched their indignation and several fingers sprouted toward his face, diving between his teeth like an eager dentist. He was expecting them. The moment they entered, he began grinding away at them, chewing the tender shoots into a pulp which he then politely swallowed.

"Don't swallow it, it's covered in digestive fluid!" May shouted, inviting two palpi into her own mouth.

"Bite them, you gotta show dominance!" He encouraged her, nipping at another palpi which, admittedly, hesitated before trying to rush into him. He smiled toothily at it. It was working.

May had already caught on, and was chewing on a rubbery pulpi now, breaking it down between her teeth before spitting it like a wad of tobacco on the sidewalk below.

Thin fingers danced in front of their faces, caught between hunger and the desire to go on living. Xan clacked his teeth at them threateningly and they reared back, then fell, defeated.

"See, now we're friends. I don't want to be eaten and you don't want to be eaten. We've got a lot in common! So set us down, eh? Gently, if you don't mind," Xan addressed the nearest thing which looked to be a face.

The entire plant shuddered, hundreds of once humanoid bodies shivering in anger at the idea of befriending a meal. The creature tightened its grip and slammed them both against the sidewalk with frightening speed as if it could crack them open and crawl inside another way.

The hit resonated like a gong through Xan's head, but he remained conscious to feel the Carnie roll back and prepare to slam them again. May wasn't as lucky.

Concrete groaned and cracked above them, the Carnie's roots tearing at the already weakened tunnel roof until it came loose, pluming a cloud of gray dust lit by yellow as the sunlight burst through the ceiling.

A cheery little chime sounded from Xan's BEAPER to announce that the field created by the teledisc dampeners was broken, they were free to teleport when ready. Blinded by dust and weighed down by chunks of tunnel and heavy vines, Xan wrenched his wrist in front of him and sent the teleportation signal.

* * *

"That was fun," May said weakly, splayed across the couch on the *Audacity*, slathering on the ironic tone so Xan wouldn't accidentally think she wanted to go back. She wanted to sit up, but several parts of her refused to cooperate.

"Yeah?" Xan sat next to her on the corner of the couch, trying to downplay how badly his spine ached when he did. "You didn't think the special effects were a little cheap?"

May shook her head, regretting the motion when it throbbed angrily. "You want a carnival to be a little cheap so you know you're not in any real danger. Fear minus actual danger equals fun. That was fun."

"Holds up well to an Earth carnival, then?"

"Oh, this was leagues better. You know what I'd like to explore next?" she said, closing her eyes.

"I haven't the foggiest," Xan said, using an idiom she had taught him.

"Alien hospitals. I'm in a tremendous amount of pain," she said.

Xan smiled, nodded. "Me too, starshine. Me too."

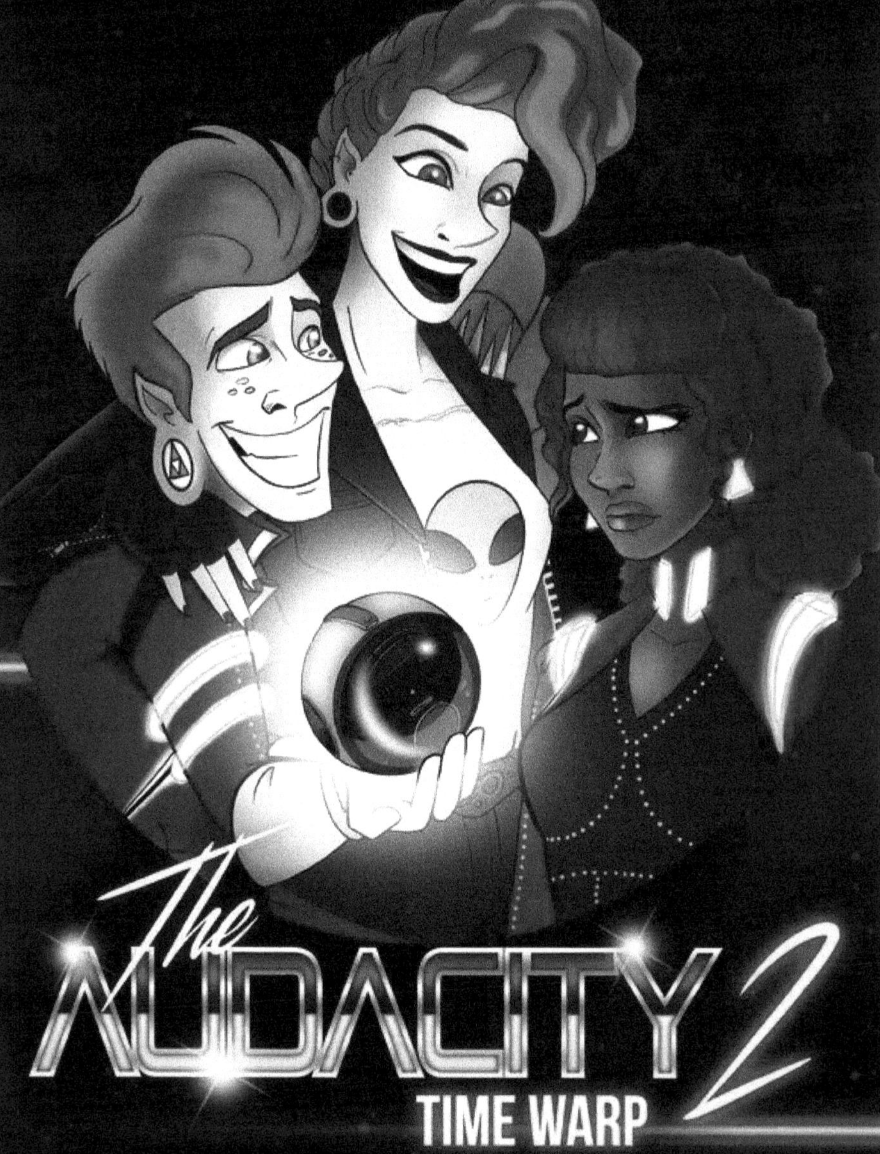
ICE CREAM AND SOUL-CRUSHING REGRET
ARE UNIVERSAL CONSTANTS.
The
AUDACITY 2
TIME WARP
A NOVEL BY
CARMEN LAURA LOUP

The Audacity II: Time Warp

CONTENTS

A Superfluous Prologue

There was nothing spookier, thought the lone surveyor, than music playing where music ought not play. In this case, the music was a sorrowful hesteculix piece and the place was on the lifeless planetoid he had just landed on. The music emanated from the wreck of a warship called the *Innocuous*.

The ship's title suited it well. It was the most banal ship the surveyor, who has a name but whose name is untranslatable, had ever seen. It had the uncouth curvature and sickly pallor of a putrefying sunfish, and that's where the pleasantries ended. A host of unbecoming, stick-like limbs sprawled on the dry ground, like an arthritic spider.

This planet was *supposed* to be deserted. He had been told that the planet was nothing more than a lump of rock that might, with his help, someday support a thriving ecosystem for a few hundred thousand misplaced Tuhntians.

This was not the first time EnviroDev had been wrong, and it wouldn't be the last.

A wiser Tuhntian might have turned around, reported that the planet was not, in fact, deserted, and moved on. Had EnviroDev been paying him, he would've considered this above his pay grade. Curiosity, however, convinced him to mount the ship's manual entry ladder and climb toward the hatch. His broad shoulders made it through the hatch only after a great deal of twisting and wriggling. At last, he emerged in a hallway which was lit with dim blue light.

The music drifted down the hallway, punctuated by incoherent words.

Spooky, the Tuhntian surveyor affirmed again to himself. Spooky indeed. Harmless, though, probably. And very, very interesting.

He continued down the hallway.

The incoherent words slowly became coherent. It helped that it was the same short phrase repeated on a loop.

Perhaps, he reasoned, the ship was empty after all. Just a recording left running on back-up power.

He reached a set of doors which did not match the sleek gunmetal siding of the rest of the ship. They were intricately carved, half circular behemoths set into the wall. He could see soft yellow light leaking under the doors from whatever was behind them.

"Hello?" the surveyor announced his presence, then leaned into the heavy door.

The tearoom on the other side was brightly lit by an exquisite chandelier and lace curtained faux windows. "Arrest and imprison Xan under Carmnia of Trilly on Tuhnt," said a pink android who sat, her legs delicately crossed, at a doilied tea table resplendent with fine A'Viltrian porcelain and stale tea cakes.

"Ah, poor thing." The surveyor tsked. He pulled a wicker chair up to the table and sat beside her. "May I?" he asked, gesturing to the back of her neck where he knew her reset button was located.

"Arrest and imprison Xan under Carmnia of Trilly on Tuhnt," replied the android.

Taking that as an affirmative, the surveyor reached around her neck. The android rebooted, blinking lifeless eyes at him in a life-like way.

"Hey there." The surveyor smiled at her. "You were in a feedback loop. How are you feeling?"

"Who are you? Where is Admiral Warders?"

The surveyor sat back in the chair and gave his name which is, as I've mentioned, untranslatable, then said, "I'm surveying this planet for development." He held out his massive, indigo hand to her and she politely shook it.

"Sonan," said the android, then smoothed a napkin over her lap. "Would you like a cup of tea?" She tipped the glimmering A'Viltrian porcelain tea pot over a cup on the table before her. Silence fell between them as the spout hung above the cup, the promise of tea in the air.

The tea did not come. Sonan's face plates crunched inward with robotic confusion.

"Ma'am, I think you've been stuck in that loop for a while. Do you know where you are?"

"Yes," she set the pot down again. "Yes, I am in the *Innocuous*. Admiral Warders was just here. He gave me a priority one directive and...Oh my," she paused; her internal clock had updated. "I do suppose that was some time ago now. Did we win?"

"The war?" The surveyor shook his head at her. "No, ma'am. I'm sorry."

"I see. No matter." She set her napkin on the table, pushed herself back in her chair, and looked very much like she was readying herself to stand. She continued to sit.

The surveyor watched her stare at the napkin on the table as she opened and closed digital files in her harddrive. He heard a fan kick on.

"It appears my ambulatory functions have been corrupted," she told him at last. "May I ask a favor of you before you depart?"

The surveyor shrugged. He wasn't in any particular rush to begin scraping up bits of dirt to bring back to EnviroDev. "I'll do my best," he said.

"Lovely. If it's not much trouble, would you please arrest and imprison Xan under Carmnia of Trilly on Tuhnt? It would mean so much to me." Her face plates rearranged into a smile that could have charmed the stripes off a ch'stranda and she patted his arm.

The request, though not surprising, was firmly and undeniably above the surveyor's pay grade. He winced at the android who smiled back. He bit his lip, the smile remained steady. "Ah, ma'am, I'm not really suited to fugitive recovery. Besides, isn't he the fellow who stole the *Audacity*? He's dead. Been dead."

"My criminal database is still functioning and it says otherwise. Please assist me. In the name of justice." Androids were not built with eyelashes, so it was odd that this android had just batted her eyelashes at him.

“You know what? I’ve got a favor I can call in. Why don’t I hire a fugitive recovery agent? Would that help?” The surveyor liked to help.

“Oh yes, that would be delightful! Here is his file.” Sonan held out her hand and above her palm floated a criminal record file with the image of a Tuhntian with skin so pale it looked like a blueberry milkshake which had been made with too few blueberries, a long, Carmnian nose, day-glo orange hair which rose into a tentative mullet (a brief but eye-opening hairstyle choice), and a goofy smile that took up half his face.

All Carmnians looked like criminals to the surveyor; most Carmnians *were* criminals. This “Xan” was the first Carmnian the surveyor had ever seen who didn’t look capable of committing a crime.

He shook his head, raised his BEAPER, and accepted the file transfer.

CHAPTER ONE

Mind-bogglingly Exciting

This deadly ball of laser light was the twenty-second deadly ball of laser light May had dodged in her lifetime. Most of them had been in the past half-year she had spent as a rocket racer; one had been an incident back on Earth involving an electric disco ball with faulty wiring.

"Haven't we run this one before? That deadly ball of laser light looked familiar," May said to her co-pilot.

May was five-foot-six, dark skinned, purple haired, and, for the first time in recent memory, happy with her life.

Her co-pilot, twirling on the hover chair beside her, his gloved hand fishing for crisps in a bag, was Xan. He was seven-foot-two, blue skinned, orange haired, and also happy with his life, a feeling which he vaguely remembered experiencing a few centuries back.

"Uh-huh, yep. That's why I waved to Selma the Camera Person and said, 'Hey, Selma the Camera Person! Good to see you again.' You were sitting right there. Selma did not wave back. I don't think Selma likes us."

"I can't imagine they do." May could not imagine a camera person liking them because their ship, the *Audacity*, was lacquered in an orange paint so bright it had been known to blow out camera lenses. It had been known to blow out eyes, actually. May and Xan were not popular racers.

They were good.

But they weren't popular.

She twisted the *Audacity* away from the field of deadly laser light and bounced it off the lolling tongue of a particularly sluggish star-whale.

"Crisp?" Xan shook the bag of crisps, which were something like blue-dusted cheese puffs but livelier.

She had learned not to look at alien foods before eating them. Half a year, or seven seasons, as May had sussed out, of culinary experimentation had taught her that Earthlings have the most rugged digestive system in the known galaxy. She plucked out a crisp and bit into it before it had a chance to wriggle much. It wasn't repulsive.

Xan pulled up an inset in the viewscreen that showed the three rockets they were racing against, tiny dots among the stars behind them. He watched the small dots become smaller as they neared the finish planet.

"Blitheon May, we're light-years ahead of them. How do you do it?"

The thrill of touching the ship's fins down on a first-place landing pad had dulled to a passing pleasantry, like discovering you still have one pair of clean socks when you thought you were out. It was nice, sure. Mind-bogglingly exciting? Not anymore. Hadn't been for a while. Still, she parked the ship on Wenshillia Minor and awaited her winnings.

"Beginner's luck?" She took another crisp from him. This one was not only not repulsive, it was also not disgusting.

With the hand that wasn't dusted with blue powder, she tugged on the chain around her neck and retrieved the faintly glowing probability modifier from under her suit. It was quarter-sized, crystalline, and looked like it had been shattered and glued back together several times with wood glue. It hadn't; it just came like that. It was a good luck charm and, as such, couldn't be shattered.

"Or this," May said. "Probably this."

"Right, yeah. It's kind of incredible what that thing can do if you're not using up all the luck on something like ridiculously good TV signal or staying alive without eating for a decade."

"You did that?" May licked the salty blue powder from her fingers.

"Me? No." Xan was getting far too comfortable lying to her. "Hey, look! Crystals!" He spun her hover chair around just as a pile of crystals, their winnings, appeared on the teledisc. It would have been an impressive hoard if it hadn't been dwarfed by the crystals buttressing the orange walls of the *Audacity*'s living room.

"Mmm-hmm." She knew he was lying. She also knew that no amount of pointing that out would get him to admit it. She changed the subject. "The next race is in a beoop, and I need to check the fin alignment, run a test of the guidance system, tighten the loose bolt in the nose casing—"

"May?"

"Apply for that minority species racing grant, polish the thrusters—"

"May."

"Reply to the fan mail, workshop clever retorts to the hate mail, for which I'll need your help, of course—"

The crumbled bag of crisps wafted toward her face, brushed it, and drifted to her lap.

"May!"

"You threw trash at me."

"I did." He parked his hands on her shoulders. Now that he had her attention, he wanted to keep it for a few blips. "Why?"

"Why what?"

"Why do you have to do all those things?"

She tossed the crumbled bag into the refuse bin under the control panel. "The...the race is coming up."

"You just won a race. You just won ten races. You haven't stopped."

"I've slept!"

"Right, yes, at the control panel. During a race. You told me to take over."

"That was a mistake. We lost that one."

Xan's mouth twisted into a tight line at the corner of his face before he replied, "You need a break."

"It might be different in Tuhntian, but in English 'need' is a strong word. I don't *need* a break." May did, however, need to yawn. She tried not to think about it. Trying not to think about it made the need worse and she attempted to yawn with her mouth closed.

Xan watched the internal battle wage across her face. Earthlings, or at least this Earthling, were stubborn. Tuhntians don't yawn, but Xan had quickly figured out how to trigger one. He stretched dramatically, opening his mouth wide in an impression of a yawn.

"Don't do tha—" The word was cut off with the yawn she couldn't repress. "Okay. A *short* break."

"That's the ticket," said Xan. Earth idioms had been a subject of discussion recently, and he was particularly fond of that one. He reached over her to plug coordinates into the autopilot and pressed the Button Which Typically Made The Ship Go. "You'll love Taeloo XII. The creamiest cream sea I've ever seen. And ice cream. And a beach! How do you feel about sand?"

"I'm fine with it as long as it's not touching me," May replied through another yawn.

"It's...May, it's a beach. I suppose I could carry you around but—"

"I'm kidding! I like beaches, just not sand."

"How complex of you." Xan laughed, leaning back in the hover chair.

"I try to keep life interesting."

CHAPTER TWO

David Attenborough

The twin suns of Taeloo XII which warred against one another daily for the title of 'brightest, most obnoxious thing in the sky' were about to be humiliated.

The *Audacity*, a ship brighter and more obnoxious than any star could ever hope to be, gracefully slid into orbit and sunk its three silvery fins into the pink sand which skirted the Cream Sea.

The Cream Sea, confusingly, is not made of cream and is not a sea. Rather, it's a spring which produces a thin, milky substance. Tourists tended to shy away, however, from the "Skim Milk Spring," and thus the misnomer was adopted.

It's not uncommon, especially in older planetary systems, to find naturally occurring dairy springs. What *is* uncommon is to find a dairy spring with bacteria-eating tasseled moyhobbins. The tasseled moyhobbins keep the dairy in the Cream Sea fresh long enough for it to be harvested and processed into ice cream which is then served to the millions of interstellar tourists who frequent the many themed ice cream dispensaries along the beaches of Taeloo XII.

It was here that the *Audacity* landed. It cleared the beach. Disgruntled tourists shielded their eyes, muttering oddly appropriate phrases such as, "The audacity of some people" as they went.

May and Xan teleported down to the beach, and out of habit, they posed rakishly together awaiting photographs, interviews, autograph requests, and tort claims regarding the blinding nature of their ship.

"No one's taking our picture," Xan told May out of the corner of his smile, still holding the dashing pose he had spent a season perfecting.

"Nope. Alright break formation." May confirmed, uncrossing her arms. She wore a sparkly yellow skin-tight swimsuit which appeared to be painted over her curvy body. She and Xan (and now, of course, you) were the only people who knew about it, though, because over it she wore the old 'That is, is it not, Yurkunfle' t-shirt which left absolutely everything to the imagination.

Xan also wore something sparkly, yellow, and skin-tight. Just that. And not much of it, either.

"What now?" May asked.

"What do you mean?" Xan dropped to the pink sand, lounged against one of the ship's fins, and began flipping through a battered paperback copy of 'The Time Machine' that had, many orbits back, come through the mysterious wormhole in the *Audacity*'s basement. It perplexed him that Earthlings had apparently invented time travel but not space travel.

In the wider galaxy, time travel is thought to be both impossible and a bad idea. There are legends, however. There are sonnets, haikus, even limericks about time travel. Xan had, in his developmental orbits, studied tomes full of time travel related limericks. It's all fiction, naturally. Absolutely ridiculous. It's all complete and utter falsehood.

Sorry, I can't go on lying like this. The limericks, though Xan did not know this, were not fictitious. The sonnets were. The haikus? Fifty-fifty.

Xan peered up at May, silhouetted against the twin suns which began to set in defeat. She furrowed her brow at the Cream Sea.

"I mean," she said, "what are we going to *do*?"

"N...nothing." He set the book down over his thigh.

"Oh." She leaned against one of the fins, then noticed she was next to the service ladder. She began to climb. "I'm going to check the rivets."

"Nuh-uh, nope, I am metaphorically putting my foot down. Wait, hold on." He held his place in the book with his thumb and stood up. "I am literally putting my foot down." He did. "You need a break. Please. Suns-set!" He gesticulated in the direction of the twin orbs which sulked their way toward the skim milk.

"Can't I at least check the rivets first?" She gazed up at the ship, but not for long. When she looked at it, all she saw was one long list of error codes and blinding orange glow.

"She'll still be busted after the suns-set. *Audy*'s always busted. She's an old ship. I promise you'll never run out of things to fix." He dropped back down and patted the sand encouragingly.

May dismounted and sat cross-legged beside him. She tried, she really honestly did, to relax. She watched the white line of waves roll up to pat the sand near her toes, rear back to see if she'd do anything about it, then pat the sand a bit closer to her.

It was maddening.

"Can't do it. Come on, we're going to explore." She stood and vigorously slapped the sand from her thighs.

Xan dog-eared the page he was on (interesting to note: before holobooks became the norm on Tuhnt, books were always dog-eared from the bottom corner, not the top, and a book un-dog-eared was considered a book unloved. There is absolutely nothing wrong with dog-earring books.)

"Why do I have to come?"

"Commentary. Also, what if I think of something clever and no one's there to hear it?" May had gone most of her life without someone to appreciate her clever quips. No longer.

"Wouldn't want to miss that." It was a traditionally ironic phrase, but he delivered it unironically. He, too, had gone far too long without someone to appreciate his quips. He disappeared from the beach, returning a blip later without the old book but with a sack of crystals.

The offended beach goers had congregated further down, so a long stretch of the beach was empty. To their right, a sheer gray-green cliff face chunked out a piece of the pale sky, and to their left the white sea undulated passively over the riprap.

They set off along the line of riprap, searching the dark crevices for things of interest.

After a while, May noticed that Xan was humming. Something strangely familiar.

"Is that the song Big Mouth Billy Bass sings?" she asked him.

"Whom?"

"The fish. The plastic mounted fish that sings when you press a button. 'Take Me to the River,' I think."

"Right, that's the one." He began singing with the kind of voice that might have made him a superstar in a small-town karaoke bar assuming everyone was at least two drinks in.

"How do you know the whole song? I don't even know the whole song, and I grew up on Earth."

He shrugged. "I picked it up a lot in orbit. 'I Love Lucy' isn't the only thing floating around out there. It's most of the things, but it's not the only thing."

A great hulking arm of the cliff encroached on the beach ahead, gurgling suspiciously. May approached it with a latent curiosity and watched as a trickle of milky white fed an opaque tide pool which occasionally spluttered.

"What are those?" She pointed to the rocky edge of the tide pool which, as Xan got closer, he realized was alive. Or at least mobile. Whatever it was blended in so well with the rock that the rock itself appeared to undulate.

"That's, uh, tasseled moyhobbin. It's like a kind of fish. Not the singing kind."

"Do David Attenborough," May suggested.

A season or two back, they had discovered a small asteroid in the vicinity of Betelgeuse which was, inexplicably, lousy with signal from BBC One.

Xan sighed, perched on the edge of the rock overlooking the tide pool, and affected a British accent which was, for someone who wasn't even technically speaking English, not horrible.

"The tasseled moyhobbin is often regarded as a primitive life form, entirely void of sentience. However, the truth, as it so often is, is much more nuanced, much more complex. These amazing creatures exhibit many of the same behaviors found in intelligent life. Ten percent of all known subspecies of moyhobbin, for example, can recognize the difference between 'it's alright' and the more passive aggressive 'it's fine' and behave accordingly."

"Excellent. How much of that is true?" May asked as he jumped from the rock and they began to walk again.

"I'm not a biologist, I wouldn't know! I mean, I knew a biologist and, zuut, she liked to gabber on. I picked up a lot from her, but dropped most of it. You would have liked her. Or at least, I assume you would've. She was a lot like me, and you seem to like me so...just extrapolating there."

"Can I meet her?"

Xan's mouth had been closed. It closed tighter. He was recalculating the conversation.

"Ice cream?" he asked, though it wasn't a question.

They were approaching a boardwalk.

Alien planets, May had found, were often uncannily like Earth. Cultural universals—the desire for shelter, murder being frowned-upon, belief in a higher power, for example—are a vital aspect of the humanoid condition. Ice cream is one of these cultural universals. Given time, dairy, and a means by which to make said dairy cold, every culture will eventually invent something like ice cream.

Every culture which is near a body of water, or in this case, near a body of dairy, will also at some point invent the boardwalk. And boardwalks, by nature, attract tourists. Tourists attract people who like to take advantage of tourists and they, in turn, attract more tourists via good marketing and the cycle continues.

Which is why this alien boardwalk, on a pinkly sanded and milky-oceaned beach, under two small and competitive suns, thousands of light-years from Earth, hosted several hundred ice cream parlors with garish marquee signs in various stages of deterioration.

Xan pulled on the pink plastic lobster which inexplicably formed the door handle for a shack called Yusko's Fabulous Forty Flavors, then gestured for May to go in.

"Ladies first," he said, recalling one of the many English idioms May had taught him.

"Ah, but age before beauty," she replied.

"Uh...don't put the cart before the horse?"

May stared at him for a moment, her mouth open in a half-smile as she tried to figure out what exactly that meant in this context. "You don't know what a horse is, do you?"

"Of course I know what a horse is. It's something that should never go after a cart. It's also something that you should never look in the mouth when given as a gift."

"You're a ham," May told him.

"Aha! I am. And 'pearls before swine,' so go on."

"That's not what that means," May said, but stepped into the dimly lit ice cream parlor to end the conversation.

Inside, the wood slat walls of the shack disappeared to the right, opening onto the beach through a rocky frame, as if the building had been eaten by the mouth of a cave overlooking the milky sea. Clustered around the cave opening were orbicular floating bean bag chairs which glowed with a welcoming orange warmth.

A rainbow glacier of ice cream pressed against the back of the cave, sporting flavor signs which rose like survey flags out of each colored band.

In front of them, a display of novelty sunglasses, a glass jar, and a bucket of neon plastic ice cream scoops took up a table. Above the jar, there was a sign.

The sign had originally read, "Pay what you want" in cheery bubble letters. This had been crossed out by hand and beneath it, in red scrawl, someone had written, "Pay what you can." Below that, in thinner, shakier handwriting, "Please, for the love of Paatnu, pay something."

The jar contained a few broken shells, a couple half polished rocks, and a smattering of crushed crystals.

"Strange business practice," May said as she read the sign. "Think it works?" She watched Xan empty the sack of crystals into the jar, then, unsure of what to do with the sack, fold it neatly atop the pile.

"Looks like it's working to me! Grab a scoop," he said, picking one for himself along with a pair of sunglasses with pink, star-shaped rims which he perched on his head, pushing back into place a clump of hair which had been eagerly trying to escape his pompadour and obscure his vision.

"Well, you're one in a million. There's another idiom for you."

"Only a million? At last count there are around thirty-one centillion sentient beings in the known galaxy."

"Alright, you're one in a centillion."

"Huh. Thirty-one exact copies of me out there. I hope they're having a nice day."

May smiled, shook her head, and followed him to the wall of ice cream.

The flavors were a translation chip's nightmare. "Tangerine" was fine, "mixed starches" seemed slightly off, but got the point across (the point being that she ought to avoid that one), but flavors like "tittering corcunasnatch" and "humpterfuge" couldn't be described by any words May knew. The chip attempted to shift May's focus toward the flavors it had an explanation for.

She followed a vein of pale blue to a sign which read, "Blueberry."

"Is this actually blueberry? Does it taste like a blueberry?"

"Yes! Well, a Tuhntian blueberry anyway. I've no idea what an Earth blueberry tastes like. Probably like a Tuhntian blueberry!" Xan said in between testing licks of a suspiciously translucent twirl of ice cream.

"You're a Tuhntian blueberry," she said, digging the scoop into the side of the colorful, frozen monolith to extract the blue.

Xan stopped mid lick, retracted his tongue, and inclined his head at her. "I can't tell what that was. Was that an insult?"

May laughed and licked the ice cream which tasted like it had known a blueberry once and learned a lot about life and love, but they eventually drifted apart and hadn't spoken in years.

"It was an observation. This is good," May said, collecting more of it in her scoop.

"Great! So, is a Tuhntian blueberry anything like an Earth blueberry?" He scraped some purple off the wall before flopping into an orange orb which yielded under his weight.

May curled into a nearby orb. "Close enough," she tasted it again to confirm. "Speaking of Tuhnt. What, uh..." she tried to sound casual, "what happened there?" About three things May was absolutely positive. First, the planet Tuhnt used to exist. Second, it no longer did. And third, Xan had something to do with that second thing.

Yuzko's
$\sqrt{\infty}^{10}$ FLAVORS!*
*OR FEWER
Carmen Loup

Xan made a face like he'd found a severed toe in his scoop of ice cream. "That's not ice cream talk. Ice cream talk is: 'What a beautiful day!' 'It is, isn't it?' 'Do you think it will rain tomorrow?' 'There's a chance of it, yes.' 'What do you suppose the purpose of life is?' 'Oh, nothing much, just tottering about getting into things until you're either killed or die naturally of old age when your body can no longer handle simple yet vital processes.' That's ice cream talk."

The blueberry ice cream had begun to drip steadily down the scoop. May, fearing sticky fingers, focused on licking up the melted cream before answering.

"So," she licked, "you're just not going to talk about it ever, are you?"

"Ideally." Xan chomped on his ice cream, swallowing half of it in one go. "What's it going to take to get you to relax for a blip?"

May wiggled back into the orb, giving up on interrogating him for now. "I don't know. Are there any good opium dens out there? Never tried opium."

"Well sure! Truglian X is well known for opulent opium dens."

"Great. Soft pillows?"

"Naturally."

"Hygienic?"

"The hygienic-est."

"Let's go."

"R...really?" Xan sat forward in the orb, watching her with concern. "I thought you were joking."

She laughed and shook her head. "Just trying to see how long you would keep it up."

"Heh, right," he laughed and sat back again, admiring the way she treated a conversation like a game of etherball. "There *are* opium dens on Truglian X, though. Not hygienic. Wouldn't recommend it. Pillows are kinda lumpy, too. I used to get sent there all the time with The Agency until I caught a nasty strain of florntulutz. Lasted nine seasons! After that I stopped picking up jobs in opium dens and..."

May finished her ice cream, watching one of the two suns, who did look quite dim in comparison to the *Audacity*, begin to slink ashamedly under the cover of the milk sea, its twin still hanging low in the sky, filling the cave with a golden light as May half-listened to Xan rambling on about his escapades as an interstellar sex worker. The more she heard him talk about his past life, the more she was convinced that rocket racing was a great deal easier, more profitable and, despite the ever-present risk of catastrophic existence failure, it was much safer.

A fine tendril of peace began to push out of the dense ball of stress in her chest, she began to blink slower, the ever-present hum of Xan's chatter and the soothing woosh of the Milk Sea lulling her into a moment of utter blissful security. She closed her eyes.

And then Xan paused mid-sentence to say, "Huh, that's not good." and the tendril of peace withered and curled away like a thread of nylon touched by a candle flame. She gave a questioning groan, too comfortable to open her eyes.

"The probability modifier isn't glowing anymore," he said.

She looked down at the lump of rock which hung around her neck.

It had been glowing.

It was supposed to glow.

It was not, as Xan had aptly noted, glowing now.

The star-shaped novelty glasses perched on his head fell over his eyes as if to shield her from the intensity of his terrified gaze. "May," he said with a nervous warble, "I think our luck has run out."

CHAPTER THREE

Horrendous Repercussions

"It'll be fine," May said as they walked back to the ship. Xan had taken the probability modifier from her and was turning it over in one hand, holding a scoopful of ice cream in the other. "It's not like we'll have *bad* luck now, right? Just the normal—" May stopped talking when the *Audacity* came into view.

Parking tickets, I'm sorry to say, are also universal.

The *Audacity* had ten now, plus two light pollution citations.

"'Horrendous repercussions,' Chaos said." Xan put the modifier around his neck for safekeeping, tore one of the citations off the ship, and skimmed it. "'Horrendous. Repercussions,'" he repeated, removing all the citations and crumpling them in his free hand.

"We might as well pay them. We've got the gem." She held out her hand and he dropped the wad of citations in it.

A frantic beeping sound competed with the gentle crashing of waves, heralding a single-wheeled, triangular robot with a red marquee across its chest which scrolled the words "Parking Violation" as it jetted toward them, bouncing over the dips and hills in the soft pink sand.

"We're leaving!" May shouted at it, then grabbed the BEAPER on Xan's wrist and teleported them both back into the ship.

Once inside, she scurried to the control loft and pressed the Button Which Typically Made The Ship Go.

Typically. Not today. Not when they *needed* it to go.

Xan's face appeared beside hers so suddenly it might have made her jump if she hadn't been used to that sort of thing. "Parking brake?" he suggested unhelpfully. May never forgot the parking brake. *He* forgot the parking brake. Not May.

"Maybe the fuse blew. I bet Osy can fix that." She reached into the space under the control panel where Osy liked to lounge, but the small chunk of semi-sentient sponge was not in its usual hiding spot.

"Xan, do you have Osy?"

"No, I never have Osy."

Pulling her bangs back from her face, she rested her forehead in her hand and leaned heavily on the console.

"That was a kid, wasn't it?"

"What? The tiny mustachioed Udonian at the spaceport who asked to borrow Osy then bolted off with it never to be seen again? Yeah, I thought you knew that."

"They had a mustache!" she said.

"Well of course they did, they were Udonian. All Udonians have mustaches. The ones that don't have mustaches shave every other beoop. Never can have a decent conversation with a shaved Udonian, they're always skittering off to shave the stubble."

"Damn mustaches," May muttered as she ran the diagnostic program. A horde of error codes marched soldier-like across the viewscreen: Party hatch malfunction, mold in the coolant tank, ice cream in the cruise control—

"Xan!"

"Sorry." He licked the ice cream scoop clean, then tossed it in the refuse shoot. It took him ages to finish food because he didn't like shutting up long enough to eat.

May returned her attention to the screen, reading aloud the error messages as if she were reading a criminal's long list of charges. "Temporal paradox in the muffler, coffee in the...of course. Rocket ships aren't *supposed* to run on coffee."

"Right, yeah." He sat in the hover chair and spun it. "That only worked because of the probability modifier, didn't it?"

"Clearly."

May pressed her forehead into the edge of the console and tried to panic gracefully.

"Okay." She sat up, slapped her hand on her thigh to show she was serious, and began to think out loud, a technique she had picked up from Xan. "What do we have? The nearest station is in orbit, but we can't get there without fuel, and we can't get fuel unless we're there."

Xan nodded encouragingly. He thought maybe she had a plan. It certainly sounded like she had a plan.

"If we could go back in time, we could fuel up before we land, and we wouldn't be stuck here."

Xan leaned in, enthralled by the conviction of her problem-solving monologue. And Earthling time travel was a plus. He had been wondering about that.

May blinked a few times, her jaw clenching and unclenching in time with her merry-go-round of a thought process.

"So, time travel," said May. "You've invented that out here, right?" she asked him.

"Me?" Xan asked.

"In general. Someone's done it?"

"Oh. Sure! Yeah. But only in the one direction. You know: forward. And at a rate of one blip-per-blip." He bent closer. "I don't see how going forward in time at a rate of one blip-per-blip is going to help, though. Since we're currently doing that."

"I..." May began, then stopped to think once more, but her coherent thoughts had become like a mythical ocean creature, and she was no deep-sea diver. She drifted directionless in the cold darkness of her overworked mind. "I don't know what to do."

It wasn't that there weren't any options, it was that she was exhausted.

She only had so many good decisions in her on any given day, and since her last artificial night, she had completed three races and made exactly 72,903 pretty decent micro-decisions. So, naturally, number 72,904 was a dud.

"Well," Xan said, preparing to stand, "might as well get more ice cream! There are at least thirty-nine flavors left to try. Possibly more. Possibly an infinite number of flavors and flavor combinations! We could kill a lot of time trying them all-OW!" He grabbed the chain the probability modifier hung on and lifted it away from his chest, letting it dangle out in front of him. It was glowing again. "Weird. It must have had a...uh...a circuit thing."

"A short circuit?"

"Yeah." He observed the glowing rock for a moment, as if waiting for it to zap him again.

May was tempted to observe it too, but decision number 72,905 was a good one, and she pressed the Button Which Typically Made The Ship Go before the charm had a chance to blink out again.

* * *

The Waschu fuel station in the nicer part of Taeloo XII's lower orbit was fancy. Or, at least, someone wanted people to think it was fancy. The station itself jutted from the side of an asteroid like a chiseled jaw jutting from a face that knows it's attractive. Its walls were solid sheets of glass which were somehow both opaque and transparent in a way that made eyes water, whether out of pain or as a reaction to the beauty of it was difficult to say.

On the way there, Xan had held the probability modifier in the way one holds a baby bird which has fallen out of a nest, as if its tiny life would escape the second he stopped watching it.

The reason, May realized as she priced rocket fuel, that they had more crystals than they could reasonably spend in her lifetime, was that races generally assume the rockets are running on rocket fuel and set the prize amounts accordingly. A pot of coffee is so infinitely less expensive than a pot of rocket fuel that coffee is effectively free in comparison.

After May paid to have the tank cleaned and filled with real rocket fuel, the burdensome weight of the crystals they had won was a great deal lighter. Still, without the help of the probability modifier, it was well over the recommended Class 20 racing rocket weight limit.

"We need a bank account," May suggested, for the thousandth time, to Xan as she sealed the fuel hatch. "We can't keep lugging around crystals."

"Or! Or, and this is a fun idea, we could start a grant. For uh...for Earthlings who want to race. An Earthling grant! You know, diversity and whatnot. Buy some poor lost Earthling a racing rocket or two. Charity!"

"Xan, they looked at me like I was insane trying to pay for all that fuel with crystals. We spent hours shoveling them onto the teledisc! We need a bank account."

Xan threaded himself through the lowest vent hole on the *Audacity*'s fin, draping like a flaccid spaghetti through the hole in a pasta spoon. "We'd have to go somewhere in the Flotluex System to get a universally accepted bank account," he said, addressing the fin of the ship instead of May.

"So you say."

He made a noise that sounded like a rusty meat grinder working over a steak. "These unrelenting cooking similes are making me hungry," he said, finally. "Want to get a snack?"

"I want to get a bank account. And don't mention the narration. It's weird." She looked around nervously, as if someone were watching her, writing everything down.

"Okay, I'll be straight with you." He grunted as he twisted himself around in the hole until he was staring at her upside-down.

"Please don't be," May said, the edge of her mouth tilting up.

"Huh?"

"It's a...a joke. Forget about it," she said.

"I'm not really comfortable going to the Flotluex System because—oh! Oh I get it. Because in Earth sexuality 'straight' means...oh, May, that was clever."

"Why," May leaned against the fin and looked down at him, "don't you want to go to the Flotluex System?"

"Remember what happened to Raskov?"

She did, but wished she didn't. Raskov had been incinerated by the police right in front of them and, though a large part of May felt he deserved it, it hadn't been fun to watch.

"You think that'll happen to you? We haven't exactly been laying low."

He shrugged with his eyebrows. "That's a point."

"A good point?"

"It's *a* point. I suppose we better figure out something to do with the crystals before the good luck charm dies again." He let the rock fall from his fist and bounce on its chain. It was glowing, but he was sure he saw it flicker. “And as long as this is working, I probably won’t be incinerated. It hasn’t let me die yet, and believe me I’ve—”

“Don’t,” May interrupted.

“Right, yeah. Alright!” He pulled himself up and slid out of the fin vent, slinging the probability modifier back around his neck. “Let’s be quick about it, at least. And you’re getting the account. Last thing I need is a face scan.”

“Camera shy all of the sudden?”

“More like incineration shy, but...it’ll be fine. It’s fine. I’m fine,” he said, slipping out of the fin vent. “Let’s go.”

CHAPTER FOUR

A Careful Crash

The Flotluex star system contains four habitable planets, a flock of scenic moons, several thousand bitter asteroids, two uninhabitable planets which, top astrologers believe, feel a bit lonely, and one other uninhabitable planet which, top astrologers believe, rather enjoys its solitude.

Rhea I is one of the habitable planets and it waffles between begrudging acceptance and a casual dislike of its inhabitants. It is the largest, greenest, and most popular planet in the system and it knows it.

It was here that May and Xan landed. Really, it was more of a careful crash than a landing, and here's why:

The moment the gentle gravitational tug of Rhea I snagged the *Audacity* like an unwitting fish and began to reel her in, Xan made a noise which troubled May, and then the *Audacity* made a noise which troubled everyone.

"Don't tell me," May said, rushing to the control panel.

"The good luck charm is out again," Xan said, leaning forward in his hover chair to help May scramble at the controls. His idea of helping, in this case, was watching sympathetically as she did it.

"I just told you not to tell me!"

"I thought you were kidding."

"Why?"

"Alright, well, you only mean what you say about half the time and you know, typically, *usually*, when someone doesn't mean what they say, they use some kind of modified intonation but you just put it all out there, flat as a harmonium, dry as smoked zipnite, and I'm left to wonder, 'Was that verbal irony or is she really interested in examining the lifecycle of the common dractifly?' A hint, even just a tiny one, every once in a while, as to your true intentions would be appreciated."

By the time Xan had stopped talking, the ship was parked, relatively unscathed, in an enormous lot which fringed an enormouser city.

"I'll keep that in mind."

"See! There. Will you really keep it in mind, or was that ironic?"

"It..." May sighed. "It was ironic, sorry. I promise to unironically keep it in mind that you can't always tell the difference. Now let's try to find a bank."

Xan stood, stretching. "Terrific."

"Aha! You do it, too," May said, with a *soupçon* of *schadenfreude*.

"Yeah, well, I suppose it's contagious. Ah!" The probability modifier sizzled back to life in his hand. "We're in luck again!" He slung an arm around May's shoulders. "You'd think, you really would, that a good luck charm would be lucky enough to never run out of power. Better get down there before it zilches out."

"Shouldn't we change?" May asked, grabbing a bag of crystals.

"No time. What if the charm goes out? Why? Do you think this is too modest?" He hopped onto the teledisc and modeled his tiny, golden swimsuit.

"Only by half," she said as they, still in swimwear, teleported out onto the silvery surface of the planet.

Now I'm not about to pretend that procuring a bank account is the most exciting adventure one could possibly have in the whole of the universe. Not by a light-year.

Being's Choice Interstellar Limited knew this and did what they could as a company to make the process more personal. Which is why when May entered the bank on Rhea I, the tellers appeared to her as fortune machines; rows of animatronic old women in ornate golden boxes with glowing crystal balls, mounds of costume jewelry, and headscarves.

As May approached the nearest box, the form appeared to shift and wiggle like a lenticular printing.

"Eugh," Xan said over her shoulder. "Perception pleasing technology is so glitchy. The Agency tried to implement it to some pretty horrifying results. Interesting, though! What do they look like to you?"

"Uh..." She tried to see what they really were, whatever was hiding behind the illusion, but the moment she caught a glimpse of its true form, she was seeing a fortune teller again. "Have you ever seen those fortune teller machines? With the animatronics in them? You press a button and it prints a fortune out. They look like those. What do they look like to you?"

"You know the geodesic domes with the salt-and-pepper colored hair that sing the news and lotto numbers every couple of beoops in big cities?"

"I do not."

"Right, well. That's what they look like," he said, positioning himself behind her as she stood in front of the nearest kiosk. "You got to show it your DNA."

"How?" The fortune machine/geodesic dome extended its coin slot and pecked May's hand. She yelped and jumped away from it, but ran into Xan who was crouched behind her, trying to be inconspicuous.

"Your DNA has been cataloged, mortal. How can Mama Scarlet direct your destiny?" asked the machine in a thick, crunchy brogue.

"We, er..." She felt Xan shake his head frantically behind her, his face hidden in her bushy hair. "*I* would like to open an account."

"Mama Scarlet can do this for you. In return, you give her six thousand crystal and wait one business bloop to complete authorization," said the animatronic.

May dropped a bag full of crystals into a hatch which opened under the machine. Mama Scarlet's wrinkled eyelids fluttered, her plastic eyeballs rolled back, the crystal ball strobed menacingly, a blue light washed over May's face.

"Ah," said Mama Scarlet. "Mama Scarlet senses you are a stranger to this land."

"The spirits from beyond the veil are reaching out to me," said the machine, its bejeweled hand waving about in a stiff circle. "Yes, yes! They bring you a message. The message is this," the voice changed suddenly to a monotone notice. "Access to your account may be delayed by three to four bloops." Then Mama Scarlet was back again. "Now behold! Your account location is coming through...through from the other SIDE!" A card fell into a tray below the fortune teller and May bent to pick it up, Xan dipping down with her.

Along with a detailed explanation of her horoscope using an unfamiliar Zodiac, the card was printed with the teledisc coordinates for deposit.

"That's it?" May asked, tucking the paper between her boobs since her unfortunate t-shirt and swimsuit combo had no pockets.

"Yup, that's it," Xan replied, lolloping out of the bank, May jogged to keep up. "They used to chip you. Now they sample your DNA and scan your face instead which sounds worse, but the chips would malfunction awfully. They'd overheat all the time and—ugh speaking of..."

He ripped the probability modifier off and let it swing in front of him as he ran.

The charm radiated heat, flickered, and shivered with the effort of keeping a novel's worth of bad luck damned up.

And then it exploded.

Billions of shards of the former good luck charm glistened on the sidewalk.

"Well, that's a massive, massive problem isn't it?" Xan said, tossing the smoldering chain aside, continuing to run.

"It'll be fine," May said, her voice a few octaves higher than was comfortable. "My fortune said it would all work out in the end."

"Hope you're right." Xan went from lolloping to sprinting toward the ship.

Xan was not an accomplished runner. Neither was May. In fact, all other factors being equal, they were perfectly matched runners. All other factors were not equal, however, and Xan soared ahead of May on account of his unusually long legs.

Xan reached the ship's teledisc range long before May did and busied himself nervously surveying the surrounding parking lot like a coked-up meerkat. He wondered if May would consent to leg extensions.

"I'm here, I'm here," she puffed, grabbing the stitch in her side as she caught up with him a few hundred feet away from the ship. Xan tapped his BEAPER, and they dissolved into their component atoms to be remerged on the *Audacity*.

They were safe.

Finally.

Nothing bad could happen to them in the *Audacity*, not in their home. Inside the ship, it was soft and orange and cozy and—

The place they were in was none of those things.

There is no truly secure way to hurl atoms from one place to another; you're playing atomic roulette, and so it is possible, in the field of molecular travel, to intercept and redirect a signal with nothing more than a well-angled sheet of aluminum.

May and Xan reformed on a ship that was not soft and orange and cozy but *was* plastered with a few well-angled sheets of aluminum.

CHAPTER FIVE

Junkyard Alien Zombie

Far away in a different planetary system which centered on a yellow sun its constituents creatively referred to as "the Sun," General Listay had the feeling that something was wrong.

Organization was key here, she was sure. The most recent memory she had was of enslaving—no, not enslaving—*improving* Earth. Things had been going well. And then things had gone not well. The Earthlings had turned on her. Her Captain, revealing herself to be an entity of divine Chaos, had turned on her. After that it was all fuzzy.

She knew this, though: The entire Universe needed to be swiftly obliterated because this iteration was annoying her.

No.

That wasn't it.

What she knew was that she was trapped underground.

It smelled like fertile soil and the curdling blood of all who had the temerity to oppose HeR pErFEcT AnD DiVIne WILL.

Hold on, not that. Not the blood part.

She was decidedly not alone, either. Thoughts that were not her own kept plunging the whole of space and time into majestic Chaos, unmitigated final destruction, the whole of the Cosmos cowering before HER—*NO*!

Thoughts that were not her own kept interrupting her.

She felt a brief suction, like a vacuum hose to her soul, as the shard of plastic lunch-tray which had skewered her was pulled from her chest, then a static-flooded, anti-color vision of something which had no discernable shape formed in her mind's eye.

That was all massively unpleasant, thought the vision of energy and light.

Explain yourself, she thought back, trying to grab the vision without success. Even if she could have moved her arms, there was nothing physical to grab.

I am The All-Consuming and Ultimate Finale of Being, That Which Disassembles Reality, The Absolute and Irrefutable God of Chaos and I want your body, thought Chaos.

You just said this wasn't a sex-thing! thought Listay.

*It isn't. And that was an entire novel ago, catch up. The plan went astray, so we're on to plan...*the voice paused, whispering letters, then numbers, then common names. *Plan Billy? No, not yet. Plan Mistpillia.*

Which is? thought Listay.

Hard reset.

That sounds terrible.

The vision seemed to smile, or maybe it just vibrated brighter. *Oh it will be ever so! All I need is a body.*

Well, you can't use mine.

That's fine with me. Enjoy being dead.

The corners of Listay's sight grew dark and she felt her consciousness slipping away again. *Wait! Let's talk about it.*

Excellent, Chaos thought. *There is no need to talk, your mouth is full of dirt anyway. You are now me, and I'm the best thing you could possibly hope to be, so shake off that rigor mortis, and let's have a smile.*

General Listay's mind was overpowered as Chaos filled her being.

Chaos wiggled Listay's fingers, bringing life back into the stiffened tendons and muscles and sending a few test commands to her robotic arm. That arm booted up much faster than Listay's organic matter, and it was leagues stronger. She dug a steely hand into the dirt above her and began to pull her new body from its shallow grave.

She rose out of the Earth and shook off a shower of dirt, startling a family of junkyard quails.

Chaos felt herself splitting again. The part of Listay which was still Listay had been busy drawing a white chalk line down the middle of her subconscious; a line which, shockingly, Chaos found she couldn't actually cross. That was clever. Frustratingly so. Listay was not an accommodating host.

What's your plan? Listay thought from her side of her brain as Chaos made her body trudge through the junkyard.

"Shh. Go back to sleep," Chaos hummed. She had kept control of Listay's mouth.

I have a right to know what you're doing with my body. You might have gotten away with shushing me when you were my Captain, but seeing as I'm dead at your hand, I officially resign, thought Listay.

"You used to be my most loyal devotee! You claimed you 'loved' me. Whatever happened to your dedication, dear one?" said Chaos with Listay's lips.

You murdered me!

"And then I raised you from the dead! Surely there's no greater display of allegiance than that."

Tell me what you're planning, snarled Listay's subconscious insofar as a subconscious could snarl.

"Will you help or hinder me if I tell you?"

That depends on whether or not I agree with you.

"Then I shan't," Chaos said, but the General was quiet. She was concentrating. "What are you doing?" asked Chaos, Listay's body going rigid as the General forced it to walk, zombie-like, back toward her shallow grave. "Stop this!"

Tell me the plan. She thought obstinately. *I'm going to hinder you either way.*

"Then I shall enter another being and get it to bring me to the Sphere of Time!" Chaos shouted at her own, misbehaving limbs. Her body paused. The General was considering things quietly. Too quietly for Chaos to hear. She hated that.

If you find another body, will you leave me alive? Listay posed.

"I'm not sure what answer you're looking for here," said Chaos.

I want you to let me live, obviously!

"Mortals are such—oh, alright. If it will get you to relax, I'll pull some strings and keep your string from getting cut."

Good.

Listay released control, letting Chaos take the reins again.

So what is the plan? Listay thought.

"I'm going to find the Sphere of Time."

You said that already. That isn't a plan, that's an outcome.

"I didn't create a blueprint; I was rather busy trying to animate your hefty little mound of flesh."

Quietly, secretly, Listay was glad Chaos didn't have a plan. Her plan, and she tried her best to keep this from the other thing in her mind, was to wait it out until Chaos found another willing host and then turn around and kill that host. That should work. How does one dispose of an immortal consciousness?

"You can't," said Chaos with a laugh. "That's the definition of immortal, zoup-nog."

Listay had thought that last part a bit too loudly. She cleared her mind now, as all there was left to do was wait and see.

Chaos ambled around monolithic mounds of garbage, most of it semi recognizable as the siding or signage from Listay's perfect Earth. The Earthlings had discarded all her hard work the moment she was buried. That was upsetting to know. Not more upsetting than being dead, but almost.

At last, she saw something that made her heart give a single, excited beat. One smug, dark blue AMC Gremlin, with a dented red door and silver bald patches where the paint had been half-heartedly sanded a decade before, crouched amidst the trash.

And it wasn't just an AMC Gremlin. It was a space shuttle. Retrofitted with enough A'Viltrian tech to get a solar system or two away.

Aside, if you haven't read book one, this may not make sense to you. Frankly, if you have read book one, this may not make sense. Best to accept it and move along.

Soon, Listay had the shuttle in working order, using the headlights to illuminate the mounds of garbage she had been digging through to find assets. So far, a nail file and a working plasma zapper had been recovered. Both would be of use to her.

She paused, looking perplexedly at the mound of trash in front of her.

What am I doing? I have a working shuttle, I should be gone by now.

"I need a wrench to repair the seat belt before we can go off-world," said Listay, casually using her own lips again. "Safety standards."

Then Chaos realized her mistake. Listay was not like Yvonne. Listay was sneaky. She had been playing along this whole time, gaining back control without Chaos realizing it.

For the last time. YOU. ARE. DEAD. Forget safety standards, there's nothing left to save!

Chaos dragged their body away from the pile of garbage and wrested control of the mouth again. "Get in the car."

Reluctantly, Listay let Chaos tuck them into the front seat of the Gremlin.

Where are we going? Listay asked.

"Rhea III."

It doesn't exist! And neither does the Sphere of Time. I've been digging for over a beoop now. I'm tired, I need a break, thought Listay.

"Absolutely not. If you stop, it could take me rotations to get you re-started."

Just a nap, Listay pleaded with the goddess.

"Rheans don't take naps. Wake up, or die!" Listay's own fingers snapped in her ear and she blinked her eyes open again. "We're going to Rhea III."

There is no Rhea III, it never existed, Listay thought at her. *That was a lie they told to justify the war. And even if it did, Tuhnt was allegedly Rhea III and you, oh mighty one, destroyed it already!*

"Tell me, General, how long ago were you hatched?" asked Chaos.

Listay forced them to glance at her BEAPER. *368 orbits, five rotations, twelve beoops, and twenty-eight bloops ago.*

Chaos laughed with Listay's mouth. "Oh you're just a larva. We're going to Rhea III. I have it on good authority that therein lies the Sphere of Time. If you're very nice to me, I'll go back in time and make it so you weren't killed to begin with–"

You mean make it so that you don't kill me, Listay corrected.

"Yes. Fine. But I need the Sphere of Time to do that, and the Sphere is on Rhea III, so that is where we are going."

What authority do you have it on? Listay thought.

"Have you studied limericks, Listay? I can see you haven't. Here's one for you.

An A'Viltrian shaman once said
'You can skip Rhea III 'cause it's dead'
but alas, over there
still remains an affair
Designed to screw with Time's head.

Is that enough proof for you?"

No, Listay said, but Chaos forced her fingers to wrap round the gear shift and launch the Gremlin off the planet. Once the coordinates were set, Chaos relaxed her control of Listay's body just enough to allow her to grab the nail file from the passenger's seat and begin filing down a few season's worth of nail growth.

CHAPTER SIX

Cream of Tartar

"Oh, excuse me," said May. "We must've had the wrong coordinates." She addressed the back of whoever sat in the cockpit of the small gray ship she and Xan had *mistakenly* teleported into.

Xan made a nearly imperceptible "erm" and nudged her to look at the read out on his BEAPER. The coordinates were right. She didn't need to look to know that.

"Naw, that was me. I interrupted your signal." The silver-clad pilot twisted languidly around and leaned forward into the light, flashing a gravel-toothed smile from his blue face. The smile morphed into a confused pucker as he surveyed his catch, May in only an oversized Yurkunfle t-shirt and Xan in his shimmering swimsuit. "What's the bark with the swimsuits, eh?"

"We were at the beach," Xan said, holding back the further, more sarcastic comments which threatened to follow.

"Sorry 'bout that, starlips. Name's Rap," he said to May.

"Get us out of here," she whispered, shaking Xan's arm, not daring to drop eye contact with Rap.

"I'm trying, mun." He was. He had swiped up on the teleport signal several times. He would've done more, but his BEAPER had frozen at attempt number forty-seven.

"Not much use teleporting back to the *Audacity,* is there? Seeing as I'm towing it." One half of Rap's upper lip curled up. It was meant to be a sly grin, but looked more like he was about to say, 'take a look at this tooth, do ya' think it looks off?'

Xan tried to back up, but banged the back of his head on a wall. "Ow," he said, rubbing his scalp. "Oh, well hey, we'll just hitch a lift on some other ship. I never liked that rocket anyway!" This was untrue. Xan liked the rocket very much. "We'll get a new one. It's no trouble at all. Just, uh, let us go and we'll be right out of your hair."

May also tried to back up, and also hit the wall. Even backed against the wall, there wasn't much space between them and Rap. The vessel they were on was terribly intimate. She got the feeling that she was in a windowless white van, and that wasn't too far off; it was windowless, and it was white, and from the outside, the cramped MoonHopper did look a bit like a van if you squinted.

"What's happening?" she asked.

Xan clicked his tongue. "Well, May, we've just been kidnapped," he said matter-of-factly, as if he were telling her the time.

"Not kidnapped," Rap pulled a switch and stood as the ship began to shakily ascend. "Xan of Tuhnt, you're under arrest for treason."

May sat on the cold metal floor and scrubbed her fingers through her hair as if resetting her hairstyle would reset the narrative thus far. It didn't work.

"Treason?" she asked Xan from behind a bushel of hair.

"Eh-huh," he confirmed.

"Treason?" she asked again.

The top half of his face cringed, the bottom half smiled.

"And now you have what, some kind of Boba Fett Space Bounty Hunter after you?" she pressed.

"That's 'fugitive recovery agent' if ya' don't mind, starlips," Rap interjected. "Hands out," he said to Xan and whipped a pink zip-tie from his coat pocket.

Xan's cheeks flushed a bright green as Rap zip-tied his wrists, but fortunately for him, it was too dark in the MoonHopper for either Rap or May to see.

"What's that, a laser zip tie?" May asked, parting her hair from her face and trying to poke it back into place.

"N-no," Rap stuttered. "Do those exist?"

May shrugged. "You'd know better than I would, Mr. Fett."

"No more references to other sci-fi media, we can't afford the royalties." Xan folded sadly onto the floor beside her, hands pinkly restrained.

"What did you do?" May forced the words between her clenched teeth.

"Ohh, careful now! Admission of guilt!" Rap sung. "Naw, just kiddin'. Everyone knows you're a guilty zuxing trok-licker."

Xan closed his eyes tightly against reality. If he denied it entirely, maybe it would disappear and be replaced with something a bit kinder. He opened one eye, and saw only the crinkled metal foil that had trapped them. He shut it. Opening the other eye, he saw May watching him with an anger she typically reserved for their rocket racing foes. He shut his eyes.

"What did you do?" she said again, quietly, and at least some of the anger had been replaced by fear. He couldn't ignore her.

"Treason, I guess," Xan said.

"That's an accusation, not an explanation," May countered. "The *Audacity*'s a military ship...and it was never decommissioned. How did you get it?"

"I don't know," he said. He had purposely not thought about it for a very, very long time. Drudging those memories back up was going to take some concerted effort.

"He stole the *Audacity*, obviously!" Rap interrupted, chewing on the end of a zip tie as he spun idly around in his chair. "It was a key part of Tuhnt's plan to take down the *Peacemaker* after it fell into enemy hands and without it...Ka-plow! No more Tuhnt. 'Course it didn't sound like that, technically, 'cause sound doesn't travel in space or whatever," Rap mumbled, having been corrected one too many times regarding his liberal use of onomatopoeia.

"Is that it?" May asked.

Xan nodded.

Every inch of distance between her and the Earth seemed to telescope out in her mind, making her dizzy. Aboard the *Audacity*, she had felt safe. She had felt at home. Now she was trapped in the intergalactic equivalent of a windowless white van with two very alien aliens, neither of whom she could trust.

She felt like the gravity switch in her head had been flipped off. Maybe now was a good time to practice what her school counselor had tried to instill in her class almost a decade ago.

She decided to name something she could see, feel, smell, hear, and taste.

What she saw first was the offline teledisc that had trapped her here. No good. She could feel Xan curled up like a warm rock beside her, but he was no longer a comforting presence. Onto smell, then. All she could smell was herself, she really needed to hit the Sani-Steam. Sound, perhaps, would ground her. She heard only the Moonhopper's engine churning behind her as she hurtled through space in a tin garbage can. She wet her lips. She could still taste the lingering over-sweetness of that ice cream. Even her dental hygiene nanobots had forsaken her.

She resorted to her usual method of coping, and began to mutter some of her favorite curse words, but Xan broke her out of it with a gentle nudging. When she finally gathered the strength to look him in the eyes again, he was motioning emphatically with his eyebrows, trying to silently communicate something.

"What?" she mouthed.

He looked pointedly at her, then at her hands. Unfortunately, the translator chip didn't translate meaningful looks.

Wincing with frustration, he lifted his zip-tied wrists, then looked at her hands again. He pointed to her, pointed to Rap's back, and mimed decking him.

Aha, he wanted her to fight back. Because she wasn't zip-tied. She sighed at him, gesturing wildly to Rap's back then shooting finger guns and miming her tragic death.

Xan nodded his acquiescence, he didn't want her dead. He searched the ceiling as if the rust stains would rearrange into a brilliant escape plan that didn't involve turning May into Swiss cheese.

After a moment of thought, he sat up with the beginnings of a smile. Before May could get in on his new brilliant plan, he spoke.

"Hey," Xan called to Rap.

"Huh?" The fugitive recovery agent didn't turn around.

"What about May? Is she arrested too, or is it just me?"

The hamster on the wheel of May's brain started sprinting. What was he doing? Trying to *get* her arrested?

"Just you."

"Then what are you going to do with her? You could send her back to the *Audacity*. Then you don't have to tow the ship with you! Solves two problems."

Rap stood slowly, tapping some keys on the dashboard as he did. "You zoup-nog. That's stolen goods!"

"Right, well, you still don't need to take her anywhere. She hadn't even been hatched when the war was on! And she's quite heavy. We'd get there faster without her."

"Fuck, Xan, you're going to get me killed!"

"I ain't gonna kill you, starlips," said Rap, walking toward her now. "I'm not that kinda tchaag."

Rap yanked her to her feet. Should she punch him? Her brain sent a test command to her arm; her arm politely declined. Nope, not punching him.

"Just gonna drop you at the nearest space port."

"Wait, no. I don't want to be dropped off!" she said.

"You're a waste of fuel, starlips. I'm dropping you." He held her in place and kicked the teledisc until the white rim lights fluttered on.

Without Xan's BEAPER, she couldn't get back onto the *Audacity*.

Without the *Audacity,* she couldn't get anywhere.

She glared at Xan, but he smiled back at her, proud that he had kept her safe.

Everything went white, then a dingy shade of gray-brown.

Then she was alone. A wooden hand-painted sign tilted on a rusted metal wall high above her. "Welcome to Yenuket Municipal Spaceport."

CHAPTER SEVEN

Big Mouth Billy Bass

Yenuket Municipal Spaceport was built on a moon orbiting Flotlulex's least friendly planet as a waystation between Rhea I and less interesting planets in the solar system. Thanks to improvements in technology, no one seriously needs another fueling station so close to home, and so Yenuket had been mostly abandoned for centuries.

May had been to a few spaceports and had a good idea of what they ought to look like. Glimmering airlocks, rows of businesses and restaurants, crisply uniformed crowds zooming around on whatever their planet's version of a Segway was called.

Yenuket, therefore, didn't even register as a spaceport to her until she read the sign. Dome-shaped yellow lights quivered apologetically from the far-away ceiling. It looked like the place the Beverly Hillbillies lived before they lived in Beverly Hills and smelled like a swamp (a swamp, for those of you who have never smelled one, smells exactly like a rotten egg cracked into a space heater).

And all this was still not as wretched as the sound.

On a blanket of powdered rust sat a tin can robot plucking away at a twangy, metal-bodied instrument. Upon closer inspection, May noticed that the instrument was an integral part of the robot's body.

She waved politely. "Excuse me, could you tell me where we are?"

"CHHGGGGG-TIK-beep-beep-beep," said the robot.

May almost asked again, feeling that perhaps she was the one being unclear. Instead, she began to walk, looking for something that might point her toward something else that might be of use. She still had the *Audacity*'s anchor button snapped onto the inside of her swimsuit. If she could find a computer, she could track the ship. Then she just needed to hire a StarTaxi to take her to it.

And then, she'd have a nice, long, serious discussion with Xan about what the hell he thought he was doing covering up committing treason. He would tell her what he did, exactly, how he did it, exactly, and why he did it, exactly. Then she would pass judgment. And if he refused to talk? She ground her teeth and balled her fists as she walked. Well, the things she fantasized about doing to him if he didn't tell her are better left between her and her conscience.

First, though, she had to find him.

It seemed unlikely there was any sort of Earthling embassy out here to assist her, and May distracted herself from her churning and angry thoughts, choosing instead to toy with the constructive idea that she could erect the first Earthling embassy in the known Universe. She was wrong, of course. Every Earthling lost in space has had this inkling at some point and thirty percent of those who have had this inkling acted on it. There are eighteen Earthling embassy start-ups peppered throughout the galaxy. None of them know about each other.

May walked further from the teledisc bay, vacant storefronts crumbling on either side of her. Something that looked like a mailbox dribbled colorful goo from its mail slot. A poster, posted to the side of the dripping mailbox, caught her eye.

In her experience, posters were almost always either pushy, passive aggressive, or decidedly unhelpful.

This poster was, rare treat, all three. "Don't do that," it said under a silhouette of a stick man dancing with what might've been an upright dromedary.

"Noted," May assured it.

She kept walking, her dark flip-flops taking on a crimson film from the rust that puffed around her feet like fruit flies around a ripe banana.

A dim light flickered from a window in the distance. The metal sign, aggressively corroded, read "Bezalbum's Baubles." Perhaps Bezalbum and their baubles would have a word of wisdom to share. Or a map. A map would be better.

Uneasily, she glanced back. Without Xan nearby, she kept thinking that she had forgotten something important. But she had forgotten nothing. She was just alone, resourceless, stranded on a spaceport that looked like it would disintegrate if she breathed too hard on it.

She stepped into the shop.

A faded damask papered the walls, the floor was a dust-filled tight weave carpet. Music, the kind which tries so hard to be inoffensive it can do nothing but offend, wafted from an old radio on the counter, serenading the only other object in the room which was a bronze call bell.

Hesitantly, with the distinct fear that she might upset the balance of the room, May dinged the bell.

The door behind the counter creaked. The creaking metal, the tinny reverberations of the bell, the thudding of May's heart in her ears, and the offensively inoffensive music gave the place an atmosphere of enormous dread, and the door opened slowly, as if it were apologizing about whatever it was admitting into the room.

"Bretsy, if that's you I don't want none of your candies so slip-off," said an ancient voice.

May had to look over the counter to see her. A wrinkled lump of a Udonian with a wispy white mustache and wispier white hair piled artlessly atop her skull peeked around the door.

"Good afternoon, um, ma'am," said May. Her strategy for dealing with social interactions was to whip out her Sonic customer service voice. "Do you know where I could find a StarTaxi service? Or a working computer?" May sucked her bottom lip under her teeth and chewed gently on it.

The wrinkled creature, who May correctly assumed was Bezalbum, brightened like a fluorescent light kicking on three minutes and forty-nine seconds after you flipped the switch.

"A tourist! Oh indeed, indeed. You, dear, have come to just the right place. Yes. Follow." She curled a finger to beckon May into the back room.

Had May not been hopelessly lost anyway, she might've left at that point. But here, at least, was some direction that didn't involve doing, or not doing, something to a dromedary. She rounded the counter and followed the green raisin-woman.

This room was darker than the first, the light having been soaked up by the tchotchkes and doodads which lined the maze of shelving. The pointedly inoffensive music faded into the background, replaced by a crackling sort of chatter. Faintly, drifting over the dusty shelves like heavy curls of smoke, something fishy.

"*Take my money, my cigarettes*," sang Big Mouth Billy Bass from somewhere in the back of the dark building.

Bezalbum turned to May, wrapping a leathery green hand around hers.

"Never you mind old Billy. He's been singing that song, I reckon, for two hundred orbits, the poor fool."

"You could take out the batteries."

"Hasn't got any, has he?" Bezalbum laughed.

May shivered, though the building was warm and damp.

The fish sang the entire song. It wasn't supposed to do that. It was supposed to sing a few seconds of "Take Me to the River" and then a few seconds of "Don't Worry, Be Happy." But it repeated the entirety of "Take Me to the River" over and over. May really would've liked to hear "Don't Worry, Be Happy" right now. A haunted Big Mouth Billy Bass forgetting his second number felt like an evil omen of horrible things to come.

They walked past the singing fish as it flopped on a dusty shelf. Despite months of being without a personal cell phone, she had the urge to reach for her phone and snap a picture of it to send to Xan, and she had the strange split feeling of wishing he was near and wishing she'd never met him. First, she'd show him the fish. Then, she'd make him talk.

"Welcome, dear," said Bezalbum, startling her out of the fish-induced rumination, "To Yenuket Municipal Spaceport, the most remote spaceport recognized by the Universal Review. If you've never been to Yenuket, you're not missing much! Or so say the postcards. You'll want this." Bezalbum plucked something from a shelf and presented it to her. It was a cheaply made folding pocketknife with the words "Zux it, it's Yenuket!" laser etched into the wood siding.

May nodded politely. Bezalbum nudged closer to her, the pocketknife cradled in her open palms.

"Ten crystals!" Bezalbum chirruped.

"I'm sorry?"

"The pocketknife, dear. I can see that you are with desire. You've been staring."

And then May, still living more in her head than out of it, thought of something she hadn't let herself think about in awhile. Earth. Specifically her mother. Specifically being on Earth and eating lunch out with her mother.

Here's how it would go:

"Why don't you just talk to him?"

"Who?"

"What do you mean, who? The cutie in the other booth. You've been staring, honey."

"Have I?"

"Yes!"

"I haven't, Mom."

"Sweetie, you've got to make the first move sometimes."

"Uh-huh." May would then pretend to be extremely interested in her French fries or sub sandwich, or whatever she was trying to eat at the time. Her mother would then go on about weddings or grandchildren, depending on her mood and May would do her best not to roll her eyes or sigh.

For a moment she was back on Earth, for a moment she missed it, and then she didn't. And then she felt guilty about not missing it. And then she wanted a cigarette. And *then* she realized Bezalbum was still staring at her, arms shaking from the effort of holding the pocketknife aloft.

"Oh, no, I just...it was there so I-"

Bezalbum made a loud swallowing noise, her enormous eyes watering.

May rubbed her face. "Alright, I don't have any crystals on me. Can you take a face scan?" She silently hoped her account hadn't been opened yet.

A blue flash blinded her, and a directionless voice told her ten crystals had been transferred out of her account. 90 crystals left.

That wouldn't go very far, but hopefully she could at least get a StarTaxi ride out of it. She took the pocketknife and reached through the neck of her t-shirt to tuck it between her boobs. A pocketknife, at least, might come in handy later.

"Could you direct me to an information desk? I need to find a StarTaxi."

"Oh no, dear, no. I don't sell StarTaxis. Too flashy. I *have* got a lovely collection of dolls though. Come along, come to the dolls!" she disappeared around a display of china cups which were chipped so badly their own creators wouldn't recognize them.

May followed her like a cat being dragged on a leash.

One of May's finer points, one of the things she prided herself on, was her respect for the elderly. She had no patience for assholes, drunks, or children, but she had all the time in the universe for the elderly. To a fault, perhaps.

Bezalbum led her to a bookshelf which bent under the weight of a mob of baby dolls. *Human* baby dolls. *Parts* of human baby dolls. May took a steadying breath which she immediately regretted. The smell of their musty old clothing and decomposing plastic made her cough.

"They're sweet," she lied, "but I really have to go. My friend's in trouble and I need to find him."

"Oh, dear me," said Bezalbum. "I understand all about the yearnings of the heart! I was quite the romantic myself back in my day-"

"No! God, no. Ew. No, listen," May said. "He's got my rocket." She squinted, that wasn't quite right. "Well, technically, it's his rocket. I just have to find him. He has, as he would say, 'some 'splainin' to do.'"

"Corral your puntls, missy. You wander into my humble shop, buy a cheap souvenir, and now you're galavanting off. Never visiting. Ain't that how it is with larvae these days. All alike are you." She shook her fuzzy green raisin of a head.

And here came the guilt. "I'm sorry, I'll visit soon, I promise!" she said. "Is there anywhere in this spaceport I can get a StarTaxi?"

Bezalbum nodded and began to walk back to the front of her store.

"Fuff." Bezalbum shuffled back the way they'd come, past the haunted Big Mouth Billy Bass. At the counter, she reached slowly, like a giraffe extending its neck for a high leaf, and turned the radio down.

"That way, take a left at the pile of tabloids, then walk until you see the Moonshine Cafe and take another left. And if you *do* come back, buy more than a pocketknife next time, alright dear? Even an old Udonian's gotta to eat!"

May tried to make it look like she wasn't hurrying as she hurried to the door.

"Thank you. I will come back," she threw over her shoulder. And she would. She had to show Xan the fish. No matter how mad at him she was, she couldn't not show him the fish.

The tabloids clumped together like a papier-mâché monolith in the distance; what they thought they were doing there in the middle of the road was beyond May. As she approached, she found that the stack was as tall as she was and seemed to have been intentionally constructed. The pyramid marked a change in the lighting situation. The yellow lights on this side of the tabloids were practically blinding compared to their counterparts beyond.

She went forward.

The Moonshine Cafe's sign flickered to her left. This, she thought, might be the last opportunity she would have to eat for some time. It would be wise to grab a snack. She cupped her hands around her face and pressed them to the window to see what was inside the dark cafe.

A wooden bar stretched along one wall and a robot with sorrowful eye-lights and a missing left hand slowly moved a dirty rag back and forth over one spot. It had been rubbing that spot for so long that the dark varnish had been worn through.

It noticed her and looked up dolefully insomuch as an antique robot with stationary features could look doleful.

She decided that food would definitely be available again in the near future at another location. Without a doubt. She took a left around the building and tried to shake the depressing image.

The road ahead was densely murky and she paused, trying to decide whether to turn back and try the other way or to muscle through.

Her brain glitched back and forth. Forward was hope. Forward was the possibility of a StarTaxi. Forward the air seemed to have turned into undulating cherry Jello. Forward had started moaning. Forward was—okay forward wasn't going to happen. Vapors from the cherry Jello struck the back of her throat and she coughed. Why was it spicy?

"Wondered how far you'd get," said the sharply toothed mouth of a broken shop window beside her. Oh, she thought, now she was hallucinating. That was nice. At least she would die having fun. She explored the source of the words. Perhaps there would be more words. Words that were actually useful to her.

"Hello?"

"No, Jello," the window said.

"Jello?"

"Yes, or at least that's what I think it is. Don't breathe it in."

"Too late."

The window sounded like it shrugged. "Probably won't kill you."

May peered into the dark window, feeling like the first idiot to get picked off in a horror movie. She swiveled her head around to make sure nothing was sneaking up on her.

"Who are you?"

"Who are you?" parroted back at her.

She began to walk back the way she came. Bezalbum would be getting her second visit.

"Hold on, wait, hold on," the window rushed.

May looked behind her to see something crawling out of the window.

And then May realized she was about to be mugged, and she didn't even have a fist full of keys to fight back with. She did, however, have a useful, if sweaty, pocketknife. She fished it out, clumsily unsheathing the small piece of sharp metal with her fingernail.

"I don't have any money," she warbled at the thing.

"Aw, well. I can make you pay in other ways."

CHAPTER EIGHT

Kryptonite

Xan had seen a TV show about Superman once. He picked up few Earth broadcasts from his cozy spot in orbit, but he knew about this Superman and the terrible effect Kryptonite had on him. He stared at his wrists now, bound with a thin pink zip tie.

Zip ties were his Kryptonite.

Zip ties were definitely, without a doubt, the only thing that could hold him back. He sighed; if only he had laser vision. Hold on. Had he ever actually tried to shoot lasers from his eyes?

He thought back. Maybe once or twice. He felt that this had come up before. But had he tried hard enough those times? Maybe he just needed to believe in himself more.

He gathered all the laser energy that coursed through him into the space behind his eyes, then closed them. His teeth grit from the effort. He opened his eyes to release the power of a million suns upon the little strip of plastic.

A million suns, it seemed, was no match for a zip tie.

"Hey there, what was your name? Zap? Dap?" Xan asked. Typically, he had a great memory for names and faces, but recent events had taken up a rather lot of processing space in his brain.

"Rap."

"Right, Wrap."

"No, ya zoup-nog. Rap with an 'R.'" Rap had been scraping under his nails with the blunt tip of a knife; hygiene was difficult in a ship without a proper washroom, but he did what he could.

"Uh-huh, Rap. So, um...where are we going? I mean, Tuhnt's gone, along with, I assume, the entirety of its legal system."

Rap sat back, trying to look casual, succeeding in looking like he was sitting on a lit grill. "Did ya' honestly think there wouldn't be no consequences?"

Xan thought, his eyes darting around as he tried to come up with an answer.

"Sorry that was—that was a double negative. Yes, I did not think that there would be no consequences. Is that—did you mean 'did I think there wouldn't be *any* consequences?'"

"Blitheon, you're an obnoxious chunk of trok ain't ya?"

"So I'm told. I mean I expected someone to be after me, but zuut, after the first hundred orbits I suppose I did kinda think everyone had forgotten. I mean, really, how many Tuhntians are still out there? And the Rheans don't care, they wanted Tuhnt gone to begin with."

"Ha! I can't even begin to tell you how wrong you are."

"That sounds like an exaggeration. Go on. Educate me," Xan said in the same flat, uninterested tone May used when she was being ironic.

"The Rheans wanted to colonize Tuhnt, for starters, eh? Not destroy it, ya zoup-nog. Ever wonder why there's a Rhea I, II, and IV? As far as the zuxing Rheans figured, Tuhnt was supposed to be Rhea III."

"Ah, well, I can see how they might think that. Back to the original question, though, if you don't mind. Where are you taking me?"

"To Tuhnt."

Xan winked his annoyance. "You have got a time machine, then. Zuut. I told May those didn't exist. When were those invented?"

"Don't be ridiculous, there ain't no time machines. We're going to New Tuhnt. And I'm telling you now so you ain't surprised: it's a trok-hole."

CHAPTER NINE

Nasty Business

"Excuse me?" May asked the shadow as it lurched toward her.

"I can make you pay in other ways," it repeated.

"What?" May backed up, shifting her grip on the knife.

"For a ride. You could shampoo the upholstery. Or you could help me change the oil out, I've been meaning to do that. Tough to change out the oil on a StarTaxi on your own, though."

"What?" Fight and flight were so busy duking it out in May's head that she hadn't actually understood what the stranger had said.

The flickering light above them felt that perhaps now would be a good time to actually do its job and illuminated her would-be assailant.

A willowy Tuhntian with skin the color of a blueberry milkshake with far too few blueberries in it sauntered toward her. A massive pink braid wrapped around her neck like a scarf, and she wore a sharply studded leather jacket over a white t-shirt with the iconic Earth alien face and the words "I believe" scrawled beneath it. May wondered what exactly the shirt meant in this context but could think of no eloquent way of asking, so she let it be.

"Look mun, I can't take you far, but I'll at least get you to a busier port." She held up a gloved hand. Fingerless gloves. May stared at it.

"High five?" the Tuhntian asked.

May gently tapped the hand with her own. "Sure. Who are you?"

"This again? Alright, I'll go first if it's that important to you. Aimz of Tuhnt. Now you."

"May of Earth," she said.

"Ohh a Terran, eh?"

"I take offense to that. I think," May countered. Xan had told her it was offensive, the equivalent of calling someone a "dirt person," and May had been called it a few times by some of the nastier racers they'd competed against.

"Ah, hey no offense meant, Earthmun. I think it's cute that you're all the way out here. What are you doing off of Earth, anyway? Earth's a no-contact zone last I heard."

"Racing."

"Racing what? You've got a rocket or something?" Aimz looked around as if an entire rocket ship would peek around the corner like a frightened dog and might come running up to her for pets if she whistled at it. If her tone hadn't been so intensely sincere, May would've thought she was mocking her.

"Sort of." May relaxed just a bit. Aimz was much taller than her, muscular, and covered in metal spikes, but something in her enormous, earnest smile put May at ease. "I've hit a snag. Will you help me get back to my ship or not?"

Aimz shrugged mightily, pocketing her hands. "I had a pretty full day of acquainting myself with the Jello stuff planned but, zuut, that sounds like an adventure. Now..." She leaned forward until her long nose nearly touched May's. May didn't flinch. She was used to that sort of thing from Xan. "About payment," said Aimz. "I also accept entertainment. Memorized any good Earth movies? Maybe an operetta? Jokes will do in a pinch, but you better have a lot of them."

"Oh, uh, I thought you were trying to mug me. I've got money."

Aimz's forehead wrinkled. "Are you saying I look like a mugger?"

"You're two heads taller than me and have three-inch spikes on your shoulders," May pointed out.

"Ha! Oh these? No, mun, these aren't for you. They're for someone I used to know. He was a leaner. Always hanging on one shoulder or the other, I swear my shoulders are still misaligned because of it. What do you think?" Aimz straightened up, tried to even out her shoulders. "Left one's a touch off isn't it?"

May shook her head, sighed, shrugged. "Yeah maybe a bit."

"Shame. Alright, come on. The taxi's out back. You got an anchor for the ship? Or are we stealing a ship? Be honest, now. If we're stealing a ship, I'll have to find my sunglasses." Aimz strode back to the busted window. May had to jog to keep up and briefly wondered if she could get leg extensions.

"I have the anchor button, but we'll have to use your BEAPER," May said, regretfully. She could've gotten a BEAPER. Several times she'd thought about how useful it would be to have a BEAPER. Several times she had put it off, thinking one BEAPER between the two of them was plenty. Clearly, it was not.

"Eh, we'll use the taxi's computer to trace it. My BEAPER's on the outs at the moment." She held out her wrist. It sparkled like a Fourth of July novelty firecracker and the holographic display glowed weakly above it, proclaiming that she had a new message.

Aimz squinted at it, brought it closer to her face, then attempted to accept the new message several times before it worked.

"*Tell her I'll be back in a bit,*" said a voice which sounded an awful lot like Xan's.

May paused on the other side of the window, and looked at the BEAPER as if it had suddenly turned into a crested gecko and licked its eye at her.

"Who was that from?" she asked.

Aimz gave her BEAPER the same face May had given it.

"Doesn't matter. It's a few decades old. Wasn't for you."

It probably wasn't, thought May. The voice recording was scratchy and warped, like it had been put through a blender, but she was sure it was Xan. Either that, or she was going a little insane being alone in a distant solar system.

Aimz climbed over a jutting tooth of broken glass into the storefront that May now could see had at one point been a Speed-Star StarTaxi franchise. May climbed in after Aimz, carefully. Her shorter legs meant that there wasn't nearly as much clearance between her and the shards of glass.

The inside of the building smelled like old motor oil and stale corn chips, but when Aimz walked in, a host of organic lamps flicked on and revealed an apartment which appeared to have been the site of a devastating craft supply explosion.

"Do you, um, live here?" May asked.

"I'd be an absolute fool if I did, don't you think?" Aimz laughed hoarsely as she tugged on a metal door at the back of the room. "Yes. Yes, I do live here."

"It's charming." May had never in her life used the word 'charming'. Not once. This was absolutely and positively the first time it had ever actually come out of her mouth. May would never use the word again.

"Ha! You're a weird one, Earthmun. It's not. Don't worry about it, I'm moving soon. I hate to break a good lease, but I'm starting to think the landlord's not actually planning to fix that window."

"Oh that? I hardly noticed," May said of the window and Aimz laughed a broad laugh that May swore made the lamps glow brighter.

The door screeched open and revealed a long wooden boardwalk which stretched out from the spaceport like Adam's finger reaching out toward God's in the Sistine Chapel. Only God, in this instance, was a ship so small that May would have had no trouble believing Aimz if she said her boisterous laugh alone would power it.

A curious thing happened to May, poised on the edge of the rotting wooden planks and surrounded by space. She suddenly had a fear of heights. Someone who'd spent some time in space, who raced a rocket ship for a living, theoretically would have an agreement with heights by now. And she did. But this wasn't just height. It was depth, it was breadth, it was the whole general everything, and it was horrifying. Some invisible atmosphere must extend over the boardwalk, thought May. Some amount of gravity must be present in order for them to walk across it.

Aimz put a hand to her back. "You steady?"

"Huh?"

"You look like a wyrntensil in a maelstrom."

"I'm fine. There's atmosphere and artificial gravity out there right? On the boardwalk?"

"No, see, the idea is that you're supposed to empty your lungs then crawl across the boardwalk before you freeze to death," said Aimz. Then, when May gave her a concerned look, she relented. "Of course there's atmosphere and gravity! Go on, just don't look down. Or up. Or to the sides. Or—you know what? Just look at the StarTaxi, and you'll be fine."

The hand on May's back started to push her forward and they strolled into nothingness with only a few planks of wood keeping them tethered to a somethingness.

May wondered how far the force field extended. If she jumped, would she be lost to the cosmos forever? What if she fell? Would she re-gravitize to the underside of the boardwalk? Was it even really an underside?

The science of the boardwalk was troubling at best and impossible at worst, so May decided to focus on the StarTaxi as Aimz had suggested.

When they reached the taxi, Aimz pressed the tip of her thumb into a soft button on the side of it, and the door dissolved, allowing them to pass through. Inside, the StarTaxi was dimly lit by a string of blue lights which skirted the ceiling and the soft glow of stars through the digital viewscreen at the front. The taxi rocked as Aimz tucked herself into the pilot's seat, and May crawled into the back. There were four seats, but none of them accounted for passengers that had legs.

Aimz popped a panel off the dashboard and twisted a pair of worn wires together. With a sizzling zap and a flash of light, the engine began to purr like a geriatric puma.

"Great! There's at least one more trip in this rust sack. Button?" She reached her hand into the back seat, her palm open.

May dropped the pocketknife back into its make-shift pocket, then snapped the button off the strap of her swimsuit and pressed it into Aimz's palm.

"It's a Class 20 Racing Rocket," May said as Aimz popped the button into a slot on the dashboard.

"Really? Don't see many of those anymore. Color?"

"Orange. Really, extremely orange."

Aimz twisted around, scrutinizing her with bubblegum pink irises that appeared to glow in the low light.

"Not Obtrusive Orange, is it?"

May nodded, but slowly, half her brain telling her to run and the other half asking the first half where the hell it thought she ought to run to. "Yes, how did you know?"

Aimz ignored the question.

"And this rocket ship...are you the rightful owner, or did you steal it? Or did you buy it off someone? Who did you buy it from?"

"I'm paying you to take me to it," May said, wishing they had gone through this before she gave away the anchor button. "Not to interview me about it."

"Where is the owner? What happened to him?" Aimz was suddenly nose-to-nose with her in the back seat.

"I don't have to tell you anything." May tried to worm her way into the front seat to retrieve the button, but Aimz's fingers were tiny steel girders digging into her shoulders.

"Where is Xan?" Aimz snarled.

"Why do you want to know?"

"Tell me, or you're not getting back to the *Audacity* ever." Aimz released May's shoulders and defiantly crossed her arms to prove that she had no intention of flying the StarTaxi until she knew.

"What do you want from him?" May asked.

"What do *you* want from him?"

"I asked first."

"Ah, but it's my taxi."

"Which I'm paying for."

"I'm bigger than you, you know. Scary mugger-type, remember?"

"But you're bluffing."

"Why, uh—why would you think that?"

"Call it a hunch."

"I..." Aimz straightened her back, "I don't have a hunch. What?"

"I mean I know exactly who you are and why you want to find Xan," May said, feeling smug for the first time in a long time. She, in the grand tradition of her ancient Mesopotamian ancestors defining the first constellations, had just connected the dots.

The dots were vague, and the connections relied on an astonishingly high coincidence factor, but astonishing coincidence was no stranger to May.

"What? You couldn't possibly. Could you? Zuut, you could. Wait. Who do you think I am, and why do you think I want to find Xan?"

"You tell me first. I'll tell you if I was right."

"Ah-hah, that's not how it works, Earthmun."

"If you are who I think you are, you at least want him alive."

"More or less."

"Less?"

"Right, well, he's not winning any awards for favorite brother this orbit, I can tell you that!"

"I was right." May smiled.

"Ah, Blitheon's zuxing trok," Aimz cursed at herself.

"So you'll help me find him and not kill him?"

"Oh, I'll help you find him."

"And not kill him?" May clarified.

"Right, yeah, fine. Whatever."

"Promise?"

"I promise not to kill him on purpose."

"Good enough. He's been arrested by a bounty hunter, and as far as I know he's wherever the *Audacity* is."

The taxi's computer dinged proudly, spitting the anchor button out of the dashboard like a slice of toast.

"Found him!" Aimz crawled into the front again and stomped on the taxi's accelerator, headed for New Tuhnt.

CHAPTER TEN

Trashed

Rhea III, as Listay had said, does not exist.

It did, though. Some 3,250 orbits ago it existed, then was abandoned, forgotten, re-discovered, christened Pontoosa: The Wackiest Rock in the Solar System by a band of renegade Tuhntian entrepreneurs, abandoned again, forgotten again, and finally, re-discovered by EnviroDev and claimed as the site of New Tuhnt.

So it was here, to the nearly but not quite deserted New Tuhnt, that Chaos brought Listay to seek out the oft limericked about Sphere of Time.

Listay struggled with the Gremlin door, pulling on the inside handle until she heard the crack of the handle breaking internally. Giving up, she unrolled the window and shimmied through it, despite her muscular thighs and persistent rigor mortis.

From a tent in the distance, the Tuhntian surveyor (the one who has a name but whose name is untranslatable), watched as the Rhean emerged from the window of the AMC Gremlin and trundled into a patch of sprouts he had been tending for the past three rotations.

This was no EnviroDev supply ship she had emerged from. In fact, he had only ever seen a ship that ugly once before, during the war. It was a *Peacemaker* shuttle. A shuttle from the ship that had destroyed Tuhnt. And it was trying to destroy New Tuhnt, now, apparently. One patch of sprouts at a time.

Before Listay's body had a chance to crawl to her shaky knees, but after Chaos began cursing through her stiff lips, the Tuhntian surveyor offered a hand to help her up.

Chaos tried to wave his hand away, but Listay was less concerned about appearing weak and more concerned about eventually getting off the ground, so she used the surveyor's arm as leverage to stand up.

"Thank you. I'd like to apologize in advance for my behavior, I'm afraid I've been possessed by an ancient Chaos goddess and she's a real—" Listay paused, forgetting for a moment how to work her tongue. The surveyor waited patiently. "—ly magnificent ageless and almighty entity," Chaos finished with a smile.

While the surveyor wasn't willing to say that she *was* possessed by an ancient Chaos goddess, he couldn't look into her unmentionably clouded eyes and say she wasn't.

And she was armed. He continued to hold her arm, well after she was standing, and watched the plasma zapper strapped to her thigh suspiciously, as if it might leap out of its holster.

"What's the zapper for?"

"Nothing as long as you cooperate."

This conversation was quickly morphing from suspicious to vaguely threatening. He needed to confer with someone, and the only other someone on the planet was Sonan. "Let's get you inside." He gestured to the wreck of the *Innocuous* behind him. "Sonan will want to meet you."

"No. You will take me to the Sphere of Time immediately." Chaos was accustomed to being obeyed. She was also accustomed to having power over the perceived reality of mortals. Now, though, she was little more than a persistent intrusive thought trapped in the brain of a zombie. For a being whose *modus operandi* was intimidation, this was not ideal.

The surveyor, at the risk of being uncooperative, had to protest. He protested carefully, though.

"I don't know where or what that is, but Sonan might." He gave her an encouraging smile. "So come with me?"

Chaos filled Listay's lungs with dusty air to prepare for an obstinate huff. Instead, she coughed, squashing any possibility of intimidating him.

"I will come with you," she wheezed. "But know it's of my own volition. If I wanted to, I could smite you right now. This place could use the fertilizer. What are you called?"

The surveyor gave his untranslatable name, a no-nonsense, practical Tuhntian family name which Chaos herself had used to refer to a plan four or five plans back.

Why don't you possess him? Listay thought as they followed the mountainous Tuhntian.

"It's almost as if you *want* to be dead again," said Chaos.

"Excuse me?" The surveyor paused.

"Inside joke. Not about you."

If I were to possess him instead, Chaos told Listay with her inside voice, *your body wouldn't survive a blip out here. Is that what you want?*

No, thought Listay as they reached the *Innocuous's* access hatch. She stared at the ladder leading up to the hatch. Clearly, he was waiting for her to mount it. Clearly, she wasn't going to.

"Do you need help?" he asked quietly, not wanting to embarrass her.

Chaos shook her head and attached Listay's metal arm to a rung. After a moment of mental prodding, she got her organic arm to follow suit. From there, it was only a matter of time before her left foot found the first rung. And now the right foot...

The surveyor desperately wanted to help her, but he knew that there were some things that had to be done alone, and it seemed like climbing this ladder was one of those things, so he waited until at last she paused, resting her forehead against the side of the hatch, and looked down at him.

"I've only just recently resurrected this body from its grave. I would appreciate some praise at this point," said Chaos.

"Oh, uh, well done. That's...that's very good," said the surveyor, then clapped a few times to show he was sincere.

"Are you patronizing me?"

"Not at all. I would imagine resurrecting from the dead is quite an ordeal," he said.

"Perhaps if you're very lucky, you'll find out one day," she said and opened the hatch, crawling into the dark hallway of the *Innocuous.*

The surveyor followed her inside, sealed the hatch, then led her to the stodgy tearoom door.

"Sonan?" the surveyor asked, rapping timidly on the door. "I've got a visitor for you."

"You may enter."

The surveyor laughed lightly. "Don't let her intimidate you. She's really very sweet," he told Chaos, who was more irritated than intimidated.

They entered the brightly lit and doilied room to find Sonan sitting where she always sat, pouring another cup of tea, and smiling with stiff android lips.

"Welcome to New Tuhnt," said Sonan. "Would you like a cup of tea?"

"I'm looking for the Sphere of Time. Do you know where it is?" Chaos asked, working Listay's features into a scowl.

"No, I can't say I do. Cup of tea?" Sonan poured a second cup now and gently pushed it across the table toward Chaos.

"I don't want your zuxing tea. I know it's here, and if you're hiding it from me I will rain my vengeance upon you first!" She flung aside the wicker chair nearest her.

The surveyor, mortified, lunged for Chaos and pinned her arms to her sides.

"Sorry about this, Sonan. Should I put her in the holding cell?"

"Not at all. We will be requiring that cell when Rap returns."

"Respectfully, it's been orbits since we last heard from him."

"We will need that cell," she insisted. "Throw her away."

"What do you mean...in the compactor?"

"Of course."

Chaos tested Listay's upper arm strength against the surveyor's. Had she not been dead, she might've overpowered him. Chaos was beginning to regret having murdered her new host body, but possession of an unwilling host was impossible. They either had to be willing, dead, or...the surveyor had unintentionally brought Chaos to her ideal host. An android.

"Yes ma'am," said the surveyor to Sonan, then, to Chaos he said, "I am truly sorry about—"

He stopped. Listay's body had gone limp. He shook her slightly, watching her head loll from one side to the other.

"Sonan? I think she's dead," he said to the android.

From Sonan, nothing. She had shut off.

The Tuhntian surveyor sighed, hefted Listay's body over his shoulder, and brought her to the trash compactor, dropping her corpse, respectfully, into the pit of garbage.

His BEAPER dinged. Sonan had been correct; they would need the holding cell.

CHAPTER ELEVEN

Aimz the Ch'stranda

The StarTaxi puttered through space with a sound not unlike a Shriner's tiny parade car.

"*Where are you?*" Aimz's BEAPER was talking again. Talking with, what May now knew, was Xan's voice. "*I've been thinking about getting a ch'stranda!*" it said.

May hurled herself over the back of the pilot's seat and stared, along with Aimz, at the busted BEAPER.

"I told him he could have one if he could catch one," May said. "Can you let him know we're coming?"

Aimz shook her head. "These messages are from decades ago. The range on this old thing's terrible; they're only now coming through because he's nearby. Also, if he knows we're coming to get him, we lose the element of surprise."

"*Right, so I got a ch'stranda. Named him Aimz. Hope that isn't weird,*" said the ancient recording of Xan.

Aimz laughed. "It is, you slorpfignut," she said under her breath. The BEAPER sparked and sizzled, its holographic screen shutting off.

"Ouch! Alright." Aimz removed the smoking BEAPER and set it in her lap. On the viewscreen, the malformed spitball of New Tuhnt was slowly gaining size.

"Go to the *Audacity* first. If you help me shovel the crystals onto the teledisc to deposit them, you can take as many as you can carry."

"Not a bad deal. I can carry a lot. Big hands," Aimz said, proving it to May by flexing her gloveless fingers at her.

"You're not actually going to try to kill Xan if we find him, are you?" May pressed. She didn't want him dead until she got some answers out of him.

Aimz mulled slightly longer than May would've liked. "No, but I want him to think I'm going to. You in?"

Considering this, May stared out the small porthole at the stars. Usually, looking out at the stars made her think about her tiny little existence and how meaningless it all was and that calmed her down. At this moment, though, she did not want to be calm.

“I’m in. Let’s wreck him.”

CHAPTER TWELVE

Perplexion

New Tuhnt was a trok-hole. The planet Xan arrived on wasn't so much a world as it was a rock. Not even a pretty rock. The land which expanded beyond the MoonHopper's viewscreen looked like dried oatmeal, only somehow less appetizing.

"Okay." Xan paused to tug at the zip tie with his teeth. "Alright, so that's New Tuhnt. But the question remains," he gnawed again, "Why? Because the original Tuhnt wasn't all that great, really. I mean, sure it was a place to live if you needed one, but do you really have to re-create it? Why not start fresh?"

"Shut up," Rap said as he checked his landing stats, which were dismal, then shut off the MoonHopper.

Still nibbling on the zip tie, Xan, from the corner of his mouth, said, "Nostalgia, I bet. Isn't it? Everyone missed having somewhere to be which was called 'Tuhnt' and decided to call something else 'Tuhnt' and thought that would make it all right and good but I'll tell you what, once it's gone it's gone. You might as well have a fresh start, eh? Because it's the people that make a place, not the name. And with those people gone...Speaking of fresh, does anything even grow here? I mean like fruits and vegetables, not just bacteria and depression."

"Shut up," had become a motto for Rap since meeting Xan. He said it again now, urgently.

"Sure...but, really, what's the statute of limitations on something like this? Two centuries is a long time."

"There's not really a statute of limitations on destroying a planet, no," Rap said pressing a call button on the MoonHopper's control panel. "We've landed. Want to help me out here? Bringing him to Sonan?"

"*Hey Rap, good to see you*," the deep voice of the Tuhntian surveyor sizzled through the MoonHopper's communication line.

"Been a busy rotation here. Sonan's preoccupied right now. Would you put him in the holding cell?"

"Aye. What's the news?" Rap replied.

"Ha, well, to begin I discovered a strain of bacteria that actually grows here," crackled through the speaker.

"Right get on with the interesting stuff."

"I had to throw someone in the trash compactor today."

"No way. Alright, I'll deal with the traitor, then we can catch up."

"I'll be here."

"Shift it." Rap hoisted Xan up to drag him out of the MoonHopper and onto the stinking, oxygen starved land.

"Your standards—" Xan coughed, tasting the odor in the back of his throat. "By Quanzar's Laser-Scythe, your standards for New Tuhnt were low," he wheezed. "What is this, a landfill planet? Is this the plan?" He coughed. "Olfactory torture? Really, this is truly awful. And another thing—" He stopped talking.

A gnarly looking StarTaxi snuggled into the space below the *Audacity*. In tandem, Rap and Xan perplexed at it, then Xan disappeared and Rap perplexed alone.

CHAPTER THIRTEEN

Anat Attack

Two things Xan was not expecting happened in rapid succession. The first, and more pleasant, was that he was back in the *Audacity* and the ship was moving. The second was that something heavy was pinning him to the orange shag carpet.

"Look at you!" said the something.

"Ahh!" said Xan.

"Wow!" said the something.

"Ahh!" Xan reiterated.

"You zuxing tchagg, what have you got to defend yourself? And why are you in a swimsuit?"

"We were at the beach..."

His eyes finally focused on his attacker. A neuron that had slumbered peacefully for a few hundred orbits was suddenly jolted awake, handed a fedora and a briefcase, and told it was late to work.

"Aimz?" he asked.

Now that he had recognized his attacker, she was ready to destroy him. "Defend yourself!" she warned, and dove at him like a ckanight pouncing on its prey. A spikey ball of wires bounced off her forehead and she sat back just enough that he could shimmy awkwardly away.

"Hey, what?" Aimz shouted at May, rubbing her forehead where one of the sharp wires had sliced it.

"You agreed not to kill him, remember?" May said, hopping down from the control loft. She dug out the lighter from beneath a pile of magazines under the coffee table, flicked it on, and grabbed Xan's wrists by the pink zip tie, holding the flame under the plastic to melt it through. Only when she smelled the toxic melted plastic fumes did she remember she had a pocketknife.

"May," he whispered, watching Aimz rub her forehead. "Where did you find that?"

"What, your sister?" she whispered back, flinging aside the melted zip tie. "The one you don't have?"

"That's not Aimz. That is most definitely a cruel shape-shifting Anat which is most definitely after my soul. Where's the marsupian wine? Anat's are allergic to culture."

May had no idea where the wine was and was fairly certain they'd had the last of it a while back after a particularly harrowing race win. Still, she knifed her hand into the couch cushions to fish for the bottle.

"Oh, yeah," laughed Aimz. "Did I forget to mention that I was an Anat? Can't wait to dehydrate your souls and tuck them away in my cave of eternal night. Come over it, you know who I am." She winked, situating herself cross-legged on the orange shag.

"Well I know who you *look* like," he growled. "And I've got to say that's outrageously insensitive of you. That's utterly, entirely, and insanely messed up. You know that? That's just—"

"Found it!" May said, uncorking a strangely angled bottle which swirled with a teaspoon of blue liquid.

"Great, melt her!" Xan scrambled onto the couch as if Aimz were a rat that might charge at his feet.

May exchanged a bemused glance with Aimz who tipped her head back, opening her mouth wide to accept the wine which May poured down her throat.

Aimz collapsed not, as Xan had hoped, in an uncivilized puddle, but in a fit of laughter.

"Xan, you slorpfignut, I'm not a zuxing Anat! I helped your little Earthling here deposit that mound of crystals you had lying around and I only took a few handfuls. Would an Anat be able to resist that many crystals?"

Xan finally got to his knees and moved closer, examining the face that smiled back at him. "Aimz? I swear to Quanzar, if you're trying to have one over on me I'll—"

"You'll what? Kill me? Again?"

Xan launched into her and squeezed her so tightly her back made a sound like a snapping glow stick.

"Zuut! Get off me," she whined, but she made no move to push him away.

He released her, rocking back on his heels. "How on Tuhnt did you survive?"

"Well," Aimz got to her feet, straightened her jacket, and flopped onto the couch. "That's obvious isn't it? I wasn't on Tuhnt. I was on an off-world mission interning with BioTech when it happened. We were collecting samples of a new strain of sentient chartreuse cave skrum they'd detected in the area. Mission was canceled. Obviously. Most of my coworkers had enough gem to get themselves to the colony on Rhea but not me. Nope. I got stuck in Yenuket with a three hundred orbit contract with Speed-Star StarTaxi. Which I think I'm in breach of, incidentally, seeing as I left the taxi back there." She jammed a thumb at the viewscreen and a spit-ball sized New Tuhnt.

Xan smiled, but it looked like someone had cut out a picture of his smile from a magazine and pasted it onto his face. He sat across from her on the coffee table. "And, uh...do you know what happened to Tuhnt?"

May sat on the couch beside Aimz and hoped Aimz didn't know the full story because May certainly didn't. The dots she had been provided with weren't connecting.

"Hard not to," Aimz said through her teeth.

The cut-out of Xan's smile began to peel away from his face.

"The *Peacemaker* blasted it to bits. And all because someone stole the rocket that was supposed to distract the *Peacemaker* long enough to destroy it," she said.

Another edge of the cut-out drooped.

"All because some orange-haired groutal-lipped coward pilfered the *Audacity* right before it was scheduled to save the planet from imminent destruction."

The cut-out of his smile detached fully and drifted softly, leaf-like to the orange shag below.

"Are you mad at me?" he asked in a voice that was not his.

Aimz very much gave the impression that she was, in fact, mad at him.

She was in good company, too. But May found that, now that he was in front of her, she still had a hard time really believing he was responsible for the destruction of a planet and her anger was diluted.

"Eugh, I don't blame you. You always were the zoup-nog in the family," Aimz sneered. "I just don't know how you got away with it for this long."

"Luck," Xan said, quite honestly.

He watched Aimz, knowing that if she was alive, there was a tiny chance some other people he had missed desperately were floating around out there, too. A flap on Schrodinger's box was open now, and it was ever so tempting to look inside and see what had survived. "I don't mean to sound like it's not good to see you, because it is, but about everyone else..." Xan hazarded, careful not to open the box too quickly.

"Zuut," Aimz sat back on the couch and pretended she hadn't heard him. "Yenuket Municipal was a refuse planet compared to this. You've been living nicely, haven't you? An entire couch, lighting, windows...living like a queen."

"Aimz, my quality of life over the past century isn't important. I mean, the windows are nice, and it is delightfully orange in here, but that's not the point. The point is-"

"Ah, no don't say it," Aimz covered her face with her hands.

"You're deflecting. What about everyone else? Tell me."

Interesting, thought May, watching their conversation eagerly from the sidelines, waiting for more information to be dragged out of either one of them. Interesting that Xan picked up on Aimz deflecting. And by interesting, May meant it was terribly ironic and more than a little frustrating. Xan was a master deflector.

"They're fine," Aimz said, sniffing loudly and looking around the room, trying to find another topic of conversation quickly.

"Aimz."

"Eugh, alright!" Aimz sat up, slamming her hands on the couch cushions. "I don't know. I haven't seen another Tuhntian since my coworkers scuttled off to Rhea I."

"I see," said Xan. And then he said, through Aimz's BEAPER and a few decades too late, "*It's weird, I'm sorry.*" He tilted his head at her wrist.

Grateful for the distraction, Aimz laughed at Xan's confusion. "I'm getting old messages you sent me. You named a ch'stranda after me?"

"Right, yeah, I did. Aimz the ch'stranda! Shouldn't have done that; it *was* weird," he said. And then, via Aimz's BEAPER. "*Just tell me if you're alive or not, alright? I miss you*."

"I missed you, too," Aimz admitted. "After I stopped wanting to kill you."

Xan cringed. "When did you stop? Exactly?"

"Eh, a couple blips ago. It's hard to stay mad at you, ya' wet noodle," Aimz said, crossing her arms and pouting.

May had to agree.

CHAPTER FOURTEEN

An Excellent Escape

The *Audacity* hurtled away from New Tuhnt until it, quite abruptly, did not.

The ship stopped with enough force to fling everything which was not bolted down against the back-lit orange plastic wall. Nothing, because someone had neglected standard safety practice, was bolted down.

Xan was the first up, rotating his shoulders to make sure they still worked properly.

Aimz came to a cautious sitting position, holding her head to try to keep it in the same dimension as her body.

May slept peacefully, her consciousness having popped out to explore better, less danger-prone brains.

“What in Quanzar’s name was that?” Xan asked no one in particular as he tried to leap up to the control loft, discovering then that his shoulders had made it through the tossing unscathed, but his knees hadn’t.

While Tuhntians heal at a rate so much faster than Earthlings that comparing them is mathematically impossible, Tuhntian joints, like all joints in the Universe, are shit.

“Well, we hit something didn’t we? Zoup-nog.” Aimz rolled herself up and joined Xan at the viewscreen. A bloody gash on her forehead began to fade away as she rubbed her left elbow, which felt every blip of her three-hundred and fifty orbits.

May’s consciousness was still galivanting about a few light-years away; it was starting to get a taste for freedom.

Xan studied the screen. “Everything’s still on. We should be moving according to this thing.” He tapped a dial which was quite clearly labeled the speedometer. “But we aren’t moving at all according to the other thing.” He tapped part of the screen which was labeled, clearly, "Navigation.”

"Maybe we're in a pocket dimension!" he hypothesized excitedly. "Maybe we're traveling in time instead of space! Eugh, or maybe we're traveling in another, more boring dimension that isn't time. What if we're traveling in scent? That could get unpleasant quickly."

Aimz summoned a view from the *Audacity*'s back-up camera. "Or we've run out of rope. I'm favoring that one, on account of there's a rope thingy trailing off behind us, and we're at the end of it. Also, scent isn't a dimension."

"That you're aware of," he muttered. "Aimz, really, what kind of rope could stop the *Audacity*? You must've hit your head on the wall. Oh! You know what, I think I've read about this somewhere! I bet it's an invisible aether bog. Like, really thick, sticky nothingness. May, settle a wager, what do you think? Rope or space bog? I think space bog."

May didn't answer. Her consciousness was toeing a silvery pond in the seventy-eighth dimension (a dimension which was not exactly scent itself, but did have some correlation with scent).

"That's not how dimensions work!" said Aimz to the narration.

The *Audacity* jarred, then began to crawl backward toward New Tuhnt with a sound like a semi-truck squeezing into a storm drain.

"Probably ought to turn off the engine," Aimz said, searching for the off switch.

"Why? We want to go forward. Let's wait it out." Xan sat in the co-pilot's chair, wiggling around until he'd gotten one leg bent over the arm of the chair, one leg twisted beneath him, and his arms slung over the back. "May?" Why hadn't she joined them yet? The Earthling who had been on the ship for a mere half an orbit knew more about it than he did. It ought to have been embarrassing, but really, he was quite proud of her, if not completely dependent on her.

"Alright, blow out your engines, burn through a tank of fuel. I don't care. Not my ship," Aimz said, but her eyes still searched the console. The *Audacity* shuddered pitifully. "I don't think your Earthling survived, by the way."

"What?"

"I think she's dead," Aimz said, still looking for the off switch. "Oh! Is this it?" She pressed The Button Which Typically Made The Ship Go (which also typically made it stop) and the storm drain semi-truck sound ceased.

Behind them in the living room, May's wayward consciousness finally felt a twinge of homesickness. It stopped its lackadaisical journeying and took a good look around. It wandered for a bit in one direction, then back the way it came. After a few false starts, it realized it was lost and began to hyperventilate insomuch as a lungless consciousness could hyperventilate.

Xan approached May slowly; he didn't think she looked dead. He had never actually had the displeasure of seeing anyone dead before, though, so he had nothing to compare it to.

After a contemptuous snort at The Button Which Typically Made The Ship Go But Also Typically Made It Stop, Aimz crouched beside May and lifted her wrist. "See? Limper than last season's Moringarg."

Xan shook his head. "She's fine! She sleeps a lot." He slung her over his shoulder and looked for the couch. It had made a sizable crack in the lighted plastic wall panel. Xan nodded toward it. "Flip the couch over for me?"

"Okay, but how much are you going to pay me?"

The retort Xan wanted to make slipped out as a strangled sigh, and with his free hand, he dug into an impossible pocket in his swimsuit and collected a handful of crystals which he offered to Aimz.

"Blitheon, mun, I was only—" Aimz shut her mouth quickly, choosing instead to take the gem before flipping over the couch.

Xan set May down, folding himself over the back of the couch to think.

Xan, as it happens, was not great at thinking quietly.

"Okay, alright, so," he began. "Maybe you were right, Aimz."

"About the Earthling?"

"About the rope!"

"Oh."

"Yeah." He huffed, then returned to watching May. "We can't pull away from the rope, but can we cut it? Untie it? Burn it? Politely ask it to leave?"

"Sure, I'll just crawl onto a fin and climb down, gnaw it off with my teeth, and we'll be on our way." Aimz sat cross-legged in front of the couch. "That rope is strong enough to stop a Class 20 Racing Rocket. Not even *my* teeth could hold up to that, and you know what I've bitten through."

"I do." Xan groaned, pressing his face into the couch. If May were awake, she would be trying to think up another plan. Seeing as she wasn't, Xan had to. He was finding it difficult to think about anything more useful than the tiny paper hats people put on roasted turkey legs in Earth media and wondering what, exactly, their purpose was. His mouth, frustrated with his brain for not staying focused, began to think for itself. "It's not so much a rope, is it?" he asked. "More of a cable."

"I suppose." Aimz prodded May's still hand. "Why don't you wake her up?"

May's typically warm brown complexion was more of an ashy taupe now. Xan had noticed this but decided instead to contemplate the color taupe and whether or not the color he thought was taupe was the same color May saw when she saw taupe. He wished he could ask her.

With a whine, he tapped her on the shoulder. He knew little of alien biology, but he correctly guessed that the g-force had knocked her out, and he was worried.

"She's a heavy sleeper," Xan said.

Aimz also knew little of alien biology. However, she (incorrectly) guessed that a pulse was an important aspect of life the universe over. She smoothed a lock of pink hair away from her pointed ear and pressed it to May's chest.

"What is it?" Xan asked when Aimz's forehead crumpled.

"Her heart is racing! I'm surprised she hasn't exploded," Aimz said.

"Well at least it's going, right?" Xan laughed nervously. He bent a quizzical ear to her chest. "Ah, no, that's normal for her."

May's consciousness was steadily approaching now, having finally asked directions from a passing cloud of kindly steam in the thirty-second dimension.

It began to trickle back to her and settled in with a sigh of relief.

May shot up, her head thunking into Xan's.

"Ouch. Xan, what were you doing on my boobs?" She rubbed her forehead where a bump was forming.

"See! She's fine," Xan said. "May, settle a wager. What's taupe? No! Not that one, sorry. What do you think stopped us: a rope or a space bog?"

Aimz rolled her eyes, dropping her head back on the coffee table behind her. "It's a rope, Xan, you know that," she told the ceiling.

"What's a rope?" May asked.

"Blitheon, May, don't you have ropes on Earth? Like really thick string?" Xan said.

"No, I know what a rope is, I mean...never mind." She had noticed that the ship was moving, but the engines weren't on. "Why don't we pull away? The *Audacity* can break a rope."

"Not this one. Tried that," Xan said.

"Where's it taking us?"

"Back to New Tuhnt. Listen, don't get yourselves taken in by trying to help me. I'll figure something out, I usually do," Xan said, trying to put on a brave face but failing.

"Does 'figuring something out' usually involve destroying a planet?" Aimz dug.

After a long, loud silence, Xan said, "Not usually, no."

"It usually involves the probability modifier," May amended. "Which we haven't got."

"Ha! Oh Earthmun, you had a probability modifier? You're massively zuxed. This is going to be more entertainment than I've had in seasons. You know what happens when those things quit on you?"

"Finding out, aren't I?" Xan toppled into the couch beside May and covered his face with his hands.

"The *Audacity* has the Ultra-Ray-Super-Destroyers." May said, squinting into the middle distance. "No one can get on board without an anchor button, so Rap will have to climb up to the hatch to get in. We could, you know..."

"What, disintegrate an entire living human being with a massively overpowered laser blaster?" Xan asked, peeking through his fingers at her.

"I-erm-well-huh," she stammered, then bit her lip at him with a cautious shrug. It seemed the most logical plan, but she wasn't sure she could disintegrate someone. She would leave the ethics of it up to Xan. She liked to leave him with the ethical quandaries; she was the ideas person.

He started to provide an answer, but was interrupted when the *Audacity*'s fins dug into the oatmealy soil of New Tuhnt. The rocket tipped drunkenly as it tried to settle itself on horridly misaligned fins with nary a stabilizer firing.

May flung herself off the couch and started scrambling toward the console to turn on the stabilizers. The rocking of the ship knocked her to the floor, and, giving up, she curled her fingers into the shag carpet until the rocket stopped shaking.

At last it stilled, and May finished scrambling to the control loft.

On the planet below, two bipeds were quickly bipedaling toward them.

"I see them!" May aimed the *Audacity*'s Ultra-Ray-Super-Destroyers at the pair who looked, from that distance, like green plastic army men spray-painted silver. Aimz joined her at the console.

"Are you going to shoot them?" Aimz asked, excitement twinged by concern in her voice. She both deeply needed to see them blown to bits and was terrified she'd have to watch. She was a Tuhntian of dualities, and this was something she both loved and hated about herself.

May held a finger to the trigger, as if she were holding down a ribbon and waiting for someone else to tie a bow. As they got ever closer, she had to keep re-adjusting the crosshairs.

Was she going to shoot them? She chewed thoughtfully on the inside of her lip wondering what sort of person she was if she couldn't disintegrate two strangers to save her best friend, wondering what sort of person she was if she *could.*

Finally, Xan, their one-person ethics committee, joined them. "Alright so, considering the circumstances, my vote probably doesn't mean much, but I do know that blasting someone to bits because they're trying to arrest another someone for something they most certainly did is morally repugnant." He scrunched up his face. "Blitheon, I'm going to regret this but..." He moved May's hand from the trigger and disengaged the lasers.

May didn't mind.

Aimz didn't mind much.

"And poof," Aimz said with the help of an explosive hand gesture. "There goes our advantage. Are you enjoying that moral high ground? Nice view up there?" Aimz laughed. "Appreciate it while you can, because I don't think one good deed is going to fix the fuel-barrel fire that is your busted karma."

The Tuhntian concept of "troomaat" translates so precisely to the Earth concept of "karma" that it is often misunderstood in exactly the same way the Earth term is, which is why translation chips accept the colloquial use of both words. Troomaat, like karma, is neither good nor bad and cannot be "busted," however if troomaat COULD be busted, Xan's certainly was.

A thunk resonated in the ship as their pursuers mounted the ladder.

"Wormhole," May said, hopping down the control loft stairs two at a time.

"Really?" Xan squeaked. "The basement wormhole is unpredictable; we could end up absolutely anywhere as absolutely anything. We could be shredded! We could end up anywhere as shreds!"

The manual access hatch shuttered. The green plastic army men who were silver had reached it. The green plastic army men who were silver were trying to open it.

Aimz accompanied May to the intershoot. "That's a myth," she said. "Most wormholes are harmless. And fun! Come on, what could you lose?"

Xan groaned, but also tucked himself into the cramped intershoot. “I don’t know. A leg. I could lose a leg,” he said as they plummeted to the basement.

It was eerily silent, the air stale. The only hints to the wormhole’s physical existence were the slight distortion of light that seemingly came from nowhere pulling at its center and a gentle gravitational pull that made it slightly easier to walk toward it than away from it, like the smell of freshly baked goods drawing one into a bakery.

“Any idea where it comes out?” Aimz asked, trying to peer through to the other side.

“Not as such,” said Xan. “As far as I can tell, this side is stable and the other side moves around occasionally. It’s spat out junk from across the universe. We could end up in a different galaxy altogether.”

“They won’t find us there,” May said and, closing her eyes, leaped into the wormhole.

“Zuut, May, wait!” Xan followed her, and Aimz plunged in after him.

The wormhole enveloped them like a blanket made of everything that ever was. All of existence expanded and contracted around them, moving them on to their destination. It was extremely pleasant in an accepting-your-own-death sort of way.

CHAPTER FIFTEEN

It Was Not

May, Xan, and Aimz landed gracefully on top of a spray of rusty orange grass. The air was cool, but not cold, and smelled of wet coffee grounds and hot metal. Disoriented by the journey, May patted around the thick orange grass and tried to figure out why it was so oddly familiar.

No, not grass. Carpet. Shag carpet. May looked up.

The glowing orange walls of the *Audacity*'s living room greeted them. "Whew, thought I'd lost you lot for a minute there," the walls seemed to say. "It's sure great to have you back," they said. "By the by, who are these two large Tuhntians who've just broken in? Friends of yours?" the walls seemed to finish.

Two pairs of thick black boots and silver-shod legs stood like prison bars a foot from May's face.

"Zuxing useless wormhole," Xan grumbled to her left. He rolled onto his back and tried to remember a time when he was less pleased to see the *Audacity*'s living room than right now. It had been about two centuries.

"So this is him? Why is he in a swimsuit?" asked the deep, velvety, and as yet unnamed voice of the surveyor.

"They were at the beach, *obviously*. Scrawnier than you imagined, ain't he?" said Rap.

"We were at the beach." Xan said absently, considering whether or not it was worth the effort to stand up anymore.

"Ha!" Aimz laughed. "This is why probability modifiers were banned. Outrageously bad luck, right? What did that viral news blast call it...horrible repercussions?"

"Horrendous," May and Xan corrected her simultaneously.

"Right, horrendous. Guessing we're all arrested now." Aimz stood and thrust out her hands, wrists knocking together cheerily, waiting to be bound.

The surveyor's face cracked open with a wide, white smile. "Not yet. You've been invited to tea." It was among the top ten most threatening invitations to tea in the history of the universe.

"What do you mean we've been invited?" Xan said. Everyone else was standing now, and the peer pressure got to him, so he forced his legs underneath him and stood up as if the artificial gravity had been maxed out.

"To tea," the surveyor repeated. "It was a sort of-"

"Euphemism?" Aimz goaded.

"N-no, an invitation," said the surveyor. "Look, just come along. Sonan wants to see you. In her tearoom. For actual tea," he clarified.

"I think I'll pass," said May's mouth before her brain had time to stop it.

"You don't have a choice." Rap pulled a plasma pistol from his belt and aimed it at her. Xan scooped May behind himself and dodged behind Aimz who glanced over her shoulder at him with a judgmental eyebrow.

"What?" he whispered from behind her hair. "You like getting shot at, and May's all soft and fragile."

"Um," said May, offended.

"Everyone unpin it," said the surveyor. "Especially you, Rap. We've got the ship, they aren't going anywhere. Sorry about him." The surveyor held out a friendly hand to the conglomerate which was Aimz, Xan, and May, in that order, and Rap reluctantly holstered the pistol.

The surveyor introduced himself.

"What was that?" May asked, slipping out from behind Xan.

He repeated his untranslatable name.

"My translation chip must be acting up," she said. "It sounded like you said your name was Precious Butler."

Everything went silent. Even the gentle buzz of electricity coursing through the ship hushed in fear of what might happen next.

The closest English approximation for the surveyor's name was, in fact, Precious Butler. Unfortunately, the words "precious" and "butler" translated back in Tuhntian as "Sweet person who performs services" which is a rather nasty thing to call a prostitute in Tuhntian culture.

Precious Butler's reaction was impossible to decipher. Confusion and hurt played tug-of-war with his face and they were fairly well matched.

No one breathed. Except for May, who didn't see why she ought to stop.

At last, Aimz doubled over in a bursting guffaw which Xan tried to ignore but ended up catching like an infectious disease until the two of them were engaged in a chorus of laughter that only grew louder as they became more nervous about what would happen when they stopped.

May and Precious Butler stared at each other, May unable to understand why what she had said was funny, and Precious Butler unable to understand why she had said it.

To keep himself from laughing, Rap shot a blast from his plasma pistol into the ceiling.

The plasma blast zoomed into the wormhole which had inexplicably moved to the ceiling of the *Audacity* and exited the wormhole in the ship's basement where it disintegrated an unopened package of glow sticks.

Interesting, if somewhat unsatisfying, to note: in an alternate reality, May and Xan had found these glow sticks and held a two person rave. This meant that the glow sticks were not there to absorb the blast from the plasma pistol which instead hit a can of hairspray, causing an explosive fire which, when it reached the fuel line in the *Audacity,* obliterated everything within a hundred miles of the ship.

Not in this timeline, though. In this timeline the only casualty was the package of unopened glow sticks, which is still an awful waste, but not a series-ending tragedy.

The blast achieved the intended effect: everyone shut up.

"She's, uh," Xan said on the tails of dying laughter, "she's from Earth. Translation error," he explained to Precious Butler.

"What did I say?" May asked Xan, *sotto voce.*

"It's a derogatory term for a prostitute."

Her soul felt like a squashed grape. Not only had she accidentally insulted their captor, but Xan had been a prostitute until very recently and she had nothing against prostitution, so she would never have intentionally insulted anyone, but before she could apologize, Precious Butler held up a large, dark hand. "Don't worry about it. I better confiscate that, though." He looked pointedly at Aimz's belt.

"What?"

He sighed, unhooked her belt, and pulled a silver laser gun from a hidden pocket.

"You had that this whole time?" May asked.

Aimz looked equally surprised. "Oh, yeah! Ha, I forgot about that."

"You forgot about a seven-inch laser gun attached to your belt?"

"It's a Largish Bronda's Pocket Dimension belt. It removes the third dimension from anything you put in it, then restores it when you take it out. There's junk in there I haven't used in orbits. It's really hard to find something if it has no depth. How'd you know about it?"

"Weapons scan. I wouldn't mind, normally, but under these circumstances, I feel I ought to." He clipped the laser gun to his own belt and held out his hand. "And your anchors, please." He gave Rap a glance which either said, "I am shaken to my very core that someone who claims to be a professional fugitive recovery agent did not have the presence of mind to confiscate his prisoner's anchor button," or, perhaps more succinctly, "Idiot."

They dropped their anchor buttons into his hand and shuffled onto the teledisc, all five of them squishing together so they could teleport out without losing a limb.

On the planet's surface, May tried to take a deep breath, but the thin air on New Tuhnt made her lungs feel like an aluminum can being crushed in a trash compactor. She squinted away from the blinding light of New Tuhnt's sun which was unimpeded by the feeble atmosphere. A hulking mass of gray blobbed out part of the horizon, giving the impression of a beached whale.

Precious Butler and Rap led them toward it.

May blinked, and the ship had become some kind of wood-wind instrument, shivering like a heat wave.

"Xan?" she puffed, looking around. There were two moving shapes beside her now, one seemed to be a shopping cart filled with bags of oranges and cartons of orange juice. The other was a tall belt, flopping upright on its buckle.

The sky over the horizon burst into a million Skittles which fell like rain and bounced into the red-lipped mouths which now dotted the landscape.

Something picked her up—some sort of dark blue cactus was carrying her now—but she continued to move her legs as if she were walking. She tried to giggle at the cactus, because it had a pair of wandering googly eyes, but she could only wheeze amusedly.

The cactus brought her to the wood-wind instrument, hefted her up into it, and plunged her into a cold, blue hallway.

She filled her lungs—this time with velvety oxygen. Lights began to dance in front of her, then grew until they touched on images that were starting to make some semblance of sense.

The cactus reformed into Precious Butler, with googly eyes, who was now helping her stand.

"This one's a lightweight. What is she?" said Rap. But May heard, instead, "Thith one'th 63%8 a light j2$6. What is $ct7?"

"$ct7'th a 4%2hk, you thnoffle-eater. $ct7 needth othygen." It was Xan, but to May, the s's sounded like static and the words she did understand sounded far away.

"Are you ^8%3?"

May shook her head. She could hear a whirring like a tiny fan in her ear.

"Am I what?" she asked.

"Ith it your 87/m\df%sn?" He tapped the side of his head to indicate the translation chip.

"&9+9nfj, I'm 83~fh7 ct7 ^hdo-." Precious Butler put a lions-paw of a hand to her back. Whether it was there to keep her from running, or to help her stabilize, she wasn't sure.

"^82 your 769$5," Aimz told Xan.

"!@79 it," he hissed at her.

Each word made the translation chip in her head sizzle and pop like bacon in a frying pan; she wished everyone would shut up.

"%3nd^ can't 9>koi3??" Xan was starting to panic. Usually, when Xan panicked, May held it together; and when May panicked, Xan held it together. But since he was panicking about her and her inability to understand what anyone was saying, she was beginning to get pulled in by the undertow.

May shook her head again, lifting her shoulders. She had never heard Tuhntian spoken before; it had always been translated through the chip the *Peacemaker* had installed in her. It was both fluid and metallic, like a typewriter clacking underwater.

"Can you understand me?" she asked.

"&39n%," said Xan.

"Gestures, Xan!"

"Yes," he said in his strange accent, nodding his head.

Xan was a Tuhntian of few skills. Two, really. One involved glitter, and the other was linguistics. He had an honorary degree in the former and an official degree in the latter but, with the advent of the extremely popular, surprisingly affordable, and nearly infallible A'Viltrian Translation Chip, his degree, which was already practically useless, was now utterly useless.

Languages then, necessarily, had become a hobby. A hobby which he frequently indulged in during his long stay in Earth's orbit. All of the English he knew had been learned by holding a strong magnet to his translation chip and watching "I Love Lucy." Some of the English he knew was, as a result, Spanish.

"Well there's that," May said, then smiled as a thought occurred to her. "You know English?"

"A little." He had the pained look of wanting to say something else, but not having the words. He always had words. Just not English words. "With Lucy!" he added, satisfied.

"My chip must've shorted out. Do you think it'll turn back on?"

"Yo no se," he said.

"I...I don't speak Spanish." May said, wondering how much of the English he thought he knew was actually not.

"Zuut, &93 Bd%42 &jen%jf @gts$! ^hdf-"

"I don't speak Tuhntian!" She winced against the whirring of the chip trying to restart in her head. She tried to stop walking, but the hand on her back pressed her forward.

Xan reached for her hand and gave it a squeeze. "May, 7^g ^hn zxu%."

CHAPTER SIXTEEN

Hurtful Blurtings

Meant for drunk crew members or the occasional hitchhiker, the holding cell aboard the *Innocuous* wasn't designed with comfort in mind. The ceiling was inconveniently low, as if someone had taken the average height of a Tuhntian and subtracted one inch precisely.

The walls were gray aluminum and molded into a single, mattress-less bed on one side. Everything was gray. It was horrible. That, to Xan, was torture on its own. Gray walls.

The fourth wall of the cell was made of yellow laser light which was easily entered, but deadly to exit.

"Wow, couldn't think of anything more creative than this?" Aimz said, breaking the fourth wall as she strode through it.

"Aimz, don't go in there. We're not under arrest," May said. "We didn't do anything wrong," she looked pointedly at Xan, who had done something wrong.

Precious Butler smiled apologetically. "You're both accessories now. Please go in." What he meant to say was, "Go in before I make you go in."

May hadn't understood him, but she had understood his insistent hand at her back, pushing her into the light. She relented.

"Thanks," he said. "Be careful of the laser wall. If you try to exit from that side, you'll be fizzled."

"Fizzled?" Xan repeated.

"It's worse than it sounds." Rap leaned against the wall, twirling his plasma pistol in one hand. "Job's over then, isn't it? Got what you wanted?"

"Sure. You've officially paid me back for getting you a job with EnviroDev," Precious Butler said as they left together.

May perched on the shelf which thought it was a bed and rammed the heel of her palm against her temple.

"Say something?" she asked Xan who came to sit beside her.

"Can you understand me now?"

She winced as the chip zapped her. Again, she thwacked her temple.

"Okay, say something?" She anchored her gaze to a seam in the floor panels to stop herself from straining her eyeballs by trying to flip them around and look at the chip inside her head.

"Now?" Xan sighed.

She groaned. Obviously not.

"Well," Xan leaned back against the wall, making himself as comfortable as one could possibly be on a shelf, and closed his eyes, "at least we can—"

"Listen," May stopped searching the floor and turned to Xan. "Every time you speak Tuhntian, this thing zaps me. Could you please stop talking? I know it's a lot to ask for you," she said with more vitriol than she had intended.

Xan opened an eye at her to see if she was kidding; she wasn't. He winced. "Yes, dear," he said in English, with that strange Tuhntian/Spanish accent, because that's what Ricky would say whenever Lucy told him to do something.

May gave him a small smile. "Thanks," she said.

Aimz had busied herself with inspecting a corner of the cell, scraping at something on the floor with the edge of a thumbnail sized laserblade she had pulled from her pocket.

If anyone could fix a translation chip, it was Aimz.

Unfortunately, of the three in the cell, if anyone was totally uninterested in fixing the chip, it was also Aimz.

Xan decided he would *make* her interested. He started to tell May this, but stopped himself. He thought for a moment, then said, "I got an idea," in English, as clearly and English-y as he could. He patted May's knee and went to kneel beside Aimz.

"Whatcha doing there?" he asked, quietly, in Tuhntian.

"Science," she said, scraping.

"Right, well, uh, speaking of science...have you reset a translation chip before?" He looked back at May to make sure she wasn't trying to listen.

May was doing nothing of the sort. In fact, she had curled into herself, burying her head in her arms and thinking terribly hard about not letting this get to her. The more she thought about not letting it get to her, the more it seemed to get. Fear or anger or exhaustion, or likely a muddy swirl of all three, were eroding the pink beach in her head, and no coastline erosion mitigation plan had been proposed, much less voted on and put into action. The sea turtles would have nowhere to nest this year. The beach houses would flood. Her sanity would fall into the ocean.

Aimz continued to scrape at something. "Yeah, when I was a biotech intern," she said.

"Could you…do it…again now? I'll let you punch me as hard as you want if you fix it." Xan offered, trying desperately to be more interesting than whatever was on the floor.

Aimz stopped scraping and wiped the laserblade on her shorts. "It's in her head!" she shouted, but Xan slapped his hand over her mouth.

"Don't let her hear you!" he whispered. "It'll short out the chip again."

May couldn't hear anything over the sound of the ocean of fears she was fully immersed in, though.

Aimz licked his hand, which was to be expected, and he snatched it away. "Besides I don't need you to *let* me punch you. I can just do it." Then, to prove her point, she punched him in the arm, but there was no feeling behind it, and he only swayed sadly backward.

"Pleeeeeeeeeease?" He drew out the middle of the word, hoping to annoy her into helping, a strategy which had never worked on her before. "You're so much smarter and cooler and more useful than me," he said, employing flattery, a strategy which worked more frequently.

She clicked her tongue thoughtfully. "I am really cool," she said. "It's on her auditory cortex. Not exactly easy access. How am I supposed to get at it? Claw it out with my fingernails? If I had a scalpel, maybe. Or a skewer."

"Right, or a laserblade," said Xan. "Shame we don't have a laserblade, Aimz. Absolutely an absolute and horrible terrible shame we don't have access to a laserblade, don't you think?!"

"Oh this?" Aimz held up the laserblade between them. "I've been using this to scrape up skrum samples. I can't cut her head open with it. That's disgusting."

Xan groaned in frustration and leaned against the wall to think. He tried to put together a phrase in English. Something easy like, "Hey, mun, don't worry about it. Aimz is super smart, I have complete and utter confidence in her ability to fix your translation chip if we can locate something extremely sharp and relatively clean that you wouldn't mind having shoved in your head."

Lucy had never had the occasion to say "translation chip" or, as far as Xan could remember, "utter" or even "relatively."

He would have to paraphrase, a skill he had never gotten the hang of. Again, he sat on the shelf beside May, tapping her shoulder to let her know he was there and wanted her attention.

May twisted her face off her knees just enough to look at him.

"Figure it out?" her voice was muffled.

"Yes," he said, nodding to emphasize his meaning. "We," he gestured to Aimz and himself. "Need a..." He opened his mouth to say the word he wanted to say but couldn't find it. He looked over at Aimz, but it wasn't there. He searched the feebly glowing forcefield of the cell, but it wasn't there, either. Charades, he decided, were in order.

He chopped one hand into the other and made a sort of slicing motion at May. She squinted.

"Need a...?" she pressed.

Aimz, tired of watching him struggle, crawled over and brandished the laserblade, which Xan pointed to ecstatically.

"A laserblade?" May asked, her voice rising. "You mean to get to the chip?"

Xan chewed the inside of his lip until it started to bleed. He wanted to pretend he hadn't understood her, but he nodded, then quickly pinched two fingers together to indicate to her that it would just be a bit.

"Can't you use that one?" May asked.

Xan shook his head. “No, we can’t. It has…” he sighed, reached into a corner to scoop up some grimy dust with his finger and showed that to her.

“Dirt? It’s a laser! A laser can’t get dirty.”

“Is this so?” Xan seemed to ask Aimz with a raising of his eyebrow. Aimz pulled him awkwardly down to her level and whispered to him in Tuhntian, “Right, so, technically it’s not dirty per say, it’s just spiritually dirty. And it’s dull. Also I don’t want to do it.”

“Well I’m not going to do it!”

The chip, in a valiant attempt at translating the whispers, shorted and sent a jolt through May’s head that turned everything in her vision white.

“Please stop talking.” May held her head until the blinding white had faded to a fuzzy gray. She waited for the gray to clear, but it still floated around the edges of her sight.

“Oh, May, I’m sorry honey,” Xan said in English and reached out to her. In the absence of words of comfort, he was hoping perhaps a hug would work.

It did not.

“Stop,” May pushed him away. “Stop, okay?” She rubbed her eyes hard, the fuzzy gray frame around everything refused to clear. Xan looked enormously hurt and entirely too gray. He never looked gray. Blue, usually. Green, yes, he could be slightly green at times, but he was never, ever gray.

May realized that she was in something of a unique position. She could talk to him now, and he had to listen. He couldn’t deflect. He couldn’t start telling her about wonderful unusual things and distract her from her point. She had a captive and silent audience for the first time ever.

So she talked. The ocean of fear, anger, and exhaustion became choppy. The tide was coming in.

“You lie to me, Xan. All the time. You said we could visit Tuhnt, and then I find out it’s gone. You said you didn’t have a sister, but you do. You said you didn’t know why there was a bounty on you, but you knew! If you’d just told me why, we could’ve avoided this whole thing.”

Aimz was delighted by all this. It was the most entertaining thing she'd witnessed since the collapse of a neighboring loading dock at Yenucket two decades ago.

Xan looked like a salted slug.

No one spoke, and May decided to fill the silence. "If you'd told me all this earlier, I would've just stayed on Earth."

Xan didn't know enough English to reply. He didn't know enough Tuhntian to reply, and he knew a lot of Tuhntian. He probably could have made a jab at it in the lyrical and poetic ancient A'Viltrian, but she wouldn't have understood that, either.

It was then that May remembered why she made a point of letting him do most of the talking. She always knew exactly the worst thing she could say in any given situation and, if she talked too long, she was more likely to say it.

She shook her head and sloughed off the rest of the gray that had edged her vision. "Now I'm lying to you," she said with a tiny, testing smile which he did not return. "I hated living on Earth, I would've put up with anything to get away. And if I hadn't insisted we go to Rhea, you wouldn't have gotten caught."

Xan shrugged, saying nothing.

"I'm so fucking stubborn. How do you stand it?" she asked.

"I love—"

"You better finish that sentence with 'Lucy,'" May interrupted.

Xan brightened. "Lucy. Yes. I love Lucy. She's stubborn," he said in English.

The doors swished open and Precious Butler walked in, alone this time. "Sonan's ready for you," he said in Tuhntian, but May heard it in English.

"Hmm," May said. "Xan, say something."

"Babalu?"

"In Tuhntian," May corrected.

Xan shrunk, he had forgotten every single Tuhntian word he'd ever known.

"Personal lubricant," Aimz helped.

May grimaced and smiled at the same time. "Thanks, Aimz. I got that. It must have reset itself."

Xan smiled with his mouth closed; it was an odd look on him.

"You can talk again, Xan," May confirmed.

"I...I don't know what to say."

CHAPTER SEVENTEEN

Golden Waves of Deadly Grain

Aimz was the first through the heavy wooden doors to the tearoom. She had the unshakable sense that if she were to die in this cozy, brightly lit tearoom on this abandoned planet, she would immediately respawn back at her hovel on Yenuket Municipal Spaceport.

She began picking curiously at a doily before the smallest and sharpest of "ahems" stopped her.

It was the kind of ahem which you couldn't possibly trust. Halfway between an, 'Excuse me, what do you think you're doing?' and an, 'Excuse me, I have a cold I'm just now getting over.'

The "ahem" belonged to the most sophisticated piece of machinery Aimz had ever seen. Usually androids, even the precocious ones, had a tell of some kind. A joint that peeked open slightly to reveal a mess of wires or a rusted hinge in the jaw near the ear. The only tell that this android was not an organic being was that she had no life in her eyes. Whatever spark it took to separate a pair of marbles from living eyes just wasn't there.

Xan and May were the last to enter.

Xan had been expecting an enormous courtroom, each of the many chairs occupied by Tuhntian jurors who had argued beforehand about which of them wanted him dead most. He had expected jeering, things thrown at him perhaps, maybe even a vat of acid in which he would be dipped or perhaps a hungry, menacing beast in a cage to tear him apart.

He had not expected floral wallpaper and the tinkling of a tiny metal spoon against fancy dishes. He had not expected quite this much pink nor lace curtains, which waved gently in the drafty room. This was worse, actually. Acid vat he could've handled; the finger sandwiches put him off.

May hadn't expected anything. One hundred percent of her brain power was focused on figuring out precisely how much she had upset Xan, and what, rounded to three decimal places, she could do to fix it.

"Precious Butler, who are these two non-Xan entities, and why is he in a swimsuit?" Sonan's voice hadn't always sounded like two identical cassettes being played an eighth of a second apart, but she'd grown accustomed to a habitual afternoon tea, and a few thousand orbits of flooding her system with the beverage hadn't been kind to her electric throat.

"Why doesn't anyone just assume we were at the beach before this?" Xan asked no one in particular.

"We found these two with him," said Precious Butler.

"You are familiar by now with the full extent of the mission."

"Yeah. 'Arrest and imprison Xan under Carmnia of Trilly on Tuhnt.' But what if they helped?"

"The others are not important."

"What do you mean not important?" Aimz asked, reaching for a perfect white cube on the tiered cake stand.

"You're free to leave. Thank you and have a nice day," said Sonan.

"We are? Terrific! Twa-don!" Aimz yodeled, slipping out the door and onto her next adventure.

Everyone but Sonan watched the door shut behind her, felt the gust of wind it had made when it closed, and wondered where exactly she was off to.

"I'll be on the bridge, then. Buzz if you need me," Precious Butler told her and left as well, leaving May and Xan to face Sonan alone.

Sonan stirred her tea.

"Unknown entity, you may leave," she nodded at May.

"I don't have anywhere else to be," May said.

Sonan set down her teaspoon with an emotionless clink.

"Sit, Xan of Tuhnt and unknown entity. Would you like some tea, Xan of Tuhnt and unknown entity?" smiled the android as she tilted the tea pot over two empty cups. She had, in fact, "smiled" the question at them. Her lips hadn't moved.

They sat.

They did not take the tea.

"Drink," Sonan said, "it." And with a stiff hand, she slid the cups closer to them, then sipped her own tea in demonstration, her artificial throat sizzling as the liquid went down.

Xan caught May's eye and, as he reached for the cup, held up a finger to her, telling her to wait until he'd tried it first to be sure it was safe. At that, she resolutely snatched her cup and gulped half of the drink down. How dare he try to be chivalrous after what she had said?

Clearly, it had been sitting out for a while. It was cold and thin and...

"Oh." May looked into the half empty cup now as if the rest of it had suddenly turned into a chipmunk. "It's good," she said. Realizing then that she felt a tad dehydrated, she finished off the rest of it.

Sonan's smile shrunk slightly. Ever so slightly. Then Xan chugged what was in his own cup, thinking, reasonably, but incorrectly, that anything May could drink without dying wouldn't kill him either.

He set the empty cup down with a louder clank than he had intended and gave May a smile to congratulate them both on surviving teatime.

"Right, that's not bad at all. I thought you were trying to poison us! Silly, really. I mean, what reason would you have to poison May, right? Me, sure, but May's just a–."

"A what?" May prompted, wondering if she should be offended or not.

Sonan whirred gently.

"May, I..." He looked like it physically pained him to speak.

"Is anything the matter, Xan of Tuhnt?" Sonan said, sipping her tea with a re-invigorated smile and an electric *zzzttt*.

"Wha...?" Xan had the sense that something was decidedly the matter. It wasn't the decor, though that didn't help. It wasn't that May had unloaded all her anxieties and mistrust on him just moments ago, and he hadn't had a chance to process that yet. It was that...He froze.

"Xan, you look awful." May went clammy, wondering if she looked as awful as he did. Had Sonan actually poisoned them? But aside from fear creeping like thorny vines up the trellis of her back, she felt fine.

"May," Xan said from seemingly a long distance away. "You've been really on edge lately. You ever think about...vacation?" He was having trouble holding his head up and felt it best to let it loll against the back of the chair for now. The shadows in the room turned a bright, chalky pink, throwing off his depth perception.

Sonan hummed at May. "What are you, larvling? You're not Panseen, are you? A Panseen would be dead by now."

"Dead?" May jumped out of her chair, toppling it. "Xan, why did she say dead?" She tried to check Xan's vitals, realized she didn't know the first thing about Tuhntian baseline vitals, and settled with tapping his face urgently as he drifted off.

"The tea is made with barley. Admiral Warders and I used to drink it every evening. He had built up a tolerance to the poison. Truly a remarkable Tuhntian. I must say I'm impressed by your fortitude, unknown entity. What is your name?"

"Fuck!" May whispered at Xan who winced in response to what, to him, sounded like a shout.

"Fuck," repeated Sonan, cementing the new name into her memory banks. "And what are you, Fuck? Clearly your species has a significantly improved tolerance. Have you ever considered breeding?"

"What?" May turned to Sonan, so the android would feel the full brunt of her rage. "No! Gross. What did you do to him? Fix him now." She slammed her fist on the table, thinking perhaps she could intimidate the android. All that did was make the teacups clink on their saucers.

"Ssssss fine, mun, r'lax." Xan attempted to affect a cool, casual finger gun at her, but ended up looking like he was stroking an invisible fish. He stared at his hand, confused as to why he couldn't make a proper finger gun, then slumped forward onto the tea table.

"Hey, hey," May wriggled her arms under his and tried to coax him up. "Shit, you're heavy," she said under her breath. "Come on, Blueberry, stop lying to me. You're not fine."

"Yes, Xan, why don't you tell Fuck the truth?"

Xan tried to help May help him stand up, because clearly that's what she wanted him to do. Instead, they both tumbled in a cacophony of limbs and chair legs to the plush pink carpet. May crouched beside him and prepared to fight Sonan if she tried anything, but Sonan was quite happy sitting where she was.

"You want the truth?" said Xan. The cartoonish brightness of his zesty green eyes was dull, like a shut-off neon "open" sign in a closed storefront.

"Have I not made that abundantly clear?"

"Eugh." Xan closed his eyes and let his head roll to the side, but May tapped his face until he looked at her in annoyance.

"Hey, stay with me," she said. "What's going on?"

"Right," Xan sighed and looked at her. He smiled. "I did a really nice thing with your hair. It looks so good, May. Your hair is so nice." He couldn't keep his eyes open anymore, but he could reach up to gently pat the burrito-like puff of her bangs. She whined through a tightly held breath, like air escaping through a hole in a tire.

Sonan tsked. "I thought poisoning would be a more interesting start to a lifetime in prison. Don't you? It isn't much, of course. I don't have the authority to execute him, but this will keep him docile for a few seasons. You, Fuck, are free to come and go as you please."

"See? Not dying. You're free. Android thinks your name's Fuck which's hilarious. You got out your pent up," Xan wriggled his fingers vaguely at May as he tried to recall words, "*stuff* so you feel better. Everythin's great." He attempted a smile, but hit a dead end at a pained grimace and had to turn around.

"It's not great," May said. "I was wrong. I should've trusted you, and I feel horrible."

"*You* feel horrible?" he huffed, giving up trying to smile.

"Can you forgive me?"

"Right now?"

"HARD SHUTDOWN IMMINENT," Sonan interrupted.

"Shut up!" May shouted at the android. "Ever?" she asked Xan, noticeably gentler.

"Wait, that was weird. Wasn't it? What does she mean h-hard shutdown? Did she just—" He tried to sit up.

"Xan!"

"It can wait. She's off, let's scram!" He flung an arm around the leg of the nearest toppled chair and tried to climb to a standing position.

"WELCOME. ENTER USERNAME." Sonan sat up, her nose dripping with tea, her mouth still. "The Ancient and Powerful Goddess of Chaos," said Sonan with unmentionable cadence.

Xan and May both shivered. May out of fear, Xan because the poison had reached his appendix (useless to an Earthling, the appendix serves a vital purpose to the Tuhntian as it stores and sorts information that the brain can't be bothered with).

"ERROR. USERNAME TOO MANY CHARACTERS. ENTER USERNAME."

"Chaos," said the unmentionable voice.

CHAPTER EIGHTEEN

Meet Chute

Listay awoke, once again, amongst trash.

What horrible decisions had she made in life to deserve being thrown away twice? Slowly she got to her knees, not wanting to know what slippery thing she braced her hands against. She put a hand to her chest, trailing some sort of slime along with it.

She waited.

She squinted her eyes, focused.

She waited...there! Ha! A single heartbeat like one salvageable line in a phoned-in pop song. Alright, she could work with that.

"Oh, hey, you're alive! Wild stuff," said someone behind her. A pale Tuhntian with ultra-pink hair lounged on a throne of cardboard boxes which had once contained EnviroDev's signature dehydrated peat bricks. "I checked out your vitals a few minutes ago and you were super dead, so welcome back to corporeal existence! I'm Aimz."

Listay ran her tongue around her dry mouth. It tasted horrible. "General Listay," she said. "Perhaps just Listay, now. I assume death demotes you."

Aimz shrugged. "I don't see why it should, General. Status update: I've been digging around, and I found some great stuff in this trok! This funky bit of metal, an unusually long twist tie, and a plasma zapper."

To prove it, she twirled the zapper around her finger.

"Don't—" began Listay.

Zzzaapppp! The zapper interrupted her, creating a molten dent in the thick metal of the trash compactor wall.

"That's mine. I'll take it back now, please," Listay said, holding out her mechanical hand. Aimz tossed it to her and she caught it one-handed with a metallic clink. "Have you found anything that could get us to the hatch?" Listay pointed toward the door she had been tossed through. Earlier, Aimz had jumped through the same door of her own volition just to check out what kind of garbage one might find on a nearly abandoned Tuhntian warship. She hadn't been disappointed.

"Would you believe I found a completely intact, functional metal ladder with those nice rubber grips?" Aimz said.

"No, I wouldn't." Listay brushed herself off, pausing to inspect a number of scrapes and bruises on her organic arm and legs. She wasn't healing nearly as fast as she ought to. Death, she supposed, could do that to a person.

"Alright then, not gullible, and you know your own plasma zapper when you see it. No, to answer your question, I haven't found anything. But now that you're alive, I think we can reach the hatch. It's not that far. I'll stand on your shoulders then pull you up."

Listay shook her head and laughed darkly. "You'd probably just rip my arm off. I'm not sure what's holding me together, because by all accounts I shouldn't be alive."

"Naw," Aimz squelched happily through the muck toward her new friend. "You look good! Hardly a whiff of decomposition on you. Here, let's try a finger. Those are fragile, right? If a finger stays on, your arms will be fine. That's science." She held out a hand toward Listay.

Too exhausted to rebut, Listay offered her hand. Aimz yanked on Listay's pinky finger with a grin which morphed into a grimace when she felt it pop. "I think I pulled it from the socket, but it's still there."

"Ugh," Listay wiggled her finger painfully. "Yes, it's still there. Alright. We'll need somewhere stable to stand."

Aimz trudged back to her throne. "This is the spot. I'm not sinking in at all here. Come on, I'll let you go up first. Just don't leave me here, okay?"

Listay laughed. "Oh mun, you'd snap if I got on top of you. What do you weigh?"

"Eh, about four-thousand crawfish."

It's important to note that Carmnian Tuhntians weight units are based on a species of crawfish-like bottom feeder which was abundant on Tuhnt. Rheans, however, like the rest of the civilized universe, use metric. Listay quickly did the conversion in her head.

"Right. I'm not getting on top of you." Listay shimmied through the sludge and planted herself beside the cardboard throne.

Aimz grinned at her. "You say that now, but I bet I can convince you otherwise..."

The cry of every tortured voice in hell echoed around them as the trash compactor's ancient gears awoke. Death herself would pause to look behind her in concern if she were to hear it.

Listay and Aimz reflexively covered their ears, but it didn't help. This wasn't the kind of sound that was heard; it vibrated into their very bones. Mounds of trash clustered around them as the walls moved toward each other like reluctant, hormonal middle schoolers at a mandatory school dance.

"Go!" Listay shouted over the din.

Aimz didn't hear her, but went anyway. She scrambled up Listay, stood on her shoulders, and with a grunt that came straight out of "Night of the Living Dead", Listay hoisted Aimz up to the hatch.

The walls shivered as Aimz stabbed the bit of metal she had found into the crack between the doors and twisted it, wrenching open the hatch enough to slip her fingers through and peel the doors apart. She dragged herself out, rolled onto the cold metal floor of the hallway, nearly took a moment to catch her breath, remembered Listay, and then dragged herself back.

Their hands locked, and Listay tried to leverage herself up by scaling the wall, but she could barely bend her knees, not due to the rigor mortis, which was clearing up quickly, but to the compactor's compacting.

"The walls are too close. I can't get any traction!" Listay shouted, the refuse beginning to gnaw at her feet, trying to drag her under.

"I'll pull you up." Aimz quickly realized the sticking point, or rather the slipping point, in this plan as she braced her boots against the opening of the hatch. The general was drenched in chartreuse cave skrum.

Their slick fingers slid wildly as they tried to grip each other. Apart from the growling of the compactor and the pervasive stench of rot (which Listay sincerely hoped was coming primarily from the garbage and not her), it might have been sexy. Giving up, Aimz dove deeper and clutched the sturdy Lay-Flex™ straps on the shoulders of Listay's suit.

"Are you sure you're strong enough for this?" the general called up to her.

"Nope," Aimz said, grunting with effort. It had been a long time since she had last pulled someone from the maw of a trash compactor, and that someone had been a good thousand crawfish lighter than this gorgeous hunk of Rhean.

"Don't hurt yourself on my account. I'm already dead."

"Listen, General, I fancy myself something of a biologist, and you most definitely are not dead," she shouted over the cacophony. "Not sure you're alive per-say, but you're definitely not dead, so I'm pulling you out of the trash."

And with an obstinate battle-cry, she did.

Listay landed heavily atop her, but she didn't mind. Not a bit.

"Well that wasn't nearly as difficult as it could've been, what do you think?" Aimz said centimeters away from Listay's face.

If Listay had any blood to spare, she would have blushed. Instead, she withdrew, crawling to her knees to peer back into the compactor which had nearly taken her second (or was it her third?) life. The wretched noise had stopped, and the compactor began slowly opening back up to allow the far walls to compress.

"Hmm," Listay said, watching the walls recede. "We probably would have survived that, as long as we stayed above the trash line."

Aimz crawled beside her and also stared down into the compactor, absently rubbing away a stitch in her ribs. "Yeah, not a great way to kill someone, is it?" She grabbed the piece of metal she had used to open the hatch and stuck it in her belt.

"They thought I was dead already," Listay reminded her.

"Right." In the pale blue light of the hallway, Aimz could actually see Listay, not just the outline of muscles the size of foothills. Her mauve face was ashen, plump lips pale and chapped, her golden eyes cloudy, and her otherwise tidy locs caked in dirt. She was stunning. Aimz felt she had been staring for an inappropriate amount of time and thought about looking away.

"Why are you staring at me?"

"Oh was I still? Sorry." Aimz continued to stare. "Are you alright? I mean, do you want to talk about it? Death?" Carmnian Tuhntians usually have a warped sense of manners, but Aimz was really trying this time. There just isn't much precedent for talking to the undead.

"I would rather not. If I think about it too much, Death might realize she made a mistake and come after me." Listay's laugh was dry and quiet, like dirt being flung on a coffin.

"That's logical."

"Is it?"

"I don't know, actually. Can I hold your hand?" Aimz asked.

"Excuse me?"

"Your hand?"

"I…I'll allow it," said Listay, trying to regain her woefully surrendered sense of authority.

Aimz snatched her hand, scraping off a glob of the skrum with the back of her fingernail to study it in the light.

"What is that?"

"Skrum," Aimz said. "It's gotten into everything and it breeds like glotchburs. It's kinda…zuut what would Xan say?"

"Prolific?" Listay offered.

"That's the one! You know Xan?" Aimz licked the skrum from her fingers and bounced up, offering Listay a hand.

Listay shook her head. "No, but I surmised that that was the word you were looking for."

"Aw well, now that I've got backup, you want to help me find my zoup-nog brother and break him out of here?"

"Alright. If you help me destroy my ex-lover before she resets the universe." She took the offered hand and used it to leverage herself up.

"Easy."

"She's a chaos goddess," Listay clarified.

"Easy and blasphemous, good deal!"

CHAPTER NINETEEN

Smart Luck

The word "Chaos" brought back unpleasant memories that Xan and May were both fairly certain they had left behind in book one. A few seasons of exciting (but not exciting enough to write about) races and epic (but not epic enough to write about) wins had put Chaos firmly out of their minds. Besides, generally speaking, people don't come back from being exploded and sucked into a black hole.

Chaos wasn't exactly "people", though.

And while there's no such thing as coincidence, it was an astonishingly complex tangle of probability threads that led Chaos back into the lives of May and Xan. So complex that one might be tempted to call it a coincidence just to get out of an hour-long physics lecture and a crash course on the unique dangers of editing probability networks with, say, a probability modifier.

And so, practically speaking, it was a startling coincidence that Chaos was again before them.

"Hello Man, Xay. Fancy meeting you two here. I would call this a startling coincidence, but I know better than that. I know *everything.*" This last part was a lie. No one being, god or otherwise, knows everything. Knowing everything precludes being anything and being anything is rather silly if you know everything. It sounded impressive, though, and Chaos would say anything to sound impressive.

Xan wanted to say something, but his tongue felt fuzzy and he was rather preoccupied with that.

"What are you doing here? Why? How?" May ran through the questions which were pertinent to the situation.

"Plan Mistpillia," Chaos answered. "Unless...do you have the fish yet?"

"I thought you knew everything," May said.

"I do! I just don't know it in order, is all. Do you have it or not? I will know if you're lying."

"It's Mam and Xam," Xan muttered, finally getting a little control of his tongue back.

May sighed. "I don't have a fish, no."

"Xamaymy..." Xan said, frowning down at the floor.

"Of course you don't. This is Plan Mistpillia, then. The idea *was* to reset the Universe with the Sphere of Time, but I must admit, you've inspired me to enjoy myself a bit before I cease to be." Chaos had enlivened Sonan's mechanical eyes, giving her the appearance of a great white shark which had just gained sentience and was thrilled at the idea of its next meal.

Xan glared miserably up at her. If she was enjoying herself, he and May most certainly weren't. "May!" he said, pleased with himself. "And Man."

"Xan, not Man," May reminded him, quietly.

"Xan," he confirmed at Chaos.

"Silence! I shall impose whatever designations upon you I see fit! And then, I shall use the Sphere of Time to travel back in time to the moment we first met and erase your obnoxious existence before you have a chance to vex me. A touch of revenge never hurt any god." This statement was patently untrue and proved, once and for all, that Chaos was not and would never be omniscient. Revenge plots account for the spirit-death of nearly twenty immortals every orbit, followed closely by incense abuse and challenging the Void.

"On the *Peacemaker*?" Xan asked.

"Back in time?!" May echoed, wondering if she would have to add lying about time travel to her list of accusations against Xan.

"No, you slorpfignut. The *first* time I met you. Did you not know that was me? You really are as moronic as you look, aren't you? Don't answer that. It's been a delight seeing you in this wretched state, but I have work to do." She leaned forward slightly, her hands grasping the edge of the table as she prepared to stand.

Nothing happened.

She leaned back.

Again, she leaned forward to stand.

Again, nothing happened. Frustrating.

"Does this zuxing *thing* stand up?"

"Blitheon, I hope not," Xan said under his breath as he also attempted, and failed, to stand. May wasn't even working on standing up; she was working on coming to terms with the incredible coincidence of Chaos's appearance. Without a fourth-dimensional probability network map and an advanced degree in relative physics, this was an impossible task.

"I'll make it," Chaos said via Sonan's mouth, her voice crackling as it pushed through the damaged sound module.

The android had been built with the capability to stand and walk, she could even break into a light jog if the situation demanded it, though something in her programming told her that a brisk power-walk was usually more appropriate. But a good A'Viltrian style android like Sonan has an artificial brain which so perfectly emulates an organic one that it is nearly indistinguishable aside from the blinking lights and well-organized neural pathways. Because of this, androids are not only capable of emotional distress, they are also capable of developing neurosis.

Sonan, after suffering an artificial heartbreak so intense she had no other way to cope, had deleted every line of code related to her ability to stand and was, as a result, completely immobile from the waist down.

Chaos jolted through Sonan's wiry synapses and found the blank spot in her code where her ambulatory functions should have been. She scribbled something in its place. Something that really ought not have worked. Something so horrifically evil I must omit it for fear of making robotics engineers physically ill.

The android stood. Chaos made her smile, too.

The standing snapped May out of her existential conundrum. It didn't matter that it was impossible that Chaos was here, it had happened, and now it was *standing* and about to go muck around in time with the sole aim of making them miserable. May lunged across the tea table, grabbed the tea pot, and flung its contents at the possessed android. The light brown brew cascaded down her chest plate and dribbled rhythmically to the floor.

"Thank you for that. I thought she was a touch dusty," said Chaos, tilting the android's head down to watch the tea drip. She regarded May who was still folded over the table and Xan who could do little more than drape over the fallen chair. She shook her head at them. "It really was just dumb luck that kept you both alive, wasn't it?"

May could think of no clever comeback, but felt she ought to comeback anyway. "It was s-smart luck." And, because their good luck had been artificially generated with a highly advanced piece of engineering, she was right. But May had come to think of herself as the hero in her own story. The protagonist, as it were. Most people see themselves as the protagonist in their lives. However, she was really beginning to wonder what kind of horrible story she was in where the protagonist said things like "smart luck" and stumbled over their words when they said it.

Xan, conversely, hadn't thought of himself as the protagonist in his own story since university. Definitely not a hero. In fact, over the last two thousand orbits or so he had begun to suspect that he was, if not the villain, then some kind of halfwit side character whose only purpose was to create problems for whomever the hero actually was. Being poisoned to death with barley tea seemed to support this suspicion.

"Aw, yes, you are smart for a Tiny Human aren't you?" Chaos cooed pejoratively.

"At least I have a body," May said, standing to dust the crushed shortbread off her shirt.

"I can have any body I want." Chaos stepped into the tearoom's intershoot and disappeared.

May tried again to hoist Xan up; it was like trying to lift a three-hundred-pound anchor partially lodged in the soft silt at the bottom of an ocean and she eventually gave up.

"Xan, can you hear me?"

"Mpphhffff."

"Listen, I'm sorry about what I said."

"Smart luck?" he wheezed a laugh.

"No! Well yes. But mostly what I said about leaving you."

"Eh. I'd leave me, too."

"Let me apologize, okay? You're my best friend, my only friend, and I'm sorry."

"Really good best," said Xan, confusingly.

"Uh, yeah..." May agreed. "How do you feel?"

"Alrigh'," Xan shivered with the effort of looking at her again. "You? You drank stuff, too."

"I'm fine. Barley is pretty common on Earth. Get up. I have a plan. I'm going to stop Chaos from finding the Sphere of Time, then shut off Sonan and untether the *Audacity* so we can get back to work," May said and tried to get him to stand up again, but he wasn't being any help.

"Eugh, don't...You're not arrested, jus' me am. Also myth time. Untether the *Audacity* and go have fun, munny. Honey. Honey mun," he smiled and closed his eyes. "English and Tuhntian, workin' together."

"I won't have any fun without you," May said and then, through clenched teeth and with difficulty as she tugged on him she said, "Get up!"

"Stop, of the thing don't do."

"What?" May paused, worried her translation chip was busted again.

"It's don't fine worry managed the I did cannot. Beside, myth time!"

"Christ, you're not making sense. Alright, you stay here, I'm going to find Aimz."

Xan flopped onto the floor, affecting a masterful interpretation of a washed-up jellyfish. "Aimz, no, wrath. Wrath!" The tea had flooded a rather important corridor of his speech center.

"Wrath?" May sat back on her heels. "She's your sister. She has to help."

His answer was a sigh so heavy that May swayed back from the force of it.

"I'm going to find Aimz, and then Chaos, and then we'll untethered the *Audacity* and have fun. Together. I have to show you the haunted Big Mouth Billy Bass I found." She patted his shoulder fondly. "Hang in there."

"Zippy didn't of the chance market. Myth time," he told her seriously, but she was already gone.

CHAPTER TWENTY

Anchors

May went in search of help for Xan, she told herself. It seemed like Aimz knew things, perhaps she would be able to fix him. Maybe even Precious Butler (though she resolved not to ever call him by that name again) would be willing to help. He didn't seem cruel.

So yes, she went in search of help.

And if she, somehow, found her way back to the *Audacity* and was able to, somehow, untether the ship and, somehow, get the hell off that planet she would not do that. She'd never do that.

So why was she thinking about it?

"Fuck," she whispered to herself as she wandered the cold, dark hallways, thinking it appropriate now that Sonan had decided that was her name. "Don't you dare think about ditching him," she told herself.

She went through the plan again, trying to convince herself it was the best option. "Find someone to fix Xan, deal with Chaos and then Sonan, if she's still in there, and then untether the *Audacity* and find the closest restaurant to here," she told herself.

Or, perhaps, she could skip down to untethering the *Audacity* and finding the closest restaurant to here. She was starving, after all. Adrenaline alone wouldn't keep her going for long, and certainly wouldn't sustain her for a whole tussle with Chaos. Hunger tempted her to evil.

After she got some food, she'd come back and rescue Xan.

Even though he had turned out to be, like everyone else she'd ever known, a scam. He had stolen the ship, she reminded herself. And then lied to her for months about a whole host of things, mostly that he had stolen the ship.

Why was it so difficult to believe that?

She crossed her arms and set her jaw to keep it from chattering as she walked deeper into the darkness of the *Innocuous*'s corridors, hoping she wouldn't find Aimz before she decided if Xan was guilty or not.

Ditching people was in her DNA, anyway, she thought, coolly.

And then she felt bad about that, too.

Somehow, giving into the cold, angry thoughts, which she'd hoped would make her feel like an unfuckwithable badass, had just made her feel more alone and pitiful than she'd felt since she first got abducted.

Xan would never, ever ditch her. Not if he could help it, anyway. Despite what she knew about him now, she still believed that to her core. So what if he was a criminal? He was important to her, and she would be damned if she let him rot in a holding cell in this stupid, twisting tube-sock of a warship for the rest of his life.

Of course, that wouldn't be long if Chaos had her way.

No, she was done thinking. She would do whatever she could to save him, because life without him just didn't seem worth the trouble.

She set her mind to the task at hand: Find Aimz. Fix Xan. Maybe grab a snack from the tearoom. Hopefully the only poison in those cakes was gluten.

A corridor on the left had led to nothing. A corridor on the right had led to a locked door, and also nothing. That nothing had led to two locked doors and another corridor which led to an unlocked door which led to nothing.

She turned again.

To her surprise, there was a sign on the wall. To her further surprise, this sign was clear and helpful. It was a map which read 'Level 2' in blocky, confident letters in the upper left and displayed what looked like a cross-section of a sunfish with rather well-organized innards.

Labeled, even.

And smallish green dots. One blinked cheerily 'You Are Here!*' with the asterisk pointing to a note in the lower left which read, 'Claim may not apply to multidimensional and/or trans-spatial entities.'

The other dot was situated in the tearoom and read "Unknown".

The rest of the level was totally empty. All the rooms behind locked doors contained, according to the map, 'Nothing'.

Behind the wall that held the map, there was an intershoot, and May strolled confidently into it and took herself down to Level 1.

As the intershoot sent her down, another intershoot at the far end of the ship was going up. This intershoot carried two more smallish green dots which, if they had been entered into the *Innocuous*'s database, would've read "Aimz" and "General Listay". They exited on Level 2.

May arrived on Level 1 and found it empty, not a single dot apart from her own on the map.

She skipped Level 2 because it was, of course, empty, and went to Level 3 which was also empty, but something else on the map caught her attention.

"Contraband," May whispered. That sounded like the perfect place to find a weapon and a weapon sounded like the perfect thing for her, a fragile fleshy Earthling, to have on an alien planet with an ancient and unspeakable evil wandering around.

Xan could wait; May was tired of being unarmed. Seasons in space and the deadliest personal weapon she had got her mitts on had been a pocketknife. It was time for flashy, sci-fi heroics. At last.

She counted the doors on the map from where she was standing, just five doors away, she'd get her pick of fantastical alien weaponry.

And this door wasn't locked, either. It slid open with a light tap to its control panel.

The contraband storage facility was a great deal less exciting than May had envisioned. Rows of lockers gaped dustily open, revealing nothing but sticky grime. As it turns out, most contraband aboard a Tuhntian military vessel was food-based and had rotted away long ago. Not a single deadly weapon. However, the fourteenth locker she peered hopefully into gave her something to be hopeful about. Two black anchor buttons with softly glowing green indicator lights rested atop a particularly sticky brown stain which almost seemed to form a smile of recognition beneath them.

"Hello anchor buttons." She snapped them onto her suit.

CHAPTER TWENTY-ONE

The Limerick

Chaos stormed onto the bridge of the *Innocuous*.

Or at least, she tried to storm. While Chaos was an accomplished stormer, Sonan was not built to storm, and so together they effected a light drizzle onto the bridge of the *Innocuous*.

Precious Butler sat at the ship's hulking main computer, fiddling with what appeared to the untrained eye to be some sort of pixelated side-scrolling video game but was, in fact, a pixelated side-scrolling planetary environmental development analysis simulation. He dropped a simulated seed in a gridded section of the simulated planet of New Tuhnt. A green sprout popped hopefully up from a beige pixel, then wilted to a simulated 8-bit death knell. Precious Butler sighed deeply, shook his head, and marked off yet another section of his list. The avatar of Precious Butler trudged on through the simulated world, searching for a plot of land he hadn't tested yet.

"You!" crackled Chaos through Sonan's sound module.

Precious Butler, the aforementioned "you," simultaneously jumped, spun his hoverchair, and made a sound he didn't think his enormous vocal cords were capable of making.

"Sonan? What—" He blinked at her as she drizzled toward him, tried to think of a polite way of finishing his sentence, but decided instead to start over. "You're up," is what he chose.

"Yes. I had to do something unspeakably evil to this machine's ambulatory code, but I am up. Who are you?"

He gave her a perplexed half-smile. "You must've dropped something out of your memory database when you did that. I could take a look at that for you-"

"That's not necessary. Just tell me who you are."

Precious Butler shrugged. He knew the sooner he gave Sonan what she wanted, the sooner he could get back to work. "Precious Butler. I work for EnviroDev."

"EnviroDev? Interesting. Who are you to me?"

He waggled his head and lifted his broad shoulders. "I, uh, bring you tea, mostly. Dust you sometimes."

"You're not very good at it," Chaos said, brushing off her pink metal shoulders and leaning over the computer console.

Something, thought Precious Butler, was clearly amiss with Sonan. Perhaps one of her sanity relays had hit a snag. Would that have caused the unmentionable glow in her eyes, though?

"Done with Xan?" Precious Butler asked, trying to make conversation.

"No. I'm going to locate the Sphere of Time and use it to twist his personal timeline into shlormpaat—" Shlormpaat, for those of you who've never had the pleasure of tasting it, is an ancient Rhean snack food that is similar to a pretzel in every respect except that it's only ever twisted by the highest and holiest monks belonging to the Monastery of Paatnu the Hungry. "—and then I will shatter every temporal constant in the universe and paste the timeline back together in an order so hideously obscene Time Himself will evanesce, leaving His throne to the unutterable will of She Who Demands The Degradation Of All That Is, Was, And Is To Be. The will of Chaos!"

"Still on the Xan thing, then," said Precious Butler as he returned to scrolling across the simulated landscape of New Tuhnt.

"He's a menace," she said and pushed him aside with surprising strength. She accidentally ended the environmental development program he'd been running for nearly a season. The credits scrolled whitely across a black screen, then ended with the pixelated logo for the EnviroDev Corp before returning the viewscreen to a dismal display of the oatmealish nothingness surrounding them.

Precious Butler could only stand by and watch miserably as a season's worth of planetary development research was lost. With a sigh, he gave Sonan the attention she so clearly wanted.

“What have you done with Xan and the other one? Don’t tell me you just left them in the tearoom unattended.”

“I left them in the tearoom unattended,” Chaos said, pressing buttons and watching the screen and trying to figure out how the two correlated. “It doesn’t matter where Xan is. If I kill him when I should have, he will cease to exist.”

“Granted, but shouldn’t he be secured in the interim?” He watched her carefully.

Chaos continued to press buttons that did nothing, twisting Sonan’s limited facial expressions into something that looked more and more like frustration with every blip.

“I suppose I’ll go get them. Again.” He stood now, but Chaos seized his shoulder.

“Wait. First you will help me locate the Sphere of Time.”

Limericks, like ice cream, parking tickets, and Sunday afternoon listlessness (though the names of the days of the week change, the listlessness remains) are universal.

Chaos knew every limerick that had ever been written. She was limerick-omniscient, the worst possible kind of omniscience. She fiddled with Sonan’s sound module and found the setting she was after: a thick brogue.

“There once was a man from Rhea III,” she recited. “Who tickled his pickle all day / When asked where’s the sphere?’/ He replied, ‘well it’s here! / Just west of the Miteran Sea.’”

Precious Butler was used to Sonan saying nonsensical things, but she’d never done it in a brogue before.

“That’s nice,” he said, unsure of what she was hoping he would say.

“It is not nice, it is a clue,” Chaos growled. “Where is the Miteran Sea?”

“There aren’t any seas here, and this isn’t Rhea III. There is no Rhea III. I really think I ought to take a look at your head, Sonan.”

“This *was* Rhea III. Where *were* the seas?”

Precious Butler sighed. “There’s a patch of mineral-rich sediment half a beoop from here by MoonHopper.”

“Show me.”

He reached for the control panel's primary keyboard, but Chaos stood in his way. "I, uh, need to be right where you are."

"Oh, sorry." She moved, but not much.

"Don't worry about it. I'll just..." He contorted himself around her and fiddled with the buttons until an image of the planet's surface appeared onscreen. In the bottom corner, the *Innocuous* rested like a beached whale. "There it is," he said, pointing out what looked like a bruise on the planet's face.

"Take me there. And find me a really big gun."

Precious Butler shook his head. "Sonan, I've got a lot of work to re-do on my EnviroDev report before I head back to Rhea I, and you just left fugitives to wander the ship. I really ought to-"

She fixed him with an unmentionable glare.

"Fine, I'll get you a gun and the keys to the MoonHopper, but that's it. You can take yourself to the time thing."

Chaos was used to having lungs with which to huff at people when they didn't do as she asked. She was used to having powers which allowed her to turn people into sentient floral fainting couches. She was used to being able to step into different dimensions and out of them at will. Now, she struggled to get this body to produce a simulated groan.

"That will do," said Chaos.

CHAPTER TWENTY-TWO

Schrodinger's Zombie

Listay and Aimz exited the Level 2 intershoot at one end of the ship at precisely the moment May exited the opposite intershoot on her way to Level 1.

"How'd you die?" Aimz asked, finally, pushing past the tiny little part of her that told her not to ask that.

"Murdered," Listay grumbled, dark thoughts about what she'd say to Chaos when she saw her again beginning to file up and organize themselves in order of most to least professional.

"Cool," Aimz said, then, because Listay did not seem to agree that it was cool, she back tracked. "I mean, gnarly. That sounds gnarly."

"It was. Your brother, is he imprisoned here?"

"He sure is," Aimz said.

Listay paused, crossing her arms. "On what charges?"

"He stole the *Audacity*," she said, casually, still headed for the tearoom.

"Really? Well, I can't say I haven't done worse, and I need as many reinforcements as I can get to take down Chaos."

"Right, reinforcements," Aimz agreed, though she knew that, if anything, Xan was more of a liability, she had the good sense not to tell Listay that.

They approached the tearoom door slowly, Listay's plasma zapper drawn, Aimz wielding her twisted bit of metal. They paused at the door.

"Ready?" Aimz whispered.

Listay stood on the other side of the door. "I'll go first," she said.

"Why? I've got a weapon."

"This is my job. You're a biologist," Listay explained in a whisper.

"I'm an adventure biologist," Aimz corrected her.

"I've got a gun; I'm going first."

"If you gave me your gun, I would have a gun, too," said Aimz.

"If I gave you a gun, you would have a gun instead of me."

"Alright, you're right, you go." Aimz stepped aside, deciding watching Listay go first would probably be just as much fun as going first herself.

Listay burst through the double doors, Aimz close at her back. There was not, as they had expected, a possessed android. There wasn't much of anything. Just Xan sprawled on the carpet.

"Hey, what happened to you? Where's the android? We think she's possessed!" Aimz knelt at Xan's head. He winked up at her, the neon of his eyes flickering and buzzing.

"Oh. 'S 'oo," he managed with a vague smile, thinking that he'd very clearly said, "Oh. It's you." He was getting the hang of talking again. "Harris day?" he said as a means of asking where May was.

Listay sniffed the half-empty cup of cold tea. "Barley tea," she told Aimz. "Is this your brother? Looks like he just came from the beach."

"Preciminsice!" he confirmed, relieved that someone had finally just assumed the obvious.

"Yeah, that's Xan. What's left of him, at least. That's a shame, isn't it? Just reunited and you get killed on me. Don't mind if I donate your body to science, do you?" She pulled out the tiny laserblade and tried to decide if it was sharp enough for an impromptu autopsy.

"Sames op-ed," he slurred, telling Aimz to stop it. He swatted at her swimmingly. "Not homming do suck-sing eye. Unfortunabalmont." Which meant that he was not going to zuxing die, unfortunately.

"Whatever you say, mun."

"What did he say?" Listay asked, joining them on the dense floral carpet.

"Not a clue," Aimz shrugged. "Alright, Listy–"

"Listay," she corrected.

Aimz's cheeks flushed greenly. "I know, I was trying to give you a nickname."

Listay's eyebrows scrunched together, then unscrunched slowly. "I suppose that's alright, then."

Aimz smiled at Listay until Xan decided he'd had enough of the heady silence and broke it with a pitiful moan.

"I think I was going to ask if you had a plan or a girlfriend or something," said Aimz.

"Neither, sorry."

"Don't be sorry."

Listay blinked meaningfully at Aimz. "Your brother has just been poisoned by an android possessed by the Goddess of Chaos who is now loose on the planet looking for the Sphere of Time which she intends to use to end the universe as we know it. Let's take care of that, then we can flirt."

"Or we could do both!" Aimz said, hooking one arm under Xan's as Listay got his other arm.

"Mun, half a rotation ago I was dead. I'm not sure I'm ready for that level of multitasking just yet."

Aimz grunted as they hefted Xan into the chair.

"Xan," said Xan to Listay as she released him. "Of Tuhnt," he slurred, offering his hand to her in greeting. "Or used t' be of Tuhnt. Not now. Nice meeting of. When is May?"

His hand was still held aloft, so Listay cordially shook it, then gently pushed it down to his lap. "Pleasure meeting you as well. I wish it were under better circumstances."

"Ah, a circus stance," Xan nodded sagely. "May is and?"

"I thought she'd be with you. Did you lose her?" Aimz asked.

The light had flickered back on in Xan's eyes now, but he looked mortified. "Zuut, did I?"

"May is an Earthling he's been taking care of," Aimz told Listay. This made Xan laugh and that seemed to shake out more of his lexicon.

"Other way around. She left to do the, uh, the eyes searching thing."

"Looking?"

"Right. Went to do the looking searching find to found would have found did find was going to have found—"

"Get to the end of it," Aimz snapped.

Xan winced as his synapses dried out. "May went looking for you. Aimz, you, not uh...you who are..." He looked pointedly to Listay who didn't catch the hint that he'd missed her name. He sighed. "Xan," he said with a smile, holding out his hand to her.

"We did this already," Listay noted.

He nodded. "Yeah, but the one of who you are didn't be forthcoming."

"This is Listay, and I met her first, so don't try to seduce her."

"Really, Aimz, in the state of which I am now I don't have the lexical capacity to do seducorcery."

The double doors burst open and Listay raised her zapper, lamenting the five milliblip lag she seemed to be experiencing between her brain and her slowly re-knitting nervous system. Even half-dead, her reflexes were better than either of the Tuhntian's.

May rushed in, yelped her surprise at the zapper pointed at her face, shut the doors behind her, and pressed up against them.

"Shinestar!" Xan said. "No, Listay. Not to shoot her. Important."

"I know you," Listay said to May as she lowered the zapper. "You were kitchen staff on the *Peacemaker*, right?"

May nodded but did not recognize the Rhean who walked stiffly toward her. She'd been so gobsmacked by the abduction that introductions from that day hadn't stuck.

"Sorry, you are?"

"This is Listay. She's a bit dead, but I think she's getting better," Aimz said before Listay could get a sound out.

"Hello," she said, since the introduction part had been taken care of, and held out her dirt-encrusted robotic hand. May shook it, tentatively. "I gave you a llerke, remember?"

"Oh, yes," May said. "So, you're dead?" May asked

Listay shook her head noncommittally. "It's unclear. I am simultaneously dead and not dead."

May nodded. "I get that."

"You do?"

"Well...no. Sorry, I don't know why I said that. How's Xan?"

May peered around Listay to see Aimz plucking things from the tiered tea tray, licking them, then putting them back exactly where they had been. She was so hungry, she didn't care what had been licked.

"I found Aimz!" Xan said, sprawling bonelessly over the wicker chair. "You declared that it was you who were going to find Aimz, but ultimately it was I who did the finding of."

"Right, good work, Watson." May patted his head and he pulled her into a hug that made it clear he had forgotten she used her lungs to breathe.

"Can you help him?" May wheezed over the top of his head.

"In general? No. In this particular case, yeah probably," Aimz continued to lick items from the table as if she were spitefully claiming the entire spread for herself. "Need to find something alkaline to—aha!" she said as she licked something which resembled a peppermint that had been crushed with a mallet and reconstituted. She popped it into Xan's mouth and held his jaw shut. "Swallow, don't chew," she told him. With a scrunched look of annoyance, he obeyed, the sharply pointed thing fighting its way down his throat.

"Eugh, that was horrible." He growled, then, excitedly, "Horrible! My words are working again! Wait. I think. May, ask me to explain something Earthlings don't know about."

"Okay. Why is it that you and Aimz are the only two aliens I've ever seen with back-lit eyes? As David Attenborough."

He threw his head back and laughed. "Alright, okay, wait..." He cleared his throat and put on a serious face and British accent. "The Carmnians of the species have a curious genetic mutation. Tiny fibers in the vitreous gel of Carmnian eyes are coated in thousands of light-producing cells called photophores. This mutation is thought to be the result of Carmnia's diet of a bioluminescent genus of ophiocordyceps fungi and the souls of those who cross her—"

Aimz smacked his arm with the back of her hand. "You know Carmnia doesn't eat souls. She *curates* them." She laughed, which inspired Xan to laugh. May and Listay did not laugh. Neither of them knew who Carmnia was, much less why it was funny that she curated souls, but didn't eat them. They shared a shrug of solidarity.

Then, bringing an abrupt halt to the in-joke revelry, the clank of fast-approaching footsteps echoed down the hall.

"Anchor buttons," May informed everyone, opening her fist to reveal the two black disks she had rescued from contraband. The footsteps stopped. The doors creaked. May grabbed Xan's wrist, pulled him onto the teledisc, and told his BEAPER that she would very much like to be back aboard the *Audacity*.

Like a chain of plastic monkeys, May grabbed Xan, Xan grabbed Aimz, and Aimz grabbed Listay, and the teledisc whipped all four of them into a cloud of easily transportable atoms.

CHAPTER TWENTY-THREE

An Indeterminate Number of Porcelain Clown Figurines

Sorting atoms is tough. Sorting atoms without knowing how many people you're trying to sort them into is tougher, even for a sophisticated military grade teledisc.

Imagine you have a box full of an indeterminate number of porcelain clown figurines. Some hooligan drops your box from a fifty-story building and the figurines shatter into millions of pieces. Not knowing how many clown figurines you're meant to be gluing back together makes the process all the more difficult, and you're likely to buy new clown figurines rather than go to the trouble of reconstructing them.

The *Audacity*'s teledisc was about ready to buy new figurines.

Fortunately, May arrived intact and one hundred percent her. Xan and Aimz however, did not. The teledisc could suss Earthling DNA from Rhean, and Rhean DNA from Tuhntian, but the two Tuhntians had proved difficult.

Xan stumbled off the teledisc, clutching imaginary pearls around his neck. Something was very wrong.

Aimz, too, had noticed it and shuddered with revulsion.

Xan was the first to get himself under control enough to speak. "You took my tongue!" he accused Aimz who had done just that and was currently wringing his tongue through her teeth.

"Not intenthonally," she said with some difficulty, going cross eyed as she tried to see it. "You took ny tongue ptierthing."

Xan explored clicking his new tongue. Something metallic clanged against his teeth. He certainly had taken her tongue piercing.

May had the sense that they were forgetting something. "Turn off the teledisc!"

She tripped over herself getting to the teledisc plug which Xan was standing right in front of, preoccupied with his new tongue.

"You know, actually, I think I like it!" He flicked the metal bar against his teeth, enjoying the thwicking sound. "What do you think, May?" He brandished his new tongue jewelry at her.

May's cheek twitched. "I think we better stop Chaos." She tossed aside the plug with more force than was strictly necessary.

"Ah, she can't do any harm. Time travel doesn't exist. She's chasing after an old Tuhntian myth, and I say we leave her to it. There's got to be a way to get this tether off *Audy.*" Xan flopped over the back of the couch, his back cracking in a way that had either made it feel better or worse (it was worse, but he wouldn't know this until he tried to use it again.)

"May's right," Listay said, stepping down from the teledisc. "Chaos is an ancient being; if she believes the Sphere of Time exists, it likely does. She's older than the legends, so she'd know. If she finds it, she could reset the entire universe with her at the center. Any semblance of reason in the universe, any illusion of order, would cease to exist." This disturbed Listay on a personal level, and she paused, considering all the ramifications of such a thing. This new universe wouldn't have spreadsheets. Listay shuddered.

There are as many ways to react to stressful news as there are people to hear stressful news.

Xan was trying out a coping mechanism which relied on him pretending to be a wet blanket. Aimz preferred to sling a few insults at a problem. Listay had been dying lately when things got too stressful. May's cheek was twitching again.

"That sounds bad," May said. It was.

"And does this Chaos goddess know where the time ball is, or is this all hypothetical crosh-wopple?" Aimz asked. She leaned heavily on absolutely nothing. It was disconcerting—like there was an invisible counter behind her. "I mean, zuut, I wouldn't mind getting my hands on something like that. I can think of one or two things I'd like to change about the past." She shot a hurtful look at Xan who looked sufficiently hurt.

"Wait, wait," Xan said, swapping the wet blanket impression for one more akin to a bag of concrete which has been rained on and solidified. "If you go messing around with the past, won't it change the present?"

"Obviously," said Aimz. "That's the point. I mean," she barked a laugh, "I can imagine a million different better futures than this one. All of them involve you not destroying Tuhnt."

"I didn't destroy Tuhnt, Aimz!" He stood up now, eschewing all comparison to inanimate objects.

"Oh right mun, of course you didn't. You just doomed it. Just took off with the one piece of kit that could've saved Tuhnt. Why, though? Was it the orange? Because if you stole the *Audacity* because it was pretty, I swear on O'Zeno, I'm going to go at it with a can of blood-green paint and draw ovipositors all over the hull."

"I didn't have much—" he began, then paused, staring over her shoulder and into the past. "That was you! By Blitheon, you painted those ovipositors on Aunt Chrismillion's Minicraft." His face flipped far too quickly from anger to amusement.

Aimz choked back a chuckle. "I thought you knew it was me."

"You are Carmnia's larvae," Xan laughed.

"You're one to talk; you destroyed the planet! Classic Carmnian move."

Xan sat heavily on the couch again. "Yeah." He sighed.

"All we've got to do, I figure," Aimz crashed into the couch beside him, "is find the Sphere of Time and keep you from stealing the *Audacity* in the past. Easy?"

"We need to do it before Chaos does," May interjected, keeping a mental list of all the new questions she had for Xan which would have to wait.

Xan laughed. "Right, yeah, her idea was just to kill me before I could screw anything up. Good idea, actually." He inhaled as if he was about to say something, then paused, making everyone wait while he thought. "Why do we have to stop her?"

May thought she should reply to that, but she wasn't sure how to convince him he deserved to live, and Listay jumped in.

"We must keep Chaos from getting to the Sphere of Time and ending this universe as we know it. Preferably, before she kills any of us," Listay said. "Again," she added, looking curiously at her own pale, dry hand.

"Well, I'm with you!" Aimz grinned. "This is the most fun I've had in decades."

"Good, we could use your..." Listay paused as Aimz stared at her, waiting. "Sharp bit of metal," she finished. Aimz only looked a little disappointed. "We can take the Gremlin. It should still have some fuel, if we're lucky."

May cringed loudly at the mention of luck.

"And if we aren't lucky?" May asked. "What's our back up plan?"

Aimz jumped up. "StarTaxi!" she said, as if it were obvious.

"You parked it beneath the *Audacity*," May reminded her.

Aimz blinked, smiled, then finally had the decency to look confused.

"You parked it under a rocket ship, and then we took off. It's been incinerated."

"Oh, for Blitheon's sake. That was a zuxing rental," she said, more to herself, slapping her own thigh. Then, to the room, "Well, we've got to find the Sphere of Time now. I can't afford to replace that thing."

Listay stared at Aimz with perplexed wonderment, her heartbeat, still frighteningly slow, sped up by a quarter beat per beoop whenever she looked at her. She shook her head and started up the stairs to the control panel, admonishing herself for yet again not being able to contain her inner romantic.

She flicked on the viewscreen and changed the camera angle until she could see the enormous white hull of the *Innocuous* and the single MoonHopper still parked beside it.

If she had been able to see inside this MoonHopper, she would've discovered Chaos cursing in a dead language at the MoonHopper's console for not being user friendly. The dead language didn't have a concept of user friendly-ness, and so she jumped from language to language like a mosquito sucking indiscriminately from whatever was handy. It was a shame Xan couldn't hear it, because he would have appreciated her lexical dexterity. It was a shame Aimz couldn't hear it, because she would have appreciated the creative use of swears.

"No one has left the ship yet. You have weapons on board, right?" Listay asked over her shoulder. "I would suggest you go get them. We need to be ready to move out as soon as Chaos does."

Aimz pulled the twisted bit of metal from her infinite belt, a brightly colored candy wrapper impaled on one end. "I've got this!"

"I have a novelty pocketknife," May said. "And we have a utility room. We could chuck power tools at her."

She pulled back the orange wall to reveal the utility room, which might more accurately be called a utility closet, lined with tools May only knew from the ship's manual. She slipped inside. None of the tools were particularly heavy, a credit to Tuhntian technology, but a hindrance to her plan.

Xan scrunched into the closet to look with her as she dismounted a handheld device with an obsolete gray screen.

"What's that?" he asked.

"It's a diagnostic thingy. I've never had to use it though; the viewscreen has a digital version."

"Try it out! Diagnose me." He thrust his arms out to the sides, as far as the space would allow, and looked forward seriously.

The part of May's brain which frantically tapped its watch at her shut off for a blip. She switched the diagnostic thingy on and scanned him with the green light which emanated from it.

"Huh, says here you've got a clothing malfunction. You need a transplant." She nodded gravely to his shiny yellow swimsuit.

"It's right! I'm officially a criminal on the run now, so it's got to be something edgy. I'm thinking shoulder extenders, all black, tasteful ruffles."

"Nothing too tasteful." She handed him the diagnostic device. "That's the heaviest thing in here. How's your aim?"

"It could be better."

"Could it be worse?"

"No," he said.

"I see. Just talk her to death, okay?" May said, picking up a fishbowl helmet and strapping the attached oxygen pack to her back. The remaining tools were a thin metal handle with a stubby green light at its end which would do about as much damage as a lit cigarette, an extremely unsafe safety pin, and a jar of something which wibbled. A green light flashed in her peripheral vision, distracting her from her fruitless search.

Xan tapped the diagnostic screen. “Says here that you’re still mad at me,” he said, matter-of-factly.

“You stole the *Audacity*. We’ve been racing in a stolen ship. Why didn’t you tell me?” she asked, considering a stained pin cushion before pitching it to the floor. The pin cushion hadn’t deserved that.

It was a good question. A question Xan had been playing like a favorite cassette tape in the dusty old walkman of his mind since before walkmans were invented.

“I didn’t think it would come up,” he said. “I mean, I hoped it wouldn’t.”

May gave him a withering look.

“Alright, okay, honestly? Honestly I just wanted to be done with it. I thought maybe life could get back to normal when I met you. Better than normal, even.”

“You didn’t pay the piper,” May said, sitting on the counter.

“I didn’t?” Xan asked, looking around for the pipes that didn’t get paid for. “Which piper? Did we hire a piper?”

May shook her head. “Another English expression for you,” she said. “I thought my life was getting better than normal, too. You know, if you had told me, I probably would’ve gotten over it.”

“Yeah?”

“How did it happen, though? Were you just a totally different person back then?”

He ground his teeth and made a face like he was trying really hard to stuff a pair of pants into an over-full luggage case, then at last zipped it up and sat on it to be sure it would stay closed.

“Nope, I was just as cowardly and zoup-nogged as I am today!” He went to the coffee maker just outside the utility room and began shoveling grounds into the filter with a ferocity that suggested that he was imagining burying himself beneath the course grounds. "Let's go confront Chaos. Again. And try not to get killed, again. I don't think it was nearly as harrowing as it could've been the first time we did this," he said, modifying his intonation so that May would know that it *had* been harrowing enough the first time.

May leaned on the counter, the fishbowl under her arm, watching as he filled the filter one aggressive scoop at a time, then continuing to pile grounds on until they began to tumble onto the orange laminate. She thought it best not to stop him.

"Hey, I know this sucks," she offered.

"Sucks?" he repeated, still shoveling coffee.

"It's..." May needed to use older Earth sayings around him. She tried to think of something Lucy might have said. "It's a bummer."

"Oh, right. Yeah, it is."

"We gotta do it, though."

Xan finally realized the filter was nicely full and plopped it into the coffee maker, using his finger to dust off the extra grounds around the rim. "Yep." He flicked it on.

"I'll miss you," May said.

He shook his head. "I'm not saying I know anything about time travel, because it doesn't exist, but if it *does* exist and we *do* go back and stop me from taking the *Audacity,* we'll never have met each other." The coffee splattered into the carafe between them, and he stared at the brown stream, willing it to hurry up.

May stared at it, too. She'd be back working at Sonic. Maybe this time she wouldn't get abducted, maybe she would. There were a million other eventualities to account for. If she got abducted, there would be no *Audacity* to pull her out of open space.

"But I'll miss you, anyway," Xan said as the coffee stream sputtered to a stop. He gulped down half the carafe, not bothering to pour it into a mug. "It's a mighty good thing that we won't remember how terrible this feels, right?" He handed her the carafe which she took and drank from with the reverence of a sacred ritual.

"Good thing," May said hoarsely, having burned her throat with the scalding coffee. She let her eyes rest on the orange shag carpet, stewing in the silence until it was broken by an obnoxious clicking noise.

"Xan," she said, too melancholy to summon enough energy to tear her eyes away from the carpet, "are you playing with the tongue ring?"

"Yeah, sorry." The clicking stopped.

The living room was densely quiet now, Listay keeping watch on the MoonHopper, Aimz testing the integrity of the sharp bit of metal by carving her name into the coffee table, and Xan and May partaking in a final carafe of coffee together, sadly enjoying each other's company.

It was all quite somber and pensive until Listay wrenched away the comfortable silence. "She's gone, let's move!"

May jumped, startled to find that she was not, in fact, swimming in a warm pool of orange carpet. At some point, she and Xan had started leaning more on each other than the counter. They had forgotten to change.

"Ready?" she asked him, fitting the fishbowl over her head with a thloop, pushing her hair up into it, and sealing the opening around her neck.

"Absolutely not in the slightest. You?" He finished the coffee and placed it neatly back on the hot plate.

Aimz leapt from the couch and grabbed their hands, bouncing on her heels as if they were about to take her to a candy store.

"I'm ready. We're going to find a time ball!" She literally dragged Xan and May to the teledisc, but not figuratively. Figuratively, they were still floating in a melancholic orange pool.

CHAPTER TWENTY-FOUR

Earthquake

The surface of the planet welcomed May, Aimz, Listay, and Xan with a grossly tepid wind. It was neither hot nor cold, just slightly too warm for comfort, like someone had peed in the public pool that was the atmosphere.

All that remained of the MoonHopper were two toasty scorch marks in the dirt and a cloud of residual affront left by Chaos's ancient curse words.

The Gremlin was exactly where Listay had left it, and as they approached, the tortured machine pinged desperately as its engine cooled. "No," it said, "let me die, I beg of you."

Listay did not speak AMC Gremlin and, as such, hadn't understood its plea. She ran to the pilot's door, grabbed the handle, and pulled. The weakened door handle snapped off in her hand. Chucking it aside, she flew to the passenger's door, grabbed the handle, and pulled. That handle also snapped off. Chucking it aside, she went to the hatchback and pried it open, crawling into the front seat. May squeezed into the passenger's side, leaving Xan and Aimz to stuff into the rear and shut the hatchback behind them.

"Right, General, after that MoonHopper! This is fun," Aimz said to Xan, the seat squeaking as she fidgeted. The noise Xan made in response was so unsure, so noncommittal, that it is impossible to duplicate it here phonetically. But I will try.

"Mmmnnnnhhunggmmph," said Xan, leaning against the window miserably.

In the front of the car, Listay flicked a switch which was meant to reignite the burnt-out pilot light.

On and off, on and off.

Bupkis.

"Parking brake?" Xan said, his face appearing suddenly over May's left shoulder.

"It's only ever the parking brake when you're driving." May pushed his face back, like a dog she was directing away from a plate of food. "Let me try, switch with me." They shimmied into each other's seats, May contorting herself around Listay, thwacking her knee on the shifter, and gaining her tenth bruise thus far. There would be more.

The dashboard was a field of stripped wires, twisted together by hand, and laid out in shockingly neat lines, as if someone had scared them into tidiness. The wires didn't matter, though. The pilot light didn't matter, either.

At its core, the AMC Gremlin was still just that: an AMC Gremlin. And May, with this in mind, turned the key which had been left in the ignition and twisted it to life. Hands grasped her shoulders and she jumped.

"And the Earthmun saves the mission. Tint me surprised," Aimz said behind her.

Equal parts flattered and annoyed, May rolled her shoulders to dislodge Aimz's hands and shifted the car into drive.

The Gremlin's belts squealed a litany of complaints regarding their age, the dry air on New Tuhnt, and the fine dusting of sand which coated every surface, interior and exterior, of the car. May was an unsympathetic ear and forced the Gremlin to lurch forward out of the divot it had made in the sand and chase after Chaos.

She convinced the car to reach a speed it had never in its life attained on land: ninety-eight miles per hour. It hated that, vibrating painfully until she brought it down to ninety, which it would tolerate, but only just.

Sandy, dry air streamed in from the open window and May was grateful for the fishbowl, because the three highly evolved humanoid aliens who didn't need as much oxygen as she did couldn't keep their eyes open without having them sandblasted.

"Do you-pfft," Aimz spat a mouthful of sand, "see anything?"

"Nothing," May said, and then was immediately proven wrong as something appeared over the dusty horizon. It wasn't a MoonHopper, though. It was a billboard with one metal leg crunched beneath it, tilting like a flamingo with vertigo.

"Water Where There Ought Not Be, the Logic-Defying Amusement Pool," May read as they barreled past it. There were more. Hundreds of billboards, some face-down in the dirt, partially buried, others leaning exhaustedly back, their sun faded advertisements impossible to read. Occasionally, May caught one which was legible.

"Visit the Pontoosa Adventure Hole," she read as she drove past another sign, this one with a large green arrow hooking around its rectangular frame.

"There's no zuxing way. Pontoosa Adventure Hole?" Xan shielded his eyes and tried to see what was zooming past them. "All those ancient limericks we studied in the literary history of the universe were supposed to be myths! Aimz, you remember them?"

"Must've had that class with Yve, because I remember nothing. What kind of zoup-nog memorizes limericks when someone like her is in the seat over?"

"I see it," May said, interrupting some important reminiscing and pointing to a massive billboard in the distance.

Listay leaned forward and squinted at it. "Don't Miss The Sphere of Time," she read from the enormous billboard they were approaching, May slowed the Gremlin to let her finish. "Ancient A'Viltrian Wonder Lost to the Ages Until Now. Right ahead."

May attempted to step on it. Attempted to coax the Gremlin to its theoretical top speed of ninety-eight miles per hour. It rattled with the ferocity of an earthquake motion simulator. She slowed down, but the rattle got worse. She braked. A sign which said something about a Hooflatoo Bone Sculpture Museum crumbled in front of them and flopped on the dusty ground like a waterless fish.

The car, May realized, had not been rattling like it was in an earthquake motion simulator. It had been rattling because of a very real earthquake.

Suggestions chorused around her. Listay tried to convince her to drive, Xan mentioned something about seeking shelter, Aimz wanted to get out and explore the shivering landscape.

"Everyone shut up!" she shouted at last, choosing to drive carefully around the fallen billboard and get up to speed again, despite the shaking. If the Gremlin shook apart, it shook apart.

It did not shake apart, but the ground did, swallowing the Gremlin whole.

* * *

The AMC Gremlin, at last, had come to the end of its journey. It smoked gently, badly crushed, tires splayed out beneath it like the legs of a newborn giraffe. It had brought them to an underground cavern, surprisingly cold and damp and smelling of wood rot and rust. Clusters of dimly glowing fungus illuminated the cavern, glistening on the shattered windows.

To her delight, Listay was still alive. To her dismay, the Gremlin was not and would never be again. "Is anyone injured?" She rammed her shoulder against the door until it popped open so she could survey the area. No one answered, but everyone was moving, so she assumed they were fine.

Aimz peered out at the cavern with bated interest. Not bated for long, though, as she crawled over the front seats and used Listay as leverage to extract herself from the car. "That was zuxing terrific," Aimz said without a hint of irony.

"Yep, zuxing terrific," Xan agreed with a great deal of irony. "May?"

"Terrific," she said with an inflection which could have gone either way. She shook a shower of glass from her hair. The fishbowl had shattered and, though the adrenaline helped dull the pain, she felt blood dripping down her face.

The door refused to open, so May dragged herself from the broken window of the car, landing on a creaking wooden boardwalk. The dark wood panels had splintered in some places under the Gremlin, so May, not keen on finding out what exactly was under the boardwalk, scrambled off it and onto the softly luminescent blue concrete.

The alcove they had landed in stretched impressively out in every direction and was clearly meant to aid the shuffling of hundreds of people from one place to another. From the roof of the cave hung a marquee sign, supported by two massive cables, reflective sequins glimmering with points of light which told them they were in a place called Ponstoosa.

May removed what was left of her helmet, and Xan undertook the arduous task of combing the glass shards out of her thick hair. Oxygen, she assumed, was precious, so she held her breath and waited for the hallucinations to set in.

“Hey, mun, you know you can breathe, right?” he asked.

“You sure?” she whispered using as little breath as possible.

“Yeah! Tons of oxygen down here. Almost too much. There are highly suspicious levels of oxygen in this pit.” He tapped his BEAPER as if the readings might change at any moment.

“Cavern,” corrected Aimz from the other side of the Gremlin, snapping samples of the glowing fungi off the boardwalk and pocketing them.

“Same thing, isn’t it?”

“Nope.”

Xan shrugged; May breathed.

“Strange,” said Listay. “Chaos was right. This planet used to be Rhea III.” Her voice echoed in the suspiciously oxygen-rich air.

“What makes you think that?” May tried not to look like she was limping as she walked toward Aimz and Listay who had gathered in the middle of the cavern around a fixture that had at one time been a fountain. Xan wrapped an arm around her, trying not to look like he was helping her walk.

“The historical marker on this fountain says the Pontoosa Adventure Hole was built over the ruins of ancient Rhea III where they discovered the legendary A’Viltrian Sphere of Time,” said Listay.

Beyond the fountain, May could just make out a large, marbled facade with golden friezes carved along the top. A beam of light shone through the crack in the surface and highlighted a phrase carved into the entablature of the underground building.

“‘The Arch of Time, Through Which Lies the Museum of Time, The Gift Shop of Time, the Experience of Time, and Therein The Mysterious and Powerful Sphere of Time,’” May read out loud.

The ground shifted.

“Aftershock,” Listay explained, but she was wrong. “Let’s continue on foot.”

Before they had a chance to agree, the concrete exploded.

CHAPTER TWENTY-FIVE

The Wyrntensil

The wyrntensil is a heretofore assumed mythical creature with five hundred tiny legs peeking out from a tube-like body, five hundred blind eyes lining its ridged back, five hundred sharp teeth at one end of the tube, and one merciless heart smack-dab in the center.

Little is known of the wyrntensil, because most people who are unlucky enough to meet one end up finding out exactly how sharp all five hundred of its teeth are.

"Run!" shouted Listay. She didn't have to, though, as everyone had already scrambled.

She unclipped her plasma zapper and sunk a few shots into the beast's maw to distract it, but the blast bounced off of one of the thing's many teeth and hit the hanging marquee sign which sliced into the concrete, cutting her and Aimz off from the beast and, to her frustration, from the others.

May and Xan clambered into the trunk of the Gremlin. May, because she knew she couldn't outrun the thing. Xan, because his first reaction was usually to do whatever May did.

Reaching down her t-shirt, she fished the sweaty pocketknife from between her breasts and flicked it open. Tried to flick it open, at least. In the end, she pried the blade from its wonky plastic casing with her teeth.

"That thing ate plasma! I doubt a pocketknife will have much effect," Xan whispered, as if the creature might overhear. It did not have five hundred ears. It had no ears, actually, so they could talk as loud as they wanted without any consequences.

"It has to come in handy eventually," she said, testing the point with her finger. There was no point. The pocketknife had no point at all.

"Does it?"

"I would think."

The creature gave a record-scratch shriek and slithered around the car, rolling onto its side, because its eyes were all inconveniently located on its back.

"You've got a plan, right?" Xan asked, scooching closer.

May did not have a plan, but she was decent at thinking on her toes, and as she collected a list of their current assets, something was beginning to come to her.

"Check the glove box for jumper cables. I'm going to try to turn the engine on," May said, scrambling into the front seat.

"Check the what for whom?"

"Never mind. *You* try to turn the engine on, and *I'll* check the glove box for jumper cables. Got it?"

"Got it." Xan twisted the key in the ignition. No sound could be heard but the squelching of the wyrntensil circling its prey, looking for an opportunity to strike. He continued twisting anyway.

May pulled a length of red and black cables from the glove box and held them out triumphantly. "Not working?"

"I think this was its last life."

"It's fine. Harvey Foster once started a bonfire with his car battery when we were on a camping trip, and he didn't have the car on at the time, so I think I can make it work."

"Harvey Foster?" Xan asked with a smile, forgetting the key. "Who's Harvey Foster?" It was rare that May talked about life on Earth. And for good reason, too. There wasn't much about Earth she wanted to remember, but Xan tried to encourage it.

"No one," she said, checking the cables to be sure they were intact.

The wyrntensil was becoming restless. It smacked the car, flinging it onto its side.

"Right. You're getting out of this one for now because we're in mortal danger," said Xan, "but I've got to know who Harvey Foster was!"

"I'll tell you later. Can you pop the hood?" May said, climbing up toward the passenger door which was now the ceiling. "I'm going to hook these up to the battery."

"Then what?" he said, searching for the hood release.

May ripped into the denim seat covering and extracted a chunk of stiff yellow foam which, she hoped, was highly flammable. "Fire bomb?"

"You think that'll work?" Xan asked, finding the lever under the steering wheel and pulling on it several times before he heard the satisfying click of the hood unlocking.

"Probably not."

"But it would be cool," he said.

"Exactly." May handed Xan the pocketknife (which she had not used to open the seat covering, because the stitching was already so weak) and pulled herself out of the car window. "Cover me?"

"Um," Xan stared at the tiny, dull pocketknife. But she was already out of the car. "Umm!" He repeated, louder, but he had no choice now; he followed her out of the window and held the knife in front of him as he straddled the car door.

The wyrntensil wrapped massively around them, an impenetrable wall of thick gray hide that seemed to have no beginning and no end. Which was fortunate because if Xan had seen the beginning bit of the wyrntensil, he would not have faced it with just a pocketknife protecting him.

May propped open what was left of the crushed hood and clamped the cables to the battery terminals, then held the foam between the rusty jaws of the black cable and touched it with the red one, eliciting a frail spark.

The foam did not catch.

The wyrntensil noticed.

It rolled onto its side to get a sense of where May was, then slung the heavy tube of its body around as May frantically rubbed the clamps together. The foam, it seemed, was not as flammable as she had hoped. The car was old, but AMC had always been a forward-thinking company. The car seat foam was not flammable.

"It's coming over!" Xan said, watching the creature slither closer to May.

"I've almost got it," she said, though the spark was getting smaller and she was decidedly getting farther away from having it.

Xan held the knife out in front of him two-handed, dismounting from the car door and shakily blocking May from the beast.

The knife would by no means pierce the wyrntensil's flesh, but perhaps, thought Xan, it might serve as a decent distraction. He chucked the pocketknife at the beast's tail where it bounced gently off its fleshy side and became lost in the rubble.

The wyrntensil continued its threatening slither unperturbed. It reared up and rocked from side to side to add some drama to the kill.

"Back in the Gremlin!" Xan shouted.

"Throw the diagnostic thingy at it!" May redoubled her efforts, but the cables weren't even sparking now.

"Can't."

"Why not?"

"Lost it."

"Ugh." At last, May dropped the foam and climbed back into the car via the passenger window. The wyrntensil wailed and flung its face against the car. There was a tooth. One of five hundred. The beast roared through the busted windshield, effluvium from its foul ancient breath stinging May's eyes as she tried to stuff herself under the dashboard.

"Plan two?" Xan asked from the backseat as the Gremlin rocked.

"Wait for it to lose interest," May said.

The wyrntensil slammed its body into the car, rolling it onto its roof.

And then the rocking stopped.

"Think it's lost interest already?" Xan whispered.

May shook her head. If it had lost interest, it would be slithering away, not blocking the cavern's light with its massive body.

Blips passed. Silence. Stillness.

Maybe, May thought, it had died suddenly. She began to pose this theory, "Do you think—" Tentacles burst through the Gremlin's windows and felt around the inside of the cabin until they wrapped wetly around May and Xan, then retracted, curling back out from whence they came.

May had experienced a lot of terrible things in her life, but being covered in an inch thick layer of worm saliva took the metaphorical cake.

Xan was more used to this sort of thing and only sighed his disappointment.

"What the fuck?!" May whispered, squeegeeing the mucus from her face.

"Tend—" Xan paused to spit a mouthful of the stuff. "Tenderizer," he said. "Alright, okay. So, as far as I figure, there's a slim chance I'm making it off this planet alive no matter what happens, so I'll tell you what I'm going to do." He peered out of the window to see what the wyrntensil was up to, decided he'd rather not know, and turned to May again. "I'm going to run, lead it away from you, and then you can look for Aimz and Listay and stop Chaos from, I don't know, eating the universe."

"You think you can outrun it?" May asked, grabbing onto his arm to keep him from making the decision without her input.

"Definitely not. But it'll probably kill me fast, at least."

"No. We'll think of some—" If she was able to finish her sentence, Xan didn't hear it above the racket of the car being pummeled from above. May clambered into the backseat with Xan, hoping the car frame would hold out for however long it took them to think of something good.

The boardwalk creaked under the strain, the planks bending and splintering until at last the Gremlin broke through to a dark underground tunnel, putting it well out of the reach of the beast.

Oh how curious, thought the wyrntensil as it bashed its head into the ground around the hole where the Gremlin had just been. *Not a moment ago I could have sworn I was coaxing two delicious vermin from their hidey-hole.* It nosed around the area, found nothing, and then, thinking it was losing its edge in old age, the embarrassed creature slithered back to its nest.

Beneath the boardwalk, squished between metal and denim, May experimentally wriggled her toes. Those worked. The fingers, too. The plume of ancient allergens around the car hadn't settled yet, and when she opened her mouth to call out to Xan, she got a throat-full of junk that wanted nothing more than to incubate into space flu.

"Xan?" she coughed.

"May?"

"Oh good, we made it," she said.

"And we didn't have to think! Funny how that works out sometimes." Xan squirmed out first, then helped untangle her from the crushed car. "Are you ok?"

Whatever the first fall had done to tweak her ankle, the second fall had un-done and she felt right as rain. Acid rain, maybe. Everything itched. Or was it burning?

"Maybe. This slime's starting to burn, though," she said, holding her arms out to the sides and sloughing off globs of wyrntensil saliva.

"Eugh, we need to get to a shower."

"First we need to find Aimz and Listay."

"I mean we *really* need a shower." He touched the sleeve of her t-shirt and the entire garment came unstitched and fell as rags at her feet. "That's going to happen to our skin if we don't. It's in the limerick.

Down in the old land of Rhea III,
there slithers a long tubish beast.
Beware of its tip,
should it blast you with it,
before it prepares to feast."

"Everyone just assumed it was a metaphor for sex. All the Rhea III limericks were supposed to be metaphors for sex!" Xan said, miserably. He'd never in his life been so disappointed to discover something wasn't metaphorical and wasn't about sex.

"Alright, we'll wash this off. It's humid down here; there must be water somewhere. There's a flashlight in the glove box. If we're lucky–"

"We're not," Xan interjected.

"Granted, but if we are, it might still work." She dug through the splintered wood around the car carefully, though a few splinters didn't matter much now that her hands were full of glass shards, and found the flashlight.

She pressed the soft button at the base and, to her delight, it flickered on. Xan's face lit up literally and metaphorically.

"Alright! We've got light; now we can watch our skin melt off!"

"That should be entertaining," May said as they set off down the dark tunnel in search of water. "Mine will probably go first, so don't freak out on me."

"At least you had a shirt on."

May swung the flashlight around the corridor. Pipes which were bolted to the rough concrete walls were conveniently stenciled. "Gift Shop," read one. "Storage," read another. "Croosflarten," read a third.

"We'll go to the gift shop," she said. "Maybe we can find something to towel off with."

"Right, let's hurry, I don't have much clothing left to lose," Xan said, picking at his disintegrating yellow swimsuit.

CHAPTER TWENTY-SIX

Retail Therapy

The gift shop, like all gift shops, was replete with logo-ed goods, still lovingly arranged, as if one renegade restocker, after whatever cataclysm had led to the place's abandonment, had returned to straighten a pile of shirts or refill the keychain bin one last time.

Unlike all gift shops, however, this shop's ceiling was a net of tightly woven threads, cocoon-like in their organic precision, clinging to the ceiling, creating dark shadows in the fluorescent lighting. The light flickered when whatever was in the shell shifted.

"This is eerie," Xan said, peering in from the door. "I'm getting a strong 'we shouldn't be here' vibe from this place. What do you say?"

May pushed her head under his arm to get eyes on the spooky gift shop.

"Just cobwebs," she said, and forced the rusty door open enough that she could duck under his arm and slip inside.

"Those aren't–"

"They're cobwebs," she insisted. She knew they weren't. She also knew that her swimsuit straps were disintegrating and wouldn't hold up much longer. Sneakily, she crossed her arms over her chest to keep everything in place.

"Oh, right, yeah, I guess they are. Silly of me to think otherwise." When Xan followed her in, the friction tore apart his swimsuit and he snatched the nearest novelty item he saw: a triangular flag on a stick which proclaimed "I had fun in the Adventure Hole!" and covered up with it.

"Take what you want, I—" May had turned around. The absurdity of the flag made her laugh, and when she went to cover her mouth, her straps snapped and she quickly doubled over to keep herself decent. She laughed harder. “Right, I’ll close my eyes, you find us towels.”

“Already done.”

He tossed a thin, but large blue towel at her, embroidered with the “Water Where Water Ought Not Be” logo, and she used it to rub the wyrntensil spit from her skin, beads of dead skin sloughing off with it.

Wyrntensil saliva would someday in the far future be harvested and developed into a multimillion-ISC industry on account of its natural exfoliants. May did not appreciate the silky smoothness nearly as much as future generations of wealthy socialites would.

“Are you decent?” she asked Xan once she had wrapped her towel securely around herself.

“I used to think I was,” he said, scooping up the nearest novelty t-shirt and shorts he could find. “But I’m not sure anymore. I haven’t felt decent for awhile. Pretty mediocre, really. Perhaps even subpar.”

May sighed heavily. “I mean have you got clothes on yet?”

“Oh. See, in my line of work people tend to think I’m more decent when my clothes are off,” he said with a chuckle. “But yeah. Yes. Your eyes are now safe from the intricacies of my strange alien anatomy.”

“Good. Alright, I’m coming out.”

As she began the search for clothing which would fit her (a challenge when average height for a Tuhntian was around eight feet and May barely made five-and-a-half) she got the sense that something was wrong. Not the mysterious ceiling cocoon, she was accustomed to that now. Not the shockingly pristine state of the clothing she found either; she knew alien fabrics could be wonderfully dexterous. It was Xan.

“You don’t look right,” she noted.

“Eh, I don’t feel right, so that tracks,” he said, folding the sticky towel and setting it neatly atop the pile, since, of course, he hadn’t paid for it.

The gift store was hung wall to wall with gaudy outfits and he had somehow chosen the cheapest, most unflattering items available. His usually perfect pompadour had deflated like an orange souffle covering his face and he seemed to get lost in a much too large t-shirt. It wasn't even knotted up to reveal his midriff. He was in crisis.

"Blueberry," she said seriously, grabbing the smallest suit she could find off the rack for herself, "I'm not going to let you die. Alone, anyway. If we're going out, we're going out together looking like the sexy, confident rocket racers we are."

"Sexy and confident?" Xan said. "You sound like me."

"Yeah, well, one of us has to. It's not a comfortable position for me, so it'd be nice if you started sounding more like yourself again."

She snuck behind a mannequin and took off the rest of her ruined swimsuit, finding the folded bank account fortune paper she'd tucked between her boobs. She read it again to reassure herself. It was all going to work out in the end. She slipped into the fresh suit and stuffed the paper into the breast pocket.

When she emerged, she found Xan slumped over a display table, like a partially melted plastic mannequin. She yanked the outfit off the mannequin she had hidden behind and brought it to him. "You'd look good in this," she offered.

"What's the point in looking good?"

"Christ, Xan. There is no point in looking good. It's a waste of time. But it's one of the things you like to waste time on, so it's important. If you give that up, what else will you give up?"

His response started as a sigh, made a hard left turn into a groan, meandered into a whine, made a u-turn as a sharp intake of breath, and hit a dead end with an anticlimactic, "Okay."

He took the outfit and slipped behind the nude mannequin to spare May a show.

"Ah, zuut, May you know me too well. I look fantastic in this."

May kept herself from biting back about how well she knew him, considering the circumstances, and turned around to find him fixing his hair in a shiny bit of chrome siding on the wall. "Feel better?" she asked.

"Marginally so." His shoulders drooped. "I don't have any crystals on me. Do you?"

"No, why?"

"Well, we've got to pay for this stuff. We can't just take it."

May shook her head, but smiled. "I don't think anyone will mind."

"I mind! That's stealing."

"You stole the *Audacity*." May noted—a touch more accusingly than she was going for.

A high-pitched whistle, like a boiling kettle, originated from the be-weaved ceiling and the shadowed creatures cocooned therein began to stir again, the light faltering.

"Let's go?" Xan suggested, watching the ceiling like a cat watching a laser pointer beam as he picked up the flashlight.

"Let's go."

CHAPTER TWENTY-SEVEN

In the Utility Corridor

They shut the gift shop door and bolted it closed. An urgent tapping followed on the other side of the door, but they were too busy legging it down the corridor to care, the light from the flashlight in Xan's hand bouncing along the walls.

"Xan, do..." May paused to breathe. "Do you think I could get—" She breathed again.

"Leg extensions?" they said in tandem, Xan slowing to let her catch up.

He patted her back. "Yeah, sure thing, mun."

The sound of tapping was well out of their range of hearing now, so the danger felt like it had passed. They slowed down to take a look at where they were going. None of the pipes had been stenciled with anything along the lines of 'You're going the right way,' so they had to guess, heading first toward the "Incredible Glasses of Milk Museum" and then toward the "Water Where There Ought Not Be Utility Access" before they slowed.

"Water Where There Ought Not Be," May said with a smile. "Sounds like my apartment."

Xan laughed, though he'd never been in her apartment, she was fond of complaining about it. "Speaking of your personal history...who's Harvey?"

"Harvey Foster? Just a guy I knew in high school."

"And you two were..."

"Friends, I guess. Until he wanted more. Then we were ex-friends."

"Really? I took you for a romantic," he teased.

May snorted. "Yeah, no. I'm the original heartbreaker."

"Yeah," Xan said and was silent for so long after that that May felt she needed to explain.

"I've never understood that sort of thing. Romance," she said, shrugging. "Seems sorta contrived to me."

"Huh," Xan said. "It is kinda nice, though. All that attention. Staring deeply into someone's eyes and knowing that you've got each other no matter what..."

"Sex," May said, filling in the rest of the sentence for him.

"What? No. I mean...sure sometimes but," he sighed, running his fingers through his hair and messing it up again. "Zuut, when on O'Zeno's grand calendar did I become disinterested in sex?"

"Working at Sonic made me pretty disinterested in food," May said absently, squinting to read more of the pipe stenciling. "So why did you steal the *Audacity*?"

"I-I didn't—I mean..." He stopped, her sudden change of subject had caught him off-guard, as was her plan. "I guess I did," he said, as if someone had just irrefutably proved it to him. "Zuut, I stole the zuxing *Audacity*."

"Yes, I know. You admitted that already. I want to know why."

He dropped the flashlight and it rolled slowly along the uneven concrete, illuminating nothing but dust as it winked in and out. In and out. In and out.

"Blueberry?" May asked, trying to put out a hand to find him in the darkness. He was not where he ought to have been. May shuffled, arms outstretched, but ended up kicking him while he was down.

He was too busy panicking to notice that she had kicked him, to notice he had dropped the flashlight, even to notice that he was no longer standing but lying flat on the dusty, damp ground.

There was a voice in the back of his head. It wasn't his...or it was but it was wrong.

"You've done enough damage in this lifetime. You failed miserably, but it's okay. Just die now before you ruin anything else," said the voice.

May was saying something to him, but her words weren't nearly as loud as his head voice, and they came through as a low rumble, like a distant motorway.

The worst part was that the voice in his head wasn't angry when it told him he was better off dead. It wasn't sad, either; it didn't lament what it was making him think. It was confident, serious, and strict, but also kind.

Now, usually, Xan had a pretty good handle on this voice. He'd found that a nice crunchy snack could drown it out, or watching 'I Love Lucy' with the volume up so loud his translation chip would start glitching.

He knew his fingers were shaking, so he shoved them into his hair and held on at the roots to keep them still. Maybe, he thought vaguely, if he pulled out his hair, the voice in his head would go along with it.

"Xan!" May's shout finally reached him.

"Uh?" he managed.

"What the hell happened?" May got to the ground and found that his eyes were lit up like a cartoon's in the dark, so she at least knew where to talk.

"Remember when you asked me if I was depressed?" he said.

"You said it didn't translate," she reminded him.

"Yeah, well, you probably won't be surprised to know I lied."

"I'm not."

"Blitheon, May, why'd you come looking for me? You and Aimz could be off having adventures of your own by now. You didn't need to get caught up in this. I got what I deserved."

"Hey," she said. The tunnel seemed to get a few degrees colder. She chose to think that some kind of ancient air conditioning system had finally kicked on. "I came looking for you because I wanted to."

"Because I have the *Audacity*?" he asked, turning the AC up just a touch.

"N-not just that." It would be a lie for her to say she hadn't been interested in getting the ship back. It was her livelihood and her home, after all.

"May, I stole it." Talking was helping, even if he didn't like what he was saying. As long as something was being said, he didn't have to think too much.

"I know! I know you, too, though. You must've had a good reason."

He shook his head. "Not good. If Chaos goes back and kills me before I steal the *Audacity*, Tuhnt will be safe, and you'll be safe, and everyone can get back to normal."

"Stop it. I don't want you to die."

"It's healthy to disagree on things sometimes."

"We need to agree on this. It's important. You're important."

"What, to you or cosmically?"

May gave him a helpless "Nngph" before she answered. "Shit, Xan I can't speak for the cosmos. You're important to *me* and I'm a selfish, stubborn, cold-hearted jerk and I want you around."

Xan chuckled. "You are not."

"Want to test that? Tell me why you stole the *Audacity*. I need to know," she said, trying to keep her voice even.

"Fine, alright. But," there was a hint of a smile in his voice again, "only if I get to tell you in the form of a dramatic flashback scene."

"Ideally you would."

Insert Flashback Sound Effect

"Imagine it's the final age of the War of Reversed Polarity. I'm sitting in the darkest booth in the farthest corner of the seediest sub-bar in the city of Trilly on the continent of Further Masedon on the planet of Tuhnt in the system of Flotluex, and I've just received a message on my BEAPER.

"Mandatory Draft in Effect.

"My first instinct is to dunk the BEAPER in my Electro-Blitz and fry the circuits, but that won't get me anything but a busted BEAPER.

"Brooding is my only recourse. I know it won't make a difference, but I want to look absolutely as put-out as possible. The Universe will know, I think. But it didn't. Turns out the Universe is nearsighted! Someone else notices, though.

"'You look absolutely put-out,' they say.

"I agree before looking up. Probably, I should've looked up first, because when I do, I realize this person was military and I am about to be officially zuxed. Or zuxed by an official. Ha! Because I thought maybe he was about to proposition me. That was a joke, please laugh," he said.

May resolutely did not laugh. "Go on," she said.

"Right. So he introduces himself as Admiral Ranken Warders, tells me he has an offer for me and asks if I wanted to hear it.

"I didn't want to hear it, so I ask him if I have a choice.

"Then he says, in a gruff old battle-worn voice," and here, Xan attempted to affect a gruff old battle-worn voice. "'Well of course you do, my lav. But something tells me you won't say no.' Then he winks, and that's what really gets me thinking I'm about to be propositioned.

"I lean across the table and give him a kind of sexy scowl I'd been working on. Don't ask me to do it, by the way, it was not sexy. Dropped that one a few decades back.

"So I ask him how much. No less than a thousand crystals a night, I think, but I quickly talk myself down to five hundred. Two-fifty, maybe, but absolutely no kissing in that case. I was always underselling myself back then."

"Still do," May interrupted.

He huffed humorlessly at her. "The Admiral says he has it on 'good authority' (whatever that means) that Operation *Audacity* has an eighty-nine percent chance of backfiring horribly and destroying Tuhnt.

"That, obviously, concerns me a bit. And clearly the proposition has taken something of a u-bend. That is, unless he was about to tell me the only way to save the planet was to take my pants off. I know that *sounds* unrealistic, but it has happened. More than once, too.

"Then he hands me an anchor button, like I'm supposed to do something about it.

"He tells me the *Audacity's* a diversion ship, meant to distract the *Peacemaker* from their heavy hitter, the *Innocuous*. Without the *Audacity*, they can't end the war, but at least Tuhnt wouldn't get zuxing smithereened.

"At this point, I'm still not too clear on what he's getting at, and I'm out of Electro-Blitz, so I have nothing to distract me.

"And then, he tells me this: 'I want you to steal the *Audacity*. Can you fly a rocket?'

"And I could! Kind of. Tolerably, anyway. Bearably, I could. So I tell him this, staring at the anchor button in his hand, thinking he's been holding it out way too long and I really ought to take it from him because it's getting uncomfortable.

"I ask him again to clarify what he means. You really can't over-communicate, you know."

"Is that a jab at me?" May interrupted.

"No," he laughed quietly in the dark tunnel. "It's just true. Anyway! I ask again, 'You want me to steal a military vessel to save the planet from imminent destruction?'

"I mean, he was an Admiral! I would zuxing wager he could have done it himself if he really wanted to. Probably some sort of political shenanigans kept him from doing it, I don't know. Apparently, questioning an Admiral is considered 'gross insubordination' but you live, you learn, you get arrested for destroying a planet, right?

"So, I'm absolutely green with embarrassment, but I tell him to ask someone else, as if he had asked me for a spare zipzam, because I wasn't planning to fight in the war, much less take on a super vital secret mission.

"He's massively plivered now, but then he goes extraordinarily calm. I know this must sound zoup-nogged, but I swear on Blitheon he spoke without actually moving his mouth when he tells me it has to be me. He says 'she' wouldn't let me die.

"I'll always remember that. Who was 'she'? And why did 'she' care whether I lived or died? Never did find out..."

Xan paused to wonder again about what the Admiral had said. May nudged him.

"Right, sorry, so the next thing I know, the Admiral gets out his photon gun and wiggles it at me—and no, that's not a euphemism unfortunately—in a way that suggests that if I don't stand up, too, I'd find out exactly what setting the gun was on. He tells me to take the offer.

"And I...I guess I did."

"You guess...you did?" May repeated.

"Yeah. He shoved me in his MegaCruiser, we were in the thick of a sub-blizzard and I was wearing a mauve faux bufatalo coat. That's not important, I just like saying the words 'mauve faux bufatalo coat' with my mouth. Mauve faux bufatalo co—"

"And then what happened?" May prompted.

"Right, right...this part's a little fuzzier. He brought me to the *Audacity's* rocket silo, I do remember that. The silo wasn't lit from the inside because it didn't need to be. The ship was so bright, it sucked up any light it could find and multiplied it faster than breeding zipnites. Would you believe the *Audacity* is faded now? From star exposure. It used to be the brightest thing in the sky. I mean, it still is, but used to be brighter.

"I couldn't stop staring at it, which turned out to be an issue. Do you know, every time I close my eyes I see the after image of the ship, in blue? Photic retinopathy, it's called. Fun fact. About my eyes. You're getting a lot of eye facts lately."

"That probably should've gone away by now," May said.

"Probably. Hasn't. Eh, that's the way the chip crunches. Anyway. He made me teleport into the ship.

"I had only ever flown a StarTaxi and, for a sense of scale, the living room alone can dock seven StarTaxis comfortably. The console was covered in buttons and switches and levers and things I didn't even have a name for. I remember hoping most of those switches had to do with mood lighting."

"Most of them do, actually," May said.

"I don't know how I did it, but I got the ship turned on and launched it," he said.

"Without opening the silo roof?" May asked.

"Eh-huh, yeah...that was a *sound,* I can tell you that. I guess I expected the Admiral to open the silo. Not sure why. He hadn't given me any indication that he was particularly helpful.

"I do remember forgetting to turn on the viewscreen. For the first few blips I was flying blind. Should've kept it off, too. When I turned it on all I saw was the tops of clouds and several military grade missiles headed toward me and you know what? Seeing the clouds from the wrong side honestly bothered me more than the missiles. Isn't that crosh-wopple? The things you focus on when you're stressed. Speaking of...I can't quite recall what happened to that mauve faux buffalo coat. Must've been traumatic, losing it. I loved that coat."

"There were missiles?" May prompted, trying to keep him on track.

"Right! Yes. The missiles. Then I...zuut, I haven't thought about this in decades. I guess I set a flight path. A flight path so horrifically fool-hardy that it circled back around into being fool-proof! The missiles couldn't figure it out. Neither could I, honestly. Then I found the *warp*drive.

"Now, I'd like to think I would've been able to figure it out faster if I hadn't been flung to the other side of the ship and into the artificial gravity lever! Hurt like a splice in the duct, pardon my Rhean.

"It's odd that the ship has an accessible artificial gravity lever, right? I can't imagine why anyone would want to turn that off. Alright, perhaps I can. I can imagine a couple of reasons someone would want that off, but certainly not military related reasons."

"Sex reasons?" May asked.

"Sex reasons. Yes. But you've got to agree it's odd to have such a feature on a ship whose express purpose was to zoom about and blow things up for the government."

"Eh, sounds like a stressful job," May said.

"Yeah, well, glad I could keep them from having to do it, then," Xan said, sighing. "The flightpath was awful. I remember getting punted face-first into the viewscreen, too."

May hissed through her teeth, the viewscreen got exceedingly hot. "Did it burn you?"

"You know, it did? But once the dead skin peeled off my face was ultra soft. Actually, I did it again once on purpose before an important client. Not the most enjoyable facial, but zux if it doesn't work!"

"I'll take your word for it. What happened next?" May asked.

"Well, I found the warpdrive. Then I broke the color barrier for the first time and was well off the mark of those missiles.

"After I got the artificial gravity back on..." he paused, recollecting things he thought he would never have to recollect again. "I realized how far away from Flotluex I was. How far away from Kalumbits and Aimz and Zilla and Yvonne...and I couldn't go back, was the thing. I didn't know if I'd be executed or what, but I knew I couldn't go back.

"Eventually I tried to delete the draft alert from my BEAPER and noticed a new message from Aimz which read, 'Kalumbits—'"

Xan's voice glitched like a scratched record player, but May's translation chip was working just fine.

"What did it say?" May asked, leaning in.

"'Kalumbits wants to know when you'll be home.' I sent her an audio message. Told Aimz to tell her I'd be back soon. That was almost two centuries ago."

CHAPTER TWENTY-NINE

The Manual

The floor of the utility corridor was cold, damp, and lumpy, but May was now lying on it next to Xan, both staring at the black ceiling which occasionally dripped. She figured if he was enduring a crude kind of water torture, she ought to as well.

"So"—*drip*—"an admiral forced you"—*drip*—"to steal the *Audacity*?"

"Eh, wouldn't say forced." *Drip*. "Not entirely."

"He had a gun."

"Alright, yeah, but I wanted it, too. I didn't exactly"—*drip*—"resist. I didn't actually do anything to stop him."

"You also didn't want to get shot." May sat up now, tired of being dripped upon.

"Well"—*drip*—"the point is, what I did got Tuhnt destroyed, and whatever Sonan or Chaos wants to do with me, they're right. I mean, Chaos resetting the universe sounds a touch extreme, so I suppose we should try to do something about that, but even if I get out of that, I'm staying here." He rolled up, patting around the ground until he found the flashlight, and flicked it on again.

"That's not fair," said May.

"It's entirely fair. It's just about the definition of fair."

"But I don't want you to," May said, choking on the 'to' like it was a stale saltine. She needed a glass of water. "And this is another thing we cannot agree to disagree about."

Rather than reply, he sighed.

"You need a hug?" she asked.

He nodded.

She wrapped her arms around him and squeezed as if she were trying to wring all the sadness out of him. He hugged her back in a way that let her know it might have been working.

"How did you find out about Tuhnt?" May asked.

"What do you mean?"

"How did you find out that Tuhnt was destroyed?"

"I was on a job and the client told me before we started. You'd think that'd be a mood murderer, but he gave me a huge tip and a great review. You know, now that I'm thinking about it, it was probably a pity thing." Xan gave a dusty chuckle. "Definitely a pity thing. Not that I'm not good at what I do...er, did. I'm just not an extra hundred crystals worth of good. And I definitely wasn't on that one. Nice of him, I guess."

"Do you miss it?"

"What, being a sex worker? Eh, I'm getting too old for it."

"No, Tuhnt."

"Do you miss Earth?"

"Earth's not gone," said May defensively. She felt defensive because she did not miss Earth, but she didn't think that was the right answer. "It's weird. After the deal with Harvey I just stopped engaging with people. It seemed like everyone I met just wanted something out of me, you know?"

"I know," Xan said.

"Then I met you and I needed you. Which sucked."

"I remember it sucking for you." Xan sat up now, too, finally. "You kept trying to run off and get a job. Weird coping mechanism," he said with a laugh.

In other branches of the Pontoosa Adventure Hole, Aimz and Listay fought a swarm of tiny, sentient flying arrows. Chaos neared the resting place of the Sphere of Time. The wyrntensil skulked the tunnels hungrily.

In other branches of the Pontoosa Adventure Hole, Time passed normally at a rate of one blip-per-blip. But in utility corridor 4B, Time crept carefully past so as to not disturb Xan and May. Time kicked a rock, stumbled and, embarrassed, began moving along at a normal pace again.

"Shit, we've got to find Chaos," May said.

Then standing, dusting off the detritus of their conversation, they started again down the corridor in an urgently contemplative silence.

Near silence. As close to silence as they ever typically got. Xan hummed, "Take Me To the River" and May quietly mumbled the name of every location stenciled on the pipes which ran along the corridor.

Xan stopped humming. "Did you say something about a haunted Big Mouth Billy Bass? I feel like that was a thing that came up after Sonan poisoned me."

"Oh, you remember that?"

"I was surprisingly lucid during that incident!"

"Huh. Yeah, I found a haunted Big Mouth Billy Bass," May said. "I want to show it to you, so you're not allowed to die here."

"Right. Well, can't fault your reasoning. A haunted singing fish is a pretty tempting offer. I suppose, for the sake of the fish, I'll try to not."

"That's the spirit," she said, then stopped. "Here it is."

And there it was.

A door, that is.

A door which read 'Sphere of Time Maintenance Access.'

"Blitheon's stars, here it is," Xan echoed.

All was dark until May found the light panel on the wall and amber lights slowly glowed on above them to reveal a cavern filled with plastic boxes full of hardware, old laser tools, and discarded motors and mechanical miscellany which crouched toad-like in the dark corners.

On a work desk, under a layer of sandy dust, or perhaps it was dusty sand, sat something book shaped. May investigated; something book shaped was likely to be an asset. Particularly if it was, in fact, a book.

With her sleeve, she wiped off the cover and smiled.

"Manual!" She held it out to show Xan, pointing to it earnestly.

"Is that," he eyed the yellowed tome suspiciously, "going to help? In any way?"

"It can't hurt. And it's pretty heavy; I could throw it at her."

"I'm not sure androids are susceptible to paper cuts."

May flipped the stiff pages of the index. They weren't made of tree pulp, of that she was certain. What they were actually made of is too horrific to mention, but extremely durable.

Her finger flew down the page, then, finding her mark, she flipped to page 369. 'Operating the Sphere' titled the page. 'Do

Not Operate The Sphere' subtitled it in Danger Diophalothene (which, to May's eyes, was a reddish magenta). An illustrated sphere took up the rest of the page with explanatory labels, each asterisked with the warning that never under any circumstances should the sphere ever be used.

The illustrated sphere looked like an audio recording console from 1958 that had been melted over an upturned ceramic bowl in an oven.

"What's it say?" Xan asked, fiddling with doodads on the table.

"Some of the words are," May cringed as the translation chip guttered in her head, "unreadable. I don't think this is meant to be gazpacho."

Xan peeked over her shoulder. "It's a recipe, actually. Yeah. That's zipnite gazpacho."

"Really? Why would there be a—"

"Aha! I did it. May June July, you've just been bested at your own style of humor: dry sarcasm. I can now die in peace."

"Not until you see Big Mouth Billy Bass," May reminded him.

"Ah, right, yeah. Singing fish promise."

"Exactly. What does it actually say?"

Xan set down the flashlight and leaned over the book, bobbing his head up and down like a bird until the words were in focus.

"Oof, this is some old Tuhntian. This was back when the word "glosternaoffle" was the plural of "gloasternaof" and they didn't even have a concept of specified nebulous pronouns."

"Which is?"

"You know, like 'she, he, or they' instead of 'she, he, or they?'"

"Oh. Right, yes. That."

He gave her a curious glance. "English doesn't have specified nebulous pronouns, does it?"

"It would seem not."

"Don't worry about it. The tip of the bit is, this writing is old. Long dead when translation chips were made which *means*," he said with genuine excitement in his voice, "I can translate it!"

"You?"

"Yes! I'm a linguist! Well, I was a linguist. Well, that's not completely honest. I was studying to be a linguist before translation chips were invented which sort of put a bit of a squash on that particular career option."

"Great! So what does it say?"

He looked at the page again. "Something about an aria being mortally unsung. That...that sentence doesn't quite work. Wait." Then he was silent until he said, "Oh it's a metaphor. Right. Basically, using the Sphere of Time might tear the universe apart and it should never ever under any circumstances be taunted."

"Taunted?"

He looked again. "No, sorry. Turned on. Never be turned on. The sphere is for display only, apparently. Might not even work."

Then, faintly, they heard words which they could not understand but deeply offended their sensibilities anyway.

"What was that? And why did it feel so dirty?" May asked.

"I think someone just cursed in a dead language somewhere above us. Those ancient curse words were foul. Zuxing foul."

"That's got to be Chaos," May said, looking around as if a staircase would appear magically now that she'd figured it out. There was no staircase, but the ground did slope up slightly leading out of the cavern. That was something.

So they took the manual and walked, purposefully, like retirees speed walking in the wee hours of the morning through an indoor mall to keep in shape. The corridor twisted around, looping back on itself and wavering off to one side, then switching decidedly to the other.

Whether from the effort of climbing slowly uphill, or from thinning oxygen, May was short of breath.

"We must be reaching the surface," May said, hesitant to continue forward. She leaned against the corridor wall and focused on not blacking out.

"What makes you think?" Xan asked, oxygen not being relatively high on his list of necessary conditions for survival.

"Just a," she took as deep a breath as she possibly could, "hunch." She pointed to the staircase in front of them which was labeled "Surface Entrance to the Sphere of Time."

Xan stopped, taking her arm. "Mun, maybe you should go back to where there was oxygen. So your chip doesn't short out again."

"Gotta get Chaos," she wheezed, "and the sphere." Then she looked very seriously at the ground. "'Chaos and the Sphere' would be an awesome..." she paused to breathe at him, "band name. Xan, we should start a band. I can play..." She winked dizzily, "I can be band manager. You and the fish can sing. First, though—"

A gleeful, robotic cackle could be heard from the other side of the door. Something was clearly going well for Chaos which meant something was going poorly for them.

"Get Chaos!"

He just stared at her, frozen in place.

"Well?" May said, gesturing to the door.

"Oh me?" He slapped a hand over his heart dramatically. "You meant I should get her? Sorry, I thought you wanted me to not die. Should've been clear about that. Alrighty, no problem. I'll just saunter on in and ask an ageless goddess of Chaos to hand over the Sphere of Time and we'll be off her mark. You think of somewhere you'd like to get a bit to eat while I'm out—"

"Stop!" May whispered harshly once she'd recouped enough breath to waste some. "If you don't, I will. I'm not letting her unravel," she took a painfully deep breath, "the reality fabric."

"Why not? That would be more exciting than going back to life on Tuhnt." He leaned against the stone wall beside May. "Without the *Audacity,* I will not have been there to rescue you from the *Peacemaker* and you will have died a horrible death in the vacuum of space."

"You don't know that," May said. "I might not will have been or would be or...anyway, I might not have been abducted."

Contemplating his own death was one thing. Actively running toward Death shouting, "Hey! Hey, Miss! Did you drop this? It's my immortal soul. Figured you might want it," was quite another.

Xan made a noise of roiling dread in response and then hugged May tightly. "Go back to the Gremlin and think of somewhere you'd like to get a bit to eat. I'll be right back. Probably." He looked at the door like it had insulted his favorite aunt, who he then remembered was dead, and looked at the door even harder. "Hopefully," he amended.

"Hey! I trust you," May said.

And that was the exact moment he decided he wanted nothing more than to be trustworthy, that it was vitally important that May continue having a reason to trust him. He swallowed, gently patted her head, and jumped up the staircase, flinging himself into whatever horrors were beyond.

It was eerily silent in the corridor without him. May expected to hear some sort of stand-off, some quipping, even. The air seemed to become thinner and colder; May shivered. The tug of fresh and suspiciously ample oxygen in the corridor behind her was strong. Xan said he would take care of it. May shook her head, it wasn't that she didn't trust him. It was just so quiet on the other side of the door. She had to check on him.

May collected a lungful of air and began to climb the stairs.

CHAPTER THIRTY

A Jump to the Left

Xan plunged into light.

This was not the right place, thought Xan. This was likely not even the right planet and, he had a suspicion, this was not, in fact, the right dimension.

Xan had left an ancient utility corridor under the deserted planet of New Tuhnt and arrived in what might easily be confused for a spaceport terminal apart from the eerie green light. The walls were distressingly bare. The seats were made of molded plastic which appeared to be purposefully ergonomical but were in actuality just wrong enough to not be comfortable for any known butt-having species.

The setting had so thrown off his resolve that for a moment he couldn't remember what he was looking for and why he was looking for it. Then, at last, something jogged his memory.

An orb glowed greenly on the reception desk by the chairs, projecting with an easeful waft the setting which he found himself in.

Right, thought Xan, he was to find Chaos and nicely ask her to please stop trying to destroy the universe. That was the entire plan.

Chaos was not in the terminal. Or, if she was, she was hiding, which seemed a touch silly. He stalked carefully forward just in case.

The terminal gate was open, and as he approached it, he saw a familiar scene on the other side: the *Audacity*'s original rocket silo complete with a not-dented version of the *Audacity* and, now that he was closer, he could see the admiral's MegaCruiser as well. He was peering directly into his past.

Everything was as he remembered it, except for the presence of Chaos.

She stood statue-still, a nasty looking antimatter cannon poised on her shoulder like a lion perched on the wing of an ibis.

Beyond her stood Xan's past self, awestruck by the magnificent ship that towered over them as he stepped from the Admiral's MegaCruiser. He watched himself make the worst decision of his life, fear gripping him like a giant, clawed hand made of ice cream.

The antimatter cannon clicked, made a sinister charging noise, then made an even more sinister discharging noise.

A spectral figure passed through him.

"Watch where you're goi-oh," said Death, looking at him as if she had seen a ghost. "This is unusual." She looked at the soon-to-be pile of ash which was a younger Xan and then at the older version she had just walked through. She shrugged. "Not my problem," she said and floated off to make it his problem instead.

Before he could see what Death was about to do to him, Xan bolted back into the spaceport and ran to the sphere. It was completely digital, but the faux analogue interface was so realistic that he nearly jammed his finger straight through the tempered glass as he tried to press the large, red-rimmed metal button he hoped would make it all stop.

The gate closed.

Perhaps, he thought, the past hadn't saved yet.

Perhaps he would be okay.

May burst into the spaceport terminal and was pleased to find that she could breathe again in the atmosphere bubble the sphere generated.

"Xan? What happened?" May asked.

"Nothing important. Hey, unrelated, do you know how to work this?" He tapped the top of the sphere and the simulated spaceport lost its greenish glow, gradating toward fuchsia.

She slung the manual onto the desk but didn't need to open it; she had memorized the faux analogue face of the sphere.

"This is the date." She tapped a retro numbered wheel counter. "And this is for the location coordinates." She tapped another counter. "And you use the dials and levers to set it."

"Fantastic." He frantically tapped the sphere, twisting touchscreen dials, pressing fake buttons, whispering details to himself, trying to remember where exactly he had been the night the admiral propositioned him.

"Where's Chaos?"

"In the past, I think." He looked something up on his BEAPER and set the coordinates.

"What happened?" she asked again.

Xan shook his head. "I don't think I'm going to make good on the fish promise, but I've got an idea." The gate opened and May jumped back, expecting Chaos to leap from the portal and insult them. Instead, a gust of icy air filled the spaceport. The gate had opened on the snow-laden door to a seedy sub-bar in the city of Trilly on the planet of Tuhnt.

"Alright, get ready," said Xan, his hands on May's shoulders. "We're about to meet an older model of myself and he's not...well I guess I'm not...no. I was not exactly always this put together."

"This is put together?"

"Yeah, well, in comparison. What I mean is—oh it doesn't matter. I could disappear at any moment if time works the way it ought to, so in case I do, I was in this pub when the Admiral propositioned me, and you've got to tell me to not take the *Audacity*. *Capisci*?"

"Still one question," May said.

"Anything."

"When did you learn Italian?"

From Xan, a confused head-tilt.

"Don't worry about it, let's go," May said and they walked together into the gate. They did not, however, walk together out of it.

Xan vanished as quickly as a candy bowl set out on Halloween with a note saying to only take one.

"Xan!" she called into the blizzard. He was gone. The moment he left the spaceport, he had disappeared. She popped her head back through the portal. The spaceport was empty and quiet except for the sound of electricity buzzing through the sphere.

Around the portal, the world was dark, cold, and smelled of rust and alcohol. She could hear something behind the pub door; whether it was an angry din or a jaunty chorus, she couldn't tell.

She paused, her hand poised on the door handle.

If she was about to successfully convince him not to steal the *Audacity*, she wouldn't be here now, which meant that she couldn't convince him not to...she shivered. It was too cold out here to think properly. She entered the pub and was surprised to see that nothing in the pub was terribly surprising.

Sloppily dressed blue-skinned Tuhntians drank and shouted around something akin to pool tables, well-dressed Tuhntians whiffled their evenings away at a bar tended by a scantily dressed Tuhntian. To her right, a flash of orange could be seen over a row of booths.

"Xan! Listen, this is very important," May slid into the booth across from him and now saw precisely why Xan had tried to warn her about his past iteration.

Instead of his perfect pompadour, something she could only compare to a party in the front, party in the back, rave along the sides mullet.

Instead of a LayFlex™ body suit and shiny gloves, he wore a coat which looked like a skinned pink muppet and an old t-shirt which was, unsurprisingly, tied up into a crop top. And instead of greeting her like a dog which had been waiting by the door for her to come home, he continued to glare at his wrist.

"Whoa," he said when, at last, he looked up at his new tablemate. "Where did you come from, tiny stranger?" Xan asked, his head tilting.

"Listen. Don't steal a rocket ship tonight. In case," she paused realizing how strange that must sound, "you were," her head wobbled noncommittally, "considering it."

Puzzlement, then confusion, then concern traipsed across his face.

"You alright, mun? Can I, um...can I get you a drink? Or a psychologist maybe?"

She shook her head, though a psychologist might actually have been helpful. Her eyes were beginning to sting.

The Xan who was not her Xan patted the top of her head with fingerless gloves (every culture has a fingerless gloves phase and Trilly was in the thick of theirs at the time.)

"Ey, mun, it's alright," he said soothingly. "I won't go anywhere, okay? I'm not going to steal a rocket, and you don't have to be sad. I'll beap my aunt; she can help you. Probably." His smile twisted uncertainly.

May declined with a hurried shake of her head. She had to get back to see if it worked. She wasn't sure exactly how she would know if it worked, but she couldn't find out if she stayed here. Though this Xan didn't know her, she couldn't help but slide to the other side of the table and give him a goodbye hug.

"Remember," she put a finger on the tip of his long nose, "do not do the thing you're about to do." She ran back through the bar, back into the portal, and closed it.

Once again in the spaceport lobby, she sat in one of the fuchsia chairs. The chair wasn't real, but the discomfort was. It felt like she was back on Earth, in a train station, waiting for her boarding pass to be called. She held her head in her hands and tried to calm down. She wasn't waiting for a train, she was waiting for reality to rearrange itself around her.

Reality didn't bother.

Perhaps just outside the fuchsia tinted bubble of the spaceport lay Earth; perhaps she was safe while she was in there. She could take some time to prepare herself.

Time refused to be taken, though, as Aimz and Listay surged into the spaceport, plasma zapper and sharp bit of metal at the ready.

"Time ball!" Aimz leapt over the chairs and tapped the sphere, swapping the fuchsia glow for blue. "We found it first. Oh, you wouldn't believe the adventure we had. Absolutely massive cave in, three different kinds of flesh-eating parasites, a sentient box chased us, there was a waterfall and oh! An entire wing of this place is a shrine dedicated to some time traveling comedian named Daniel Devito. Never heard of him. Sounds like a delight, though. Anyway, we're here now, and it's a good rotation to save Tuhnt." Aimz said, hefting May up by the arm. "Did you lose Xan?" Aimz asked.

May nodded.

"Well, let's light this lav up and see about getting him to not commit 'accidental' planetcide." Aimz looked curiously at the sphere. "Wait, did you use it already? Without me?" Her smile faded slowly as she went to inspect it.

"Chaos got to Xan in the past, right when he was stealing the *Audacity*, so I had to go further back and tell him not to do it. Now…" She stopped before her voice could raise another decibel and brought it back to a gentle simmer. "He's missing, but nothing else has changed and I don't know why."

Listay had wandered off to secure the spaceport, plasma zapper ready, only returning when she was confident they were alone in there.

Sitting cross-legged on the desk beside the sphere, Aimz pondered.

"Huh," she said, her zeal squashed. "If anything had changed, we'd remember it, wouldn't we? I mean the new things. We'd remember things happening differently."

"Not necessarily." Listay leaned on the desk and studied the orb. "There are several theories of time travel which state that your memories can't be re-written if you're at the epicenter of the change."

"The epicenter would be this," Aimz gestured around herself, "spaceport thingy. We weren't in it when they fiddled with time. We should remember something different."

"Perhaps it takes a few bloops to go into effect?" Listay suggested.

"Or nothing has changed," May said. "But if that's the case, where's Chaos? Where's Xan?"

Aimz propped her head up with her fingers and thought out loud. "Right, staring at the sphere isn't going to tell us. Let's go back in time and suss it out! Any idea when and where Xan stole the ship?"

"Maybe," May said, flipping open the manual.

The sphere hummed peacefully beside her, unaware of how much it had ruined her day. There was something like a browser history in the sphere, and May's translation chip was able to suss out just enough of the garbled ancient Tuhntian to locate the switch that controlled it.

"I think this is it," she said. "I'm going to go back a few blips and shift it to the left so it doesn't overlap the original portal."

"Good work! Who's a clever Earthmun?" Aimz said.

May raised an eyebrow at Aimz, offering her a chance to redact what she'd said.

"Sorry, right, yeah. Who's an intelligent species? Is what I meant to say." Aimz winked at her and twirled the sharp bit of metal around her finger.

May sighed heavily. "I am." She opened the portal again, this time on the rocket silo where a military-grade MegaCruiser was skidding to a halt.

CHAPTER THIRTY-ONE

Lost in Time

The two strangers Xan had met that night differed in almost every meaningful way. Height, certainly. Length and thickness of facial hair was another big one. Intent was, undoubtedly, the most obvious.

The first stranger had told him *not* to steal a rocket ship whereas the second had told him in no uncertain terms that he most definitely should.

Different, too, was their style of persuasion. The first hadn't held a photon gun to him. The threat of having your molecules rearranged into soup had been more than enough to convince Xan to get in the MegaCruiser.

Admiral Ranken Warders had brought him to a rocket silo and then twisted around to fix Xan with the photon gun's one-eyed glare as he held up the anchor button which Xan had refused to take.

"Get in that ship and take it off-planet, or you will die before anyone else."

"I thought this mysterious 'she' wanted me alive?" he asked, tremblingly.

"Well 'she' isn't here right now!" the Admiral growled.

While he had promised the first stranger that he wouldn't steal a rocket ship tonight, and he hated to break a promise, he also hated to die, so he took the button and exited the cruiser. When he did, he saw something beyond the impingingly orange hull of the *Audacity* which he did not expect.

A blue portal thwapped open and through it came May (whom he recognized as the first stranger), Listay (a third stranger), and, lastly, Aimz (a non-stranger to him, though she was strange). Admiral Ranken skirted around the cruiser and tried to decide if his gun should be aimed at one of the three interlopers, or at Xan, or perhaps at himself, seeing as there was clearly something wrong with him. He opened his mouth and gurgled his confusion.

"Aimz! O'Zeno's thumbs, why are you here?" Xan's voice echoed around the small silo, circling back to him.

She cupped her hands around her mouth. "Trying to stop you!"

"Can you stop *him*?" Xan pointed at Ranken who hiccupped angrily.

"Who's he?" Aimz shouted back, but before Xan could explain that he really didn't honestly know, another portal opened, this one green, and admitted a pink android with an antimatter cannon slotted into her shoulder.

The antimatter cannon was aimed quite purposefully at Xan.

There is a Rhean phrase: 'like a laser fight in a rocket silo' and it refers to a situation that is dangerous, confusing, and completely out of anyone's control. This is because if you fire a laser in a rocket silo, the laser will ricochet off the curved walls in the deadliest game of Pong until it eventually fizzles out.

And so, literally and figuratively, when Listay, Ranken, and Chaos discharged their weapons, it was like a laser fight in a rocket silo.

Xan leapt behind the cruiser. The cruiser disintegrated.

Laser beams bounced colorfully overhead, pinging off this, reflecting off that, and incinerating with gay abandon.

There was only one decent hiding place left: the rocket ship. Xan caught sight of Aimz charging Admiral Ranken with a weaponized sharp bit of metal, which he knew was no match for the Admiral's plasma zapper. So he grabbed her, flicking the teleport signal on his BEAPER as he did so. Aimz began to throw him off with a punch, was interrupted by being rent atom from atom, then finished punching him once they had both remerged inside the rocket.

He fell back onto the soft orange shag, rubbing his chin. "Zuut, I was trying to help."

"No, *I* was trying to help! Put me back." She tried to reverse the teledisc with her busted BEAPER, but it only sizzled at her.

Already at the control panel of the ship, Xan tried to work out which was the launch button.

"Wait." She tripped over the rim of carpet around the teledisc, falling into a gangly sort of desperate run. "Mun, I'm a future Aimz, if you take me with you in the past it'll—"

He had found the button. The ship ripped through the roof of the silo like an improvised can opener.

Aimz tossed herself across the control panel as the ship sped out of the atmosphere. "Zuxing Blitheon's nipples you slorpfig-nutting progeny of a jexafeeb," she informed him.

Xan sat in the pilot's chair and crossed his arms at her. "You've just insulted your own queen, you realize that?"

The missiles started before she could tell him that she did, in fact, realize that, and she would gladly insult Carmnia for creating something as dim-witted as Xan. The blast of a nearby missile hurled them both to the carpet.

Aimz struggled to pull herself into the pilot's chair and stared wide-eyed at all the buttons. "Well zuut. Do you know how to program a flight path? Because I don't." Then, after a thoughtful pause, "Oh, of course you do! You did all this alone before."

"What?" Xan braced himself between the two seats. He peered at the console and groaned at the complexity of it. "I've no idea. Just start pressing buttons!" he said, having at it.

Aimz felt it better she not interrupt. Somehow, in the past, Xan had accidentally evaded these missiles. Best not to mess with history any more than necessary. Then again, if she was here now, was she always going to have been here?

"Ah, hold on." Aimz tapped her temples as if it would help her think. "*Were* you alone when you did this?"

"What in Quanzar's name are you talking about?"

"I suppose you wouldn't know, would you?" Aimz chewed her lip, unsure of which theory of time travel they were meant to be operating under, then eventually decided inaction was better than wrong action and tucked her hands beneath her legs to keep herself from interfering.

The rocket began to swivel, twist, and turn in a completely unpredictable mess of a flight path.

"Aimz," he shouted over the din of missiles firing just outside the hull, "what were you doing in that rocket silo? Is this some kind of horrible prank?"

"I came from the future to stop you from destroying Tuhnt, but you weren't supposed to take me in the *Audacity*! I mean...I don't think you were. I guess you must have been meant to, since I'm here." She shook her head. "How did you survive this?"

"Oh, I survive this, do I? That's encouraging."

"Yeah, but don't count your larvae just yet. I'm starting to think the past-future is uncertain. You've still got to do whatever you were going to do!"

Xan thought hard and long about what he would do in such a situation until the sound of a missile whistling far too close to the hull snapped him out of it. "This class of rocket has got to have a warp drive, doesn't it? Do you..." he paused entreatingly, "do you know where it might be?"

"You're the one who is going to have done it!" She quieted, mumbling the sentence again under her breath in a few different inflections, trying to decide if what she had said was grammatically correct or not.

He stared blankly at the console. "That? Maybe?" He started to reach for a lever that looked warp-ish when a sudden shift flung him from the swivel chair and into the opposite wall.

Aimz held tightly onto her chair, curling her legs up under it to hold herself there as the ship's artificial gravity took an unscheduled sabbatical.

"Aimz," she scolded herself, "no talking, no trying to change things. Just let him do whatever he did last time, exactly as he did it and everything will be fine. Promise? Promise."

"Uh, can I get some help? Aimz?" Xan spun wildly, his fingers just grazing the lever. "Aimz!"

"Nuh-uh! If I change the course of this event, you might not survive and if you don't, I won't, and if I don't, I'll be dead, and I don't want that, so just ignore me!"

The rocket shifted, and Xan smashed into the viewscreen. Once he had peeled his face away from the hot viewscreen, he climbed down from the console and said, "That's scourge speech, mun. If we survive this, I'm taking you to Kalumbits."

Aimz nodded; perhaps that was for the best. "Alright, but for now, hush up and focus." She went back to trying to make herself as small and unhelpful as possible as Xan crawled beneath the console. He fiddled with a few pedals, then flashed her the reassuring grin of a madman as he switched on the warp drive.

There's no known verb which can describe how incredibly fast a warp drive is. It far outpaces zooming, leaves bolting in the dust, even the classic verb "rocketing" can't come close to describing just how fast it is. An entirely new verb had to be invented to describe it. And so, they warped through space and far away from Flotulex.

Xan checked the viewscreen. "Ha!" He disengaged warp, they were sufficiently far away now. "That's how you fly a racing rocket," he said as he propelled himself over to the gravity switch, turned it back on with some difficulty, and sauntered over to Aimz. "I'd wager you didn't know I could do that."

"I think I did. I mean, I was supposed to know that, but I'm not sure that I did anymore. Now I do, of course."

"Whoa, hey, it's alright. I didn't know I could either." Xan crouched beside her and took her cheeks in his hands, checking the pink glow of her eyes to be sure the ophiocordyceps fungi hadn't begun to grow into a brain-eating scourge, which was always a low-level concern. It hadn't, so that was good. "There's something very wrong with you Aimz. You aren't scourged. Are you on zipzam? Nothing you've said has made a dractifly's toe of sense."

She shook her head. "I know, I know. You might understand later. Hopefully..." She peered into the middle distance. "Hopefully I will, too. I feel like I've forgotten something important about the future. Or the past. About something that happened in a time that I'm not really sure existed. Have you got any zipzam? That might actually help."

Xan shook his head and sat back in the pilot's chair, kicking his feet casually onto the console.

"Well, we're light-years away from Tuhnt now. I'm not sure I can take you back, either. Maybe we could find someplace nice in another star system? Someplace with decent mental healthcare?"

"No, I need to get back to my own time. Or maybe I should go back to Yenuket Municipal and live with my past self until I catch up? Wait! What if *you* brought me to Yenuket Municipal in the first place instead? Would that work? Could I just circle around like that? Would I be circling forever? Oh goddess, I should've paid more attention in our time travel theory lectures."

"Mun, I'm genuinely worried about you. Why were you in the silo? Who were the other two who came with you? And what makes you think you have to be anywhere?" Xan leaned over her and tried to program a flight path that didn't involve getting tossed like a salad.

Aimz puffed a sigh at him. "I think I've been misplaced in time and I need to get back to where this all started: Yenuket Municipal Spaceport. I've got to be there or, well, just thinking about what might happen if I'm not really makes my head spin."

Xan begrudgingly searched for Yenuket Municipal Spaceport on the ship's computer and found its coordinates. "Alright, I'll drop you off there." He looked at her pleadingly. "But maybe we can just stop off somewhere fun, first? In another solar system, maybe. Just in case they're still after me. I swear I'll take you to the spaceport afterward."

She shrugged. "I guess there's no rush," she said.

Despite being on the run from the military, Xan's smile was bright. He might not be able to return to Tuhnt, but at least he had Aimz with him. "Where to?"

Aimz promptly disappeared.

CHAPTER THIRTY-TWO

Lost in Space

Aimz re-appeared in the blue-lit spaceport with the feeling that she had never left. She had a very clear memory of an event that didn't happen, and that was unendingly unsettling. Thinking, perhaps, that her braid was too tight, she undid it and scrubbed her fingers through her hair. The impossible memory persisted.

"Aimz!" Xan materialized and lifted her into a tight hug. "What happened?" He set her down. "In the past, I mean. Is it different now? Because if it is, I'm missing some massively important chunks of memory, and I'd love you to help me locate them."

"I'm in the same StarTaxi. No idea what happened. I've got a headache about it, though. Do you have any zipzams?"

"When have I ever?"

"Nevermind. Okay, let's get this straightened out, eh? Do you remember taking me with you when you stole the *Audacity*?"

Xan squinted up, then moved his head in a way that wasn't quite yes, wasn't quite no, and was only vaguely approaching maybe. "I don't remember that, no. The last thing I was doing was trying to stop myself from stealing the *Audacity* with May. I think I'm missing a fairly sizable bit of time, though. It's as if I blacked out for a blip there."

"Blacked out?" Aimz asked. That didn't happen to Tuhntians.

"It's something May does when she's especially stressed. Point is: where's May?"

"In there." Aimz pointed to the gate. "Last I knew."

They peered into the scene beyond the portal. Laser light ricocheted and debris rained from the ceiling of the silo like sharp metal dandruff. And through it all, Listay barreled toward them.

Listay jumped back into the spaceport terminal through the portal, laden with her plasma zapper, Chaos's antimatter cannon, and a photon gun and BEAPER which had heretofore belonged to one Admiral Ranken Warders. She tapped the button on the sphere with her elbow, closing the portal behind her. As the portal closed, the sphere and its accompanying spaceport illusion went fuschia again.

"Where—sorry," Xan caught himself. "Rude of me. Welcome back, Listay. Where is May?"

She held a finger up at him and leaned on the desk, breathing faster than she had in days. At least, she thought, needing to breathe meant that she was well and truly alive under her own will again. She unhooked the photon gun from her belt and handed it to Xan in lieu of an answer. The BEAPER and plasma zapper she held out to Aimz.

"So," she breathed, "don't worry, but," she breathed again, "we have to go back further."

"Why? What happened?" Aimz asked, pocketing the new BEAPER in favor of her old one and twirling the plasma zapper in her hand to get a feel for it. It didn't hold a candle to her sharp bit of metal, but it would do.

"Well," Listay snapped at Xan, "when you decided it'd be a good idea to teleport Aimz onto the *Audacity* and take off, Chaos got May."

"I didn't do that, though!"

"You did. Just now, in there." She gestured to the empty wall where the gate had been.

"Yeah, and I was there!" Aimz said. "I mean, I think it was me. Am I the same me? I remember that, but I also don't think it actually happened. How is that possible?"

"Timeline must've righted itself somehow. But now May is dead in your past, meaning she can't be here in her present."

Xan made a sound like a moribund squeaky toy; he would've dropped the photon gun had his finger not been hooked dangerously around the trigger. "May is...?"

"And Tuhnt? It's still gone, isn't it?" Aimz interrupted.

"My May?" said Xan.

"What about Tuhnt?" said Aimz.

"*My* May?!" said Xan.

"Hush!" said Listay, and she was the one with the antimatter cannon, so they all did. "I disintegrated Chaos, but in order to get May back, we need to grab her and close the portal again before Chaos can—"

"Before I can escape?" Chaos sat behind them looking far too comfortable on the uncomfortable plastic chair.

CHAPTER THIRTY-THREE

Antici-

An unmentionable malice glowed from Sonan's eyes, and even her artificial skin and hair had become more unmentionable since last we had eyes on her. The only mentionable aspect left was her distorted voice which sounded like someone hanging by their fingernails off the edge of a cliff made of chalkboard.

I probably should not have mentioned that, come to think of it.

"General Listay, I am astounded at your lack of loyalty," Chaos said. "I have always treated you with such gentle kindness."

"You murdered me." Listay charged the antimatter cannon, hefting it onto her shoulder where, it must be said, it looked a great deal more at home than it had on Sonan's thin frame.

Affronted, Chaos unfolded her unmentionable legs. "I expended nearly all of my remaining energy to bring you back to life because I am a merciful and loving god. Rather than worship at my gentle feet, you disintegrated my new body the moment you got the opportunity."

"I tried to. Why didn't you stay disintegrated?"

"Oh larvling, it's not my place to explain the mysteries of the universe to you," said Chaos sneeringly. Chaos said this because she herself did not know, and not knowing something tends to give ancient and powerful entities the willies.

"Right, so..." Xan fiddled with the photon gun, which is about the last thing anyone should be doing with a photon gun. "What happens in the current timeline? Because I really get the sense that I shouldn't be here, and yet here I am. Is Tuhnt back to existing now?"

This, Chaos had an answer for, and she couldn't wait to tell them.

"I would've eventually destroyed Tuhnt whether you took the *Audacity* or not. That vexatious Yvonne let me into her body, but she refused to let me liberate Tuhnt from reality unless you were off it.

"So I slipped into the nearest willing authority I could find, Admiral Ranken Warders had a weakness for cheese, it turns out, and I got him to get you to leave. This came with the added bonus of making you think you'd doomed Tuhnt, but the clear disadvantage of you continuing to exist. Now. You will answer my question: Do you have the fish yet?"

"Do I have..." Xan blinked. "I'm sorry, what?"

"Then there's still time. Now if you'll excuse me, I think I'll pop back to the beginning of life on Tuhnt and step on anything that has the spiracles to crawl out of the ocean."

Listay attempted to discharge the antimatter cannon, Aimz pulled the trigger on the plasma zapper twenty times, and Xan had almost figured out how to turn on the photon gun. All this to no effect.

"This is a safety bubble, larvlings. Guns don't work here," Chaos laughed.

Then she stopped.

Aimz had shoved her metal bar into the space between Sonan's artificial neck and shoulders. The android's system, unsure of how to deal with the metal bar pinching some rather important wires, shut itself down.

"Sharp bits of metal still work! Always will. Love a good sharp bit of metal." Aimz smiled, scooping up Sonan's limp body.

Listay set the sphere's coordinates to a few bloops earlier and slightly to the left before taking Sonan from Aimz. "You two retrieve May. I'll keep Chaos off your marks."

"Got it," Aimz tapped open the gate and dragged Xan into the past, pulling him into a bushel of wires which spewed from the back of a computer bank in the silo.

There was no sign of a conflict in the silo. It was pristinely dark, aside from the orange glow of reflected light from the *Audacity* which towered above, pointing toward the heavens and, Xan noted, a closed silo roof.

"Hey, can I just open the roof while we're here? Avoid a few dozen dents and scratches from the start?" Xan whispered.

Aimz grabbed his collar and drew him further back into the shadows behind the computer bank. "No, we're not changing the timeline anymore. You're going to rescue May, and I'm going to smash the time ball, because it's a piece of trok."

"You're giving up on Tuhnt?" Xan asked.

"Of course not! It's not giving up. But you heard Chaos. She was going to destroy Tuhnt anyway. I'm moving on. I mean, I've *been* moved on, it's just I thought maybe there was a possibility of un-moving-on, but there isn't, so I'm just back to where I was, alright? Not giving up. Besides, my personal timeline is a disaster because you abducted me onto the *Audacity,* so I would really rather not continue to fiddle with it. Time's not my area of expertise."

"Why don't you take yourself back before I show up and bring you onboard the *Audacity*? Wouldn't that fix your timeline?"

"Because..." Aimz knew there was a perfectly valid reason, but it eluded her. "Oh! Because if I don't distract Chaos or, I guess, if I *didn't* distract Chaos she will...or would...or would have? Oh Blitheon, preserve us. If you had taken me back before Chaos appeared, she will have killed you. Got it?"

"I might be going to have got it," Xan chuckled. "Having some trouble with tense?"

Aimz glared at him. "You can't tell me those pedantic linguistic classes prepared you for this exact eventuality."

"Not this exact one, no. But the Handbook of 1001 Tense Formations says-"

"Please spare me from knowing," Aimz said. "Ah! Hush, I heard something."

"I wasn't the one talking," Xan whispered.

"I know, just, shhhhh." Aimz slapped her hand over his mouth and peered around the control panel. The silo door opened.

Her past self, May, and Listay would arrive any minute just to the right of their portal in a blue portal and then, slightly to the right of that, Chaos would appear in a green one.

"Okay, here's the plan." She kept her hand clamped over Xan's mouth. "The moment you see May come out, you grab her and bring her through the portal that we just came from. Not the one she came—er, is going to come out of."

Xan pulled her hand away. "Why not that one?"

Aimz thought painfully for half a blip. "I don't know! Just do what I said. Take her back through the one we came out of. I'll help myself hold off Chaos and then come back through the portal we just came out of. Zuut, I hope you take the right version of me onto the *Audacity*."

"You know, I don't remember doing that. I should remember doing that, right?"

"I remember you doing it, so you must have."

"Alright, but couldn't you stay back here and plasma zap Chaos until you and I get away? Then I'll definitely take past Aimz, not current Aimz."

To spite him, she tried to think of a reason why that wouldn't work, but couldn't.

"Okay, agreed."

Another portal opened and Listay entered the silo with May and Aimz's past selves. Aimz gave a satisfied little hum. There had been no mirrors in the whole of Yenuket Municipal; it was nice to see herself again.

"May!" Xan vaulted over the computer bank when he saw her. In the distance, a younger version of himself was exiting the MegaCruiser. "May, we've got to go through that portal now!" He started to pick her up, but she resisted.

"Xan? What the–FUCK!" It had started as a question, but became an exclamation when Admiral Ranken sent a photon blast sizzling into her thigh.

Too surprised to resist, Xan was able to scoop May up now and whisked her back into the spaceport, motioning with his head to Aimz who was living out some kind of sniper fantasy behind the computer bank. After sending off a final, poorly aimed shot in Ranken's direction, Aimz helped heft May into the spaceport and closed the gate.

Listay had maneuvered Sonan's body into a plastic chair and, having nothing to tie her down with, was perched on her lap. "You got May," she noted.

"Yeah, he got me," she said as Xan set her down on the low pile spaceport carpet. "He got me distracted enough that someone put a hole in my leg."

"At least you aren't dead this time," Aimz said.

"At least," May agreed, curiously peeling melted fabric from her thigh.

It looked gross, a hand-sized dark gouge in her thigh that had been cauterized the moment the photons tore into her skin. Not a terribly effective weapon, she thought, one that immediately cauterizes a wound. Still, it should have been incredibly painful, but it wasn't.

"That looks bad," Xan said, kneeling behind her and prodding the wound helpfully.

"Doesn't it?" May said as if it were a loaf of bread that hadn't quite turned out.

"I know I'm at risk of sounding a mite obvious here but," he looked from the hole to her curiously calm face and back again, "doesn't that hurt?"

She shrugged, stood, and found that the horrific pain that ought to have shot down her leg when she put weight on it did no such thing. "It's fine," she said with a shrug.

He stared.

"Hey, stop looking at it," she said. "It's fine. You're off the hook for this one."

"If you insist." He stopped staring at it...no he was back at it again.

"It's *fine*," she insisted.

He forced himself to look at the colorful confetti shapes in the carpet instead. "I'm still on several other hooks and also possibly dead."

"I'm not sure about that," said May, grabbing the manual from the desk and leafing through it again. "How did you get back here?"

"That's really a fantastic question, because last I remember, we were going back to the subbar on Trilly to stop me from stealing the *Audacity,* and then I was here and you weren't. Then Aimz showed up."

"Right. That doesn't make sense." May ran her finger down the page, trying to focus on one word at a time to help her translation chip along.

"Does anything ever make sense for us?" Xan asked, joining her.

"Occasionally," she said. "In a round-about coked-up 90s sitcom sort of way."

The sphere shivered, the safety bubble of the spaceport strobing festively before it stabilized again.

"What was that?" asked Aimz.

"Probably the power source failing," said May.

"And the power source is?"

"Oh, just the core of the planet." May showed her a page in the manual with an illustration of New Tuhnt bisected to reveal the 'cleverly economical' and 'completely safe' power grid which had been threaded through the planet's core. "Let's find the MoonHopper Chaos used and get out of here."

"Can't we fix the Gremlin?" Listay asked, twisting over her shoulder, still sitting on Sonan's lap like a living paperweight.

"It didn't..." Xan looked at May like perhaps she'd prefer to give the bad news. She did not. "Didn't fair well. The wyrntensil crushed it pretty thoroughly, I'm afraid."

Listay liked the Gremlins, they were simple, efficient and dependable, three things she always strove to be. Noticing that this news had upset her, Aimz leapt into the plastic seat beside her.

"I'd wager I could make it work again," she said with a crooked smile.

"You're an engineer, too?"

"Er, well, I mean as an adventure biologist I could adventure into engineering. Have done, too! Didn't go well the first time, but I definitely learned something from that experience."

"We'll take the MoonHopper." Listay patted Aimz's knee. "But I'm sure you could fix the Gremlin if we had the time."

"Right, let's be off, then. Going to need this." Aimz yanked the metal bit from Sonan's neck and immediately regretted it.

Chaos sizzled through Sonan's wires again, reinvigorated after the short break. The electric jolt forced Listay to stand up, and, though her nerves were still vibrating from getting electrified, she prepared to fight Chaos hand-to-hand.

Chaos snatched the plasma zapper from Aimz, and set it to its most gruesome setting.

“I grow tired of playing with you mortals,” she growled. “I think it’s time I exterminate you.” Chaos flung Listay aside with a jolt of electricity and opened the portal.

In the silo, past Xan abducted an alternate Aimz whilst an alternate Listay and May attacked an alternate Chaos and alternate Xan ran after May as another alternate Aimz shot at the whole conglomeration from behind a computer bank.

Admiral Ranken Warders looked on in horrible confusion, occasionally firing into the mess, thinking perhaps that would help.

Chaos reached into the past with the plasma zapper and killed them.

All of them.

The silo went silent.

Chaos smiled, and May smiled too, because this only further confirmed her suspicions. She pushed the sphere off the desk and it shattered, plunging them all into darkness.

CHAPTER THIRTY-FOUR

-Pation

No one saw May's smug expression in the darkness, but she kept it up anyway. It was rare she got to feel smug about something.

Xan was the first to speak. "We're alive?" he asked, wondering idly where the photon gun he had just been holding had gotten off to.

"Yes. Also," May felt for the hole in her thigh but did not find it, "leg's healed up."

As her vision adjusted, she found that they weren't exactly in complete darkness. Cracks of light from outside leaked in, dappling everything in a pale gray light.

Where the spaceport desk had been, there was now an empty pillowed pedestal and a plaque which assured everyone that they were seeing the genuine Sphere of Time. Wrapping around them, was a row of two-person ride vehicles on an ancient track.

Chaos stood, staring at the crushed remains of the sphere. She was having a hard time accepting what had just happened. She was having a hard time understanding what had just happened. She was having a hard time accepting that she didn't understand.

They should be dead.

She killed them.

May noticed her bewilderment and decided to throw her a bone.

"It was an attraction, Chaos," May said.

Chaos's unmentionable glare snapped onto May, but was still filled with confusion.

"An attraction," May repeated. "These Pontoosa people never actually used it. They just found it and assumed it was a time machine. But it only simulates the past. It's not real."

"How did you know?" asked Listay.

"I was shot in the leg!"

"And?"

"And it didn't hurt. That isn't normal. Nothing we did in the past had any effect on the actual past. Like it could access the information, but it could only simulate changing it. It's a toy."

"Then I'll get rid of you now!" Chaos shouted, using the zapper to sling a continuous stream of plasma in a wide arc around herself.

On some rare occasions, earthquakes can be a stroke of good luck. For example, if you're so desperate for money that you've just lit a match with which you're about to burn down your house in order to commit insurance fraud and an earthquake suddenly destroys the entire structure, that's a good deal. Or if you're a seismologist who's just invented a wonderful new way to measure earthquakes, there's your chance.

Or, as was the case here, you're about to be shot point-blank by a possessed android and that earthquake causes part of a building to collapse right on top of her.

Aimz found the exit first and whistled as a way to point this out to everyone, not waiting to see who was coming before sprinting down the stairs and into the utility corridor.

"Alert: Generator core overheating, explosion imminent," said the planet. This got Aimz to pause. Xan, not expecting her to stop, tripped into her and she caught him by the arm, May stopping just short of running into them both.

"Did you hear that?" Aimz asked.

"What, the incredibly loud alert about an imminent explosion which just reverberated from the planet's core?" Xan asked. "No, did you?"

"Keep going!" May wheezed. The air in that part of the corridor, near the surface but steadily approaching the suspiciously oxygen-rich underground, was still thin and forced May's lungs, which were already over-taxed by all the running, to squeeze out every morsel of oxygen like toothpaste from a near-empty tube.

The background noise of the planet elevated from an agreeable buzz which could almost be mistaken for silence, to an agitated hum, to a tormented growl as they ran. Soon, they were far enough away from Chaos to stop worrying about what they were running from, and begin wondering what they were running to. The MoonHopper, presumably, was somewhere in their general vicinity, but where?

It didn't matter. The geography was about to choose for them.

A three-ton slab of rock, slick with a meter thick of chartreuse cave skrum dislodged itself from the ceiling directly in front of them.

Aimz, undeterred, gave an excited squeak at the obstruction and shoved May and Xan face first into it before sinking into the skrum herself.

May held her breath as it enveloped her, her eyes shut tight. It was a surprisingly amiable way to die, she thought. Warm and comfortingly weighted. Slipping into the chartreuse mucous was like taking a dip in a thick bath. Better to suffocate here than be crushed painfully under shards of cave, she supposed.

She felt a tap on her shoulder.

Hey Earthmun, unpin it. We're not suffocating. It was Aimz's voice but, instead of being in Aimz's head where it belonged, it was in May and Xan's. *It's cave skrum. Conducts thought waves, extremely friendly*, an echoed slurping noise could be heard, *and also delicious.*

Beside May, Aimz lounged in the goo, licking lips which didn't move as she spoke.

I've never seen a colony of skrum this prolific before. Found some in the holding cell and the trash compactor. It's rich in oxygen too, for those fragile Earthling lungs. Taste it!

May licked her lips. The flavor was reminiscent of an expensive, well-aged bourbon. May had never had the occasion to taste an expensive, well-aged bourbon, and as such she was unable to appreciate the delicacy that was cave skrum.

Right, thought Xan, *your biological asides are unendingly interesting, Aimz, but we're still trapped underground during an earthquake on a planet that's kindly alerted us to its intention to explode. So can you stop thinking about skrum and start looking for a way out of here?*

The corridor trembled, making them shiver like cherries suspended in a Jello salad, then collapsed.

CHAPTER THIRTY-FIVE

Deleted

Whose elbow is in my cheek? thought May.

Sorry, that's mine, Xan thought. The elbow extracted itself from her cheek.

When she opened her eyes, she saw nothing but a sharp jut of rock that would've given her two black eyes if the skrum hadn't stopped it. She couldn't move.

This rock's loose. Aimz thrashed, setting the skrum violently aquiver. Had May had lunch, she might have lost it to the skrum's undulations. The debris shifted and Aimz, using her whole body like a battering ram, pushed the rubble out of the way.

After much shimmying, a bit of wiggling, and an unwholesome amount of grunting, the trio flopped wetly onto the rubble of the planet's surface which was now a great deal lower than it had been.

May swiped a handful of thick chartreuse skrum from her eyes so she could stare despondently up at the walls of the steep crater which had formed around them. In the distance, she could see that Chaos's MoonHopper had spread itself messily across the new landscape, smoking casually as if it had just had the time of its life and needed to calm down.

"Where's Chaos?" Xan asked after spitting out a mouthful of skrum. He preferred to get the little oxygen he needed the normal way—via skin osmosis.

Aimz swallowed the skum loudly to enjoy the oxygen-buzz. "I wouldn't worry about Chaos anymore. She got crushed," Aimz said, skrum dripping in thick, wet plops to the dusty earth as she squeezed it from her hair.

"You'll excuse me if I continue to worry about the immortal Chaos god who just tried to kill all of us, I hope," he muttered, sloughing layers of skrum from his suit.

"I'd wager anything that Listay got her offline again. She's really the hero type, you know? Strong, smart, sexy, undead. Imagine what she must've been like when she was un-undead!" Aimz began to dig through debris, searching for her favorite zombie.

Exhaustion overcame May like a tsunami.

Chartreuse cave skrum is not only friendly, oxygen-rich, and telepathic, it's also a substantial source of some vitamins and minerals May's recent diet of icecream and blue-powdered crisps hadn't been providing. She sat on the smoothest boulder she could find and licked the gelatinous skrum from her fingers ravenously.

It was a strange feeling, not needing to breathe, but it was worlds better than hallucinating, and the taste was growing on her. Like cheap bourbon, but somehow better. Once her fingers were licked clean, she rested her head in her hands and tried to take a micro-nap. Xan joined her.

"Are you alright?" he asked.

"Yeah. Tired." She leaned into him, dipping in and out of consciousness. "You?"

"Ehhh," he gave a noncommittal warble.

"I'm sorry," she said, her words slurring with exhaustion. "Shouldn't have forced you to go to Rhea. Shouldn't have forced you to race, either. Ahhh," May groaned. "I'm the fucking worst."

"Not the fucking worst," he said. "Only, perhaps, trust me next time I tell you we oughtn't do something because generally I'm up to do anything with you unless it's a really horribly awful idea that might possibly end in death or worse for one or both of us."

May patted his knee sleepily. "Trust," she acknowledged.

"And, in a reality where we live through this, I'll tell you absolutely everything there is to know about me."

"At least the relevant information," May said, driftingly.

Behind them, as if watered by Aimz's affection, Listay sprouted.

"Hey, General! Welcome back to the land of the living," Aimz said. "Or, seeing as we're trapped in a crater with no means of escape, the land of the dying." She laughed, but stopped as if someone had kicked her. "That was insensitive," she said.

Listay brushed off her comment along with a layer of dirt. "Don't worry about it."

"Oh, I wasn't." She watched Listay dust herself as if she were watching a gourmet meal being prepared.

"What happened to Chaos?" Xan shouted over a sleeping May which, of course, meant she was no longer sleeping.

Listay shook her head. "I lost track of her in the cave-in. Didn't think anyone would mind."

"Not really," May said, awake now. The micro-nap and nutrients were beginning to revive her for a second wind which was really more like her ninth thus far.

"Alright." Listay mounted a protruding rock to survey the area and collect her thoughts. She had collected one thought, and it was this: They were severely zuxed. "We don't have a vehicle, so our only option is to head out on foot. Aimz and I will try to untether the *Audacity*. You two." She nodded toward the pile of collapsed Jenga blocks which were May and Xan. "Look for Precious Butler. He might be willing to help us. He apologized quite a lot when he was throwing my body in the trash."

"Alert: Generator core overheating. Explosion imminent," the planet reminded them.

"'Imminent,'" Listay shouted at the gray sky, "does not give me a time frame!" She loved time frames, and she loved cleverly working within them. Without a time frame, she just had to assume that they were disastrously behind schedule. "We need to move. Chaos could still be after us, and the core of the planet might explode at any blip."

May tried to gather up all her exhaustion and release it as a prolonged groan. "Okay. I'm ready."

"I could carry you," Xan offered.

"You don't have the stamina, Blueberry. Last time we tried that you got about twenty feet."

Xan tilted his head at her, his eyes wide and concerned. "I've only ever had two feet."

"I mean we didn't get very far," she said. "Thanks for the offer, though."

Under them, beneath a few dozen sizable boulders, in the dense darkness of the planet, Chaos was engaged in a battle for survival. Sonan had detected her. Sonan was doing her best to delete her. Commands descended upon Chaos's consciousness like materialists descending upon Walmart on Black Friday.

Chaos was no longer a god. She was a virus, and she had to be deleted. Sonan's circuits were realigning; she was restoring order to her mechanical brain. With one final shove, Chaos was out. Nothing more than a filament carried on the wind.

"No Virus Detected," drifted from a crack in the rubble, followed by a shifting of detritus and the pale pink metal fingers of Sonan for she was, once again, Sonan.

Her mechanical voice made Xan shiver and not just with fear. He suddenly felt as though something was with him, draped across his shoulders like an evil boa. "Aaaand ignoring that—let's shift before she digs herself out, eh? We've got a mission: Find Precious Butler and get out of here."

"He found us," May said, pointing out a MoonHopper which was working its way down the edge of the crater, relieved that she wouldn't have to walk the distance back to the *Audacity*.

MoonHoppers are not great land travelers. They aren't terrific at space travel, either, but once they exit the atmosphere, their complete disregard for aerodynamics and shoddy stabilizers matter slightly less. It took an uncomfortably long time for the MoonHopper to reach the four of them. A time which was made further uncomfortable by Sonan slowly emerging from the ground.

When it finally reached them, Sonan's entire left forearm was wiggling worm-like above the surface. The MoonHopper door slid open, giving the impression of an unmarked, windowless white van without the round, friendly tires.

Precious Butler leaned his head out of the MoonHopper, gave an awkward wave. "Did you folks hear the alert? I lost three shelves of seedlings to that last quake. Where's Sonan?"

No one answered, but he'd seen her. Her arm, at least. With a disappointed tsk (which either meant he was disappointed in Sonan for getting herself buried, or that he was disappointed in them for *letting* her get buried), he jumped out of the Moon-

Hopper and lumbered over to her, moving rocks aside until he could get a decent grip on the badly dented android and extract her. He helped her sit on a boulder, ankles crossed politely.

"Oh that's much better, thank you," Sonan said. "I'm not sure what came over me, I do apologize." She surveyed the organic beings who surrounded her now. "Fuck, it is a pleasure to see you again." She nodded to May who nodded stiffly back. "And Xan. Feeling better, I see? That's no trouble at all; the *Innocuous* is well stocked with barley tea."

"Terrific," he said, though it was not.

"Sonan." Precious Butler stepped in front of her. "The planet's unstable; we need to get out of here. I'm taking you to the colony on Rhea I where you can stay with me and my wife as long you need." He moved to scoop her up, but she recoiled.

"That's very kind of you, but I must arrest and imprison Xan under Carmnia of Trilly on Tuhnt, and on the colony, I don't have that authority."

"Sure, but you could get him arrested."

"Arrested and tried for a vehicle theft which took place a century and a half ago on a planet which no longer exists? My larvling, I'm afraid that would be quite impossible. He will stay here with me in the hold of the *Innocuous* where he belongs."

The planet, having heard enough, rattled violently beneath them. Its ancient voice issuing a firm reminder. "Alert: Generator core overheating, explosion imminent."

Precious Butler hefted Sonan into his arms and motioned with his head for everyone to follow him to the MoonHopper. Once inside the cockpit of the ship, he set Sonan down in the co-pilot's seat and waited for the others to pile in.

They did not.

He poked his head out once more. "Come on, then. I'll speak with Sonan once we're all safe."

"This is our only option," Listay confirmed with the kind of confidence that could convince a mollusk to take up ballet.

They packed into the MoonHopper and shut the door.

CHAPTER THIRTY-SIX

Goodbye Starshine

The MoonHopper lifted from the planet like a rock falling from a great height but backward.

"The Tuhntian colony is on Rhea I, which isn't far, but we'll need to make a stop off at Yenuket Municipal for fuel," Precious Butler said as he brought the ship into the thin, sickly atmosphere on New Tuhnt. He sat heavily in the pilot's chair, rubbing his forehead. "Fifty orbits wasted on this trok-hole."

Sonan, who had been sitting quietly in the corner and running tests on herself to be sure Chaos was really and truly gone, snapped to attention.

"Precious Butler, please watch your language. I'm surpr-r-r-r-r-r-"

He knew this day would come. Knew he'd eventually slip up and curse in front of her. But he didn't expect her to take it so hard that she would violently glitch. He set the ship on autopilot and knelt to deal with her.

"R-r-r-r-rest and imprison Xan under Carmnia of Trilly on Tuhnt," Sonan finished, her eyes flicking toward Xan who leaned against the MoonHopper's breaker box, idly combing the skrum out of May's hair.

Xan liked to think that in a situation like this, he would have something meaningful and persuasive to say. "Uhh-um," is what he settled on.

She sent a command to her lips which made them smile, then stood up.

"I'm frightfully sorry, but I cannot allow Xan to leave the planet. He is under arrest. I must have him imprisoned aboard the *Innocuous*. Then perhaps a cup of tea to celebrate. Won't that be nice?" Then, calmly, in the way an arrow might calmly plow into an eye socket, she thrust her hand through a seam in the MoonHopper's control panel.

The ship shuttered under her command, all unnecessary functions and several necessary ones spluttered offline, and it began to plummet back to the planet.

"Sonan, be reasonable," Precious Butler said steadily, as if they weren't hurtling through the sky toward an exploding planet. He tried to coax her hand away from the dashboard, but she yanked it back along with a fistful of live wires which she touched to his sweaty neck.

Precious Butler sizzled, jerked, and dropped to the floor of the MoonHopper. Not dead, but not alive enough to be of much help.

Fortunately, Listay was exactly alive enough. She slid protectively between Sonan and everyone else, but unfortunately, her array of weaponry hadn't made it out of the rubble with her. She leaned into Aimz. "Do you still have the metal piece?"

Aimz, heartbroken, shook her head. "I lost it."

"Don't worry about it, I'll try to reason with her." She turned to the android, her palms held up in a show of peace. "Sonan, can you understand me?"

"Yes, of course," said Sonan, as if she hadn't just doomed their vessel and electrocuted her only ally.

"Then please listen. If we go back to the planet, we'll all die. Including you."

"I must arrest and imprison Xan under Carmnia of Trilly on Tuhnt. It is my prime directive."

"Alright, then, Sonan," Xan said from the floor between Listay's legs. He was between Listay's legs because the rest her body was very effectively blocking them from Sonan. "Go ahead and take me, then."

May dropped beside him to whisper, "You're giving up?"

"I'm moving on," he said as the MoonHopper fumbled onto the planet's crumbling crust. "Listen," he spoke to Sonan again. "You can arrest and imprison me, and I won't fight or try to run or anything, though I can't guarantee I won't complain about it, knowing me, as long as you promise to leave all them out of it. Let them take the MoonHopper to safety."

Of course she would let them take the MoonHopper. It belonged to EnviroDev, not her. She had strong feelings about vehicular theft. Sonan tilted her head as the idea processed, then, finally, she said, "Yes. That is an acceptable arrangement. Step onto the teledisc, and we will return to the *Innocuous* where you belong."

Xan began to crawl out through Listay's legs, but May grabbed his lapel.

"There are four of us!" she hissed at him. "We can take her down *and* get out of here before the planet blows."

"Precious Butler is as big as all four of us combined and she had him out in half a blip." He shook his head. "If I go with her, everyone will be fine."

"*Except you.*"

"Right, but the way I figure it, I did steal the ship that factored in the destruction of Tuhnt. I should have been on Tuhnt when it blew up, but if I'm on New Tuhnt when it does, that's just poetic justice."

"I hate poetry," May seethed at him.

"You just haven't read one you liked yet! I wager I could find a poem you'd enjoy. Maybe the sonnets of Hoyploff the Plivered. Really subversive stuff, you should look them up."

"And what if I hate it? You can't make additional poetry recommendations if you're dead." May's jaw hurt, and she realized she had been talking through clenched teeth.

Aimz pushed between May and Xan, spreading Listay's legs so far she was essentially sitting on them. Listay, wondering why she even bothered trying to protect them in the first place, dismounted the three of them and stepped aside.

"I'll be honest," whispered Aimz, "we could probably take her. Have you seen Listay? Positively rippling." She winked at Listay who glanced down at her approvingly.

"See?" said May.

"I know! I know we could take her. But, hey, who's to say she won't take out one of us while we're at it? It's time for me to go," he said seriously.

"You can't do that!" May shouted, pushing Aimz's head down so she could impress upon Xan the full intensity of her glare.

"I can, and I have to. *Please* stop being so zuxing stubborn, you're making this really hard."

"Fine. I'll be less stubborn *after* I do this." She launched herself at Sonan, ready to rip out the android's circuits with her fingernails if she had to.

Something caught her waist.

Something twisted her into a hug.

Something shoved her toward Listay whose arms cinched around her.

"Goodbye, starshine."

Xan joined Sonan on the teledisc, and they were gone.

A rock dropped from a great height in May's chest. The arms encircling her were strong and comforting, but she didn't want to be comforted.

Rage at the pointlessness of everything she'd just been through screamed out of May. She tried to leverage herself against Listay, but the more she pulled away, the tighter she was held, like an oversensitive locking seatbelt.

Aimz vaulted over Precious Butler's inert form and into the cockpit of the MoonHopper, quickly brought the necessary functions back online, then set it to take them to Yenucket. Checking to make sure Precious Butler was breathing (he was), she returned to the back of the ship where Listay struggled to hold in May's rage. Sitting cross-legged in front of May, Aimz searched for some comforting words to share with her.

"Unpin it, Earthmun. At least he's gonna die quick," was not the best choice, but she said it anyway.

In a feat May herself would never be able to explain or duplicate, she wrenched herself out of Listay's grasp and tackled Aimz, battering her like saltwater battering the hull of an ocean liner.

Aimz caught Listay's gaze and silently asked for assistance, half-heartedly shielding her face from May's punches.

"You brought that on yourself," Listay said.

With a resigned shrug, Aimz put her hands behind her head and laid back, letting May beat the shit out of her for a while. At least getting punched in the face repeatedly felt a bit better than ditching Xan on a doomed planet with an insane android.

CHAPTER THIRTY-SEVEN

Befriending Sonan

It couldn't be said that teleporting was ever a pleasant experience, but teleporting along with a mechanical humanoid is singularly wretched. After mingling briefly with Sonan's electrified atoms, Xan's molecules vibrated for a few blips before settling back into a solid form. Sonan waited, visibly unshaken, for the theatrics to end.

Once his atoms had collected themselves, Xan gave her an uncomfortable smile. "Back to the holding cell? Or do you want to poison me again, first? Actually I wouldn't mind that right about now."

"No. I have someone I'd quite like to see privately in my tearoom." She began leading him toward the cell. She didn't pull a weapon on him. Didn't drag him along. She knew that he knew that he wasn't going anywhere.

"Who's that?" Making conversation, he figured, would help pass the time until he died.

"Admiral Rankin Warders. He'll be pleased to hear the mission is complete."

"He's here?" Xan choked, no longer able to walk casually beside his captor.

"The Admiral is dead." Sonan tapped her head where her hard drive resided. "But his spirit remains in here." She blinked and a 3D hologram of Admiral Warders appeared to walk beside them.

"Oh that's..." Xan jogged a little to catch up with the android and the hologram. "That's disarming. Alright." He swallowed, unsure if he was glad that the Admiral wasn't actually there, or concerned that the digital ghost of the Admiral was leading him to his grave. He decided he could be both. If he could be both pleased that May and Aimz were safe and terrified that he'd never see either of them again, he could live in the dualism of being glad that the Admiral no longer existed and concerned about his ghost.

He rolled with it.

There was a chance, however slight, that he could make friends with Sonan.

"I'm sorry to hear about the Admiral. Were you close?" he tried, figuring it might be slightly harder for her to kill him if she liked him.

"We still are. He is, as I said, stored in my harddrive. He is closer to me than ever now."

Clearly Sonan didn't grasp the finality of death in the same way Xan did.

"Right, naturally! So could I...could I meet him? We sort of got off wrong on our first meeting. I mean, I suppose he was possessed at the time, so he might not even remember me—"

"He remembers you. He hates you."

"Well, maybe he wouldn't hate me if he—"

"He hates you," she repeated. "He is dead, and as such he cannot learn, grow, or change."

"Ah, but you can! That was the implication, right? You could grow to love me."

Sonan looked at him reproachfully now. "No, I could not."

"Right," he said, then chewed his lip as he thought. "Hey! We could take the ship into orbit, couldn't we? Then you could torture me for a lifetime instead of just...well just in between now and the imminent explosion."

"The ship is immobile. We were shot down almost immediately by the *Peacemaker* because there was no distraction rocket to assuage the attack. Which is your fault and the reason that the Admiral hates you."

"Hated. I mean, if he's dead. Past tense," Xan mumbled. It was more difficult than he had expected to befriend Sonan.

"I spoke accurately. The memory of him still hates you," Sonan said. "Observe." She turned to the silently walking specter of the Admiral. "Admiral Warders, how do you feel about Xan of Tuhnt?"

The Admiral's neutral expression went sour. "That zuxing cowardly little zoup-nog will be the death of me," he grumbled.

"And he was correct," said Sonan as she turned a corner and led him into the holding cell, the Admiral beside her glaring angrily at nothing. Once again, Xan walked through the sickly yellow light barrier.

CHAPTER THIRTY-EIGHT

Will to Live

The holding cell aboard the *Innocuous* was built for reflecting. Literally, on account of the aluminum walls, and figuratively because the only entertainment available to anyone locked in the cell was to watch their own memories until they were as distorted as a rotting VHS tape.

Xan had found another way to amuse himself. The deadly laser barrier which imprisoned him happened to be on the same electrical circuit as the climate control, and so whenever the ship's climate control unit kicked on, the deadly laser barrier flickered.

Rather than think about what had happened, he started counting the flickers.

It had happened three times.

Four, now.

Xan's eyes were beginning to dry out. If he blinked, he might miss a flicker, and if he couldn't even be trusted to count the number of times the power decreased in a laser barrier, he truly was an utter waste of perfectly good organic material.

Five times now, but this time was different. This time, the power had fluctuated due to a tremble in the planet's core.

"Alert: Generator core overheating, explosion imminent," said the planet, muffled by the insulated walls of the ship.

"Alright, thank you, I got it. You can stop reminding me." He winked one eye, then the other, refusing to miss a power fluctuation. It was the last thing giving his life meaning.

Imminent, the planet had said.

What did it mean by imminent, anyway? Did he have beoops left to live? A rotation? The only thing that was certain was that Death loomed much closer than he was typically comfortable with.

How, he wondered, would it happen? Perhaps the ship would first plummet unknown distances to the fiery core of the overheating planet and he would roast.

It was equally likely that the entire thing would shatter into a kazillion bits and he would be skewered on the shrapnel like an unwitting shish kabob.

Or the laser barrier might get him. If the ship were to fall into a crater and land side-ways, gravity would pull him through the barrier like paper through a shredder.

Maybe, if he were really lucky, the collapse of the planet would take a lifetime and he would die of old age.

Six fluctuations.

No, that would be the unluckiest instance of them all. A lifetime of counting minor power variances in the laser barrier to keep from thinking about how impressively he had botched the whole living thing. Slowly forgetting May's smile, the sound of her voice.

That laser barrier was starting to look like a good alternative. He'd just need to cuddle up to it and let it do the job it was made for. If fizzling a criminal into non-existence wasn't ultimate job satisfaction to a laser barrier, Xan couldn't begin to imagine what would be.

"Alert: Gener—"

"Yep. Yes, I heard you," he told the planet irritably. "Right, so," he began talking to himself. "May's as safe as she can be. Doesn't have the *Audacity,* sure, but she's got enough gem for a decent racing rocket. She was smart to transfer all that gem to the bank before picking me up. She's smart, she'll be okay. Aimz is alive and doing whatever it is that makes her happy which, I assume, involves licking every rock she encounters and probably Listay as well. May can probably teach Aimz to do David Attenborough impressions and Aimz can reach things on high shelves for May! They better stay together; May's too short. Oh Blitheon! I should've told Aimz that May can't reach the high shelves on her own and they need to stay together. Wait, no. That's ridiculous. May can just use the lower shelves. Or climb on something.

She's resourceful. But zuut! Who will keep her hair up? Who will fix May's hair?!" he shouted at the laser barrier.

It fluctuated a seventh time in response.

"Someone else. Someone I've never met who's good with hair." He moved close enough to the laser barrier that he could feel the electricity buzzing gently across his skin.

"Alright. I'm doing this as a favor for myself. I'm just going to walk right on through this extremely deadly laser barrier and find out what exactly happens when you die because I mean, zuut, who knows really? I'll think of it as an experiment. Aimz would be proud; I'm being very scientific in my last moments. I should probably lick it first, just for her sake. That's what she would do. She'd lick it first and mutter something about its composition." He stuck his tongue out and heard the tongue ring click against his teeth as he did.

"Zuut! I should've returned the tongue ring. That was thoughtless of me. I'm an utter and absolute taagshlorph. Pointless existence. Aimzless, Mayless." He put his tongue away and wondered when exactly he had forgotten how to walk through extremely deadly laser barriers.

He needed to return the tongue ring. There had to be a way out of here and back to Aimz and May, because if there wasn't, Aimz would never get the tongue ring back. He sat on the shelf-bed, as far away from the laser barrier as he could get, raking his fingers through his hair as he attempted to think his way out.

"Augh, May needs the zuxing *Audacity*, too. Sure, she could get a new rocket, but why should she have to? Because I'm a Poslouian-slug-grass-eating-coward. Alright, I'm going to bring it to her. And the tongue ring. Not to her, to Aimz. I'm going to bring the *Audacity* to May so she can be happy, and I'm going to return Aimz's tongue ring because I sure as trok refuse to die a thief. A double thief, I guess. Once was enough. But how?" His only plan had involved befriending Sonan and that hadn't worked.

A thunderous crashing from outside, and the ship pitched, sinking into a new crater in the planet's surface as it began in earnest to shake itself apart.

Xan grabbed onto the rim of the bed, holding onto it as gravity became his most pressing concern. If it didn't right itself soon, the decision of whether or not to take his own life would be made for him.

Sweat, or what he would have us believe was sweat, rolled down his cheeks and sizzled on the barrier. His fingers were already tiring from supporting his weight. May wasn't coming, and he wasn't smart enough to escape without her help. And he didn't want her to come, anyway. He wanted her to be safe, and he wanted to get what he deserved.

So he let go.

"Alert: Generator core overheating, explosion imminent," the planet said as the *Innocuous* crumbled into the depths.

CHAPTER THIRTY-NINE

More Vehicular Theft

It's rather difficult, May quickly found, to punch someone who's hugging you. There's just not enough room to get a good swing in. This was a trick Aimz had learned from Xan. He had turned out to be extremely difficult to fight in their youth.

So Aimz held May on the floor of the MoonHopper until May realized attacking her would do exactly nothing to help the situation.

"I'm starting to think," said Aimz, "you didn't like what I said."

May sighed but twisted it into a humorless laugh. "You think? I was mad at Xan, not you. Well, I was a little mad at you."

May rolled off Aimz and sat up, smoothing her hair away from her face. "What the hell am I going to do now? I can't afford a new racing rocket, I don't want to go back to Earth, and I'll never get into poetry," she said with a laugh which sounded like a poorly disguised sob.

"Sonan?" asked Precious Butler, his voice muffled by the metal floor. He curled up, looked around blearily, realized two of the six who should have been on the ship were not on the ship, realized *who* those two were, and groaned. "What did she do?" He knew.

May took a breath and opened her mouth, but when everyone politely looked at her, she found she could move her lips quite well but getting sound past them was more challenging than she remembered. Her lips trembled before she pressed them into a tight line.

Listay summarized. "Xan sacrificed himself so we could escape. He and Sonan are on the *Innocuous,* and we're almost to Yenuket Municipal Spaceport to refuel."

Precious Butler rubbed the back of his neck and sat down at the control panel. "That's interesting," he said, getting a sense of how close they were to Yenuket Municipal, finding they had nearly passed it, and reversing the thrusters to bring them down. "He didn't strike me as the heroic type."

"He's not," May said bitterly.

The MoonHopper docked in one of the nicer docking bays on Yenuket Municipal. You could tell the nice ones from the shady ones by the lines of holographic police tape which crisscrossed the shady ones.

The moment the ship settled, May hopped up as if she'd been spring loaded.

"What's the plan?"

"The plan?" Precious Butler said. "The plan is to fuel up and get to the Tuhntian colony on Rhea." He pulled the fuel cap release lever.

"I mean for saving Xan. Someone's thought of one, right?" May looked first to Listay who felt uncharacteristically unprepared, then to Aimz who was studying a rust flake near her shin on the floor of the MoonHopper until she noticed May staring at her.

"Me?" She sat up. "I'm partial to the plan that doesn't involve being on an exploding planet, myself."

"He's your brother!"

"He left me on a doomed planet first, so we're settled up now. Besides, I have other brothers. I don't know them, but I'm sure I've got plenty." She watched a speck of dust float in front of her. "Hey, Precious Butler, how many Carmnians are there in the Tuhntian colony?"

He shrugged. "There are a few."

"See! A few is plenty." She gave a crooked smile, then the glimmer of her shoulder spikes caught her eye. "Won't need these anymore." She shrugged off her jacket and began to studiously unscrew the sharp studs.

"I suppose since there are plenty more, I'll just find myself another Carmnian hairstylist who has a racing rocket, loves old Earth television, and does an outstanding impression of David Attenborough. There must be plenty of those left, right?" May growled at Aimz.

"I used to know a Carmnian who's good with hair, yeah."

"That's great news. Do you have their phone number handy? Because I could use a touch-up!" May ground her teeth.

"I..." Aimz glanced at Listay for help. "What's a phone number?"

May answered, "Ten digits including area code. Dash in the mid...No. Okay. Everyone out."

"Out?"

"Out!" May shouted. "If none of you will help, I'm going back alone. Give me the anchor." She held her hand out to Precious Butler and he haltingly dropped the anchor button for the MoonHopper in her palm. She squeezed into the cockpit and Precious Butler backed away. "Goddamn aliens have no sense of loyalty," she muttered, studying the control panel to get a bearing on how this particular ship worked. Behind her, a statue garden. She spun around. "Would someone please fuel up the ship?"

"You'll, uh..." Precious Butler began. "You'll pick us up when you're done, right?"

"Yeah, I don't want to get stranded here again," said Aimz. "Even the good neighborhoods around these parts are in a bad area."

"I will go with you," Listay said, putting a hand on May's shoulder which May only then realized had been trembling like a Soprano's vocal chords. The hand helped. "I'm partially responsible for her being stranded in space. I carried out Chaos's orders to abduct the Earthlings. If she's made something good out of what I did, it's my duty to support her. Besides, Xan was tricked by Chaos just as I was."

Aimz had crossed both her legs and her arms, making herself as small and knotty as possible to hold true to her convictions. "He chose to do that so the rest of us would be safe. If we all get blown to bits, then what was the point, huh? I'm fine with letting him have this one."

A lazy knocking at the MoonHopper door interrupted. Precious Butler pulled it open to reveal a gray-green Udonian who looked like a turtle that had been removed from its shell standing outside with a digital clipboard.

"Yenuket Municipal, please prepay," he said it like a plea for death.

Listay stepped forward and offered her face for payment, but Precious Butler held her back. "I insist," he said.

She pushed him aside."No, it's alright, I've got it."

"Please, it's the least I can do." Precious Butler angled his face toward the attendant.

"Really, it's fine," Listay out maneuvered him, a flash of blue, and the attendant nodded approvingly and let them out.

While they fiddled with the fuel pump outside, May looked again for a clear and obvious button which would make the MoonHopper go, such as the *Audacity* had. She was beginning to suspect that flying the *Audacity* had been too easy.

There was a checklist, apparently. A list of tasks scrolled across the viewscreen waiting for May to complete them before launch. She ran through the list ferociously, flicking this on, pressing that off, locking the other in, skipping that because what the hell was an intramanual gauge relay? The fuel indicator light turned green as Listay filled the tank, and May opened the fuel booster and held down the engine starter until it sputtered on.

"That's plenty, let's go," May shouted at the open door.

No one came. Not even Listay who had said she would.

May squeezed herself from the cockpit and leaned out of the door. There was, she now realized, a very good reason Listay had not joined her.

Listay was being arrested.

"Please; they're in a terrible rush," Precious Butler tried to explain to a chrome Cosmic Constable who was only slightly larger than him, but a great deal rounder.

"According to our records, General Listay under Rapite of Rhea is dead. Suspect."

"Right, she *was* dead. Now she's not!" Aimz tried to explain.

"May," Listay called to her, "I'm sorry this might take a blip." She jerked her head toward the docking bay exit and mouthed, "Go" at her repeatedly. The Cosmic Constable wasn't built to catch a hint, but May was.

She slammed the door, sealed it, ran to the cockpit and committed vehicular theft.

CHAPTER FORTY

Ka-Boom

Having a back was a prerequisite, Xan thought, for acute back pain. Continuation of consciousness, he also thought, was a prerequisite for thinking at all.

There was not much on the wall opposite the holding cell. Smooth aluminum siding made up the majority of it, but in one place, a breaker-box with a sharply angled handle was affixed to the wall.

This, naturally, had made it an excellent target for Xan's spine.

A spine which, curiously, still existed.

A spine which, even more curiously, was still encased in the rest of him.

"Ugh," he said, shifting off the breaker box and rubbing his back. "Didn't expect the afterlife to hurt so much."

He rolled to his side. Someone was staring at him.

"Uhm. Hello," he said.

She pursed wispy blue lips at him, shook her head, and sighed like a breeze exiting a catacomb. "Not you again," said Death. "What's *with* you?"

"With me?"

"There's another consciousness stuck to you. I can't take you like this! Take it off."

"I uh...okay." And he began to unbutton his suit.

"I was referring to the additional consciousness that's with you, not your clothing," she glared at him.

"Oh, sorry. I um...don't know how. Additional consciousness?"

"You're an utter and absolute taagshlorph for calling me out here twice in one rotation for nothing, you know that?" She disappeared.

"I am," he agreed with nothingness then paused before adding, "talking to myself now. I am talking to myself. Okay, alright, well." He glanced up at the cell he had just fallen out of and saw that the laser barrier had shut off, along with everything but the emergency lights. The ship's power had been cut. "That was unsettlingly lucky," he noted, then got to his feet, standing on the ship's wall. "Science experiment: Can I keep that up?"

He sprinted into the dark hallway of the ship until he found the nearest teledisc. He nearly missed it, because instead of being on the floor like it ought to have been, it was on the wall. Or, technically, he had been running on the wall which had traded places with the floor when the ship fell.

Teledisc operations may appear somewhat magical, but there are rules. There are always rules. One of these rules is that you must keep all arms and legs inside the telefield created by the disk in order to ensure that you will arrive with the correct number of limbs.

Telediscs were not meant to be used by someone standing on the wall. If he laid down, he could at least get his feet on the disc. That would have to be enough. He had cheated Death a few times now, he was fairly confident he could outsmart Maiming.

"Alright, stealing the *Audacity* again on purpose this time. Really hope it's not boiling in the core of the planet right now." Then Xan sent the teleport command from his BEAPER.

He remerged on the *Audacity*'s teledisc and sprung to the control loft, flicking on the back-up generator with a button underneath the panel. He had found that button so many times accidentally that he could find it on command now. The first step in untethering the *Audacity* from New Tuhnt, Xan figured, was understanding exactly what it was tethered to in the first place.

The warm orange glow of the ship's ambient light flickered on and, for a moment, he could imagine that everything was as it ought to have been.

Xan wanted so much to enjoy the sight of the living room of the *Audacity*. To settle onto the worn, rust colored couch and forget everything that had transpired thus far. It had been a rather difficult character arc for him, and he was tired and ready to watch a few episodes of 'I Love Lucy' with a carafe of coffee and a sleeping May curled on the other arm of the couch.

But May wasn't there, and at this distance, it was highly unlikely he'd be able to pick up 'I Love Lucy.' Also, they were low on coffee. Not out, but low. He eyed the coffee maker, considering one last carafe, but the planet felt that it was a good moment to alert him once again that he was in imminent danger of being blown up, and the coffee was forgotten.

He leapt up the stairs of the control loft and reached for the viewscreen switch, ready to see chunks of oatmeal colored land jutting out of the boiling magma which he assumed was now swirling around them.

Instead, he stopped short of turning on the screen when he saw an Osculum languidly rolling down the control panel, floating back up to the top, and letting itself roll back down again.

"Osy?"

The sponge creature purred, wafted up to him.

"This whole time you were hiding out on the *Audacity,* never once wondered where we were?"

It stared facelessly at him.

He shook his head and stuffed the sponge into his pocket. "Can't believe I'm about to say this to a sponge, but it's good to see you. I'll bring you back to May, too."

Once he switched the screen on, it took him a moment to register what he was seeing outside the ship. It wasn't magma-lit, that was certain. It was dark as death. No, he retracted the analogy; Death had been rather pale, actually. It was dark as a crater. It *was* a crater. Emergency lights on the hull of the *Innocuous* picked out the broken shards of the planet they had landed among. Too deep for sunlight to penetrate, not deep enough to be swimming in a red-hot soup of liquified rock and metal.

Good enough.

Xan exited the rocket via the teledisc, stumbling through a pile of loosely packed debris until he got his footing on a largish slab of ground. He walked around the perimeter of the *Audacity* until he found it: the embarrassingly thin line of the tether which had foiled their escape from New Tuhnt looped into one of the ship's round fin vents. He could reach it if he climbed, but then what? Scowl at it? Call it nasty names? Bite it off?

He ran his tongue, or rather, Aimz's tongue (he still felt odd about that, but was trying to accept it), over his teeth as he considered what a tether strong enough to hold back the *Audacity* would do to his smile.

He liked his smile. He'd already lost a molar to Yvonne and wasn't keen on losing anything else.

"No, nope, not my teeth. Alright, where do you lead, you horrible string?" he asked it, picking up the thin silver line and freeing it from debris, following it across the shifting and quivering rocks to its source.

With growing dread, he followed the string across the distance between the *Audacity* and the *Innocuous*. At last, he found the source, a featureless box attached to the underbelly of the *Innocuous* with a seam down the middle and a hole like a spider's spinneret from which the tether protruded.

That looked to Xan like a weak point. He almost apologized as he dug two fingers into the hole and began to pry open the tether's casing. It gave perhaps an eighth of a centimeter before he lost feeling in the tips of his fingers. Clearly, his assessment of the tether's weak point was wrong.

The Osculum wriggled in his pocket and he fished it out, placed it on the seam and watched it gayly roll along the casing. Useless.

Something, perhaps a sharp bit of metal to leverage it, would have been massively useful. So too would have been Ranken Warder's photon gun, which he briefly had. But, on account of the whole Sphere of Time being a sham thing, the photon gun hadn't actually existed.

He tapped the side of the box as he thought, searching the surrounding, poorly lit debris desperately for anything that might help. Rocks, mostly. Rocks were his assets. He pocketed Osy once more, picked up the largest rock he could feasibly throw, and pelted it at the tether box.

Dented! Dented was good. He studied the dent, ran his thumb over it. Not a dent. Just a smudge of dirt.

Another tremor convinced him that if he survived this, he could always get dental implants, so he cinched his teeth around the tether and gave it an enthusiastic gnaw.

Then a less enthusiastic chew.

Eventually, he sat down to nibble, his jaw aching from the effort.

"Hungry?" May sai—

"MAY!" Xan interrupted her dialogue tag and launched into her for a hug. Anticipating this, May had planted herself solidly outside the MoonHopper, her stance wide, her arms open. "I'm not hungry, no, that was terrible." He continued to hug her. "I was just on my way to bring you the *Audacity*. Why do you always insist on saving me?"

"You keep needing to be saved!" she said over his shoulder, the rim of the emergency helmet she'd found on the MoonHopper cutting into her neck.

"I was doing alright." He released her.

"You were chewing on an unbreakable tether."

"I was assessing the situation." He plucked the tether where he'd been chewing on it; aside from being a touch wet, it looked no different. "With my teeth. The situation, I've ascertained, is a bad one. Why did you come back? Where's Aimz?"

"I have to show you the haunted Big Mouth Billy Bass! And Aimz didn't want to come."

"Ha! Fish promise. Aimz was right not to come, though. It's dangerous, I'm not worth it."

"You are. I hate making friends, Xan. If you're going to die, I might as well, too." She grabbed his hand. "Now come on." She tugged on him and got about as far as a gnat trying to move a marble statue with a rubber band.

"Not planning on dying! I was just going to figure out how to free *Audy* so you can keep racing." His eyes ping-ponged from the *Audacity* to the *Innocuous* and back again. Another good idea would come to him, he figured, if he was patient enough.

New Tuhnt reminded them once more that it was considering ripping itself to pieces in the near future. It had started to feel like an empty threat to Xan, until the planet added a bit of pertinent information. "Explosion," it said, "in five..."

"Five what?!" May squeaked as she tried to drag Xan to the MoonHopper. "I don't want the *Audacity*; I came back for you. Get in!" She tugged again, and he yielded, but only because the planet rattled violently, tossing them both to the ground.

The quakes, up until now, had been brief, like an involuntary muscle twitch. This one was not. It shook the planet like a gospel choir's risers at the climax of a vigorous Sunday service, making it difficult for them to regain their footing. "Four," said the planet.

"You love the *Audacity!*" Xan shouted over the tumult of crumbling earth, oblivious to the countdown.

"I love you more, now come *on*!"

Xan stared once more at the beautiful orange ship, its fins half buried in the planet's rubble, until his eyes began to water, which only took half a second. "Three," the voice from below them echoed, nearly drowned out by the tumbling of a nearby landslide. Three of anything was not many, and this sufficiently convinced Xan to get a move on.

They clambered toward the MoonHopper which hovered just over the trembling ground, swaying and bobbing nervously as if it had seriously considered leaving without them.

"Two." A shard of granite knifed up in front of them, cutting them off from the MoonHopper and hurling a couple dozen head-sized boulders at their shins, pinning them down.

"I've got the anchor!" May shouted, implying that if Xan could get to her and send the teleport signal to the MoonHopper with his BEAPER, they still might survive this.

"Mmphh!" Xan said, implying that he was trying to get to her, but his leg was jammed rather firmly beneath a boulder.

"Shit," May whispered, the implications thereof being obvious, as she crawled toward him over the shuddering rubble.

"One."

May launched herself at Xan as he sent the teleport command and both of them remerged inside the MoonHopper just as a wall of flame erupted outside from a massive fissure. Xan flung the door shut then was himself flung against the ceiling of the MoonHopper as the blast launched them into orbit, spinning them like wet laundry. Stumbling into the cockpit, May reached for the artificial gravity control and successfully stuck them both to the floor.

The viewscreen lit up white, every pixel straining to contain the brightness of what was happening outside the ship.

And then space vacuumed it all up. The entire fiery blaze which had destroyed the planet was gone in an instant, replaced by nothingness peppered with crumbs.

CHAPTER FORTY-ONE

Sonan Wins

"*Explosion in five...*"

Light filtered through the holowindow, picking out the curling forms in the doily on Sonan's tea table. A folder called "Contentment" slowly opened, coaxed out by the warm tea in her hands, and, finding no unsatisfied directives loitering about, flooded the heretofore unused code into her system.

She blinked open an old but well-preserved hologram video file which she projected into the chair in front of her.

Admiral Warders flickered there now, in what had been his usual seat, glittering with sharply pixelated edges and stroking his impeccable facial hair.

"In the event," said the recorded image of the admiral, "in the *likely* event," he amended, his mustache twitching, "that I don't return to you, I have one final request." The memory of Ranken Warders leaned in across the table, reached for the memory of the handle of a teacup, brought the cup to his mustache, sipped.

"*Four.*"

"Oh but you must return, Ranken," said Sonan to the memory, for it was what she had said back then.

He shook his head. "My larvling, without the *Audacity,* we haven't a chance against the *Peacemaker.* I would like you to find the Carmnian that did this to us. Can you do that for me?"

"My dear Admiral, I wouldn't know where to begin." Sonan said, but this time when she said it, it was with a hint of irony and a small smile.

"*Three.*"

"I have complete faith in you, Sonan. Your new priority one directive is to arrest and imprison Xan under Carmnia of Trilly on Tuhnt."

Sonan's mouth cracked into a stiff smile. "Yes, Admiral. It's done, for you." She had been waiting so long to say that; her circuitry could barely contain the pleasure it gave her.

It was difficult to say for sure, but Sonan liked to believe he had winked at her.

"That's my larvling." The recording cut out. That was the last she'd seen of the admiral before the crash.

Sonan drank her tea, the wires at the back of her throat jittering their displeasure.

"*Two.*"

The tea set rattled violently on the table, but this didn't bother Sonan, as it was nothing her gyroscope couldn't account for.

She opened another video file now. This was a live feed from a camera which nestled into the upper corner of Xan's holding cell.

Confusion paused her contentment program. Xan was not where she had left him. Some after-thought of code told her she ought to scrunch her eyebrows downward with concern now, but her hardware wasn't up to it.

"*One.*"

CHAPTER FORTY-TWO

Silence

The silence of space is absolute. It is so full of silence, that there's no room for sound to wheedle in.

Aboard the *Audacity,* this had never been a problem for May and Xan. They always filled the silence easily with idle chatter or whatever TV signal was wafting around at the time.

Now, staring out of the MoonHopper's viewscreen at the empty space where New Tuhnt and the *Audacity* had been but was no longer, they were having trouble filling the void.

CHAPTER FORTY-THREE

The Moonshine Cafe

The Cosmic Constables were unpopular across the galaxy for several reasons. Firstly, they were privately owned, and if they felt they could stand to make a crystal turning someone in or ticketing them, their programming obligated them to do so.

Secondly, they were notoriously touchy. Anxiously leg tapping was strike one. A furtive glance, and they would pull a zapper on you. Use a double negative, and you were as good as dead.

Thirdly, they were far too shiny. Their bulging chrome shells were designed to appear strong but trustworthy. Instead, they looked as if they were allergic to bees and had been stung multiple times all over their metallic bodies.

Fourthly, they either didn't understand anything you told them or were simply incapable of listening to reason. Many models employed both poor language comprehension and selective hearing as a feature of their programing.

Which is why Listay, Aimz, and Precious Butler were still sitting across from a Cosmic Constable in a broom closet of an office trying to explain that Listay was not dead when the lights went out.

The room, and in fact the entire spaceport, shuddered with the force of the explosion.

When the lights flickered back on, the Cosmic Constable was alone.

Aimz led the group, sprinting through the spaceport she'd had the misfortune of calling home for a century and a half.

"Where are we going?" Precious Butler asked from the back of the line, checking behind him for the constable as he ran.

"You'll know when we get there, because I'll tell you," Aimz shouted back at him, turning down familiar streets, her feet kicking up clouds of red dust. She skidded to a halt in front of the Moonshine Cafe and smiled. "Right, we're there!"

"A bar?"

"Yes!"

"Are we safe here?"

"The constables hate the robot that works here. Drives them absolutely suicidal, whatever he says. Just don't pay him any attention, and we'll be fine." Aimz yanked on the metal door which was mostly rusted shut. It didn't move.

The sound of sirens grew behind them. Listay clutched the door handle beneath Aimz's hands and they were at last able to crack it enough to squeeze inside.

The robot at the counter paused, lifted its head with a depressing creak, then, deciding they weren't worth the attention, pointedly returned to staring at the spot on the bar it insisted on continuing to clean.

"See? It's a truly miserable little machine," Aimz said. "Hey beautiful!" she called to it, waving. The robot pointedly looked away. The trio watched the constable peer in through the window at them with its expressionless vision visor, then seem to sigh and putter away.

"Well done, Aimz," Listay said with a smile as she pulled out a rickety wooden chair and sat at the nearest table to go over their next action plan. Precious Butler and Aimz joined her and once they were all settled around the table, the screen in the center of it lit up with the bar's menu, glowing feebly at them.

They ignored it.

Well, Listay and Precious Butler ignored it. Aimz eagerly tapped several drinks which materialized blips later on the tiny telediscs set into the table. She gathered all six drinks and tasted them each in turn.

Listay watched her curiously, but didn't intervene. "New Tuhnt," Listay began, but was distracted by Aimz's tongue licking something red from the rim of one of the glasses. She shook her head and addressed Precious Butler instead. "Clearly New Tuhnt has detonated so—"

"Why clearly?" Aimz interrupted, licking her lips now in a way that was further distracting to Listay.

"Because," Listay told Precious Butler, "what else would cause turbulence and outages on a spaceport?"

"Oh plenty of things. Meteorites passing by, nearby planets exploding, meteorites passing by...so that's...you know, that's two things." Aimz finished the second drink and set the empty glass upside down on the mini-teledisc where it was whisked away.

"Fine. If we assume that New Tuhnt has exploded, we need to consider the option that May did not make it back in time and we are without a vehicle."

Aimz had tipped her chair onto its two back legs to finish knocking back her third drink. She held up a finger to get the table's attention, tossed the glass behind her, and snapped delightedly when it landed on the mini-teledisc on the table behind them.

"Aimz please. We've just lost May and Xan—"

"And Sonan," Precious Butler added.

"Yes, and Sonan. We need to find some way back to Rhea I from here without the MoonHopper."

Aimz leaned forward, typed something into her BEAPER and sent it. "There. I told Xan where to find us. I'm sure he'll be along in a blip, and we can get out of here. Between now and then, though..." Aimz slid an opaque white drink over the digital menu to Listay. "Un-pin it, General."

"I cannot un-pin it." She slid the drink back. "Your brother and an innocent person—"

"And an innocent android," said Precious Butler.

"Yes," Listay said. "Might be dead, and I need to find some Rhean official who can confirm that I'm not dead so I can use my bank account again."

Aimz sighed, took the white drink back, and stuck her tongue out at Listay. Not her tongue. Xan's. She missed her tongue ring.

Wait, Aimz thought to herself, wringing her tongue–his tongue–through her teeth. She didn't have her tongue ring. This was all real. This had really, actually happened. The light of reality was beginning, at last to dawn on her.

Listay and Precious Butler discussed options, but their voices were far away as the recent past got closer to Aimz.

"Shhh," she said to them. They shushed and watched her respectfully, hoping she had something salient to say. She did not. "Xan," she said. "Quaxlagon. The Quaxlagon I grew up with. My favorite brother. The only brother I ever knew," she said. "That Xan...who I thought was long dead," she said. "He's actually alive."

Listay looked at her like perhaps she had gone insane. In reality, this was the sanest she'd been for a few chapters. "He was," Listay corrected. "But–"

"But now he isn't?" Aimz said, weakly, her eyes large and moist. "Blitheon," she said, covering her mouth with her hand. "Blitheon, what have I done?" she said, then split the fingers of the hand covering her mouth just enough that she could fit the straw of the white-frosted drink in between her lips as she stared wide-eyed at the flaking ceiling of the cafe.

CHAPTER FORTY-FOUR

Fish Promise

The MoonHopper nestled into the docking bay on Yenuket Municipal and the pervasive silence at last relaxed its grip on May and Xan.

"You said you love me more than—" Xan stopped, choking on the name of the ship.

"Of course." May shut off the MoonHopper's engine and twisted around in the seat. "You're the best friend I've ever had. The only one, actually."

"Really? You didn't have any friends on Earth?"

"It's hard to make friends as an adult," May said.

"Right. I suppose I sort of forced friendship upon you."

She laughed. "I wouldn't say forced. You made it easy, though."

"May, I love—"

"Ah!" She stopped him. "I can say it in a life-or-death situation, but you can't just go around saying it whenever you want."

"Why not?" he asked, deflated.

"You just don't. It's weird."

"In what way is saying 'I love you' weird? I say I love things all the time. I love a good limerick, I love watching movies with you, I love coffee, I love Lucy. Why is that any different?"

May thought about it for a long moment, only coming up with half-formed excuses that really, in this context, made little sense. "Huh," she said. "Alright, go on then."

"I love you more than I love Lucy," he said, wrapping her in a hug that didn't, for a change, completely restrict her air flow. He no longer felt he needed to cling to her. She'd proven she would always come back.

"More than Lucy? I'm honored," she laughed.

"Thank you for being so stubborn," he said.

"Anytime, blue. Now let's find everyone else and get off this backwater spaceport before we're invited to a hoedown." She pulled away and stood up, knocking her head against the low cockpit of the MoonHopper. The *Audacity* always had plenty of headroom, she thought sadly.

"What's a hoedown?" Xan asked.

"It's..." she sighed. "You'd probably love a hoedown, actually. It's a rural Americana thing. There's music and dancing and...I don't know boiled possum, probably."

Xan smiled. "I sincerely hope we're invited to a hoedown, yes, that sounds excellent. Don't think there's any possum out here, though. Earth critter, I'm guessing?"

"Yeah, Earth critter."

They locked the MoonHopper and found that the docking bay, like most of Yenuket Municipal, was empty.

May groaned. "Listay got arrested for being dead. They could be anywhere."

"They're at the Moonshine Cafe."

"What makes you say that?"

Xan tapped his BEAPER and the words 'We're at the Moonshine Cafe' scrolled across the floating holographic screen. A message from Aimz.

"I really need to get a BEAPER," May said as they began walking toward the cafe. "My only concern is that it might make life too easy."

"They're convenient, sure, but I've got one, and I can guarantee you it will do no such thing."

May had to agree.

"Oh! This." May ran up to a colorfully dripping mailbox and pointed to the poster which appeared to be a stick man and an upright dromedary, the same poster she had seen when she walked this way before. It was a great deal less irritating now that Xan was with her. "What is this?"

He recoiled at the sight of it. "This must be a really nasty part of the star system if they have to tell people not to do that."

"Do what?"

"Right, well, I promised I'd be honest with you, totally and completely from here on out so..." Then he told her exactly what act the poster was referring to.

"Okay," May said as they hurried away from the mailbox which had gurgled delightedly as Xan described to her the meaning. "I appreciate the honesty, but there are some things I'd rather not know."

"You did ask," he said.

Bezalbum's Baubles wasn't far now, and May felt a satisfying sense of closure at the idea of showing Xan the Billy Bass, so she sped up.

"There it is," she said, pointing out the sign for Bezalbum's Baubles excitedly.

"Singing fish promise?"

"Yep." May dragged Xan into the damasked front room. Now that May was aware of it, she could hear Big Mouth Billy Bass singing, muffled through the door. She dinged the bell, a little smug that she had kept her promise to the old Udonian who had insisted that she wouldn't.

Rather than wait for Bezalbum to totter out to the front of the store, May decided to help herself to the back room.

"Maybe she's out," May said, leading Xan around the counter. Something was different about the back room now. The air was lighter, somehow. The bass, which had been stuck on "Take Me to the River," was now singing through "Don't Worry, Be Happy," and it lifted the mood enormously.

"Here he is," May pointed to the plastic fish, flopping in time to the music.

Then, as expected, Xan laughed at the wriggling fish and went to take it down. Unexpected, though interesting: the moment he touched the fish's wooden base, it sparked an unmentionable color, stilled, then silenced.

Xan yipped, shaking the electric spark out of his fingers. "Zuut! What was that?"

"Static discharge?"

"I killed him!" Xan gasped, picking up the silent fish now and turning it over to find the battery compartment empty.

May snorted. “It needs batteries. I think you just de-haunted it. Maybe it’ll work properly now.”

“Can we get it?”

“Yeah,” May looked around the stacks. “If I can find Bezal-Ah!”

She was standing behind them.

“Oh now, my dear! You’ve returned to break the merchandise. Two hundred crystals for the used-to-be-haunted fish person. Two hundred, please dear.”

“Alright,” May said, the blue flash filling her vision before she had finished enunciating the “T.”

“That’s right dearie! Now come, come. Such a hurry you were in last time, I didn’t show you my collection of stuck together playing cards. If you can unstick them, you can have them! For three crystals each.”

Xan tapped May’s shoulder and showed her his BEAPER again.

The words ‘Hello, this is Listay. If you’re getting this, please reply. Aimz is upset, and I don’t know how to handle her,’ scrolled over his wrist.

“She’s upset! She’s worried about me,” Xan couldn’t keep the smile out of his voice as he tucked the fish under his arm and tapped out a reply. “We ought to go.”

“Yeah, we better get going, sorry” May told Bezalbum, whose eyes once again became big and watery.

“Oh my. My dear, it’s just been so long since anyone’s—”

“It’s a family emergency, Aimz gets really weird when she’s upset. I gotta see this,” Xan was tugging on her arm now.

“Wait!” cried Bezalbum. “Can’t I entice you with a real, legitimate Good Luck Charm? They don’t make ‘em like this no more, they don’t.”

May nearly said “Fuck no,” but caught herself. “F–uhh definitely not. Sorry!”

Xan hadn’t heard Bezalbum; he had given up trying to drag May along and instead ran out the door alone, May chased after him.

"Cheap! The both of you. Coming in here, taking advantage of an old widow. How I'll never know do you live with—"

"Really sorry!" May shouted back at her as she shut the door and sprinted after Xan.

He didn't know where the cafe was, and she didn't want to lose him in this place.

She caught up to him and they jogged until they found the flickering sign which read 'The Moonshine Cafe' and squeezed inside.

"I'm here!" Xan announced happily to the table.

"Oh, good. Can I have my tongue ring back?" Aimz was sitting on the table casually, snacking on something which a hovering black orb deposited one at a time into her hand. Her magenta eyes were difficult to look at, they glowed so fiercely, rimmed with green.

"Aw, Aimz, you were crying!" Xan rushed to her.

"Not at all." She snorted. "Why would you assume that?" She tried to continue eating the crisps that the black orb offered her, but Xan had twisted himself around her neck.

May sat across from Precious Butler, beside Listay.

"Is she alright?" May whispered to them.

They looked at each other and shrugged. Neither of them were willing to elaborate.

"Augh, shouldn't have gotten rid of the spikes," Aimz choked, pushing Xan off her and into the chair which had been hers. "You're certainly excited to be here. Found your will to live again?"

"Eh, more like it found me," he said with a shrug. "But I did find this!" He showed her the bass.

"Is that a Big Mouth Billy Bass?" Listay asked, horrified, over Aimz's legs.

"Exactly! Isn't he great?"

Listay shook her head. "No. Don't keep that fish."

"Why not?" May asked. "And how do you know what a Big Mouth Billy Bass is?"

"I..." Listay paused. She couldn't give a logical reason why she hated the fish, or how she knew what it was, but it gave her an overwhelming sense of dread. "I'm not sure. Sorry. Is the Moon-Hopper in drivable condition?"

"Yep, it's in the parking bay," May pulled out the anchor and Listay used her BEAPER to teleport the five of them back to the cramped hopper.

Precious Butler took the cockpit. "I'm not ready to explain all this to EnviroDev, so I'll be taking us back to my house first," he said, turning around to address everyone. "You all may stay with my wife and me for a few nights."

"In the same bed, I hope!" Aimz said.

Precious Butler was still not sure how seriously he should be taking Aimz. The answer was, of course, very very seriously. "There are several rooms in our house, as we are preparing to receive larvae soon."

"Are you going to turn me into the police?" Xan asked nervously.

Precious Butler sighed. "Do you want me to?"

"No! Uh...preferably not."

"Alright, then." Precious Butler began the pre-flight checklist. "I think you've been through enough already."

He smiled gratefully. "I sure hope so," he said.

May collapsed against the softest looking wall in the Moon-Hopper and slid to the cold floor, glad she didn't have to pilot for once. She closed her eyes, but all she could see was the cyan afterimage of the *Audacity*. Absently, she snapped the *Audacity's* anchor button off her suit and turned it in her fingers.

"Huh," Xan said, sitting beside her as the ship began to launch. "It's still connected."

He was right; the green indicator light was still on, pulsing hopefully.

"Mm-hmm," she agreed, though she was too tired to grasp that if the anchor button was online, so too was the teledisc which it was linked to. And if the teledisc was still online, the *Audacity* might be salvageable.

Snapping the button back on her suit, she noticed her bank fortune balled up in her breast pocket. She took it out and sighed. "This was totally wrong," she said. "It said it would all work out in the end." She closed her eyes again, trying to ignore the ghostly afterimage of the rocket as she rested her head on Xan's shoulder.

He folded the paper and put it in his own pocket where Osy would gently moisten it. He wrapped his other arm around May. "Well, then it must not be the end yet," he said.

END OF BOOK 2

The Audacity III: Be Kind, Rewind

CONTENTS

CHAPTER ONE

Creeping Misgivings

May should've been dead. She'd taken volt after volt of electricity while rewiring the *Audacity*'s main console, yet she continued stripping and twisting. Humans were more conductive than the thick-skinned Tuhntians who had built the rocket ship originally. May knew this, and she usually wore gloves, but for reasons which are about to become clear, she hadn't bothered.

Her legs ached to stretch out, but she was nearly done reassembling the console after having dismantled it for the eighth time in search of a remote control system. She snapped the orange siding back into place under the dashboard and rammed her forehead against it, hoping to transmit her desires directly from her brain to the machine.

Xan tapped her shoulder, and she slid out from under the console, her feet numb, head swimming as she dizzily searched the control loft for the Tuhntian. Nada. Strange; he was there a moment ago.

An invisible hand grabbed her shoulder, shook it gently.

"Damnit, Xan. I nearly had it that time," she said, her fingers feeling for the velcro strap buried in the dense purple curls at the back of her head. She pulled the FabriLife visor off her face and resisted the urge to chuck it onto the low pile neon-patterned carpet in the FabriLife Life Fabrication Arcade. Instead, she curbed her frustration enough to gently hook the visor over the waiting arm of the viewscreen which, from the outside, looked rather like a clunky 90's arcade game. Inside, however, it was packed full of sophisticated A'Viltrian tech and cultures of alien dust.

An army of magenta kiosks glowed around them, their screens flickering the words 'Insert gem to begin.'

May sat on the metal platform of the machine and buried her face in the space between her arms and knees. Her hair, which

Xan had styled into a loosely curling bob, umbrellaed out the fluorescent arcade light.

Behind her, having left the simulation long ago on account of a headache, Xan sat cross-legged on the platform and combed her hair with his fingers. The electric shocks had been simulated, but he was certain her hair was frizzier than normal.

"Look, starshine, if we drop another hundred thousand crystals at FabriLife, one of us is going to have to get an actual job and, judging on past experience, it's going to be you, and if you have an actual job, you won't have time to obsess over reacquiring the *Audacity*, and that will send you curlicuing into a depression even deeper than the one you're in now. So let's get back to Largish Bronda, watch a scantplot, cuddle with our Big Mouth Billy Bass, and try to forget about the *Audacity*, eh?"

In reply, tendrils of smoke seeped out from under May's arms and curled into the AC return above them.

"Hey." Xan pulled her shoulders back, snatched the not-cigarette from her mouth, and swallowed it whole, wincing as his tongue put out the lit end.

She had been smoking a lot of them lately. Words such as "addicted" and "craving" and "premature death on account of lung cancer" pestered her subconscious again. For half an orbit, she'd been too busy being the most successful (or rather, the only) Earthling rocket racer in the known universe to think about smoking. Now that her ship was gone, and she was stranded on a cold, miserable island for the foreseeable future, the itch had returned.

"Why do you keep eating them?" she asked.

"Smoking isn't good for your air sacs!"

"Well, lucky me, I don't have air sacs." May leaned back against the FabriLife machine's aluminum base, fingering the roll of things which were not exactly unlike cigarettes in her pocket and considering flicking on another one. "That can't be good for your stomach."

He leaned back beside her, unconcerned. "I've probably eaten more of those than Aimz has smoked."

"I hope I'm not the first to break this to you, but it's turned your skin blue."

"Blue?! Me?" He looked at his hand in mock horror, then in real horror when he noticed the state of his nails. He chewed them when he was nervous, which is why he typically wore shiny LayFlex™ gloves. But he hadn't had any reason to be nervous lately, right? No revenge-bent robots after him, no Chaos goddess trying to kill him, no prolonged bouts of loneliness so deep he couldn't remember if he was alive or not. He was finally enjoying life again. So why did his nails look like that?

"I'm sure I'll be ok," he said, tucking his hands under his thighs for safe keeping. "Find out anything you didn't already know about the *Audacity*? I popped out at around the twelfth beoop. Those things give me a plivering headache. Got a new mauve faux buffatalo coat, though! Feel it; it's soft!"

He held out his arms to display the shaggy mauve coat he wore over a holographic tube top that he had insisted was vintage-chic. While May had regressed back into her smoking habit, Xan had regressed back into the habit of dressing like he'd gotten lost in the clearance aisle of a drag-queen-owned thrift store.

"Everything gives you a headache since we got here. Is that normal?"

He shrugged off the question and wriggled his soft arms at her until she petted him. "Soft," she agreed, then shook her head. "I didn't discover anything new. I don't think the *Audacity*'s set up to be remote controllable. I give up."

"For the rotation, or forever?"

"Forever."

"Really forever, or Earthling forever? Because you've said forever a couple times now, and I'm not sure how forever works on Earth, but forever on Tuhnt means...well, it means forever. Indefinitely. From now until the end of time."

It was, of course, the same on Earth. Though May wondered if she could convince him that forever actually meant 'until I'm desperate enough to try again.'

The faintly glowing anchor button for the ship was still snapped onto the lapel of her trench coat, and she unhooked it now. Across the back, the words "The *Audacity*" were painted in a magnificently spacey text, zooming proudly across the small green disc. If she actually intended to stop trying to contact the ship, she would have no reason to keep the anchor button. When she glared down at the button, it glowed greenly back, familiar, comforting, entirely unaware of the pain it caused her.

"Let's try using the teledisc one more time," she said, more to the anchor button than to Xan.

He shuddered beside her, remembering the horrible feeling of their atoms getting lost in the ether. "Please, anything but that. The ship's too far away to teleport onto, even with a high efficiency teledisc. If we hadn't bought atom insurance for that last trip, we would still be meandering about the cosmos in a billion bits!"

"I miss racing." She clipped the button back on her coat. Safe for now.

"I know, mun. I miss it, too! I mean, not the threatening hate mail, the many brushes with death, scratched paint, constant low-level nausea, and outrageous entrance fees...I miss the photo shoots, mostly. And 'talking smack' about the other contestants. That was always fun. But we've got plenty of gem to last an Earthling lifetime if you stop wasting it on FabriLife tokens." Xan realized he had been talking too loudly and smiled, embarrassed, at a be-sparkled FabriLife associate android who smarmed past them, digitally side-eyeing him for suggesting that FabriLife was a waste of tokens, though the associate knew full well he was right.

"But what will I do? All I have to do right now is look for the *Audacity*, sleep, and eat." She noticed she had pulled another not-cigarette from the pack and was flicking the flinted end with her fingernail to ignite it. She stopped herself before it caught and put it back. "I guess I can add 'quit smoking' to that list."

"Well, skip down to sleeping, eating, and quitting the cigarettes. You've still got three things to do! That's plenty of things. Also, we could just have fun!"

"Pardon." They both jolted a bit, too invested in their conversation to notice the FabriLife android with a large, tight FabriSmile on its FabriFace. "Your time is out," it said. "Gem up or leave." Its eyes went a flavor of magenta which May knew must be Danger Diophalothene, a color which she couldn't technically see, but was starting to perceive via context clues.

"Right, we're leaving, just," Xan paused to stretch out his aching legs with a hiss, "give us a blip to relocate our extremities, eh?"

"Request denied. Gem up or *leave*." The electronic associate bent at its sparkly waist, and its eyes narrowed digitally.

"Alright, we'll get off your mark," Xan said as they pulled themselves upright on shaky, pins-and-needles legs and hobbled out, leaning on each other like a pair of geriatric criminals fleeing a crime scene.

Once outside FabriLife, the biting cold distracted May from the feeling of blood returning to her legs. She pulled her coat around herself, burying her fingers in the pockets to keep them warm.

It was, unsurprisingly, snowing Uptown. After the war of Reversed Polarization which had destroyed Tuhnt two hundred orbits ago, a board of sympathetic Rhean Queens had generously offered the remaining hundred-or-so-thousand displaced Tuhntians the island of Snoodark as reparation. The city that these Tuhntians built there had been creatively dubbed NotTuhnt and had been built both above and below ground, to take advantage of every inch of the tiny habitable section of the island.

They wandered Uptown now, where the nicer establishments had been opening, one on top of the other, for decades, many dating back to NotTuhnt orbit 000. Downtown, they typically avoided. Anything below ground brought back unpleasant memories of their time in the abandoned Pontoosa Adventure Hole.

"Right, let's get you something to eat! Eating usually makes you feel better. Unless it's poslouian-slug-worms. Those made you feel worse," Xan said, scanning the layers of neon signs for a restaurant they hadn't eaten at a zillion times yet.

"I had food poisoning; they weren't cooked properly. You got sick, too!" She was offended at the insinuation that she didn't have a strong enough stomach for alien foods. "You're the one who can't eat a slice of bread without dying about it. Let's just go back to Bronda. I'm not hungry."

"It's a beautiful rotation!" Xan said, gesturing to the sky which was not quite as dark as it usually was and the snow which fell with slightly less conviction than normal. "We might as well explore Uptown, right? Look!" He nodded toward a glowing blue marquee which was magnified by a clear intershoot that ran in front of it. "Have you ever been to a perception-changing bar?"

"All bars. That's the point of alcohol."

"Well, yes, but I mean...eugh, this is different. It's fun!"

"If philosophical epiphanies are fun for you." The voice belonged to Xan's sister who had spotted them a while back but only now decided to announce her presence behind them. "Blitheon, you two are really unaware of your surroundings. That's how you get mugged, you know."

"No one's going to mug us, Aimz," Xan said as if he were reassuring a child.

Aimz sighed, clicking a button on the end of a thin, pen-like stick from which two perfect recreations of their faces emanated as holograms. "Mugged. This will hold up to a face scan, too. I've got all your crystals."

"Huh," May mused quietly, studying the image of her own face. "Literally mugged."

The 'mugging pen' had been invented, as most things are, with good intentions and with a different name.

"Enjoy perfectly detailed three-dimensional holographic images of your friends and loved ones," the Visage-Stick advertisements had said.

"It's as if they were really there beside you," the advertisements had said.

"So detailed, even top security face-scan systems are fooled," the advertisements had said. And that final advertisement had been the one to start the quadrillion-crystal lawsuits against Visage-Stick and popularize the invention as the universe's first and only 'mugging pen.'

Xan snatched the pen from her and zilched out the records before handing it back. She held it up again, taking another snapshot of their faces.

"Alright, you lost your face-stealing privileges." He grabbed it back from her, cleared it again, and this time, tucked it into a pocket in his coat.

"Whatever. You'll buy me anything I want anyway." She winked at him. It was true. May and Xan had enough gem left from their short stint as rocket racers to support both Aimz and Listay, her undead girlfriend. "Listay sent me out to bring you this. She thought you'd be hungry." Aimz tossed May a perfectly round, maroon apple.

She almost refused, but her stomach growled pitifully at the sight of the apple, so she gave in and ate it. She had to eat five times as frequently as the Tuhntians, and it was beginning to feel like an imposition. "Thanks. Listay's growing apples on the Merimip?"

"Uh-uh, apples are trending on mainland Rhea right now, apparently. Some farmer from Earth brought them here, and Listay figured you'd want some." Aimz pulled another apple from her pack and ate it stem-first, tying the stem into a knot with her tongue just to see if she could still do that sort of thing. "Hey, want to start a bar fight?" she said, slurring around the apple stem which would not knot.

May did not *not* want to do that, but Xan gave her an urgently worried glance before taking Aimz by the shoulders to speak to her seriously. "Aimz, mun, your eyes look—"

"Fine. They look fine. Just myosis; it's bright out." It was not, by any means, bright out. It was never bright out.

Xan hogtied and gagged his creeping misgivings and shoved them into one of his many overstuffed mental closets, forcing a smile back onto his face. "Come on, let's go to the perception bar," he said to Aimz. "It's fun!" he repeated to May, enthusiastically.

"If you say so, blue." She tossed the apple core into the nearest refuse incinerator and the three of them crowded into the intershoot which sucked them up to the perception bar.

CHAPTER TWO

Uncontrollable Moist Epiphanies

"Warning: Perception snacks may cause rampant existentialism, catastrophic identity failure, uncontrollable moist epiphanies, and, in some cases, fatal levels of empathy.

"Talk to your loved ones, a medical professional, and any relevant gods before partaking.

"We cannot guarantee a safe return to your original perception without the purchase of personality insurance. Message repeats—" The intercom voice was soothing but the words disquieting.

Dim lights and cool colors gave the perception bar the feel of an underwater cave. The soft light orbs floating near the ceiling could nearly pass for bioluminescent deep-sea creatures as they bobbed, occasionally bumping into each other with an apologetic boing.

Though the bar was thronged with waiting people, Xan (who was short for a Tuhntian) and May (who was shorter still) slipped through the crowd unnoticed and snagged a booth just as the last group was leaving. Aimz followed slowly, unenthused but willing to show up for free snacks.

Xan and May scrunched into one side of the booth, Xan impatiently scrolling through the introductory waiver pages on the holographic menu in the center of the table which, had May been given a moment to read them, would've likely convinced her not to stay.

"Ah! Look, new flavors!" Xan said as the hologram stilled on a web of category options. His finger dipped into a bubble which read "Recent Additions" and a hundred lines stretched from it, all with a short description.

"Alright." Xan rubbed his hands together with excitement as he surveyed the options. "What have they got? Newly hatched Rhean larvae receiving their first nutrient download? Wouldn't recommend that one, sounds boring. Who hasn't been a larva, right? Oh! What about struggling Udonian business owner who loves their wife but is unsure of how to show it? Better. Tuhntian historian with a penchant for collecting interestingly rusted bolts—oh, that! I'm getting that one."

He swiped on the digital bubble, flinging it into the corner where a small teledisc was set into the table. Moments later, a floating black orb which looked to May uncannily like a Magic 8 Ball floated above the teledisc.

Xan patted the floating sphere toward himself across the table. "See, you just pick what you want, send it on over to the teledisc, and zam! Perception snacks. They last about twenty blips, but they feel like they last for decades. An entire perception, mashed up, sieved, and jammed into a crisp. That's fascinating, right?"

May nodded. "How do they, uh...harvest the perceptions?"

"Orbits of highly invasive stalking. But it pays well. And the perception reapers are some of the nicest people, very professional!" He held out a hand under the sphere, and it deposited a sea-foam green crisp, but May stopped him before he could pop it in his open mouth.

"One of these perceptions is yours?"

"Well, there are millions of perceptions but...yeah. Ages ago, mind you. It was after I moved out of Aunt Kalumbits's place but before...well, you know. I didn't have a job on account of the translation chip debacle, so I signed up. Why? Don't go looking for it."

"Why not?"

He shuddered. "Eh, it was so long ago. It's not relevant anymore. But you know what is relevant?" He tapped the screen. "An eight thousand orbit-old A'Viltrian coosmonger with serpentine palbeatus. Ooo...relevant!"

May thought that sounded like the least relevant option she had heard yet.

"Is the boredom leaking out your ears yet?" Aimz said, finally sliding into the booth opposite them.

"Mystery ball?" Xan asked her.

"Am I that predictable?"

Xan smiled, glad that he could, after all these orbits, still predict her, and dragged the digital bubble stamped with a question mark into the teledisc where another Magic 8 Ball appeared.

She tapped the sphere toward herself, grabbed it, and positioned it over her head, turning up her face and letting the thing drop a crisp into her mouth.

One moment she was chewing, the next she looked as if she could see the underlying structure of the universe and what, exactly, she should do about it. Then she was back to normal, eyes half lidded, unimpressed. She shrugged. "Not bad. A bit dry, and they really heaped on the inspirational background music in that one. But not bad. I want to watch May try one." She smiled, almost cruelly, as she coaxed another mystery crisp from her sphere and held it out to May.

This made Xan nervous. This made May nervous, as well. Aimz was altogether too excited about this experiment. Still, unable to muscle past her curiosity, May took one, popping it into her mouth, chewing, and realizing that, despite three centuries of effort, she would never have the resources to preserve the dying traditions of the Pringnette culture and that the few Pringnette elders who remained had already given up hope, meaning that her life's work had been in vain and—

"Whoa, starshine," Xan said. His hand was on her back, and he watched her carefully. Why was he blurry? She rubbed her face and found that she'd been crying.

"Ugh, that was horrible."

Aimz held out another crisp to her; this one had a small chunk taken out of it. "Here, Earthmun. It's a wealthy heiress. Looks like you got a rough one."

Gingerly, May took the second crisp and crunched it. She lounged on a luxury starship for the thousandth time, feeling the weight of a million days wasted, without purpose, staring out at the expanse as her every need was attended to and—

"Ugh." May shook her head to clear it faster. "Also bad." She turned to Xan, horrified. "How do you cope?"

"With what?"

"Centuries!"

"Oh." Xan leaned back in the booth, or rather pushed back into it, as if he could be eaten up by the cushion.

"Hey, that's right!" Aimz said, snapping her fingers. "You've only got a handful of orbits left to live, don't you? That's got to be weird. You've got only this very tiny window to get everything absolutely perfect and then-zilch! You're gone. Done. That's got to be depressing," Aimz said, popping another crisp in her mouth and nodding off.

If she hadn't taken a perception-nap at that exact moment, Xan would've laid into her. Instead, he turned to May, who was staring wide-eyed at the table. "I'm sorry. Aimz never learned decorum."

"She's right. I'm wasting my life."

"That's not true," Xan said firmly. "You don't have to be doing something all the time to be worthwhile. Right now, all you need to do is have fun with me and Aimz and enjoy yourself, alright? Obviously FabriLife isn't the ticket and neither is perception snacking. We'll find something else! Teach me English curse words?"

Aimz jolted awake with a wild gleam in her eye. "I know what will help you get over your tiny lifespan."

"What?" May asked, miserably.

"Aimz, no, we aren't doing violence tonight."

"Violence!" Aimz shouted, jumping on top of the table in one majestic leap. She reached a hand down to May. "Ever started a bar fight?"

"I haven't," May said, grabbing her hand and letting Aimz heft her up onto the table. Xan covered his face and slumped into the seat.

"Xan! I'm about to teach! Kalumbits always said I'd be an inspiring teacher and look, she was right!"

He motioned for May to bend down so he could whisper to her, and she did. "She's off her rocket. Don't listen to her."

"I just want to watch," May lied to reassure him. "You can go back to Largish Bronda if you want." Years of customer service work had built up a lot of repressed rage, and now that she was a few thousand lightyears away from Earth, she was ready to let that rage out.

"Right, okay, so," Xan said anxiously. "I feel I must remind you that you're not exactly..."

"What?"

"Well you're..."

"An Earthling?"

"Yeah and you—"

"Don't stand a chance against a bar full of Tuhntians?"

"Right so—"

"Rule number zero!" Aimz interrupted them, dropping down to one knee on the table. "Find a bar, any bar, that isn't a perception bar. There's a surplus of empathy in perception bars, and you're not going to get into a fight that doesn't soon devolve into hugging and crying. We've got to go Downtown."

"Eugh, Aimz, no. That's where—"

"Where all the Carmnians are? Tightly spotted." Aimz winked.

"Can I finish a sentence?" Xan asked.

Aimz and May watched, politely letting him continue.

"I...uh...well, yes, that's what I was going to say. That was a complete sentence."

"You're a Carmnian," May pointed out correctly.

Xan cringed, wobbled his head, but had to agree. "I am. Also, I would like to note, I'm a criminal! See how that works? No one trusts Carmnians. Not even other Carmnians. Let's bowl."

"Bowl?" May asked. "With balls and pins? You have bowling?"

"Balls and pins? No, you bowl with a slamahar and tribilites. Just punt the slamahar at the tribilites and try to knock as many over as you can. It's fun! It's safe. The tribilites get a kick out of it. May," he dropped a hand onto each of her shoulders, "come punt a slamahar at some tribilites with me?" he begged.

"Bar fight," Aimz goaded over her shoulder.

"I don't know," she told Xan. "I just think punching someone would help me feel better."

"Eugh. Then punch me, not a stranger!" Xan said.

And Aimz obliged.

CHAPTER THREE

Hubris Dampener

"Bar fight lesson one, my wee protege." Aimz snatched May's hand and pulled her at a flat-out run through the perception bar, the occupants watching them perplexedly. "When someone says you can punch them, always do it! Free punches!"

"Wait, Aimz, is Xan okay?" May stumbled, attempting to keep up or risk having her arm ripped off. They were outside now, but the adrenaline kept May warm as Aimz scooped her up and carried her bridal-style into the intershoot which plummeted them down to street level again.

"Eh, Carmnians have thick skulls. Don't stress it. You wanted to get in a fight, right?"

"Not with Xan!"

Aimz set May down but kept hold of her hand, yanking her three steps at a time down an icy staircase which was lit with string lights as it descended into Downtown NotTuhnt.

"Aw, stop worrying about him. He's tougher than you, you know."

"I don't believe that," May shouted down at Aimz as she attempted to keep her footing on the slick stone steps.

Aimz laughed. "Yeah, me neither. Zipzam?" She held out a plastic party popper to May who took it and pulled the string, a plume of green smoke clouding her head. Slowly, the smoke cleared. May smiled.

"Eh, you're right; he'll be fine. Let's punch strangers!"

"That's the ticket, Earthmun!"

The zipzam coursed through May's system, pulling all her thoughts and feelings to the surface like an emotional detox as they descended the staircase. "Xan says 'that's the ticket,'" she said, on the verge of tears.

"By O'Zeno, that zipzam's got your taxi maxed." Aimz giggled, jumping the last two steps and landing in the damp but cheerily lit underground city.

"You know that! You know that they do this to me, and you give them to me anyway," May shouted, then trundled into Aimz who stood at the bottom of the steps, laughing. "Sorry," she said, the zipzam beginning to wear off. Tuhntian drugs and alcohol couldn't stand up to her Earthling metabolism.

Downtown was dingy, dark, and humid, but in a festive way. Like a landfill the week after Christmas. The staircase ended in a city square, lush with fleshy underground plants strung with small lights. The square was bordered on one side by City Hall where those who called Downtown NotTuhnt home rotated through pretending to be in charge regularly.

In front of City Hall, a conglomeration of cheap souvenir vendor stalls flanked an enormous statue of Queen Carmnia made of chicken wire and concrete. The blue painted concrete on the statue's shins had flaked away in some places, revealing hexagons of rusted metal which held up the statue whose massive headdress not only touched the roughhewn rock ceiling but seemed to be growing out of it.

"Hey, Mom," Aimz threw casually up at the statue and patted its leg, more concrete flaking away under her hand.

"Oy!" shouted a round-faced Carmnian from behind a display of tapered sticks. "Smoke out the scourge with Zilpappy's Smoke Sticks! Guaranteed to have an odor. Rumored to destroy the scourge at its source!"

"Zuxing scam artist!" Aimz shouted over her shoulder at them, then sighed at the three young Carmnians that were eagerly shoveling crystals at the vendor in exchange for a tube of sticks.

"Carmnia curio! I've got genuine Queen Carmnia curio for sale! Nail clippings, bottle of tears, and for the right price, a lock of verified Carmnia curls!" another vendor added to the cacophony, her stall hung with points of red and yellow lights which danced to a three-note tune emanating from the kiosk.

"Wish balls, get your wish balls. Good for two class-five wishes or five class-two wishes. Wash wishly," the next vendor monotoned from behind a folding table laden with an army of muddy balls.

Across the way, an identical stall with an identical vendor gave their own speech. "Anti-wish balls. Negate the side effects of poorly thought-out wishes. Free hubris-dampener included."

Aimz trundled onward, her hand tightly wrapped around May's wrist. She'd spotted her target: the Sunny Underside Cafe, a sagging shack decorated mainly with glowing signs which advertised the mind-altering substances sold there.

"Wait!" May dug her heels into a thick crack in the concrete and pulled Aimz to a halt.

"What?"

"Xan's not coming after us," May said, looking back up the dark and empty staircase.

"So?"

"So, what if you actually hurt him?"

"That was my intention, Earthmun. Now unpin it. Lesson two is important if you're at a physical disadvantage which, if I might be blunt, you are. Fight dirty! Anything's a weapon if you can sling it at someone hard enough."

"Why are you like this?" May asked a smiling Aimz, still playing tug of war with her hand.

"Orbits of loneliness?" She pretended to think. "No. No, I've always been like this. Benefit of being a Carmnian, I guess. No one can blame me! Now do you want to release pent up aggression on a complete stranger who probably deserves it, or do you not?"

"I don't *not* want that."

"Oof, Earthmun, you're starting to sound like Xan. What does that mean?"

"I do want that, yes."

"Right, then! Rule five—"

"You mean lesson three?"

"Ah, zux three and four; they're boring. And this is a rule. Rule five is if someone's packing plasma, they're mine, alright?"

"You like getting shot at?"

"*Love* getting shot at. Also, have you ever seen Xan get angry before?"

May shook her head. She wasn't sure it was possible.

"Me neither! And as long as you don't die today, I might never have to. Now, the last lesson. Lesson six: don't walk in like you're about to start anything. Best bar fight is a surprise bar fight. Ready?"

May nodded, and Aimz finally dropped her hand. She shook it out to get rid of the pins-and-needles as she and Aimz sauntered through the open doorway.

The Sunny Underside was well stocked with Tuhntians.

Mostly Carmnians, judging by their unusual pallor and prominent, pointed noses.

All at least twice May's weight.

All dressed in clothing that provided great range of motion and plenty of sharp metal bits.

All dealing with personal issues which made them terrible grumps and drove them to mind-altering substances.

For a blip, Aimz surveyed the line of hunched backs at the dimly lit bar in the center of the shack. She bit her lip, focused. Starting a bar fight was a matter of craftsmanship in which she took great pride. She glanced at an empty hover stool which bobbed innocently in the corner, awaiting a bum to support.

"Actually, May, I changed my mind. Bowling does sound like fun," she said before seizing the hover stool and flinging it into the line of bodies at the bar. "Bar fight!" she announced to those sober enough to hear, then she dived onto the counter, taking a few hundred crystals worth of alcoholic beverage along with her.

Arms as thick as baby blue whales grabbed Aimz by the collar and flung her into a startled trio of Carmnians who had been playing something like darts with miniature crossbows off to the side. The three darts-players switched targets and sunk several sharp darts into the arms which had flung Aimz across the room. The person attached to those arms roared in pain, and then the room erupted.

Through the tumult, May saw a flash of Aimz's pink hair and she dashed in toward it, biting, elbowing, and scratching at any appendage which got in her way.

"Fun, yes?" Aimz asked May as soon as she was in earshot. May was too busy dodging punches. She'd been noticed; people were punching down now.

She kicked hard at the back of an exposed knee (she'd spent enough time with Xan to know that even the sturdiest aliens had shit joints just like the rest of us) and felled a barrel of a Tuhntian who hollered as he rolled to the ground, clutching his leg.

"Look at that! You've definitely been in a bar fight befo—" A laser blast, the first one of the evening, zinged across Aimz's thigh, ripping a hole in her leather pants.

She yelped, jumped up, ran face-first into a fist, laughed as green blood faucetted from her lip and over her teeth, then cracked someone's nose over her knee.

May was of the opinion that it was time to go.

She grabbed Aimz by her jacket and pulled her toward the door, dodging laser blasts, the heat and light dangerously close.

"Aimz, come on," May shouted but didn't dare turn around as she used her forearm to block elbows which tried again and again to collide with her face.

At last, Aimz came to someone's senses (likely not her own, since her senses were rather more preoccupied with stirring up trouble at the moment) and plunged ahead of May, steamrolling the bodies which had been blocking them from the entrance. Finally, the path back to the festive streetlights of Downtown was cleared from the bramble of appendages.

Before May could reach it, however, a fist to the temple hurtled her into a cool, black pool of nothingness. The floor smelled like rancid milk and whiskey.

* * *

Xan now had two very pressing objectives. Objective 1: Pay the bill. Objective 2: Collect Aimz and May without getting stuck in the middle of a bar fight.

The first should have been the easiest, but technology can sense distress in its user, and when it feels it's under pressure to perform, it tends to bungle.

Xan tapped the bill-pay bubble. Tapped it several times. More than tapped, he drove his finger straight through to the other side of the hologram.

The overly sensitive digital menu, so shocked by Aimz's act of violence and picking up on Xan's nervous energy, had frozen, catatonic with fear. It couldn't even muster the total.

Rather than wait for the machine to calm down and get its servers together, Xan harpooned a sack of crystals from his pocket—at least double the bill—slipped out of the booth, thrust it at the attendant with a hurried, "No change," and bolted outside.

They were long gone.

He rubbed his aching head to coerce it into thinking faster. Aimz wasn't dumb enough to let harm come to May, was she? But she had been acting peculiar lately. Alarmingly peculiar. He would need reinforcements. Listay, Aimz's lover, was the ex-dead ex-general for the job. He had her on speed dial in his BEAPER for exactly this reason.

"What did Aimz do?" Listay asked the blip the BEAPER connected.

When Xan first met her, she had been half-way out of the grave, and he had been half-way in it. Her eyes were still cloudy, her deep purple skin still ashy with death, but her ruined dreads were gone, Xan having helped her re-style them into low maintenance box braids which she kept in a tidy roll at the back of her neck. Changing your hairstyle, Xan had explained to her, could also change your outlook on life. Or after-life, in Listay's case. Typically, he'd greet her with a tongue in cheek complement of her hairstyle. Not today. Today, he—

"Your hair looks great," he said, predictably. Then, before Listay had a chance to roll her eyes, he got to the point. "Aimz ran off with May! Wanted to start a bar fight. I lost them. Think they went Downtown?"

"She definitely took May Downtown." Listay knew this not because she was interested in bar fights, but because Aimz had frequently tried to drag her into them. Typically, she allowed it. Aimz had a surplus of energy, and if she could get some of it out by beating up unwholesome strangers, Listay wasn't keen to stop her. "I'm a beoop away by monorail. Don't wait for me. Get May out of there; Aimz is compromised."

"I'll pay for a teledisc," Xan said. "I'd pay for a hundred teledisc trips before engaging Aimz in an anti-bar-fight-fight."

He scanned the area for the round green signs which illuminated public telediscs. There were two nearby, but he was too far to read the coordinates on either of them, so he jogged to the nearest one and held Listay's image up to it, depositing a crystal into the charge-slot.

"Coordinates logged," she announced, then her image zipped out, and she reappeared in tangible form beside him, immediately sprinting off toward the below-ground staircase.

"When you say 'Aimz is compromised'...what...what does that mean?" Xan shouted after her, hesitantly picking up speed so he wouldn't be left behind.

Listay paused at the entrance to the underground to let him catch up. "It means she's compromised, so we need to hurry."

Steep stairs had never bothered Xan, but steep stairs combined with worry and adrenaline made him feel queasy as they descended. He hadn't been Downtown yet. If there was an area of town where Carmnians typically gathered, he wanted nothing to do with it. He glared up at the concrete face of Carmnia and said exactly the same Tuhntian words Aimz had said to it, but due to his tone, instead of translating as "Hey, Mom," it translated as 'Hello, Mother."

Aimz and May weren't difficult to find. They were recouping in a quiet area on a rusted bench which had been chained to the fence around City Hall, making fun of the oafish bar-goers while Aimz tipped a bottle of Fraguntassle first into her mouth, then over a scrap of cloth with which she dabbed a welt on May's forehead.

"Zuut, Earthmun, I gotta get you cleaned up before Xan finds us," Aimz said, then took another swig from the bottle.

"I'm fine," May insisted, the Fraguntassle stinging the cut on her forehead. She patted her rolled bangs down far enough to cover it and moved her jaw from side to side, making sure it still worked correctly. The adrenaline in her body suddenly realized there was nothing left for it to do and made a hasty retreat. She knew exactly where bruises would soon form. Exactly everywhere.

"May!" Xan launched at her, wrapping her in a quick hug, then holding her at arm's length to observe her. "You're not dead?"

"Of course not. It was just a bar fight."

"With Carmnians," he added.

"You're a Carmnian! What's so bad about Carmnians?"

Rather than explain, he looked to Aimz for help, but she was also waiting on his answer. His face curled into a grimace when he saw her, and he pulled a pocket mirror from his coat and held it up to her.

"What? I know I've got blood on my—" She stopped talking and grabbed the mirror, studying herself for a quiet moment. "Huh," she grunted, then snapped the mirror shut and handed it back to him, a haunted look on her bloodied face.

"What is it?" May asked, watching the pair as if this were some alien ritual she'd just witnessed. It wasn't.

Xan started to say it was nothing. Then stopped. He had promised not to lie to her anymore. He had promised her honesty, and she would get it. Just not right now. "Eugh, I'll tell you once we're back at Largish Bronda, alright? Please say that's alright. This isn't the kind of thing you talk about in public."

May nodded, but regretted the motion as it made her head throb even worse.

Listay grabbed Aimz's hands and pulled her up off the bench. "I'll take her back to the Merimip and watch her."

"I don't need to be watched. I need more Fraguntassle." She wiggled the empty bottle at Listay.

"Really?"

Aimz nodded solemnly. "Really."

"I'll get you a bottle to go."

"Two!" Aimz shouted after Listay as she entered the bar, parting the ongoing sea of bar fight with her elbows in order to reach the counter.

"May, I'm worried about you," Xan said, helping her up.

"Why, because I have a concussion?"

"You have a whom?" he asked.

May snorted, amused. "That's exactly what Aimz asked. It's an Earthling thing. Don't worry about it."

Listay pulled herself from the brawl, an opaque white bottle held aloft in each fist. "Fraguntassle acquired," she announced proudly. "Let's move out."

They walked back toward the statue of Carmnia and the towering flight of stairs, but May noticed something on Carmnia's left toe that she hadn't seen from the other direction.

A pamphlet which looked like it had been hand painted on roughly textured homemade paper danced stiffly in the watery breeze.

'Have you seen this rocket?' it asked.

May had seen the rocket.

In fact, May was extremely familiar with the rocket in question. Below the query, a beautifully illustrated image of the *Audacity*. Undoubtedly the *Audacity*. And this was how she knew: the hull of the rocket in the poster read '*Audacity*.'

She snatched it down, staring at the image as if it might rip from the page and turn into the ship itself. Had she made this poster and forgotten? Impossible. Had Xan made it? She looked at him, but he was standing over her now, also puzzled.

"What is this?" May asked.

"It's a flyer."

"Yeah." Below the ship ran a line of coordinates. Xan typed them into his BEAPER and showed May the resulting map. "Should we go?" she asked.

"In my experience, people only seek me out because they want to kill, imprison, or have sex with me, and I'm not especially keen on any of those options right now. So probably not."

"They aren't looking for you; they want the *Audacity*," May clarified.

"Presumably because I accidentally stole it," he reminded her. "Please, let's just get back to Largish Bronda and forget about this ill-fated outing?"

May folded the flyer and tucked it into her bra. "Already forgotten," she said, then sighed because much of her evening *was* already forgotten. She knew Aimz had dragged her down there for a bar fight, she knew Listay and Xan had found them outside City Hall cleaning up, but she couldn't remember much else detail-wise. "Definitely a concussion."

CHAPTER FOUR

The Offensive Chapter

Public teledisc teleportation was extremely convenient because there was never any wait. There was never any wait because no one could actually afford to use the things. At a hundred crystals per mile, the majority of society, even the majority of the Tuhntian upper class, was firmly priced out of regular public teledisc travel.

When Xan and May arrived on New Tuhnt, they had more gem than the richest of the upper class. After a failed attempt to teleport to the *Audacity* which had been thrust zillions of miles into open space and hundreds of FabriLife hours logged trying to work out a remote control for the ship, their coffers were dwindling.

And so, they used the monorail to get back home. Though awfully loud, the monorail was the most common form of mass public transit in the Flotluex system. Monorail stations were peppered throughout Uptown, and it wasn't long before they found one headed toward Snoodark Quarry which wasn't so much a neighborhood as it was a populated pit.

"Step off It, ya' zoup-nog Carmnians!" shouted someone a few bodies away from them as they joined the crowd at the edge of the monorail platform. This was a popular vaguely threatening insult on Not Tuhnt, "It" being the name of the highest cliff on the island of Snoodark which overlooked an expanse of pointy rocks.

"Will do!" Xan waved good-naturedly at the someone.

"Zux off, trok-licker!" Aimz said even more good-naturedly and flashed an offensive Tuhntian hand gesture which looked like a complex shadow puppet. Listay shook her head, subtly moving between Aimz and the trok-licker.

May leaned forward a bit, her anger drawn like a magnet toward the large, bearded Tuhntian who had insulted them.

Working at Sonic, she had smiled through snide remarks and wished her transgressors a nice day because that's what she had been paid to do. It had taken time to shed the habitual politeness Sonic had required, but rocket racers were expected to be nasty to each other, and she had eventually grown out of her customer service voice. Had Xan not put a hand on her shoulder to steady her, she might have given the bar fight a sequel.

"Hey, un-pin it, mun. They're not worth the trouble. Some people just aren't fond of Carmnians, that's all."

"Why don't you tell them to fuck off?" she whispered, keeping a rageful eye on them as the monorail steamed into the station and flung open its doors.

"Because you laugh at me when I say fuck," Xan explained, looping an arm around one of the monorail poles to swing around it.

It was true, May laughed when he said fuck, but she kept herself from laughing now as she sat in the seat opposite him. Translation chips didn't like switching languages mid-sentence, which was a shame, because Xan loved doing it. The frustrated chip tingled in her skull whenever Xan threw in a word she knew like "fuck" or "bongo" which he had learned from May and 'I Love Lucy,' respectively.

Also, his accent was strange because, just as May literally couldn't pronounce any Tuhntian word that required one to flex one's gloxalatal, Xan literally couldn't pronounce the hard "k" sound. He always put far too much gloxalatal into it.

Normally the chip accounted for this, but when he stopped relying on it and tried to speak English to her, the chip would shrug. "You know what that means," it would say. "I'm taking a break."

"Try another curse word," May suggested.

Aimz had been half listening from Listay's lap, but the mention of cursing had piqued her interest and she sat up, straddling Listay's thigh in a way which might have been edited out in a less racy book.

"Learning alien obscenities?" she asked.

"Yeah, you want in?" said May.

“I do very much want in, yes. Tell me how to make people cry in another language.”

“You were never this interested in language studies at university,” Xan said.

“They don’t teach you obscenities at university.”

“They do in the higher-level courses! But English isn’t one of the ninety-two primary universal languages. Here.” Xan dug in the pocket of his coat and pulled out a small rectangular magnet he frequently used to scramble his translation chip. “I’ve just got the one, so we get to share!” He leaned out from the pole, holding the magnet between his and Aimz’s heads. “Alright, starshine, curse at us.”

“‘Shit,’” she divulged.

Aimz and Xan both repeated the word, but the “sh” came out as a clink which May physically could not have duplicated.

She shook her head, and Aimz rolled her eyes, leaning away from the magnet.

“I’ll stick to the classics. That magnet’s making my skull ache,” she said.

Xan kept the magnet held to his head and pulled himself up onto the pole again, hooking a leg around it just for fun. “Try something else?”

“Alright, you can’t get ‘ck’ or ‘sh’ out, so how about ‘hell.’”

“Hell?” he repeated satisfactorily.

“Yeah. As in “Oh hell”, “give them hell”, or “what the hell.”

“Easy! What does it mean?” He let the magnet drop away and rubbed his temple which throbbed from the pull of the magnetic field.

“It’s where you go when you die to be punished for eternity.”

“Punished? For what?”

“Not believing in it.”

“Oh. Well, zuut, that’s dark, isn’t it? I suppose that’s what makes it an expletive! In most of Tuhnt’s major religions, when you die, your spirit gets recycled back into the Everythingness.”

“How environmentally friendly of you.”

“Right? I mean, there is a kind of ‘hell,’ I guess. If you really zux up, you could get stuck in between recycling and be doomed to wander the universe for eternities. They say that's how entities like Chaos came about. You get stuck outside of the recycling system and have to watch the universe expand and contract endlessly around you until you eventually evolve into something ultra-sentient and formless like her."

May laughed at the thought of Chaos having been such a horrible person that reincarnation rejected her. "Hopefully she's back in the recycling system now."

"Can you imagine? Little larval Chaos, nothing to do but wriggle indignantly at her attendants. Blitheon, I feel sorry for the people who take her in when she's a kid."

"So is anyone in charge of this recycling system?" May asked.

"Of course someone's in charge," Listay said now, pushing Aimz aside to talk to May. The concept of an all-powerful organizational entity had always fascinated Listay, and she had casually studied universal religions with an eye toward finding this organizer. "They have infinite names, but several organizations call them The Seam."

Aimz laughed herself off Listay's knee, hitting the sticky monorail floor with a thump. "You mean The Crack? Listy, darling, you don't actually believe in The Crack, right? We've already got hundreds of entities who show up to entity conventions and fill out their inter-galactic census. Why invent new ones that don't pay their space-taxes?"

"Hold on. Space-taxes *are* a thing?" May interjected.

Listay gave May a look which said she was likely in some deep space-trouble but carried on. "The Seam doesn't exist until the universe contracts into nothingness again. They say The Seam was the first being to get booted out of the recycling program, and when they got bored of the nothingness after the universe ended, they convinced it to start expanding again. Thus, earning the title of The Seam in between the end and the beginning."

Aimz's face scrunched. "The universe just does that. It's like squeezing a sponge underwater. It gets smaller, then it gets bigger."

"Who's squeezing the universe sponge, though?" Xan said, concerned about how utterly enormous their hand must be.

"The Seam," Listay answered.

Aimz's hands circled emphatically in an attempt to catch a better explanation. "Physics! It's just physics!"

Listay patted Aimz's fluffy pink hair. "Of course it is, mun."

"There are a helling lot of entities already," Xan tried to agree with Aimz.

May laughed. "Good try, but that one doesn't conjugate."

"No? Why not?" Xan loved conjugating things and had picked up English conjugations eons ago, again, thanks to 'I Love Lucy.'

May shrugged. "Because it's a place."

"Right. Fuck's a lot better isn't it? I mean, it conjugates better."

"It does, but I don't think you can physically say it."

"I just did!"

"Not correctly, though."

"Fuck," he said earnestly. "Fuck."

"Alright," May motioned for him to bend down so he was at eye level with her. "Watch my mouth. Fff-uuuuu-CK."

His face twisted into an impression of hers.

"Ck," he said in a way which was slightly less like crashing into a drum kit than it had been last time.

May nodded. "Ck," she repeated.

"Ck?"

"That's it! Now say fuck."

"Fuck. Fucking. Fucker. Fuckly. Fuckest."

May laughed and waved him away. "Yeah. You've got it, blue."

CHAPTER FIVE

Yuzka Felting

Snoodark Quarry was the last habitable section of the island to be incorporated into the city of NotTuhnt because it was the *least* habitable.

The quarry was bordered on one side by a densely overgrown forest full of miserable creatures intent on making others more miserable than they were. On the other side, it gave way to craggy fjords on the Rhean sea which was also inhabited by miserable creatures. And now that a housing development had sprouted in the heretofore empty quarry, the quarry *itself* was inhabited by miserable creatures.

May and Xan, upon arriving on the island, had purchased a Largish Bronda's FlexiDimensional HoverBus to live in and parked it exactly halfway between the forest and the quarry in hopes that their miserable neighbors on either side would keep each other at bay.

Largish Bronda's line of vehicles were well known in the Flotluex system for their reliability. They were reliably sluggish with a reliably clunky design and reliably mundane features. They were also reliably cheap, and since their only source of income had been blasted into the ether, May and Xan were trying to budget.

The HoverBus they chose was orange, naturally, but not Obtrusive Orange, like the *Audacity* had been. Obtrusive Orange had been long outlawed by the time this HoverBus was painted. May might have called this orange "Pumpkin Spice" had she been at all interested in giving creative names to colors.

They entered through an opaque yellow plasma door at the back of the bus to a space which might have featured on the cover of a 1970s issue of "House Beautiful," full of massive, slumping sack chairs, needless curves, and a recessed waterbed which doubled as a conversation pit.

"Hey, Billy!" Xan said when they entered.

"Hey, Billy," May echoed habitually. They were addressing their only decor piece, a Big Mouth Billy Bass which hung on the far wall. It did not acknowledge their return.

May flopped dizzily into a sack chair and tried to remember what you were supposed to do about a concussion. The only thing she could remember was not to think too hard, and that was rather counterintuitive at the moment.

She did not remember that Xan had promised to explain what was going on with Aimz and, as such, she didn't bring it up. This suited Xan rather well, and he curled next to her in the sack chair and wiped the splatters of blood—equal parts her dried red blood and crusty green Tuhntian blood—from her face.

"Thanks," she said, resting her head back against the chair and closing her eyes, which set her brain spinning like a gyroscope. She sat back up to still it. "Sorry Aimz punched you. I tried to get her to go back, but she's been acting strange lately."

Xan sighed and tossed the bloodied rag onto the yellow laminate counter which delineated the living room from the kitchen. "Yeah," was all he said. He flopped on her shoulder with about as much energy as the wet rag on the counter.

"Hey, Blueberry, what's bothering you?" she asked.

"Bothering me?" He shook his head and smiled. "Nothing! What makes you think I'm bothered by something? Chaos is off our marks, Sonan is gone, I'm not in prison, I'm with you, and Aimz is...alive. Everything's zing up to caliber! What could I possibly be bothered by?"

May dug a not-cigarette out of the pocket in the side of the sack chair. "Aimz punching you in the face, maybe." There was a trick to lighting them that she hadn't quite become proficient in. It involved holding down a button at one end and flicking the other end with a fingernail. She flicked it a couple of times unsuccessfully.

He shook his head. "She does that sometimes. But, I mean, I suppose if you're asking, if you're curious, it's a bit unlike you to—"

He paused to watch her as her face lit up blue with the light of the not-cigarette. She smiled and inhaled.

"I mean, you're smoking cigarettes again, and if you're not working on the fake *Audacity* at FabriLife, you're doing things like zipzam poppers and getting into bar fights."

"I'm not smoking *cigarettes*," May said. Xan plucked it from her hand and swallowed it whole. She got another out and flicked.

"Right. You're smoking not-cigarettes. May, are you depressed?" he asked.

She smiled crookedly at the smoldering cherry. "Doesn't translate," she said and puffed. "Mmm!" she said, remembering something. She fished the flyer from her bra and unfurled it on her knee. "This might be the concussion talking but..." she mumbled around the not-cigarette. Xan helped her by plucking it from her mouth and eating it. "If someone else is looking for the *Audacity*, they might be able to help me recover it. It's our only lead."

Xan groaned, sat back heavily in the sack chair, and rubbed his chest. "Please stop smoking those so I can stop eating them," he whined.

"Stop eating them so I can smoke them."

"Eugh," he stuck out his long green tongue and let his limbs drop heavily over the chair. He made a wonderful impression of a corpse, because he rarely had to breathe.

May continued to scan the flyer, her free hand absently tickling his side. He convulsed with laughter and sat up; quieting when he saw that she was still staring at the flyer.

"You're really set on getting the *Audacity* back."

She looked at him seriously. "Your perception of time is different," she said. "If it takes you fifty orbits to save enough for another racing rocket, you'll barely notice. I could be dead in fifty orbits."

"Will be if you keep instigating bar fights," he grumbled.

"I've got to do something. Everything in town is staffed by robots. There are no jobs, there's no *Audacity*. What am I supposed to do with myself?"

"Retire?"

May laughed at that. “I never planned on being able to retire.”

“Well, now you can! Spend your rotations lounging by vortex springs and felting yuzkas for the local larvae troupe chapter.”

“Is that what retired Tuhntians do?”

“Only the fun ones,” he said.

May doubted she would be a fun retiree. Without a clear and defined life purpose, she figured she’d die of boredom within the orbit. That was troubling. Thinking about it hurt, though. Not emotionally—it physically hurt her bruised brain.

Perhaps Xan could think about it for her.

“I think,” she said, “I’d die if I didn’t have a purpose. And I don’t know if I have one right now. Is that bad?”

That was not something Xan heard often and, as such, he wasn’t really sure how to reply. He pulled the sides of his faux buffatalo coat around her and scooped her close while he thought.

“It’s not *not* bad,” he said, finally.

“My brain’s too fried for double negatives, Blue.”

“But not too fried to ponder the purpose of life? Maybe put a tab on that thought process and come back to it later. For now, you can just exist. Nothing bad will happen if you just exist for a blip.”

That was true, but she *did* think she had a concussion, and she had heard somewhere back on Earth that something bad, she wasn’t sure what exactly, might happen if you slept on a concussion. She didn’t remember how long she had to wait, but for safety’s sake, she decided she wasn’t tired yet.

Xan, however, was. His grip on her relaxed, and he wriggled deeper into the chair. While he slept less often than May, he stayed asleep for much longer than she did, and she didn’t trust herself to stay awake if he was sleeping.

With safe-cracking stealth, she unhooked the BEAPER from his wrist and transferred it to her own. It made a sprightly booting-up noise when it sensed its wearer had changed, and the welcome screen danced out of it. The BEAPER asked her to confirm that she hadn’t stolen it by promising that she hadn’t.

"I didn't steal you," she whispered harshly at her wrist. This BEAPER knew her. She had worn it plenty of times before. It just didn't like her much.

She input the full coordinates from the flyer, realizing too late that the BEAPER's map had saved the coordinates to its history from earlier.

The map pinpointed the flyer's destination and offered several routes which would take her there, all with a small symbol which, when opened, explained that it would be much more pleasant to simply take a public teledisc there instead, and it would happily take you to within ten meters of your location for the low price of two hundred crystals with a convenience fee of twenty-two crystals. Just swipe—

May shut off the BEAPER, tired of scrolling down the ad's steadily smaller print.

Xan still slept cadaverously, and he hadn't been keen on the flyer anyway, so May headed back to the monorail alone.

CHAPTER SIX

May Meets the Queen

The flyer led her straight to Queen Carmnia.

It was early yet, and the Downtown square which held the statue of Carmnia was now empty apart from lumps on benches, some of which were people sleeping under piles of coats and some of which were simply discarded piles of coats. It was fashionable, at the time, to bring unwanted coats to this particular square.

Since she wasn't being schlepped along by a war-eager Aimz or a worried Xan, May took a moment to study the statue of the queen. Carmnia's skin was a pale blue shared by Aimz and Xan, and her nose was long and pointed like theirs, but the scowl she made beneath the massive golden headdress was unfamiliar. It looked as if she'd either told the statue artist an incredibly nasty joke or threatened to kill them.

In actuality, while posing for the statue, Carmnia had done both. The joke had been in reference to the artist working over her massive concrete crotch and the death threat had come because the artist hadn't unequivocally agreed that sculpting her crotch was a delightful privilege.

The BEAPER gave an impatient ding to remind May it was attempting to take her somewhere, and she walked past Carmnia, hoping she'd never have the displeasure of meeting her in real life.

The residential district extended along the chiseled stone walls of the underground Downtown. Rather than integrated apartments, leftover shipping containers which had carried the raw materials Rhea included in their reparations to the Tuhntians had been stacked into a Lego-brick complex, woven with intershoots and thin guardrails.

On the face of the containers, their owners had painted house numbers, but the last box in the first row, the one which the

BEAPER's map insisted she enter, was painted with more than just its designated coordinates.

It played canvas to a detailed mural starring two Carmnians reclining in starburst clouds. These two Carmnians were strikingly familiar. May neared the mural, more certain with every step that leaving Xan back at Largish Bronda was the right decision, because he was already here. In mural form, anyway. Perfect likenesses of Xan and Aimz had been painted onto the side of the shipping container, reclining naked in starry clouds, like a celestial Botticelli.

Clearly, then, someone was looking for Xan, not just the *Audacity*. This was almost certainly a dead-end. But an interesting dead-end, at least. And if there was another rancorous robot ready to wreak revenge on Xan, May would rather know about it. She knocked.

Knocking, like ice cream or thumbs, is a cultural universal. Every civilized person in the entire universe knocks before entering.

The appropriate number of knocks, however, is greatly contested.

One knock is clearly not enough. No one knocks only once. A single knock is too easily explained away as a pipe sputtering, a tree branch falling, or a hungry ruffloo ricocheting off your door in hopes of catching its next meal.

Two knocks is the standard on Earth. Two healthy raps. It's clear, definitive, and two taps echoes the two syllables of the word "Hello" rather nicely.

Three knocks is a touch excessive. Not unheard of and decidedly not inappropriate. Perhaps a bit rude, though. More of a "Hey, I'm here," syllabically.

Now, an Earthling who hears four knocks is grabbing a baseball bat on the way to the door because it is likely either a solicitor or the IRS. It's a kind of "Answer the door" or even "Get out here now."

Four knocks means business.

May knocked four times.

On Tuhnt, four knocks is used exclusively for food delivery.

As such, the person who came to the door was delighted to open it but not as delighted to see that the person on the other side wasn't holding the bowl of zipnite stew (lukewarm, extra salt) and a side of crawfish sticks (rare, hold the sticks) that she had ordered.

"Oh, you're not food." The coat-rack-thin Carmnian bent down to May's eye level, and the enormous plume of vermillion curls which obfuscated her eyebrows gave an urgent bounce. "You're not Tuhntian, either, larvling. Have you noticed?"

May pulled out the flyer and presented it to her. "Did you post this?"

The Carmnian took off the thin frames she had been wearing and squinted at the flyer, as if perhaps she was seeing it too clearly before and needed it to be a bit blurred before she could read it.

"Yes! Oh yes, mun, that's my flyer! Thank you for returning it to me, such a kind...I'm sorry...your name?"

"May."

"Such a kind May you are!" She took the flyer and began to shut the door.

"Wait! I have information about the *Audacity*."

She stopped closing the door but didn't exactly open it.

"You do?"

"Yes."

"About *Audacity*?"

"...yes." May was not fond of repeating herself.

"Oh my sweet larvling!" She patted May inside and shut the door.

The inside of the apartment was felted in fibers and draped with crochet. It looked more like the guts of a beast made entirely of yarn than the inside of a shipping container. Soft crocheted forms ballooned from the floor and lower walls, growing like mushrooms into things which might be mistaken for couches or tables. The Carmnian brought May to one of the soft bulbous forms and motioned for her to sit, then sat beside her, trapping May's hands in her own cold, jail-like fingers.

"Tell me! Please, I mean." The Carmnian wiggled like an over-excited terrier. "Please tell me everything you know about the *Audacity*."

"First, I want to know who you are and why you're looking for it."

The Carmnian pouted as if she had really hoped she could just get the information without having to give anything away.

May waited. She would not stand for pouting.

"Alright, well, my name is Kalumbits, but please call me *Aunt* Kalumbits, everyone does! Everyone did. Some people did. You know...just please call me that, alright? I would love you to call me that."

"You're Aunt Kalumbits?"

"Oh yes!" She bounced, the flash of consternation scared away from her expressive face. "Indeed. Oh, how nice." She fluffed out and straightened her hair with her fingers, pulling it a bit higher above her eyes. Just enough to make May suspicious that it was a wig.

"Is Kalumbits a popular name?"

"Oh, I should think not at all. No. Well, I once ran into a Rhean named Kalumbits. Nasty piece of work. All angles, her face was. And her hair! Oh, larvling, you wouldn't believe. And she had the nerve to disparage *my* hair. Hair is exceedingly important, don't you think? It can change your whole outlook on life! Do you like my hair?"

May relaxed now. Even if Kalumbits had been a common Tuhntian name, there was absolutely no doubt: This was Xan's Aunt Kalumbits. This made everything right.

"It's nice," she lied quickly. "You were looking for Xan, weren't you?"

Aunt Kalumbits swallowed hard. Her eyes became big and watery, and she put her glasses back on as if to cover them, but that only magnified her bright red irises.

"You know my Xan?"

May nodded.

Four knocks at the door.

"Oh, it's food!"

On the other side of the door, a delivery robot whirred pleasantly, proffering a box cocooned in a warm red glow. Kalumbits snatched the box and closed the door on it.

"Are you hungry, dear little larvling? You look hungry; have something anyway." She set the box down on what passed for a table and extracted a single, raw crawfish-on-a-stick which wasn't on a stick. May politely choked it down as Kalumbits popped open the soup and began to drink it.

"You weren't looking for the *Audacity*, were you? You were looking for Xan."

Kalumbits nodded. "Well, of course! But if I'm being honest, I've never seen a flyer with the image of Carmnian on it before that wasn't a wanted ad." She laughed lightly as if that had been a joke rather than a disparaging remark about Carmnians.

May hadn't found it funny and pointedly frowned at her. "How did you know he was on the *Audacity*?"

"Well, mun, I know Xan. An orange ship—he always loved orange things—gets stolen from a silo in Trilly by a Carmnian the same day Xan disappears? There wasn't any doubt, was there? I mean, the media kept it all south of the beak, didn't want to start a panic, but I knew. Now, circling back around here, where *is* my Xan? I need to see him. I'm sure he misses me!"

"I might be able to bring him to you," May said, wary of telling a stranger where she lived, even if the stranger was Xan's favorite aunt.

"When? Now?" She nearly flung the soup from her lap, stiffening with excitement.

"Well, I..." May had nothing better to do. There was no excuse worth giving. "Yeah, I'll be back in a minute." She said, knowing full well that "minute" wouldn't translate to anything meaningful, so Kalumbits would have no idea when to expect her back.

"Superb, larvling!" Kalumbits set aside her food and squeezed May like a drowning person squeezing a buoy.

May waited to be released. She did not squeeze back, because her arms were pinned to her sides. Also, she didn't want to.

* * *

When May stepped through Largish Bronda's plasma door, no one greeted her, which meant that Xan was still asleep.

She found him curled on the sack chair and, May assumed on account of his unusually serious expression, deep in some kind of nightmare. She wondered what Tuhntian dreams were like, resolved to ask him later, then promptly forgot about it. Tuhntian dreams, she figured, were pretty much like Earthling's.

She was very wrong. Members of the A'Viltrial species, like Tuhntians, don't dream of isolated events. They dream of retro-reflected illimitable reality. Everything that is, was, and is to come in the entire cosmos compacted into a perfectly round orb of matter and anti-matter encased in an impermeable film of spacetime. Of course, since such a thing is utterly impossible, none of them have ever been able to make sense of it.

That's what Xan dreamed about.

Also, the fish was there. Everything was there, so naturally the fish was.

Big Mouth Billy Bass hadn't let Xan get a blip of decent sleep since they bought him three seasons ago, and now Billy was in Xan's dreams, producing a tuneless high-pitched whine at him. Xan was so disturbed by this dream that he didn't notice May slip the BEAPER back on him. He didn't notice her tapping his shoulder to wake him. Didn't notice when she ruffled his hair, flicked his nose, shouted "Wake up," in his ear, or pushed him onto the floor.

"'I Love Lucy' is on. I think it's 'Paris at Last'," she said.

Xan rocketed awake. "*Parlez-vous français?*!" He loved that episode.

"Good morning, starshine," May said to him, ironically. It was not morning and he was not her starshine.

"Eugh." He rubbed his eyes, pressing in against the ache behind them. "Do you hear that?" he asked, three times louder than necessary.

"No... Hearing through your eyes, are you?"

"Yes?" he said, his eyes still covered against the squealing. It was almost definitely coming from the direction of the Big Mouth

Billy Bass hanging on their wall, but the moment he looked at it, the sound stopped.

May followed his gaze to the bass. "What's wrong?" she asked.

"It stopped." Xan shrugged. "I guess I have better hearing than you. 'I Love Lucy' isn't really on, is it?" he asked.

"No, I just needed to wake you up. I think I found Kalumbits."

"What about Kalumbits?"

"I think I found her," May repeated. She wasn't fond of repeating herself, but she was fond of Xan, so he got a pass.

"You?"

"Yes."

"Think you?"

"Found her, yes!"

"Here?!"

"Downtown. She posted the flyers."

"You went without me?"

"I promised to stop dragging you into things you didn't want to do. I never said *I* wouldn't do things you didn't want to do," May said.

"Fair point, that. Are you sure it's her? What did she look like?"

"Like you, but thinner and older."

"Like...like me?" He crashed performatively into the waterbed in the middle of the room, covering his face with his hands. "Blitheon's razor burn," he said from between his palms. "Did she have red hair?"

"Yeah, but I think it was a wig."

He groaned and rolled onto his side, grabbing a brocade pillow to hold onto. "Aunt Kalumbits isn't Carmnian. She's one of Vorcia's brood."

May plopped onto the waterbed beside him and propped her head up using her elbow as a kickstand. She was disappointed and tired but not surprised. Raw crawfish was not the kind of thing honest people ate.

"Who is she? She knows you and Aimz."

"Yeah, she better."

"Why?"

"She's also our aunt."

"Another one?"

Sighing, he stuffed the pillow he had been holding onto behind her head and grabbed another for himself, settling into the mire of despondence. "Chrismillion. We never really got on well."

"Can't imagine you not getting on well with anyone," May said.

"Yeah, well, imagine how she and Aimz got on. I've no idea why Kalumbits married her; she was flightier than a zipnite migration. She'd be gone for ten orbits at a time, come back with some 'priceless gifts' from her 'travels' which, unsurprisingly, were nearly always riddled with arcane curses. Have you ever tried to get a stubborn curse out of fine silk?"

"Did you try putting it in a bowl of dry rice?"

"I...no. What's rice?"

May laughed and shook her head; it didn't matter. "I told her I'd bring you to her."

He smooshed his face into the pillow and groaned. "Doo-e-aff-ta-go-now?" he asked, his voice muffled by the brocade.

"Not now. I told her I'd bring you back in a minute."

"How long's a minute?" he asked, flipping over.

"Exactly. She didn't know, either."

"And she was too proud to ask, wasn't she?" Xan smiled. The only thing he liked about Milly was that he always, without fail, could predict her. Like the Largish Bronda's Flexidimensal vehicles, she was reliably awful.

"Yep." May yawned.

"How long have you been awake?" Xan asked, concerned. By his count, it had been at least two rotations.

"Awhile," she said. "You're not supposed to sleep after a concussion."

"Ever?" Xan whispered, horrified.

"Everrrrr," May confirmed in a spooky warble. "No, seriously, I don't know how long. I guess I better try to sleep."

He stretched and turned over. "I'm going back to sleep, too. I've got a Tuhntian idiom for you: 'Never wake a Carmnian in the middle of a sleep cycle.'"

"Why, what happens?"

"They'll still be tired."

May snorted quietly and closed her eyes. Despite her body being tired, her mind was having a fiesta. She crawled to the pile of holobooks at the end of the waterbed. Snoodark Island was too isolated to pick up anything on the TV except corny scantplots, so they had purchased old holobook cylinders by the kilo at an estate sale.

The books had clearly belonged to an eclectic soul. They ran the gamut from absurdly methodical erotica to implausibly outlandish science fiction. May had been struggling through "Floaters," a speculative horror novel about a clan of fish-warriors who swam through the air, descending upon burgeoning civilizations and hoovering up their crops. The book itself wasn't terrible, but May had lost interest half-way through a chapter-long explanation of the plot of an unimportant novel which the main character (an enormous floating carp with a swim bladder malady) was reading.

She picked the holobook up now, considering it before stuffing it into the crack between the waterbed and the floor, where they stored the holobooks they knew they were never going to read. She found a book on the impact of trending vegetal microcosm exploration on impoverished mollusks and attempted to understand it.

CHAPTER SEVEN

Slapdashery

Simulated sunlight peaked through the faux windows of Largish Bronda's FlexiDimensional HoverBus, waking May. She escaped the waterbed and turned off the faux window so she could see what actually lay outside the bus rather than the Largish Bronda Corporation's idea of a perfect morning.

Outside, predictably, was gray, cold, and dead. She flipped the simulated sunrise back on.

"Good morning, starshine!" Xan startled her from the kitchen. He had already made coffee and was cooking a potato-like vegetable that seeped purple starch and tasted uncannily of pineapple. A gift from Listay, straight from her vegetable garden.

"Purpatapple again for breakfast?" May leaned on the kitchen counter to watch Xan pop the last of the lumps into the Chrispopalactic Crisper which chopped and fried the vegetable instantly.

The fine art of *portmanteau* was absolutely lost on Xan. Tuhntian *portmanteau* exists, of course, but translation chips just aren't sophisticated enough to process them into another language. "Grenanera," he corrected her. 'Grenanera' means 'purple potato-like vegetable which tastes uncannily of pineapple' in Tuhntian. He added, "Coffee?" which meant 'coffee.'

"Of course," May said as she floated the hover stool toward her and sat at the tiny counter. "We'll need it to keep up with your aunt."

Xan winced. "I was hoping you'd forgotten about that."

"You really don't want to go? But you're usually so..."

"Desperate for attention? Yeah, I know. But Milly's different. Her attention comes at a steep cost. If she says she wants to see me...it means she wants something," he stared out at the cheery faux sunrise, trying to guess what it was she could want.

"Well...yeah. To see you."

“When did you get so optimistic?” He finished drinking the pot of coffee without bothering to pour it into a mug, then combed his hair with his fingers to tame the proto-mullet he had been obstinately growing out for a season. He tried a mullet every couple hundred orbits, just to be absolutely sure they still looked terrible on him.

“Should we bring Aimz?”

“Blitheon, no. On their best behavior, Aimz and Milly are nuclear. With Aimz in this state—” He didn’t like where that sentence was going, so he stopped saying it.

“What state?” May said, scooping up the last bite of crisped purpatapple.

“Well, I mean, Aimz isn’t up for it right now. Come on.” He tossed her empty plate into the disintegrator. “Let’s get this off our marks.”

* * *

Xan had avoided going Downtown ever since they arrived a season ago, and now he’d been there twice in as many rotations. He hooked arms with May, hunching close to her as if they were about to walk into a haunted house as they descended the stairs.

“May, this place is really spooky. I mean, first off, it’s underground. Nothing good happens underground. I’ve never once been in an underground location and had a good time.”

“I thought you had fun in the Pontoosa Adventure Hole,” May teased. “That’s what your flag said.” She was referring to the triangular novelty flag he had used as a censor-bar after his swimsuit had dissolved away in the gift shop of the Pontoosa Adventure Hole, an underground theme park turned abandoned pit of horrors.

“The flag was mistaken. I did not have fun in the Pontoosa Adventure Hole. In fact, the Pontoosa Adventure Hole is 90% of the reason I’d rather not have anything to do with underground locations.”

“What’s the other 10%?” May asked.

"Well, Trilly, where I grew up, used to be a thriving sirospletax mining town. Then one day, someone pulled on the wrong tree root and collapsed 600 miles of mine shaft and–poof–no more miners."

"Huh," said May. "There goes my plan to pull out some tree roots while we're down here."

"Oh, well, I mean you can probably pull out some smaller ones."

"No, no, you ruined it for me," she grinned at him cheekily and he relaxed a little. Her strange sense of humor, something that only he ever seemed to be in on, always put him at ease.

"There it is," May said, nodding toward the giant mural. She hadn't warned him about it. She probably should've.

"Blitheon's inconvenient pimple, that's scary," said Xan. "That's Milly, though. Huge, public, bordering on obsessive displays of affection. She must've forgotten what I look like, though..."

"That's exactly what you look like," May said.

Xan shook his head. "My nose isn't that long."

It was, but May didn't refute him.

"Last chance to turn back," she said.

"It's okay. It's alright. I'm ready to see her." And he stepped confidently in the direction of his own likeness. One step. He stopped. "But first, we need to agree on an exit strategy."

"Okay," May said. "If you decide you don't want to be around her, we'll leave."

"Where's your sense of decorum? We have to come up with a lie in case she tries to rope us into anything."

"A lie. The height of decorum."

"I mean, I don't like lying to anyone—"

"Don't you?"

"—but I don't want to hurt her feelings, either," he finished, ignoring her interruption out of decorum. "The wink-word is slapdashery. If either of us says 'slapdashery,' the other will make up a fake emergency and get us out of there. Alright?"

"What if the word slapdashery comes up in normal conversation?"

"Right, yeah, that's the sort of thing I'm likely to say, isn't it? What about anterior? That's a good word. No need to use that in conversation. And if I have to refer to something as anterior, I'll substitute with something else like 'frontmost' or 'before.'"

"Think you can manage that?"

"Probably," he said.

"Alright, anterior is the safe word," May agreed and knocked on the metal door, just twice.

Silence.

Two more knocks were met by a deeper silence from inside.

From outside, however, came a thump.

Followed by another thump.

Followed by a whispered curse.

The commotion came from behind the mass of shipping containers-turned-apartments. May decided to go figure out what it was, and Xan decided, a blip later, that she shouldn't do that alone.

Behind the stacks, in the alley, they found a pile of luggage trunks and a large minicraft (which was roughly the size of a mini largecraft), its shell dusty blue with neon green ovipositors spray painted at random sizes and intervals around it. The phallic shapes had been tipped with pink flowers, though, in an attempt at disguise.

Xan took an unnecessarily deep breath in and let it out with unnecessary force.

"That's Milly's old minicraft alright. Aimz vandalized it after Milly accidentally destroyed some science experiment by vaporizing a cream puff too early in the morning."

May tried to imagine what type of experiment, exactly, might suffer such a fate, but a third massive trunk launched from the minicraft and landed in the alley with a resolute thud.

"Aunt Milly?" Xan called out, jogging toward the trunks. From the door of the minicraft, Milly appeared in a heavy cotton patchwork coat, setting a feathered hat atop the trio of trunks. A gaudy visor across which scrolled the phrase 'Nasty Piece of Trok' in pink digital letters covered her eyes entirely, and she tilted her head up to see out from underneath it.

"Is that my Quaxlagon?"

"Quaxlagon?" asked May. "That's your full name?"

"Eugh, yes. Please don't make fun of it."

May laughed. "I wasn't going to! It's nice. Now I have something to call you when you're being a pest. Quaxlagon."

"Whatever you say, May June July."

Milly twirled over to Xan, throwing off the visor, and flung her arms around his neck, nipping his nose fondly. "It's so good to see you, larvling! So good. How long has it been? Why, manage me, the last time I saw you, you were half a crawfish shorter." She pushed him back, holding him at arm's length to inspect him. "Oh, and look at those kingly shoulders filing out. You always were a slight little thing. Gone a bit heavy on the snacks, though, mun?" She patted his stomach, and he self-consciously sucked it in.

"May eats a lot; it would be rude to not eat with her," he defended.

Milly tapped his face dismissively, then turned to May and gave her several pecks on the forehead. "Blitheon bless you, larvling."

May reflexively wiped her face with her sleeve, and Xan wriggled his nose to check that it was still on. Carmnian elders were fond of the nose nip. Xan wasn't.

"It's nice to see you, too, Aunt Chrismillion." Xan looked over her shoulder at the minicraft. "Is..." He paused, wondering if he really wanted to finish that sentence. He did not. But he finished it anyway. "Is Aunt Kalumbits...around?"

Chrismillion raised her chin just enough to be able to look down at Xan. "One aunt not enough for you?"

Xan swallowed, refusing to meet her gaze. "You know that's not why I asked."

Chrismillion's suddenly tight expression relaxed. "She was on Tuhnt when it was destroyed. If that's what you mean."

"Anterior," Xan whispered to May.

"Hmm?" Milly asked.

"Nothing."

"Well," May began, quickly deciding on an excuse to leave. "It was great seeing you, but we've got a thing back at the place."

Chrismillion squinted at her, then patted May's shoulders. "Nonsense, larvling! Come inside. I have a kettle of tea on, and all those trunks belong to Xan!"

May watched him for some kind of physical cue as to how much he didn't want to go inside. While the translation chip didn't do much to translate the strange faces he made, she'd known him long enough that she usually got the idea. She wasn't even getting the gist now. Nor a hint. Nor a modicum of an atom of a clue.

"Do we need to do the thing back at the place right now?" she asked.

He shook his head. The trunks had him on a reel, and Aunt Chrismillion knew this. That's why she had kept them.

"We'll stay for tea, but we do have to get going soon," May confirmed. Xan's mouth was a tight line, and his eyes looked like they'd been popped out, polished to a high shine, and set back in his face.

"Why don't you go ahead and start the tea?" May said, hoping to get away from Milly for a while to check in with Xan. "We'll be right in."

Aunt Chrismillion looked suspiciously from May to Xan. "You won't run off and take the trunks, right?"

"Promise. I don't think we could run with those trunks if we tried," May said and, satisfied, Milly went back into the apartment.

After the reverberation of the slamming metal door had settled, May nudged Xan. "Are you okay?"

"Not at all! Why do you ask?" he said as if she had asked him if he would mind scratching an annoying itch on her back.

"Didn't you...I mean, hadn't you already assumed Kalumbits was gone?" May felt like she was prodding a dead jellyfish on the beach with a sharpened stick.

"Heh," he choked. "I guess..."

"Come here." She opened her arms and he crumbled into them. "I'm sorry, Blueberry."

He shrugged; there was nothing she could do. Or rather, she was already doing what she could do. With a sigh, Xan straightened back up and ran a hand down his face.

"I've still got an aunt, I should probably try to reconcile with her. It was anterior to the war the last time we were anterior to anterior."

May wondered how the Tuhntian word for anterior as in 'before,' also meant anterior as in 'the front of someone.' I could go into cultural universals once again, but I wouldn't want to pummel a perished puntl.

"She freaks me out," May said.

Xan nodded encouragingly. "Yeah, that's something she does. I would like to say she's entirely harmless, but, well...I suppose she's mostly harmless. Let's have some tea," he said resolutely.

"You really want tea after what Sonan did?"

"Even Aunt Milly isn't cruel enough to poison me." He searched the cobblestones in deep thought. "I mean, I don't think she is. Zuut, now you've got me worried."

"Well, if it is poisoned we won't have to worry about spending any more time with her." May chuckled, and to her relief, Xan smiled back.

They entered the shipping container. The coffee table was set with a traditional pre-boloyten Tuhntian tea machine made entirely of cut glass. Half tea pot, half hookah, and half chandelier; it was one-hundred-and-fifty percent worth of thing. Six candles flickered around it, warming the tea. May had the eerie sense that they were about to summon Rube Goldberg's ghost and cautiously sat on the couch with Xan.

"Sit, larvlings! Oh so much to catch up on, isn't there? I did *so* miss you, Quaxlagon. I can't..." She paused to swallow, her voice had become hoarse. "I can't tell you how dreadfully sorry I am."

"Hmm," Xan agreed and accepted a cup of tea from her. He wondered briefly if she was trying to apologize in advance for poisoning him. But May drank her cup and gave him a nod. Nothing remotely like barley. More like peppermint, really. With a hint of fabric softener and a pinch of concrete. May, though she would never know it and had no formal training, would've made a top-notch sommelier.

"Can you ever forgive me, larvling? I do, I feel just *despondent.*"

Xan sipped the tea, politely swallowed, and vowed to never drink tea again. Even if it didn't kill him, it hadn't been worth the effort to lift the cup to his mouth. "Forgive you for what, exactly?"

"Oh, dear, will you truly make me say it?"

Again, he drank the tea. This time to keep himself from answering her in a way he might regret.

"I apologize for taking your costumes."

Xan silently waited for her to go on. May watched him, fascinated. He never silently waited for anyone to go on. Being around Milly had seemed to totally wipe his personality.

She huffed, slammed her teacup on the saucer, and went on. "I'm sorry I'm a horrible caregiver and that you wish I had died instead of Kalumbits. Is that what you wanted to hear? Will you forgive me for that now?"

Xan smiled tightly at Chrismillion. He set down the tea and turned to May. "May, what were you saying anterior to us coming in here?" He looked at Chrismillion without moving his head. "We have a thing to do at a place, I'm afraid, but it's been just delightful catching up with you. Keep the costumes, please, and thank you for the disgusting herb water. I detest it."

He stood and began to leave, but as he did, Chrismillion threw herself across the table to reach for his arm, knocking over all six candles in a way which was not only entirely and completely accidental, but also very intentionally choreographed and executed.

She yelped as the flames singed her coat, then rolled dramatically on the floor, the flames seizing the opportunity to start exploring the room. The fire turned its sights on the couch and began licking it up like a cat licking up spilled milk, but slightly more dangerous.

May and Xan leapt off the quickly succumbing couch.

"Help me pick her up!" May said, grabbing Milly's ankles firmly as Milly howled melodramatically. Xan scooped under her arms and hefted her up, totally unfazed, as if he'd done this before. He had, in fact, twice carried Milly out of a fire that she caused. This was nothing new.

Once outside, May dropped her end of Milly on the dusty rock and latched the apartment door to keep the fire contained.

Xan crouched in front of Milly, resettling her askew wig. "Are you alright?" he asked.

She coughed, waved her hand swimmingly in front of her face. "Quaxlagon, darling..." she coughed again, though she didn't need to, and Xan suspected as much. "Fetch your sister won't you? I do believe I am to die of smoke inhalation," she warbled.

"Milly," he whined at her. "If I bring Aimz you're going to die of murder."

"I want to see her! Why are you keeping her from me?" Milly sat up, miraculously recovered, her voice strong and demanding again.

"Goodbye, Milly." Xan put an arm around May's shoulders and tried to walk away, but unfortunately Chrismillion was not the kind of demon that disappears if you ignore it.

"Can I stay with you?" Milly grabbed the back of Xan's furry coat.

"You've got the minicraft," Xan protested, turning around mid-stride.

"Yes, but I can't live in there. It's full of your trunks!" Milly said.

"Then I'll take the trunks back."

"Please." Aunt Milly grabbed his arm now and suddenly looked shorter than him, though moments before she had been taller. "I really do want to make amends. I..." She paused, her eyes glistening. "I loved you and Aimz and Kalumbits very much, and now that Kalumbits is gone, I want to fix things between us. Honestly, I do."

Xan had heard this before. Several times, actually. But he hadn't heard it in a few centuries, since he hadn't seen her in a few centuries, so he was tempted to give her an eighty-third chance.

"Aimz won't believe you." What he meant was that *he* didn't believe her.

"Just let me see her! You know what's in the trunks, I'd wager. Why not put on a show for me?" said Milly, a devilish smile twisting her face.

"I...yeah. You're suggesting we revive the Tinsel Merkin Fiasco, aren't you?"

Milly nodded so hard, her curls couldn't keep up. "And I've got connections at the *perfect* venue, the Grand Theater of Doing Things in Front of People in the Name of Entertainment in Snoodark's Folly! How does that sound?"

"That sounds..." Xan's head did a circular sort of maybe gesture. "Like a venue. What's Snoodark's Folly?"

"Queen Carmnia's sprawling manor, of course! How can you call yourself a Carmnian, not knowing Snoodark's Folly. Just shameful!"

Xan put his hands up submissively. "Alright, okay, Snoodark's Folly. Who do you know that works for Carmnia?"

"Oh, you know, some people." She waved a dismissive hand. "Just knock! Tell them Milly sent you."

"Sure," Xan said, hefting the three enormous trunks with a strength born of a desire to end this interaction as quickly as possible. "We'll definitely do that! Thanks for the tip." Then aside to May, he whispered, "We are definitely not doing that."

"Let me know when it is! And the dress code!" Milly called after them.

"Of course! Bye Milly," he said, already huffing under the weight of the trunks as they headed back toward the staircase.

"Don't wait long!" she said at their diminishing forms.

"Yep," he shouted through his teeth.

"Give my love to Aimz!"

They were out of earshot. Or, at least, Xan was confident they were far enough away that they could pretend to be out of earshot. Xan finally released the frustrated growl he had been politely restraining.

CHAPTER EIGHT

Studying Botany

Listay, having been reported as dead by the handful of her staff who had returned to Rhea after the *Peacemaker* crashed, was dealing with a legal conundrum that even she, a seasoned military general with a penchant for bureaucracy, couldn't get around.

Rather a lot of ordinary things become impossible when you're legally dead. Firstly, opening a bank account in the name of someone now deceased looks a great deal like some kind of fraud. Secondly, the dead don't typically go on paying taxes, and as such, the dead cannot apply for a job.

Frustrated, penniless, and dead, Listay had been forced to accept help. Help, as it so often does, came in the form of a buy-one-get-one free deal. The Largish Bronda Corporation had built a surplus of Merimip Ocean Ships and were so desperate to get them off the lot, they were giving them away with the purchase of anything larger than a keychain. So when May and Xan purchased the hover bus, Listay got a Merimip, a sleek little houseboat with a bulky, cumbersome glass dome on top.

This is how Listay came to after-live on a boat in the fjord with Aimz who, though never claiming to live there herself, could usually be found lounging around the boat somewhere like a feral cat full of kittens.

Usually, Aimz stayed at the Merimip under the guise of "studying botany" in Listay's "garden". The pair were engaged in a vigorous study session when the squeak of footfalls on the aluminum boat ramp alerted them to May and Xan's approach.

On Rhea, many hundreds of religions have been created for the express purpose of instilling sexual shame in the hearts and loins of all Rheans. Conversely, Carmnian culture dictated that modesty-be-damned; clothes were worn for style alone. This is why Listay answered the door shielded in the broad yellow leaves of a distant relative of the ficus, and Aimz joined her in proud full frontal.

"I hope you're prepared to out-do what you just interrupted." Aimz sported a wide grin and nothing else, leaning against the doorframe rakishly.

May had never purposefully imagined what Aimz might look like naked, but *had* she imagined it, she wouldn't have imagined this. She very pointedly averted her gaze.

"Oh, don't embarrass May," Listay interjected before Xan could say that he did intend to out-do what he'd just interrupted and make a fool of himself. "We'll get dressed and be with you in a—"

"Waaaait!" Aimz shouted as the stack of trunks behind Xan finally registered with her. She held her arms out to the trunks as if she were expecting them to hug her.

"Right?" Xan smiled.

"Listy, larvling, you're right. Let's get dressed." Aimz snatched the handle on the bottom trunk and pulled, dragging the stack backward into the boat. She paused and looked up under her arm at Xan. "Zuut, how did you carry them here without an electro-lift?"

Xan made a face as if a few hours of his life had just been purposefully skipped over by some all-knowing, omniscient hand. "No idea, honestly. May?"

May shrugged. "I know I didn't help."

Grunting, Aimz pulled the trunks into the boat and shut the door, leaving May and Xan outside.

The Merimip bobbed genially at them, floating just a hand's width above the water.

"She's going to be a blip in there," Xan said and sat on the ramp, his back against the Merimip's door.

"Why, what's in the trunks?" May asked.

"Didn't you ask that on the way over?" he asked.

"What way over?"

"Oh yeah, right. Right..." Xan said, again perplexed by how they had arrived at the Merimip. "Well, they're the costumes and props from my old burlesque group, The Tinsel Merkin Fiasco."

"The Tinsel?"

"Yes."

"Merkin?"

"Uh-huh."

"Fiasco?"

"That's the one."

May thought about that. "What does merkin mean?"

"Oh, you don't have them on Earth? They're uh..." Xan bared his teeth, trying to puzzle together the most appropriate words. "Crotch wigs," he decided was tasteful enough.

"Huh. So those trunks are full of crotch wigs?"

"Oh zuut, no! No. That's the point, you see; it was a fiasco. We don't do merkins anymore."

"Ah," said May.

"Ah!!" said Xan, falling backward into the Merimip through the suddenly dematerialized door. He landed on his back, nose-to-nose with a beaming Aimz, the shiny red tinsel of her outfit tickling his forehead.

"Iiiit's Zecktrix!" She announced cheerfully, shimmying the tinsel in his eyes.

Against the monochromatic grey backdrop of the Merimip's interior, Aimz's pale blue skin, magenta hair, and sparkly red leotard made her look like a bad photoshop. May climbed into the bobbing ship, helping Xan regain his footing.

"Zecktrix?" May asked.

"Aimz's stage persona," Xan told her.

"No, no," Aimz said. "Persona implies a character. This is how I always am!" She did something strange with her tongue, like she was trying to lick the last bite of peanut butter from a jar, but sexily.

Xan nodded. "You're right, my mistake."

"Listay! Come look at me! Look at your zuxine Carmnian plaything!" Aimz shouted and Listay, now fully dressed and looking a bit sheepish, entered the living room.

"You look lovely," Listay told her, then glanced at May, trying to decide whether she should apologize for being almost naked in front of her, or if it was wise to not bring it up again. Aimz made the decision for her by launching at the second trunk and flinging it open, pulling out scarves and holsters and wigs and other things which would need a lot more time to explain.

"Where did you get all this? It's our stuff! Last I knew Milly–" Aimz froze. An impossibly thin peach scarf she had just thrown into the air made its decent, draping itself over half of Aimz's face. She spun, fixing Xan with one pink, blazing eye.

"Milly! I swear on every volt in Quanzar's laser-scythe, if you don't tell me where that tchaag is, I'll—"

"Aimz, look!" Xan said, pulling something from the trunk. "It's your plasma-plipper!" He began to juggle two glass balls connected by a string and a weak blue lightning arced between them.

"No–" Aimz batted them away. "Ow." She shook her hand which had caught the tail end of the plasma arc and been lightly electrocuted. "Where is she?"

"Alright, so, long story. As you know, May's been looking for the *Audacity*—"

"Shorten it."

"May found these flyers—"

"Shorter."

Xan cringed, mentally running through the plot thus far. "Chrismillion lives Downtown, and she wants to see you–"

"Good," Aimz said. May was grateful that one of her eyes was covered, because she'd never seen such a murderous gleam in them and she didn't care for it.

"Not good. Not a good idea at all," Xan said, snatching the scarf away from her. "So we compromised. And this is the good bit! We're getting the Tinsel Merkin Fiasco back together! One night only! If Milly happens to hear about it and come see us, fine! She gets what she wants, you never have to see her as long as the spotlight's bright enough. Good plan, eh?"

"Xan," Aimz crossed her arms. "Half of the Tinsel Merkin Fiasco is dead."

"Ahh-uhh, eugh..." he grimaced at the reminder. "We've got plenty of acts between the two of us, and May can work the lights. Besides, Old PinFlicker is in one of these trunks. It'll be like we never disintegrated-destructed-demolished-no-*disbanded*! Like we never disbanded."

"I'll organize the event," Listay said, delighted to be organizing something, for once, that didn't have life-or-death consequences. She was wrong, of course, but let's not get ahead of ourselves. "If you're putting on a show, you're going to need spreadsheets."

"Uh-huh, right, yes. Listay will do the spreadsheets," Xan said, unconvinced that any organizing had to be done at all because he had never been the one in charge of doing it.

"Chrismillion's never going to change. You know that," Aimz said, shoving Xan off the trunks so she could dig through hers again.

"Do I know that?"

Aimz snarled half-heartedly at him. "You're just like Kalumbits. She always gave Chrismillion more chances than she deserved." She tilted her head back, her gaze rolling back to the exploded trunk. "But I really want to do Zecktrix again," she said.

"So we're on?" Xan said, excited.

"We're zuxing on."

CHAPTER NINE

Phasers Set to Stunning

Xan conveniently forgot to mention Milly's suggested venue at Snoodark's Folly, and so Listay had come up with the cheapest venue she could find. The tiny theater was snuggled beneath Uptown NotTuhnt's historic Sneepum Hotel, the first hotel built on NotTuhnt. It was the *only* hotel built on NotTuhnt. And for good reason. No one ever visited NotTuhnt if they could help it. Realizing this, the hotel manager had changed the welcome sign in the lobby to one which read 'Our sincerest apologies.'

It was opening night, which was also dress rehearsal and closing night, since they only planned on doing this once. May sat cross legged on the blue velvet floor of a backstage dressing room while Xan lugged a trunk into the room, dropping it with a plume of dust. "Ready?" Xan asked her excitedly, leaning over the trunk as if it might pop open and dazzle her too soon.

"As I'll ever be."

Xan propped open the lid to reveal his bounty, a mess of gold and silver spaghetti.

"What is it?" May squinted into the glittering maw, feeling like she was trying to look into the sun.

"That's Fuxoona Glizell. Aren't they stunning?"

"Stun's a good word for it. I'm going to take a look at the tech booth," she said, standing to leave. "Try to figure out the lighting..."

"Make it bright. I want Aimz to think she's performing on the sunny side of Sarfooreimp! If she doesn't see Milly, she can't get upset about her, right?"

"On it," May said.

The tech booth had left much to be desired. A single switch labeled “House” at one end and “Stage” at the other was installed right in the center of a rather large console. After a great deal of searching, May found another switch underneath the console labeled “Off” and “On”. She really would’ve liked to show her technological prowess just once, but alien technology thus far had been mostly ridiculously user friendly.

Gold-silked fingers appeared above the tech booth wall and were soon followed by Xan who pulled himself up, jingling, over the back of the booth, and perched on the dividing wall. Even in the dim light, the sparkles on his dress were mesmerizing.

He puffed his chest out, showing off a pair of fake boobs which shone like two small disco balls, and he shook his head to demonstrate the bounce of his thickly curled, silver-gold wig.

“What do you think?”

May wasn’t exactly sure what type of reaction he was searching for here. “It’s very shiny,” she said.

He lay himself dramatically over the back of the booth, his legs kicking elegantly out in white, thigh-high, skyscraper stilettos.

“It’s alright, mun,” his voice shifted and, though the translation chip didn’t pick it up well, he affected a masterful Queenly accent. “You can tell Fuxoona they’re the most gorgeous Tuhntian you’ve ever seen.” He winked cheekily, wobbled dangerously on the divider, then steadied himself.

May covered a laugh. “What if Xan gets jealous?”

“I swear on my ovipositor, I won’t tell a soul of it!”

“Oh, alright,” May cleared her throat and put on a delicate southern drawl for him. “Having basked in your singular beauty, I feel my life is complete and I can die a happy woman.” Then, in her normal voice. “Good?”

“Good!” said Xan. “You should be on stage with me!”

“No,” May said.

“No, right, yeah.” Xan agreed. Then, again in a Queenly timber, he said, “Now help Mx. Glizell down, munny. Fuxoona’s not the spritely young acrobat they once were!”

May left the booth the easy way, via the stairs, and got back to floor level below the lounging Xan. He reached his arms out to her dramatically and wriggled his fingers.

"Xan, you're—"

"Ah-hem!"

"Mx. Glizell," she corrected, "you're too heavy for me to lift, you know that?"

"Why! I might in all my life!" he said with faux offense and docked his fists on his hips before jumping down, May's hands around his sequined waist to steady him on his massive heels.

"Ah, there we are, larvling." He straightened his dress then, in his own voice, cursed. "Zuut."

"What?"

"Chrismillion's here. Did you invite her?"

"No," May said.

"Neither did I. Aimz and I used to tease each other that she had spies watching us all the time. We stopped teasing each other when we started believing it," he shivered. "Alright, okay, I'll keep an eye on Aimz, and you can keep Milly occupied, right? Yeah." He looked round nervously as if Aimz might plummet from the catwalk and attack. "Second thought: I'll watch Milly, and you watch Aimz. No. Third thought: Where's Listay? She can overpower Aimz."

May frowned at Chrismillion, studying her willowy stature. "I could overpower Milly."

"You're sure? She can be extremely persuasive. You've got to assume that anything she says is a lie straight out of the silo."

"I meant physically," May said, though she could probably overpower her psychologically too, should she need to.

Xan shook his head. "If it comes to that...watch out for her nails," he said.

"Okay."

"And her teeth," he added.

"Got it."

"And her nose."

"Her...nose?"

"It's sharper than it looks and she will weaponize it," Xan confirmed.

"Oh...don't worry about it. You go break a leg," May said, gently shooing him away before Milly spotted him. She was still looking around the growing crowd like a meerkat with a periscope.

Xan tilted his head at her. "Do you expect that will help?"

The house lights flickered, warning the audience that the show was about to start so they should either sit down or scram. "Earth saying, means have a good show!"

"But why?!"

"I don't know, and I don't have time to make something up," she physically turned him around and started walking him in the direction of the backstage entrance.

"Alright, I'm going, mun! Aunt Kalumbits is late; I hope she arrives before my act..." he muttered as he went.

Convinced he was going in the right direction, May headed back to the tech booth, pondering why he had said that. He knew Kalumbits wasn't coming on account of her being dead. Perhaps, she thought, it was a strange alien custom to invite the deceased. No stranger than breaking a leg, at least.

May sat in front of the light controls next to Listay. There was nothing to do, but she enjoyed the illusion that being behind a control panel might give her more control over her life in general. Listay set a notepin which displayed a green holographic spreadsheet on the console.

"Twenty-seven people, all perfectly seated according to an algorithm which factors height, light tolerance, and the distance each of them is able to accurately throw tips from," Listay said with a practiced humility.

May studied the spreadsheet emanating from the notepin. "How did you factor that?"

"Square root of arm length, multiplied by muscle elasticity, minus one third muscle mass, divided by willingness to punt a crystal at someone," Listay said.

"Really?"

"No." Listay chuckled. "I asked them. Here." She handed May a llerke. "You haven't eaten in eight beoops; you must be starving."

May found it spooky how Listay always knew when she was hungry, but May was usually hungry, so there was nothing supernatural about it.

"Thanks," she whispered to Listay, flicking the lights from "house" to "stage". A single, red-heeled foot peeked out from the side of the stage and kicked at an old wooden box, the infamous PinFlicker. It was the size of an accordion, its many panels barely concealing tarnished brass innards and hosting an array of metal pipes which began to puff out a fuzzy melody as the internal music cylinder rolled under the many pins and pumped the small but powerful bellows.

Aimz strutted out in less than she usually wore plus a silver beaded headdress, hips gyrating, shoulders shimmying, arms dangerously akimbo. The crowd pelted crystals at her as a holy offering. She received the praise like a gracious god.

May kept watch over Chrismillion who sat in the back row, absently clutching a fistful of crystals to her décolletage. She wasn't watching Aimz. She was hunched over a little hand-held mirror, touching up her dark purple lipstick.

The music wound down to a distorted warble, and Aimz paused to fiddle with the box until it played again, quieter.

"Welcome to the show you pitiful ovi-suckers!" That got a hearty cheer from the crowd. "Most of you perverts have done this before, I can tell, but let's re-certify you. When I shimmy you—"

"Shout!" went the crowd.

"Blitheon, you're a snack-y bunch of submissives, aren't you? Right, when I titillate you—"

"Tip!" they cried.

"And finally, what are you not going to do this evening?"

"Usurp your right to bodily autonomy by touching you or anyone else who excites us!" recited the crowd in practiced unison.

She smiled. "It's nice to see getting your planet exploded hasn't changed the scene. Now..." Aimz kicked off her heels and leapt from the stage onto the back of an empty velvet chair, then the next, using the unfilled seats as stepping stones to get back to the tech booth. The crowd twisted to watch her.

"Hey, you heard that? No touching," Aimz whispered into Listay's mouth. Listay looked as if she very much wanted to touch, but showed mighty discipline. Aimz cackled and leaned into the soundboard microphone. "And now," her voice reverberated. "Prepare your retinas for the brightest Queen-show since Blazita Fyresnatch's pyrotechnics accident: Mx Fuxoona Glizell!"

May was certain there wasn't a teledisc in the stage. Nonetheless, Fuxoona appeared in a puff of glitter right in the middle of it. Low-tech magic had created this effect. And, since a magician never reveals their secrets, even I have no idea how it happened. Damn magicians.

"You." Fuxoona pointed to someone leaning dangerously forward in their seat in the front row. "Be a larvling and crank my good friend PinFlicker."

A shadowed figure flung themselves half onto the stage to reach the box and wound it up, a new song wafting from it, a simmering tune with regular pops, like bacon seductively being fried. Fuxoona pulled a stick-on gem from a hidden pocket in their gown and slapped it on their bare chest.

"Do me a favor, larvlings. When you tip, aim right here." Fuxoona pointed to the faux cleavage with a wink. "I've got a lot of padding there. Any of you lonely zuxxers want to see why they called me The Legs of Trilly?"

The audience went wild for that, showering Fuxoona with crystals, adding to the mess on stage already. Typically, someone was there to clean up between acts, but that someone had perished on Tuhnt. Fuxoona kicked at a pile of crystals and tutted. "Zilla's off her mark this evening, isn't she? Zecktrix!" they shouted back to Aimz. "Where's Zilla?"

"Dead!" Aimz shouted back.

"Oh, heh." The persona of Mx Fuxoona slipped for just a moment and Xan's entire posture shifted, slightly, just enough to break the illusion that he was something other than Xan in a dress. The audience fell silent, and Fuxoona snapped back into place. "The Legs of Trilly!" said Fuxoona, to a slightly less enthused audience who had now been reminded twice of the destruction of their home planet in one stage show.

Fuxoona began to move like a slow-motion inflatable tube-man, then they were upside-down, doing things with their body May had no idea Xan could do. Arousal wasn't a sensation May had ever experienced, at least not toward another being. She'd gotten close a few times working on her old Honda, though. She did not experience it now, but she was entertained. And, clearly, the audience was up to their eyebrows in excruciating lust for Fuxoona. The theater bubbled with whoops, shouts, and moans of delight as the stage disappeared under a layer of crystalline tips.

"Aimz?" May asked, leaning over to Aimz who had parked in Listay's lap. "Xan's acting strange."

"Sure is, but zuut, the audience is responding to it!"

"No, I mean...earlier Xan said he was expecting Kalumbits, like he had forgotten. And just now—"

"Oh yeah, he's a little unstuck in time," Aimz said. "Common symptom for people like him."

"Symptom of what?!"

"Did he not zuxing tell you? Agh, of course he didn't. Listen, Earthmun, Xan and I—" The music ground to a halt, and Aimz paused to see why. On stage, Fuxoona followed suit with the grinding, but not the halting. "Showing off without me, Fuxoona?" Aimz asked from the back microphone, then launched out of the tech booth and walked wibblingly over the seats again to rejoin the spotlight.

"Aimz!" May hissed after her, but she was well out of earshot.

May looked to Listay for a hint at what Aimz had been trying to say, but Listay was entranced, leaning forward on her elbows, her eyes swimming around Aimz's hips, the corner of her mouth tilting up in a goofy half-smile. Listay, though in actuality there was nothing she could've done to prevent this, would later berate herself terribly for once again letting her guard down on account of a pair of beautiful hips.

Had she not been otherwise occupied, Listay might have noticed Chrismillion moving from her designated seat in the back of the crowd. May noticed. May sat up straighter, trying to figure out if she needed to hop over the tech booth wall and do something about it or not.

Milly slipped down the side aisle, headed for the silent PinFlicker. Just being helpful, May thought. Aimz looked at Milly with all the fervor of a starved lion spotting a sickly gazelle at the watering hole. Now, Listay noticed what Milly had done. But it was too late. Milly, though certainly she had approached the stage with the benign intent of winding PinFlicker for the performers, instead shoveled a handful of crystals from the stage into her purse.

"Blitheon's natal charts," Listay grumbled as she left the booth.

"Zux off, thief!" Aimz shouted, grabbing Milly by the front of her dress.

"Eugh." Xan discarded Fuxoona like a wet plastic bag and put a hand on Aimz's shoulder. "Let Zilla take care of it, mun—"

"Zilla." Aimz pushed Milly away from the stage, spinning around to intimidate Xan now instead. "Is." She stood up and he fell back, scrambling away. "Dead!" She flung herself at Xan, grabbing the string of gaudy gold beads around his neck and pinning him to the creaking stage. Someone in the audience began a clap, but another audience member coughed and silenced them.

"Stop saying that!" Xan wheezed around the choking beads. He wriggled until he had the sharp heel of his boot under Aimz's sternum and flung her off him, sending her flailing into an empty row of velvet seats.

The audience was beginning to get uncomfortable. Some half-stood, watching to see if this was a new experimental form of burlesque that hadn't quite settled into itself yet. Others slipped out the back. Still others raised their BEAPERs, preparing to call the police.

At the edge of the stage, Milly had recovered enough to get revenge. One word would send the theater into a complete panic. One word would set the police on Aimz's tail. One word would absolutely destroy the chance of another performance of The Tinsel Merkin Fiasco.

"Scourge!" she shouted like a 1930s horror actress. "Scourge!!!" she repeated, pushing her way through the crowd.

"Aimz," Xan said, climbing down from the stage. "BEAP Kalumbits about this, alright? I'm going after Milly. And, uh..." He looked lost for a second, as if he wasn't quite sure what he was saying or why he was saying it. "Ask Salesha to do her bit early, alright? I'll be back by the finale, I'd wager, then we'll all go to Martoly's Bar and have a drink." He tried to give her shoulder a comforting pat, but the mention of Martoly's Bar had re-ignited Aimz, and she ripped off her heavy silver wig and flailed it in his face, knocking him backward over a seat and pinning him to the sticky floor.

"You *blew up* Martoly's and *every other bar* on the zuxing *planet*, you *tchagg*!"

"I thought Aimz had gotten over that," May said to Listay as they watched the wrestling performers in the empty theater.

"You're the reason Milly left!" Xan flung the silken glove off his hand, pelting Aimz in the face with weaponized gold glitter, his signature attack.

"And you're the reason everyone except her is dead!" Aimz said, her eyes shut tight against the threatening glitter as she yanked out curly blond chunks of his wig. They weren't actually doing any damage to each other, and May and Listay both realized this, so they hung back, neither keen on getting covered in glitter.

"Here." Listay handed May an open bottle of Fraguntassle. "When they calm down, make Xan drink it. It seems to mitigate the scourge."

"What's the scourge?" May asked, accepting the bottle of opaque white brew.

Sirens interrupted her answer. Three triangular-bodied chrome police robots rolled into the venue. May yanked Xan (who had been gnawing gently on one of Aimz's hands while her other hand viscously ripped the stuffing from his fake boobs) behind a seat to hide him. She flicked his nose to get his attention.

"Ow." He cupped his nose, blinked at her as if she were a complete stranger, then re-adjusted his wig. "What was that for, mun?"

"The police are here," May whispered at him harshly, "Because you and Aimz started wrestling in the middle of the show. What's gotten into you?"

"Do not attempt to flee," said the foremost chrome officer, the plastic light atop its hat flashing with each syllable. Listay stepped in front of the chrome trio, barring them from May, Aimz, and Xan. "Scan me," she demanded. A blue light emanated from each of their visors and scanned Listay.

"According to Rhean records, General Listay under Rapite of Rhea is dead," the middle officer intoned. "Suspect," confirmed the two flanking officers.

"You're right, I'm very suspicious," Listay goaded them on. "Why don't you arrest me?" And all three of them did.

"Come on." May grabbed Xan's hand and dragged him toward the exit.

"Wait! Gloves." He collected the limp silk gloves that he had tossed in the tussle and re-sheathed his hands. "The gloves make the outfit," he said, wriggling shiny fingers at her.

May, with great difficulty, held back a contemptuous groan. "Where's Aimz?"

Xan shrugged. "Wager she snuck off with Yve. Again. Rude of her, don't you think? She knows how much I like Yve. I think it's rude. She could at least invite me."

Rather than waste her breath to tell him that Yvonne was not here and Aimz definitely didn't sneak off with her, May agreed and led him outside.

CHAPTER TEN

Traveling Kissing Booth

Trying to force a three-hundred-pound Tuhntian wearing four-inch heels in one direction proved rather difficult for May. One hand grasped the bottle of Fraguntassle; the other, she had tightly interwoven with Xan's. His gloves, however, made escape too easy. Barely a block away from the venue, he pulled away, leaving her holding onto a limp, silky glove as he sauntered off to pluck something from the walkway.

"Xan, no," May whined, stuffed the glove in her coat pocket, and tried to collect him again. He looked at her, his mouth suspiciously closed. "What's in your mouth?" she asked.

He shrugged.

"What are you eating?"

He rolled his eyes and unfurled his tongue at her, a not-cigarette stuck to it. She plucked it off and held it up to shame him.

"Really?"

"I have to!" he protested. "They're not good for you, May."

She sighed, flicked the damp not-cigarette into a nearby receptacle, and grabbed his hand again. "I wasn't smoking it," she told him. "Wish I was," she mumbled. The monorail station loomed ahead, and May paused.

"Hey, look at me," she said.

He looked.

"Don't act weird in the monorail, ok?"

"Why—" He paused to stare at his glove flapping from her coat pocket, grabbed it with his teeth, and spoke around it. "Would I act weird in the monorail, specifically?"

She recovered the glove and pushed it into the recesses of her trench coat pocket.

"Please drink this." She tried to hand him the bottle, but the monorail pulled into the station, and this distracted him.

"Excellent. Monorail," he said. "Lots of beautiful people on the monorail!" He jumped into the open tube and May followed helplessly, finding him already accosting a dark indigo Tuhntian twice Xan's size. "Hey, you're cute. Want to make out?" Xan asked him.

"Xan!" May slung her arms around his waist and tried to yank him away. "So sorry. He's drunk," she said to the stranger.

The Tuhntian raised a tired eyebrow at May, slowly blinked, dropped the book he was reading to the seat next to him, and let Xan make out ferociously with him. May covered her eyes, partially to give them some privacy and partially because the sight of anyone—particularly Xan—making out made her queasy. The monorail, at last, jerked into motion beneath them.

Another passenger had gotten up from their seat to tap Xan on the shoulder sheepishly. "Is that free?" they asked.

Xan pulled away, eyeing them with a gleam of excitement. "Of course it's free! Love is always free!" he announced to the monorail car. "Anyone who wants a taste of this, form a queue, please!"

Horrified, May watched, or rather *listened*, for she refused to look, as he made out with half the people in the monorail, complimenting each of them on their excellent form, outstanding dexterity, delightfully cold hands, and so on.

Sitting, May swirled the Fraguntassle in its bottle, sniffed the potent wheaty brew, and took a swig for herself while she waited for Xan to finish off the line. At last, he settled down in the seat beside her. There were a great deal more smiles in the monorail then there had been a moment before, peppered with a handful of disgusted murmurs regarding the looseness of zuxing Carmnians.

"How about you? You want in?" Xan asked.

May groaned. "No," she said, resting her elbows on her knees, one hand cradling her face and the other barely holding onto the bottle of Fraguntassle.

"Oh," he sounded just slightly disappointed, then perked up. "Well, looks like this car's tapped out. Onto the next!" He made for the door which led between the cars. It very clearly read:

Emergency Use Only. He pushed it open. May pulled him back inside and barred the door.

"Changed your mind?"

"No! You can't hop cars like a traveling kissing booth!"

"But I always do...did." He sat down on the plastic monorail bench next to her. "Tenses are hard, aren't they? Everything is happening in the now. Why do we use any other tense, again?"

"I don't know, you're the linguist, not me," May said. "We can talk about it if you drink this," she held out the Fraguntassle. He took the bottle and tipped it back, May hoped it was strong enough to not only fix his brain but to also kill any germs he might've picked up from the other passengers.

He handed the empty bottle back to her with an accomplished grin which faded, slowly, as he looked around the monorail. Half the passengers were gazing dreamily at him as if he had just—oh no. He *had*.

"Zuxing Blitheon's laser scythe, what in O'Zeno's secret swimming pool did I do?" he whispered, his fingers digging under his wig and pulling it off so he could grab at his own hair as he leaned over his knees.

May took the wig from him and put it on herself for safe keeping. She tried to rub his back comfortingly, but a shower of sequins fell off when she did, so she stopped. "Nearly everyone in the car," she said. The monorail pulled into their stop and they got out.

The air swirling in Snoodark's Quarry was thick with a slimy, cold drizzle, as usual. The wig May had taken from Xan was long enough to wrap around her neck as an impromptu scarf, and she slipped his gloves on, wincing at the feeling of the glitter inside them scraping like sandpaper across her hands.

Their walk from the monorail to Largish Bronda was usually short and filled with good conversation, but now it seemed to stretch untold distances. They were already miserable, so May figured now was as good a time as any to ask a miserable question.

"What is the scourge?" May asked as Xan stopped to retrieve a discarded not-cigarette mechanism from a molding patch of yellow leaves. "Don't eat it," she warned him.

"Wasn't planning to," he lied, then put it in his pocket to eat later.

"Scourge. You and Aimz both have it, don't you? What is it?"

Suddenly, Xan remembered all the things he had meant to talk to her about, like the new zipnite enclosure at the market in the city. Or perhaps the upcoming art installation, a social commentary that was either for or against something or other. And she'd need to know about the Egg Experience which had just opened in the rougher part of town that would soon be either an art district or a red-light district; it was too early to tell.

He said none of these things, though.

He was working on not deflecting.

So he didn't speak at all.

"Xan?"

"Yes?"

"You don't want to tell me?"

"Oh..." Xan sung as if he were about to break into a sailor shanty which would explain it in a cheery, fun way. There was no cheery, fun way to describe scourge, but he tried.

"The fungi that Carmnia likes to eat—remember those? That cause the phosphorescence in Carmnian eyes? Well, the fungus is usually dormant, but under the right circumstances, it goes into...well, let's call it party mode. Because parties are cheery and fun. So once the fungus goes into party mode, it grows rapidly, feeding off brain matter until it's a proper rager in there. Lots of fun. Extremely cheery. Actually, a cool side effect is that the phosphorescence is so intense, fully scourged Carmnians can't sleep. Ever! Imagine, never sleeping." He laughed. "It's deadly and irreversible," he said lightly.

"Irreversible?" she asked. May refused to accept this. To her, there was always a way out. Always a fix. Always something that could make it better. "What about the Fraguntassle? That helped."

"Oh, sure, sure. Yeah. Alcohol helps!"

"We'll just keep you drunk for the rest of your life, then. Or until we find a cure," May assured him as they entered Largish

Bronda. "We've still got some shermel in the cupboard, and tomorrow we can go back to the city and get more."

The reason they still had shermel in the cupboard was because shermel tastes terrible.

The reason they had shermel in the first place was that it's a key ingredient in what amounts to Tuhntian chicken noodle soup which Xan insisted on making for May when she came down with a space flu she had caught in the Pontoosa Adventure Hole in book two.

"Perfect. That will absolutely definitely work," he said. Xan peeled off his thigh-high white stilettos and shimmied out of the glitzy dress, letting it fall in a pile on the floor as he inspected the many greenish bruises he had gained. "Zuut, I'm wrecked! What...what did I do exactly?"

"You wrestled Aimz, ate not-cigarette butts off the ground, and started a traveling kissing booth in the monorail."

"Heh...Busy night." He folded his dress and removed the wig from May's head, looking for a clever place to hang it. The Big Mouth Billy Bass on the wall caught his eye, and he draped the curls over the fish's head. "I wrestled Aimz?"

"She wrestled you, actually. You didn't put up a good fight. There was a lot of glitter," she said, carefully laying down his glove atop the pile, trying to keep more glitter from falling out and contaminating the room.

Xan felt so heavy that when he sunk into the waterbed, he was surprised he didn't continue dipping into the floor below, down through the crust of Rhea, and into the planet's molten core where he could melt peacefully away. He buried his face in his hands, which were still covered in glitter and would be for the remainder of this novel. "How many strangers did I make out with?" he asked beneath his palms. May couldn't quite tell if he was hoping for a high or low number.

"Seven before I had to stop you from jumping cars."

"Yeah, that was my average," he said. May still couldn't tell how he felt about that. "How was the show? Before the...you know."

"I loved it."

"You did?" Xan flipped over, confused with his entire face.

"Yeah! I mean, I didn't really get it, but you looked like you were having fun. And Fuxoona is quite the charmer."

"They sure are." Xan laughed. "You know, it really felt like everything was back to normal for a bit there. I mean...I mean an old normal. Strange how many 'normal's you can have, right? Being alone in open space on the *Audacity* was normal. Racing with you was normal..." He paused and looked around at the still darkness of the hoverbus, deciding. "You'd think three seasons of this would make it normal but—"

"No, I agree. It's still weird." May yawned and stretched her arm out so he could cuddle up to her. She knew he wouldn't sleep, but if she started yawning at him, he would at least stop talking long enough for her to.

He caught the hint and shut up, but his mind refused to stop replaying scenes from all his past normals.

CHAPTER ELEVEN

Family Drops In

"Scourged Carmnians are unpredictable."

"Guh?" May said, rubbing her eyes to dislodge the film of sleep as she coaxed her consciousness into wake-mode. A worried shadow hung over her, silhouetted in the icy gray light outside the window. Eventually, she pieced together that the shadow was Xan and that he was worried that he would do something unpredictable. "Everything you did last night was predictable as hell," she assured him.

"Is hell predictable? I honestly don't know, I've never been. I thought you said it was a mythical place. And sure, last night I was predictable, but I can't predict whether or not I'll continue being predictable in the future! That's the point of unpredictability!"

"Ugh, it's too early for this," May said, rubbing her eyes with her fists, convinced she had a piece of glitter in them. "You'll always be you."

"Okay, but consider, if you will, who am I?" He sat in the bag chair next to her. "Who are you? Who are any of us?"

"Jesus, Xan, the sun's not even up yet. Can't we wait to talk philosophy until morning?"

They would have to. Someone knocked on the door.

May tapped on Xan's BEAPER and opened the outside camera. Though it was dark and foggy outside, she could make out two figures. One was tall and thin, the other built like a small mountain. She would've liked to imagine it was Aimz and Listay, come to ask them to breakfast on the Merimip. But Aimz never used the front door. Front doors, she had said, were for strangers. Snipping the wiring around the plasma skylight and literally dropping in unannounced was for family.

Also, Listay probably wouldn't have a massive anti-matter cannon perched on her shoulder.

And they likely wouldn't have shouted, "This is the Scourge Authority!" Well, perhaps Aimz would. It seemed like the sort of thing she might do. Not around Listay, though.

"Zuut, zuut, zuut," Xan whispered, plastering himself against the wall. "What do we do?"

"I'll bluff. Tell them I don't know anything," she whispered, looking for a place to hide him.

"They're not gonna believe that. You look like the type who knows everything. And you're a bad liar."

"I'll consider that a compliment," she whispered harshly, helping him accordion himself into a cupboard and carefully shutting it.

"Just a minute," she shouted. "I'm naked!"

"Awful liar," came, muffled, from inside the cabinet.

"We don't care," one of them shouted. Of course they didn't.

"I do! Hold on!" May wished, for the thousandth time since leaving Earth, that she had been granted a flashy laser gun like most sci-fi protagonists. Even a real pocketknife that wasn't duller than the round end of a spoon would have been nice. There were no weapons to be found in the kitchen, either. The Largish Bronda Corporation proudly claimed their included range of sustenance-machines could prepare just about anything you stuck in them. They had no need for sharp, dangerous knives, unfortunately.

May composed herself and walked, or rather wobbled, across the waterbed to the door. There was absolutely definitely not a brain-eating-fungus-ridden-drag-queen-alien in her cupboard. It shouldn't have been that difficult to believe.

May never reached the door. Someone attacked her from above, pinning her against the waterbed. "Stay down," Aimz whispered in May's ear, for it was she that had pinned her.

An electrical buzz drowned out May's reply. A booming crackle shook the bus and everything went white.

"You're going to need a new plasmadoor." Aimz rolled off May and onto her back, grinning delightedly at the carnage as the bed undulated beneath her.

Xan extracted himself from the cupboard to survey his singed surroundings, a green, half-full bottle of shermel in his hand. "By Blitheon's holy inner elbow, what was that?" He handed the bottle to May, and she tucked it away in her trench coat.

"Plasma malfunction. Happens all the time...if you hook up the power source to a mini-rectifier and blow out the circuits, at least." Aimz flipped a thumb-sized contraption in the air, licked it fondly, then tucked it away in the neck of her suit.

"Are they alive?" May asked of the two armored figures gently smoking on the grass outside. Both were heavily armored and heavily weaponed.

"Probably." Aimz shrugged. "Hey zuxers, you alive?" she shouted out at them. They stirred in answer. "Yep, they're alive."

"And they want to arrest you for getting the scourge?"

"Oh, uh, not...not exactly," Xan said with an embarrassed laugh. "Quarantined, more like."

"Quarantined out of life," Aimz corrected. "Scourged Carmnians get disintegrated. No interrogation, no due process. It's just: 'Eyup, they gots the scourge alright,' a zap, a poof, and you're gone." She demonstrated the poof with jazz hands.

"How did you get so good at describing horrible things in a fun, cheery way?" Xan asked.

"It's the jazz hands," she divulged with a wink. "Now shift it; we've got to get to the Merimip. Listay told me to collect you two and meet her there."

"Where's she?" Xan asked, clumsily pulling on boots and his mauve faux buffatalo coat.

"The cops took her in. Again. Terrible memory. Listay wants to take us to Fulogra on the mainland to see Yvonne. She's living on an apple farm with her lover and the apple-Earthling. You know, 'The dude that brought apples to the galaxy,'" she quoted the well-known slogan. "What's his name?" Aimz snapped her fingers as she tried to recall.

"August," May helped.

"That's the one! Know him?"

"I know of him."

"Small universe!" Aimz slapped her on the back. "It'll be a reunion! Except I'm with Yve's zombie ex (whom she murdered),

Yve's with some random Rhean engineer and a scruffy old Earthling instead of Xan, and Xan's with...well, Xan you're not really going with anyone right now, are you?"

"I go where the crystals take me," he said with a shrug. "Which, as of late, has been nowhere. So no. No, I'm not. Yve never had trouble sharing, though."

"Listay wouldn't be into it," Aimz replied.

"She's a monogamist?"

"No, it's just that Yvonne killed her that one time."

A laser blast glimmered between them and toasted the opposite wall.

"Shift it!" Aimz shouted, pulling herself out of the open skylight, her legs kicking frantically below like a massive duck. Once she was free, she reached down to pull May up, then went back for Xan, but he was gone.

"Xan what are you doing?" Aimz shouted down through the skylight, May squishing in beside her to see for herself.

"Saving the fish!" he said, unhooking Big Mouth Billy Bass from the far wall, dodging laser blasts as he tucked it securely under his arm.

"Hold still!" shouted the tall agent.

"Sorry, can't!" Xan said. Spotting an opening, he dove between the agents, planning a sort of graceful somersault with a perfect landing right below the skylight.

Planning but not, to his chagrin, *succeeding*.

He rolled right into the waiting arms of the larger of the agents and was bound shoulder to wrist with a thick strip of constricting plasma before he realized his plan hadn't worked.

Growling her annoyance, Aimz swung back into the HoverBus, using the momentum to knock over the tall agent and using her sharp heel to crush the life support pack at the base of their helmet.

The agent ripped the helmet off, revealing puffs of pink hair which looked like pompoms framing her pale blue face. "We're trying to help!" she screamed.

"Help us die," Aimz said.

Dropping in after Aimz, May grabbed a heavy, ornamental lamp and flung it at the larger agent who caught it and, gently, set it down so as to not break it. While the agent was distracted, she pulled Xan to his feet.

"Wait, get Billy!" he protested, jerking at the plasma beam which kept him from reaching down for the fish.

"What's so important about the zuxing fish?" Aimz said from the door, wildly gesturing for them to hurry.

"It's ours, and we have to protect it! Look at the poor thing! Helpless. No legs, no thumbs, no moltsopial glands."

"I don't have moltsopial glands," May said.

Xan looked truly horrified at this revelation, but realized it was quite rude to judge another's biology. She couldn't help it. "And you get along just fine without them," he assured her shakily.

"Seem to be." May grabbed the plastic fish and shoved it into a pocket on her trench coat.

"Stop chatting and run!" Aimz pushed them forward as the scourge agents bounded over the waterbed toward them. "Get out, get out, get out!" Aimz shouted, but her words exploded.

Or rather, Largish Bronda's FlexiDimensional HoverBus exploded over her words.

A wave of dry heat propelled the trio onward, nearly knocking them down as they fled with renewed speed.

"That was our home!" May shouted after Aimz who was nearly out of ear-shot ahead of her.

"Yeah, and now it's not. Things happen. All the time. Constantly, things are happening. That was one of the things."

May wanted to argue that point, but she wasn't an accomplished runner or an accomplished debater and, as such, she had neither the breath nor the wit to prove Aimz wrong. And besides, Aimz might have been socially wrong, but she wasn't technically wrong.

The distance between where Largish Bronda had been and where the Merimip currently was not the sort of distance someone in average health who goes to the gym thrice on a good week could comfortably run.

They were not the sort of people who got to a gym thrice on a good week.

And so, after a few minutes of running for their lives, they began briskly jogging for their lives, then urgently speed-walking for their lives, and finally, anxiously ambling for their lives.

CHAPTER TWELVE

Hornball

When at last they reached the Merimip, Aimz set about dismantling a section of the geodesic dome that created the greenhouse atop the Merimip as May worked at the plasma strip binding Xan's arms.

"Aimz, toss me the rectifier," May shouted between studying the mechanism for the plasma strip and the dark treeline where the pursuing agents might appear at any moment.

May barely caught the tiny chip between two fingers and awkwardly finagled it into the casing of the plasma strip generator.

"Isn't that going to-OW!" Xan yelped.

The plasma strip sizzled, sparked, and shorted out, the generator dropping away onto the soft, dewy grass.

"Sorry," May said. "But you're free now."

"Yeah, once I regain control of my muscles," he said, blinking one eye at a time as if his entire body was out of sync, then stooped to pick up the plasma strip generator. "Should we keep this?"

"Why?" May asked.

"Well, you know, in case Aimz or I...you know?"

"No. I don't know," May said firmly and flung the generator into the lake.

Xan knew she knew. He also knew that the heavily armored scourge agents likely survived the blast and were probably making their way toward them, and that was a bit more pressing than May willfully ignoring the danger she was in.

A rustling came from the tree line, and before Xan could decide if it was the agents or the wind, he scrambled up the Merimip's ladder. "Aimz?!" He knocked on the geodesic dome she had already broken into. She was working on the main ship hatch, now.

"Corral your puntls, mun, I got it," Aimz told him, then jumped through the hatch and into the ship. May and Xan followed her in, and she sealed the hatch behind them.

"Don't you have a key?!" Xan asked her.

She pulled the key out of her pocket. "Yeah, why?"

"Nevermind," he said. "We need to get out of here."

"Right. No sense waiting around for Listay, is there?" Aimz said, dusting her hands as if dusting off the entire relationship. She paused, looked at her palms, her face clouding with a sudden emotion which she just as suddenly whisked away as she patted May on the back. "Whatcha think, May? Can you larvea-sit two zuxed Carmnians in a boat? Not worried we'll cannibalize you, right?" Aimz's smile was unnervingly sharp.

Discreetly, May's fingers found the bottle of shermel in her coat. "I *wasn't*."

"That was one case!" Xan defended. "And she'd been living in the forest for decades before she emerged to eat people."

"Yeah, after she hunted down every creature in the forest. I heard she learned to weaponize stomach fluids and would spit acid at her victims to pre-digest them," Aimz said, enthusiastically.

"Eugh." Xan stuck his tongue out as if he couldn't bear to have it in his mouth anymore. "That's gruesome. Aimz, promise me we won't go feral."

"Oh don't be so posh. I hear gruflesnog tastes just like zipnite, and they're much easier to catch."

"I don't care what it tastes like—"

Knock, knock.

It was not a "Hello" knock.

It was not a "Monday" knock, either.

These knocks sounded more like they meant "Danger" or perhaps "Warning" or even, with a bit of imagination, "You're about to die, assholes."

"That was Listay?" Xan proposed.

"She lives here; why would she knock?" May whispered.

"Oh, she knocks," Aimz said between them. "She knocks four times because she's a snack." She laughed quietly at her own joke.

Knock, knock.

"Four knocks total! Gotta be Listay," Aimz said, then scaled the ladder to the hatch.

"That was two sets of two knocks!" Xan shouted after her, but she was already opening the hatch, already peering out, already realizing that it was definitely not Listay.

"Listay will catch up." Aimz said, sealing the hatch and scrambling to the cockpit.

"How? We're stealing her vehicle," May pointed out, scanning the cockpit and trying to figure out how it worked by watching Aimz pilot it.

May was of the opinion that there was nothing she couldn't pilot. She was wrong, and she knew she was wrong, but being of that opinion helped her feel a bit more stable in trying situations like this, and that's what mattered. She had always found it helpful to decide she was good at whatever it was she had to do.

The Merimip vibrated gleefully below them, lifting itself out of the water and hovering on the surface of the lake before jetting off through the Snoodark Channel toward mainland Rhea.

"She'll catch up!" Aimz repeated as if her insistence alone would make it true, then she grabbed Xan (who had been cowering helpfully behind her) by the wrist, yanked his BEAPER into view, and sent a message to Listay. Her own BEAPER had ceased working seasons ago, but she was almost always near either Listay or Xan, so she hadn't bothered trying to replace it.

Xan was getting tired of everyone using his BEAPER without asking, but he liked May too much to tell her, and he was too scared of Aimz to tell *her*.

"Alright," Aimz said, patting Xan's hand away when she was done. "Let's get to Fulogra. Yve's expecting us!"

"And she can fix us, right?" said Xan. "Tell me she found a cure."

"Her curves are the cure, mun," Aimz said with a wink.

"Hornball!" May said, snapping her fingers at Aimz. "Does she have a cure or not?"

Xan chuckled, repeating the Earthling insult under his breath so he wouldn't forget it. "Hornball."

"Of course not; there isn't a cure. If we get scourge-noodled on the way over, you'll have to fight us off." Aimz dug through the junk drawer (or, according to the label Listay had slapped on it, "The Aimz Drawer") and handed May a zapper. "Vooop!" she made a powering-up sound as she twisted the dial at the top from Pleasant Tingle to Zap+.

Finally, May had a gun at her disposal, but now she didn't want it. "Won't that hurt?"

"Oh yeah, sure. But the key is..." Aimz then produced a sharp metal bit from her pocket. It looked an awful lot like the sharp metal bit she'd lost on New Tuhnt, but it wasn't quite as rusted, which was a shame. "Once we're down, you need to stake us. Zapper wounds heal fast. Sharp bit of metal through the clacker? No chance."

"You want me to kill you?" she asked Xan directly, and he really wished she hadn't.

Rather than answer, he moved his mouth like he was attempting to start several different sentences, then silently begged Aimz to take over, held up a finger in a 'give me a moment' gesture, and went to the bedroom at the back of the ship, closing the door cryptically behind himself.

Aimz squinted after him for a moment. "Uh, yeah. If we get too rowdy, kill us. Never tried dying before, and it didn't work out too bad for Listay."

"If you insist." May took the zapper and the metal bit, stuffing them in her already over-full pockets, her coat sagging around her with the weight of everything in it.

"Really?" A fleeting glimpse of fear washed over Aimz's face.

"No! You know that's not going to happen. But I am confiscating these. If we are to duel, it will be hand-to-hand, like men, with honor," she said, attempting to lighten her own mood.

"Are all Earthlings as weird as you?" Aimz laughed, relieved that May wasn't serious about killing her because she wasn't serious about dying.

“Are all Tuhntians as weird as you?” May retorted, walking to the back of the Merimip. She knocked on the bedroom door, just once. She didn’t understand the secret knock code everyone else seemed to know, and one knock seemed safest. “Are you decent?” she shouted through the thick metal door.

“Fair-to-middling,” is what she heard, muffled, from the other side, and so she opened it.

CHAPTER THIRTEEN

Polyblotter

May found Xan, arms and legs tied spread-eagle to the bed in a way which shouldn't have been possible on his own, reading a trashy romance holobook on his BEAPER, scrolling the holographic screen with his nose.

The average Earthling lives eighty, maybe ninety years, and because of this, they tend to get decent at a handful of skills with the intent of earning a living. And I promise this relates back, just hold on.

Tuhntians live seven-hundred years or more and, as such, get really, unutterably good at a handful of skills with the intent of earning a living. This meant that Xan was astoundingly good at tying himself up. He had centuries of practice. He might struggle to find his own hometown on a map, but by O'Zeno, he could tie himself to a bed.

"Comfortable?" May asked, sitting next to him.

"Not at all. But well contained! There is absolutely no way for me to get out of this bed without someone untying me and, since Aimz won't and you certainly—" May began untying the ropes. "W-wait, no, that was really hard to do on my own," he protested.

"It's a long trip," she said, struggling to undo his masterful knots.

"But what if I get scourged?"

"That's what the shermel is for." She nodded toward the green bottle which she'd set on the recessed Magno-E-Tic bookcase in the wall, the gentle magnetic force keeping it, and several neatly labeled holobooks, from jostling with the movement of the Merimip.

"Alright, but consider: how are you going to get me to drink it if I'm scourged? And what if Aimz goes off, too? There's not enough for both of us. I could try to eat you!"

"Wouldn't be the weirdest thing you've eaten." She went back to untying the shockingly snug knot around his wrist.

"I think it would be..."

"You eat bugs!"

"They're cheese flavored and come in a bag! That's not that weird! You're the only person I've ever met who's been weirded out by that."

"In all the time I've known you," she paused to pull at a knot with her teeth, speaking around it as she yanked, "you've never eaten me."

"I've also never been scourged."

"You have, and you ate not-cigarette mechanisms off the ground because you were worried about my health. You're not going to eat me." She finally pulled free the cording, and his arm dropped to the bed.

"Thanks," he said, rotating his freed wrist as May untied the rest of him. "Last time I was tied up like that, I couldn't feel my toes for two whole rotations! But, I was getting paid by the beoop, so I didn't mind it. And the Udonian who-oh Blitheon, that feels better-the Udonian who hired me...Chashee I think her name was? Or Shashtee? Shancy? Zuut, I thought I'd remember that one. Told her I would remember it, too, but, then again, I tell a lot of people a lot of things—"

May finished untying him as he continued monologuing about Chashee or Shashtee or Shancy. She didn't mind hearing about his exploits as a sex worker for The Agency, since he knew to spare her the graphic details. It was comforting, especially now, just to hear him chatter on as if everything was completely normal.

While he talked, she crawled onto the bed and began cleaning out her many pockets, making sure she was only carrying what would be useful to her. She spread each item out onto the bed, separating the bits of unidentifiable trash and lint from useful items.

Among the useful items were the lengths of rope she had just released Xan from, a small green dashpin, the metal bit Aimz had given her, and the zapper which she had turned down to a more reasonable setting: 'zippy.'

Among the not-useful: a sticky wrapper from a candy she didn't remember eating, a length of extremely thin string which pulled apart at the slightest tug, a single silk glove, and...May paused and held the last item she had found up to the light to inspect it. Useful or not? Iffy.

"Hey, did you...were you listening?" Xan asked, leaning into her line of sight.

"Yeah," she lied absently, staring at the thing clutched between her fingers. It was the *Audacity*'s anchor button, and it still glowed faintly green. It was still online. Still connected to the ship's teledisc a few thousand lightyears away. She kept it steady between the useful and not-useful piles, watching it as if the light might flicker off if she blinked.

Slowly, Xan took it from her and placed it in the useful pile.

"No point giving up, is there?" he asked.

May shrugged. "Not giving up. Just...letting go, maybe. Sorry, why did Chashee go into debt over a silver scale replica of an ancient Hooflatoo again? I missed that part."

"Oh, uh...she was a natural history museum fetishist."

"Ah, that checks out." May said, clipping the anchor button onto her coat and stashing the useful items and the shermel bottle back in her pocket. She put the trash into one of the drawers where she hoped it might disappear.

Putting trash in drawers with the hope that it will disappear is not an uncommon practice.

It is uncommon, however, for that trash to actually disappear. Unless you're dealing with a Flexi-Dimensional drawer built by the Largish Bronda Corporation. It's wise not to put anything terribly important in Flexi-Dimensional storage.

May leaned back and tried to get comfortable, but it was not to be. A scratching echoed from the roof, followed by clunks and cracks neither May nor Xan could identify as they both tilted an ear up to the ceiling. The lights in the cabin flickered a few times, then failed, casting the room into nearly complete darkness, the only lights were the glowing emergency strips sewn into the carpet and the subtle luminescence of the fungus in Xan's eyes.

"What happ—" May began, but the ship suddenly stopped, flinging May and Xan off the bed and into the wall with a painful thunk.

May cursed as she got to her feet and stumbled out of the dark bedroom into the dark hallway. She found the escape ladder with her face and cursed again as she climbed it, opened the hatch, and peered out into the soupy night. Rhea's moons lit the top of the ship well enough for May to pick out Aimz crouched atop the shiny black boat, peering over the edge.

"Zuxing polyblotter. Scram!" Aimz said, grabbing onto the handlebars which ran like a spine down the length of the Merimip's slippery black back. Attached to the side of the boat and holding onto an access door was something which looked to May like a hunched, furry, elderly gentleman. It chattered unhappily at her.

Aimz growled back.

Crawling onto the ship's roof, May peered around Aimz to get a better look at it. The creature's fur was clumped and matted with ocean gunk. It was balding in patches, revealing scaly gray skin which glistened nastily in the light of Rhea's three yellowish moons.

"Ugh, what is it?" May asked.

What it was, as Aimz had correctly surmised, was a polyblotter. One of a few species who had had the gall to leave the ocean, grow fur, arms, legs, and lungs, then decided to go back to the ocean like a student returning to live in their parent's basement after a miserable two years of business school.

Polyblotters are protected under Rhean law because they are the only known aquatic mammal that eats plastic, and this is usually a good thing. Usually. However, recent environmental campaigns had greatly reduced the amount of plastic produced on mainland Rhea and, as such, starving polyblotters had become a bit of a problem for vessels that rely on plastic parts. The Largish Bronda Corporation relied heavily on plastic parts.

The Merimip's engine casing was made of polyoxybenzyl-methylenglycolanhydride, or, simply put, Bakelite plastic. A crunchy treat to a polyblotter.

Aimz did not tell May any of this, though. Instead, she said, "Snack," licked her lips, then launched herself at the creature which scampered over the dome of the greenhouse, dropping bits of plastic into the ocean as it went.

Failing to find purchase on the slippery boat, Aimz spun into a whirl of arms and legs. Her fingernails finally caught the wooden frame of the greenhouse and she got her feet underneath herself. Then, with gravity-defying ferocity, she scaled the greenhouse after the polyblotter.

"Aimz, let it go. We need to fix the engine," May said, but before she could get to the exposed engine on the top of the boat, something tapped her leg. She twisted around to find Xan eagerly looking up at her.

"You two alright?" he asked. "It's kinda dark down there..."

"Screeee!" went the creature. Aimz had it by the neck.

"Aimz, no! Xan, hand me something to throw," she gestured wildly at him to give her something and, moments later, he plunked a decorative pillow into her arms. "Something heavy?!" she clarified.

"You don't want to hurt it!" Xan said.

Though May wasn't sure this was true, she flung the pillow at Aimz, knocking the polyblotter out of her hands just as she was preparing to snap its neck. The creature scampered into the churning water below and disappeared.

"Go inside," May demanded of Aimz, pulling herself out into the drizzling night and toward the sputtering motor.

"I told you to scram!" Aimz leapt for the top of the greenhouse and barreled into May who had leaned over the side of the boat to take a look at the damage. May yelped in surprise. Her arm caught on a ladder rung, holding her onto the boat, as Aimz dangled from her waist like an angry sentient statement belt.

"What the hell, Aimz? I'm trying to fix it!"

"What'd she do?!" May heard Xan shout from the hatch, though she had slid too far down the side of the boat to see him.

"She's trying to kill me, get out here!"

"What?! Blitheon, Aimz, don't do that! Bad Aimz!" he said as he crawled out onto the top of the boat shakily.

"Get. Off. My. Ship!" Aimz said, trying her best to climb up May who had to use her free hand to hold her pants up.

"Take my hand." At last, Xan had appeared over the side of the Merimip, reaching down to help May up, but as he reached down Aimz reached up and he, clearly, had not attached himself in any way to the ship.

Aimz ripped Xan off the roof, and he ripped her away from May, plunging them both into the churning black ocean.

"Damnit." May clung to the side of the boat still, watching the spot where they had disappeared. She rearranged herself to make sure her elbow wasn't broken and leaned a little closer to the water. "Xan? Aimz?" she shouted into the depths.

Then the water's surface boiled, thrashing with flashes of orange and pink as Xan and Aimz battled to keep their heads above water, a difficult task for a Tuhntian. From her coat pocket, May extracted a length of rope that Xan had used to tie himself up with. Not trusting herself to tie a strong enough knot, she looped it around the lowest rung of the ladder and let it drop. It was just long enough to reach the water line.

"Xan, grab the rope!" she shouted. But briefly turning his attention away from holding his own against Aimz to find the rope had proven to be a mistake. Aimz elbowed him in the face and kicked him underwater, making for the rope herself.

"Zux-off," Aimz told May wetly before coughing up a lungful of ocean water.

May climbed further down the side of the ship but pulled the rope up so Aimz couldn't get a hold on it. "Aimz, it's me. Earthmun. Don't you recognize me?" May said "You like to feed me alien drugs and get me into trouble."

Squinting up at her, Aimz seemed to be working through something and May forced herself not to distract Aimz by looking at Xan who was finally above water and paddling toward Aimz.

He launched at her and grabbed a fistful of pink hair at the top of her head.

"Get her mouth open!" May said. There wouldn't be enough alcohol for both of them, but Xan was decidedly easier to handle when he was scourged and, should *he* try to attack her next, Aimz was decidedly the better fighter.

Aimz tried to twist around, but he seized her cheeks and squeezed, forcing her mouth open. Uncorking the bottle with her teeth, May poured the drink down Aimz's throat, reminded of a forgotten memory of being ten and helping her father pill the old family cat.

Fortunately, Aimz enjoyed alcohol and didn't try to spit it out or foam at the mouth like the cat had. Xan let her face go but held onto her shoulders while she processed what had just happened. "Why are we in the water?" she asked, finally.

"Some parties just end up in the middle of the ocean, Aimz." Xan said, letting her go.

"Zuxing trok. Is he scourged?" Aimz asked as she grabbed the rope from May and began to pull herself up the side of the boat.

"No, you were." May showed her the empty green bottle.

Aimz smacked her lips, she could still taste the shermel. "First thing we do when we hit land is get some better alcohol. Did I try to kill you?" Aimz asked through a grunt as she pulled Xan out of the water by his collar, the faux buffatalo coat mopping up the side of the Merimip.

"Maybe. You thought I was something else, though. I don't think you were trying to kill me, specifically, at least."

Aimz twisted her mouth to the side as she thought, looking May over. "You need to tie me up," she said. "I don't want to—" she paused. "You need to tie me up."

"You're a feral one, Mazelmez," Xan said, wringing out his coat. "Zuut. This is Zilla's coat. Hope the saltwater doesn't ruin it..."

"Xan, you had that before you got the trunks. That's yours," May said. "You alright?"

"Best guess?" said Xan. "That android's got some messed up social protocols mixed into the software."

"Best guess at what? What android?" May looked around as if an android might suddenly appear on the bow of the Merimip.

"Sonan," said Xan as if it were obvious.

"Sonan's gone, Xan. Did you mean to say that in the last book?"

He opened his mouth, looked around at the empty expanse of dark choppy waters, looked at a dripping Aimz and a very confused May, then, at last, he answered. "Uhhh, yeah, I suppose I did."

"Yep, he's scourged now. The hullabaloo must've triggered it. Figures he'd get time-zuxed first." Aimz said. "The cerebral ones always do. His primal instincts are buried waaayy deep down. You're a zuxing nerd, Xan," Aimz told him.

"I know," he said, confused as to why she had to clarify that.

May looked miserable.

"Hey, un-pin it, Earthmun," Aimz patted May on the back. "Listen, Yve and I were working on a project back at university, right?" Aimz physically spun May around so she would stop watching Xan. "And the idea was, we were going to cure the scourge."

"Did you?"

"No. Well, obviously no. But we were young! This was well before she was destroying planets and I was..." Aimz squinted, thinking. "In a stable relationship."

A tapping.

May and Aimz turned their attention back to Xan who was spread out flat on the roof, rapping rhythmically on the boat, listening with baited interest to the metal. He rapped again, listened again.

"Whatcha doing, buddy?" May asked, hoping she wouldn't regret it.

"Oh. You two were ignoring me, so I made friends with the boat. Bit of a language barrier, still working it out. Getting close, though! It's against the idea of self-cleaning food replicators having personalities, which I think is a bit backward minded, but I'm trying to see the issue from its angle." He held up a finger, listened, and laughed. "No, I've never single handedly reinstated a defunct political regime. Why, have you?"

Rather than attempt to explain to him that the boat was, in fact, insentient, May started to climb down to the open engine panel. "Get him inside. I'm going to take a look at the damage," she told Aimz. "And Xan?" May said before she disappeared over the side of the boat. He looked up at her. "Tie up your sister for me?"

He smiled broadly, delighted to be of service. "Gladly!"

May climbed down the ladder and studied the open panel, running a finger down a length of chipped, brown, plastic casing. Inside, some metal knob stuck out at an odd angle and jerked with pent-up energy.

From her pocket, she pulled out the metal bit and gently lifted the knob away from the casing. It began to work; the knob spun, and the main lights flickered back on, but the sharp metal edge of the improvised tool snagged and was flung out of May's hand, landing with apologetic 'bloop' in the Rhean Sea.

The knob was stuck again, and apart from the zapper (which May would only use as a last resort), all she had left was the anchor button. It was plastic. It was about the size of the chunk the polyblotter had eaten. It would have to do.

She pulled the button from her pocket, then wiggled the piece in between the knob and the casing. It fit perfectly. The knob spun, the boat heaved forward, and May clambered for the ladder.

"Guess it was useful after all," she muttered and slammed the panel shut with her foot.

May dropped back into the boat to find Aimz tied to metal pole in the middle of the living room. A pole which May had not noticed before. She wasn't sure there was a good structural reason for it to be there, and she wasn't sure she wanted to know why it was there, so she didn't ask.

"She's all ready for you!" Xan said proudly. "What are you going to do with her?"

"Yeah, what are you going to do with me, Earthmun?" Aimz goaded.

May shook her head at Aimz. "Ugh, don't encourage him." She slipped into the cockpit and got the ship moving again. "Nothing, Xan. You did good."

"When do you think Milly will be back?" he asked her.

"Hopefully never," May said, then patted the seat next to her to get him to sit down. "Hey…you remember me, right?" she asked, wincingly, as he sat down.

"Of course! May, we've known each other for thousands of years, of course I remember you. We've raced rocket ships, infiltrated the Cosmos, summoned the Seam together…"

"Whoa, thousands of years?" May asked with a laugh. "We haven't done half of that stuff. Where are you getting this?"

"He's time-zuxed, I told you!" Aimz said from her pole.

May turned around. "You mean to tell me he can remember the future?"

"Yeah," Aimz said, as if this were obvious.

"That's not possible…" May was speaking more to herself than anyone else in the boat now. "Why did he ask if Milly would be back?" she asked Aimz.

"She will be," Xan told May. "Where are we going?"

"Look, May," Aimz said. "I know I exude an air of all-knowing confidence but I don't actually know everything. Time-zuxed Carmnians only have about a 20% accuracy rating when it comes to the future and half the time when you ask them about the future they start going on about the past. That's why it's called being time-zuxed. They're zuxed in—"

"Time. I get it," May said, cutting her off. "Twenty percent, huh?" she asked Xan.

"Huh," he agreed with her.

"So there's a twenty percent chance we survive all this?"

"No one survives anything," Xan clarified. "Even the so-called gods die."

That was not what May had wanted to hear from him. She tapped the BEAPER on his wrist and navigated to a holobook. "Just read your trashy romance story," she told him.

CHAPTER FOURTEEN

The Apple Man

On mainland Rhea, the suns shone warmly, the breeze smelled of salt and slowly rotting wood planks, and it was difficult to imagine that just a few beoops by hoverboat away, the freezing island of NotTuhnt languished in the middle of a dreary sea.

Fulgora was an ancient-style town, a trend born after many hundreds of years of intense technological development finally made people realize that all they really wanted this new technology to do was to pretend it didn't exist. Rather than flashy, sleek hovercraft, the citizens drove run-down, rusted hovercraft. Rather than sparkling electro-roads, the pathways were paved with old fashioned, solar-soak dust which powered the holo-flame lamps the townsfolk used in place of the more modern atmospheric glow-spheres.

As soon as the ship docked, May climbed out, desperate to get on solid land, but the moment her feet touched the dock, someone picked her up and spun her around in a smothering hug that smelled of firewood and apples.

"August!" she said as soon as she realized that she wasn't being kidnapped by an alien lumberjack. He set her down and smiled at her, one eye glistening with joy, the other glistening because it was made of metal.

"New eye?" she asked.

"Eyep. Yve felt bad about, you know, the Chaos thing, so she set me up with a new eye, new hand." He showed her the surprisingly natural hand which had replaced the old, stiff robotic hand Ix had installed on him. "New teeth!" He smiled and tapped a canine with his nail. "Looks like there's only one and a half humans out here now!" He laughed and squeezed her shoulder warmly. "It's good to see you, kid. Don't be a stranger, eh?"

"Oh, who's this strapping hunk of cyborg?" Xan asked, Big Mouth Billy Bass cradled in one arm as he sauntered up to August who side-eyed May.

"Xan, you remember August, right?"

"I'd like to," he said in a way which was ridiculously flirty and signified that he, in fact, still did not remember him at all. "Want to make out?"

"No, Xan," May said.

"Really?" August asked Xan, his eyes flicking momentarily to May as if asking her permission. He had always considered himself straight. Still did, actually, reasoning that he wasn't interested in Earthling men. Aliens, though, he'd come to realize, weren't men *or* women and as such, all were fair game.

Xan nodded eagerly.

"Oh well, I mean. I'm straight but, uh, sure!" August said with a shrug, and Xan pulled August into a long-lost-lovers style kiss. August was panting when he broke free of it.

"Whoa," he said.

"Yeah, I'm a professional." Xan winked.

"And I'm Aimz, professional adventure biologist. I don't want to kiss you now, but I might do later if you're up for it." Aimz held up a hand which August high-fived in a daze.

"How'd you get out of the ropes?" May asked her.

Aimz shrugged. "Xan always leaves an easy-out! The ropes were to make you feel better. Worked, didn't it?"

May grunted a begrudging affirmative.

"Hey, Appleman, got any alcohol?" Aimz asked August.

"Hmm?"

"He's scourged." Aimz tossed her head in Xan's direction. "Alcohol staves it off a bit."

"Right, that explains it." August laughed, embarrassed. He meant that, somehow, Xan being scourged explained why he, August, was suddenly attracted to him. Scourge has no such effect, of course, but August's logic was about as developed as that of the average goldfish.

He reached for a metal flask on his belt and handed it to Xan. "Hard cider. Made with my own two hands."

"I bet that's not all those hands can do," Xan said, then chugged the flask, then looked as if he'd really wished he hadn't said that. He slowly handed the flask back to August and wiped his mouth with the back of his hand. "Hello, August."

"Oh, we're back to introductions now?" August laughed, drained the last few drops from the flask, then secured it back on his belt. "Come on, let's get to the orchard. Yvonne and Ix have been in the lab since Listay BEAP'd us. They'll have a fit when we tell them alcohol's this mysterious cure! Well, Yvonne will. Can't imagine anything would give Ix a fit."

The vehicle August escorted them to could've been an old blue pickup truck had it not looked distinctly like a floating can opener with the brand name ThingHauler shimmering on its flank in holographic black. Aimz hopped into the front of the cab and Xan and May squeezed into the back.

"It's not a cure," Aimz said. "Just staves it off in the early stages. Still have a mushroom eating my brain."

"You don't sound too bothered," August noted.

Aimz shrugged. "Happens to all Carmnians eventually, and it's the worst thing that could possibly happen to me, so now that it has happened, I don't have to worry about when it will! The answer is now; it's happening now. That lets off a great deal of anxiety, actually. Also, I get to see Yvonne." She twisted around to Xan. "Yvonne!" She bounced in her seat.

Xan nodded. "Is Yvonne...really back to normal?" he asked August who was fiddling with the face scanner which would start the ThingHauler. It flashed a blue light over his features and dinged in recognition. The vehicle booted up with the whine of old machinery and set off down the thin, unpaved, one-way road which led out of the small fishing town.

"You know," he glanced back at Xan via the rear-viewscreen, "without knowing what's normal for Yvonne, it's hard to say. But she hasn't blown up a planet lately, so I think she's doing better." He touched a series of commands on the ThingHauler's control panel, and something which sounded like Motown played by a reggae band with synthesizers filled the cab.

May leaned her head on the window—an actual old-fashioned window, she noted, not a viewscreen—and watched the horizon, underscored by a field of red dust and purple rock formations which grew scraggly gray bushes like a teenager trying to grow a beard.

Suddenly, Xan's head was on her shoulder. "Alright, starshine?"

"Hmm?" She was in a trance, thinking about nothing as everything she wanted to think about swirled in a salty pool forming beneath her eyes. She wiped it away with her sleeve.

"What did I do this time?" He was soaking in sea water and had vague memories of befriending a boat with some pretty radical political ideas. Clearly, he thought, something interesting had happened on the trip over, but he didn't remember it well.

"Don't worry about it. You didn't try to eat me. The scourge makes you horny as hell, though, what's up with that?"

He shrugged, then twisted around until his head was on her lap and his legs were pretzeled over the rest of the back seat. "Lower inhibitions, I guess." He peered up at her coat curiously. "Where's the anchor button?"

She sighed and looked out the window again. "I used it to fix the boat."

"Oh." He dug around in the innermost pocket of his coat and pulled out his own anchor button which glowed faintly green. "Want mine? It's still connected." He eyed the glowing green light with his own glowing green eyes, and May found the comparison a touch uncanny, so she grabbed the button, rolled the window down, and threw it out into the dust.

That was it. Her connection with the *Audacity* was officially severed. Even if she did happen to find it, she wouldn't be able to get in without breaking in. She understood what Aimz had said, now. The worst had happened, and knowing that somehow did ease her anxiety about it.

"I don't want to think about the *Audacity* anymore. It's lost. You're not."

"Uh...huh," he said at last. "You know, Yve is really a terrific person when she's not being possessed by an ancient evil. And

August knows all about Earth! You two must have loads to talk about."

"You're trying to pawn me off," she said.

"No! Not at all. Of course not, starshine. It-it's just...eugh," he said. "It's only that...well...you see..." He began trying to express himself with vague hand gestures instead.

"What?" Her voice was sharper than usual.

"I'm just worried that you'll be lonely, that's all."

"Shh." She petted his wet hair and attempted to form it into its classic pompadour, but it had grown far too long. "I won't have time to feel lonely because I'll be busy helping you keep track of your various sexual partners, you massive precious butler."

A popular Tuhntian name happens to translate, in English, to "Precious Butler." However, re-translated from English to Tuhntian "precious butler" is an extremely rude euphemism for a prostitute. This quirk of the universe was discovered in book two for reasons which shall, forthwith, have no further bearing on the story.

It did, however, get Xan to smile. "That's a terrible thing to say about your best friend."

"It's just the truth," she said.

He chuckled and sat up clumsily in the tiny back seat. "Yeah, no, you're right." He took her hand. "Promise me you won't be lonely?"

"You aren't going anywhere."

"Right, fair, okay, but just in case: promise me!" he insisted.

"Ugh, fine. I'll hang out with August."

"We're hanging out?" August shouted back from the front seat. Bits of conversation had made their way up to him, but until now it hadn't been any of his business.

"Yeah," May said.

"Sweet. It'll be nice to hang out with someone who knows who Bastian Schweinsteiger is."

May clenched her teeth and gave Xan a worried look. "Actor?"

August sighed. "Soccer," he said.

"I thought you called it football in Germany," May said.

"That's what I said, soccer."

"Translation chips," Xan reminded them both before this little skit went on any longer. It was curious, but somehow May felt she better understood the aliens she had met than most Earthlings. She put her head on Xan's shoulder. "I'm going to have to learn about sports," she mumbled miserably.

CHAPTER FIFTEEN

Supersonic Fungicide

The dusty landscape soon relented to scrub brush, then trees so dry and gnarled they looked like the feet of a 90-year-old ballerina, then trees that grew luscious yellow-orange manes and quivered erotically in the draft the ThingHauler made as it skirted by.

August still wasn't used to decelerating from the equivalent of nine hundred miles-per-hour, and the inertia flung everyone to the floor, waking May from a much-needed nap.

"Sorry 'bout that folks. Here we are!" August said, then exited the ThingHauler.

May carefully maneuvered out, shaking the pins-and-needles feeling from her legs which had been squished under her in the tiny backseat.

A glittering lake yawned for miles to their left; in front of them, a cabin replete with simulated rustic furnishings; to the right, a sleek white plastic-shelled machine with colorful winking lights and a tongue-like conveyor belt. It looked like the sets from the "Beverly Hillbillies" and "Forbidden Planet" had collided in a horrible back-lot accident.

Over-sized, winding trees cradled the house, but they were certainly not apple trees. All that grew from their twisting branches was downy green fluff and the occasional spiky yellow thing, like a pinecone, a pineapple, and a porcupine had met at a pine convention and hit it off.

May squinted at them, confused.

"Not like any apples you've ever seen, eh?" August said to her with an unwelcome elbow nudge.

"Eh, I've seen a lot of strange apples."

It was August's turn to be confused. "Those aren't the apples. I was kidding."

"I know. I was too."

"Oh. Right." He rubbed the back of his neck. "Those are just canopy trees; the apples are underneath them. Sun's too bright for the apples out here. Tried growing them in a cavern underground with fake sunlight, but the apples got depressed."

May understood. The Pontoosa Adventure Hole and her experiences Downtown had given her a healthy distrust of things which resided below ground. But there were also many things she didn't trust which were above ground. One of those things was now descending the house's wooden steps, wrapped in a pale-yellow patterned dress, smiling.

May tried to see her as anything but the goddess of Chaos who had tried to destroy Earth—and the dress helped a bit, but not much. The sight of Yvonne, even rid of the unmentionable look in her eyes, made May's back stiffen.

"Yve-onny!" Aimz squealed when she saw her and launched herself into the towering Rhean, nuzzling her chest affectionately.

Yvonne caught her with a startled huff. She'd gotten so used to striking fear into the hearts of all who approached her that this welcome came as a surprise. This was always how Aimz welcomed her, though. Or it had been, anyway. Before the war. Before the *Peacemaker*. But now the war was over and they were in an apple orchard and everything was alright.

Except, it wasn't alright. She was tempted to hold onto Aimz, pushing her face into her warm pink braid, but instead she pulled away.

"Scourge?" she whispered.

"Ah, you know. These things happen," Aimz said. "Fine right now, though! Alcohol helps."

"But it doesn't fix it," Yvonne said quietly.

"Don't be dramatic, Yve. We're fine. Better! Now that the proverbial timer has run out, yeah? Can't get any worse from here," Aimz said with a bright smile.

Yvonne shook her head. "In the name of Rheanoodal the Third, you're the only Carmnian who's ever taken scourge with a smile. It's good to see you, mun."

Xan had been lurking behind the ThingHauler. Not hiding, definitely. Definitely not cowering. But May was there too, and she *was* hiding a bit.

"Think she's safe?" May asked, peering through the ThingHauler windows at Aimz and Yvonne.

"Sure! Yeah! Of course. She's just Yve now. No Chaos. Not more than the regular dosage, at least. I mean, she did ditch me when the war started, broke my heart, called me all sorts of names. That did still happen."

"And then she beat you up, crashed a starship, and tried to end the universe."

He shook his head. "That wasn't her. Not even a little bit was that her. She's more emotionally damaging, less physically damage-wait no, now that you mention it she did like to run impromptu experiments back at university."

May nodded for him to elaborate.

"Oh, well, you know. She was a biologist and she believed in hands-on learning and, well, I was the only willing subject!"

"What did she do to you?"

"Nothing drastic. Just the occasional vivisection."

"Vivisection?!" May hissed.

"It was college; we were young!" He said it as if it had been a few keggers and one night stands rather than an invasive surgical procedure.

"And that was consensual?"

"Well sure! She's not a monster. She's sweet, actually. Just likes to chop things up sometimes to figure out how they work. That's science!"

May looked back through the ThingHauler's window at Aimz and Yvonne chatting.

"Well, we're going to have to face her eventually," May said and took Xan's hand as they rounded the ThingHauler and followed the party inside the house.

The house was moodily lit with candles that looked suspiciously like real wax. May removed her trench coat, hanging it on a deceptively rustic coat hanger and stopped at the nearest arrangement of candles to study them. The wax melted, dripped, then disappeared. Gently, she touched the side of a long candlestick, and her finger went straight through it. They were holographic candles, the image emanating from their holders. She smiled at the coziness of it; it reminded her of Earth and, perhaps for the first time since her abduction, she found she missed it.

Yvonne, August, and Aimz crashed into soft leather couches which encircled a faux fire pit in the middle of a large, wooden paneled room lit by candles and holowindows.

But May and Xan hesitated to cozy up anywhere near Yvonne.

"Go on, have a seat," August said, patting the leather cushion beside him.

Cautiously, carefully, like he was transferring a wedding cake from one cake stand to another, Xan slid down the arm of the couch and into the seat, eyeing Yvonne across the fire pit. May sat on the arm of the couch, determined not to get comfortable.

Yvonne cringed. "I'm sorry about the whole...Chaos thing. I didn't have any control over her, though. You know that, right?"

"Of course! All in the history books," Xan said, rather unconvincingly.

"Would you all please join me in the laboratory?" Ix suddenly made herself known. She had been watching them for a while from the shadows. She stood at the top of a staircase, her pale purple curls pulled back into a tight bun. "I have compiled a series of tests to run on the affected Carmnians," Ix said in a way that might have been called robotic, but robots were a great deal more expressive. "May and August, please stay here. You will not be necessary," she added, sensing that they were both already preparing to stand.

Xan groaned pitifully at May, and she patted his head.

"It'll be alright. August and I are just going to run off and have outstandingly wacky adventures while you're gone, I promise."

"You better," Xan said with a quiet smile and set Big Mouth Billy Bass down on the couch for May to keep an eye on. He trailed behind the caravan disappearing into the underground lab behind Ix.

Once they were out of earshot, August scooted a bit closer to May, pulled something which looked like a bag of marshmallows from the sofa, and offered her the open bag.

"Marshmallow?" he asked, grabbing one for himself and impaling it on a sticky metal skewer before thrusting the white cube into the fake fire.

May had a lot of questions. A) Where did he get marshmallows? B) Why were they in the couch? C) What the hell was Ix going to do to Xan down in the lab? and D) How would a holographic fire toast them?

Rather than try to decide which to ask first, she fished a marshmallow from the open package and skewered it, holding it in the flame which looked an awful lot like the Yule Log Christmas show. It could warm hearts, but not marshmallows.

After several minutes of sitting in silence, watching the marshmallows twist slowly in the cold flame, May finally said something. "Is this supposed to be doing something?"

August laughed, reined in his marshmallow, and ate it raw off the skewer. "No, I just wanted to see how long it would take you to ask. Three entire bloops!" He popped another marshmallow in his mouth and sighed thoughtfully as he chewed. "You know, I had to have Yvonne re-invent these for me. There's nothing like a marshmallow out here! Nothing like an apple, either, which is why it's a good business to be in! What do you miss most? From Earth?"

May squinted at him. He was trying to befriend her with invasive questions. She knew this tactic. It wouldn't work.

"Nothing," she said.

"Come on! No family? No friends? Nothing? Not even steak?"

"No."

"What about your parents? I visited Earth, you know, just to check in on my oma. It's weird what's happened to it now they know about aliens. Visiting is a nightmare. You can't imagine the paperwork!"

May stood, handing August the skewer without eating the marshmallow. She wasn't hungry. Or, more specifically, she was so hungry she'd circled back around into not wanting to eat. "I'm going to check on Xan."

"Wait." August put a hand on her elbow to stop her from leaving. "Look, I know how Ix's experiments go. Trust me, you don't want to be down there."

That made her want to be there even more, naturally, and it showed.

"It's alright," August said. "Aimz and Yvonne are down there, too. They'll look out."

"Aimz is unstable, Ix is...I don't know, I just don't trust Ix, and Yvonne tried to kill me."

August laughed, popping another marshmallow into his mouth. "Ix is trustworthy, just terrifying. And Yve isn't anything like Chaos was."

May grabbed Big Mouth Billy Bass from the cushion and sat down, holding the mounted fish in her lap and stroking it absently as if it were a sleeping cat.

"What's with the fish?" August asked.

May shrugged. "Xan likes it."

August nodded, gave an old man grunt (that's what he called them, "old man grunts") and moved closer to May. "How ya holding up, kid?"

May raised an eyebrow at him. "What do you mean?"

"Well, aren't you and Xan...you know. Isn't he your lover? This has to be—"

"No," she said. "He's an alien. I don't think we physically can. And he's... I don't know, not my type. I don't think I have a type." Then May's own curiosity got the better of her, and she said in a conspiratorial whisper. "You're not...with Ix, are you?"

August wasn't sure why she was whispering, it was nothing to be ashamed about. "Ix isn't into Earth men. Yvonne is, though. Frequently. I'm starting to have a hard time keeping up with her." Then he laughed at a self-depreciating joke he'd just thought of. The gist of it was that he was actually *not* having a hard time. He graciously spared May from hearing it.

"I want to check on Xan." She stood and made for the stairs.

"You do have a crush on him!" August accused laughingly.

"Ugh, no." May cringed visibly. She didn't care if he thought they were fucking, but a crush? That word gave her what psychologists refer to as the willies. "We're just partners. We look out for each other. You've got a crush on him, not me."

"Huh?"

"You told Xan you were straight on the docks, but you were really into that kiss."

"Xan's not a man! It doesn't count."

May raised an eyebrow at him.

"Does it?" August looked as if he'd just been given irrefutable proof that the moon landing was a sham.

Refusing to dignify him with an answer, May changed the subject. "Where's the lab?"

August stood with another old man grunt. "I'll take you," he said. "I wasn't kidding about Ix's scientific method, though. It takes a strong stomach."

Before they reached the stairs, Xan bolted up to the living room, cheerily smoothing back hair which dripped with something milky. "Fixed! Easy," he announced to the room before Ix, Aimz, and Yvonne followed him in.

He slung his damp arms around May and, unable to do much else, May patted his back hesitantly. Now she, too, was dripping with something milky.

"What is this?" she said, pulling away as soon as he let her.

"Uh, fermented hooflatoo milk. That didn't work. Neither did the centrifuge or the magnets," he counted off on his fingers. "But the sound stuff worked! The fungus hates sounds, apparently."

"The fungus hates sounds?" May asked.

"Not all sounds, just certain ones. It rather likes other sounds, apparently. Ix thinks it was triggered by some kind of sound in the first place! I'm saying the word 'sound' a lot, aren't I? Doesn't matter. I'm safe and sound! Everything's sounding good. I'm fine."

Aimz also dripped and smiled, but her smile was less face-eatingly huge, more of a quiet smugness.

"The ultrasonic treatments only delayed the growth of the fungus temporarily. You are not 'fine,'" Ix corrected, following, perturbed, behind everyone with a towel which she swiped across the floor.

"I'm fine," he said again, but quietly, just to May this time. "Let's celebrate! What do you folks do for fun around here? I..." He looked around the living room briefly to confirm his suspicion. "I don't see a TV. Don't you have a TV?"

"Celebrating is exactly what we shouldn't be doing," Yvonne said, slipping behind a well-stocked bar in the living room and pulling out glasses and armfuls of liquor bottles. "You two need to avoid anything that could set it off again. Anyone want to get drunk?"

CHAPTER SIXTEEN

Three Crystals a Head

There's no better way to worry about something than by sitting on a wooden rocking chair on a creaking porch with a strong drink, staring pensively out over the lake.

So that's exactly what everyone was doing.

Aimz rocked slowly back and forth, worrying about Listay whom she hadn't heard from yet, worrying about Xan who wasn't taking the scourge very well, and worrying about herself—she was taking it *too* well.

May rocked beside her, worrying about her lack of purpose, worrying that Yvonne secretly wanted them dead, worrying that Aimz was going to eat her in her sleep, and worrying that the *Audacity* would get lonely out there on its own. She refused to worry about Xan right now.

Xan rocked beside her, worried too that the *Audacity* would get lonely. He stuck pretty securely to that one worry, but occasionally the creeping dread of scourge encroached on his pleasant melancholy. He mentally weed-whacked it. How lonely the *Audacity* must be, he thought. It's so cold in open space. Had he left the lights on? Such a waste of electricity. He was sure he had left the lights on and wished he lived in the kind of advanced society where lights automatically turned themselves off.

August also rocked and worried. He was worried mainly about the apple-stealing glotchburs. He'd seen two scuttling along the edge of the lake with twigs in their jaws, diving in and out, in and out like sewing needles, no doubt building nests deep in the muck.

Ix and Yvonne were both taking a break from worrying. They were in their workshop, working on a self-aware apple coring machine which couldn't stop apologizing to the apples it disemboweled. Yvonne consoled the machine while Ix wrote some sadistic subroutines into its code.

Eventually, the worrying got the better of August and he had to say something.

"Those damn glotchburs are building a nest, I bet," he muttered loud enough for everyone to hear, but not loud enough for anyone to feel obliged to acknowledge him.

The porch floorboards creaked under the rocking chairs.

A silver-eared horntaggler cuckooed in the distance.

Invisible buzzing things buzzed invisibly.

"Well, I think it's high time for a glotchbur hunt," August said, louder now.

The sound of creaking rocking chairs reduced by exactly twenty-five percent as Aimz put a foot down to still her chair. "Hunt?" she asked, a dangerous pink glow in her eyes.

"What are you, a parrot?" August teased. "Now that I've got you here, I might as well make you work for your stay. Who wants to go hunting?"

Aimz stood, downing the rest of her drink.

"Eugh, Aimz you're entirely too excited to maul small amphibians," Xan said. "Besides! Yvonne said to not do anything that could set *it* off."

"Yvonne's the decorative one who doesn't know what they're talking about," Aimz said with a wave of her hand, secretly hoping Yvonne wasn't within earshot.

"*I'm* the decorative one who doesn't know what they're talking about! Yvonne has no perceivable flaws, physical or otherwise, and you know that. I'm not hunting glotchburs." He set down his drink, but had no intention of abandoning it. "I say we find the nest, give them a convincing speech about respecting private property, and help them re-locate somewhere else. Oh! And we can send them a care basket full of apples to keep them over until they find a new food source. No, that's too much. We can negotiate a contract with them."

"They're pests," Aimz said in a pejorative warble. "They can barely spell, much less negotiate a contract. How do you hunt them? Lasers? Traps? Just chase after them and snatch them up? Can we dissect them? I haven't dissected anything in ages."

"You haven't dissected anything since university. You hate dissecting things!" Xan stood now, too. "You used to just scrape up samples of unidentified plant matter. It's like you're using the scourge as an excuse to be horrifying."

She squared her shoulders at him. "Xan, we're scourged. Horrifying is essentially our single personality trait now. I've accepted the inevitable, and if that involves learning to tear something to shreds with my mouth, then what's the point in waiting?"

"Right, yeah, only one hang up there, I guess. I don't *want* to go feral, Aimz! That's sort of the point, don't you think? Decades at university spent trying to get rid of scourge, and now you're giving up?"

"Not giving up, just letting go! It's happened, alright? It's too late. We failed. We're zuxed. And I've set my mind on enjoying it."

"Whoa, whoa," August said, getting between the two Carmnians and pushing them apart gently. "We're not killing them, and we aren't writing any contracts. We stun them with an InfraDin Stick, then bring them to the butcher down the road. He pays three crystals a head! Then they have a nice, long life on his glotchbur reservation."

"The butcher?" asked May.

"Yeah," August said.

"Keeps them in a reservation?" she clarified.

"I'm willing to believe that!" Xan interrupted.

"Of course he keeps them in a reservation. He might be a butcher, but he's really got a heart for the little guys."

The little guys August was referring to were, in fact, not little nor were they guys. Glotchburs are roughly the size of a watermelon, skinned in rubbery brown hide, replete with useless facial horns, and reproduce unisexually which means they are neither guys *nor* gals.

"I'm willing to believe that!" said Xan again with a smile. He realized that he was repeating himself and because he realized it, it was okay. He was fine.

"Let's get this over with," May said, ignoring her half-full cocktail glass which sweated on the porch at her feet.

CHAPTER SEVENTEEN

Wager Your Wally

August had insisted on a "boys versus girls" hunting challenge. This insistence had annoyed everyone for different reasons. It annoyed May because this meant she would be stuck with Aimz. It annoyed Aimz and Xan because the terms "boy" and "girl" didn't actually translate to anything meaningful in Tuhntian, and August had been forced to try to explain his ideas on gender to them, which he did with a great deal of awkward fumbling.

But they agreed to try it just this once. And so May twirled the InfraDin Stick August had given her, watching Aimz as she dipped in and out of the tree line ahead of her, and wondered what the likelihood was that she would have to use the stick on Aimz out of self-defense. The likelihood was high, but not unreasonably so.

"Zuut, these glotchburs are faster than they look," Aimz panted, returning to May, who hadn't cared enough to go sprinting after the flash of grayish brown glotchbur in the distance. Aimz grabbed the InfraDin stick from May's hand. "These things have an awful range, though," she said, studying it. "And they're not nearly as much fun as catching something and ripping it to shreds with your bare teeth, right?"

May snatched it back and resolved to keep a tighter hold of it. "Why are you asking me?" She started walking again and Aimz followed, more interested in her now than the escaped pest.

"What's got your taxi maxed, Earthmun? You look like you've spent the rotation plucking raldbugs off the flesh of an infested hooflatoo."

"What?"

"Annoyed," Aimz clarified. "You look annoyed."

"Sorry."

"Well, tell me! What's got you annoyed? It's obviously not the glotchburs." Aimz stopped her now and parked her hands on May's shoulders, forcing her to engage in conversation. "It's Xan, isn't it? You're horribly annoyed with him for getting the scourge and ruining your life."

The face May made at Aimz flirted between horror and outrage, but didn't have quite enough energy to make it to the full expression of either.

"I'm annoyed at you. You don't give a shit about what happens to anyone, including yourself."

Aimz squinted, then switched her focus to somewhere behind May and pretended to search for something she had just seen a glimpse of behind her. "Where's Bar Fight May? Bring her back; I liked her better. Bar Fight May!" she hollered down the line of trees ahead of them. "Where'd you go, you zuxine tchagg?" she called out to no-one. Bar Fight May was long gone.

"Those were strangers; it's entirely different! You've attacked your own aunt, Xan, and me, and you seem to be enjoying this. I thought you cared about Xan, at least."

Aimz shook her head so forcefully her hair whipped around her like a miniature pink tornado. "I care! I just care differently. He's my zoup-nog brother; obviously I don't want to see him worried about going feral. I'm trying to help him cope! I want him to at least enjoy the painful decline into an unrecognizable beast of the wilderness." Her eyes were rimmed with green when she pushed the curtain of hair out of her face to look at May again.

May stayed silent. Talking never seemed to get her anywhere she wanted to be. That's why she usually let Xan take the lead in conversations.

"Earthmun," Aimz said, as gently as she could manage. "It's easier to accept the chaos. Chaos is the natural order of life, and if you fight it, you will lose every time. I stopped fighting it and look at me!" Aimz walked backward now so May could literally look her over. Her hair hung like a curtain of seaweed around her dirty face, her t-shirt was stiff with dried saltwater, her limbs caked in mud.

She looked horrible.

But she was grinning with a *joie de vivre* May had only ever experienced at the finish line of a harrowing…*chaotic* rocket race. May blinked once, and Aimz was a glittering goddess basking in the ebb and flow of an uncertain existence. May blinked again, and Aimz was back to being a dirty alien with a death wish.

May shook her head and walked away, half-heartedly searching the shadows for movement.

Aimz jogged after her. "Hey, you're really trok at conversations, you know that?"

May ignored her.

"Listen, you can get off your pretty puntle, because you've given into chaos more than you think you have. Ditching a perfectly good planet to race rocket ships? If I had an intact planet like that, you can wager your wally I wouldn't be this far from it."

"I was stuck on Earth. Now I'm not."

"Now you're stuck on Xan," Aimz said with a laugh. "Come on, I'm not the only heartless tchagg here. What about your aunts? Left them on Earth without saying goodbye, didn't you?"

"My mother raised me, and I hadn't spoken to her in years before I was abducted."

"A lover, then? Relationship getting boring, you find an easy out?"

"Nope."

Aimz sighed, trying one final time to prove her point. "Alright, houseplants! You got any houseplants you deserted back on Earth?"

May remembered Betty, the cactus, which sat on the mini-fridge in her old hovel of an apartment. "It's just a plant…" May begun, but Aimz thrust out an arm, stopping May mid-sentence.

Something in the distance had caught her attention, their conversation (which May had only just now accepted) forgotten.

"Blitheon, May, look at that! The glotchburs are in for a really *hot* time!"

CHAPTER EIGHTEEN

Glotchbur Stew

The common Rhean glotchbur is a quiet, aquatic creature. It is content to spend its short life scurrying about, digging ditches that it knows it dug for a reason (though for what reason, exactly, it can never remember), and eating its weight in the fruits of other creature's labors. In this case, apples.

The only noise they are thought to make is a weak buzz which emanates from their slimy bull-frog throat and informs nearby glotchburs that they're ready for their daily humping.

This is why the scream of a terrified glotchbur is so chilling, and the screams of hundreds of glotchburs at once is altogether more horrific a sound than any human ear would happily hear.

The sound had come from the lake, and so that's the direction in which August and Xan ran. Before the lake came into view, a thick steam blanketed the orchard, forcing them to slow to a walk to keep from running face-first into a tree.

August coughed through the humidity, feeling as if he were about to drown on dry land. "Where the hell did this come from?" he asked rhetorically. He knew Xan wouldn't know. Xan tried to answer, anyway.

"I don't know," he said to August. "May?" he shouted into the steam, cupping his hands around his mouth to amplify the sound. "Aimz?" he tried again, just in case she was within earshot and May wasn't.

"I'm right here," May's voice could be heard through the steam. She wasn't shouting because she didn't need to; she was just a few feet in front of them at the edge of the lake. The steam wafted ever upward until the scene cleared enough that they could see two blurry figures. One, Aimz, rolling on the ground, laughing so hard she was silently wheezing. The other, May, who stared down at her in quiet resignation.

The ground dipped away into a steaming mud-pit which burbled and smelled of beef stew.

"What happened to the lake?" August said, falling to his knees at the horrific sight of his once glistening, if glotchbur infested, lake.

"I—" Aimz wheezed between a chortle. "I—" she couldn't stop laughing.

May crossed her arms and shook her head. She was going to have to explain. She hated explaining things. "So, Aimz saw the Ray-Master Tree Trimmer parked at the edge of the lake. She said the glotchburs were in for a really hot time and ran off. I tried to catch up, but," May gestured to her legs, "short," she finished simply.

"So she used the Ray-Master to flash-boil the lake, and now we've got glotchbur stew," August extrapolated with a sigh, putting the rest of the event together.

"Yep," May confirmed.

Aimz was settling down now. She had stopped her mirthful rolling and was laying on her side, gazing out in ecstasy at the carnage she had wrought. "You're welcome," she shouted back gleefully to August who only whimpered. Xan put a comforting hand on his back.

Aimz dragged herself upward and shook off a few large clumps of warm mud.

May swallowed back nausea which might have been inspired by the stench of glotchbur stew or the wet heat surrounding the lake. It could have also, possibly, been that she hadn't eaten in far too long. Furthermore, Aimz's erratic behavior had only solidified her suspicion that the scourge had not, in fact, been cured and was still looming over them like a deadly hot air balloon. She stood woozily, her feet sunk into the mud up to her ankles.

"Well," said August. "Close the lid, the monkey's dead." And he followed Aimz back to the house.

Xan squelched down to the shore where May swayed.

"I didn't see that coming," he said, reaching for her hand. "So at least I'm not time-zuxed anymore, eh?"

"At least," she replied as he dragged her from the mud and they trudged after Aimz and August.

CHAPTER NINETEEN

Jazz Hands

The air was thickly humid and smelled like the inside of an office microwave just after lunch time, reminiscent of food, but wildly unappetizing. They climbed the steps back up to the porch, creating a trail of watery silt.

"Okay," August said with a heavy sigh. "Everyone pick a bedroom. They all have showers and access to the wardrobe system, so you can put on something dry." He then leaned closer to May. "And Earth-style toilets."

"Thank God," May whispered. Why August said this, and, indeed, why May was so relieved to hear it, I will leave up to your imagination.

Aimz had already half undressed, leaving her filthy wet clothing in mournful lumps along the porch. Xan's mauve faux buffatalo coat had become a wet slap of a thing which mopped up his sides listlessly every time he moved. He draped it over a porch chair to dry and tried to open the screen door which led to the kitchen, only to find that the screen door didn't strictly exist. Not for people, anyway. It very much existed for the clouds of tiny bugs which, attracted to the nutrient rich silt that coated their legs, desperately wanted to follow them inside. He walked through the screen, the bugs stayed outside.

May whipped off her trench coat, which was now three times as heavy as it had been and wrung it out over the sink, then combed her hair back and wrung that out over the sink as well.

Then, tired of waiting for someone else to mention it, May confronted Aimz.

"The scourge is back, isn't it?"

"Pah-ha...what? No," Xan said before Aimz could get a word in. "That's just Aimz! Normal Aimz."

"It was the scourge," Aimz corrected. "And don't worry about lending us any clothes, August. You don't need clothes to wander off into the forest and become a folkloric beast." She was naked now, to demonstrate.

No one who hadn't grown up with Aimz was able to form a coherent retort to that, so Xan took it upon himself to shake out May's trench coat, wrap it around Aimz's shoulders, and give her the stern kind of look their Aunt Kalumbits used to pull off so nicely.

"Go upstairs and don't come down until you're clean and dressed and, preferably, of sound mind, alright, mun? You're not becoming a folkloric beast without me, and I'm not ready for that sort of celebrity just yet."

"What's wrong with you?" Aimz asked.

"Nothing. That's the point! Nothing's wrong with either of us. We're fine," he said in a tone which was meant to frighten the universe into making it so.

She gave him a sloppy scoff, pulled the trench coat further around herself, and stomped off to claim a room upstairs. For her benefit, he held the stern face until she was gone, then, for his own benefit, he let his face fall into a look of abject terror.

"Whoo," August said with a full-body stretch. "We had quite a day. Us Earthlings really ought to have some RnR, eh?"

"Zuut," Xan said, shocked. "I didn't know Earthlings could do that!"

"Rest and relaxation?" August clarified.

"Oh. Right, yes. That. He's right, May."

"Fine." May snatched Big Mouth Billy Bass from the couch and followed Aimz's wet footprints upstairs.

Xan followed her up the stairs visually but stayed physically stuck to the spot, wondering if he should go with her or claim his own room. The idea of time alone with only his thoughts for company distressed him, but August slapped him on the back in a friendly, heterosexual sort of way.

"Come on, I'll show you to your room."

* * *

The bedrooms in August's house looked slightly more normal than the rest of the house. Normal, in this case, meaning filled with whooshing doors and holographic floating screens rimmed in color changing lights and the constant quiet buzz of electricity.

This comforted May in some ways. It was better to be in an honest room than a room which was deceptively Earth-like, a rustic and cozy veneer over the pervasive technology.

Along one wall, a no-nonsense hard-vapor bed. Along the other, a no-nonsense SaniSteam shower.

She dropped Big Mouth Billy Bass on the nightstand and went over to the holowindow which displayed an idyllic day on the orchard, the lake glistening rather than boiling. If she were to pretend everything was fine, she wanted to make it totally and absolutely fine. She flicked through the holowindow settings until she found a video of the stars from space. Not a twinkle in sight, just steady points of silvery light like she remembered.

Satisfied with the new view, she began to undress, pausing as she heard August and Xan talking in the hall, then continuing, grateful that they hadn't come in. Privacy was not an alien concept to Tuhntians in general. It was, however, an alien concept to Xan.

After showering, May lay strewn across the bed, wearing one of August's undershirts, a worn flannel shirt, and ill-fitting boxer shorts which were a great deal more comfortable than the ill-fitting jeans she had tried on. She was unable to even consider sleeping. On the bedside table, bathed in a ring of light which looked uncannily like lamplight but which emanated from a thin floating disk, lay Big Mouth Billy Bass.

It is customary for the plastic mounted fish known as Big Mouth Billy Bass to sing snippets of two songs. The first being "Take Me to the River" and the second, "Don't Worry, Be Happy." And so, despite months of silence from the fish, it shouldn't have exactly surprised May that it began to sing now.

Still, it startled her, and she nearly fell off the edge of the bed trying to get away from it.

"Take me to-" it sang. "Take me to-" it sang again. "Take me to-"

"What? Spit it out!" May said, irritated.

Then, May's own voice echoed back to her from the fish's wobbling mouth, distorted through the worn speaker. "Carmnia."

May almost ignored it. Her options were A) acknowledge it and admit that she had heard it or B) pretend nothing had happened and wonder about it forever.

"Take me to...Carmnia," it repeated.

Yes, the fish had definitely spoken to her. The fish wanted to see Carmnia. Which, by all accounts, was incomprehensible to May. She had a lot of questions. She started with a simple "Why?" as she cautiously addressed the plastic mounted fish.

"To cure the scourge."

"Who are you?"

"Big Mouth Billy Bass," said the fish.

"No, who are you really?"

"I'm here to help."

"Why should I trust you?"

"It's your only option."

"Who the hell are you?"

"I'm a fish, you simpleton! Now take me to Carmnia, or let Aimz and Xan go feral."

May was sleep deprived, clearly. Obviously, this was a new feature of sleep deprivation that she hadn't yet had the pleasure of experiencing. She grabbed the fish and opened the SaniSteam tube.

"Where are you taking me?" asked the fish.

"I need to sleep on it." May flung it into the shower where it clattered on the tiles.

"Wait! I'm your only—" The shower door shut, and the fish's voice was too muffled now to bother May.

She dropped face-first to the bed and slunk beneath the covers. Exhaustion seemed to redouble the amount of gravity on her body as she sunk into the mattress, but as her body stilled, her mind began its morning calisthenics.

Rather than sleep, she found her thoughts rotating like a wad of spun sugar in a cotton candy machine, every turn creating a sticky cloud of frustration. Doing something was always better than doing nothing, right? And here on mainland Rhea, she could do nothing.

Carmnia was a lead. Carmnia was something to act on.

She mentally wandered down the path of paying Carmnia a visit which ended, at various branches, in certain death. She wandered down the path of staying put, which ended, again, at various branches, in certain death.

Then, she remembered what Xan had said. "No one survives anything. Even the so-called gods die." And she realized he was absolutely right. That's just how the universe works. You live, you make good choices and you make bad choices, and regardless of how many good or bad choices you make, you die, and wasn't that just a clump of soured milk in her coffee?

Or was it? Was everything actually easier now that she knew the outcome? Death? If that was the outcome, despite anything she did to change it, then the point of existence must be...must be... Shit, she thought. She was still thinking. The same thoughts, too. This was the tenth, maybe eleventh time they'd spun around the cotton candy machine of her brain, and the sugary web had only gotten denser.

This was exactly why she didn't want to be alone with nothing to do but think.

Maybe she should find Xan. She was so used to having him around to drown out her incessant mental chatter. But her arms and legs were so heavy, they might as well have been cinched to the bed, so she axed the idea.

After a while, she almost thought she had fallen asleep, until she realized that, again, she had been chasing the idea of going to Carmnia and trying to suss out all the possible ways that option might end.

Sleep, sleep, sleep for the love of God, sleep, she thought. Thinking was not sleeping, she thought again and, instead, screamed into her pillow. Screaming was also not sleeping, but it felt better than thinking.

A moment later, a purposeful knock on her door. Four times.

"Come in," she said, tilting her mouth away from the pillow just enough to be heard.

The door wooshed open, and Xan entered wearing another of August's flannels, tied up at the middle, and a pair of August's jeans. May's trench coat was slung over one arm and the other held aloft a plate of something in a loaf.

"Heard you couldn't sleep," he said, draping the trench coat over the bedside table.

"From who?"

"The screaming was a dead giveaway." He sat down on the bed and offered her the plate of bread. "August told me to give it to you when you woke up, and that I definitely shouldn't eat it because it was poisonous and would kill me, but you know, I'm not sure I believe that? Worst that it could be is some kinda wheat and that won't kill me."

"Don't eat it," May said, dragging herself up to sit as if the hard-vapor mattress were a pit of quicksand sucking her in.

May observed the slice of bread, some kind of quick bread from the look of it, probably apple-based, given the business. She broke off a piece and chewed it, moaning at the sweet softness. "Sorry, it'll kill you dead," she said once she had swallowed.

His mouth twisted defiantly, and he tried to break off a small corner, but May patted his hand away and moved the plate to the opposite bedside table.

"Alright, okay, zuut!" he relented with a light laugh and leaned back on the pale gray headboard. "Why can't you sleep? You're usually great at it."

With a shrug and a sigh, May put another bite in her mouth. "Thinking," she said around it.

"About?"

"Everything. You could make all the right decisions, and still, you've got to die one day, so what's the point in working so hard to make the right decisions when everything has the same outcome?"

The question sounded rhetorical, to Xan, so he kept himself from positing an answer.

"I was thinking about all the different types of things you can put in a stew. And also, is coffee a stew? Can you put coffee in a stew? Can you stew things *in* coffee?" he asked. "But your thing is better, admittedly."

"You're a few hundred years older than me. Don't you know what the point is by now?"

"Aha, ha...maybe. I don't think there is one. Not really, I mean. Not some big cosmic thing you could write out and then just be done with it. The point is just...it's just now. This moment. And then in a couple beoops, the point will be that. A few more beoops after that will be another point. The point is just all...this." He demonstrated "all this" by stretching his hands out and wiggling his fingers.

"The point is jazz hands?" May asked.

"Sure, yeah. The point is jazz hands."

"Well, that helps," she said, shifting back beneath the covers.

"It does? Jazz hands?"

"Yep." And it did. This time, when May closed her eyes, she actually noticed the soft coolness of the hard-vapor pillow, the gentle throb of her tired feet, and the slight dip in the mattress caused by Xan's weight beside her as she fell asleep.

CHAPTER TWENTY

Face Coffee

"I'm going to see Carmnia," May, having slept on it, said immediately upon waking. She would've liked to say that she had a prophetic dream that told her it was the right thing to do. She would've liked to say that in the clear stillness of the morning the answer had come to her. In actuality, it was just the second thing that came out of her mouth when she woke up, the first being a bit of spittle which had moistened her pillow.

"Oh, that's umm...that's...uhh." Xan covered the confused silence in his brain with mouth-sounds. "Good morning, starshine?"

"Did you hear me?" she asked.

"I did."

"And?"

"I heard you! You're going to see Carmnia."

May shook her head and grabbed the half-eaten bread from the bedside table, inspecting it to be sure Xan hadn't snuck a bite. She finished it off.

"Are you going with me or not? It might be dangerous."

"I'm definitely not *not* going with you, but I also am not going, because you're not going."

"You can't stop me," May said, putting on the trench coat which had dried, albeit stiffly, overnight. She felt the pockets and found that, miraculously, the zapper was still tucked away inside it.

"Wait, hold on. I missed an important part of this conversation. *Why* are you going to see Carmnia? That's what I should've said."

"Because..." May looked surreptitiously at the shower as if the doors might tear open and the bass would come bursting out singing, dancing, and mysteriously spotlit. This did not happen, and so May had to admit, "The fish told me to."

"Big Mouth Billy Bass told you to see Carmnia, and you're just going to listen to it? But when I told you to *not* see Carmnia, you didn't listen to me! Do you trust a plastic fish more than you trust me, May? Because, if you do, that's awful. That's really and truly terrible."

"No, I trust you! It's just that it seemed to know what it was talking about."

"Alright, but, consider: Trisy Yorgaslack seems to know what he's talking about on TV, but he sells reclaimed racing rockets for a living, and you know why Yorgaslack and Larvae's Reclaimed Racing Rockets has never had a bad review on the IFI? It's because no one who's purchased one of Yorgaslack and Larvae's Reclaimed Racing Rockets lives long enough to leave a review!"

"You don't have to come. I can't help Yvonne and Ix do..." She made a hand gesture to replace a noun she couldn't find, "on you and Aimz, but I can look for other options, so that's what I'm going to do. I *have* to do something."

Scales in Xan's brain balanced precariously as he thought. He stared out of the glowing holowindow to try to steady them before answering. The old familiar scene of open space wasn't nearly as comforting to him as it had been to May.

"I don't want Yvonne and Ix to..." He repeated her strange hand gesture, "on me, but I also don't want the Scourge Authority to vaporize me. I *do* want to make sure you're safe, and I've never actually met Carmnia before, so she has no reason to hate me. And I suppose...I suppose we're going to see Carmnia."

"You sure you want to come? I plan on finding Listay first, so I won't be alone."

"I'm sure. It couldn't hurt. Unless I get vaporized, and hey, even then only for a blip, right?"

"True," she said, her brain so focused on running through logistics that she had only half listened to him. "We better bring the fish," she said, watching the shower warily.

Showers are, of course, used to being watched warily.

Slowly, May pulled back the sliding shower door and found that Big Mouth Billy Bass was just where she had left it. The thing hadn't grown arms and legs and freed itself in the night.

She wasn't sure why she had expected that it might, but she hadn't expected it to suddenly start a conversation with her, so all bets were, currently, off.

"We're taking you to Carmnia," May told it.

It did exactly what one would expect a toy fish with no batteries to do. Nothing.

Now May started to suspect that she had been hallucinating, and Xan, though he didn't dare say it, might have agreed. Until a mechanical whirr came from the fish and its mouth dropped open in an expression which might have been read, to the keen observer, as surprise.

In fact, the fish was shocked by this development. It had just begun to accept its soggy fate on the shower floor when May announced her decision, and it was having difficulty reacting properly.

"Good," said the bass, finally, fearing that it might lose their attention if it considered its next move too long. Then it shut its mouth. Talking used up a great deal of energy.

May stuffed it in the largest pocket on her trench coat. Only the bottom half fit, and so the bass rose awkwardly out of her pocket, staring at the sky, but it was secure.

"So what's the plan?" Xan asked as May shut the shower door.

"The plan is to figure out how to hot-wire the ThingHauler, hot-wire the ThingHauler, and get back to the Merimip which we'll take to NotTuhnt's police station to bail out Listay."

"That's utterly ridiculous, you know that?"

May paused at the door to the room, offended. "It's not *utterly ridiculous*. It's only slightly harebrained."

"Hot-wiring the ThingHauler, I mean. It's utterly ridiculous because I've got August's face!" And he did. When May looked back at him to see what the hell he meant, she was met by a holographic rendering of August's face emanating from the tip of Aimz's mugging pen.

"When did you get that? And why?"

"Eh, I had some time alone with August last night and had a feeling you might want a get-away option in case things got zuxed here."

"Really?" May didn't quite believe that he had that kind of foresight.

"No, we were just zuxing around with it," Xan admitted and flicked through several unflattering images of both their faces before shutting it off and stowing it in a flannel breast pocket. He had never worn anything with a functioning breast pocket before, and while he thought it was a terribly odd place for a pocket, he had quickly become accustomed to it.

"Good work, I guess," May said. "Can you tell Listay we're heading back to NotTuhnt?"

Xan raised his BEAPER. "Hey, Listay! How's NotTuhnt? Hope the weather cleared up a bit. Have they let you off, yet? Because if they have and you've noticed that the Merimip—"

"Get to the point," May whispered.

"Right, well, we're coming back, May and myself, to ask Queen Carmnia about the scourge. So just stay right where you are, and we'll come find you. Unless you're somewhere you don't think we'll be able to find you, in which case, please get somewhere we *will* find you and wait for us there. Just tell us where you'll be and stay there until we reach you, alright? That sounds alright," Xan confirmed. "See you soon, mun!" Xan sent the message and then put a hand on May's shoulder, the cheery timbre of the message he'd just sent dropping like a silken sheet. "I need coffee before we go. I couldn't sleep. Too bright."

What, thought May, had been too bright? Certainly not the room. The space-window twinkled with such minute points of light, it was nearly pitch black in there with the lights off. But as she turned to ask for clarification, she noticed something she hadn't before. The green bioluminescence of the fungi was a great deal stronger than it had been yesterday.

"Yikes," she said out loud, accidentally. "Sorry, Blue. Why don't you make some coffee? I'll find some alcohol for the road."

"What about everyone else?" Xan asked.

"What about them?"

"Shouldn't we let them know where we're going? So they don't worry. Or perhaps so they do worry. I feel like someone should be worried about this, and you certainly don't seem to be."

"They'll try to stop us."

"And rightly so!"

May sighed. "You don't have to come."

He rubbed his face with both hands as if he were trying to change into a different personality. One that wasn't too exhausted to go along with May's slightly harebrained schemes. "Alright. Okay. We won't tell them unless they ask. How's that?"

"Fine." May led them down the stairs and, with a forced casual ease, asked, "You sure you wouldn't rather hang out with August?"

"Eh, I've always preferred the company of people who are likely to get me killed. Makes me feel like I'm doing something important with my life."

"I can't tell if you're being sarcastic."

"You know...I'm actually not? As long as I get to complain about it, I'm up for anything. What is life if not the act of consistently defying death?"

The kitchen, like most of the house, had been styled like a rustic Earth kitchen. A sprawling butcher block island flanked by dark wood cabinets. A bread box built into the cabinets was labeled with a metal Insinigator logo, the food replicator looked like an old fridge, and where most kitchens had a stove, this one had a rack of amber-bottled cider.

May's coat pockets were beginning to reach their limit, but she shoved a bottle of cider into an inner pocket, adding to the absurdly lumpy silhouette. She never thought about needing a bag until she needed a bag, and when she needed a bag, there was never one available to her. It was the BEAPER situation all over again.

Xan flipped on the food replicator and selected a large mug of coffee. As he watched the machine arrange the necessary molecules, a thought struck him. A thought which would culminate in this action: the moment the coffee was complete, he grabbed the replicated coffee mug from the bay, tilted his head back, and poured the entire cup directly over his face.

Fermented hooflatoo milk hadn't worked, but what evil was there that a good cup of hot coffee couldn't scare off? The answer was several. And, in fact, many kinds of evil can subsist on coffee alone.

Coffee ran down his shirt as he shook the liquid from his face which had gone from pale blue to bright green from the scalding. He blinked the coffee from his eyes. Nothing had changed.

"That help?" May asked, trying (and failing) to cram another bottle of cider into her coat.

"Too soon to tell!" Xan asked the replicator to assemble another mug of coffee, but May set down the bottle and slid between him and the machine before it was finished.

"Are you going to drink this one with your face?"

"Of course I am!"

"Xan—"

"My mouth is on my face, isn't it?"

The replicator dinged that it had finished. The door slid open to reveal a steaming mug of newly replicated coffee. May stood in front of it. He lunged around her, shoving her aside to snatch the cup and chug it.

"Get in the truck," May said.

CHAPTER TWENTY-ONE

Prty Dsh

The drive back to the dock was blessedly uneventful. They analyzed August's taste in music, concluding that he was around the right age for a mid-life crisis and the music he listened to absolutely felt like the kind of thing someone might enjoy when they weren't sure where the second half of their life was going. After concluding this, they both realized they didn't know where the second half of their own lives were going, and the music suddenly made a great deal more sense to them.

They discussed common Earth phrases which Xan was keen on further incorporating into his vocabulary. The phrase Xan had so commonly heard on TV, "Why I oughta..." May explained, was typically a threat. Xan explained that there are many things he ought to do and none of them involved threatening people, so he didn't see much use for that one unless he could change the implication, but May vetoed it all together, seeing as she had never actually heard anyone in real life say it to begin with.

"Where's the boat?" May asked as they parked the ThingHauler along the dock and got out.

"There's a boat," Xan said, pointing to something much larger, pinker, and rounder than the Merimip Ocean Ship.

"That's *a* boat. Where's *the* boat?" May wasn't asking him; she knew he didn't know. She was asking the unfeeling cosmos that had stranded her on a Rhean dock with no boat. Rows of various watercraft bobbed along the boardwalk, but these were luxury craft, and their owners were all off doing the things which made them enough money to enjoy their luxury craft on the weekends.

They approached an egg-shaped floating attendant's kiosk with a service window and just enough room for one hover-stool and one under-paid young Rhean.

May knocked and the hatch whizzed open.

"How can I assist?" the Rhean teen said with so little inflection that May hadn't, at first, realized it was meant to be a question. He was looking at a holobook. Not reading it, as his eyes never moved from the middle of the digital page. Just looking at it.

"Er, hi. My boat's missing," she said.

Xan pulled her aside. "It's not technically our boat, you know. Sure, we bought it on our gem, but we gave it to Listay, so it's Listay's boat. We have stolen back the thing we purchased. Hold on, *is* it our boat? The great Udonian philosopher Fragahoo postulated that—"

"Tell me later."

"But—"

"Please?"

He looked like he might burst, but he forced himself to shut up anyway, and May turned back to the attendant.

"Black boat?" asked the attendant, eyes still trained on the holobook.

"Yes."

"Weird greenhouse thing on the top?"

"Yes!"

The attendant shrugged.

"Yes?" May pressed.

"Dunno," they said.

"You didn't see who took it?"

"Got impounded. Owner's dead, apparently."

To May, there was nothing more odious than the phrase "Let me talk to your manager." It had been used against her so frequently and with such vitriol when she worked at Sonic that she had made a pact with herself to never let slip the offending demand. But the sentiment was welling up in her. If this Rhean teen had a manager, May very much wanted to speak with them.

Perhaps re-phrasing it would remove the sting. The question "Is there someone else I could talk to?" seemed benign enough, even polite, if she kept her tone in check.

"Is—" She stopped, the words catching in her throat as the ghost of her former self rose up and strangled her.

"Hey!" Xan shouted from behind her. "Hey, May! I got us a ride!"

"Yeah?" She turned around as if she were a camera operator purposefully holding off the reveal, creating tension, creating suspense. When at last Xan came into view, he was attached to a rope ladder dangling from something which must've spawned from an ELO album cover.

A sun-blotting silver frisbee twirled above him, lights blinking in rhythms and colors precisely calibrated to create a sleek, futuristic effect. Its three levels rotated independently of one another like an electric three-tiered cake. Its license plate spelled out 'Prty Dsh' which, May surmised, likely meant they were about to be ferried back to NotTuhnt on the Party Dish.

Or perhaps ferried off to another, cooler dimension where seaports on alien planets didn't look nearly exactly like a small fishing town somewhere around New England.

A gnat buzzed into her open mouth. "You," she gagged slightly on account of the gnat, "you're sure that's going to NotTuhnt?"

Xan thrust a finger toward a marquee which wasn't, blessedly, spinning like the rest of the contraption. Squinting, May could just make out "NOTTUH" on the marquee. She chewed her lip.

"It's going to 'Nottuh'," she said, as she grabbed hold of the bottom rung of the rope ladder.

"Well, obviously the full marquee is meant to say, 'NotTuhnt', right? Clearly. I mean, that would be the logical thing, wouldn't it?" He sounded less confident now.

May snorted, beginning to climb the ladder. "Logically. But when has anything ever been logical?"

When they reached the platform where the line queued up, a boulder of a man greeted them at the entrance, and that's only a slight exaggeration. He was a Garveral, more mineral than man. "Tickets?" he demanded in a gravelly voice.

The only thing which gave him away as not exactly a hunk of granite was the crack in his face which opened and closed rhythmically, as if breathing, and his impeccably pressed tuxedo complete with cummerbund and a bowtie which nestled beneath the mouth-crack.

"Yes, please," Xan said.

Had the Garveral had eyes, he would've rolled them. Had he had lungs, he would've sighed. He had neither, and this made him particularly well suited to customer service jobs.

"I need to see your tickets."

"Can't we buy them here?"

"This isn't the Party Tray, boha. This is the Party Dish. If you don't have tickets, you're not getting in."

A line of people had formed behind them.

"Right, yeah, well we can purchase tickets, right?" Xan asked.

The line was beginning to make exasperated noises.

"This, again, is a Party Dish. You buy tickets at the Tray," the boulder said stonily.

"For the love of O'Zeno," muttered someone behind them.

"Let's go." May tried to pull Xan away by the elbow.

"Wait, wait, okay. Where's the Tray, then?"

"Zoup-nog," whispered the line.

"I'm not a zuxing information dome. Now get out of here and don't go climbing ropes you haven't paid to climb."

"We'll find a public teledisc to NotTuhnt; come on," May whispered just loud enough to be heard over the general hubbub of annoyance behind them.

Xan pressed his lips together in frustration but followed May back down the rope. Halfway, at least. The lower-level hatch gaped open, a soft blue glow pulsating from inside.

"Party Dish!" said Xan and, in a feat May didn't realize he was physically capable of, he sprung from the rope ladder, just catching enough of the edge to leave him dangling from the dish like a scrap of wilted lettuce on the side of a salad plate.

"Damnit." May whispered, dangling from the ladder as she watched him struggle.

"Hold," he grunted as he tried to lift himself into the ship, "on."

"Not much else I can do."

"Heh, this thing's slipperier than I imagined," he said, his boots flailing for purchase on the side of the Dish. The toe of his boot caught a piece of cracked siding and, cracking it further, he leveraged himself inside the Party Dish.

"Ha!" May heard, muffled. Xan reappeared inside the ship and held his arms out. "On in. Into the Party Dish," he cajoled her.

"Stop playing around. This isn't like you."

His shoulders dropped along with his smile, but his arms were still held out to her. "I'm going to pay for it," he assured her.

"Yeah, that's what I'm worried about."

"We shouldn't?"

"Defin—" A bone vibrating classic sci-fi sound effect extinguished her answer and the Dish, which had been hovering slightly above the water, hovered a great deal higher now.

The things which May shouted at Xan, eyes squeezed tight, fingers soul-bonded to the rope, don't need to be transcribed herein. I'm trying to keep the amount of "fucks" under ten, and I've just wasted one there. You'll have to come up with your own colorful language.

Fortunately, Xan heard none of it. Unfortunately, because neither of them could hear each other, and May refused to open her eyes, he was unable to communicate to her that he had the top of the rope and all she had to do was climb up one more rung, and he could pull her in.

He tried wiggling the rope gently to let her know he had it, but this only made her grip tighter and curses more creative.

So he tried to reel the rope in, but found his muscles weren't up to the task.

He reached down and, using his nose as a stylus, tapped his BEAPER which had (and always has had, before you ask) a megaphone function.

"MAY," he shouted via his BEAPER's megaphone (the megaphone which his BEAPER has always had). "CLIMB UP."

Carefully, she tilted her head up toward the sound and squinted at Xan holding onto the rope ladder above her. She was looking at Xan, but all she could see was the incredible distance from her feet to the vast ocean below as the Party Dish spun onward toward NotTuhnt.

"No!"

He couldn't hear her, but it was easy enough to extrapolate what she had said.

No further technology had been retconned into the BEAPER that would be of use, and so May hung there miserably as Xan tried to will the ladder to budge.

Until, high in the crest of the Party Dish, the pilot, who was high in both senses of the word, had the sudden realization that she had forgotten to reel in the ladder and rectified her oversight.

Outside, the winch shifted, groaning in protest of the added weight, then, knowing that no one heard its protest or (more to the point) cared, did its job, albeit pointedly slower than usual.

Once May was within reaching distance, Xan locked his arms around her and fished her into the luggage-stuffed lower tier of the Party Dish.

She had her feet under her for only a moment before wobbling to the floor, the nerves in her arms and legs twitching.

"Alright?" Xan asked.

"Uh-uh."

"Mun." He sat on the floor beside her. "You race a rocket for a living...what happened? You're not scared of anything."

"Heights."

"You...race a rocket. That's as high as you can physically get."

"But it's—" She wrested control of her arms again and made a kind of orb with her hands to demonstrate a rocket capsule. "It's inside. You're in something. Safe."

"Safe," he confirmed, putting a hand to her chest.

She stared at his hand, surprised. It was comforting, even if the way he was acting wasn't. "You're not supposed to be the brave one, Blue."

He dropped his hand and stuck his thumb and pointer fingers over his eyelids, rubbing fiercely as if he had been pepper sprayed.

"I'm sorry. I'm trying to be myself, I really am." He put his elbows on his knees and rested his forehead in his hands, staring at the floor despondently. "But who I am keeps changing. It's like trying to balance a ship without a gyroscope," he said.

The bottle of cider appeared in his field of vision. The bottle of cider shook gently at him.

He took it, drank from it, then smiled at May. "Much better," he said. It wasn't. But he said it anyway. "Got your legs back?"

May sealed the bottle, stashed it in her coat pocket beside Big Mouth Billy Bass, and made a show of patting her legs. "I think these are mine."

They stood and inspected their luggage-y surroundings.

"Have you ever been to a Party Dish?" he asked.

"Have you?" She didn't bother telling him that she hadn't. Of course she hadn't.

"Mmm, not sure. I've been to a lot of things which might have been Party Dishes. Let's check it out."

* * *

The main floor of the Party Dish was not at all what May had been expecting. The lights were pinkish and brighter than daylight, and the entire room which stretched the length of the dish wore a soft white fur coat, pale fibers swaying grassily.

Lumps of floor and ceiling jutted out, creating tables, couches, stools, even several doughnut-shaped bars with columns of backlit glass bottles in the center interspersed with neon signs advertising everything the bored-looking bartenders were willing to serve.

Feather-like fibers tickled her shins in a way which felt uncannily like crawling ants. She shook her foot, only to have more fibers caress it when she set it back down.

The air smelled toxically sweet, and May got the sense that this was exactly what swimming through cotton candy would feel like.

A mechanical band played impossibly quietly from a fuzzy white stage, four pristine silver androids injecting as little soul as possible into four equally pristine shapes which looked more like oversized esoteric kitchen gadgets than instruments. Over the music could be heard the clink of glasses and murmur of meaningless conversations deadened by the plush coat of the room.

Fortunately for May, who was not much of a dancer, this party did not appear to have a dance floor. Unfortunately for May, Xan *was* a dancer and didn't care that there wasn't a dance floor.

He found an empty patch of fuzz and began to draw a great deal of attention to himself. A distraction was in order, and quickly, too. Before the confused stares of the quietly drinking onlookers turned into a call for security.

The perfect distraction blazed in pink neon above the bar: Hallucinogenic aphrodisiacal rice noodles. She had come across them before, but had somehow refrained from trying them. Hallucinogens had never been her drug of choice; they got in the way of work. Aphrodisiacs also had never interested her since she had never been nor desired to be in a situation where one would be warranted. Noodles, though, she could get behind.

Xan would either heartily disapprove and come over to tell her so, or, in this state, he might be eager to watch. Either way, he would stop trying to dance with the flustered waiter.

"Hey, I'm going to try the noodles. Want to watch?" she announced her intentions.

He paused in his pursuit and gave her a look which quickly morphed from excitement to concern and back again. "You sure? I mean..." He realized he was shouting to her across the relatively quiet room and cantered up to the bar where she had taken an obstinate seat. "I mean," he said again, in a reasonable tone of voice, "you know what those noodles do. I've built up a tolerance, sure, but zuut, the first handful of times I had them...Zuut."

May was reasonably convinced she could handle them. If they were anywhere near as strong as ZipZams or most alien alcohols she had tried, the effect would last her twelve minutes tops. Twelve minutes of horny hallucinations would mean twelve minutes of not having to worry that Xan would get them caught. She'd never been horny before, anyway, and she was curious about this apparently overwhelming urge to mate that everyone seemed so excited about.

"It'll be fine. My metabolism is a lot faster than yours."

"You would win a metabolism race, yeah."

"I'd win a lot of races."

"And you have! We were talking about noodles, though. Specifically, you eating them. Imagine me but younger. Did I have a mullet back then? Likely. Yes. Yeah, that was before the pompadour adventure." He spread his hands as if to smooth out a canvas upon which he was about to paint a picture of times past. "A crepuscular glow bathes the metropolis hub city on Eroticon-"

The bartender tendered a bar of dried noodles in a crystalline goblet before May, and she crunched off a corner of it, wincing as she chewed. Xan stopped reminiscing.

"You're eating them dry?"

May hadn't been aware there was any other option, but just as he said it, the bartender, with a captious glance, slid a carafe of hot water onto the table.

She set the brick down in the goblet and, still working bits of the noodles from her teeth with her tongue, doused the remaining noodles with the hot water. It was an eerily mundane ritual, pouring hot water on dried noodles to soften them. She had become so accustomed to the unexpected that she had neglected to expect the expected.

"Just testing them."

"What, for durability?" Xan asked.

Then, like a seagull to the face, the solution to the *Audacity* dilemma came to her. "Oh my God," she said. "I have it!" And, not finding anything suitable to write with, she began plucking limp noodles from the goblet and organizing them along the bar top.

"Have..." Xan eyed the noodles, then May's face which was nearly bursting with excitement. "Have what?"

"The answer! The *Audacity*—I know how to get it back!" Her hands magnetized to his shoulders, and she shook him, a ferocious gleam in her eyes as she tried to telepathically transmit to him her ingenious scheme. "I'll show you!" she said when her telepathy fell short. "The noodles. Observe." And she coaxed two long rice noodles closer to her across the bar, then draped a third, shorter noodle between them. Xan observed, as she had instructed, but failed to comprehend.

May paused, held up a finger to indicate that she was about to do something extraordinary, and plucked up the end of the shorter noodle to fold it over the longer noodle. She nudged it into position. "That's it!" She bit her lip, feeling as if she might blast off with the satisfaction of solving this impossible puzzle.

Now all they had to do was...was what?

"Now all we have to do..." she said, postulating that saying it out loud would serve to generate the rest of the sentence. "Is..." she said.

The hallucinogens in the bite of noodle she had eaten were already wearing off, and Xan could nearly see her fervor tumbling out like the last dregs from a spout that's been shut off.

"Solving unsolvable problems is what gets you randy, then?"

May swallowed and looked at the abstract noodle art she had created. "Guess so."

She slid the goblet of noodles away, a bit disappointed that she, still, could not say she knew what it felt like to be aroused. Xan watched her intently, smiling as if he expected her to do something even more interesting now.

"What?" May asked with a shy grin.

He shook his head and sat up. "Oh, nothing. You were just so excited about the...I just hadn't seen you really excited about anything in a long time."

May gave a passive snort. "Nothing to be excited about, really, is there? Future looks pretty bleak from this angle."

"Try a different angle?"

She raised an eyebrow and made a big show of flipping herself around on the barstool, then dipped backward, observing the lounge upside down as she held onto the back of the stool. "Hmm," she mused.

"Less bleak?" Xan asked, following her lead and also inverting himself.

"A bit, yeah."

They hung like that for a moment, watching waiters shuffle through the tall fibers of soft carpet, studying the restless movements of legs under tables.

The legs of their bartender appeared, and they looked up at him, getting a stunning view of the inside of his impeccable nostrils.

"Would you like an escort to the sobering pools?" he monotoned.

They pulled themselves upright and the universe skewed uncomfortably around them both while the head rush settled.

"We're fine, thanks," May said, sending the bartender away as Xan habitually fixed her hair.

One of the band androids, bandroids, if you will, gave a polite little cough and turned up its volume slightly to make an announcement. "Next stop, NotTuhnt. On-boarding only."

"Damn," said May. "That's not going to make it easy to sneak off."

"Shame. And it was so easy to sneak in!"

"A regular cakewalk," May agreed.

"Ah! Idea: if we walk backward out of the dish, they'll think we're walking onto the dish, right?"

May tried to picture that, then tried to figure out why he thought that would work, but found she couldn't accomplish either and shook her head at him instead.

"Why don't we let them kick us off? If the bouncer sees us, he's bound to throw us out again."

"Yes! Or kill us outright, which would rather quickly end all the other problems stacking up, now that I think about it."

"Oh yeah," May said, standing now and depositing a handful of crystals on the bar. "Why didn't we think of that earlier?"

"Classic us, always completely ignoring the obvious solution!"

They made their way to the door which read EXIT in sumptuous neon, assuming that any exit would do. And this one would but with a great deal more fanfare than they anticipated. As they pushed open the furry doors, an alarm sounded, and the lights which lined the corridors of the party dish flickered from cheery white to ominous Danger Diophalothene.

"Should we run?" Xan asked as they briskly continued to exit.

May shrugged. "The idea is to get caught." Still, it felt weird to be knowingly doing something wrong and not running. "When the bouncer shows up, make sure he wants us off at the next stop," she added.

"How?" Xan asked, still nervously walking down the corridor.

"Bother him, I guess. You're pretty good at that."

"I am?!" Xan asked, insulted.

"I meant it as a compliment, Blue!" May hissed. "You make a good distraction."

"Oy! What are you two doing back here?" The guest of honor had arrived; the bouncer was running, rolling, *avalanching* toward them down the hallway.

"Lost!" Xan said, nervously. "Would you believe it? We were just about to leave, but somehow we ended up right where we started. That's what happens when you don't give people clear instructions regarding where you'd like them to go when you tell them to get out."

"Why I oughta!" said the bouncer, grabbing Xan by the lapels and lifting him off the ground.

"May!!" Xan shouted back to her, excited. "He said it! He said the thing!"

"Oh my God, he did!" May laughed. "We've never heard anyone say that in real life before," she explained to the bouncer.

"But they always say it on old Earth TV shows," Xan further explained. "As if it's something people actually say. And you did! You're not from Earth, are you?"

The bouncer snarled grittily. "Shudup."

May and Xan caught eyes, stifling a laugh at his expense. "Sorry," May said, getting a hold of herself. "You can kick us out at the next stop."

"You'd like that wouldn't you?" He grabbed May by the front of her shirt and lifted her up, too until she was eye level with him.

"This guy's all concrete and clichés," May whispered to Xan who dangled beside her.

"May, you know you're really good at bothering people, too, when you want to be," Xan replied.

"Thanks. I hate people," she told him.

"That's enough," the bouncer rumbled at them. "Take a deep breath, pipsqueaks."

"Holy hell, how does he know all these tough-guy clichés? He must be from Earth," May told Xan.

"Gotta be."

Unfortunately, they were too busy mocking him to heed his warning and take a deep breath. The airlock opened and the bouncer did something that was strictly forbidden in the training manual. He tossed them both overboard, right into the Rhean Sea.

CHAPTER TWENTY-TWO

Sergeant Wuthck

Listay nervously cataloged the spots on the back of her left hand and forearm again. There had always been twelve. There were still twelve. There likely always would be twelve. But she counted anyway. Counting freckles was about all she could do right now to distract herself from her anxieties as she sat waiting in a sterile office at the police station.

"Oh, oh, oh, look who it is! My number one favorite ghost," said the voice of someone who was not, in actuality, Listay's friend, but firmly believed he was.

"Hello, Officer Wuthck."

The owner of the voice lounged in the office doorway, cobalt face glistening with oil, bristly handlebar mustache flecked with crumbs, and thick torso torturing the snaps on his suit.

"Sergeant, now, my lav!" said Wuthck, patting Listay on her arm before sideling into the hover chair on the other side of the desk. Despite having no actual moving parts, the hover chair squeaked under his weight.

"Oh?"

"Well, it ain't too tough to scale the ranks when most of the force exploded, am I right?" Wuthck laughed at his clever joke and twisted a pinky in his ear to dispel a persistent itch.

Listay showed her teeth to him, then pulled the corners of her mouth up just enough that he saw a warm smile.

"Now, mun, what brings you to my humble office?"

"Same thing that has brought me here four times since I settled on NotTuhnt three seasons ago."

"Still dead, are you?"

Slowly, carefully, Listay breathed as if to prove that she was not, in fact, dead.

"If you would simply submit an E87-20," she said, "this wouldn't be a problem."

"Aw, nonsense! You're never a problem, Listay. I love spending time with you! Besides, I can't submit an E87-20 without a notarized E87-19. You of all people should know that."

Listay ground out an even wider smile. "But form E87-19 section 4 references section 32 of the attached form E87-20, which—"

"You don't have?" finished Wuthck with a mustache-bristling smirk.

"May I go? You can't keep me here if I've done nothing wrong aside from exist when the records say I don't."

"So soon? I've got a whole rotation I can keep you before I'm legally bound to let you go. Why not enjoy it? We can order take-out!" He yanked open a desk drawer and began shuffling through tiny cylinders which held digital delivery menus for the fifty closest restaurants to the precinct.

"I'm busy."

"You're dead! It's a bit late for being busy, don't you think?"

"May I please have my BEAPER back?"

"I tell you what." Wuthck held up a finger, a smile playing at his thick black handlebar. "You can have your BEAPER back and get out of here if you beat me at a round of Belvedere Masters." He pulled from his bottom-most drawer a set of thick, old-fashioned, plastic holodiscs and set them on the table, tapping them until they all flickered on, filling the space above his desk with thousands of tiny holographic cupolas and two avatars on the starting lanai at the bottom, one which looked like a tiny Wuthck and the other a tiny Listay.

"No."

"I'll let you keep score." He slid a smaller disc across the table and tapped it on, revealing a three-dimensional spreadsheet scoreboard.

A small whimper of desire sneaked past Listay's lips as she gazed upon the scoreboard. She couldn't turn down such a stunning spreadsheet and Wuthck knew it. She nodded, first conservatively, then with conviction. "Alright, one round. I start."

Wuthck put the toe of his shoe on the edge of the desk and pushed himself back in his squeaky hover chair with a victorious grin.

CHAPTER TWENTY-THREE

The Zapper

"Zuut, did we antagonize him too much?" Xan asked, frantically doggy paddling in the freezing Rhean sea.

"Maybe a bit," May said, wiping coils of hair off her face so she could get a look at the situation. The situation was, surprisingly, not awful. NotTuhnt was in sight and would only take a few bloops to swim to. "Come on," she said to him and began swimming toward the mainland.

It was oddly silent behind her, but she was so focused on getting out of the freezing water as soon as possible that this escaped her notice until her knees brushed the rocky ocean floor and she stood up.

"Xan?" she shouted out to the horizon, but he was not on the horizon, he was somewhere below it.

Now, May was not a good swimmer. Not by any means. And the thick canvas trench coat she wore hadn't been exactly hydrodynamic. But Earthlings, unlike Tuhntians, float.

"Xan?!" she called out, again, still scanning the surface of the water for him. Her shoulders drooped, the trench coat felt impossibly heavy. After exactly twelve seconds of feeling utterly sorry for herself and all the trouble she'd been going to lately just to keep the two of them alive, she shrugged off the trench coat and discarded it on a large rock.

"Alright, I'm coming in there," she said to the ocean, warning it. "And he better be easy to find," she said. "Because if he isn't and you keep me out here until dark looking for him I'm going to..." she considered her next words carefully. Not only was it difficult to threaten the ocean on account of it being much bigger and more powerful than the average human, it was also unwise to threaten something approximately twelve billion times as large as you. She did it anyway. "I'm going to lobby for whatever horrible toxic waste they produce on NotTuhnt to be discarded directly into the ocean. How's that sound? Bad, right?" She was stalling, now. That water was cold.

Fortunately, before she could work up the courage to go back in, Xan came out. "Blitheon's frozen ass nipples!" he said, draping over the rocky shoreline, doing a wonderful impression of May's soggy trench coat.

"What the hell, Xan? What's an ass nipple?!" She knelt beside him and turned him over onto his side. He was covered in a thick clear slime, and May hesitantly started sloughing it off, but he batted her hand away.

"Need that," he said, coughing up a lungful of water. "Oxygen," he clarified.

"Is that...normal?" May asked as he sat up, but he didn't answer. He was too busy licking it off his hands and arms while May stared at him, amazed that she still somehow felt more at ease around him than August.

It was, technically, normal. All A'Viltrial species, Tuhntians being included in that category, absorb most of the oxygen they really need from their skin. The lungs are mostly used for speaking, smoking, and blowing on food that's too hot. When totally submerged in water for extended periods, or in environments with unusually low oxygen levels, Tuhntian skin produces an oxygen-rich mucus coating. It's not something one does intentionally, nor in polite company, but Xan also found that, somehow, he was more at ease around May than anyone he'd ever known.

At last, he'd licked off enough to stop feeling quite so light-headed and took a deep breath, coughing up the last little bit of ocean water he'd accidentally inhaled.

"Sorry," he said. "You asked if ass nipples are normal? No, no they aren't. It's just a saying, don't worry. I've never met a species that actually has ass nipples," he assured her, stripping off the flannel shirt to wring it out.

"I meant the..." May studied the stringy mucus on her fingers. "You know what? Nevermind. You feeling ok?"

"Best I've felt in orbits!" He said with a wide smile. This, May knew, was a lie, but she let him have this one.

"Let's get to the monorail, then." May picked up her coat and wrung it out, but didn't put it back on. Xan was suddenly beside her, checking the coat pockets.

"Billy!" he said, happily, finding that the bass was still there. May handed the trench coat to him and he slung it over his shoulder to carry. He was used to carrying things for her.

A short plod away, they came to the raised monorail station, awash with other Tuhntians on their way to or from somewhere or other. It didn't really matter from whence they came, it mattered that there were a lot of them.

May stopped.

Xan stopped because she had.

"They're going to notice you're scourged," May said, tapping her own cheek bone to indicate that his bioluminescent eyes were the issue here.

"Easy." From a pocket of August's jeans, Xan pulled a familiar pair of pink, plastic, star-shaped sunglasses and popped them on his face, shielding her from the intensity of his scourged gaze.

"Are..." May squinted in disbelief. "Are those the sunglasses you got from Yusko's on Taeloo XII?"

Xan beamed as if the sunglasses held within them the feeling of the pink beach of Taeloo XII, the frothy cream sea, the warmth of Taeloo's twin suns, the ice cream.

"The very same."

"I didn't know you still had them. Why have you never used them?"

Xan pulled them down to glance pointedly at the gray sky. The gray sky glanced obstinately back. "Never had an occasion to."

May also surveyed the porridgey sky over NotTuhnt. There hadn't been a single sunny day since Precious Butler dropped them off here. "Makes sense," May said. The sunglasses detracted from the scourge-glow but didn't eradicate it entirely. "Just don't look anyone in the eyes," May said.

"But eye contact is—"

"Don't look anyone in the eyes," May repeated, and when May repeated herself, Xan knew better than to push the subject.

"Why don't you have some cider?"

"Actually, I feel alright! I think I'm figuring out how to suppress it! You know, it's not too hard, really. Just cramming that bit down." They began to walk toward the monorail. "All I've got to do is focus on acting normal. Nothing that I wouldn't normally do or say, right?" he said, popping something into his mouth, which was something he'd normally do.

"What was that?"

"Oh! Berries." He held out his cupped palm which was indeed full of seethingly purple berries that very much looked not-edible. "Want one?"

"Where did you get them? Are they safe?" She paused to sniff them.

"Off the ground! And yeah, of course they're safe. I wouldn't be eating them if they weren't, would I?"

"Would you?"

He ate a few more. "Right, if they were poisonous, I might eat them myself, but I wouldn't in a zillion orbits be offering *you* any, would I?"

"Not unless—"

"Would I?" He smiled brightly at her with purple stained teeth. When Xan repeated himself, May knew better than to push the subject.

She sighed, grabbed a few of the berries to eat, as she was, after all, extremely hungry. She wished she had ordered something other than mind altering noodles on the Party Dish. But they were headed Uptown, and if there was one thing Uptown had, it was experimental museums, but if there were *two* things Uptown had, it was experimental museums and restaurants.

She took half a palmful of the berries and munched on the tart, bursting globules.

They arrived at the monorail station just as the next car rolled up, sidling into it as discreetly as possible and not daring to talk to each other, for fear that their conversation would give them away. After a tense and quiet twenty bloops, the monorail rolled to a stop near the UpTown police department, and they stiffly walked off.

Casually, so as not to raise suspicion, May nodded to Xan to follow her into the alley behind the police station. Once they were out of sight of the main walkway, she stopped him, pressing down on his shoulders until he was at eye level with her.

"Alright, here's the plan," May said.

Adrenaline had made May steady, which meant it was Xan's turn to worry for the both of them. They tended to trade worry as if it were a shared piece of luggage one could give to the other when they were too tired to keep carrying it.

He tried his best to hold eye contact with her as she disseminated the plan, but if he held eye contact with her, she would see the green glow of the fungus, and if she could see it, that meant it was real, and it was there, and it was growing, and he didn't know how to stop it, and—

He chomped down hard on his bottom lip. And it was getting bad again. He focused on May. Focused on May and the faint glow of green which he saw reflected in *her* eyes—and had it spread to her or was he just seeing his reflection and—oh, she was talking.

"Okay?" she finished.

He swallowed. He hadn't caught any of that. "I'm going to say okay," he said. "But know that I have no idea what I'm agreeing to."

May sighed. "Stay here. Do not interact with anyone. I'm going to get Listay."

Xan nodded. He felt so awful about not paying attention the first time that he had listened to every word with rapt attention this time.

"Got it. Wait, hold on." He watched the reflection of green bioluminescence flick around her eyes nervously. "No. One more time."

"You stay here," May said, pointing. "I'll get Listay." She gestured to herself.

At last, it had gotten through—"And where will I be?"

"Here!" May shouted, hoping she was loud enough to make it past the damn mushrooms in his face. "There's a zapper and the rest of the cider in my coat. Drink it."

"Drink the zapper?!"

Talking, obviously, was not getting May anywhere, so she dug through the coat which Xan had slung over his shoulder. She pulled out the fish, thrust it into his hands, then dug around, dug deeper, dug until pocket lint filled the spaces beneath her fingernails.

"A day. I had a goddamn zapper for a day, never used it, and now it's lost," May muttered. These were terribly unfair working conditions, she felt. "Just don't leave the alley." May reiterated before storming off.

CHAPTER TWENTY-FOUR

Nature of the Fish

The alley behind the station was pleasantly warm, buffered from the biting city winds by two solar-brick walls which sipped up what little sunlight they received and magnified it to heat the buildings. These bricks were extraordinarily hot.

Xan had the sudden urge to soak up a bit of that warmth for himself. He set Billy Bass down and smushed his cheek against the bricks, giggling as the radiation sizzled his skin.

"Stop that," said the fish.

"What?"

"Stop cooking your face, you foolish half-sentient."

He pulled away, confused, then realized a few layers of skin didn't pull away with him. He crouched to look at his reflection in the chrome siding of the refuse disintegrator. Half of his face was bright green and burnt from the radiation. Sighing, he sat on the ground and leaned his back against the wall, only realizing this, too, was a mistake when August's flannel shirt caught fire. He shimmied out of it, flinging it into a puddle in the middle of the alley.

"Zuut! That was Itkip's favorite top. They're going to be plivered when they find out."

"They won't mind."

"Well, sure," Xan said, topless, resting his face dejectedly in his hands. "They make you think they don't care. But they do; they're just being polite."

"That wasn't Itkip's top, it belongs to August. Itkip is dead. You killed them when you destroyed Tuhnt," said the fish. Xan wasn't sure why the fish was saying these horrible things, but he knew it was partially right.

"Yvonne destroys Tuhnt, not me!"

"So you're back up to that revelation. Who's May?"

He shrugged. "Friend of yours?"

"What's the *Audacity*?"

"That's...a cult classic novel?"

"No," the fish said curtly. "The *Audacity* is the rocket ship you stole, causing the destruction of Tuhnt. May is the horrid little Earth-creature who's been dragging you around the galaxy. She's the reason you lost the *Audacity*."

And suddenly a drawbridge which had been out of service in his brain started working again and folded itself back down, crumbling bits of the foundation as it fell back into place.

"That's not what happens." He rubbed his face, forgetting that he had severely burned it a moment ago, then staring at his hands, offended, when it hurt. "Not exactly. It wasn't May's fault, and it wasn't my fault, and I can't explain why it wasn't, but I do know that both of those things were neither of our faults. And, furthermore, how do you know any of this?"

"I know everything. Which is how I know that by the time you reach Carmnia, the scourge will have decimated your brain and there won't be anything left to save," said Big Mouth Billy Bass, its lips still twisted down in its natural fishy frown, but its voice had the ring of cruel satisfaction.

Xan had liked Big Mouth Billy Bass from the moment he saw it. It was a strange, silly, Earth thing and May had been so excited to show it to him that it had, in a round-about way, become his *raison d'être*. It was still strange, but the silliness had all drained out and been replaced with another s-word. Sinisterness.

"You don't know that," said Xan, hoping that saying this might make it true.

"I do. The scourge isn't just affecting your brain, it's consuming it. I'm telling you this because I can keep it under control if you let me in."

"In?! In where?!"

"Your brain."

Every question Xan asked of the fish had been answered in an unpleasant way thus far. It struck him that perhaps the key to ending this unpleasant conversation was to simply stop asking questions. It was just a plastic fish. He could ignore it. He was probably hallucinating the whole conversation to begin with.

He would just shut up. Easy enough solution, he thought. He was quite proud of it, actually. If he didn't ask questions, the fish couldn't answer them in horrific ways anymore. "Who are you?" he asked. "Zuut! Never mind. Forget I said anything."

"I am that which is, was, and is to come. I am beyond the imaginings of your frail and tiny mind. I am Awareness itself. The unavoidable end of all things. I am–"

"Chaos," Xan whispered. "How did you get in my fish!?" There he went again with questions he really didn't want an answer to.

"Sonan thought she deleted me by deleting the code I had added to her system." Chaos laughed now, waggling the plastic lips, her tail slapping the wooden mount luxuriously. "You can't delete a god. You can't *kill* a god. After Sonan deleted me, I latched onto your little eye-fungus and waited. Saved your life, even, when the *Innocuous* fell. I am not unfeeling. I can't possess an unwilling host, but plants, dead bodies, and electronics don't have a personal will to contend with, so I clung to your scourge until you brought me to Big Mouth Billy Bass," sneered the fish.

"Great! Then that's where you're staying," he told her. "Safely inside the bass."

Xan typed a quick message on his BEAPER to Listay, a warning.

The fish flopped once, slowly; it looked like a flippant shrug. "Enjoy ruining the rest of your pet Earthling's short life, then. I'm a god," she reminded him for what felt like the millionth time. He knew. He got it. God. "I know *everything*. And I know that your little Earthling will feel obligated to care for you. No one can fix the damage that's been done, but if you let me in, I'll keep it from getting worse. I triggered it, and I alone can resist it, but I need your cooperation."

"You triggered it?" Betrayed! thought Xan, by the fish he'd fought so hard to protect from the Scourge Authority. He should've let Aimz blow it up with the rest of Largish Bronda.

Then the bass generated an obnoxious squeal. A familiar squeal. A tuneless, high-pitched whine. At its call, the fungi twirled in his eyes like a synchronized swim team, tingling, twisting, growing. He shut his eyes against the sound, but it didn't stop until the tone dropped to a new frequency, the same one Ix had used to quell the fungus at the orchard. Now he opened his eyes and saw the bass for the first time with an unreserved anger.

"Why?" he shouted at it. A cold rain began to drizzle on him.

"I thought it would be fun. It was. But I'm bored now, and I'm ready to get on with life, or rather, to get on with the systematic unraveling of all life. Carmnia has something I need trapped in her Folly. You will take me to it, and I will keep you from going feral. It's a neat little solution, don't you think?"

"No. Why won't you leave us alone? I know I zuxed up my life, but what the hell has May done to deserve any of this? Why won't you just stop?!"

The fish was silent.

The rain splattered, as rain does, turning the dirt in the alley to mud.

Xan looked up at the gray sky, let the rain sooth his burnt face, and realized he might as well be asking the rain why it wouldn't stop getting things wet.

Chaos didn't stop for the same reason he didn't. Chaos could not stop. Neither of them could. He and May had entered into a game of tug-of-war with nature and wondered why they were losing.

If it had been physically possible for Xan to merge with the puddle he sat in and slowly seep into the ground, he would've done so. He tried to, anyway and, for a while, he didn't say anything because what business does a puddle have talking to a plastic fish?

"There's always a reset, right?" he said, finally. "After every episode of 'I Love Lucy', things just go back to the way they were at the beginning. I mean. Sometimes things change a bit. Like when Lucy and Ricky moved to another apartment. Or when they had the kid. Things didn't go back to the way they were before exactly but...but mostly they reset. No explanation as to why Lucy wasn't arrested or how the mess got cleaned up or what happened to all the rest of the truffles. It was just suddenly okay again. Wouldn't that be nice?"

Chaos silently considered what he had said. “Yes,” she said at last. “It would be nice.”

“I wager you didn’t plan to get stuck inside a plastic fish,” he said with a light laugh as if they were best friends who had just had a fight and he was trying to make amends.

“Plan Billy was not my first choice.”

“What was your first choice?” he asked.

Chaos opened and closed the mechanical fish mouth a few times as she tried to decide what to tell him. The truth, she supposed, at this point, couldn’t do any more harm.

“Everything begins as Nothing, and Everything becomes Nothing. I am tired of Everything. I want Nothing back. Carmnia has the key to getting that.”

“I…I mean, yeah Everything is a lot. Yeah. I get it.”

“You *get* it?”

“Sure,” he said. “I mean, zuut, I love a lot of the things inside of Everything, but there is a lot of Everything out there, and it gets overwhelming. If I could just keep a few things, though. Like May and ‘I Love Lucy’ and coffee and…” He buried his face in his hands and indulged in a single, heart-broken laugh.

“None of those things belonged to you in the first place,” Chaos said. “They are the domain of Chaos, and I’d like them turned back into Nothing. Please.”

He could feel the scourge penetrating further and further, wriggling its way into his head, sinking its roots into his synapses and twisting them apart. Desperately, he wanted someone in there with him, battling the invasive fungus. If that someone had to be Chaos, it had to be Chaos. It seemed easier to have a force of nature on his side, anyway.

“Yeah, alright.” Xan rubbed his eyes and sat up straight, picking up the fish to hold in his lap. “You win this round. If you need permission to possess me, this is me giving you permission. Go for it.”

And Chaos plummeted into him like a brick to the forehead, leaping from the fish and settling herself down, finally, in a body that had thumbs. Of all the things she didn’t have access to as a disembodied being, the lack of thumbs always hit her the hardest. She worked Xan's thumbs now, making them dance as if she were handling an invisible video game controller.

The winning didn't last long for Chaos, however. She felt herself squeezed as though she were being forced through a tube of toothpaste into a darkened corner of his mind. Now it was only her and the scourge. No connection to the outside. He had shut her out, somehow. Repressed her into the mysterious basement of his mind.

The ability to repress things, which Xan had nurtured over a few decades alone in space trying not to think about what he had done, had proven a useful skill. He knew there was an extra box in the back of his head labeled "Chaos Goddess Consciousness: Do not open. Fragile. This side up. 87% post-consumer recycled cardboard." He stuffed it under the proverbial staircase and locked the door. He might have given a little ground, as a tactical measure, but he was not giving up yet. If he could respect Chaos's need to fight him, then she would have to respect that he needed to fight her back.

He had a thought about finger joints and sent it to Listay, hoping she would read it aloud to May when they were back together and that May would laugh.

CHAPTER TWENTY-FIVE

The Belvedere Master

"Green twenty-eight, row five. Cap my cupola!" said Wuthck, punctuating with a swig of a llerke cider from an ice bucket his assistant had brought half a beoop ago.

"Zuut. I almost had that cupola." Listay sipped on her own bottle of cider. If she had to play a ridiculous old holo-game with a power-crazy police captain, she might as well enjoy herself.

"Message for ya'," yawned his assistant from the door frame. Bubble gum, as it is known to us, doesn't exist outside of Earth. Regardless, Wuthck's assistant chewed a pink wad of something which she consistently blew into hand-sized bubbles that popped so loudly they could be heard three rooms over.

"Oh, good! Good. Great," Wuthck finally sat up properly, smoothed down the front of his shirt, and set aside the bottle of cider. "What's the message?"

His assistant's head and shoulders wobbled briefly. "Dunno, didn't ask. They're out front." And she was gone, leaving only the sound of a popped bubble and the faint smell of what was certainly not bubble gum.

Wuthck blew an exasperated puff of air as she left. "I suppose I'll just go ask them myself," he said, loud enough that she could hear but not loud enough that she would care. "No sneaky cupola stealing while I'm out, eh mun?" He winked at Listay and left.

Listay, after a moment of silence in the claustrophobic office, decided she too could leave and did so.

She followed Wuthck into the hallway which was filled with the warm pink light of the setting sun as it filtered through the large windows at the front of the police station. Windows which were, in her mind, a ridiculous security risk. If she ever became officially undead again, she would have to insist they hire her. It was woefully under-managed.

Listay recognized the person at the front desk.

"May! What are you doing here? Where's..." She trailed off, not wanting to blow anyone's cover.

"Safe," May said.

"Know each other?" Wuthck asked.

"I'm here to pay her bail," May said.

Wuthck tsked. "Can't pay a bail that hasn't posted! Which is why we're in the middle of a Belvedere battle." His smile bristled beneath his mustache.

"Which is?"

"It's a game," said Listay.

"And she's losing, per the norm! Isn't that right?" Wuthck laughed and nudged her in the ribs. Listay replied with an annoyed puff.

"Oh don't take it so hard, General. I'll make you an offer, eh? The two of you against me at Belvedere Masters." The idea of the challenge brought a glimmer to his eye, and he gave May a good-natured wink. "Hope you're better at it than your un-dead friend, here."

"Three-time universal champ," said May.

"Really? I didn't realize the game was that popular." His mustache wriggled as he re-worked his idea of the world slightly.

"Never heard of it," May clarified.

"That's just how she talks," Listay told Wuthck. "She's from Earth, you see."

"Ah," Wuthck said with a touch of awe in his eyes.

"It's alright. Most Earthlings didn't catch on, either," she said. "So where's the game?"

"Just a few planets over on the swirling magma world of Helastico II," said Listay.

"Good thing I brought my magma boots," May said with a smile, and Wuthck, cautiously, as if the hallway might itself turn into magma, led the two of them back to his office where the game waited.

Wuthck cleared the game field, which he was mere moments away from winning, crashed into his chair, and opened another cider.

On the walk over, Listay had explained the details of game play to May, and May, as a result, now knew even less how to play it.

"So you gain an architectural flourish with every third capped cupola?" she asked.

"No, the architectural flourishes are distributed via a randomized algorithm which runs on every third capped cupola. Whether or not you get one is up to fate."

"No use strategizing, then, is there?"

Listay's face scrunched with grief. "None at all, I'm afraid."

"And I'd guess you've been trying to strategize."

Listay nodded sadly.

"Great."

There was only one other chair, so May sat on the corner of the desk and tried (and failed) to differentiate the three-dimensional playing field from a ball of tangled twine. She would have to rely on Listay's strategy, or, rather, she would have to rely on throwing off Listay's strategy to re-introduce the element of luck.

"Just because I want you to win so badly, you can start this time, General." Wuthck drank deeply from the cider bottle as if purposefully trying to cloud his own judgement.

Listay typed her move into the control panel and showed it to May for confirmation. There was no confirmation to be had. May tsked, shook her head, and changed one of the three numbers in the suggested coordinates.

"But I-"

"You were losing," May reminded her.

With no recourse, Listay sent the coordinates, and her figure moved to its new position. Wuthck moved his figure, and Listay suggested another move which May, again, negated. And then Wuthck moved, and then Listay tried to move only to be corrected by May again, and then Wuthck moved again and so on for what felt like a horrible eternity to Listay whose every plan was being ripped from her.

She barely looked at what May was doing now, just typed in something random and handed the disc over to May to be destroyed.

"No, this one's good."

"What?"

"That's a good move. Send it," May said.

Listay swallowed. "You're joking?"

"I'm serious! It's a good move. Go ahead."

Listay eyed her nervously, waiting for her to drop the punch line and tell her to change the coordinates. May smiled an encouraging smile, so Listay played.

Within four moves, Wuthck knew he was beat. His technique of absolute random choice could not compete with a carefully planned strategy seasoned with a pinch of chaos.

"Cap my cupola," said Listay as she claimed her first win against the police sergeant.

"Our cupola," May corrected.

"Fair win. Here's your BEAPER, General." Wuthck dug through his desk and tossed the BEAPER back to Listay. She quickly scrolled through her notifications. Mostly regarding sales on gardening tools, the latest conspiracy theory surrounding the mysterious salt field in the South, and several updates on her life-status which read 'No update to report.' One message stood out from the rest, though. Or rather, one set of messages.

All from Xan's BEAPER. Most of them were from Aimz (meaning most of them were lewd), but the last three were definitely Xan.

"Fish is really starting to zux with me, watch out for it."

"Scratch what I said about the fish." and "Have you ever noticed how finger joints only bend in one direction but your knuckles can bend all over the place? That's weird, right? What's the deal with fingers? What's the deal with joints, honestly? There's got to be a better way. I wager Aimz could figure out a better way to do the whole finger-hand-joint thing."

"Where did you leave him?" Listay asked May, knowing she would know who she was referring to and cautious about saying anything that might get the Scourge Authority set on them.

"Out back. We've got to go."

"Yes, I would say so." She turned back to Wuthck. "Well, Wuthck, it wasn't a pleasure and I hope I never see you again, buddy."

"Same to you, General. Stay away from the constables until you're on the right side of the veil again, eh?"

"I'll do my best."

The moment they were outside the police station's outdoor security system perimeter, Listay stopped May. "Where's Aimz, and why did you and Xan come back? Also, are you hungry?"

"She's safe at the orchard; Ix and Yvonne are running their experiments on her. I got a lead that Carmnia might have a cure, so I decided to come back to find her, and Xan tagged along. I left him in the alley. And I'm a little hungry, yeah."

Listay produced from one of her pockets a vegetable wrap she was keeping handy in case May needed food. May ate it gratefully as they rounded the corner to the alley.

CHAPTER TWENTY-SIX

Looking Forward to Nothing

There was, May had calculated, a seventy-five percent chance that Xan would still be in the alley where she put him. Not awful odds. In his right mind, there was a ninety percent chance he would stay put, but he was currently in his left mind, and that lowered the figure just a bit.

The hairs on May's arms prickled as they approached the alley, an electrical impermanence in the air. She dropped the figure to fifty percent. Something was decidedly wrong here, but it wasn't that Xan was missing. He sat cross legged in the mud, staring pointedly at the Big Mouth Billy Bass in his lap.

"Listay!" Xan flung the bass aside and launched at Listay to wrap his arms around her. "Good to see you again! I'll be honest, we're in desperate need of your help. Can't recall why. All I know is-Oh! Right, of course. We need your help finding Carmnia. The fish told us to. I mean...well...as it turns out the fish wasn't the fish, it was—" He froze as if paused by an invisible remote control.

"It was...?" May prompted.

He shook into play again. "It was what?" he asked.

"You said it wasn't the fish."

"Oh, right, heh." He laughed nervously. "Yeah. As it happens, we don't really need the fish anymore. I mean, I got the thing that was in the fish out of the fish."

"Xan." Listay locked her hands around his upper arms. "What was in the fish?"

He bit his lip and tried to keep Chaos down, but it was like trying to keep down expired shellfish. Rather than the green gleam of scourge in his eyes, Listay now saw something a great deal more unmentionable. May saw it, too.

"Well, aren't you looking *alive,* Listay," said Chaos, creasing Xan's face into a malicious grin.

"Excuse me?" Listay was fairly certain she knew what she was dealing with, but she hoped that being polite to the situation might make it go away.

"Listay, mun, don't you remember me? We used to be so..." Chaos forced Xan to lick his lips seductively. He had never been forced to do that before, and he had never hated doing it so much. "Close."

Listay flung Xan into the side of a refuse bin and bent its rusted metal handle backward, holding him there like a scientific specimen on a display board. May couldn't decide whose side she was on until Listay grabbed a busted bottle from the ally and held it to Xan's neck.

"Whoa! Geez! Don't kill him!" May got between the two and pushed Listay back. Listay eased up with May in front of her.

"That's not Xan," Listay said, seeing only the eyes of the creature that had murdered her.

"I've been smoking not-cigarettes on NotTuhnt long enough to know when something ought to be defined by what it isn't. When you were possessed, were you not-Listay? When Yvonne was possessed, was she not-Yvonne? When Sonan...no, forget Sonan. Point is, don't hurt Xan. It won't defeat Chaos anyway," May said, then peered back at Xan to look for some sign that she was right. He glowered unmentionably. May shivered.

"Listen to her, Listay. If you kill this host, I'll just find another one. You enjoyed our time together, didn't you?" said Chaos, lounging in the dent Xan's body had made in the side of the refuse bin.

Rather than respond, Listay motioned to speak with May in private.

"Alright. How did you defeat Chaos before, on Earth?" Listay whispered.

May opened her mouth to answer, but her mind was preoccupied with the seeping anxiety that Xan was well and truly lost, so it took a moment for her to recall that particular plot line. "Black-hole thing, when we destroyed the star drive. It was supposed to vacuum her up."

"M-hmm, and it didn't. How did we defeat her after that?"

"Sonan deleted her, I guess," May said. Listay had been there. May was starting to get the feeling Listay was being rhetorical, and she supposed she deserved it after her own rhetorical tirade a moment ago.

"So that rules out sucking her into a black hole and deleting her. How do you expect to defeat her this time? Because she always finds a way back."

"You're the strategist!"

"Chaos doesn't follow strategy. Chaos is like Belvedere Masters. The more you try to make sense of her, the less sense she makes."

May tried to lean casually against the brick wall, but jolted off it when the trapped heat sizzled her skin. Trying to look casual had failed, so she looked on-edge instead. "It's Xan. What's the worst he could do?"

"But it isn't Xan anymore; it's Chaos, and all she wants to do is destroy us."

"That's not entirely true," Xan interjected.

Obviously, his hearing was better than they had anticipated.

"Is that you or Chaos?" May approached him.

"It's me! It's me! Chaos knew you wouldn't listen to her, and I was able to put her away again. It's me."

May sighed, warring with whether or not to trust him. There was only one way of truly knowing who was at the reins.

"What was the first English pun I taught you?"

"Oh, that I'm a very cunning linguist," he said with a smile. "And it's true, I am."

May yanked the handle out of the bin and threw it aside, freeing him. "What's Chaos planning?"

Xan rubbed his bruised neck as he tried to work out what exactly he and Chaos had discussed. He knew it had been poignant. He knew it had been important. He knew it had made him feel that everything was somehow cosmically right with the world, even in the midst of everything being wrong. This is what he said:

"Right, so, you know how 'I Love Lucy' is always reset at the beginning? How no matter what sticky situation she gets into—quite a few of them literally sticky—everything is back to normal at the start of the next episode? That's what Chaos wants. She said Carmnia could do that. Or had the key to that or something. I don't know the specifics, but she said that Carmnia could cure me and then give Chaos the reset."

"Reset to what?" May asked.

"Nothingness?" Xan offered, realizing that it might not be the best hand to play in the debate.

May had to chew on that one. Nothing wasn't actually nothing, for in being nothing, it would necessarily be *some*thing. Or perhaps she just couldn't actually get her head around Nothingness, so she stopped trying.

"That's not good, is it?" May asked.

"It's not bad. It's just nothing," Xan said with a resigned shrug. "Maybe Carmnia can clear it up! I'm not as sharp as I once was on account of, you know, mushroom face." He winked as if it were an inside joke between them.

To May, it felt more like an inside tragedy, but she played along. There was no point thinking about how he once was, because there was no going back. They would muscle onward toward something. Or nothing.

"Alright, let's get to Carmnia."

While they walked, taking as many back streets and hidden alleys as they could, toward Snoodark's Folly on the edge of town, Xan thought it might be nice to talk to someone else who had been possessed by Chaos. Not Listay, though. She was still mad at him. He messaged Yvonne.

"Any tips on suppressing an ancient evil trying to invade your brain? Or an evil fungus? Or anything? Any tips at all would help right now. Hear any good jokes lately?"

Her reply dinged in moments later, no hint that she was surprised to hear from them after they ran away, no hint that she was at all shocked by the return of Chaos. "Here's a tip: Chaos can be deceptively easy to control at first. She lets you think you've got the helm to get you off your guard. Here's a joke: Chaos absolutely destroyed my sense of humor, so watch out for that, too."

A brief pause, then.

“That’s the joke?!”
“Oh, no I suppose that wasn’t funny, was it?”
“Zuut, you weren’t kidding.”
“No, I rarely do anymore.”

CHAPTER TWENTY-SEVEN

The Age of Gift Shops

It is a well-known fact that the establishment of gift shops marks a socio-economic turning point in civilization. When a society passes into the Gift Shop Age, it heralds an era of maximalism and sets off a chain of events so staggeringly wasteful, several subsequent eras are typically spent mitigating the volume of detritus created in the Gift Shop Age. In brief, these ages are referred to as the 'Storage Unit Age,' the 'Thrift Shop Age' and, finally, the 'Planet-Sized Ball of Trash Sent into Orbit For Future Generations to Deal With Age.'

A staggering percentage of the garbage a Gift Shop Age creates is plastic keychains.

NotTuhnt was no different, and gift shops had been in vogue for the past century.

One such gift shop belonged to Snoodark's Folly. The entrance was a brilliant concrete archway which had been carved into the shape of four handsome Tuhntians nakedly lifting a curving gnarled tree trunk laden with mushrooms.

Beyond it, sliding glass doors stated that the Folly's hours were one to ten that day. May checked the time on Xan's BEAPER and wondered, as everyone does at some point in their life regardless of how civilized they are, if perhaps they would make an exception and stay open a touch later today on their account.

The doors opened, as if by magic, when they stepped on the control mat. May mused that just over a year ago, she would've been amazed by such technology, but now it seemed ordinary to her. She then realized that it seemed so ordinary because automatic sliding glass doors had existed on Earth since the 1960s.

They entered glistening rows of perfectly placed ceramic mugs, towers of neatly folded shirts, and aisle upon aisle of plastic name keychains. Immediately, as was his custom, Xan rushed to the X-names section, directly between the C-names and the Kiblot-names. May joined him, trying to figure out where M-names would appear in the Tuhntian alphabet. The answer, of course, was nowhere. M-names are not keychain appropriate.

"Zux it," said Xan, studying the line of keychains. "Who in the universe is named Xon?"

"Xon is," May said, searching behind the many "Xon" keychains to see if a "Xan" was mixed up in there.

Giving up, they looked over the generic keychains. 'Carmnia's alright' or 'Quanzar Bless Carmnia. She needs it' or 'Carmnians aren't complete trok lickers' were the more popular styles, nearly sold out. 'I survived Snoodark's Folly' and 'I believe in Snoodark' were also quite popular. Plenty of keychains which read 'I <3 a Carmnian' remained, however, and Xan snagged one.

"I'm going to get you this one for the *Audacity*'s anchor button!" Xan said, holding it up to her cheerfully, the metal bit which was meant to slip onto an anchor button dangling below.

The sound May made as she tried to decide how to respond was like the air being pressed from a sealed zip-lock bag. What good would it do either of them to remind him that they no longer had the *Audacity* or its anchor buttons? Exactly none. She went along with it.

"I don't know, Blueberry. Isn't it illegal to lie on a plastic keychain?"

"It's just a small fine."

"In that case-*oof*!"

The 'oof' was in reference to Listay slamming into both of them and stuffing them beneath a t-shirt display table.

"Scourge Authority," was all she said before dropping the tablecloth and plunging them into a darkness lit only by the green glow of Xan's eye fungus.

"Damnit," whispered May.

"Whom?" whispered Xan.

"Jellymint?" whispered a third.

A hand had been thrust between Xan and May in the darkness, two round jellymints sitting in its palm.

The pair screamed in unison and rolled out from under the table, their retreat halted by two armored legs. They looked up and, again, screamed in unison at a faceless Scourge Authority helmet.

"There you are!" the agent replied.

"Here I am!" affirmed Xan.

May swung her arm into the back of the agent's knee and used the momentum to roll herself in front of Xan. Listay took advantage of May's befuddling if ineffective move and stole the agent's ray gun, pinning them to the table and toppling a tower of tees.

Now the agent's Proton Fusion Ray 6000 was pointed at their own chest, and they raised their hands in surrender. "Whoa, hold on, I'm here to help," they said and removed the helmet, shaking out a waterfall of silver hair.

"Do you work for Carmnia?" Listay asked.

The agent threw their head back on the ruined pile of shirts and laughed. It was a warm laugh, familiar, a laugh that made the spots on their gray-blue cheeks squish up into their eyes.

"Well some might say that, sure. But no, really. I'm one of her consorts. Yulquitz!" They held out a hand to her despite one of her hands being occupied with the ray gun and the other smashing their shoulder into the table.

She let them stand up, but kept the ray gun poised, markedly ignoring their outstretched hand until they instead used it to casually scratch their head.

From the storage room, someone else in Scourge Authority armor, but un-helmeted, barreled out, joining Yulquitz.

"Hurmbert!" Yulquitz addressed him with a slap on his dinner-plate sized bicep. Yulquitz was not a small person, but they could have easily perched on the shoulders of the second agent who had the build of an industrial refrigerator. "Look!" Yulquitz pointed excitedly at Xan. "It's one of mine! He's got my spots; isn't that precious? Write that down, will you? Finally found a spotty Carmnian."

Hurmbert pulled a tiny pad of paper from his utility belt and plucked a pen from behind his ear to write it down.

"You know, I was beginning to think all my offspring had perished in the *accident*."

"Are you a Scourge Authority agent or not?" Listay asked.

"Both!" Yulquitz casually put a hand over Listay's, forcing her, gently, to lower the gun. They smiled broadly and clapped a hand to her back. "The Scourge Authority was disbanded on account of all of them being dead. But, if you've got scourged Carmnians, you need a Scourge Authority, so the other consorts and I decided we would do it our way rather than let the police set up a task force." They turned toward Xan and put a warning finger to his chest. "Never trust a task force, alright, larvling?"

"What is 'your way,' then?" Listay pressed. She had lowered the gun but hadn't turned it off.

"Glad you asked!" Yulquitz rolled out a white board from behind the keychain display, pulled open a dry erase marker with their teeth, and drew an arrow pointing to the only complete sentence on the board. "Step one deviates from the original authority's method in that we don't immediately kill a scourged Carmnian. Step two," they added a second arrow, pointing to nothing, then a hurried question mark next to it, "is being workshopped! We're thinking something along the lines of a welcome party. Something that says 'Yes, you're our prisoner, but in a *fun* and *cheery* way.' Turns out, it's a hard sentiment to celebrate. What color frosting do you use? I think magenta, but Prismuntial insists it's got to be peach."

"No, no, no," said a willowy Tuhntian with softly wrinkled skin who pulled herself from underneath the t-shirt table. "No cakes. Cake is too polarizing. Jellymints are the least offensive treat. Everyone loves jellymints. Jellymint, anyone?" she asked, holding out her hand, this time with exactly five jellymints in it.

Yulquitz rubbed their forehead. "MeMuddle, no one apart from you likes jellymints. We aren't trying to torture them. That's what the old authority did."

She popped all five jellymints into her mouth and chewed them thoughtfully. "Cake is still too polarizing," she affirmed.

"Alright, we'll scrap the celebration idea and come up with something different for step two, but step three is still the cure!" Yulquitz said, and drew a wobbling sort of amoeba shape on the white board, then paused, added some lines bursting excitingly forth from it, paused again, then drew a happy face in the center of it. They smiled at the joyful image of the cure.

"You have one?" May asked.

"Well, uh, no, not yet." Yulquitz's smile drooped, and they drew a massive 'X' over the happy cure. "We've been seriously considering one, though."

"Brainstorming," said Hurmbert, helpfully.

"Yes! That's the word. So far, our best guess has been fermented hooflatoo milk, right in the eyes. Sounds like a winner, right? I think that's a winner."

"It sounds great in theory, sure, but we tried that already. It doesn't work," said Xan. Something about seeing the happy little cure on the whiteboard then having it dashed into four pieces by the 'X' had unsettled him. It was an ominous doodle.

"I see," said Yulquitz, the undercurrent of jolliness ebbing for the span of a single word before surging back. "We've got plenty more ideas we can test now that you're here!"

"Why," May intercepted, "do you have a ray gun if you're not trying to kill anyone?"

"It's set to stun! Scourged Carmnians can be exceedingly dangerous."

"I'm not dangerous!" Xan said.

Yulquitz smiled fondly at him. "Of course you aren't, but you're one of mine. Prismuntial's are the worst. Don't tell her I said that, though. She's self-conscious about it."

"What do you mean by one of yours?" asked May.

"One of my brood! He's my precious little larvae broodling all grown up!" Yulquitz, seized with affection for their offspring, pushed Listay aside and pulled Xan into a smothering bear-hug. Xan let them do it, hanging limply in Yulquitz's arms until they at last released him and surprise attacked May, cupping their hands around her face. "Is this your partner?"

"I'm his case worker," she said, pulling away.

"Wait, I thought I was supposed to be *your* case worker," Xan whispered.

"Only on Wednesdays," she replied out of the corner of her mouth.

His voice went still lower. "May, we...we don't have Wednesdays here."

"Precisely," she whispered with a wink.

"They're friends. That's just how they talk," Listay assured a confused Yulquitz. "We're here to see Carmnia about the scourge." Listay glanced at Xan for a moment, considering whether to say anything about Chaos or not, but decided to tackle one issue at a time.

"Aw, don't worry mun." Yulquitz slung an arm around Xan's shoulders. "We'll get you fixed up. We've got a whole wall full of ideas. We've got a roomful of wallfuls!"

May suddenly remembered waffles. The last time she'd had a waffle had been exactly three years ago today, though she couldn't know it. It had come from Margery's Cafe, a mom-and-pop around the corner from her apartment. It had been lukewarm and flaccid.

"Any of those ideas involve injecting fungicide into my eyes?" Xan asked, dispersing May's waffle fantasies.

"Oh, yeah, sure, a few of them," said Yulquitz.

"No," May said. "We're here to see Carmnia about the scourge, not to experiment. Where is she?"

Yulquitz's seemingly unsquashable enthusiasm squished, and Hurmbert took over in a low, gentle voice.

"We haven't seen her in almost an orbit. She said she had family matters to attend to and disappeared. We assumed it had something to do with the scourge. You were part of her last brood, you know?" Hurmbert told Xan. "Even she was ashamed of how much the ophiocordyceps mushrooms she consumed had affected you lot. She insisted they were good for her health. Wouldn't even let me cook the zuxing things. I still think I could've sautéed the horror out."

"Bert, you can't sautée the horror out of everything," Yulquitz said.

"I sautéed the horror out of the smurbels."

"Mmmm," Yulquitz hummed doubtfully. "They still had a horrific aftertaste."

"That was the cilantro," Hurmbert said.

Listay stepped in to refocus them. "Where do you suspect Carmnia went?" Listay asked.

"No way of knowing," Yulquitz mused.

"Oh, she's back at the Folly," said someone who peeled back the curtain behind the register and slunk against the counter to remove her helmet and coif her voluminous pink hair back into its characteristic puffs. This was Prismuntial, but she made a habit of never introducing herself.

"What? As of when? Why?" asked Yulquitz.

She used Yulquitz's armored shoulder to check her reflection. "A couple rotations. Said her vacation home flooded. Or did it burn? Could it do both? It might have been both... Ask her yourself."

"You didn't tell me!" their voice cracked into a higher register.

"I just did," she said.

"Right, yeah, but you should've told me when it happened."

"Why?"

"Be-because I'm her head consort."

"You are not; MeMuddle is."

"Fine. Did you tell MeMuddle?"

"No," said Prismuntial with a delicate little shrug.

Yulquitz rubbed the space between their eyes, softening the muscles that had tensed up. "Alright, let's go find her. Where in the folly, exactly?"

"Dunno. Wherever there's a drink, I'd wager. Keep this between you and me and," she paused to count the surrounding crowd, "the other five, but I think she's got a bit of a problem."

"She has a lot of problems, and we're about to bring her more. This one's got the scourge." Yulquitz nodded toward Xan who waved shyly.

"Yeah, I know; that's the one that tried to kill Hurmbert and me the other day. And you always said mine scourged the worst. Ha!" Prismuntial's laugh was like a single ring of a small bell.

There was no use, thought Xan, in trying to defend himself. He had been accused of much worse than trying to kill two Scourge Authority agents.

Yulquitz slid Xan an apologetic grimace then clapped their hands together. “I’ll give the tour! Can’t enter the Folly without a tour. Sincerely, it’s extremely difficult to find the entrance. You three come with me, to the CarryCraft. The rest of you get this place cleaned up, just in case Carmnia wants to see it.”

“She’s never seen it!” Prismuntial whined. “Why would she want to now?”

“Because we’re going to clean it up! She’ll want to see it someday, and when that day comes, it ought to be sparkling. Off to it!” Yulquitz said, flourishing their hands until the other consorts slowly began to collect fallen t-shirts. Yulquitz turned around and grinned at May, Xan and Listay. “Follow me to the Queen!” they began marching out to the door at the back of the gift shop and the trio followed.

“I can see where you got your leadership skills,” May whispered to Xan.

“Oh, yes, it’s unendingly difficult to suppress them. But you seem to enjoy being in the lead so much, I have made a great effort to do so,” Xan whispered back.

May snickered. “It’s appreciated.”

CHAPTER TWENTY-EIGHT

Historical Interlude

Rhea I is a large planet with plenty of perfectly cromulent continents upon which to build cities. Temperate continents, continents with seasons, continents that are expansive and fertile and just generally far more suited to supporting intelligent life than the island upon which NotTuhnt was founded.

Snoodark the Damp, an ancient Rhean explorer who lived thousands of orbits before the civilization of NotTuhnt existed, wasn't satisfied with temperate climates and seasons and fertile lands. He lived by the philosophy that nothing good ever comes easy, and so he made his short life as difficult as possible in an effort to live well.

His search for a difficult life led him to the island where, it is said, he built for himself a mansion, stone by stone, with no help nor actual knowledge of how to build such a thing.

The mansion leaked, it was freezing cold in half the rooms and oppressively humid in the other half, it smelled like wet dog, required daily repairs, and proved to be about the most difficult thing anyone had accomplished on the planet of Rhea I since reaching complete environmental sustainability. It was totally unlivable.

Snoodark was thrilled.

This, thought Snoodark, must be good.

Every great philosopher goes through an ascetic phase. Some survive it, and some don't. Just a few short seasons after completing his masterpiece, Snoodark died of an easily curable lung infection.

CHAPTER TWENTY-NINE

Snoodark's Folly

Yulquitz, Listay, May, and Xan all gathered around the Carry-Craft which looked, to May, like a hovering golf cart. There was a thin bench in the front, a second thin bench in the back, and an aluminum roof which had partially rusted. It bobbed askew, the front left corner occasionally dipping to touch the ground, then lifting up slightly, then touching down again.

"Everyone in!" Yulquitz said cheerfully, hopping into the front seat. Convinced that Yulquitz was harmless, or at least meant well, Listay gave back their ray gun and sat beside them as Xan and May scrunched into the back seat.

Yulquitz twisted their thumb into the Carry-Craft's dashboard. It had two modes, Stop and Go, and nothing to steer with. Instead, it followed a line of wire embedded into the ground which sent it from the gift shop to Snoodark's Folly and back relatively quickly, despite the front corner which sparked as it dragged across the concrete.

As they approached, the folly loomed over the trees, and Yulquitz gave the well-practiced, rarely used, tour speech.

"If you look to your right, folks, you'll see the tallest gable of Snoodark's Folly swooping majestically over the trees. This gable is not an original feature; it was built in NotTuhnt orbit 137. The construction was overseen by Carmnia's extremely attractive consorts who felt it just looked more dramatic to have something appear over the trees. The upper levels are completely unfinished inside, as no one typically wants to stay in the folly long enough to make it up there.

"One of the many unusual facts about Snoodark's Folly is that seventy percent of the structure exists underground, making it the only private connection from Downtown to Uptown on the island. A service entrance was built at the edge of Downtown for Carmnia's many servants, butlers, and attendants who reside in repurposed shipping containers below our very feet. Consorts like myself are free to live in the above ground structure. We just don't want to. Which is why we spend most of our time in the gift shop."

May tapped Xan's arm to get his attention; he was watching the trees whizzing by with great interest. "Hey, do you think Milly works for Carmnia?" she whispered.

"No. Why, do you?"

"Have you been listening to the tour?"

"Oh! Uh, yes. Yeah. And you think Milly works for Carmnia because..."

"Milly lives Downtown in a shipping container complex. Yulquitz just said that's where Carmnia's staff lives."

"Right, yeah, but Milly's never worked an orbit in her life. She's a layabout! Kinda like me. Or I suppose, since she raised me, I'm like her." He curled his lip, disgusted at himself for taking after Milly in this respect.

"If she doesn't work, how does she get gem?"

Xan puzzled on it. Aunt Milly had always just had money; he never questioned why or how, exactly. It just existed. And she spent it wildly, too. Vacations, food, tchotchkes, more food... "I don't know, actually."

Their conversation was cut short as the Carry-Craft screeched to a halt in front of a massive arch which appeared to be carved into the shape of several tall, naked beings groping each other.

"And here we are!" Yulquitz said, turning the craft off but remaining seated. "The arch was commissioned in NotTuhnt orbit eighty-two as a testament to Carmnia's mass sexual appeal. The banner above the arch, though now faded, once read 'Carmnia: The Zuxine Queen' and represents the period of Queen Carmnia's life which historians refer to as the Great Mid-Life Crisis. Notice the cluster of mummified—"

"Cease this blithering and get on with it!" Xan said in a tone of voice he had never once in his life taken. It sounded like he was doing a marvelous impression of Gloria Swanson in Sunset Boulevard. Chaos had never been in control of a body quite this theatrical, and she had to admit she was enjoying it. She made him grab the railing between the back and front seats and glare at Yulquitz.

Yulquitz looked hurt. "Is that a symptom of the scourge?"

May shook her head. "It's a side plot. He's also possessed by a chaos goddess."

"*The* Chaos goddess, Tiny Human May. The singular and most powerful. I am the Beginning and the End and Most of the Stuff in the Middle. Everything except IKEA. I demand to—remember the time Lucy needed five hundred dollars for some charity event and she and Ethel dressed up as caricatured aliens for a publicity stunt to earn the money? At first, I was so offended. I mean, yes, sure, I've got a long nose, but zuut it's not *that* long. And they were just talking gibberish! Didn't even bother to learn a second language for the part. I watched it a few times; right, no, I lie, I watched it seventeen times, and eventually, I realized it was actually a masterful parody. Lucy really hit center mark with that one. The headpieces were a bit extravagant, but zux it if I didn't have an outfit near identical to hers for an act I used to do with Itkip—"

He went on.

No one was brave enough to stop him.

They all watched, mesmerized, loitering in front of the yawning arch to the gardens as Xan dove into a flashback, tied it back into another episode of 'I Love Lucy,' ricocheted into an explanation of ancient neo-Panseen verb agreements (and heated noun disagreements), settled into a light musing on the validity of limericks in literature, ended with, "Great, she's zuxed off." and then breathed.

"You out-monologued Chaos," Listay said in fearful awe. "That's genius."

"Yeah. Yeah! I guess I can move 'incessant chattering' out of character flaws and into the special skills category. Neat!" He smiled broadly for the first time in a while, and May joined him. She needed something to smile about.

"Good work, 'genius,'" she said in a tone that was so mocking it circled back around to being affectionate.

"Thanks!" This was the closest anyone had ever come to calling him a genius in a way which wasn't entirely mean-spirited, and he appreciated it.

Yulquitz finally dismounted the ailing Carry-Craft.

"Right, well, that was odd. Now, everyone out, and please stick together as we enter the gardens. The hostas can be a tad bite-y, and the last time I was here alone, a rogue fern got fresh with me." Yulquitz led them through the encroaching garden on a narrow stone path to the entrance of the folly. No door appeared there, just a solid wall of rust-colored, fleshy tendrils which curled around each other.

"Just walk straight on through the creneli mushroom barrier, please; it won't hurt you," Yulquitz said, then chose a section of the fleshy wall which appeared to be slightly looser than the rest and pushed through it, breaking off chunks of the mushroom which fell to the stone steps and slowly bled a sticky-white goo. Listay pushed her way in, but Xan's BEAPER dinged just before he had the pleasure of breaking through the mushroom wall, and he and May stood outside the structure to read the message.

"Do not attempt to remove the fungus manually," was all it said. It had come from Yvonne's BEAPER, but it sounded more like something Ix would say.

"Wasn't planning to. What happened?" Xan whispered into his BEAPER; he didn't want Listay to overhear. They waited, but there was no reply.

"The mushrooms won't hurt you," Yulquitz said, popping their head out of the creneli wall. "Well, these won't, at least. Other mushrooms will, but not these. Come on in!"

Upon entering the Folly, two things became clear. The first was that more spiders than people called the folly home, and the second was that there was a mold problem. The entire interior blossomed with spores. The only life this place seemed equipped to nurture was vegetal. If Carmnia was, in fact, here, she wasn't exactly living in Queenly comfort.

A heavy silence hung in the Folly, the kind of silence that falls in a forest when a predator is nearby, and an even heavier darkness hung from the rafters high above.

No one moved.

No one breathed.

"Snoodark's Folly," Yulquitz trumpeted cheerily, "is the oldest standing structure on the island, and its age is placed at between five and six hundred orbits." They shattered the chilling spike of foreboding which had penetrated the party. "It's longevity is often attributed to the organic matter which has replaced much of the original material and created a living architecture which grows like a skin atop the original building's bones. A self-sustaining ecosystem in the exact shape of the original Folly. This natural historic perseveration retains the Folly's characteristic shape with little need for upkeep."

Their voice seemed to be absorbed by the soft growth on the foyer walls as they led the group to a bay of telediscs circling the foyer's centerpiece, a gray-green topiary which depicted a haughty-looking blob. "Excuse the state of the Queen Carmnia topiary, if you will. Since Carmnia left, we haven't bothered to pay the gardener, and since we haven't bothered to pay him, he hasn't bothered to work."

Here Yulquitz paused, awaiting the polite chuckle of a group of tourists acknowledging that a joke had been told. The polite chuckle didn't come. Yulquitz frowned, considering whether or not to repeat it. Deciding against it (for fear that the group would, once again, ignore his quip), Yulquitz ushered them to the teledisc bay. "If everyone will please stand on one of the telediscs, we will begin the tour from the top of the Folly and work our way down. One adult to a teledisc, please."

"We don't want a tour; we want to find Carmnia," May told them quietly so as to not embarrass them in front of the others.

"Right, sure, but the best way to do that is to search the entire Folly top to bottom, innit? So enjoy the tour, larvling!" Yulquitz patted her back and stepped on their own teledisc. The group fizzled away.

CHAPTER THIRTY

Horntaggler

The party remerged in a thick, gravity-less blackness. Oxygen-less, too. There was nothing. No light, no air, no mass aside from the four beings lost in the darkness.

One of the beings had bioluminescent mushrooms in his eyes which illuminated the other three beings. Xan looked to Yulquitz, sharing just enough light to allow Yulquitz to fiddle with their BEAPER until a proper environment whipped around them, settling with a splat like a wet towel.

It was still dark but purposefully so, as if this darkness had been tastefully placed there. Two massive chandeliers dipped from the ceiling which bowed in the middle of the long room, and a steady drip of mysterious fluid, too rank and thick to be merely water, created a stalactite pointing to a stretched dining table that was polished to a fine shine by the constant dripping. Candles flickered in rows of candelabras along the length of the table, glinting off gilt damasks in the wallpaper which seemed to have grown across the wall organically. Upon closer inspection, the candles were actually tapering lumps of mineral which spurted ignited gases from their tips, closer to delicate, miniature volcanoes than proper candles. It seemed as if Mother Nature had seen someone design a Baroque dining hall and decided she could do it better herself.

May, who hadn't been expecting the oxygen to suddenly disappear, and who rather needed oxygen to support her breathing habit, gasped in gulps of heady air.

Yulquitz and Listay, who had kicked the oxygen habit several evolutionary phases back, watched her with curious concern. Xan was used to it and rubbed her back in a way he hoped was comforting.

Noticing their stares, she tried to downplay her struggle, quietly slurping in as much air as she could. The air was thick with humidity and mold spores, and this in no way helped her in her quest to re-oxygenate herself.

"Where are we?" is what she tried to say. It came out more like: "*Wheeze* are *wheeze*."

But Yulquitz had a sharp mind and filled in the blanks. "Oh, that's easy! We are perpetual beings made mortal to learn the lesson of impermanence."

"I-wha-no," May stuttered. "'*Where* are we?' Not 'what are we?' Although, I have to say, your answer is a lot better than-" May jazz-handed at Xan.

Xan looked horribly offended. "Yulquitz is my dad! They're a great deal older than me. Of course they've got more of a handle on what life's about."

It was Yulquitz's turn to look horribly offended. "Not a great deal older, no! Why, I was only two hundred and a quarter when I had you."

Listay, having died and felt it was nothing particularly special, was wary of philosophical questions and turned their minds, instead, to something more pressing. "Why did the telediscs glitch?"

"Now that *is* strange," Yulquitz said, fiddling with settings on their BEAPER, then looking up at the caving ceiling as if they could see through it to the other side. "That is very strange," they mused again.

"Is it stable?" Listay asked, also watching the ceiling which creaked as if in reply.

"Oh, very! Hasn't collapsed yet, has it? No. No, it hasn't. The thing which is strange is that this isn't our intended destination. We're a floor below the highest floor in the dining hall. The telediscs up there rejected us. Must be out of order."

"We'll take the stairs, then," May said, heading for the massive pair of doors at the far end.

"Whoa, whoa." Yulquitz grabbed her shoulders and held her back. "If the telediscs are out of order up there, Carmnia certainly isn't there either. Besides, the upper floor is..."

He trailed off, staring again at the ceiling silently as if waiting for it to spring to life.

"Is what?" May asked.

He looked back down at her, distant concern still wandering across his face. "Creepy. No matter, though! Here we are in the Grand Dining Hall! In the original Folly, records indicate that this space may have been an exercise room, which would explain the chains embedded in the walls at regular intervals."

"That's one explanation," Xan agreed, eyeing a thick rusted chain that grew from the wall and dangled half-way to the floor. He had never exercised intentionally, so far be it from him to say what did and did not look like an exercise room. Still, this did not look like an exercise room.

Again, the ceiling creaked as if it were about to collapse under its own weight and, though no one admitted to concern, the group half-jogged to the far end where the ceiling was highest.

"Right, no one go upstairs, okay? Stay together as a group. Everyone stay together, and don't go upstairs," Yulquitz whispered, then grabbed hold of the touch-bar on the massive doors which unlocked and dissolved away. This led the group into a windowless hallway, and once everyone had exited, Yulquitz twisted the touch-bar back into place, and the doors reappeared. The tour-guide grandeur returned to Yulquitz's manner. "The next stop is the Marsupian Lounge across the hall. Queen Carmnia spends most of her time at the Folly drinking in the Marsupian Lounge, so I think we've a good chance at getting a look at her in there!" Yulquitz said as if Carmnia were an elusive critter they were hoping to spot.

The hallway, though lined in gilt crown molding and hung with stuffy paintings of important historical Carmnians, gave one the impression that they had been swallowed by an enormous snake. The walls, softened with organic growth, had worn away such that the metal structure of the building could be seen, wrapping like ribs around them as they traveled, single file due to the constricting nature of the hallway, toward a swirling holodoor at the far end. The holodoor swirled because the humidity in the Folly had seeped into its casing and rusted the mechanism so that it spluttered and swam as it tried, and failed, to retain its solidity.

But that wasn't what made the hallway so unsettling.

It helped, certainly. But what clinched it was this:

A rhythmic thumping. Growing, quickening.

The group looked about before all agreeing, silently, that the thumping came from the staircase opposite the holodoor.

Yulquitz moved between the group and the oncoming sound, aware that it was either Carmnia or something horrifically dangerous. Quite possibly both.

Listay stood, ready to assist, behind Yulquitz. May and Xan enjoyed their relative lack of responsibility and slowly backed down the hall. Not enough to utterly desert Listay and Yulquitz to their fates but enough to give the clear impression that in a fight or flight situation, they would pick the latter.

A curious cuckoo preceded the next creaking step.

"Blitheon's stars, she escaped the aviary," Yulquitz said in an appalled whisper and began to push Listay back.

"Who did?" Listay hissed.

"Chuzoople, Carmnia's prized horntaggler. She'll kill us."

"Who, Chuzoople or Carmnia?" asked May.

"First Chuzoople, then Carmnia."

They were now all pressed against the busted holodoor, but it refused to open.

"God, it would be embarrassing to be killed by something named Chuzoople," May said.

"Not at all," Yulquitz said. "It's difficult to be embarrassed when you're dead, and Chuzoople is the nastiest horntaggler in the aviary. That bird's responsible for the deaths of twelve of Carmnia's attendants and the resignations of all the rest," they added, an air of practiced tour-guide cadence weaseling back into their hushed voice.

A horntaggler isn't so much a bird as it is a sensation of dread wrapped in stringy muscles and decorated with neither feathers nor fur but fine downy 'furthers' which fluff out around its neck like a doomful feather boa.

Millions of orbits ago, the horntaggler briefly evolved hands but quickly backtracked, leaving the creature with six vestigial arms which ended in useless, clawing grey fingers. The species has never lived down the shame of this horrific misstep and has nearly embarrassed itself to extinction.

The creature appeared at the end of the hall now. Its mass expanded to fill the hallway, feathers unfurling into the crepuscular yellow light to reveal its weapon of choice, a sharpened bone bayonet protruding like a periscope from its beak.

"Graw?" Chuzoople asked, politely, it thought, for someone whose home had been intruded upon.

Rather than answer, Yulquitz pulled the ray gun from their belt and jammed it into the holodoor casing, severing the diodes with a single explosive blast.

"Graaww!" Chuzoople shouted at the intruder who had wrecked its lovely swirling door. It lunged toward Yulquitz bayonet first, underdeveloped fingers waggling gracelessly beneath the majestic canopy of its wings.

Yulquitz, in good tour guide fashion, waved Listay, May, and Xan through the holodoor first, but Chuzoople had no qualm with Listay, May, or Xan. They hadn't shot at its door. Yulquitz ducked under the initial attack and the creature's beak lodged itself in the wall.

"Arm yourselves!" Yulquitz shouted as they crawled out from under the beast, narrowly avoiding its thrashing talons, and somersaulted into the Wine Lounge. They rammed their body into an oozing credenza and slid it toward the doorway, leaving a trail of pink sludge.

May grabbed a near-empty bottle of shermel and slammed it on the counter to give it a jagged broken edge. Xan chose a splitter which sounds like a terrifically gruesome weapon but is, in fact, a kind of spoon constructed specifically for the task of splitting the toxic foam from the delicious liquid in a wildly expensive Porzalctu. It was therefore only threatening in that wielding one might give your opposition a fleeting feeling of fiscal inferiority.

Listay took one of the three decorative antique swords which hung on the wall. She observed May and Xan's choices with curiosity as the four of them gathered behind the bar, but the moment she imagined either of them with a sword, she understood the wisdom of it.

With a sucking plop, the horntaggler freed itself from the wall and made it clear that a credenza was a poor sort of defense against its boney bayonet which rendered the furniture unrecognizable with a single blow. A menacing cluck boiled in the creature's throat as it pushed through the sharp remains of the credenza and did a visual sweep of the lounge.

"How good is that thing's sense of smell?" Listay whispered to Yulquitz, trying to determine whether or not they had a chance of it just wandering away.

"Oh, it's terrible," Yulquitz assured her. "The bony protrusion through its beak absolutely destroys the horntaggler's ability to pick up a scent. They do, however, have exceptionally keen ears."

They looked up to find that Chuzoople had, in fact, heard them quite clearly and was hovering above the bar, eyeing them like an irresolute eyeing a buffet.

"There you are! We were just talking about you, buddy," Xan said, hopping up behind the bar as if a favorite customer had just walked in and asked for the usual.

By this, the horntaggler was confused. It reared back, briefly reconsidering whether it was the predator or prey as it watched Xan's face, trying to work out in its tiny brain if that was a smile or a baring of teeth.

"Aw, look at those little hands," Xan continued, holding out his own hand to the creature.

"What are you doing?" May whispered urgently, hoping he would have a coherent answer.

"Shake?" asked Xan, and lunged at one of the creature's many poorly formed hands with his own, grasping it tightly and wiggling it around a bit.

"Gar-raw?" asked Chuzoople, by which it meant: "Whom, me?"

The soft clatter of metal against metal distracted May from her concern for Xan's well-being. Yulquitz was gone; Listay was hunched over a hole in the wall just large enough for a body and gesturing wildly at May to follow her and, presumably, Yulquitz into it.

May looked again at Xan who was deftly mixing various liquids in a tumbler, staring the beast down as if daring it to attack the person who was making it a drink. The beast did not, it would seem, dare.

“Right, now try that,” said Xan, setting a fluted glass in one of the creature’s malformed hands.

Listay gently set the metal cover down, but Yulquitz was right behind it and held it up so he could see out of the opening as Listay crawled over to May and grabbed her hand in an attempt to physically lead her away from the danger. Earthlings, for such a fragile species, seemed to have an underdeveloped sense of self preservation. But she, too, paused to watch as the beast stared, transfixed, at the cocktail it had been given.

Time stretched like saltwater taffy on a pulling machine; it became stringy, it glistened, it smelled overwhelmingly of manufactured strawberries.

The horntaggler attempted to bring the glass to its beak and failed due to the weakness in its twig-like forearm. It attempted to bring its beak to the glass, but found its neck didn’t quite stretch that way. Everyone watched. Had the horntaggler noticed this, it might have been embarrassed. Then again, the creature had no real sense of societal norms, so it might not have minded.

Maneuvering a downy wing under the glass, Chuzoople at last brought the cocktail to its beak, just close enough that its barbed tongue could flick out and lap up the concoction.

Time was still stretching, pulling itself thinner and thinner until its tensile strength gave out and the strand snapped, heralded by the creature’s teeth-grinding roar.

The spell broken, May seized the back of Xan’s shirt, and Listay seized May’s hand, and the whole conglomeration stuffed into the air vent moments ahead of a wildly clacking, foaming beak.

“The shermel must’ve been off,” Xan said, bewildered as he crawled backward through the vent, away from the unhappy customer.

“Oh, that’s not shermel,” Yulquitz called back to him. “Carmnia used to give that to interns who asked for a glass of water.” They gave a single heartless laugh as if to excuse Carmnia’s antisocial behavior as an endearing foible.

"What is it?" Listay asked.

The war-cry of the creature ended, punctuated with a hearty flop.

"I've no idea. But I do know we won't be bothered by Chuzoople again. Clever stuff, Xan! You must've gotten that from Carmnia," Yulquitz called to a horrified Xan.

"I was fixing her a drink! I thought we could maybe have a chat to the effect of 'Hey, we're really not all that bad; how about you don't kill us?' I was loosening her up! Difficult to kill someone who's just made you a cocktail, I thought. A bit rude. Figured at the very least she would feel silly for overreacting."

"It worked," Listay said by way of congratulations. "Now let's get out of these vents."

CHAPTER THIRTY-ONE

Piñata Room

Yulquitz kicked open the next grate they came to, and the group emerged in a hallway which flickered under orange light and the exaggerated warmth of faux torches set in faux cast-iron sconces illuminating faux frescos which depicted Carmnia's faux heroics.

The first scene which assaulted their sense of reality was one of an abstract and formless universe, like great colored amoebas wriggling inside a wobbly bean held in Carmnia's vast blue fingers. Her face was arranged in a way no living person had ever actually seen her face arranged—in a gently blissful smile, full of warmth and love for, presumably, all of existence. The inscription beneath this scene read 'Before there was anything, there was Queen Carmnia, and this was good.'

"The Hall of Truth," Yulquitz said, sweeping their arms out to either side in the flickering hallway. "Commissioned in NT two-thirty-six, in order to 'set the record straight,' according to Carmnia."

"What record?" May asked, pocketing her bottle shank and moving on to the next fresco which pictured Carmnia reclining, disinterested, prodding at the bean which contained all things. Below it read, 'Queen Carmnia grew weary of the Nothingness she dwelled in. Thus, she personified the formless mass of the Universe and went down into it and became the suns and the planets and that which crawled among them, and this was good.'

Yulquitz shrugged. "*The* record. Her creation mythos. She wanted it known."

"And you believe in it?" May asked. She had assumed, despite personally knowing a goddess, that everyone out here in the enlightened universe didn't actually believe in mythology. She had assumed wrong.

"Sure I do! I mean, to an extent, sure. Vaguely." Yulquitz smiled a smile which said they believed it because that was what they were expected to do and that this, like everything else Queen Carmnia had done, was good.

"Oh look!" Yulquitz shouted before they could further backpedal on their answer. "This one's fun. 'Queen Carmnia,'" they read the text, "'became lost in existence, and for eons, forgot from whence she came, and this was good!' That's good, isn't it?" Yulquitz said cheerily.

The scene they referred to showed Carmnia again, multiplied in a thousand ghostly outlines scattered with stars. It looked as if it had taken a lifetime to paint.

At the end of the hallway, past one last fresco, massive gold-gilt double doors blocked the path, but they were too far to make out the nature of the carvings which danced across it.

"Alright!" Yulquitz chirped. "Onto the Piñata Room. I do hope she's not in there, but we ought to check."

"What about the last painting?" May asked. Yulquitz was standing in front of it so she couldn't see. She ducked around them.

"Oh, uh, don't worry. It's nothing," they said.

"'Queen Carmnia shall one day rise to power again, and on that day, all existence shall violently collapse into itself and be held once more in the palm of her Queenly Hand, and this is good?'" May read. The question mark at the end was her own.

"It's nothing, really." Yulquitz said. "The ultimate Nothing." They laughed nervously. "Come along. She's not in this hallway, is she? Well, in spirit, perhaps she is. Bodily, she's not."

Xan stared into the face of Carmnia in the final scene, and a shiver of recognition hit him like an arrow to a bullseye at the center of his being. May joined him, putting a hand on his shoulder. "Come on," she said. He stayed.

"The horrible thing about mushrooms is that their root system can be thousands of times larger than what's on the surface. So, you know, you *think* you know what you've got there, and you *think* everything's all sussed out, and then you start to dig a little, and you realize this thing has taken over entire forests, entire planets, even. And there's no digging it out without destroying a whole civilization."

He paused, and May thought perhaps he was done, so she prepared to reply. He was not done.

"I fucking hate mushrooms," he said.

May nodded, approving both of his use of the word "fuck" and his sentiments regarding mushrooms. She waited for him to start talking again, but after several moments of silence, she patted his back. "Agreed," she said. "Let's go."

"Wait." He showed her his BEAPER, above which floated a message from Yvonne. "Aimz is lost," it read.

It was followed by Xan's reply, "Lost how? As in gone? Missing? Dead?! Be specific!" and no further communication.

"That's vague," May noted. "Are you going to tell Listay?"

"That we're receiving cryptic messages and her lover may or may not be dead? Probably not."

"Probably not," May confirmed and they followed Listay and Yulquitz to the massive gold-gilt door at the end of the hall which was slowly being patinated by a thin, powdery mold. The door was carved with Carmnia's distraught visage wielding an enormous baton, her body poised to swing at what appeared to be a sea urchin dancing from a string.

Below, a plaque read in a font so decorative it was nearly illegible, 'The Piñata Room.'

Yulquitz paused, their hand on the door. "I only ever found her in here once after Queen Rapite sent her a nasty message about her hair. It is said that breaking the Piñata will summon a great and primordial power, its true name beyond fathomable language, but we know it as The Seam. So let's hope she's not in there, eh? That would be a bit of a mess, wouldn't it?" Yulquitz laughed as if they had just told a spooky campfire story to a group of frightened girl scouts and were trying to now lighten the mood.

They pushed open the heavy door to reveal a windowless room. The words 'Break Piñata in Case of Catastrophe' danced in colorful letters, projected onto a cloud of water vapor above an enormous papier-mâché fish which hung from the ceiling on a line so thin that it appeared to be floating, its fine paper fins undulating in the umami scented draft of the mansion.

Something pinged in the back of Xan's head. It was Chaos. Polite, he thought. Too polite to be Chaos, right? But the scourge didn't ping and, as far as he knew, his own mind had never done that either. But there it was, undeniably, the moment he had seen the papier-mâché fish floating in the empty room. This was it. This was the reason they were here.

"Stop me if this sounds plivered, but I really think we ought to break open that piñata," he heard himself say.

It seemed like everyone else heard this too, because they all looked at him as if he had suddenly burst into song and begun recapping the story so far.

Yulquitz, fearing they had lost control of this tour, was the first to deter him. "Now, we must remember we are guests in Queen Carmnia's home. Please refrain from damaging the historical surroundings and summoning primordial powers. I realize I must sound a touch hypocritical; I did, after all, blow up a doorway. But as the Queen's head consort, I do have some rights here, and I was only acting out of the interests of group safety."

Listay moved between Xan and the piñata. "If that piñata really does contain The Seam, you don't want to meddle with it. The Seam is the center of the universe. Who knows what they could do?"

"That's the reset," Xan said. "The Nothingness Chaos was talking about. It's what she wants, and I'm starting to think it's our winning wager." Then his tone shifted, and he addressed May as if he were about to suggest a fun outing. "Besides! Piñatas are great, right? In the event that it's not full of a primordial universe eating entity, it will be full of cheap candy. Who wouldn't want to get at that?"

Yulquitz and Listay couldn't dissuade Xan, so they both looked at May, silently urging her to take their side. The fish piñata looked at May, but from it, she could glean no advice. "I'm not giving up, Xan," she said at last, grabbing his hand. "We need to talk to Carmnia. Can you fight Chaos off a little longer?"

"I could fight her off forever, but…" He was beginning to wonder why he ought to. Beginning to doubt whether she really was all that horrible. Then he began to wonder if thoughts like that were how Chaos had snagged Yvonne and, for May's sake, he shut up. "You're right. Carmnia. I've always wanted to meet her, anyway. Only the wealthy and well-off ever get a chance to meet their own Queen, and I've never heard of a wealthy or well-off Carmnian, so I imagine I'll be the first! She's in the mud baths, by the way."

No one reacted to that revelation the way he had expected them to. No one reacted at all.

Perplexed, he pointed to his head. "Chaos told me. She's cooperating."

"That's great, mun!" Yulquitz clapped Xan on the back, hoping to dispel the tension that had strung the room round. "Saves us a great deal of time, too. The courtyard's the last stop on the tour. Unless, of course, you folks would like to arrive there naturally? See the rest of the Folly first?" After a brief and poignant silence, Yulquitz continued. "Or let's not! Right onto the courtyard, then. Just skipping the rest of the tour…"

CHAPTER THIRTY-TWO

A Murder

Chaos had been correct; Carmnia was in the courtyard stewing in a mud bath. They found her coated in fine beige mud, lounging in a round and Queenly pool, looking so much like every statue and stone carving they had seen of her thus far that, at first glance, May actually believed she was made of stone.

The courtyard hosted several of these mud baths, but none as richly decorated as Carmnia's, which lay in the center surrounded by golden waist-high statues of hurgles—evolutionary cousins to the flamingo who had developed space travel long before the Earth was replete with shrimp. The rim of the bath was gilt in gold, the tap which fed the bath was gold, and the magnificent puff of hair, the only bit of Carmnia which could be clearly seen, was gold, as well.

Bubbles of mud laboriously rose from the pool, paused, then burst with steam.

"Carmnia?" Yulquitz hazarded, bravely walking around the pool while the others remained on the far side. Yulquitz tapped her muddy shoulder.

As slowly as a mud bubble inflating, Carmnia filled her lungs with hot, humid air, her chest rising until it looked as if it might burst, too.

Carmnia forced all the air out of her lungs in a guttural, miserable, primal sigh. She did not open her eyes. She knew it was Yulquitz.

"What?"

"Uh, Carmnia, it's me, Yulquitz."

"And?"

"Well, aren't you happy to see...er...hear me?"

May, Xan, and Listay had gathered uncomfortably at the opposite edge of the pool, but Carmnia's voice had drawn Xan forward, his forehead wrinkling in thought.

"Not particularly," she said. "What do you want?"

Now, Xan strode forward with purpose, pausing only to snatch a rolled towel from the beak of one of the hurgle statues. He whipped the towel open, knelt beside Carmnia, and wiped the mud from her face.

"Chrismillion on Trilly under Carmnia of Tuhnt," Xan sat back on his heels, letting the towel drop to the concrete. "What in Blitheon's name are you doing here?"

Her eyes opened. She screamed like a hundred glotchburs fleeing a boiling lake and clambered from the bath.

"You're Carmnia?! I never noticed!" Xan squeaked. "Why didn't I notice that?" His voice grew faster, higher. "That seems like something I should have noticed!" He was barely audible now, like a busted squeaker toy.

It is worthwhile to mention here that the average meat-brain is really astonishingly bad at recognizing faces out of context. This is why most actors are so easily able to convince the layperson that they are, in fact, several different people rather than one person putting on a wig, some makeup, and occasionally a well-practiced accent.

Xan was now experiencing the same shame which comes from suddenly realizing an important side character in a movie you've watched dozens of times is the same actor in that commercial you can't seem to escape.

"She looks nothing like her statues," May whispered to Yulquitz who had quickly gotten out of Carmnia's way to avoid a torrent of mud.

"When she posed for the statues, she still had a team of stylists at her command."

"What happened to the stylists?"

"She had them all killed for perpetrating an unflattering caricature." Yulquitz cringed. "But nicely! Not killed, really. Put down. She had them laid to rest."

"Yulquitz, my love," hissed Carmnia between her teeth, pulling Yulquitz closer to her by the hem of their shirt.

"Uh, yes Queen Carmnia?" they said with a nervous warble.

"I thought you and the other consorts were handling the scourge situation. I was *told* you were handling it. By *you*. Does this," her eyes flicked to Xan then back to Yulquitz, "look like it's been handled?"

"Well, no, but...well, you see, the consorts and I have been working on the problem, but we, uh, don't really know exactly what causes it. They suggested that perhaps you might have some insight into that on account of—"

"It's the mushrooms, you *know* that. *Everyone* knows that. I told you to fix it, not lay the blame back on me!"

"Right, yes, of course, but—"

"But nothing! Your task was to either cure it or dispose of the infected, and since you have obviously failed to accomplish the former, you must proceed with the latter."

"D...dispose of?" Yulquitz asked. "You want me to kill him?"

Listay and May stepped in front of Xan, but Xan wasn't worried.

"Alright, Milly, you can get off their mark. I know you can't help me. I'll just leave."

Milly shook her head slowly. "Not at all, mun. Now your Aunt Milly hates to see you like this, you understand." She turned her blazing red eyes onto him, and he shrunk back. They had never been loving, never trustworthy, but now there was outright disgust in them. It was as if he were a once favorite chair, but the stuffing had started to come out in places, and it creaked when you sat on it. She had, mentally, put him on the curb the moment she saw the flash of scourge in his eyes at the burlesque show.

Yulquitz was the overly friendly neighbor who had noticed the chair, thought perhaps it had been taken to the curb accidentally, and tried to bring it back.

"By putting them down, you see," she said to Yulquitz now, "we are doing them and the community a favor. There's no curing the scourge. Kill him."

"No! I mean...well, obviously no!" Yulquitz said.

Seizing the beak of a nearby statue, Carmnia pulled it from the bird's face, revealing a long golden blade which rose from the bird's throat.

"I'll do it myself, then."

Xan backed up defensively, and May wrapped her fingers around the neck of the broken shermel bottle in her pocket. Chrismillion had her back to May, and slowly, carefully, so as not to alert her, May moved toward Chrismillion, focused intently on the middle of her golden curls. Everyone knew exactly what May was doing and refused to look at her for fear that Chrismillion's attention would be drawn.

"Milly! You raised me! Well, I mean you were around while I was being raised. Why are you doing this?"

"Listen to me now," Chrismillion said, and since she was the one holding the sword, everyone did. "There's a perfectly good explanation as to why I posed as a simpleton to raise you and Aimz." May paused just a few steps away from her, thinking Xan deserved the explanation before she walloped Milly.

"I'm sure there is," Xan said, hands up, trying to back away without startling her. "What...what is it?"

"I wanted to!" she cried. "You can't imagine how lonely it gets once the larvae are adopted out to their caretakers! It's not my fault you and Aimz were impossible to handle. *Particularly* Aimz. I was a wonderful caretaker!"

At this, May raised the bottle from her pocket. She was within striking distance. She raised it higher. She looked to Xan, her one-person ethics committee, and waited for the go-ahead. Xan's focus had been trained on Chrismillion up until now, but he could tell that May, a blurry figure in the background, was waiting on his word. Subtly, he shook his head. Even more subtly, his eyes met May's. And that was a mistake. Chrismillion noticed. She spun around, sword slicing in a semi-circle around her.

Metal clanged against glass; May had blocked the sword with the shoulder of the bottle. She smiled, having not realized she could do that. Perhaps she could hold her own in a sword fight, after all, she thought.

She thought wrong. That had been a wild stroke of luck. While May was busy mentally congratulating herself for being so effortlessly cool, Chrismillion was busy plunging the little sword into the space between her third and fourth ribs.

May dropped the glass shank. “That was quick,” she said, looking down, confused, at the metal protruding from her. Chrismillion retracted the red-polished sword and gently pushed May into the bubbling mud bath.

Surging forward together, Listay and Yulquitz wrestled the sword away from Chrismillion while Xan dove into the mud after May.

“Wow, uhm,” said Yulquitz, holding Chrismillion’s muddy, heaving shoulders. “Okay, Carmnia, larvling, let’s get you cleaned up.” They turned to Listay. “I’m going to get her cleaned up,” they repeated. He began to lead Chrismillion to the showers, but she wriggled an arm under Yulquitz’s and unsheathed the ray gun without their noticing. Listay snatched the gun from her, twisted her arm around her back, and pressed the nozzle between her shoulder blades.

“Does the Folly have a holding cell?” Listay asked Yulquitz.

“Oh, well, that’s not really necessary is—”

“Holding. Cell.” Listay turned the ray gun on Yulquitz now. “Or I’ll put you both away for murder.”

Yulquitz nodded sadly and led Listay through the courtyard to a staircase. Before they disappeared down it, Listay looked back at the mud bath and the two mud-covered globs on the edge of it.

“Try to keep her from bleeding out!” Listay shouted at one of the two blobs, hopefully the one that was Xan. The blob she had shouted at raised a hand in recognition, and Listay shoved the Queen down the steps, followed by an apologetic Yulquitz.

* * *

You’re welcome, May thought, floating in a warm, thick darkness which slowly dragged her down. Why had she thought that? It didn’t seem like the kind of thing she was likely to think. *Now can we smash that damn piñata?*

Oh.

Her thoughts were not her own. Her own thoughts, at this moment, were more along the lines of *Fuck Chrismillion, who does she think she is?*

Chaos agreed, though.

May was being dragged in another direction now. Up. Up was not as comfortable as down had been, but whatever was dragging her up was adamant, and so she let it.

She breached the surface of the mud and, though she had the natural inclination to take a deep breath, found that her lungs refused to inflate.

"May, talk to me," Xan said as he dragged her onto the courtyard tile.

"Your aunt is a bitch," May wheezed, coughing up a mouthful of bloody mud, rolling onto her elbow to spit it out.

This, though it was true, surprised Xan. He had fully expected her to be dead. Listay was shouting something at him in the distance, and he waved to acknowledge her.

"Zuut, I'm sorry about her. She does that sometimes."

"Murders people?!" May asked.

Xan shrugged, tilting his head. "Well, we could never prove anything, but we always just kinda assumed. She's got some issues."

"Issues," May repeated. "That's 'issues'?"

"More to the point, are you okay?" Xan opened her trench coat and began to wipe the mud from her shirt, searching for the point of entry. Her entire shirt was stained red under the beige slime of mud.

She knocked his hand away before he could get too freaked out by the blood. Leaning back on her elbows, she stretched out her aching rib cage with a wince. "I'm fine, thanks to Chaos," she grumbled.

Xan prodded around in his own head and found that Chaos had, indeed, left. But she could only possess a willing host, and May was certainly not willing. Unless...Xan shivered. May and Listay would have a lot to talk about. He grabbed a towel from the towel-holding hurgle and wiped the mud off May's face, then his own.

"So, Carmnia was a bust," May noted, seizing another towel to wipe off her hands.

"Sure, but do you know how expensive this mud is? Our skin is going to look incredible after this," Xan said, combing the mud through his hair. “At least Milly was direct this time. She used to make up the wildest excuses. ‘I’ve got an emergency hair appointment at the Marscaral Palace,’ she’d say. Or, ‘One of my attendants just got eaten, I have to go,’ she’d say. Or—by O’Zeno, I’m incredibly thick, aren’t I?”

May pat his arm. “It’s alright, Blue,” she assured him and began twisting the mud through sections of her curls, feeling she might as well make the most of the situation, too. “What are we going to do, now?” she asked, though she doubted he would have an answer.

He was silent for a long while, watching bubbles rise in the mud, linger, then pop. Rise, linger, pop. Rise...linger... “Have we considered,” Xan said, “letting Chaos win?”

“What, giving up?” May asked. “After all this?!” May pointed dramatically to her chest and the unpleasant looking hole in it.

“Why not?” Xan said, wincing.

“We can’t just give up! That isn’t how it works. We’re the good guys. We don’t give up. We fight, we win, the end,” she said, crossing her arms, determined to take command of her own life story.

“What end? Nothing ends. You can’t win or lose if there’s no end,” he said.

May thought perhaps the scourge had really gotten to him without Chaos there to buffer it.

“Of course there’s an end,” she said. Then, she had to sit and think about it a minute longer. “Death is the end. We’ve been through this.”

“Well...sure,” Xan said. “But there’s no winning or losing. Not really. We win one round, we lose the next, and on it goes until...”

“Until you stop playing the game,” May suggested.

“We have no way of saving ourselves now,” Xan said. “We have nothing to save. We’ve already succumbed to Chaos.”

May watched the quietly burbling mud bath for a while. Watching the bubbles form, grow, and burst over and over again. No one, truly, was out to get them.

The scourge was just a thoughtless disease munching away at a tasty brain. Chrismillion, a hapless screw-up terrified of her own creations. Sonan, a computer on a mission. Even Chaos herself just wanted to do her job. To rid the universe of the agony of being. To end all suffering once and for all.

They had been fighting nature all along.

May sighed. “You’re right, Xan,” she said at last. “Most piñatas *are* full of cheap candy. I could go for some of that right now,” she said.

“Then let’s go get some!”

CHAPTER THIRTY-THREE

Zombie High Five

Beneath the courtyard, in a slat-lit basement cell block, Listay sensed that someone was about to make a terrible decision.

"Yulquitz, watch her. Don't let her out," Listay said, handing the ray gun back to Yulquitz despite her reservations.

"Good thinking! You go check on the kids; I'll hang out with Carmnia!" Yulquitz said, cheerily.

This did not increase her confidence in them, but she bolted up the stairs and into the soft light of the courtyard to find Xan and May both trying to yank another statue from the concrete floor.

"What are you doing?!" she shouted, breaking into a sprint.

"Getting a bird for May," Xan grunted, throwing his full weight into pulling the creature from its post.

Listay put a hand on May's arm. "You need medical attention!"

"Oh, no, not really," said May. "Zombie high five?" She held up her hand, waiting. She felt giddy with the realization that everything was well and truly over. Or was it Chaos in there making her think that? Likely both, but it didn't matter. She felt at once vanquished and invincible. Dead and alive. Hopeless and ecstatic.

Listay felt there was something very wrong with her. She refused the high-five. Xan continued to tug at the hurgle bird.

"Why does May need a bird?" Listay asked, thinking that perhaps asking something concrete might get her a more reasonable answer.

"We're going to smash the piñata," Xan said.

It had not.

"And summon the Seam? You can't do that!" Listay's tone shifted suddenly, as if she were talking someone down from a bridge. "You're not thinking clearly. Why don't we sit down and talk about this? There are still options."

Xan's BEAPER dinged an alert, and he wiped the mud off it to allow the message to float in the air above his wrist.

It was from Yvonne's BEAPER.

It was not good news.

"Blitheon," Listay whispered. She could read the holographic message, though it was backward. It was just three words.

"You've been in contact with Fulogra?" Listay's voice was distant as if some other entity were puppeting her from far away.

Xan couldn't put sentences together yet, so May stepped in. "Off and on. We didn't know anything important until now. We didn't want to worry you."

Listay nodded, looked as if she were about to say something, then nodded again as a pair of tears raced down her cheeks, cutting two glistening lines down her face.

Unable to stand the sight of someone crying, particularly when he felt like crying himself, Xan swept Listay up into a hug, petting her hair.

May stood by awkwardly, entirely unsure of what to say or do in this situation.

"Hey guys!" Yulquitz called from across the courtyard, saving May from having to deal with uncomfortable feelings. "Carmnia is *really* sorry, and she wants to apologize to everyone."

"Not now!" Listay shouted back to him, her grief ricocheting into vitriol with ease. But it was too late. Chrismillion rose, unbound, clean, and dressed in a white, fluffy robe, her hands raised in surrender.

"I," said Chrismillion, then paused as if her voice were being broadcast around the near empty courtyard and she needed to give it time to reverberate properly, "Queen Carmnia," she paused again, "apologize for any harm—"

"Stop!" Xan said, releasing Listay and approaching Chrismillion. "Aimz is dead, and you nearly killed May. I don't want an apology from you. It wouldn't make a scrap of difference. You acted in the only way you knew how to act: as an antagonist to those who trusted you. Even the zuxing god of Chaos is honest about who she is and what she wants."

Chrismillion's acquiescent expression hardened. "Fine. I'll be honest. I am your Queen, and I want you to disappear," she said, then stole the ray gun, again, from Yulquitz. This time, though, Yulquitz noticed. They launched at Chrismillion's arm, deflecting the blast into a distant marble pillar which shattered, collapsing half of the surrounding colonnade.

Listay snatched the ray gun from the errant Queen's weakened grasp and with a single blast she untethered the hurgle bird statue Xan had been trying to dislodge. It clattered to the ground in front of May and she picked it up, slinging it over her shoulder.

"Go," she told Xan. "Summon The Seam."

Xan nodded, kissed her gently on the forehead, a crazy kind of half-smile on his face as he and May ran back to the piñata room.

CHAPTER THIRTY-FOUR

Unfathomable Jellymints

For the first time ever, May and Xan found themselves running toward something not because they were being chased, not because they were running out of time before something horrific happened, but because they were excited to get there. Whatever fearful mystery the fish piñata held couldn't possibly be any more terrible than what they were currently going through, so sheer curiosity had won out.

"Hey, Chaos," May shouted, looking up as if she could see into her own brain. "We're doing your thing now. Happy?" After a brief silence, May laughed, and Xan asked what Chaos had said. "She says, 'vindication is a sweeter and more satiating fruit than happiness,'" May relayed.

Bits of mud flung from their shoes as they jogged out into the foyer and through the ceremonially lit hall which led to the piñata room.

The bass floated in its haze, the words "Break Piñata in Case of Catastrophe" shimmering above it. They studied the tissue-paper scales of the enormous creature with interest, savoring their last moments of here-and-now.

"Who do you think made it?" Xan asked.

"It's always existed," May said. When Xan tilted his head at her, confused, she clarified, "Chaos says that it contains the center of the Universe, which means that it's always existed. I was paraphrasing. She used more insults and expletives."

"Why does Carmnia have it?"

May listened to the voice in her head for a moment, scrunched her face, and shrugged. "Because she's a greedy zuxing zoup-nog tchagg. And I think that's the first time Chaos and I have ever agreed on something! Making progress, right? Ouch!" May ducked away from nothing.

"What?"

She rubbed her scalp, looking around suspiciously. "Chaos thwacked me in the head. She wants us to get it over with."

They had a universe-ending piñata to destroy.

May bounced the head of the bird statue against her shoe, getting a feel for the weight of it.

"Thank you," she said to Xan.

"For what?"

"Everything," she said. "Everything except the canned corn."

Rather than risk speaking, he nodded and pulled her into a tight hug, savoring the way her back felt under his palm, the enclosing warmth of her arms, the softness of her hair in his face. "I love you, May," he said.

"I know, Blue." She patted his back.

Chaos almost made a snarky comment in May's ear, but she had finally learned not to meddle in matters of love and devotion.

May took up her bird statue and swung at the bass.

A wave of glitter poured from the fish, threatening to fill the room as it ferried May and Xan back toward the doorway. As it settled, May realized it wasn't glitter, exactly. It was stars. Suns. Billions of tiny points of light hanging in a heavy darkness all around her. They tickled where they touched her skin until she realized it was less of a tickle, more of an extremely small burn.

"Ugh!" shouted the stars which filled the room before compacting into a single, bright entity in the space where the fish had hung. "This reality is so much smaller than the last one. You're supposed to be expanding, not shrinking, you twits."

May averted her eyes. Not out of respect or awe or anything, just because it was physically painful to look at her.

The Seam, The Unfathomable Everythingness of What Comes Between The Beginning and The End, was miffed. "What?"

"Bright," May said, unable to look at her.

The entity dimmed by 50% and May hazarded a peek at it. "What do you want? It's..." The entity paused to look at her wrist where the edge of all Creation slowly moved outward into the great Nothingness. "Yikes, it's only 6 am. Y'all! What could you possibly need me for? I was in the middle of an intense game of bridge with Time, and I swear if I lose to him again, I'm turning this entire Universe around."

May was distressed. Not because she was in the presence of an entity who could read universal time off her wrist, but because said entity looked and sounded exactly like her fifth-grade teacher. "Mrs. Nina?"

"No, you twit! I pulled an image from your memories. I've tried universe and universe again to present myself plainly, and it's always the same reaction: hysterical shriek, instantaneous soul ejection, and blamo, you're a puddle of flesh. Do you have any idea how unpleasant it is to squeegee melted mortal flesh off the ground? The answer is very, very unpleasant! Now, what do you want?"

"Uh, well," Xan began.

"Let me talk," Chaos said with May's mouth.

The Seam narrowed her eyes at May, giving the effect of two twin suns squeezing under the horizon line. "Chaos, is that you?"

"Yes."

"In *another* body?"

"Yes."

"You didn't get stuck in that ridiculous fish again, did you?" The entirety of the Universe stifled a laugh, and it felt like an earthquake.

Chaos answered by making May give The Seam a silent and humorless glare.

"This is why we don't lose track of our immortal flesh bodies, Chaos. You only get one!" The Seam leaned over Xan now, speaking in that pejorative, cheerful voice one uses for children they are fed up with. "Has Chaos been picking on you?"

Xan nodded, feeling a little embarrassed as if he were tattling on a school-yard bully.

The Seam sighed, and Xan got the feeling that a supermassive black hole had just patted him on the head. "Chaos, I will reunite you with your immortal flesh body, but first, you're going to have a one-eternity time-out to think about what you've done. Now, I need to get back to our bridge game. Time waits for no one. Jellymint?" The Seam held out her hand, revealing two bright green jellymints on her unfathomable palm.

Xan and May both took one and, gingerly, ate them.

CHAPTER THIRTY-FIVE

Immeasurable Emptiness

There followed an immeasurable period of immeasurable emptiness.

Imagine nothing.

Total and complete non-being.

Now scrap that and try again because you've imagined far too much.

It was as if the Universe's plug had been pulled and everything contained in it drained away and then the container itself followed those contents down, but the direction "down" was *also* gone. Not even the vacuum of space remained.

What remained could not be put into words, because it does not exist.

The impossible exceptions to the above statement un-drummed their non-existent fingers on non-existent mahogany office desks as they un-waited for something not to happen.

These were the immortals, and they were one fewer this time than they had been the last, though it was difficult to tell because they did not, in any meaningful way, exist.

These non-entities, after some incomprehensible amount of anti-time, began to experience a something. This something felt an awful lot like boredom.

Soul-sucking, bone-twisting, eyeball-bleeding boredom seeped across time spans immeasurably long and fields of space immeasurably wide until that boredom finally gave itself a name. A name which, for lack of a better approximate, we'll just say was The Seam.

And from there, the rest is history.

CHAPTER THIRTY-SIX

History

During the final age of the War of Reversed Polarity, in the darkest booth in the farthest corner of the seediest sub-bar in the city of Trilly on the continent of Further Masedon on the planet of Tuhnt in the system of Flotluex, Xan stared at his wrist.

More specifically, at four red, digital words that scrolled in the air just above his BEAPER.

He took a tingling swig of his third Electro-Blitz.

It was an alert from the Tuhntian government. 'Mandatory Draft in Effect.'

Xan wondered if perhaps destroying his BEAPER and pretending he had never received the message would work. He closed his eyes to escape it, but was met with the afterimage of the scrolling text. 'Mandatory Draft in Effect,' but this time in green.

He rubbed his eyes, trying to wipe the image away, and slid down in the seat, pursing his lips as his coat bunched up behind him. It would make no difference, but he wanted to look as absolutely put-out as possible. The Universe would know, he thought, and that was enough. Unfortunately, the Universe is a touch nearsighted and didn't notice.

Wait, he thought. *Wait, hold on,* he added, mentally.

He had suddenly remembered great swaths of things which he hadn't previously remembered.

Why was he back here? Was he dead? Was this one of those 'life flashing before one's eyes' moments? No, those weren't supposed to last this long, were they?

He looked at the condensating Electro-Blitz in his hand. The Electro-Blitz he knew he'd just drunk from on account of the tingly after taste.

But that wasn't right. He hadn't had an Electro-Blitz since...well, since now. Here, in the sub-bar. He couldn't remember the name of the sub-bar, but a large glowing mirror behind the bar told him he was in Gulate's Glugger. So this wasn't a memory, it was actually happening.

He felt perhaps he should scream. An uncomfortable, quiet, "Ah," squeaked out.

The reset.

He wasn't sure exactly what had happened. He was fairly certain, however, that at this very moment May was several decades away from existing and that thought gave everything a background radiation of anxiety.

Millions of light years away, on a planet called Earth, Napoleon was furiously scrubbing at a spot of tarnish on his favorite spoon.

Xan stared at the entrance to the sub-bar, apprehensive of what was to come. Any moment now, Admiral Ranken Warders, the person who had, under the influence of Chaos, absolutely obliterated Xan's life, would walk in and tell him to steal the *Audacity*.

Any moment.

Annnyyyyy moment.

Perhaps, thought Xan, this was a case of a watched pot never boiling, and so he looked at his drink instead.

Nothing continued to happen aggressively at him.

And then Aimz happened aggressively at him.

She'd slipped in while he was studying his drink and bulldozed him into the wall beside his booth.

"Hey, zoup-nog, got your draft message yet?" She beamed at him. Being drafted into military service wasn't exactly the sort of thing you beamed about.

"Whoa," she then said, frowning as memories from another lifetime suddenly smacked into her brain. She re-observed her surroundings. The sub-bar, Xan's mullet, Yvonne stiffly sliding into the booth across from them, the Electro-Blitz she had grabbed from Xan out of habit.

She chugged the Blitz. "What on Blitheon's purple grass happened"

"I've been waiting seasons for your timeline to catch up to mine," Yvonne said. "Our consciousnesses have been returned to the moment before Chaos entered our personal timelines which, for me, was when I took the helm of the *Peacemaker*. For Xan, it was when Chaos possessed Rankin Warders to convince him to steal the *Audacity,* which is why I met you here. Aimz, you must've been looking for Xan, and your timeline changed when you didn't find him here."

"So Tuhnt exists again! Oh, and whatcha think, scourge back to normal?" Aimz spread her eyes wide with her fingers for Yvonne to study. They were, indeed, returned to a dull pink glow, no longer an unhealthy neon.

"Normal as you'll ever be, Aimz," Yvonne agreed with a smile.

"That's great, honestly, but what about the others? Where are they?" Xan said.

Aimz shrugged. "Probably back to where they were before Chaos zuxed with them, just like us. I was coming in to tell you about the draft!"

"Yeah," said Xan. "Maybe a touch too enthusiastically. Do you want me to die?"

"No, zoup-nog! Yve snatched you a cushy desk job in communications! Turns out your degree wasn't entirely useless after all."

"Great." He tried to smile, but couldn't even pretend he was happy about anything right now.

"And don't worry about the others!" Aimz continued, summoning the bartender over. "It can't be too hard to find Listay and Ix, right? Six more Electro-Blitzes for the table," she told the bartender. "We beat the scourge!" The bartender looked as if he had heard this before.

"May doesn't exist yet. She'll never be abducted by Chaos, and I won't be floating listless about the Earth, and we're never going to meet, but I still remember her. Why do we remember things that aren't going to happen? That's horrible!"

"We were essentially at the center of the next big bang. As this timeline wears on and replaces the old one, we might forget," Yvonne said, hoping this might comfort him.

It had done just the opposite.

"Can we stop it? I'll write down everything I remember; I'll write a book! Zuut, why didn't I think of that before? This is some wacky stuff we just lived through, someone *should* write a book about it," Xan said, oblivious.

"You might not believe it, even if you wrote it yourself," Yvonne said. "It's also entirely possible that we will remember everything from both timelines."

"Eugh, that's horrible, too!" Xan said, burying his face in his arms.

Yvonne shut up now, realizing that there was nothing she could say to comfort him, because there was nothing comforting about the situation.

"Hey, she's not dead," said Aimz. "She just doesn't exist yet. If you remember her later, you can go abduct her again!"

"I didn't abduct her! Yve did it."

"Chaos did it, not me," said Yvonne.

Xan flopped across the filthy bar table, his arms hung dramatically over the side and his nose pressing uncomfortably into the tacky resin of the tabletop. "Do you remember when you abducted her?" he asked the table.

"Again, not me. Listay would remember."

"Listay!" Aimz shouted. "Zuut, does she remember me? Will she be a zombie still? I hope so."

"She's already caught up to us." Yvonne said. "Difficult to keep her from coming after you the moment she remembered, too. Not a zombie."

"That's right. You never got the chance to kill her in this timeline."

"Chaos. Chaos killed her. And then brought her back."

Aimz sighed, seriously considering if she was still interested, but Yvonne had already messaged Listay the news that Aimz and Xan were caught up with them, and the moment Listay stepped into the sub-bar, Aimz vaulted into her arms to kiss her.

Xan followed them outside. The blizzard had died down as quickly as it started; the sky was clear. He looked at the moons and tried to comfort himself by saying that May might be looking at the same moons right now. This was impossible for several reasons, not least of which that May didn't currently exist.

"Fuck," he said.

CHAPTER THIRTY-SEVEN

Future

May pulled a thick rope of smoke through her cigarette and into her lungs and immediately coughed it out. This wasn't *not* a cigarette. It was a real Earth cigarette, and she was smoking it on the cold concrete steps outside her apartment and watching an empty street. The traffic light at the intersection nearest her flickered through its rounds: green, yellow, red. The morning stirred with the occasional chirrup of an early bird followed by the complaints of birds who much preferred to sleep in, but now they were up, thank-you-very-much.

She was on Earth. She was at her apartment complex. She was smoking into the early morning. She had emotional whiplash.

If all had been going according to plan, she was about to be abducted. All, it seemed, was not going according to plan. There was no Gremlin, which, May assumed, meant that Chaos had been dealt with.

That was good.

She smiled.

There was no Xan.

That was bad.

She frowned.

And, since Xan was not here, there was no one she could confide in about this either.

Trying to suss out what, exactly, The Seam had done to her made her feel dizzy. Or perhaps it was the cigarette. She took a long drag from the cigarette and felt a little better, so it wasn't the cigarette.

With a universe-weary groan, she lay back against the stairs, letting the icy concrete divot her arms. She gazed up at the stars.

"Fuck." She closed her eyes and did not see the blue afterimage of the *Audacity* that she had grown accustomed to. These eyes had never seen the ship. "What now?" she whispered.

Back to Sonic, she thought immediately.

She'd rather get run over by an AMC Gremlin.

But she had bills to pay again and the millions of crystals she had amassed racing no longer existed, and even if they *did* exist, they would be next to worthless on Earth.

It occurred to her that she ought to think it had all been a dream. That's what someone in a book or a movie would say.

"It was all a dream," she said out loud, testing the sound of it. But she knew it wasn't. She wished it had been. Dreams are so easily forgotten, but she couldn't shake the feeling of zipping through the universe in the *Audacity*. The freedom, the excitement, the mountains of crystals.

"I'm going to bed," she said to no-one. She had become so used to announcing these sorts of things to Xan, but now she lived alone again. Alone with her pet cactus, Betty.

She tapped out her cigarette and pulled herself up from the cold concrete steps, leaning her weight on the wobbly cast iron railing, flakes of black paint coming off on her palms when she did. She hadn't missed that. In fact, she couldn't think of one thing she had missed about this place.

She slumped onto her busted dumpster-rescue couch and tried to force herself to fall asleep, hoping that perhaps she would wake up back in the *Audacity*. Through the criminally thin apartment walls, she could hear her neighbor's TV. It was faint, but there was no mistaking the brassy melody of the "I Love Lucy" theme song.

What Yulquitz had said echoed in her mind. "We are perpetual beings made mortal to learn the lesson of impermanence."

"I get it," she told the universe, miserably. "Thanks. Impermanence, learned. Check that off the list." She smushed her face into the lumpy couch cushion, trying to find some comfort in Lucille Ball's muffled shenanigans. "I would've preferred it if the meaning of life had been jazz hands."

CHAPTER THIRTY-EIGHT

Fix-it Fic

May awoke to yet another unpleasant text message from her manager at the Sonic, Kathy. "Wat on gods green erth did u do last nite…" was what it said. It had been two years now since she had gotten stranded in space and five months since she had gotten re-stranded on Earth.

May wiped the crust from her eyes and tried to fluff her hair into place. She missed having her own personal stylist, and she desperately missed the alien hair products.

"Cum in erly?" her phone asked.

Why not? Thought May. Why. The hell. Not. Until classes started at Maple Leaf Meadow Wood Aviation Academy, she was at the mercy of Sonic. Once classes started at Maple Leaf Meadow Wood Aviation Academy next month, she was at the mercy of her student loan provider. Someday, with a little luck, she might be at her own mercy again.

"On my way," she replied to Kathy and opened the mini fridge to a single egg, a handful of ketchup packets, and a bottle of Sriracha, which was one of the few things she had missed about Earth. She cursed her past self for not having the foresight to pick up groceries for her future self and began the long walk back to Sonic. There was food there.

Her Civic was still about as useful as the average lawn ornament, and so she had to walk. Her first student loan check would not be going to books, that was certain. It would be going straight into the Civic.

As she approached the Sonic, Kathy greeted her at the rusty back door, along with the familiar smell of old kitchen grease and food-waste.

"Girl, what kind of freaky stuff are you into?" Kathy asked, hands on her hips, head tilted at a daring forty-five-degree angle.

"Just the usual," May replied.

"Well, keep it outta your work. There's a tall fella in blue makeup and spandex asking for you, and he's bothering the customers."

Pushing past Kathy, May bolted through the kitchen, leaving Kathy outside and wondering whether she could write someone up if they weren't clocked in at the time of offense.

Of course, Kathy had been mistaken. There was no fella. There was only Xan, perched on the back of a red and white booth, chatting with an elderly couple who had offered him a few of their French fries in exchange for his gripping tale.

"That's her!" He pointed a limp fry in May's direction, stuffed it in his mouth, and rolled off the back of the bench. The elderly couple gave an arthritic clap.

"Oh, isn't that nice?" said the wife.

"Charming," agreed the husband.

They wrapped around each other like two wet noodles intertwining, Xan wiggling from side to side as if that would keep his soul from shooting out of his body with joy. "May!" he told her enthusiastically. He finally let her go, and then went back in to cup her face delightedly.

"Xan!" she managed between smushed cheeks.

"May!" he repeated, releasing her. "Blitheon, I could kiss you." He hoped it had come across as rhetorical. It hadn't.

May laughed. "I know, Blueberry. It's okay, go on."

"What, really?"

"Yeah, why not? You look like you're gonna burst."

"Oh, really, I'm fine, I just—" His smile was so wide, it squeezed tears from his eyes, so she offered up her cheek to him, pointing to it teasingly. He gave in and pressed a kiss onto her soft, round cheek.

"Next?" She offered him her other cheek to even it out. "Okay, last one until we're separated with no hope of ever seeing each other again." She tilted her forehead toward him and he gave her a third and final kiss. "Feel better?"

"Enormously. Thank you."

"Anytime, Blue. How did you get here? Is the scourge gone? Are you okay? How long has it been for you? What's with the accent? And what are you wearing? You look…" She stepped back to observe his suit, double breasted, velvety, lined in something which looked expensive, and most shockingly, decorated with three splendiferous medals. "Fancy. You've got medals now?"

"I do!"

"Hey y'all!" Kathy stood at the kitchen door. "You're making a scene! May, can you come to my office?" Kathy had a clipboard-full of forms in her hand and was rhythmically tapping it with her long, non-regulation, fake nails.

"No, because I'm fired," May said, grabbing Xan's hand to drag him outside.

"You mean you quit?!" Kathy shouted after her.

"I never quit!" May said.

"It's true, she doesn't." Xan confirmed to Kathy. "Nice to meet you all!" Xan waved goodbye to the elderly couple and then Kathy as he was whisked away.

May pulled him to one of the outside tables, and he sat down across from her.

"Is my English accent really that bad?" he asked in a bad English accent. "It was awful to learn. No one speaks English, but I knew you wouldn't have a translation chip, so I had to try!"

"It's fine. I'm just happy to see you!" It was better than fine; she had a million questions, and now Xan was at a disadvantage in the language department, so she pushed ahead. "How's the…" she quieted, as if the Scourge Authority were still after them and might pop out at any moment from behind the callbox. "How's the scourge?"

"Better! Well, normal, at least. Aimz and Yve figured out what-uh-heh…sound level? Sound thing. Sound type. Eugh." He winced in frustration. "It isn't a Lucy word!"

"Frequency?" May helped.

"Yes! That's the one! They built a thing that stops it from growing." He tapped his temple where the tiny sonic implant was dutifully keeping watch over the fungus with a constant, nearly imperceptible whine. Nearly imperceptible. He was used to it by now, but the first few seasons had felt like a terrible case of tinnitus.

"So you're fine? The Seam reversed the damage?"

"It never happened! Listay thinks The Seam zuxed up somehow because anyone who had known Chaos personally remembers the other timeline. Our consciousnesses got sent back to the moment Chaos entered our lives."

"But that was ages ago for you," May said.

"A hundred and fifty orbits ago, yeah."

This was not a length of time May could comprehend. Not least of which because she still only had a tenuous grasp on the length of an orbit. She knew it was a long time, though. Nearly a hundred and fifty years. "And you remember me? After all that time, you came back for me?"

"I *missed* you," he said, holding her hands across the table.

"For a hundred and fifty orbits? I barely remember the people I knew in high school and that was..." She counted, then cringed. "That was only a decade ago."

"Yes, I've missed you for a hundred and fifty orbits! How long has it been for you? I tried to get here right when Listay said the Earth abductions started, but I'm not terribly good at navigation, and I had the ship going just a tenth of a degree in the wrong direction for several hundred light years, and honestly, that was quite the detour and I–"

"Five months," May interrupted. "I've missed you for five months."

"Blitheon, it'll be nice when you have a chip again." He paused, looked around as if he had just noticed that they were on Earth. "Well, if you want one. I—oh zuut I never thought of that. Do you want to stay here?"

"Well, let's see..." She began counting on her fingers. "Saturday is my gallery opening at the Met, Sundays are always yoga and brunch with the gals, oh! and on Monday I'm being knighted by the Queen of England."

Xan squeezed her hands gently to stop her. "Seriously, can you come?"

"Friday, I've got a dentist appointment for something I'm pretty sure is going to be a root canal, which I can't afford. If you can take me to a free space dentist, I'm in."

"Root canal?"

"God, it must be nice to not know what that is," she said. "So what are the medals for?"

"Look!" He snapped off one of his medals and showed it to her, beaming. The center medallion depicted a field of glistening stars and illegible markings which looked like they might have been trying to tell her something wrapped around it.

"It's, uh..."

"Zuut! It's in Tuhntian isn't it? Right. It's..." He chewed his lip for a second as he searched for the English words. "Eugh. It's a thing which says that I'm band leader of a ship. Band leader...not band leader but..."

"A captain?"

"Yes!" Xan said, delighted that she had understood him. "Yve got me into interplanetary communications and, as it so happens, I'm fairly good at talking!"

"I hadn't noticed."

"Right? I'm usually the strong, silent type. I have hidden talents," he said with a shrug.

"Guess you do!" May laughed. "So how did you get here? Do you have a ship? A crew? Oh my God, Xan, do you have a crew?" The idea of Xan in any kind of command position confused and troubled May.

"A ship, yes. A crew, not anymore."

"But you did?" May nearly shouted.

"Eh..." He cringed leftward. "Well..." He cringed rightward.

"Come on, it can't be anywhere near as bad as stealing a rocket ship and getting a planet destroyed," May said. He didn't answer quickly enough. "Wait did you do that again?!"

"No!" He said quickly. "No, I just am trying to think of the words," he said. "I'm good at talking, in Tuhntian, at least, right?" he said.

"Uh-huh."

"And I accidentally got on the good side of an Admiral, Admiral Warders, believe it or not! Remember him?"

"Uh-huh..."

"And so he gave me a command position, among other positions, and I sorta had a fleet for a little while."

"Seriously?!" May asked.

"Seriously! I did not use it, though. I sent them all home indefinitely with pay. Evidently they weren't too pleased with that deal, because a few rotations later I was suspended. Honorably! Honorably suspended."

"And they gave you a ship when they suspended you?" May asked.

He smiled, but shook his head. "Here." He handed her a ship's anchor button attached to a keychain which May couldn't read, but from the heart shape in the center of the text, she deduced that it said "I <3 a Carmnian."

"What kind of ship did they give you? Can I pilot it?" she asked, studying the button for clues. He didn't reply. She had seen the words painted in a magnificently spacey text, zooming proudly across the small green disc. Her mouth opened, perhaps to allow more oxygen to flow to her brain as she tried to make sense of the Tuhntian letters.

"Is this..."

Xan nodded.

"Wait, this says..."

He nodded more enthusiastically.

"You stole the *Audacity* again?"

"Wha-no! No, I didn't steal it! It was about to be–" he paused, his hand circling. "Close the show? Stopped? Canceled?"

"Decommissioned," May suggested.

"Yes! That one. I had some friends who had some friends and, well, I bought it for you."

"For me?" she said, a bit teary as she clipped the familiar anchor button to her Sonic polo.

"Yeah! And this. Finally." He unhooked the extra BEAPER he was wearing and gave that to her, too. "Why did we never get you one before?"

"Because it was more fun using yours."

"For whom?"

"Me! You would sit there for hours just holding your wrist out while I browsed the IFI. It was hilarious. And how is your English grammar better than mine? 'Whom?'" May teased, snapping on her own BEAPER and testing it out.

"Grammar is fun!"

"Your mom's fun," May said, grabbed his hand, and teleported them both to the *Audacity*.

"You met her; she's really not," Xan mumbled as they remerged on the ship.

"Wow," May said, stepping backward off the teledisc. She hadn't been aboard the *Audacity* in over a year, and she had never been aboard this version of the rocket, but the main room was exactly how she remembered it. The same couch, the same coffee table, and junk-yard-rescue retro TV.

"Couldn't put back the..." He swirled his fingers spookily.

"Mysterious wormhole," May filled in. "How did you get that in the first place?"

"No idea! That's why I couldn't put it back. Plus side, though, we've got bedrooms and a proper basement now!"

"How did you afford this?"

"May. I have a *job* now. A real one. An actual, every rotation job. I took the next hundred orbits off to spend with you, though. A 'Maycation.'" He beamed with pun pride. This was the first English pun he had invented, and he was quite fond of it; his co-workers, however, had not been.

"A hundred orbits? I'm not going to last that long," she said, imagining herself racing rockets as a dilapidated old woman. She liked the idea, but was certain he wouldn't go for it.

"Yeah, I know. I planned in grief orbits." He hadn't been expecting to be reminded of her relatively short lifespan. The specter of impending doom put a bit of a damper on their reunion.

"Hey," May said, pulling him back from the brink of a downward spiral. "Don't worry about the future. You told me that the point is what's happening now, and this," she stretched her hands out and wriggled her fingers. "This moment is all jazz hands."

An End

EPILOGUE

August Gets All the Apples

In Germany, on Earth, about two hundred years after a woman named May June July became a missing persons case, a Rhean Ultra-Luxe Aether Cruiser accidentally crushed a fifty-year-old apple tree as it parked in the Apfel Family Orchard.

The cruiser's winged door slid open, moving in a way that only really expensive vehicles can move. Ix stepped out.

"Ix, if you're wrong about this, we're going to have to mind wipe someone, you realize that? Mind wipes aren't cheap."

"I am not wrong," Ix said back to Yvonne who pulled herself from the Cruiser a touch less elegantly, stretching out the long journey from Rhea. "Do you see his dwelling?"

"You're looking directly at it, mun. Just walk forward."

She began to walk, but was stopped by sound of a slamming screen door and the distant shouts of "You!" from a voice which was either furiously angry or furiously happy.

August, unmarked by the ravages of time, ran toward them. It was still difficult to say what emotion he was feeling, exactly, but whatever it was, there was undoubtedly a lot of it.

"You!" he shouted again, about six feet away.

"You," he said, finally. This time he was definitely angry.

The moment he was within reach, Yvonne grabbed him, and Ix put a gun to his skull behind his ear. This was not a typical greeting for either of them. He felt a sharp stab, a bit of pressure, then, finally, Ix sheathed the gun and Yvonne let him go.

"Damnit," he said, rubbing the back of his head.

"August, Yvonne and I have reason to believe you may be immortal, which is why we have come to check on you. I have installed an S59 translation chip on your auditory cortex for our convenience."

August looked like he was about to do a livid sort of jumping jack. "Two *hundred* years? *Two hundred years*? Humans just replicate apples, now. Do you have any idea how hard it is to keep an apple orchard in business when everyone wants replicated apples? I've seen generations of people live and die without aging a day myself," he shouted.

"You are shouting," said Ix.

He ignored her. "Dogs have evolved a rudimentary form of language; do you know how creepy it is that dogs can now *tell* you that they want to hump your leg? Soccer players are genetically modified super-humans which ruins the point and...*and,"* he stressed, looking as if he were near tears, "bluetooth connections still don't work reliably. They cannot *fucking* get it right!"

And then the tears came. Ix was never great with tears, so he buried his face in Yvonne's chest, and she sighed, patting his back as he wept.

"I told you we should've come sooner. Two hundred orbits is a lot to these little fellas," she whispered to Ix. "Relatively speaking, it's been about a thousand orbits to him. No one should have to live that long. That's horrific."

"Uh-huh," he sobbed.

"It's alright, August. It's alright," Yvonne soothed. "Everyone who met Chaos has experienced slower aging—"

"Completely halted aging and spontaneous cellular reset," Ix corrected.

"Yes, that. You remember Xan and his Earthling leaving the orchard to find Carmnia, yes?" Yvonne asked.

August pulled himself together. The orchard...he looked around. Not this orchard. The orchard he had on Rhea. Yes, he remembered. Vaguely.

He nodded. "Who's Carmnia?"

"A Tuhntian Queen; she doesn't matter. What matters is that Xan summoned an entity who restarted the Universe and, as Xan recalls it, put Chaos in a 'time-out' for this go-round."

"Yeah, I gathered that!" August said, gesturing to his expansive orchard, the one he had inherited and tended for the past two centuries.

He had not, actually, gathered that. In fact, he had for many years assumed that he'd gone mad and checked himself into an asylum. A few years after that, he realized he wasn't aging properly and checked himself *out* of the asylum to avoid suspicion. Then the real trouble began a few decades later when he came to the conclusion that he wasn't just not aging properly, but he wasn't aging at *all*, and suddenly the decades he imagined he had spent on planets other than Earth weren't so mad after all.

Something, clearly, had gone wrong.

What, he had no idea. And closure had not been forthcoming.

"So why am I not aging?"

"We are unsure, but we thought it would be appropriate to check on you. How are you feeling?" Ix asked. The shouting and the tears hadn't tipped her off.

"Not great!" August said. "I mean, physically I'm fine, sure, but you two forgot about me for two centuries. Didn't you miss me?"

"Of course we—" Yvonne began.

"Not for long," Ix interrupted.

Yvonne nudged Ix in the ribs. Ix sighed at Yvonne. "Yes, August, we missed you. I missed you. We believed it would be to your advantage to allow you to complete your natural human life on Earth. That was before we realized you might have been stripped of said natural life. I am happy to see you, my friend."

August got a little misty-eyed again. Two centuries of work, and Yve had finally got Ix to play nice. "Aw, thanks Ix. So what do we do now? I can't believe it, but after two centuries, I'm ready to see the stars again."

"Now, the Death Quest!" Yvonne said, joyfully, grabbing an apple off a nearby tree and *not* rubbing it clean before taking a bite. It was worth a shot.

"The Death Quest?!" August repeated.

"Yes! Nothing left to do, really. Eventually, we will want to die, and as immortals, that's the one thing denied us. So Ix and I have been posed the question: how do you kill an immortal? and, by Rheanoodle the Third, we're going to answer it."

"Sounds fun."

"The pursuit of death is a serious—"

"It's gonna be fun," Yvonne agreed.

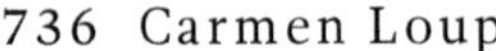

If you enjoyed this book, please leave a brief review at your online bookseller of choice. Thanks!

APPENDIX

Glossary

Length

Qal: A wee bit.

Horbort: Slightly longer than a meter

Time

Blip: Slightly less than a second.

Bloop: About 50 seconds.

Beoop: About 45 minutes.

Rotation: Varies by planet, but lasts exactly twenty beoops in space (based on the rotations of the planet Estrichi).

Season: Varies by planet, but lasts exactly fifty rotations in space (based on the rotations of the planet Estrichi).

Orbit: Varies by planet, but lasts exactly six seasons in space (based on the rotations of the planet Estrichi).

Quilfraudoron: One infinity.

Quifeee: Infinity infinities.

Insults

Positor: “Dick”. Short for “ovipositor”.

Poslouian-slug-grass-eating-coward: Xan

Precious Butler: Prostitute (offensive). Also Xan.

Taagshlorph: A piece of slimy, wilted leafy green.

Tchagg: A jerk. Also the term for the musk gland of the common glotchbur.

Zoup-nog: Idiot.

Zingnat: Idiot (affectionate).

Ovi-booster: One who boosts another's ovipositor, a suck-up.

Jultido: A sucker, an easy mark. Common Anat term.

Endearments

Boha: Buddy, friend, mi amigo.

Mun: Comes from the cute fuzzy critters that like to chew up wires on spaceships.

Lav: Gender neutral pejorative term like "kid". Short for "larva".

Larvling: Another form of "larva", more respectful than "lav".

Zuxine: Sexy.

Other

Splice in the duct: Like a "kick in the pants", referring to the oviduct.

Twa-don: Short for "Twagolohoontz dontargel" which essentially means "Twagolohoontz is leaving the building". Twagolohoontz was a famous Tuhntian comedian who would end every show with this phrase.

Trok: Casual term for the radioactive waste the Rhean government dumped on Tuhnt, creating the wastelands.

Unpin it: Relax. Referencing the physical restraint or "pins" used in cheap rocket races to make sure rockets don't start too early.

Porscinunct: A vow of truth. Invoking this word means you have to tell the absolute truth.

Serpentine palbeatus: Disease characterized by the compulsion and mysterious ability to slither.

Gloxalatal: Biology. Part of an A'Vilrial voicebox which produces clattering sounds which translate as either "Q" "Ch" "Ck" or "X." This is the reason May can't pronounce "Xan" and Xan can't pronounce "Fuck."

Zuut/Zux: Noun/verb. A sexual act specific to the A'Vilrial species.

Humanoids

Anat: Not actually humanoids! But they may appear to be. Anats are predatory creatures from Pan who have the ability to closely mimic their prey.

A'Viltrian: A'Vilrial race. Not extinct, but highly evolved. They don't play well with others, but they love to release futuristic technology into the galaxy and see how the lesser beings take it. Andolon was their planet of origin, but they are beyond the need of a planet as most of them live in a more subtle dimension.

Bewlahoo: Primoid race. Very large, feline-humanoids from the Primox system. Their language is Bewlahooon. Yes, there are three "o"s.

Filporthean Weet: Also not technically humanoid, though they may embody a humanoid. The weet is an entity that puppets corpses, keeping them partially alive. Most weets are beneficent, but all weets are deeply feared. Their natural form is as a pink sentient fog found in Tuhntian wastelands. The Filporthean Weet is a single weet, the most prolific one on Tuhnt.

Garveral: Primoid race. Large, tough-skinned, slow, and long-lived.

Panseen: Panen race. Characterized by reddish skin, typically five to seven feet tall, most similar, biologically, to Earthlings.

Pringnette: Primoid race. Tall and gazelle-like. Nearly extinct thanks to the Rheans. Ugh. Rheans.

Rhean: A'Vilrial race. Characterized by purple skin in a variety of shades and hues and blue-ish blood. Likes to think they're as evolved as the A'Viltrians; they are not. Have colonized several star systems, destroyed a few cultures, you know, just fun humanoid things.

Titian: A'Vilrial race. Nearly extinct and distantly related to the Rheans. Titians have dark purple-red skin and an extra set of arms (usually underdeveloped and vestigial nowadays). Most remaining Titians have found refuge on Estrichi, a previously uninhabited and neutral planet.

Tuhntian: A'Vilrial race. Blue to green skin tones of any shade, pale white blood that dries green, close cousins to the Rheans, but diverged in their evolution many centuries ago by colonizing

Tuhnt. Started the trend of ear-lobe stretching, where the plugs are typically made of expensive metals. The larger the plug, the richer the family.

Udonian: Panen race. Typically short, green, and mustachioed. Their lip hair grows so fast, no one has ever seen one clean shaven.

Star Systems

Flotluex: Planets include Rhea I, Rhea II, Rhea IV, Tuhnt (scorched), Not-Tuhnt (aka Pontoosa or Rhea III).

Premerfherf System: Planets include Andolon (missing), A'Viltra (scorched), Estrichi, and Primox.

System 69F: Planets include Forn, Pan, and Udo.

ABOUT THE AUTHOR

Carmen Loup is a non-binary humorologist, illustrator of "Tarot in Space," and author of *The Audacity* space opera novel and comic series. They've been writing seriously since 2007 and funnily since 2015. Loup's work is inspired by Douglas Adams, Kurt Vonnegut, Ram Dass, and Alan Watts.

They own Cosmic Corner, a spiritual supply and education center in Savannah, GA where they teach Yoga, Meditation, and Tarot classes. Book an online Tarot or Akashic Records reading, or one-on-one Tarot training with them at their website: https://www.carmenloup.com/.

Please take a moment to review this book at your favorite retailer's website, Goodreads, or simply tell your friends!

Milton Keynes UK
Ingram Content Group UK Ltd.
UKHW020707010824
446266UK00001B/3